Same Face Different Place
Visions

By Helen J. Christmas

I dedicate this to my mum, Elizabeth, whose passion for gardens and beautiful places gave me so much inspiration for this novel.

I also dedicate this book to my dear friend, Beryl Kingston (author), whose fight to save Blake's Cottage in Felpham has inspired me. Visit her blog to read about the deterioration of a historic house in need of repair. berylkingstonblog.wordpress.com

INTRODUCTION

Visions is the second book of the series, 'Same Face Different Place,' a saga, which spans four different decades of British history, from the 1970s through to the opening years of the 2nd Millennium.

In the first book, 'Beginnings,' set in the criminal underworld of 1970s London, a mysterious conspiracy to end the life of a British MP unleashes a chain of events yet to be resolved.

Book 2, 'Visions,' leaps into the 1980s; a decade characterised by a new era of politics under Margaret Thatcher's Conservative government where the face of Britain is set to change dramatically.

It should be noted that any political opinions expressed by characters in this book are not necessarily my own, but as a silent observer, I have paid homage to the changing political climate that characterised this decade, in the same way as I have featured music, popular TV shows, 80s culture and newsworthy issues close to people's hearts.

Acknowledgements

I would like to express my thanks to everyone who has helped and inspired me, especially my mum and my sister, Jocelyne, for taking the time and trouble to read the first draft and for inspiring me to continue writing.

Please note: This novel contains adult content which includes frequent strong language, as well as one scene of sexual violence which some may find upsetting.

Prologue

September 1986

The seconds passed quickly as Perry turned to close the door, trapping them all inside.

But in precisely the same instant, Eleanor had flown to her feet and grasping Elijah's hand, shot away from the table.

Moving towards the darkest corner of the lounge, she backed into the folds of the long velvet drapes to conceal herself. Her dark clothes and long dark hair merged into the shadows, her golden eyes shining like orbs as she held her son tightly in front of her.

Yet even from a distance, Charlie could see she was shaking.

With Perry Hampton standing in the centre of the room, gazing at each person in turn, his wife and son positioned themselves on both sides.

Together they formed a menacing trio.

Their eyes raked over the residents and for that moment no one really knew how to begin.

As Eleanor stared at Perry though, there was little doubt in her mind where she had seen him before. His thick hair appeared to be more white than blonde, eyes pale as frost glaring out of a familiar florid face. She closed her eyes, assailed by memories. They took her right back to 1973, to that devastating press conference where she had vowed to make one last stand against her enemies.

In her mind's eye lingered the beautiful lounge of the Grosvenor Hotel; the two men in dinner suits sat around that table and the heated discussion, which had finally brought her face to face with this mysterious man. It happened moments before she had uttered those fateful words:

'All I know is that his friend, Andries, spoke the truth when he told you Jake witnessed something. Just follow the clues!'

And never in her life would she forget the crazed reaction the man had exhibited. She could visualise him now, tearing at his collar and tie as if choking, his face turning purple.

Wasn't it always her intention to find out who he was?

Yet regrettably time had run out. The revelations of that press conference had unleashed the truly intimidating power of Dominic Theakston, whose threats had driven her away before she had a chance to discover more.

1

Eleanor shrank deeper into the shadows, feeling the chill of fear in her veins. Sensing the fragility of her son, she hugged him tight against her body. His small, thin frame felt warm against her chest, the bones of his shoulder blades jutting beneath his T-shirt. They remained very still but as her eyes continued to drink in the image of Perry Hampton, words of that conversation from thirteen years ago echoed in her head like a tape recording…

Seeing this man now brought everything back to her with a sudden clarity. Eleanor knew without any doubt this had to be the man who had organised Jake's murder all those years ago.

For several more minutes she was rooted to the spot. Desperate not to draw attention to herself, she pressed her eyes shut, filled with a sense that past and present had just collided. And as the harrowing scene unravelled itself, she found herself recalling a more recent chain of events; one which had led right up to this pinnacle in time…

PART ONE
The Fate of an English Country House

Chapter One

November 1985

It had begun almost a year ago, a day she and Elijah had arisen to another crisp, wintery dawn. Filled with a craving to grab some fresh air, they had set out on a long country walk.

It occurred to her she had not seen James Barton-Wells for a very long time, not even in the weeks of fruit picking.

Such thoughts sent her mind reeling back to the day she had arrived here, the memory vivid as ever. Eli had been just a baby. She would never forget that pivotal moment when she had stood by the gates of Westbourne House, relishing the beauty of the village. Filled with a sense she would be safe at last, she was recalling the moment James Barton-Wells had appeared, marching down the drive towards the gates with his magnificent home soaring in the distance.

With a scattering of clouds allowing shafts of sunlight to peep through, Eleanor had wrapped herself in a long woollen overcoat, thinking it would be a good day to pay him a visit. Elijah accompanied her, jogging beside her in an attempt to keep warm, gloved hands shoved inside the pockets of his duffle coat, his breath escaping in clouds. Autumn leaves carpeted the ground from the many beech and horse chestnut trees and as they continued their journey, Eleanor found herself recapturing the highs and lows of the last twelve years...

It seemed a little unnerving at first, that someone as noble as James would allow her to install a caravan in his field. Feeling like some sort of waif though, this marked the opening chapter of a brand new way of life.

From her very first week, an ironic twist of fate had brought her into contact with an old friend from boarding school. She too lived in Aldwyck. Her name was Judy, enthralled to learn how Eleanor had ended up living here, especially with a baby.

"So who is he?" she had whispered excitedly. "I see you're wearing an engagement ring. Who's the lucky guy and when is the wedding?"

Relating the truth however, left her shell-shocked.

There was a time when Eleanor and her beloved Jake had dreamt of getting married; a plan that relied heavily on their escape from London to reach Jake's home town of Nijmegen in the Netherlands. Except it had all gone tragically wrong; that on the night they planned to leave their bedsit, a hired killer had

4

invaded their sanctuary and shot Jake in cold blood. Hidden beneath the floorboards, she had pledged to protect their unborn child at all costs.

Plagued by memories too painful to dwell on, she had focussed on renewing their friendship. The local pub, 'the Olde House at Home,' provided a perfect oasis for their social life while neighbours, Marilyn and Tom Harper, were happy to babysit. On other days they enjoyed many afternoons relaxing in Eleanor's caravan, chatting and listening to music, or watching TV around at Judy's home when her parents were out. And sometimes they ventured beyond the village, the nearby town of Rosebrook tempting them with larger shops and a cinema.

There were times when Judy hungered for an opportunity to go clubbing, especially in London; at which point, Eleanor's sense of adventure dried up, leaving her friend confused as to why she seemed reluctant to set foot inside the capital.

Making the excuse she found big cities intimidating, what she never wanted to admit was her deep-rooted fear of running into notorious crime boss, Dominic Theakston; a man whose cruel threats had driven her from London when she had stepped too close to exposing the men behind Jake's murder.

So for the last twelve years, Eleanor stayed well away, but with two exceptions.

Once a year she contacted her solicitor, hankering for news of her missing father.

The only other reason she was willing to take the risk was to visit a special park in Poplar. For here, she had installed a tiny memorial stone; a token of her enduring love for Jake. And during these trips, she also seized a chance to visit the Merrimans. Closer than a foster family, they lived a short distance away in a delightful suburb named Forest Haven.

As the years drifted by however, Aldwyck had become her own haven. The locals gradually got to know her and in time, came to adore her. Eleanor had discovered a passion for village events and was ever keen to get involved, earning herself a reputation for being an excellent cook, acclaimed for her luscious home made jams and chutneys. Her cakes too became legendary; light sponges and rich fruit cakes which appeared on the stalls of summer fetes and Christmas fairs.

The way things stood, her presence was widely accepted by the locals, a strong community who genuinely felt she belonged here. Some even feared for her protection, unsure it was safe for a young girl to live in such isolation. And their fears were not unfounded.

No one was ever going to forget the incident when Eleanor's safety had been compromised; how in the autumn of 1979, a group of upper class young men out for a day's pheasant shooting had descended on the 'Olde House at Home.'

Three of them lingered. But after several hours of sustained boozing, working their way through a range of potent country wines, washed down with numerous bottles of champagne, they had just begun to turn unruly when Eleanor walked in. Gliding up to the bar to buy a bottle of cider to take home and crisps for Elijah, there was no mistaking her fragility. The chilly autumnal breeze had drawn a flush to her face, her gleaming dark hair loose as it hung down her back in ripples.

Capturing their eye, she would never forget the unpleasant way they had leered at her, their conversation lowering to whispers before they summoned her to their table. But the plummy drawl of their voices irritated her and brushing them off rudely, she had fled from the pub.

She was later to hear how they quizzed the locals. Most villagers said nothing, apart from one man who could not resist speaking out; a gentleman farmer, Herbert Baxter, renowned for being a heavy drinker. As one of the few villagers who disapproved of Eleanor's lifestyle, he was quick to broadcast that she was *'some gypsy girl, living in a caravan in a field.'*

Eleanor had been tucking her six-year-old son into bed when the sound of a fist came pounding on her door. Guessing it to be the three drunken 'Hooray Henries,' she ignored it. But the pounding grew worse. Eli started to cry. To her ultimate outrage, a brick was hurled, cracking one of her window panes. Incandescent with rage, Eleanor had grabbed an axe used for chopping wood and wrenched the door open. For a second she stood there braced, the weapon held high as the three of them swayed outside, braying with laughter.

Fearing for her safety, as well as her child, she had swung the axe, praying it would drive them back. Her attempts were met with a stream of profanities, at which point she started screaming, the axe in her hands flailing. Her screams had lured villagers from all directions; the pub, the farmhouse and even residents from the cottages on the green. If nothing else, the incident proved to Eleanor that she had the support of almost an entire village, as one after the other, people appeared in the field. The police were called, the young men arrested, but from that night onwards, the villagers had been resolute in protecting her from such dangers.

The memory of their proposal arose, just as the beautiful building loomed close.

Surely she would be safer working and living at Westbourne House.

James being the kind man he was, had wholeheartedly agreed. Inspired by her cooking, he would have happily employed her in his kitchens, if only his mean-spirited wife hadn't objected. Threatened by Eleanor's beauty though, Avril Barton-Wells was convinced she was some *gold-digger* set to take advantage of his good nature and had refused to let her in the house, never mind accommodate her. Thus Eleanor's secluded existence in her caravan continued, though Tom Harper had insisted on fixing metal mesh screens to her windows.

Two years later she had exchanged the caravan for a larger, sturdier model, using money from an inheritance bestowed by her father's late employer, Sammie Maxwell.

Two years after that, she had embarked on a career in nursing, which brought her right back to her present situation.

The distant fragments of memory turned around in her mind like the leaves swirling at her feet and just as they were taking their last steps towards this exquisite country hotel. Ascending a flight of steps supported by a stone balustrade, they were guided past ornamental urns filled with box balls, right up to the heavy oak doors.

But Eleanor smiled, fuelled with the satisfaction Avril was long gone. She had left James almost two years ago, which meant she could visit at any time she liked.

II

Stepping through the door, they were straight away struck by how quiet the place was. The emptiness seemed eerie. Apart from two elderly gentlemen resting by the windows, drinking coffee, the hotel lacked its buzz, devoid of the continuous movement of staff and guests, Eleanor was used to. She froze on the threshold, allowing the door to swing shut. It emitted a boom which echoed through the interior, causing the two men to glance up.

But within seconds a sound of footsteps came racing across the floor from the restaurant area. It was James's daughter, Avalon, who shimmied over to greet them.

"Eleanor!" she gasped. "How nice of you to come and see us!"

Eleanor leaned forward to kiss her cheek. "Nice to see you too, Avalon."

Avalon's eyes lowered to Elijah. "Eli! Do you know you get taller each time I see you..." she beamed at Eleanor, "and isn't he getting handsome!"

Elijah's cheeks flared pink and he looked away shyly. No one could deny what a good looking boy he had turned into, Eleanor reflected. His complexion radiated a peachy glow like hers but the fine facial bone structure originated from his father. He possessed lovely eyes too, not so large as hers but longer with feathery lashes, a soft olive shade, flecked with pigments of green and gold. He offered Avalon a quick smile.

"Thanks," he mumbled nervously and with the flush in his cheeks spreading, he glanced away.

"Come and sit down," Avalon insisted. "I'll ask Elliot to bring some coffee. Would you like to sit in the library? It's nice and peaceful in there with plenty of books for Eli if he gets bored."

"Great," Eleanor replied thankfully. "Is your brother not around?"

"William's back at school," Avalon muttered, "and you may have gathered we're a bit short staffed. We're having some major building work done at the moment..."

Eleanor watched as she dialled from the desk to order coffee. Without another word, they walked through reception to the library, passing two ornate staircases before they got there. Eleanor was further shocked to see the ghostly dust sheets enshrouding one of them.

Breathing deeply, she savoured the smell of furniture polish and leather upholstery, mingling with a slightly fusty aroma of old books. With a fire crackling in the grate and the room bathed in a glow of table lamps, they lowered themselves into one of the Chesterfield sofas.

Minutes later, Elliot appeared; a distinguished man in his fifties employed as butler. Crossing the room with his usual straight-backed grace, he greeted them politely then left them.

"So," Eleanor mused, settling herself against the cushions. "How are things with you, Avalon? You'll be sixteen soon..."

"Hmm," Avalon sighed. "Yet I feel older."

"Hardly surprising," Eleanor said gently. "You've got a lot more responsibility, since your mum left. But it was brave of you to leave school to help James out. I remember when I was sixteen. I'd only just left school and I found myself having to grow up very fast..." She took a gulp of air, knowing it was the year she had met Jake. "How is your love life?"

Avalon lowered her eyes. "I-I've just started dating someone..." she faltered. Subconsciously fiddling with her hair, she started twisting it, separating the ringlets.

"Go on," Eleanor probed, "you can tell me."

Glancing up, Avalon bit her lip. She seemed to be struggling to get the words out.

"Ben!" she finally blurted. "His name is Ben. He's twenty-one and blonde... drop dead gorgeous, in fact. Said he even worked as a model..."

Eleanor held her gaze, seeing none of the enthusiasm she would have expected.

"So he's twenty-one and drop dead gorgeous. What's the problem?"

"It's hard to explain," Avalon continued. "H-he can be very intense... a little obsessive even. I mean, he took me to this really expensive restaurant and that but..." her brown eyes clouded over with anxiety. "I-I'm not sure I want to carry on dating him. For one thing, he hates William! Every time I mentioned him, there was this flash in his eyes, something scary..."

"Go on," Eleanor kept coaxing her.

"On the evening we met, William was with me. We visited their house in London and Ben was showing off his fancy motorbike. He took us out for a spin... then William just took off on it."

Elijah could not resist the urge to giggle. William had always been impulsive.

Eleanor nodded. "And I'm guessing he wasn't impressed?"

"Well, he definitely wasn't expecting it," Avalon smiled. "He had no idea my brother knew how to ride a bike. William thought he was challenging him, but you should have seen his face. They don't see eye to eye. They don't even like the same music."

"That's hardly a reason to hate him," Eleanor argued, "William's adorable. Are you sure this new boyfriend isn't just a little jealous? And are you going to see him again?"

Avalon hesitated, her eyes widening. "It's going to be hard not to," she let slip. "Dad's about to enter into a business partnership with Ben's parents."

"Oh," Eleanor whispered. "What sort of partnership?"

"Oh God, you haven't heard, have you?" she gasped. "Our house needs some major work. We've had to hush it all up, because it meant closing the hotel... but one of the main staircases is being rebuilt."

"I did notice," Eleanor pondered.

"I can't say too much," Avalon continued guardedly, "but Dad is struggling to meet the cost, which is where the Hamptons come in..."

"In what way?" Eleanor pressed.

Avalon turned very still. "They've offered to help us restore it - but in exchange, they want to take over the management of the hotel and expand its business potential."

Chapter Two

Avalon closed her eyes, thrown back in time.

It had been a beautiful autumn day. The sun hung low in the sky as birds flitted between the trees. The gardens of Westbourne house buzzed with guests. As far as her father was concerned their visit could not have come at a better time and with the last days of summer dwindling, he welcomed this extra tourist trade, as well as the boost to his income.

The quaint village of Aldwyck often drew visitors. But on this occasion, a small coach party had taken a trip to a local vineyard and to round off their tour, were about to enjoy an afternoon tea in the grounds of their country house.

She remembered hovering by his armchair, swooping down to kiss his cheek.

"The coach party's here, Dad."

Offering her a slow, sleepy smile, he appeared to be surveying her, as she wandered out onto the lawn. It extended beyond the patio to the ornamental gardens. And despite the autumnal haze veiling the wooded hills, the weather was surprisingly warm.

The tables were already set up with snowy white cloths and vases of freshly picked roses. Though the tourists didn't seem in any hurry; content to amble around the gardens, admiring the roses that still bloomed in the perennial flower beds...

Avalon paused as the black and white wings of a magpie sailed overhead. Its raucous chatter seemed loud as it settled into one of the trees. Yet despite the caressing warmth of the sun on her skin, she felt a shiver - watching in a dream as a smartly dressed, middle-aged couple settled themselves down at one of the tables.

Working under the supervision of patisserie chef, Bryony, the staff continued to weave around them, laying out crockery made from delicate bone china.

Soon, they would bring out silver pots of freshly brewed tea; buttery home-made scones served with strawberry jam and Cornish clotted cream. Avalon pushed her hand behind her head and shook out her ponytail, lifting the mane of long golden brown ringlets to waft cool air around her neck. She had been right to tie it back.

The side door from the kitchen swung open with a bang before a tea trolley was wheeled out onto the patio. For several satisfying moments, Avalon had relished the scene; listening to the hum of conversation emanating from their guests - watching as the catering staff began to pour out the tea, the subtle fragrance drifting as it spilled into the cups.

James had just materialised inside the frame of the patio doors. Stepping carefully over the threshold, he caught her eye.

If that brief moment could be suspended in time, it would have captured an atmosphere of calm; the delight on the faces of the guests and the loveliness of his grounds. It depicted a perfect English country scene, one of such serenity, you could almost taste it.

Regrettably, the moment was shattered by an explosion of breaking crockery. Someone gasped. Several heads spun in their direction and Avalon watched in horror as her father fell to the ground.

Within seconds, she had flown to his side.

"What happened?" she yelped at the people sitting nearest.

"I'm not sure, my dear," muttered an elderly man. "I think he may have tripped."

Avalon dropped to her knees. James lay motionless, his face as white as the table cloth clutched in his hand. She touched his face. His skin felt cool but a film of moisture misted his forehead. She was dimly aware of Elliot hovering as she knelt among the wreckage of broken china. Bryony was fussing over the guests, reassuring them nothing was wrong.

Except something was wrong; her father had just collapsed.

"It's probably the heat..." Elliot whispered, dipping his head close.

Clasping James's wrist, he felt for a pulse. She could sense the tension but the moment passed. There was a noticeable sag in his posture as he caught her eye and nodded.

From behind them however, Avalon could hear the murmurs of disquiet fluttering among the guests. She could feel their eyes; a force of scrutiny she found intrusive.

"I think he's just fainted," Elliot said quickly.

"Can't we at least move him indoors?" Avalon muttered under her breath.

How she longed to get him away from the guests, some place they would no longer be staring at them like a crowd of ghoulish spectators in the wake of a car crash.

"Here, let me help you..."

Avalon sensed the looming presence before she saw him - caught the glimpse of a dark blue sports jacket and an old school tie. She breathed in a scent of aftershave, subtly reminded of pine forests and damp earth. But before another word was spoken, she turned, observing a flushed face and thick white-blonde hair. Without hesitation, the man had assisted Elliot and together they carried James towards the patio doors.

At least, they were back inside the house.

"Shouldn't we call an ambulance?" This time a woman's voice pierced the silence.

Avalon turned, staring at the stranger now lingering inside their lounge. Possibly in her forties, there was no mistaking her glamour. With platinum blonde hair cut in a severe jaw length bob, her eyes shone a pale aqua-marine. She seemed gracefully tall, perhaps an illusion created by her high-heeled shoes.

"It's okay, we'll look after him," Avalon mumbled, unable to drag her eyes away. "Please, enjoy your tea... the scones will be served soon. I'm so sorry about this."

"Don't apologise," the man said softly.

They laid James down onto the deep, floral chintz settee. To Avalon's relief, she thought she saw a little animation stir his features.

"Anyone can see he's not well. This is the least we can do."

"You're very kind," Avalon said, touched by his concern.

It had never occurred to her that it might be unusual to see a couple like this on one of the coach tours. The majority of people were of retirement age. Yet this man possessed an air of authority that overwhelmed her and straight away, he seemed to have placed himself in charge.

They were on the verge of calling a doctor when James spoke. "What the devil..."

"Dad!" Avalon gasped, spinning away from the strangers in their lounge. "Are you okay?"

"I think so," James sighed. His eyes peeped open. "What's going on?"

"You collapsed, James," Elliot answered him. "We've only just managed to get you inside."

James swallowed and for a moment he looked scared. The pallor in his face was disturbing enough but there was more to it than that. As Avalon gazed into his soft, brown eyes, she saw a torment that lay deeper. He looked as if he had been about to say something when his eyes honed in on the mysterious couple still hovering.

"They're guests, Dad," she enlightened him. "They helped us carry you indoors. I'm sorry, perhaps you could tell us your names?"

"Perry Hampton," the man said.

He extended his hand and Avalon accepted his handshake.

"And this is Rowena, my wife."

Avalon gazed up again. She had stepped right into the lounge where James

12

lay convalescing.

"Mr Barton-Wells isn't it? Owner of this stunning house? I've heard so much about you..."

"Have you now?" James smiled. "Well, I hope I haven't disappointed you. It must be age, though I have had a lot on my mind lately... Won't you sit down?"

Without a moment's hesitation, the man lowered himself into an armchair. Avalon couldn't fail to notice how their eyes kept sweeping across the interior, as if drinking it all in.

"Why don't you tell me what's troubling you?" Perry probed, picking up the thread of James's last sentence. "Anything you want to offload?"

"Only the stress of trying to uphold the maintenance of this place!" James confessed, "nothing I wish to bore you with. What field of business are you in, Mr Hampton?"

The man stared deep into his eyes. "Property and please... call me Perry."

Avalon could not resist studying him. Older than his wife, possibly in his late forties, his narrow eyes shone a cold silver grey; they seemed pale in contrast to his florid face.

"Property," James mused as if thinking aloud, "an interesting field of work."

"Work?" Perry said. "Property is my passion! Old as well as new."

Avalon could see he had completely captured her father's attention. Lowering herself onto the arm of the settee, she was sharply aware of his wife again. She had stepped further into the room, high heels clicking on the polished oak floor, before an ornamental rug muffled the sound. She paused by the hearth with its classical marble surround. Avalon shifted, slightly unnerved by their scrutiny. Yet they had shown no hesitation in helping her father. Looking at him now, she sensed he was intrigued by whatever this gentleman had been about to say.

"I don't suppose you have dealings with period property?" James pressed.

"Indeed, I do," Perry replied in a soft and caressing tone, "especially in the area of *restoration*. The oldest property we restored to its former glory was a two-hundred year old cottage!"

James's features drew into a frown but as the words turned in Avalon's mind, she could sense what he was thinking; their house was probably about the same age.

"Two-hundred years... what did that involve?"

"Mostly timber work," Perry kept drawling. "We replaced the inner beams, which were infested with woodworm. After that, it was simply a matter of re-plastering the interior and installing a damp course. Pretty much standard stuff in old properties. Why?"

"I'm not sure if I should be telling you this..." James muttered.

He paused as if teetering on the brink of a decision. Even Elliot seemed guarded as he averted his gaze from Perry.

"Is something wrong, Dad?" Avalon pressed.

"I'm afraid so," James sighed. "I'm sorry, Avalon, but it's been brought to my attention our house requires some major work. I won't deny I'm a little worried."

"What sort of work?" Avalon blurted, seeing Rowena advance towards the sofa.

James closed his eyes. "Last month a hotel inspector visited. Mentioned one of the staircases was unsafe and suspected woodworm. He advised that if we wanted to keep the hotel open, we should consider a structural survey."

She felt his distress. Yet at the same time, her eyes were drawn to the man resting in the armchair, his expression almost tender.

"Mr Barton-Wells," he began, "if this is your only concern, I may be able to help you."

"Go on," James responded sadly.

"To begin with, I can recommend a surveyor. One who specialises in listed buildings and I'm assuming this house is listed?"

"Of course," James said with the first hint of a smile. "It was built in the late 1700's."

"And it's exquisite if I may say so," Rowena's voice chimed from the other side of the sofa.

Observing the ceiling, she seemed to savour the detail; the ornate cornice lining the top of the walls, a standard feature of houses from the past.

"Call me," Perry urged.

Gazing into James's eyes in a manner that seemed almost hypnotic, he fished into the top pocket of his blazer for a business card. James accepted the card without question, turning it in his fingers. From her position, Avalon observed the spidery black script which bore the name *'Peregrine Hampton, BA Hons, PPE.'*

Just the flick of an eyebrow revealed her father was impressed. But Perry had not finished, his persuasive voice echoing around the walls like a mantra.

"It would be my honour to assist you. You need have no further worries, Sir. It seems our meeting today may be the answer to your prayers."

"Thank you," James replied. No one failed to notice the break in his voice. "Let me have a think about this and maybe we can discuss it in a few days time... when I'm feeling a little better. I'm sorry, I don't know what came over me. I hope it didn't ruin your visit."

"Far from it," Rowena soothed, beckoning her husband. "It has been a pleasure to meet you, Mr Barton-Wells and I hope you recover soon."

Finally, she turned to Avalon, her aquamarine eyes softening.

Avalon smiled, pushing aside any lingering feelings of unease. Their words brought her father comfort and for that, she had felt indebted to them.

II

"That was the day we met them," Avalon added softly. "You've yet to hear about the restoration work... b-but maybe you should ask Dad to explain that bit."

Eleanor shook her head as she sagged against the sofa cushions. "Avalon, this sounds like some sort of deal with the devil!"

Her voice rang across the room and in precisely the same moment, she flinched to the sound of the door creaking. All three of them glanced up as James appeared in the doorway. He fixed them with his piercing stare before a smile of pure joy warmed his features.

"You're talking about me," he said accusingly. "I thought I could feel my ears burning. Eleanor, what an absolute pleasure. Do you know I've been dying to talk to you..."

With all conversation suspended, James reached the table within a couple of strides. Eleanor and Elijah leapt up. James took one look at Eleanor and drew her into an embrace.

"How are you, my dear," he mumbled, releasing her, "and how's little Elijah?"

Elijah extended his hand, which James shook lightly.

"Not so little any more, I see," he added with affection. "Now, what were you lot talking about before I came in? 'A deal with the devil?' You wouldn't per chance be talking about the *Hamptons* would you?"

"Dad, you need to tell Eleanor what's going on," Avalon said. "In fact, I'll leave you to it." Placing their empty cups onto the tray, she turned to Elijah. "I was going to have a look around the walled gardens to see if there were any vegetables that need picking. Why don't you come with me? Leave the adults to talk alone..."

"Okay," Elijah replied with undisguised delight and within seconds, they had flitted to the other side of the library, disappearing through the door.

"James," Eleanor sighed. She gazed at him through narrowed eyes, though traces of her smile lingered. "Where have you been? I didn't catch sight of you all autumn, not even when Eli and I were helping with the harvest!"

"I know and I'm sorry," James mumbled, lowering himself into the chair Avalon had vacated. "I would so much like to have seen you. I even went looking for you one day."

Eleanor stole another glance at his face. Shocked by his pallor, she could not fail to notice the extra lines threading their way across his forehead, nor the

15

spreading greyness of his hair. She knew he was getting old but what plagued her more than anything was his gauntness.

"Now what's this about your house?" she dared to ask him."Avalon's just told me about these people who visited, but she also mentioned a survey..."

He bowed his head. "Eleanor, these last few weeks have been more stressful than you could imagine. It started before the summer ended..." He broke off, looking at her in alarm. "I don't wish to bore you."

"Oh, James," Eleanor whispered. "Don't be so humble. I've got nothing better to do on a Sunday and Eli seems happy. Just tell me what's troubling you."

"I gather my daughter mentioned the restoration," he relented at last. "I should have said something *before* we met the Hamptons, but by the time they left, it was too late... She quizzed me endlessly. So did William. My greatest fear though, was the deterioration of the staircase might not be the only defect. It's woodworm, Eleanor, which causes irreparable damage and I wasn't sure how badly it had affected the rest of the house. Cracks are starting to appear in the outer walls too. Repairs that could run into thousands..."

Reaching into his trouser pocket, he pulled out his pipe but laid it to one side.

"It was Avalon who urged me to get in touch with the Hamptons again," he added. "It's just a survey, I thought, so what did I have to lose?"

Eleanor watched with trepidation as a tear glittered in his eye.

"How could I explain what was really troubling me? This is not just any old house but their ancestral home and I am passionate about saving it. All I hope is that when it is eventually passed down to them, the building will be in sound structural condition..."

He broke off, leaving Eleanor to digest this. Yet there was more, she could sense it, something that hung in the air like fog. Embracing the silence, she yearned to hear what he was struggling to say to her.

"It soon emerged it would require an *extensive* restoration," he shivered.

III

Yes, this was how it started, James reflected, oblivious to the turmoil yet to be unleashed.

Avalon was almost sixteen, which left him wondering where all that time had gone. It didn't seem so long ago, she had been the plump, gurgling baby who had brought such joy into his life. Leaving school at fifteen, a wealth of opportunity lay ahead of her. Yet she insisted her heart belonged at Westbourne House, more so in the absence of her mother..

The Barton-Wells were a small family, James born in 1923, the youngest of four children. Tragedy had struck when his two elder brothers were killed in World War II, leaving James and his sister, Nancy, the only survivors. Nancy regrettably, had never married. In fact, few members of his family lived to a ripe old age.

James's first wife, Lilian, had suffered an asthma attack, whilst walking the dogs, from which she had not survived. Crucified by heartbreak, he shut himself away, pouring his time and energy into his estate. He had always taken his home for granted but with his life left empty, found his true calling. Built in reddish-brown stone, its splendour lay in its symmetry, the East and West wings perfectly balanced beneath identical double pitched roofs. On one side of the house, the walls were cloaked in ivy and Virginia creeper. It enriched the stonework as the foliage changed colour with each season. Yet this very feature drew his eyes to the grounds.

With lawns scattered with trees, from ancient beeches and oaks, to the peaks of evergreens and cedars, James was hit with an impulse to make pathways and from this vision, arose another. His desire to create formal gardens would be a fitting tribute to Lilian who shared his passion for flowers. Her roses still bloomed outside the patio doors, but James had sculpted new flower beds - added box hedge borders and park benches - urns spilling over with ivy.

Next, he commissioned a Parterre to be built, where nothing added more beauty than an ornamental fountain with paths radiating out from the centre.

Yet his energy held no bounds. Pleased with his efforts, James turned his attention to the walled gardens, which had provided food throughout two world wars. With huge areas laid to waste, he divided the land into quarters. First came the orchards planted with fruit trees. Later came the rows of vegetables, fruit bushes and fragrant herbs, then finally he restored the glass houses.

Clematis flowers in soft blues and purples competed with sprawling jasmine and wild roses climbing up the walls. The area looked so idyllic, he was inspired to install more benches and lastly, a brick and flint Orangerie. Tall glass windows allowed the light to flood in, a place for residents and staff to enjoy a drink in the summer months.

As every corner of his estate flourished though, so arose opportunities for the villagers. Many were employed as gardeners, others drafted in at harvest time. James even took his enterprise a step further, renting squares of land for them to grow their own produce. With an unfailing, selfless desire to share all he possessed, everyone prospered - and from each harvest, a surplus of produce found its way to the market stalls of Rosebrook, a tradition that continued to this day.

But as James's sister, Nancy, reminded him, 'they needed to generate an income' and from those words sprung the idea of starting a hotel. With Westbourne House quickly gathering a reputation as an exclusive country house, it didn't seem long before it attracted paying guests.

James had reached his mid forties by the time he met the enchanting woman who became his second wife. Deemed one of the finest estates within reach of London, it was at one of their private balls, James had danced with the lovely Avril. Strikingly attractive with bronze ringlets tumbling around a face that resembled a statue, her easy going charm had endeared her to him.

Married in 1969, she had delighted him by announcing her pregnancy a year later; the promise of the heir he so desperately craved. The origin of her name too, was inspired by Avril, since she was captivated by the legend of King Arthur; a passion James indulged by reading to her in bed from one of the massive, illustrated volumes from his library.

'Avalon was the name of an island where King Arthur was taken to heal from the wounds of battle - a magical place where the powerful sword, Excalibur, was forged.'

James smiled, recalling the adorable infant he had held in his arms.

Avril on the other hand, was devoid of any maternal instincts. In her role as lady of Westbourne House, she considered such roles as childcare demeaning; more so when their son was born in 1972. So, as the years progressed, they drifted apart. Avril had never shared James's passion for Westbourne House, not even after the premature death of Nancy, aged fifty-nine.

By the time James approached his sixtieth birthday, both children were conveniently tucked away in private schools, releasing her to new avenues of freedom. This was the life she had always craved and it wasn't long before she was drawn into a number of illicit affairs.

She was living in the South of France now with a new husband. Yet James was surprised how little it upset him, having long recognised the rift that had breached their relationship.

He was thankful his children had chosen to stay with him, which brought him back to the dilemma he was suspended in now.

Reality blinked as he gazed at his surroundings; the light airy lounge where he sat frozen, his mind wandering down a labyrinth of past memories.

Yes, he cherished his children - even more so, given the threat overshadowing their home. With the echo of Avalon's words resonating, the lure of Peregrine Hampton's business card had been impossible to resist. He saw no reason not to trust him; a respectable man, whose only suggestion was to recommend a surveyor.

James thought about it long and hard, until curiosity won him over. He had made that call.

Never could he have imagined this might turn out to be the worst decision he would ever make in his life.

Chapter Three

I

Thinking about that survey drew a chill to James's bones. By the time it took place, the weather had turned colder; the threatening clouds and violent gusts a bitter contrast to that warm, balmy day in September. The colours in his trees had been resplendent too, a tapestry of plum reds and rich golds.

Yet the cutting winds had torn away the leaves without mercy.

On that same day, he had noticed several more streaks of white threaded into his light brown hair. But following the advice of his butler, he agreed to visit his doctor, Albany Price, who insisted on running some blood tests.

There were already more people in the grounds than usual. With the arrival of October, the trees in the orchard hung heavy with fruit, waiting to be picked by the locals. He wondered if Eleanor would be among them, a thought that brought a smile.

As for the surveyors - crisp and businesslike in pin-striped suits, one possessed a friendly face which immediately put him at ease. The other, more senior of the two was taller and of heavier build. With glossy silver hair and a smooth, pink face, he introduced himself as Edward Booth, proprietor of the company.

"With a property this size, our survey will require more than one visit," he began in a monotone. "You mentioned a problem with one of the staircases..."

James noticed it was the more amiable of the two, Jonathan Trussler, who undertook the detailed examination work. Digging into the delicate woodwork with a pointed awl to look for signs of infestation, he said very little at first.

But James was beginning to feel restless.

"So," he piped up, just as Jonathan extracted a large magnifying glass, "I gather you've done quite a lot of work for Mr Hampton. How long have you known him?"

"Perry and I go back a long way," Edward drawled.

James thought he detected a glint in those unsmiling cold eyes.

"Have you ever had a survey done?" He stretched out his arm as if to specify the whole house.

"Not in my lifetime," James blurted. "That's not to say I've neglected my home. We've had plenty of work done over the years, but nothing major."

"Hmm," Edward murmured, moving towards the corner of the first landing. "It could be you have left it a little late then."

James tensed, not liking the disdain creeping into his tone.

"I wouldn't normally discuss my findings until the survey was complete but..." he allowed his words to hover. "This staircase shows evidence of a wood-boring beetle infestation, likely deathwatch beetle. Damage to the balusters and stair treads. In some areas, the wood is very soft."

James allowed his eyes to travel down the stairs where the tapering grace of the vase shaped balusters struck him as being particularly beautiful; an open string formation punctuated at intervals by newel posts. The entire construction, built in dark wood, had retained its charm for over two centuries. Yet Edward's words delivered an unanticipated prick of anxiety.

"Regrettably, it has become lethally dangerous, Sir."

"Dangerous?" James echoed.

Ramming his hands into his trouser pockets, it was hard to stop them shaking.

But Edward had not finished. "The woodwork is starting to crumble. To be honest, I'm surprised one of your guests hasn't put their foot through it."

James followed his gaze, observing the carpet, which trailed down the path of the stairs.

"This staircase cannot be used," he added. "Say, one of your older guests grabbed the handrail for support... if one of those balusters shattered, the result could be disastrous!"

"Are you trying to scaremonger me?" James whispered in horror.

"Not at all," the other man replied, unfazed, "though I insist you close off this staircase."

"But it's the only access to the west wing," James spluttered, "and to the guest accommodation. If I close off this staircase, I might as well close the entire hotel!"

"I'm afraid that may well have to be the case," Edward sighed.

For several taut seconds he fell silent as he continued to scrawl out his notes. But eventually the tension broke; his words more damning than James could have predicted.

"You cannot jeopardise the safety of your guests. You could replace this staircase at a cost of about £2,000 but given its present condition, you might be sued ten times that amount if, say, a healthy adult suffered a fall. In the event of this happening to someone elderly though, the outcome could be fatal. That figure could run into millions! Do you really want to run the risk?"

"Of course not," James whispered, his voice drained of strength.

As if that nightmare had not been awful enough, worse was to come...

The first consultation left James depressed, relieved his children were not around to witness him in such a dark place. Behind the scenes however, the survey progressed with growing momentum. Yet a whole torturous week passed before their analysis made its way to his mailbox.

Observing the package from Booth Chartered Surveyors, James experienced a groundswell of trepidation. He took the decision for Avalon to be present with no further wish to exclude her. Settling into their lounge, he stole an admiring glance. In some ways, she took after her mother, her slightly square face reflecting the classic beauty of a sculpture; a shapely mouth with generous lips, a delicate nose in comparison. Although her big hazel eyes were identical to his own.

"Open it then," she chivvied him. "Let's see what it says..."

And as the hefty report thudded onto his desk, even he could not believe the defects unveiled in those next pages.

The first issue was the roof. Rainwater had seeped through the timbers, causing a penetrating dampness and decay. Given the recommendation *it would be more cost-effective to re-roof the whole property*, his heart started to pound.

Next came the condition of the ceilings; areas of bulging plaster and cracks. In some rooms, the wallpaper was peeling, a further indication of dampness.

"Oh my lord," James whispered, knuckles whitening.

"I did notice some rooms needed redecorating," Avalon said in a tiny voice.

Many windows would need replacing, one frame so badly warped, it had started to twist away from the wall. But as the building's architectural and historical secrets were revealed, James was faced with the deeper problem of woodworm in the main structure. He knew about the staircase but it didn't end there. Evidence of deathwatch beetle was noted to the timbers, where a creeping advance of damp and fungal decay had weakened them to the core.

James shuddered.

The suspended timber ground floors too, would need replacing and a damp course installed... James could not imagine it could get much worse until he reached the last page, describing the state of the outer stone walls. Serious action was needed to ward off a potential collapse. Yet by the time he read the survey's final recommendations and costs, he had turned giddy.

The cost to put his property in sound structural order lay in the region of a quarter of a million, more than double what he had feared.

"I don't think I can save it. I'm sorry, Avalon, we simply cannot afford it."

Tears filled his daughter's eyes. Her first response was to suggest a loan - but with the inevitable closure of the hotel, how would they meet the repayments without any income?

Clasping James's hands though, she was not one to cave in. "Listen, Dad, maybe we have to close the hotel but it won't be forever. The downstairs is usable. What about the restaurant? The ballroom? We could host some posh supper parties, maybe a dinner dance..."

"Ah, ever the optimistic one." James forced a smile. "It's the hotel accommodation that brings in the bulk of our income, but maybe we could consider auctioning some family heirlooms…"

This last resort tactic was all he could think of. Failing that, only one more possibility lingered; he would be forced to put Westbourne House on the market.

Drifting around in a daze, James resigned himself to accept the gravity of the situation. He faded in and out of sight like a ghost, leaving Elliot to handle his affairs. Most distressing was having to break the news to the staff. Westbourne House was to temporarily close; the inevitable consequence being that some employees would lose their jobs.

Given they could no longer honour their bookings, deposits too, had to be refunded.

James would have moved heaven and earth to avoid this scenario, but when a letter arrived from his doctor with an appointment to visit Rosebrook Hospital, he used the opportunity to do something positive. Visit the council and submit a planning application, so that work could commence on the staircase.

Guided by the council, as well as Edward Booth, James took the first tentative steps to get the ball rolling, enlisting a firm of restoration specialists he had recommended.

He also needed to make an inventory of their more valuable assets. There was even talk of including his two classic cars. His beautiful black jaguar nestled alongside an impressive 1955 Glacier Blue MGA which he had willed to William. James wrestled with his conscience. Could he honestly bring himself to consider the sale of his son's inheritance?

Before the horror of the survey had receded though, nothing surprised him more than an impromptu call from Perry Hampton.

"How did it go?" he asked benignly. "You know you can confide in me."

Fear coiled around him like a noose before he disclosed the worst details of the report.

"I'm sorry," Perry reacted. "Would you like to meet up and discuss it? Dinner at my house. Bring your children. I've got a son of my own. A change of scenery will do you good."

James felt a little humble to begin with, but it took Perry's fine skills of persuasion to talk him around. Thus, a date was set.

II

Avalon couldn't deny feeling nervous. Her father had only met the

Hamptons once and at a time when his untimely collapse made him vulnerable. Still, at least the dinner party took place on a weekend William was at home.

"You look smart, Dad!" he grinned. "When was the last time you went out?"

She felt an unexpected flood of joy. William had the most arresting eyes, almond shaped and heavy lidded. He was gifted with the type of looks that would break hearts, his golden-brown hair windswept. James had insisted they dress up, though, and she would never forget his smile. Her green velvet dress clung to her curves and with her hair pinned back with combs, she felt sophisticated and confident.

Little had she known at the time, she would be meeting Ben for the very first time.

Elliot had offered to be their chauffeur, so that James could enjoy a glass of wine or two; but with family resident in London, this was an ideal opportunity to visit them.

Perry's house lay in Pimlico, an area of London in the City of Westminster known for its grand garden squares and splendid Regency architecture. Three storeys high with chalky white walls, it nestled within a terrace, guarded by wrought iron railings. They noted the pillared entrance, just as the front door swung wide open.

And there, Perry and his wife loomed in front of them.

Yet all eyes were drawn to an aloof young man lounging by the pillars. His white blonde hair contrasted with his gothic clothing; black jeans, a T-shirt, which at first glimpse bore the image of a skull. William was quick to recognise it as the emblem of the band, 'Iron Maiden.'

"That must be their son," James whispered.

"A heavy metal fan, I guess," William muttered from the corner of his mouth.

Perry stepped forward first. Casting James a benign smile, he seized his hands.

"James!" he exclaimed, unable to disguise the delight in his voice. "How good to see you again and what a lovely evening for this time of year!"

His oozing, upper class voice brought a smile to Avalon's face.

Yes, the weather had indeed improved, with soft shafts of sunlight spilling through the gaps between the buildings.

Yet it didn't seem long before she was the centre of attention, then William.

"What a charming boy," Rowena breathed, "and you haven't met our son..." Turning to the fair haired youth who loitered unsmiling in the background, she beckoned him over. "Come now, Ben, don't be shy."

Finally, he stepped out of the shadows. His eyes flickered over them briefly before sliding back to Avalon. Tall and of slender build, he lacked the powerful presence of his father. Avalon felt her breath catch in her throat. There was

23

something almost angelic in his face. His high cheekbones were perfectly matched to a shapely mouth, but most mesmerising were his eyes; pale blue in colour, they stared intensely back at her, stirring a wave of empathy.

"Nice to meet you, Ben," she said. "My name is Avalon."

"A beautiful name," he drawled, his handshake light, barely noticeable. "Any connection to Camelot?"

"We have her mother to blame," James piped up. "She loved the stories of King Arthur."

Next they found themselves at the nucleus of a most stunning residence. Avalon unbuttoned her coat, which Ben immediately slipped from her shoulders to hang on a stand. Over the next few minutes though, no one could have been more attentive, coaxing James towards an enormous striped armchair that practically swallowed him.

"I'm so glad of an opportunity to introduce our son," Rowena whispered, as they hovered on the shore of the lounge. "It's nice for him to meet new people. He is so very shy, you see and lonely."

Pushing aside their tension, both children inched their way into the lounge to join their father. The glittering pendants of a chandelier accentuated the hardwood floor and carved furniture, yet Avalon found something a little harsh about it. Decorated in bold, aggressive colours, it lacked the tranquil ambience of their own lounge.

At first, they engaged in small talk; from life in the Capital to the state of Britain's economy, though there was little in the news to bring much cheer. Unemployment was high, especially among the young. A bout of rioting in the inner cities had culminated in the horrific killing of a police officer.

Avalon shifted in her chair, unnerved by the undercurrent of violence. Fortunately, Rowena lightened the conversation by mentioning the fashion designer, Laura Ashley, who had died recently. Furthermore, she was one of the more notable residents here in Pimlico. Such a subject brought a smile to Avalon's face as she revealed her love of Laura Ashley's style; the almost timeless fabrics which had given her so much inspiration and before she could stop herself, her thoughts were hedging towards the re-decoration of their own house.

James sipped his wine. "Only when the work's done, sweetheart," he said gently.

The room fell into a crushing silence. Rowena glanced at her son, hovering behind James and about to top up his wine glass.

"Ben," she muttered. "Why don't you show William and Avalon around? I'm sure they'd love to see the garden while there's some daylight left..."

It seemed hard to imagine that within a very short time, Avalon would be relating this story to Eleanor - but as Ben led them through the house and into the garden, she had been drawn into a world almost surreal. Mainly given to topiary, the arrangement of writhing shapes sculpted in the foliage left her spellbound... a moment her brother spotted the shed.

"What's in there?" he asked, pointing towards a white-pebbledash outbuilding. "Bikes?"

"Something a lot more exciting," Ben smirked. "Come and see..."

For there masked in shadow, crouched a motorbike like a magnificent caged beast; a torso of gleaming chrome and black leather.

"My pride and joy," he added with pleasure.

"A Harley Davidson?" William spluttered. "Oh, cool!"

Before Avalon had a chance to restrain him, he shot across to Ben's side. He stroked his palm over the leather seat, his face aglow, a smile that spread even wider as Ben proceeded to wheel it from the shed.

"C'mon, let's take it for a spin," he muttered.

With a hasty glance at his watch, Ben rolled it down the path and through a little garden gate, William darting along beside him, practically hopping with excitement. Then in a single flash of motion, he leapt onto the leather saddle. Staring at William, he patted the space behind him.

"Hop on then!" he said with a lop-sided smile.

"Just be careful," Avalon fussed, as her brother hauled himself up onto the pillion.

Her words were drowned as the engine exploded into life and without further delay, Ben surged down the backstreet with William riding pillion. But if Ben was expecting William to show fear, he would be disappointed. His mouth curved into a euphoric smile as he clung to the hand grip at the rear of his seat, his head tilting backwards to feel the breeze wash over his face.

For several minutes, she stood there, thinking the boy's father would go berserk. In fact she was just beginning to panic when the rumble of an engine signified their return.

"That was fantastic!" William shrieked as Ben pulled up to the gate.

"Jump down," Ben ordered him curtly, "let your sister have a ride!"

"Oh, I'm not sure," Avalon faltered, her lip caught between her teeth.

Ben extended his hand, his eyes penetrating, daring her to jump on.

"Go on, Sis!" William teased her. "Don't be a chicken!"

So she had allowed Ben to haul her up onto the saddle, conscious of the clingy material of her dress as it rode up her thighs. He revved the engine. She closed her eyes, gripping his waist as the powerful machine began to move. Yet as he followed the circuit at a gentler pace, her initial fear was replaced by exhilaration. She felt a smile of pleasure spread across her face - the rush of wind, which blew out the long tendrils of her hair as they sailed along the street.

"See!" Ben laughed, as they returned to the gate. "That wasn't so bad, was it?"

"I love it," William interrupted, rushing up to them. "Is it easy to ride?"

Before she knew it, he was giving a demonstration; encouraging William back onto the saddle, pointing out the controls. William turned the key in the ignition.

"Yeah, you get the idea," Ben said. "Gear pedal's down by your foot... One down and four up, clutch on the left, front brake on the right and this here is the throttle, see!"

He twisted the hand grip, causing the engine to rev a little... Yet neither expected William to release the clutch on the other side of the handlebars and surge down the street.

"Hey!" Ben cried out but his words were lost.

"Oh my God," Avalon whimpered. She touched his arm without thinking where every tensed muscle felt like iron. "I-I'm so sorry. My brother can be a real prat at times!"

"Shit," Ben whispered under his breath.

Avalon froze, unsure how to respond. Although it didn't seem that long before William reappeared. Turning the bike through an unused side street, he was grinning with delight.

Ben on the other hand, was not smiling. Catching his eye briefly, Avalon witnessed that first sinister flash.

"Brilliant," they heard William splutter. "It's great, Ben..."

"Let's get you back inside before you cause any more trouble," Avalon said coolly. "You're an idiot, William!"

Together they assisted Ben, wheeling the motorbike back into its shed before he calmly locked the door. He pulled a box of cigarettes from his pocket and lit one.

"You two go in," he said quietly. "I'll join you in a minute."

But Avalon was still watching him. There was a clipped quality to his voice that had not been there before. Throwing him a smile, she prayed her affection would win him over; relieved when he smiled back.

As both families settled in the dining room, Avalon felt on edge, noting the same brooding colours as before. With the room magnified by a ceiling-to-floor mirror, an array of candles flickered in heavy brass holders, the effect almost hypnotic.

Avalon and William looked at each other but neither said a word. They slid into chairs, one each side of their father, and by the time Ben showed up, he seemed visibly more relaxed.

James did not usually allow William to drink, his behaviour prone to being a little silly at the best of times. But as if detecting his unease, he slopped a drop of red wine into his glass, following it with a wink.

"Good boy!" Perry muttered, smiling wolfishly. "Never too young to appreciate a fine wine."

In swept the housekeeper. A young woman in her twenties, she did not talk or look at them as she flitted in and out of the kitchen to deliver each course; a starter of wild boar pate, followed by a succulent beef wellington. Finally, they were served individual desserts. Each strawberry soufflé stood in a perfect cylinder, dusted with sugar and surrounded by a red berry coulis. Avalon had seen Bryony create similar masterpieces.

But as they dipped their spoons into it, the conversation inevitably crept towards their home. Perry seemed keen to discuss the survey.

"We knew about the staircase," James said, "the reason I had the survey done, if you remember. But it was infested with deathwatch beetle."

"One of the greatest foibles of period property," Perry muttered darkly. "Have any other parts of your house been affected by this unfortunate anathema?"

"They detected a more serious presence in the main structure," James confessed. "The worst affected timbers will need to be cut out and replaced. It will be expensive..."

"Any other problems?" Perry grilled him, swirling the dark red wine in his glass. "You mentioned something about the roof."

James seemed to crumple under his stare.

"Why are you so interested in my house?" he asked him.

From the other side of the table, Rowena tilted her head to one side. "This is Perry's area of expertise," she answered, keeping her voice mellow.

"There's no need to feel uncomfortable, James," Perry added. "As Rowena says, I have extensive knowledge of old buildings and the way they deteriorate. The condition of your home, given its age, is nothing unusual, I assure you."

"How old is your house?" Ben's voice drifted from the other side of the table.

James offered him a sad smile. "Over two-hundred years, Ben. It was built in the late 1700's."

"I see," the boy nodded. "So how long has it been a hotel then?"

"Since the 1960s... It's something I started with my sister after our parents died. There weren't many of us left to uphold the tradition of running the estate, so when we opened some of the rooms to paying guests, it seemed a good way of utilising the space. It's a beautiful place, Ben, I'd like to invite you all over one day. But I'm not sure when that day will be. We've been forced to close the hotel, while work is in progress and this is what grieves me more than anything."

Ben stirred his coffee, his eyes never leaving him. "How long do you think the work will take then?" he kept probing. "You're having a new staircase built and a few beams replaced. You'll be up and running again in no time."

"There's more," James muttered, "as your father has just reminded me, it's been recommended we re-roof the whole property. Damp has affected the trusses, tie-beams. A fair few windows need replacing and the floors..." He betrayed a shiver. "I don't think we'll be *up and running again* for a very long time."

Quaffing his wine, he lowered his glass carefully back onto the table, his hand shaking. Yet still Ben's stare didn't waver, a frown narrowing his eyes. He shot his father a subtle glance.

William on the other hand, had finished his wine and feeling a little braver, helped himself to another drop.

"William!" Avalon snarled under her breath.

"Sorry," he croaked. "Can't you see how much this is upsetting him?"

"It's okay, Dad," Avalon said, covering his hand with her own. She stared across at Rowena. "You must appreciate this has come as a shock but we'll cope! I've already said to Dad there are other ways we can attract business. People visit to see the gardens. I've even thought about advertising our restaurant for fine dining."

"Really?" Perry drawled, his fingers steepled together on the table top. "Well, I admire your optimism, my dear and you know you can draw on my expertise..."

Resting back in his chair, he threw James a look of sympathy before locking eyes with his son.

"Listen Ben, how about you leave us grown-ups to discuss this alone." His voice had turned a little calculating. "This is heavy stuff. Young William looks as if he is about to fall asleep..."

"No, I'm not," William protested.

"Why don't you go off and have some fun?" Rowena interrupted. Her voice rose rapidly as if to stifle any argument. "You can play some music or watch a video... my son has a fine collection. We just want you to enjoy yourselves!"

Chapter Four

I

No sooner had they vanished when Perry sauntered over to the drinks cabinet. Selecting a vintage port, which he brought to the table, he also offered James a cigar.

"Better not," he said. "I've only recently given up. Doctor's orders, so don't tempt me."

"Well, I hope you'll join me in a glass of port," Perry persisted. "How *is* your health?"

"I'm still alive," James smiled back. "I had some blood tests at the hospital, but while I was in Rosebrook, I thought I'd visit the council for advice on planning permission."

"Hmm," Perry pondered. "Then let's hope it's nothing serious and as for planning permission; I wouldn't have thought you'd need it."

"It's a listed building, Perry, so I have to do things right. Especially if I want to get the ball rolling."

Sipping his port, he captured Rowena's eye. She offered him an enchanting smile.

"Have you chosen a building company?" she asked sweetly.

"I have," James nodded. "Your surveyor insisted on a firm by the name of 'Heritage Building and Restoration.'"

"Excellent," Perry said.

Hovering behind his chair, port decanter suspended, James did not see his expression.

"A reputable building firm is worth its weight in gold. Now, may I ask how much this is likely to cost you?"

James stiffened. "I'm not sure I want to tell you that."

Rowena allowed a light laugh to tinkle into the room. "Why ever not? Come on, James, don't be shy. You're among friends, at least, I'd like to think so."

James loosened his tie, his face turning hot. "Seems a little vulgar to bring up the subject of money," he muttered in defence.

"Is it more than a quarter of a million?" Perry pressed.

"It *is* a quarter of a million..." he spluttered. "How did you guess?"

"I know the cost of restoring old buildings," Perry smirked, lowering himself into the chair next to him. "Given the size of your property, I suspect it's worth somewhere in the region of one and a half million, especially in the

29

area it's located. Am I right?"

"I've never taken much interest in property prices," James snorted, taking another sip of port. "I've had no reason to until now. I always imagined I would live at Westbourne House until the day I died and my children would inherit it. But that all depends on whether we can save it."

"And if you can't?" Rowena inquired.

James shrugged, desperate to avoid the inevitable.

"I think what my wife is asking," Perry added, "is that in the event that you couldn't meet the cost of the restoration, would you consider putting it on the market?"

James gave a shrewd nod. "I see... That being the case, am I assuming you would be an interested party?"

A mortifying silence ensued. Perry cleared his throat.

"Listen, James. If the worst came to the worst, yes, we'd be interested. Rowena and I think your house is exquisite... But that is *not* the reason we invited you here. What we've been wondering is if there was another way we could help you..."

"Why?" James faltered. "I hardly know you. What's your incentive?"

Perry exhaled a sigh, topping up their glasses. "I am a man of property. Old buildings fascinate me, they are the very fabric that distinguishes our fine country and if we cannot save a beautiful historic house such as yours, I fear the character of Britain may change."

"But you can't be doing this out of altruism..." James argued.

"I have a proposition," Perry butted in. "One that enables you to *keep* your home without worrying about the restoration costs. Would you like to hear it?"

James sagged in his chair, wary of mounting pressure from both sides.

"So, what is your plan?" He forced a smile.

Perry's face however, remained sombre.

"The idea came to me shortly after our visit. What I saw that day was a remarkable property whose potential is yet to be realised. Yes, it has the reputation of being a very nice hotel. But what Rowena and I were trying to work out was why you've never thought of tapping into the corporate market. Your property lies within an easily commutable distance from London."

Already James had started to frown. "Where is all this leading?"

"We're wondering if you'd consider a business partnership," Perry disclosed. "Say, we relaunch your establishment as a corporate venue... and invest the funds for its restoration *in full*."

James could hardly take it in. Gulping another mouthful of port, he felt quite drunk now.

"Your daughter mentioned the fine dining angle," Rowena intervened, "and it is not just the wealthier classes of society who appreciate nouvelle cuisine!

This is a flourishing market, especially in London. Some restaurants charge up to £100 a head for a unique dining experience."

James stared dazedly back. Her face swam like a mirage yet as the words sunk in, he was beginning to realise, albeit begrudgingly, that what they were proposing made sense.

"We take care of the business side," Perry smiled. "All you need to do is look after the house and the estate."

"But what's in it for you?" James whispered. "I'm sorry, but I have to know where your motivation lies, Perry."

"Oh, it's quite simple," Perry replied, his tone as soft and persuasive as on the day James had met him. "If I am staking an investment in your property, all I ask for in return is a share of the profits. You get to keep your home. We embark on a lucrative new business. I have to say the idea excites me, do you not feel the same way?"

His pale eyes bore into him with an intensity James had never seen. He felt a shiver roll over him, struck with a feeling he was being drawn into a Faustian pact.

"You're really serious about this, aren't you?" he whispered. "My only concern is the impact this will have on our lives, especially the children."

"I see no reason why we cannot work out a solution that is amicable for both parties," Perry drawled, inclining his head.

James found himself nodding as the idea infused. No words could express how much he loved his home and he was not quite ready to give up on it. Yet if there was a way he could remain there, without making his family bankrupt... He glanced at Perry.

"We have plenty of time to discuss the finer details," he concluded, "draw up a legal contract. Maybe the next step would be to talk to a solicitor. Will you consider it?"

"Of course," James muttered. Yet he still felt as if he was flailing in deep water.

II

Hidden away on the top floor, Avalon and William were blissfully unaware of the fate of their house being negotiated around the dining table. Avalon looked anxious - perhaps wondering how her father would cope in the presence of Perry Hampton.

Ben on the other hand, had drawn them into his own personal lair, knowing all too well of his father's predatory nature. Intent on getting to know them better, it was up to him to entertain them; though given their expressions, they looked as if they had been spirited into another world.

Maybe they had never seen anything quite like his living quarters; a spacious area where the entire attic had been converted into a suite. There was something futuristic about the decor; the walls a cool slate grey, the blinds reflecting the light; it displayed a style so typical of the 80's. With a preference for black ash, a desk dominated one corner, along with a swivel chair in black leather, an extendable pewter desk light casting a puddle of white light across the floor boards.

Avalon seemed restless, drawn to the Athena prints, which provided the only splash of colour in the room. His eyes fell upon her delicate features.

"I take it your father's quite upset about the house."

"I'm afraid so," she replied, turning to him. "Sounds like it's in a terrible state."

"Don't worry," Ben responded, his tone light. "My dad will give him all the help he needs."

Avalon intrigued him, especially as she became more animated. Unable to resist studying her, he inhaled her perfume as her glossy curls swung around her neck.

"So, what about *your* Dad, Ben? I must confess, he seems a little forceful. Did he encourage you to follow in his footsteps?"

"Not entirely," Ben faltered. "You're right though, he is very ambitious but he only wants what's best for me..." He lowered his eyes.

Forced to bite back what he really thought of his father, he felt the touch of a shiver.

Perry was more than forceful. He was a brute.

Ben tried hard not to think about his frequent outbursts. Not only had they blighted his childhood but it seemed evident some of that aggression would rub off on him.

Barely eight years old, he had been expelled from prep school for bullying another pupil... He knew his personality was flawed. It took one glance at the questioning young faces in front of him to realise he had to change the subject fast.

So he had switched his attention to the one asset he knew would fascinate them; his enviable collection of Hi-Fi equipment.

"Forget about the adults!" he announced, springing to his feet. "It's time we put some music on. Come and see my sound system."

William seemed particularly curious as he pointed to his impressive stacking system. Running his hand over a sleek, silver box perched on top, he pressed a button - out slid a tray.

"Wow!" William breathed. "A compact disc player?"

"A Phillips," Ben boasted. "One of the first to come out. What music do you like?"

This question inevitably led to their polarity in music preferences.

Avalon preferred music from the early 80s, Depeche Mode and The Eurythmics...

William on the other hand, had expressed his passion for the transgender artist, Divine.

Ben sneered. "I prefer music with more balls, like rock and heavy metal. The only electronic stuff I like is Vangelis. Or maybe Jean Michel-Jarre."

Avalon watched mesmerised, as he plucked out a CD. But there was no doubt they were blown away by the sound, each guitar note resonating with crystal clear precision.

As he sampled more music, time seemed to pass faster - and when they finally settled down to the haunting notes of 'Tubular Bells,' the subject moved on to films.

He listened with pleasure as Avalon voiced her love of fantasy; films like 'Lady Hawke'.

"Must be something to do with your name," Ben murmured.

Fighting the urge to stroke her smooth skin, he was lost in his secret thoughts.

Avalon was a stunner and if his father really did stake some sort of partnership deal with James...

Ben knew that before the evening ended, he would definitely ask her out for a date.

"What do you do for a living?" she asked, distracting him from his daydream.

"I've just completed a degree in financial management," he said proudly, "I want to train as a stockbroker. What about you?"

Avalon shrugged. "I just love running the hotel," she finished with a sad smile. "Our family is very close. I'm never going to abandon Dad, even if our house can't be saved."

III

James felt dizzy, struggling to imagine that Perry was offering to bankroll the entire restoration.

Perry meanwhile, seemed unfazed. Empowered by his enthusiasm, he was convinced they could make it work - hankering to learn about Aldwyck, a location where property prices could skyrocket - a village ripe for development.

Such a concept left James uneasy. The village already served the needs of the community with a large country pub, a beautiful church and its parade of pretty shops. He had no wish to relay that the locals were deeply suspicious of development for fear it would ruin its character.

"By the way," Perry remarked, "the day we visited your house, I couldn't help but notice a bunch of new age travellers parked in that field opposite your gates!"

"Yes, that's right," James nodded.

Picturing the field with its medley of vehicles, Eleanor's caravan among them, he was intrigued to wonder where this was leading.

"Don't you think those people are a blight on society?" Perry growled. "Damned hippies... and in a beautiful village like Aldwyck! Surely the locals are up in arms about it."

"Well, some are," James admitted, disturbed by the venom creeping into his tone.

"So what are they doing about it?" Perry demanded.

"To be honest," James said, "most long standing residents are not bothered. They are camped on the far edge of the village, so few people even notice them and those who do are the newer residents; people who have paid a high price for their homes and consider it their duty to drive out anyone who doesn't quite fit in."

"Quite right too!" Perry continued to rant. "I have to agree with them, James!"

"But they're not doing any harm," James protested. "Why are people offended by the sight of a few folk who choose to lead a slightly alternative lifestyle?"

"They're a nuisance," Perry said nastily, puffing on his cigar. "What if more turn up? They'll have that whole field converted into a hippie commune before you know it!"

"No, they won't," James argued. "Most only stop for a couple of weeks and move on. In fact, there is only one permanent resident, a lovely young woman. She has lived in our village for over ten years and is very much accepted as one of us now..."

"Really?" Perry sneered, his eyes turning cold. "Well, I'm sorry to disagree, James, but I don't really approve of gypsies. This is not a lifestyle that should be encouraged, especially in this day and age. I don't understand why the landowner hasn't evicted her."

"I own that land," James smiled.

Perry almost dropped his cigar. Turning to James, his eyes narrowed, betraying his prejudice; *splinters of ice*, James thought as he stared dazedly back at him.

"It used to be a field where people kept ponies, but the couple who live in the farmhouse have no interest in horses, so it stands empty. It's just one caravan, Perry, why does it bother you?"

"People take liberties," Perry said. "Some of us work bloody hard to aspire to a better standard of living. Why should others help themselves and live off the land for nothing?"

"Nonsense!" James laughed. "She does work - and besides, I offered to help her! When Eleanor arrived from London, she was being intimidated. She needed a new home, a place where she and her baby son would be safe!"

"She's got a child?" Rowena breathed.

"Yes, she has," James replied, a little taken aback by their disdain.

Perry had turned strangely silent, the cigar held loosely in his fingers. A curl of smoke spiralled upwards as he appeared to lapse into a daydream.

What James hadn't realised was the impact those words might strike, clueless to what he was thinking.

His gaze slid back to James. "You say she came from London?"

"Yes," James sighed.

The sound of feet thundering downstairs tugged them out of that tense conversation.

As James raised his head, he was delighted to see the return of his children, Ben trailing along in their wake.

He didn't see the way Rowena and Perry glanced at each other, nor that Perry had turned a little pale. James's eyes were on his son. Eyelids drooping, violet shadows gathered in the hollows. But with time approaching 11.00, Elliot was due to collect them.

"Well, we'd best make a move," he said, staggering out of his seat. "This has been a most enlightening evening... and I'll think about what we've discussed, I promise."

"Thanks for a lovely meal," Avalon added warmly, clasping Rowena's hands. "I hope we can return the favour and invite you back some time."

"It would be our pleasure, Avalon," Perry murmured. "I look forward to our reunion."

Stepping out into the dark street, just as Elliot was pulling into the curb, they had no idea this was about to be a turning point in their lives.

IV

By the time his story drew to a close, James was staring at Eleanor intently.
He had purposefully omitted to mention that final part of the conversation.
"Oh, James!" she gasped, covering her mouth with her hand.

"The trouble is," he added, "much of our wealth is tied up in this house and it's falling apart! The only choices left are to take out some exorbitant loan or put it on the market, which is why I am considering this third option."

"I see," Eleanor pondered, "but how is the business partnership going to

35

work? You love running the hotel! Are you sure this isn't just some thinly veiled take over bid?"

"Ah, always the suspicious one," James smiled, pulling his hip flask from the pocket of his tweed jacket.

"Well, aren't you suspicious?" she challenged him.

"A little," James shrugged, "but I have to be pragmatic. Given the choice, I don't want to sell my home, especially if there's a chance my children can still inherit it. If the only way to hang onto Westbourne House is to allow these Hamptons a degree of business control, then it's not a bad deal is it? They might have some really sound ideas!"

"But what's in it for them?" Eleanor pressed. "Do they expect a lion's share of the profits?"

"Well, I suppose so," James agreed, "after all - if they're about to stump up a quarter of a million to save my home, it would certainly elevate them to the status of shareholders..."

"A quarter of a million?" Eleanor breathed.

"I'm afraid so," James said. "But this is what it costs to restore an old building inside and out. It's a listed building. Everything has to be built like for like. That staircase alone will cost three grand! So now do you see my dilemma? This partnership might be my only option."

"But how long have you known these people?" Eleanor whispered. "How can you be sure they're trustworthy?"

"Oh, Eleanor," James sighed. He took a sip of brandy. "If it's any consolation, they are not short of money. This man is a successful property developer. They live in a beautiful house, situated in one of the most exclusive parts of London and I assure you, he is absolutely minted! That aside, I would never commit to any deal until a proper legal agreement was drawn up."

"Well, thank God," Eleanor relented, drooping back into her seat. "Look, I know it's none of my business but shouldn't you at least check this man out? Find out if anyone else has had dealings with him. Don't just take a giant leap of faith."

"Why do you distrust people?" James said gently.

"I have my reasons," she muttered.

Eleanor closed her eyes, rocked by another memory; a day when Jake had been alive. Except she was no longer thinking about the criminal community.

She had only just learned of her inheritance and a professional looking man had pledged to help them. *Councillor Robin Whaley.*

How could they have known he would betray them to the very men who were after Jake?

"Let's just say some people are not always who they seem," she finished.

"I'd be cautious of anyone who seemed a little too eager to help. If I were you I'd do a bit of digging."

"Fair enough," James smiled and sneaking another sip from his flask, he offered it to Eleanor. She shook her head. "You're frowning again."

"Just thinking about what you said about the staircase," she mused. "Three grand seems a hell of a lot. It's only wood, surely..."

"Yes, but every baluster has to be individually shaped with a lathe," James argued. "The expense is in the labour, not to mention the assembly."

"I know someone who might be able to help you," she blurted before she could stop herself. Her smile brightened. "A friend of mine lives in Rosebrook - a highly skilled builder and he's passionate about architecture! The company who employed him went bust, but he's started up on his own. He'd be fascinated by all this. In fact, why don't you let me talk to him?"

James seemed delighted. "Alright," he responded, "although I can't put the Hamptons off just yet. They're due to come over to lunch next week and take a tour of the house. But I'd be more than willing to get a second opinion."

By the time they tore themselves away from Westbourne House, the air had turned noticeably colder. Layers of cloud crawled ominously across the sky, dulling the landscape.

Elijah rammed his head down between his shoulders. Considering what Avalon had said, he was gripped by a chill that had nothing to do with the plunging air temperature.

"Avalon told me about the house," he mumbled, "some people who say they're gonna pay for it all..."

"I know, James told me," Eleanor said. "Something doesn't feel right and this is the reason I want to talk to Charlie."

Elijah gaped at his mother.

"Do you think Charlie'll be able to help?"

Eleanor nodded.

It had been a very long time since they had hooked up with them, never able to dispel the vision of Margaret's frightened face. How could he forget that day last winter? A day they had skated across the ice on the frozen green; a day she had divulged her worst fears and he had divulged his... both children drawn to the consensus *there were bad people in the world,* which had ultimately reminded him of his own father. He had never known how he died.

"Charlie understands historic buildings," Eleanor added.

Elijah blinked, snapped out of his reverie.

At least Charlie represented safety, a man who radiated goodness and quite possibly the only man they could confide in.

Chapter Five

A day later, Eleanor was still thinking about Charlie. *Charlie who had lost his adorable wife eight months ago; Charlie who lived in a rented house in Rosebrook with his two children, struggling to make ends meet as they limped from one crisis to another.*

At least he seemed to be adjusting. It had been a while since Anna's funeral, yet there were still times when the grief of losing her swept over him in waves. Charlie had thrown himself remorselessly into his work, where the determination to succeed in his own business was the driving force that kept him going. But with James's momentous story thundering in her ears, Eleanor was desperate to get in touch with him.

"How are things?" she smiled

They had settled around a table in one of the larger pubs of Rosebrook. Enlarged with a beautiful conservatory lounge, the wall to wall windows allowed a river of sunlight to pour in, warming the interior. Eleanor had finished her morning shift as a nurse at Rosebrook Hospital. Charlie had been over to the council to follow up his latest planning application.

"Not too bad," he shrugged. "Andrew's at college, which has left me out on a limb. I was hoping there'd be a decision regarding this new job... but other than that, life ticks on."

He looked less haggard these days, though an enduring sadness prevailed; those doleful dark eyes that had never quite recaptured their sparkle.

"So what's the latest project?" she dared to ask. "Have you got much work on?"

"Not as much as I'd hoped," Charlie sighed, swilling the beer in his glass to disperse the froth. "That's the trouble with being self-employed; business is up and down. This latest job's for a couple looking to convert their garage into a Granny flat. Why do you ask?"

"We went to Westbourne House yesterday," Eleanor mused. "Do you know it's been ages since I visited the Barton-Wells family. Do you remember me telling you about them?"

"Of course," Charlie said, his gaze meeting hers. "How was your visit?"

"Interesting," Eleanor whispered. "The house is in need of major restoration work, which is why I wanted to talk to you... James could do with some advice."

At last a smile broke through the gloom in his expression. "Well, that's very sweet of you, Eleanor. I'd be delighted to talk to him. A substantial part of my degree was focussed on older buildings."

"James had a survey done," she added darkly. "He gave me the impression the whole house was falling apart! Though I couldn't really see much wrong with it."

"Hmm, does this mean the inner structure's deteriorating?" Charlie pondered. "Not uncommon in period properties. Unfortunately, the remedial work can be very expensive."

"That's what James said," Eleanor sighed. "But he can't afford it. He's very short of cash. Worse, he seems to have aged terribly since I last saw him. But there's something else..."

"Go on," Charlie encouraged her.

"Don't let on I told you this, as it's confidential. He's thinking about entering into a partnership with someone, but at a price. If James allows them to take over the management of his hotel, they're going to bankroll the whole project."

Charlie's first reaction was not how she expected. "It doesn't sound like a bad deal," he shrugged. "He should consider himself lucky to be offered such a bail out package."

"That's not quite how I saw it," Eleanor pondered. "I mean, we're talking six figures. It seems like a considerable amount of money, given he hardly knows them! I warned him not to enter into any partnership until he'd checked them out first."

"Did he mention any names?" Charlie probed, draining his beer.

"Yes," Eleanor divulged. "A successful property developer from London. Charlie, have you ever come across the name *Hampton?*"

Charlie lowered his glass slowly to the table.

"Hampton," he whispered. Suddenly his eyes looked haunted beneath their thick brows, as if a storm of emotions was brewing.

"Well, have you?" she frowned.

The expression on his face shifted from shock to loathing. "Eleanor, if this is who I think it is. it's the man who bankrupted Dick's company," he shivered.

Charlie pressed his eyes shut, the memories pouring in fast.
Yes, he knew the name Hampton. How could he forget?
"So when did you meet him?" Eleanor's voice rose.

"About a year ago," he murmured. "It marked the beginning of all our troubles..."

Yes, there was no denying it. The first occasion he'd bumped into Perry Hampton had turned into a dreadful day. Yet nothing could compare to the harrowing chain of events in the aftermath. He could hardly bear to think about it; that ominous confrontation - the descent into poverty that would forever change their lives. Charlie shook his head, unsure where to begin.

"What happened, Charlie?" Eleanor pressed him. "I need to know. Not for my sake, but for James. Can you remember?"

"Oh yes," Charlie sighed.

Hampton.

And with no further hesitation, he decided to tell her.

I
October 1984

Everything was trundling along just fine until that day.

Charlie had not only spent a lifetime working in the building trade, but was one of the most efficient foremen Oakwood Construction had employed.

Buildings had always fascinated him; an interest that inspired him to take an Open University degree in architecture. He was not yet fully qualified, but his employers held him in high enough esteem to embrace his designs for a housing project commissioned by the illustrious property developer, Peregrine Hampton.

A typical day working on site, he had dreamed of the glittering future ahead of him. Thinking about his wife, Anna, he guessed she would be picking up their nine-year-old daughter. On any other day, they would have returned home; a basic three bedroom rented house with pebble dash walls painted an insipid mud brown. Except Margaret had been dying to take a peek at the show home, mesmerised by his intricate line drawings.

They had lived in Bromley for nearly five years, a pleasant suburban district of south east London. But as the area became more prosperous, so the more exclusive housing estates were developed, such as the one Charlie was working on then.

The site was distinguishable by a surround of billboards, the aggressive black and purple logo of *Peregrine Hampton Property* emblazoned above an artist's impression. There, in the centre of a vast field, teetered the first stage of the development, and flaunting itself majestically stood the show home; a soaring white building, sliced through with exposed beams.

Charlie felt a shiver of excitement.

From the outer edge of the field, he had spotted their orange Volvo. Anna had been stepping from the car with Margaret, who immediately raced across the field. Her little face could be seen peering through the chain link fence, cheeks flushed pink from the exertion of running, her dark blonde hair hanging limply. Her brown eyes shone like buttons.

"So, here we are," Anna smiled. "Is Andrew around?"

Andrew was their son. At sixteen, he had opted to leave school and following in his father's footsteps, was overjoyed to have been taken on as an apprentice.

"He's up there on the scaffolding, doing some brick laying," Charlie answered.

He stole a furtive glance around the site, then beckoned them to follow him.

As they crept towards the show home, he heard Anna gasp. Not only did the house look exquisite but featured a Georgian pillared entrance and beautiful bay windows. Best of all was the circular tower built on one side. It concealed a spiral staircase, the one feature Margaret was most curious to see. Charlie unlocked the door.

"Can I go in?" Margaret whispered.

"Okay," Charlie indulged her, "but wipe your feet!"

She paused on the doormat, grinning. Silky festoon blinds puffed around the leaded bay windows, whilst barely visible through a door on the left, she saw the staircase. Its helical path coiled right up to the top floor.

"Wow!" she breathed, running towards it. Grasping the hand rail, she ducked inside the space to stare through the treads. "It's fantastic!"

"Okay, love, can you come out now," Charlie called from the doorway. "We don't want to get into trouble..."

"It's great, Dad!" she lisped, backing away from the staircase. "If you ever build us a house, I want it to have a spiral staircase just like this one!"

Her comment sounded so innocent, Charlie reflected. *If only the bosses hadn't arrived.*

Such a situation drew Andrew to the same spot, a boy who looked very much like him.

"Dad, the gaffer's here and so is Mr Hampton!"

A stab of anxiety jolted him. This property developer was not only rumoured to be ruthless, but was fuelled by ambition, hankering to get these properties built and quickly.

"I've got to go, love," he muttered. "Andrew, be a mate and smuggle them out, preferably without being seen. I'll see you at home. One of the lads can drop us off."

"It's okay, I'll wait," Anna insisted.

Without another word, Charlie spun on his heel and strode back towards the hub of the building site. Shooting a glance over his shoulder, he was relieved to see his son steering them cautiously around the back of the show home. A footpath ran along the edge of the field, overlooking the lovely Kent countryside. Dense woods hovered close by, a brook trickling along the boundary, where several weeping willows bowed their branches over the banks.

Yet the men had been drawing closer... Charlie clocked three pairs of smartly shod feet picking their way across the track.

41

"Good afternoon, Sirs," he greeted them.

Mr Hampton fired a glare in his direction but icily ignored him. Charlie felt deflated. All he could hear were figures spilling from the man's lips. *But of course, Mr Hampton had no interest in the likes of him.* Regarded as no more than 'cogs' in a larger mechanism of profit-making, the invisible workforce behind this project would generate him more than a million.

With a sigh, Charlie turned away. Yet he had only just returned to the half-built houses when a movement caught his attention. He could still see his daughter, skipping ahead of Anna, but from another direction he saw the menacing shape of a motorbike. It seemed to materialise out of nowhere, ridden by some insane character clad in black leather.

Charlie wasted no time. Pelting across the field, he heard the motorcyclist rev the engine. Yet it was hurtling towards Margaret. He heard Anna scream.

"Look out!" Charlie roared, throwing himself into the path of his wife and daughter.

As they stood there paralysed, the powerful Harley-Davidson skidded to a halt, showering him with mud. Disaster had been averted in a second. Grabbing Margaret's hands, he swung her out of the way then turned and glared at the driver. He was removing his helmet. Young, possibly in his twenties, he shook out his fair hair, inclining his head to get a better look at him. His intensely staring blue eyes conveyed an almost crazed expression.

"What the hell do you think you're playing at?" Charlie bellowed. "You bloody hooligan! You could have killed her!"

The youth looked surprised, offering him an apologetic lop-sided smile.

"She's okay, though, isn't she?" he said in a drawling voice. "I am *so* sorry. I thought this was a private field. Is my father here by the way? Oh, Mr Hampton, that is."

The words drained the blood from Charlie's face. Gathering his panic-stricken daughter into his arms, he felt a rage frothing, which he was having great difficulty suppressing. From the corner of his eye he glanced at Anna. She looked petrified - the young man hovering as if sensing his superiority - and then the dark suited figure of a man striding up to them.

"Hello, Father," the motorcyclist greeted him coolly.

"Ben!" Hampton replied before pinning his gaze upon the distraught family. "What the hell is going on? Just who do you think you are, Sir, rounding on my son like that?"

"I'm sorry," Charlie spluttered, "I didn't realise he was your son, but he shouldn't be racing around on a motorbike like that - not when there's children around."

"Children should not be playing around a building site," Perry retorted. His eyes cut into him like silver blades. "And this is private land."

Charlie clammed up. This wasn't his direct boss but someone far more powerful. At the discretion of such men, the company could either keep someone employed on a project or remove them from it. With Margaret crying softly, he had slid her into Anna's waiting arms, fearful he was about to lose his job.

"My daughter only wanted to see the spiral staircase," he added gently.

"Really?" Perry sneered. "Are you not aware of the dangers that exist around construction sites?"

"Of course..." Charlie started to say but the other man cut him off with a raised palm.

"Second, is it normal practice to entertain family members during working hours?" He gave a deliberate pause - long enough for Charlie to feel the force of his stare. "What's your name?" he added in a low, dangerous tone.

"Charles Bailey," he answered boldly. He was fighting to retain his composure. Yet something about the smug look on the face of his son enraged him.

"Charles Bailey, eh?" Perry echoed, the blades of his eyes cutting deeper. "Tell me, would you happen to be the architect responsible for the design of my new homes?"

"Yes, that's correct," Charlie snapped.

As Perry Hampton surveyed him, he saw a cunning look; one that suggested he enjoyed the feeling of power, the fate of his entire family rolling around in his palm like a marble.

"Well, well," he drawled. "It's good to put a face to a name. Luckily, with your architectural skills you surpass yourself! Perhaps we should put this little misunderstanding behind us for now." He turned to his son. "And Benjamin, I must implore you to be more careful. Have I not warned you that you ride that motorbike of yours too damned fast?"

Charlie felt the tension drain from every muscle. Words failed him but what could he say? He felt no gratitude towards this man. He may not have fired him, yet nothing could repel the horror that his reckless son had almost mown his daughter down.

"I am glad you like my designs," he said, gazing into the man's eyes, "and I hope the standard of building work meets your approval. But please be rest assured, I will keep my family well away from now on..." He threw another glance at Ben. "As you say, one cannot ignore the dangers that exist around construction sites."

Charlie shuddered at the memory. Sneaking upstairs some time later, he had finally voiced his anger. He remembered how the kids had collapsed in front of the TV to watch Grange Hill; how Anna had caught his eye, lifting a half bottle

43

of white wine from the fridge.

Her slow, seductive smile followed him. *"Go up and have a shower, Charlie. You're covered in dust and muck. I'll join you in a moment..."*

How could he ignore the loving undertones tucked into her voice?

She had never been a raving beauty in the classical sense yet he found her adorable. A youthful pink flush bloomed in her cheeks, her snub nose cute and appealing. What Charlie had loved more than anything was her mouth, her sweet, plump lips, quick to smile and a pleasure to kiss. Savouring her face, he ran his fingers through her sleek hair; it gleamed like polished brass in the light of a table lamp.

"Oh, this is better," he murmured into her neck, "so much better. Sod Oakland Construction and screw Peregrine Hampton! I'll tell you what, sweetheart, as soon as this project's over, I want to move on..."

He had meant it too! Their lives had never been easy. Anna had endured an ordeal of failed pregnancies after Andrew was born and as one miscarriage followed another, she had withdrawn into a shell of grief. At one time, she had almost given up on the idea of another child, for the next pregnancy had resulted in a still-birth.

But then came the *Winter of Discontent*; the nation ravaged by strikes and power cuts. Long evenings spent in candlelight and too many early nights had resulted in a fifth pregnancy. Just thank God she had survived full term, overjoyed to deliver a gorgeous baby daughter.

All he could promise was their lives would get better; that the only reason that vile man hadn't sacked him was because he needed him. Charlie would have no problem getting another job with his skills, but where would Peregrine Hampton find himself another architect at short notice, not to mention a damn good foreman?

****

"God, Charlie," Eleanor breathed. "You're starting to worry me."

She was about to replenish their drinks. Though from what Charlie had described so far, this Hampton character sounded utterly heartless... and this was the property developer James was about to go into partnership with?

"It's the same man, isn't it?" he probed, picking up her stream of thought.

"Maybe," Eleanor said. "You mentioned *the son*. The clue is in the motorbike and you said his name was Ben."

A shimmy of cold crept over her. This was surely the same young man Avalon was dating, the echo of her words still resonating... *there was this flash in his eyes, something scary.*

"So how did he make your boss bankrupt?" she pressed.

44

"You're going to wish you'd never asked," Charlie smiled sadly back. "Fancy a top up?"

II
November 1984

Regrettably, no one could have predicted that Perry Hampton's splendid new development might be doomed from the start. Three weeks on from that harrowing day, Charlie had received a phone message, urging him to call in at head office. He had no idea why he was being summoned, but the first sight of his MD, Dick Harrison, should have warned him. He would never forget the way he had slouched in the light of the window, face dewy with perspiration. He was accompanied by Christopher Farrin, his assistant manager. Then the terrible news unfolded.

Despite the underlying requirements for a housing scheme to go ahead, Hampton had failed to follow the procedures. Work had begun before the planning consultancy had reached completion; and while some officials had verbally agreed to the development, the land had not been thoroughly assessed.

"A structural engineer was drafted in," Christopher said gravely. "Unfortunately, their report revealed the site to be unsuitable for a development of this scale. It's too close to the river, which is a tributary of the Thames. Charlie, these houses are being built on a flood plain."

He stared at them in disbelief. Yet nothing brought more horror than the announcement that every one of those houses had to be demolished.

"What about the show home?" he protested. "Can't the land accommodate even one house?"

Christopher shook his head. "It's no use, Charlie. Where land is prone to flooding, the underground movement of water will cause the foundations to sink. We have no choice."

Forced to bite back his anger, Charlie was tempted to add that it was far more likely Hampton had slipped some planning officer a back hander to get the nod, then recklessly gone ahead anyway. He should be liable to prosecution, surely?

"I'm afraid I no longer have the energy to take on someone like Peregrine Hampton," Dick whimpered, "which brings me to the worst news of all..."

This project might have been one of their more profitable ventures, but had taken priority over the smaller jobs. Perhaps it was down to Dick's poor management that the company finances were put at risk. Yet it was the untimely termination of Hampton's scheme that had ultimately brought about its collapse.

"Your dissolving the company?" Charlie whispered in dread. "What about my job?"

"Charles, you have no idea how much this pains me," Dick bleated, "but I'm ruined!"

The memories kept swirling. Charlie had spent the next part of the day in a daze, barely able to think straight. With traffic flowing in all directions, people flitted in and out of buses to join the faceless lines filing their way along the pavements. The weather was freezing as great clouds of fog were exhaled out of the ground. To his greater dismay, he knew Anna was working. But how he wished she could be at home to comfort him in his darkest hour.

Loitering by the bus stop, he wondered how Andrew would take the news. So lost in his thoughts was he that by the time the bus transported him to his neighbourhood, he stepped up to the front door with hardly any recollection of how he had got there.

From the moment he let himself in though, he was struck by a sense of emptiness. Unused to such solitude, the well of silence left him tense with nothing but the slow torturous drip of the kitchen tap to keep him company. He switched on the radio to drown it out before sinking into an armchair. Except he couldn't relax. Memories of that fateful conversation kept bouncing around in his mind. He couldn't deny he felt a little sorry for Dick Harrison. He had worked damned hard to build up that company and perhaps down to one fatal error of judgement, he had lost it. Yet the inherent problems concerning Hampton's project had driven the final nail in the coffin.

The anger inside him swelled. So much so, that for one insane moment he was tempted to look up Hampton's number and have a bloody good rant down the phone.

A copy of the contract was printed on one of Hampton's own letterheads. Charlie glared at the logo, tormented by the sullen tones of black and purple. It depicted the head of a Peregrine falcon - *the hunch of its wings, the cruel curve of its beak, so harsh and predatory just like Hampton.*

Yet what was he even thinking?

He could never take on a man like him, not with his connections in the construction industry. Spotting his portfolio slumped alongside his manuals on architecture, he was instead struck by a better idea. With his intricate line drawings still in there, it wasn't too late to take photos, especially while the show home was still standing. He had about half a roll of film in his camera. It would be enough.

Leaping onto another bus, he had headed for the outskirts of Bromley.

With the site lingering in the winter gloom, he felt a lump rise in his throat as the houses materialised behind a veil of drizzle. The first pictures he took were of the development in its transitory phase, but the rest of the film was for his show home…

A sad smile crept onto his face as it loomed before his eyes. He took pictures from all angles, capturing its grandeur, from the pillared entrance to the curving bay windows. Maybe this wasn't the end. One day he would design another house like this. He still had the drawings and now the photos, to prove the visionary skills he was capable of.

On returning to the exit however, he froze, as the hazy impression of two men on motorbikes took shape behind the mist. The Harley Davidson he recognised; the unmistakable figure of Ben Hampton. There was another man with him. Charlie was struck with the impression of *Hell's Angels* but with a prickle of unease, he took another step forward.

"Bailey, isn't it? Charles Bailey!"

Charlie was silent. There were no words he could think of to say to him.

"I think you owe me an apology," Ben mocked before inhaling from a cigarette. "I didn't appreciate that bollocking you gave me a few weeks ago. Maybe this is your chance to make amends, especially if you wish to carry on working for my father."

"I owe you nothing," Charlie said, too stunned to take in the full meaning. "You nearly ran my daughter over."

Ben's eyes narrowed. "What are you doing here anyway?"

"Taking a last look at the houses," he muttered in sadness, glancing back at the half-finished development. "Before they pull them down."

"Yeah, pity," Ben said tactlessly. "All that work! You must be gutted but never mind…"

Charlie's anger flared. Just one glance into his taunting blue eyes suggested he was deliberately trying to provoke him.

"I've had enough of this," he spat, "I'm going…"

The second he passed through the exit however, Ben's sinister looking companion stepped in front of him. The man smirked. Charlie hesitated - one in front, one behind, he was trapped.

As if this day could get any worse.

Yet he stood his ground, determined not to be intimidated. Okay, so if they were looking for an excuse to beat him up, so be it. At least he could bring charges against the little prick for assault.

For a few seconds, nobody moved. Charlie glanced back at Ben then smiled.

"So what's all this?" he joked. "Aren't you going to introduce me to *your boyfriend*?"

Ben's eyes blazed. "His name is Nathan and he's my security guard!" he spat, stamping his cigarette butt out on the ground.

Charlie let out a splutter of laughter. "Security guard!" he echoed. "What do you need hired heavies for, son?"

"I'd watch what you say if I were you," Ben warned. "Now, let's start again shall we, because you're not making a very good impression."

"I'm not going to grovel to you!" Charlie gasped.

"Well, you might consider showing me some respect if you want my father to employ you," Ben added, "especially if you're looking for a new job..."

Charlie gaped back at him with incredulity. He sensed the movement of the second man. He had been hovering close, so close, he could feel a flutter of breath against his neck until another thought struck him. How did Ben know he needed a new job?

Did this imply they knew about the bankruptcy of Dick's firm?

The reality struck him brutally, just as the slam of a car door broke the silence. Yet he hadn't quite finished speaking. Stung by such insensitivity, he glared at Ben with explosive fury.

"I would rather starve than work for your father, you little shit!"

The moment passed in earth-shattering silence, the chill in the air glacial as Perry came strutting across the grass.

"What did you say?"

"You heard," Charlie whispered in hatred. "Your son is being obnoxious!" With a look of devastation, he turned and glanced across the meadow again but what did he have to lose? It looked like a graveyard, where the frames of those half-built houses resembled skeletons. "Do you seriously have any idea of the chaos you've caused?"

"You're just not playing ball, are you?" the other man said, his tone lowering with threat. "When I bestow someone with the accolade that *with your skills you surpass yourself*, I mean it! My son has approached you, specifically to inform you I am willing to offer you work. I do not expect that offer to be thrown back in his face!"

"After what you've done," Charlie snapped, "you are the last person I'd want to be employed by!"

"Then you are a fool!" Perry shouted back. "Most would consider themselves lucky! Have you any idea who you're dealing with here?"

The words left Charlie choked. "You're not superior to me and you are *not* my boss. My boss is the man whose company went bust today, thanks to your recklessness!"

"I cannot be blamed for the way Dick Harrison mismanaged his finances..."

But Charlie refused to listen. "You call me a fool, Mr Hampton, yet I didn't choose to build on a flood plain! You've got no right to shout at me; not when you've brought about the ruin of a company, never mind the men who've lost their jobs! People like you destroy lives!"

"Then why refuse my offer?" Perry barked. "That paltry development was just the tip of the iceberg! I have all sorts of projects in the pipeline, *highly lucrative* projects where I could use a good foreman, as well as an architect!"

"In other words, exploit my skills to make yourselves a big fat profit!" Charlie thundered. "Forget it, I'm not interested, okay? You can take your offer and shove it!"

He felt so angry, he was ready to take whatever violence they had in mind; in fact, he almost relished it... He turned to face Nathan.

"Now are you going to let me pass or what?"

Smiling evilly, Nathan stepped aside.

Without another word, Charlie marched away from them, assailed by the chill of freezing fog as it continued to waft from the ground. Yet he could no longer ignore the feeling that not only had he lost his job today but made some deadly enemies.

****

"That son of his was an evil piece of work," he muttered.

Reading the fear in Eleanor's expression, he didn't want to elaborate further. He felt sure he must have told her the rest... *what that confrontation had led to.*

For the one thing he had counted on was he would have no problem finding another job - despite the pessimistic mood proliferated by the masses, who desperately sought work during the Thatcher era of the 80s. Yet forced to live on benefits, whilst scouring the boards at the Job Centre, Charlie had failed to find employment.

But that was just the start. Next came the descent into poverty, visits to the DHSS, the nightmare of social housing, which to Anna, felt as if they had been dragged into the darkest recess of hell.

"Everything went wrong after that day," he whispered. "I should have known better than to turn him down. Anna might still be alive... but he was so nasty, Eleanor."

"Don't say that," Eleanor said softly. "It wasn't your fault."

She seemed eager to comfort him, her hand hovering above his. But Charlie didn't respond. Immersed in grief for his beloved Anna, he remained very still.

"Hampton has got a hell of a lot to answer for. Okay, I can't blame him for Anna's death but maybe things could have been different..." Finally he raised his eyes. "And your friend is considering going into partnership with him? Eleanor, you have got to talk him out of it!"

She stared at him in shock. "But what am I going to say? James hasn't got a quarter of a million to restore his home. He's got no choice other than to take out a huge loan."

"Even a loan would be preferable to dealing with those monsters," Charlie added, "and I doubt if they're acting out of altruism. I bet they've got some other motive. This terrible situation with their property is a game to people like them. How close is he to agreeing to the partnership?"

"I-I don't know," Eleanor faltered. "Why do you ask?"

"Hampton is not a man to cross," he shuddered. "I'll never know for sure, but I'm certain he brought about my ruin. I know what he's like when he doesn't get his own way and he can be very dangerous..."

Chapter Six

If only Charlie understood Perry's rage. Or at the very least, witnessed how that dialogue had left him shaking with vindictive hatred.

Yet how ironic Perry was reliving that same confrontation.

The River Ravensbourne had burst its banks recently, as reported in the news. He closed his eyes, slamming down his paper. Did anyone consider how devastated *he* felt, especially when Councillor Dean had exposed the deep-rooted problem with that land? It was his finances that had funded the project; thousands of pounds, for which he would see no return and yet the impertinence of Charles Bailey...

Little did he know he had recognised his potential on the day of the motorcycle incident. Not only was Charles an excellent foreman but the entire housing development was modelled on his designs. So Perry had made a decision; as soon as his project reached completion, he intended to head hunt him for his own company.

People only had to hear his public school accent or recognise the fine cut of his Savile Row suits to realise he stood at the highest echelons of the construction industry. Men like him held the whip hand. So how dare Charles Bailey belittle him! His initial plan to ensnare him had failed and for that he would pay dearly. Fuming in silence, Perry was counting on the fact that by the time Charles had been refused employment by every construction company he had dealings with, he would be begging for an opportunity to work for him.

But Perry had more pressing issues on his mind besides Bailey.

His current train of thought took him back to the night of the dinner party, that earth-shattering disclosure about the new age travellers. It had been tugging at his mind for days; the concept of a young woman living there for over ten years.

Eleanor came from London...

A painful memory popped in his mind like a flashbulb. It transported him back to a confrontation that had taken place in the summer of 1973.

Eleanor.

The name brought him out in a cold sweat.

London.

It couldn't be her, surely? So powerful was his sense of foreboding, he was inspired to make contact with Robin Whaley. He knew Whaley worked for

Rosebrook Council; a man who had as much to fear from this young woman as he did.

"Perry!" Robin greeted him. "How the devil are you?"

With a shared interest in politics and Perry's proximity to Westminster, they occasionally met to converse in the public gallery. There was a time when Perry had been a member of the Conservative Party - Robin, a ward councillor in East London. Yet both men had shied away from politics through fear their reputation could be destroyed by just one person.

Neither man could forget; *an invitation to a press conference to discuss the suspicious death of a rock musician from Holland.* Yet just at the point when they felt they had been exonerated of any blame, Eleanor Chapman had sprung out in front of them.

"Something's come to light," Perry said icily. "You're the only person I can confide in."

"What's troubling you?" Robin questioned.

"Do you know about the new age travellers camped in Aldwyck Village?" he demanded.

"Of course I know about them," Robin replied in a voice of disdain.

It took several more minutes for Perry to express his interest in Westbourne House.

"In other words, I want them out!" he finished nastily.

"Perry," Robin sighed. "Rosebrook Council doesn't have the power to evict travellers. The land is private. Only the land owner has the right to remove them..."

"Well, if the council can't do anything then perhaps you can," Perry added in a sinister undertone. "You do still have connections don't you? If these hippies won't leave of their own accord, then perhaps we should resort to more heavy handed tactics."

The other man hesitated. Perry could sense his unease.

"I hope you're not implying what I think you are," Robin faltered. "The criminal underworld doesn't quite run the way it used to, not since they exposed the corruption..."

"You must be able to track down one crime boss we know of," Perry persisted.

"Violent intimidation is not acceptable in this day and age," Robin answered. "We'd be putting ourselves at risk. For a start, do you have any idea who else resides in that field?"

"I do now," Perry said with a hiss. "The Chapman girl! Are you telling me, you've known this all along?"

"Indeed," Robin replied silkily, "and to this day, her presence in that village has not posed any threat to us, so let's just leave it that way!"

"But I don't want her living in Aldwyck!" Perry protested.

"And I don't want her living in Rosebrook," Robin argued. "The truth is, we got her out of London. She is stuck in the middle of nowhere, where she lives as an outcast..."

"Except there is one thing that still bothers me," Perry kept pressing. "All those years ago, she spoke of a *secret file*; a set of documents that could implicate us..."

"There has been no further mention of it and neither will there be," Robin assured him. "The Chapman girl may not fear for her own safety but she cares very deeply about her son. She would never do anything to endanger him, which is the one hold we have over her."

"You're sure about that are you?" Perry relented.

"Oh yes," Robin murmured. "That girl lives a very isolated existence... but if there's ever a day when she integrates back into society, that is the day we need to watch our backs."

II

Eleanor had never considered the possibility that some might call her an 'outcast.' Returning to her caravan, early afternoon, she was imagining the scenario through the Baileys' eyes.

A lump rose in her throat as she recalled the terrible area they had been living in. Some might say *they were lucky to have a roof over their heads*, but little did they know the reality; the grim surround of factory units, the walls scrawled with graffiti... According to Charlie, gangs of youths loitered until late at night, Anna and Margaret too scared to step outside.

They had met on a day Charlie yearned to set his sights further afield and the small town of Rosebrook had delighted him - anything to put a smile back on Anna's face.

But even that had ended in disaster.

Momentarily breaking away from his family to look inside the Job Centre, Charlie had no idea their fate was about to take a turn for the worst. Anna thought she was safe. Waiting by an archway, set back from the pavement, she hadn't spotted a figure lurking in the shadows, nor the predatory eyes honing in on her handbag. Without warning a small, but wiry youth in a hooded sweatshirt had barged through the gap. But not only had they snatched Anna's purse - but the callous way they had shoved Margaret aside caused her to stumble.

Seeing the child splayed across the pavement, head clutched in her hands, her screaming mouth wide open, Eleanor made her first tentative approach...

"It's okay, I'm a nurse."

Suspicion flashed in Anna's eyes. Nurse or not, some found her appearance bizarre; whether it was the glittering nose stud, or her training dreadlocks dark as earth, she had done everything to reassure them. Her first concern was for Margaret. On stroking her hair away from her forehead, an egg sized lump had begun to emerge. She wasn't badly hurt. Yet fearing the possibility of concussion, Eleanor urged them to let her escort them to the hospital where she worked.

She had already finished her shift, her only concern to get away in time to pick up her son from his art class. Charlie's gratitude however, held no bounds. Insistent on driving her and Elijah home, it seemed obvious their journey to Aldwyck had made an impression.

Eleanor smiled, recalling the awe on their faces as Charlie steered his car down the country road. It gradually became more winding, enveloping them in a tunnel of trees. But the moment they cruised into Aldwyck, the interior of the car ran silent as they took it all in; the swathes of forest cloaking the hills - the surrounding trees in their stark winter beauty, spidery branches silhouetted against the sunlight. Passing a row of shops, they gaped at the village green embraced by its horseshoe of cottages. The oak beamed country pub stood on the periphery.

By the time they pulled up outside her caravan, Eleanor could never have known what they were thinking, not until they were inside.

Her home possessed an aura of charm none of them had expected, from the velvet upholstered seats arranged around a pine table to a scattering of cushions.

Eleanor stepped inside, lowering her bag onto the work surface. Head still fuzzy from the cider she had consumed with Charlie, she had not yet absorbed the impact of *his* story.

Her mind was lodged in the past, remembering Anna.

How she loved the decorative throws on the beds, the cast iron burner breathing a comforting warmth into the air, an aroma of wood smoke. A smile curved her lips as her eyes drifted towards the hand-carved shelves stacked with home made pickles and chutneys. More shelves were packed with books and ornaments, candles in brass holders where trails of old wax oozed over the rims. A faded Turkish rug added extra colour, but in a world blighted with darkness, this was Eleanor's sanctuary where all she could do was make it homely.

Lowering herself into the seating, she closed her eyes, recalling their conversation. But as the Bailey's offloaded their troubles, she was inspired to share some of her own; waiting until the kids had disappeared for a wander, before she dared mention Elijah's father.

Even that had been inspired by Anna, her eyes drawn to Eleanor's photographs.

One displayed a hippie-like family. *The Merrimans*.

"I think of them as my foster family," she had enlightened her. "Those wonderful people looked after me when I was pregnant with Eli. It's thanks to them, I ended up here!"

A mature, white-haired woman beamed out of the frame.

"Rosemary gave me their caravan. This one is newer but as Eli grew bigger, we needed more space, see."

As they continued to study the photos, Eleanor had pointed out her late mother; a beautiful black woman with alluring dark eyes and a halo of afro hair.

"Can you believe I'm a quarter afro-caribbean? Martina Chapman. She was a night club singer but tragically knocked down by a drunk driver. Dad was heartbroken..."

The next photo showed a striking looking man in a suit, gifted with a mane of light brown hair, his eyes an unusually pale shade of amber. If the photo had been black and white, one would assume they were blue.

"Is your dad still around?" Charlie had asked her.

Eleanor felt a sting of tears. "He went missing in 1972. Disappeared abroad but there's been no word of him since... Sorry, I mustn't dwell. At least once a year, I contact my solicitor with the hope there might be some news..."

One face however, stood out in particular.

"Is that Eli's father?" Anna had asked.

Only then did Eleanor drop her guard. *She had to tell them.*

"Jake came from Holland. I met him shortly after my dad disappeared and we fell in love. He was quite simply the most remarkable person I'd ever met. Sadly, he is no longer with us..."

She would never forget the shock on their faces.

"I-I am so sorry," Anna mumbled, almost tripping over her words.

"Don't be," Eleanor said. "I wanted to tell you. I just didn't want Eli to be around when I did but I feel I can trust you..."

Eleanor sat gazing at the picture; a young man whose features were pale and handsome. The resemblance to Elijah must have been obvious, from the slim dark eyebrows and wide forehead to the smiling, beautifully shaped mouth. His auburn hair was longer and sleeker although it was obvious where those reddish glints came from. An unusual stone pendant dangled from his neck, the same pendant as Eleanor wore now.

"What a lovely looking young man," Anna had mused.

"He was beautiful," Eleanor murmured, "and a lovely person. He played in a rock band. 'Free Spirit.' I've got a recording somewhere..."

"Is the band still around?" Charlie asked.

Eleanor shook her head. "They split up not long after Jake died. They played in a number of music festivals across Britain in the early 70s but sadly, they never did make it to fame."

"I'm sorry, I haven't heard of them," Charlie said. "So what happened. How did he die?"

Eleanor caught her breath. For the first time in years, she had met someone she could confide in. There was something about Charlie and Anna she couldn't quite define; a force of inner goodness which in a way, reminded her of the Merrimans.

"Jake was murdered," she confessed in a barely audible whisper.

Anna shook her head in horror.

"Please, keep this to yourselves," Eleanor added softly. "It isn't something I talk about. It's my son I'm trying to protect, see... Jake was killed before he was born."

"We won't say anything," Anna pledged. "I'm sorry! It must have been terrible for you."

"It was," Eleanor shivered. "Losing Jake was the most painful thing I've ever had to survive through..."

"So why was he killed?" Charlie probed.

Eleanor paused, contemplating how much to tell them.

"You don't have to explain - it's just - he looks so innocent!"

"He was," Eleanor nodded. "Jake was a good man but he was killed by some very evil people. If time had been on our side, I would have exposed them! But they were also powerful. Worse, they threatened to harm Elijah..."

"What?" Anna gasped, her eyes widening.

"They threatened to harm your child?" Charlie echoed in disgust.

"Eli was just a baby," Eleanor said, hearing the hate creep into her tone. "This is why we had to get out of London and hide ourselves away in the country. My little boy is all I have left now and I couldn't bear it if anything happened to him. So please keep this a secret. If he knew the truth, he'd only start asking questions and that could put us in danger."

"Your secret is safe with us," Anna murmured in sympathy.

A melancholy mood dragged the air as Eleanor recalled that fateful press conference. No one could have ignored the venom that seeped around the boardroom table; Whaley, Hargreaves... and there had been another man but she could barely remember him.

Eleanor shivered, despite the warmth discharged from the wood burner. "This photo was given to me by Jake's parents," she continued. "The Merriman boys took me to Nijmegen."

Tears beaded her eyes. To her greatest regret, she had never attended Jake's funeral although she had visited his grave. Meeting his family had been awkward. Rigid with grief over the loss of their son, they seemed unsure how to handle her, despite the fact she had borne Jake a son. At least they were sympathetic enough to give her the photo as a keepsake.

The fellow members of Jake's band however, had been strangely absent and even to this day, she had never discovered what happened to them.

Eleanor's eyes sprang open. It seemed impossible to imagine that two months later, Anna would be lost to them forever. But from that day onwards, she knew she had discovered a kindred spirit, not only in Anna but Charlie. The mugging incident had triggered it, an all-consuming sense of empathy...

How rare to meet anyone whose company had put her so much at ease.

She recalled the blossoming friendship between Elijah and their daughter too. Elijah possessed a placid nature, but years of being bullied by other kids for what they perceived as his 'gypsy' lifestyle had done nothing to aid his confidence; no more than the constant belittlement of the teachers. Having complained to the authorities, there was a time when she considered taking him out of school altogether. Yet this notion led to a sinister warning; it wasn't impossible her son could be put into care if she rebelled against the system.

Such a notion sent her mind reeling, a sense that those in power still controlled her.

Meeting the Baileys had brought a renewed sense of purpose, where listening to their story proved how they too, had fallen victims to a heartless society. Processed and shunted through a faceless system was how they had ended up in the dump they were living in.

Eleanor hated injustice and despite the traumas of her own past, felt a stirring from deep within her heart. It seemed the Bailey family had been just as vulnerable as she was...

But today Charlie had unmasked a monster, a man who had quite possibly brought about the ruin of his own life.

James had confided in her with regards to his dilemma; Westbourne House.

And there hovering between the two, appeared to be the same family. They were proposing to take on the restoration *and* fund it, but why? Who in their right mind would invest a quarter of a million pounds in a project, unless they had some deep underlying motive?

Gaining access to a telephone at the first opportunity, Eleanor wasted no more time.

She had to warn him.

Chapter Seven

"James, these are the last people on earth you should go into partnership with!"

Eleanor's words left James cold.

So, it appeared her friend, Charlie, had fallen foul of the charismatic Perry Hampton. Eleanor had shakily relayed the details yet her first concern was for *him*. It seemed hard to imagine how one man could be such a dominating force in both their lives.

Unfortunately, the Hamptons were due to visit. James didn't have the heart to postpone their engagement, in the light of their own hospitality. He would be a fool to ignore Eleanor's warnings, though. Today was an opportunity to study them; take them on a tour of the house and grounds, observe their reactions and listen to their plans.

At least the news of his health had uplifted him. There seemed no adverse reason for his decline. But only now, James sensed how vulnerable he had been on those first encounters. Perry may seem outwardly charming, though he had glimpsed a hint of his true nature when he had brought up the subject of the travellers in his field. He would never forget the malice slipping into his voice; nor the prejudice he had shown towards Eleanor.

With a sigh, he ambled into the room where they would later enjoy lunch. Due to the sensitive topic of the meeting they needed privacy, some place away from the general public. Their family dining room, situated in the east wing, possessed its own special beauty. Tall graceful windows dressed in olive silk drapes blended harmoniously with the pastel green wallpaper. A magnificent dining table had been laid out, a vase resting in the centre filled with a beautiful arrangement of flowers. James breathed in their scent, the roses picked from his very own gardens, despite the onset of winter.

Yet still the echo of Eleanor's words kept haunting him.

He felt a chill slip down his spine, his concerns not just about Perry, but his son, who sounded quite evil... It left him with a sense of foreboding that he couldn't shake off, especially in the light of Ben's blossoming relationship with Avalon.

Avalon too, had her reservations. Frozen in front of her full length mirror, she felt no desire to dress up - more a hankering to dress down. She slipped on her black ski pants and a loose-fitting jumper. Pulling her golden brown curls away from her face, she tied them back with a bow. She also chose to wear little makeup.

William bounded into the room dressed in combat trousers and a checked flannel shirt. With his bronze hair ruffled, he looked as casual for the occasion as she did.

"What's up, Sis?" he muttered. "You're not worried about seeing Ben again are you?"

"A little," she said, forcing a smile.

"What about your date? Did he turn up on his Harley Davidson?"

"No, he did not," Avalon smiled, feeling her tension lift. "He turned up in a lovely silver Mercedes sports car, driven by his chauffeur. Though I have to say, *he* was scary. His name is Nathan. Ben employs him as some kind of bodyguard, but seriously, you would not want to meet him in a dark alley..."

Avalon shivered. She could not deny Nathan scared her. With eyes like chips of lead, he possessed a face that looked as if it was chiselled from rock, his skin tight and tanned. Furthermore, those menacing looks were distinguished by a pencil-thin beard that extended from his chin to his jaw. She turned and looked at William who was watching her beadily.

"I-I'm just a little nervous," she confessed.

"Who, of Ben or his bodyguard?" William pressed.

"Both," Avalon said. "Look, don't say anything to Dad b-but I don't want to go out with Ben any more. Something about him scares me and I don't know how to handle him, especially with the partnership at stake..."

William shrugged and rose to his feet. "Just say you like him as a friend," he said, "that you're not ready for anything heavy. He'll understand."

For all his faults, at times like this Avalon realised how much she loved her brother.

II

Perry meanwhile, advanced along the twisting country road in the same fawn Mercedes Benz he had driven on their first visit. Square and solid, this car exuded dominance and there was no denying the feeling of power that consumed him today.

He had been craving another opportunity to scrutinise Westbourne House; a chance to liaise with James, intent on manipulating him to embrace his own plans. Already the stark beauty of the countryside had started to unfurl; an expanse of hills undulating beneath a pale winter sun, the enveloping cloak of woodland growing denser.

Yet Perry took in none of it.

He was engrossed in his scheming. With the survey complete, which James had swallowed whole and a building firm of his choosing in control of the restoration, little did he know that Perry already held the whip hand. He sailed past the village sign crossing into Aldwyck, aware of Rowena sat next to him, writhing with excitement.

A flicker of a smile touched his lips.

Thrown back in time, he was remembering the vast manor house in Berkshire where he had grown up; a dark and eerie place enclosed by high stone walls. After his father had died, Perry had been desperate to sell it, in order that the estate could be dissolved and shared between himself and his two older half brothers. But Perry had always been the shrewd one, investing his share in property and with the escalating house prices of the 70s, he had amassed a small fortune before he reached the age of thirty.

In roughly the same era though, he had planned to make his mark in politics.

Yet his insatiable desire to be an MP had drawn him into a bitter feud with a member of the opposition; a man whose rise to power threatened his future to such a degree, Perry was forced to take drastic measures. Such actions had put his future at risk... So he had concentrated his efforts on developing property.

Rowena meanwhile, forever craving a higher social status, clung to her dream that one day they would reside in a beautiful country house. Ever eager to appease her, Perry felt sure he could turn that dream into a reality. And if he could keep Rowena happy, one of his many lifetime goals would be fulfilled.

This very concept drew his attention back to Westbourne House and to James. The man possessed a crumpled, worn out look that reminded him of an old shirt that had undergone too many spin cycles. Primed with his own plans to maximise the potential of his hotel, he might even be doing the old man a favour. He was surely close to retirement.

There were, however the children. No one really knew the darker side to his strategy; that over time and as the partnership took root, he would eventually drive the family out. The boy was only fourteen. With many more years before he was old enough to make his own way in the world, Perry would quiz him about his future.

Eyes drawn to the driver mirror, he caught a reflection of his own son. Ben gazed back without expression, though Perry had long sensed his animosity towards William. Loath to admit it, the boy was more charming than Ben had ever been at that age, but he warned him to show respect.

For never was it more essential to win their trust.

As for the girl... Given his aptitude for spotting people who might be useful, he saw Avalon as a fine catch, especially for Ben. Not only did her beauty enchant him, but her potential for being the perfect hostess. Her passion for fine cuisine had endeared her to Rowena, so it was time to nurture that passion and encourage her ideas.

Perry crept past the shops and green, seeing the church looming in the distance. They had almost reached the edge of the village but as the gates of the house drew close, his gaze drifted to the field where Eleanor's caravan lurked.

Reliving his conversation with Robin Whaley, he had never intended to divulge his master plan. But the thought of her presence bothered him. It took him right back to the one and only time they had clashed. The vision had never stopped haunting him, her floating towards the board room table, her golden eyes lit like flames...

"Why are you here tonight? Do you know the truth? I have a feeling you do..."

A wave of hatred rose, which he could no longer suppress. Pausing by the field, he could hear Robin's reassurances, but perhaps he was right. Never was it more essential to keep this young lady under control, given the likelihood they would be neighbours.

III

"Right everyone, they're here," James announced.

His hand fell away from the curtain. They formed a forbidding trio as they spilled out of their Mercedes.

No sooner were the heavy oak doors thrust open when Perry swept into reception. He was tailed by Rowena who displayed her own flair for power dressing. Resplendent in a blue silk suit featuring huge shoulder pads, she could have stepped out of an episode of 'Dynasty,' James thought. He caught a flash of white blonde hair as Ben followed.

"Good morning," Elliot greeted them, "Mr Barton-Wells is expecting you. He's waiting in the lounge if you would like to go through. May I offer you something to drink?"

"In a minute," Perry snapped, barely acknowledging him.

Without further prompting, they turned towards the lounge.

"Hello, people," James smiled warmly.

Clocking the surprise on Perry's face, he eased himself away from the bar. But James was on his own territory today, empowered to face him with confidence.

Perry grasped James's hand. "Well," he drawled. "You seem to be in good form! Any of the work underway yet?"

"Only the staircase," James said, "but I'll tell you more about that later..."

Perry's expression changed to one of thinly veiled triumph as he lowered himself into a chair. Elliot swooped towards them again and avoiding the man's superior stare, asked them if they would like some coffee.

The instant Avalon wandered into view, Ben sprung to his feet. She knew her brother couldn't be far behind her.

"Avalon," Ben murmured with undisguised pleasure.

"Hello, Ben," she said softly.

His eyes slid down the length of her body. "You look gorgeous," he drawled, "but then you always do."

From his concealed position in the hallway, William was leaning over his stomach, cheeks bulging, pretending to be sick. Avalon resisted the urge to giggle.

Seconds later, both families had congregated in the bar. But where Rowena seemed overly affectionate, Perry's interest seemed to lay elsewhere; especially when he started to grill William. He was quizzing him about his private school when Avalon caught his eye.

"Avalon!" he greeted her. "Your father's been telling me about your first gourmet supper evening. I hear it was a great success!"

"Yes, it went well," Avalon faltered. "We're putting together a mailing list..."

"Excellent idea," Perry smiled indulgently. "You have a good business head on your shoulders, my dear! Perhaps you could include myself and Rowena on your list. We'd be more than willing to support your venture." His eyes latched on to her father. "Now James, what are your plans? Rowena and I cannot wait to see the rest of the house."

"In a moment," James responded, "but for now just relax, Perry. We have the whole day ahead of us..."

Avalon sensed he was stalling; that despite Perry's overburdening pressure to get started, he needed a little more time to prepare himself.

So he kept them talking, curious to know about their lives in London.

Perry, on the other hand, turned his attention back to William. There was something strange about the way he kept interrogating him and for some reason, his ambition to join the army delighted him.

"My two older brothers were in the army," James reflected, "both lost their lives in the war. Thank God we live in times of relative peace."

"But the next war could be nuclear!" Avalon gasped in horror. "It's hardly a wonder there are so many protests!"

"Nuclear weapons are a deterrent!" Perry interrupted, more sharply than he perhaps intended.

The scene collapsed into stony silence.

"I think Avalon just fears for her brother's life," James tried to explain.

No sooner had they finished coffee, the tour started. James knew he couldn't put this off for any longer. Guiding them from reception into the corridor to the library, he could sense Perry's agitation. With Perry pushing to the front and William hanging close to James's side, Avalon lingered at the back. Ben fell into step beside her, but apart from his predatory sideways glances, neither spoke.

Perry's mood warmed as they entered the library. Nodding in appreciation at the Chesterfield furniture and oak panelling, he voiced its potential for exclusive board meetings.

From the library, they proceeded towards their private lounge, which Rowena recognised, her eyes popping out like a zoom lens.

Finally, they threaded their way through the restaurant and into the ballroom. Even James was stirred by their enthusiasm. The magnificent hall dominated the entire north-west corner, with exposed beams and a stage, framed by long, theatre-style drapes. The cabaret style seating was ideally suited to dinner dances.

A calculating smile took root on Perry's face as the grounds materialised behind the windows. His eyes glittered. Yet he seemed to be staring way beyond the grounds - farther than the lawns that trailed towards the hills - the woods reaching far into the distance...

He clamped an arm around James's shoulder. "You do know you are sitting on a gold mine here," he muttered. "Companies would pay a fortune to host a function in this place!"

His voice thickened with avarice, leaving James unsure what to say.

Completing their tour of the ground floor, they wandered into the grounds. Perry had no idea how secretly James was monitoring him, but his eyes flitted everywhere. In fact, the manner by which he drew in the magnificence of his estate seemed beyond obsessive. Passing through the yard where several vehicles were parked, they continued to the back of the estate.

Yet Perry was gazing towards the hills again. The air ran silent as they drifted towards the walled gardens and straight away, James anticipated something he had been dying to ask.

Perry inclined his head.

"May I ask how much land is attached to this estate?" he dropped out casually.

A ripple of anxiety passed through him as he remembered Eleanor's warnings...

Charlie thinks he must have some other motive.

"My estate includes the house, the outbuildings and grounds," he answered. He waved his arm in an arc as if to indicate the lawns, which stretched as far as the encircling woodland.

"So, how much land do you actually own, James?" Perry kept on furrowing.

"About two thousand acres," he replied in earnest. "Why do you ask?"

Perry levelled him with his gaze. "With an estate this size you could expand. Have you ever considered adding an extra building? I was thinking about a conference centre, maybe, and as for all this land... There's enough space to build a golf course."

"Hmm," James pondered. "Well, I never doubted you would have some sound ideas, Perry, but first let me show you my estate in its current form."

Stepping up to the walled gardens he felt a lump in his throat. The bricks here possessed a faded quality, a myriad of terracotta shades, a pretty wrought iron gate enticing them inside.

Even Avalon's eyes became a little misty as she turned to Rowena. "Now this place really is special," she whispered to her. "Come in and look."

The rectangular area concealed a network of intersecting paths. Rowena allowed Avalon to lead, high heels clicking as they marched past rows of green vegetables. She gazed at the orchards where the crimson glow of a few wizened apples still lingered, refusing to drop.

Footsteps dwindling, a look of confusion spread across Rowena's face.

"What's all this?" she frowned. "A fruit and vegetable garden?"

"That is exactly what it is," James enthused, sidling up to them. "Original Victorian kitchen gardens! I reinstated them when I was younger. Much of our produce comes from here."

"Interesting," Perry pondered. "This is a substantial plot of land, James."

"I know," James nodded, "which is why I maintain it. The soil is very fertile and produces beautiful crops..."

"Surely you're not so hard up that you have to grow your own vegetables," Perry mocked.

"Not at all," James bristled. "Why do you say that?"

"Isn't this all a bit labour intensive?" Perry continued to grill. "It must take a battalion of gardeners to manage this lot and harvest it all!"

"The locals come here to do that," James reassured him. "I pay them a modest wage and a pick of the proceeds."

"But all this space..." Perry drawled in disdain.

"I also rent some of it," James argued. "There are people who derive great joy from being able to grow their own vegetables and the rent they pay me is income. What point are you actually trying to make here, Perry?"

"Forgive me for saying this," Perry sighed, "but I can't help thinking there are better ways you could utilise this area."

James felt his jaw clamp, struck with a bayonet of hurt; not only from the pride he had taken in reinstating the gardens, but the importance they played in his estate and the village.

He considered his next words carefully. "These gardens are a much loved feature of Westbourne House, Perry, and people travel miles to see them…"

"Maybe," Perry replied in his sharp, businesslike tone, "but if we are looking to maximise the potential of the hotel, you might want to consider redeveloping some areas. I've only got your best interests at heart here, James."

"Oh, Perry," James said, his voice a sigh in the breeze. "Westbourne House has always served a greater purpose. Former generations of my family have looked after the people of Aldwyck. It's a rural community and if you cannot find it in your heart to embrace our customs, I fear this partnership will be very difficult."

"But I'm a property developer, James," Perry pitifully reminded him. "There are so many opportunities to be realised!"

"And this is an old country house that has its traditions," James persisted. "I appreciate you have good intentions, Perry, but I have no wish to alter its character."

"I wouldn't expect you to!" Perry laughed, rapidly back-pedalling.

"Why don't we go to the Orangerie," Avalon interrupted to break up the conflict.

Perry turned to look at her. "Orangerie?"

"Traditionally, it's a glass house where citrus trees are grown," she enlightened him, "but a very nice place to relax. Hotel guests often sit here in the evening to enjoy a glass of wine and as it faces west, you can watch the sun set…"

"Sounds like bliss," Ben murmured, honing in close. "I would love to sit out here and watch a sunset with you, Avalon."

Seemingly lost for words, she lowered her gaze. James could imagine her anxiety, perhaps wishing there was a way she could discourage Ben's affections. She flashed a hasty smile.

"I have to agree. This Orangerie is quite charming," Rowena's voice oozed from behind. "Ignore my husband, James. I think your gardens are delightful."

"Well, thank you," James responded, feeling his tension slip. "In which case, I'll take you back through the formal gardens. Follow me… and try to keep up, William!"

William had been lingering further and further back. He too appeared to be biting back his annoyance. Only as the others lingered on the path though, admiring the Orangerie, did he surreptitiously catch his eye. He gave a subtle wink.

William on the other hand, felt on edge.

Disturbed by Perry's interest, unable to expel his fear every time Ben's eyes raked over Avalon, he detected something downright creepy about all of them. The very thought of his father going into this partnership didn't bear thinking about, despite the money they were prepared to throw into the restoration.

He caught up, just as Avalon was pointing out a concealed exit; a section of wall cloaked in ivy where the wild roses clambered over the top. An identical facing section created the illusion the two were joined, until you stepped into the gap where a column of daylight was revealed.

"Incredible," Rowena murmured as they walked through the parallel sections.

Back in the grounds, the formal gardens shimmered before them like a watercolour. James led them along meandering paths, past crisp lawns edged with flower beds. Grecian urns exploded with white cyclamens and purple pansies, while neat lines of box hedging provided enough dark foliage to allow the last of the roses to radiate their beauty.

But as they completed their journey, Rowena further aggravated James. Voicing her surprise that he allowed the public in for free, she adopted the same calculating tone as Perry.

"You should charge an entry fee, surely? Is it wrong to make a little profit, especially given the funds about to be invested in repairing the house?"

"It's the gardens that attract them," James protested gently. "People often stay for lunch in the restaurant or afternoon tea. The only fees I accept are from the coach parties who visit throughout the summer, as you yourselves did in September."

"Listen, James," Perry intervened. "I appreciate your ideology but it is the hotel which is going to save you, not coach parties of old ladies visiting for cream teas."

James's eyes flashed. Yet it was William's quick thinking wit that diffused the tension.

"I would never have described you and Rowena as *old ladies*," he grinned. "Didn't I hear Dad say that *you* attended one of our tea parties?"

Perry bellowed with laughter. "Your boy has a sense of humour, James!"

"C'mon, folks," James sighed, a smile crinkling his eyes. "Let's go inside and have a spot of lunch. It's getting cold out here..."

Chapter Eight

Elliot felt a knot of unease, as soon as James led them back into reception. Observing his face, he recognised the same panicked look from the night of the dinner party.

These people were draining the energy out of him.

Pushing aside his worry, the tour of the house ensued with growing speed. Elliot followed, keeping several paces behind as they swept up the stairs to the first floor.

All he could hear was Perry's voice as it boomed through the corridor, quizzing James about the guest accommodation. An adjoining passage linked the east and west wings, accessible via a door. But James seemed to have difficulty unlocking it, his hand fumbling with the key.

"Allow me," Elliot said, gliding over to assist him.

Crossing the central section into the west wing, the Hamptons' scrutinised every corner.

Elliot unlocked the doors to display the bedrooms but as the magnificence of each one was unveiled, their individual beauty did not fail to impress Rowena. Clapping her hands, she was unable to hold back her smile.

"This one is simply delightful," Elliot heard her gasp.

"It is, isn't it?" Avalon echoed. "It's hard to believe they're in such a poor state of repair. You'd hardly notice unless you looked closely..."

Perry's eyes narrowed. "What did the surveyors report, James?" he probed.

"It's like Avalon says," James replied, "you can see the odd crack in the ceiling and areas of bulging plaster. Once we re-roof the property, they'll need re-plastering. Apart from that though, there is one serious crack in the outer wall... but let's not talk about that now. I did mention I was having the staircase rebuilt, didn't I?"

Ambling a little further, they reached the staircase. Only on this occasion, the treads were cloaked in dust sheets and it was roped off at both ends, denying access.

"Every individual component has to be re-built," James explained. "Balusters, newel posts, handrails... I do hope it won't take much longer. We can't keep the hotel closed forever."

Perry said nothing as they turned to make their way back.

He threw one final glance at the staircase buried under its deathly white shroud. But if James had been observing him more closely, he might have spotted the cunning look in his eyes...

The moment was short lived. Settled around James's fine dining table, Perry temporarily forgot about his secret agenda. Rowena was in her element. Not only did she adore the room but the food; a starter of wild mushroom soup finished with truffle shavings. Even more enjoyable were the lobster tails, succulent and sweet, enveloped in shells of meltingly light pastry.

On Perry's right hand side lounged William, laughing at one of his own jokes.

Ben meanwhile, sat in silence. William seemed destined to annoy him, engaging his father with his silly humour. Pouring himself a glass of wine without thinking, he sipped it slowly as the conversation bounced around the table.

To his delight, Avalon was seated next to him but he could think of nothing to say to her. A wall of tension loomed. Ben fiddled with his napkin, twisting it in his hands.

By the time dessert arrived, his father had resumed his interrogation of James. The topic turned to finance, one of Ben's areas of expertise. He might have spoken up if his mother hadn't started raving about the beautiful 'crème brûlée' with its crown of frosted berries. The words dried on his tongue as she bashed her spoon through the caramel glaze. Ben followed suit although he could barely swallow a mouthful, compelled to leave half.

"Are you alright?" Avalon asked him.

He turned, comforted by her tenderness. "I'm not that hungry," he said. "In fact, I could use a little fresh air... perhaps another walk. Will you come with me?"

He saw the flicker of doubt in her eyes before a smile broke through.

"Okay," she answered, "although it might be a little chilly..."

She rose from her chair, which Ben politely pulled out for her.

"We're just going to take another walk," she announced boldly.

Throwing a glance at her brother, their eyes met. How Ben managed to retain his composure presented the ultimate challenge, as they sauntered from the room and down the stairs.

Avalon snatched her black woollen overcoat off a branch of the coat stand. From the other side of reception, Elliot appeared to be watching them.

"Just going out for a stroll," she called across. "But if we're not back before dark, send out a search party."

"What's that supposed to mean?" Ben demanded as they stepped into the crisp cold air.

"You don't know the scale of these grounds, Ben," she said. "If you don't look where you're going, it is easy to get lost. Believe me, I've done it!"

She proceeded to lead the way, chatting away like a schoolgirl.

Ben gazed at the back of her head, his eyes drawn to the bow confining her lovely hair. He was filled with a sudden urge to unclip it. Watch the mass of ringlets tumble free. But shoving the thought aside, he rammed his hands into his pockets, wishing he had worn a thicker jacket. The air was indeed beginning to turn icy.

Plumes of mist were exhaled from Avalon's lips as she spoke. Absorbed in the formal gardens, the paths gradually drew them to an area of trees. The undulating lawns stretched ahead of them, pale and glistening with dew, as the land rose up to reach the forest.

"This is a circular walk," her voice rang out. "Let's stick to this path and it will lead us to the grounds on the opposite side of the walled gardens, then back to the house..."

As the path wove through the forest, Avalon strode at a brisker pace to ward off the cold until at last, Ben caught her up. Wandering along beside her, they slipped into a light but forced conversation.

"It must be cool to own all this land."

"Yes," Avalon replied. "The grounds are lovely in all seasons. I love the winters here, especially when we get snow."

Ben smiled, his eyes focused on her face. She looked almost childlike, a radiant glow to her cheeks, the cold air turning her generous lips even pinker. Lowering his gaze, he didn't want her to catch him staring. Seconds later however, he froze when his eyes fell to a rabbit skull lying on the path. Ben poked his toe up against it, absent-mindedly kicking it away. He watched it roll into the thick grass on the other side of the path.

"Blasted things," he snapped to himself.

Avalon frowned. "Not a big fan of wildlife then?" she responded airily.

Ben shrugged. "I thought rabbits were vermin."

Avalon paused, her eyes fixed on the skull. "Then how do you imagine your family will take to life in the country? Won't this all seem a little quiet compared to London?"

Ben gave a shrug. "London's not that far... half an hour on the train maybe, but crowded. I like the open space out here."

They carried on walking. Yet as the mantle of silence hung heavy again, he shocked her totally by asking if she participated in blood sports.

Pausing mid-step, Avalon seemed to pick her next words carefully. "Our family doesn't actually support hunting."

"I thought all you country folk were into hunting," Ben teased. "What about your father?"

"No way!" Avalon gasped. "It's something our mother got involved in but Dad hated it! When the local MFH asked if they could hold a meet in the grounds, Dad said he would rather lose popularity than allow a load of horses to gallop across his estate, not to mention hounds crapping in his gardens!" Her words unexpectedly bubbled over with laughter.

Captivated by the gleam in her eyes, Ben also laughed. He felt his affection soar, his senses swimming from that one glass of wine. Convinced Avalon was as thrilled about their blossoming relationship as he was, he clasped her hand.

"This partnership's going to be fun, isn't it?" he prompted her. "We'll be able to see so much more of each other…"

"You're thinking of living here?" Avalon gulped.

Ben faltered, his grip on her hand tightening. He didn't fail to notice the look of anxiety dilating her eyes but for that second, chose to ignore it.

"We're bound to be on site occasionally," he purred, "especially if my mother has her way! My father was even thinking of buying a cottage here. But as you know, their only interest is in managing the hotel!"

"I see," Avalon whispered. A faint smile curved her lips. "So what about you?"

"I'll be working in the city," he smirked. "My home is in Pimlico."

He saw relief flood her expression, yet still he dismissed it. Refusing to read the signals, he felt a gradual stir of desire…

"I can still come down at the weekends," he drawled.

Hanging back in anticipation, he awaited her response - filled with a hope she might display *some joy* from that statement. Yet her face remained frozen and unsmiling. With a sigh, he let go of her hand, watching it drop to her side.

"Is something wrong?" he asked.

She turned away, leaving his eyes wandering to the back of her head again.

"Avalon?"

"What?" she demanded curtly. This time there was no mistaking her irritation.

Ben felt a peculiar giddiness. A sense of rejection darkened the air, which left him wondering if he was imagining things… *Females adored him.* How could it be that a girl he had really fallen for could suddenly be so aloof?

"Look," he sighed, rushing to her side. "This partnership won't restrict your life in any way. Is that what you're worried about?"

"I never said that," she answered in a gentler tone.

"That is, unless there could be something between *us*…" he added silkily.

She backed away and his eyes followed her. Clocking the trunk of a beech tree lurking, he was just waiting for her to slam into it.

And with a cool smile, he sauntered towards her, ready to make his move…

Wary of the sudden charge in her heart, Avalon watched him take another step closer. But with one hand resting on the tree trunk, just inches above her head, she felt trapped.

His pale blue eyes bore into her with an intensity that chilled her.

"Ben, please," she said quickly. "You're starting to scare me..."

"There is no need to be scared," he murmured. His hand brushed her cheek. Avalon flinched, although his touch was light. "Don't you like me?"

"Of course," she blurted. "You're one of the best looking men around..."

"So, what's the but?" he snapped.

Avalon closed her eyes. "I-I'm too young for a serious relationship. Can't we just be friends?"

"Didn't you say you were sixteen?" Ben pressed.

"Not quite," Avalon faltered, "b-but it's not just that. We haven't got a lot in common have we? We don't even like the same music - or - or films! It's not a great start..."

Pressing herself against the tree, she couldn't quite fend off her panic. He stood close, so close, she could see the dots of stubble lining his jaw.

"How do you know this won't work unless we give it a try?" he said. "I want more than friendship. I've barely stopped thinking about you since our date..."

Avalon swallowed, dreading the words she was about to say. "Look, I'm sorry, Ben, but I honestly don't feel the same way."

The smile dropped from his face. What terrified her even more, though, was the flare in his eyes, as if he had transformed into something demonic.

"This is down to William isn't it?" he hissed. "I bet that snotty little brother of yours has been bad mouthing me..."

"William hasn't said a word!" Avalon breathed. "Not even after the business with your bike. He was worried he might have offended you!"

"Oh, that upset me alright," Ben said. "Do you know how much that bike cost? Stupid idiot could have crashed it."

"But *you* were the one who showed him how to ride it," Avalon retorted. "Why do you hate him? And you do, don't you, which is another thing that bothers me about our relationship..."

"Oh, come on, Avalon!" Ben sneered. "You can't deny your brother is annoying and a right little show off! Everything he says and does is designed to piss me off!"

Avalon released a sob, twisting her head away. "That's not true! You're being ridiculous! I love my brother. We've grown a lot closer since Mum left, now stop being so paranoid!"

Ben's eyes narrowed. With his hand on her face, he took her chin and tilted it, forcing her to look at him.

"Maybe I'll have to find some other way to convince you then," he murmured.

Without warning, his lips crashed down, dragging over her mouth in a way that was not unpleasant, but sent her senses reeling. She could not move, paralysed with fear as the kiss ensued. Avalon began to fight, hands flat against his chest as she strained to push him away.

Except his mouth pushed down harder, forcing her lips apart. Avalon's struggle turned frantic and before she had a chance to wriggle free, he had grabbed her wrists, his lean body rammed against hers. There was no doubt he was aroused. She tried to scream, which seemed to do the trick. He froze, then straight away pulled from the tree, releasing her.

"I'm sorry," he panted, "I didn't mean to get carried away..."

"You're sorry?" Avalon spluttered. On touching her lips, they felt bruised.

"It was just a kiss, Avalon," Ben protested.

"Don't you *ever* touch me again!" Avalon said, her voice lowering to a snarl.

With a cold, lop-sided smile, he raised his hands in defeat.

Avalon backed away, breath shaking, as she began to retreat along the path in the direction of the house. Ben, who was still watching her, followed, keeping several paces behind.

But as they walked in silence, the atmosphere grew tauter.

"I never wanted to fall out," he snapped. "But admit it, Avalon, you've been stringing me along. Ever since my father offered to pay for your restoration..."

She released a long, unhappy sigh as the house crept into view again, magnificent against the deepening skyline. For a moment, she paused to stare at it, struck with a sense of utter desolation.

"You were the one who asked me on a date!" she threw back at him, "and I never gave you any reason to imagine I was *stringing you along*. Now can we please go back to the house... I have nothing more to say to you."

No sooner had they returned, Avalon was relieved to discover the Hamptons were on the brink of leaving. Yet she hid her emotions well.

"Well," Perry expressed with pleasure, "this has been an enlightening visit. I sincerely hope we can press ahead with our plans. How would you feel about meeting next week, James? I'll contact my solicitor and perhaps you could do the same. I think the next obvious stage would be to discuss the legal terms of our agreement, don't you?"

"Of course," James replied, keeping his voice light. "Would it be alright if I called you on Monday? In the meantime, enjoy the rest of your weekend."

As the door swung closed, Avalon took a few more steps into reception, then pelted up the stairs. Stumbling into her bedroom, she nearly fell over, quietly closing the door and lowering herself onto her bed. Heart thumping wildly, she revisited that scene in the forest. The click of the doorknob made her flinch. But whirling around, she was thankful to see only William.

"What happened?" he demanded. "You look upset."

Her bottom lip started to wobble, as she gripped the folds of her bedspread.

"When I-I told him I wasn't interested," she shuddered, "he - he got really nasty..."

What she didn't know was that James had momentarily paused outside her bedroom. Returning to the dining room, he had been about to collect a few empty glasses. Yet as fragments of her story drifted beyond the door, his face turned hard with fury.

"He frightened me, William... I never want to see him again!"

James shook his head. As if he needed any more persuasion to disconnect himself from those Hamptons. Eleanor's friend was right, they were pure evil and the sooner he disassociated himself from them, the better.

The more he thought about it, the more he should have guessed all along. Wasn't Perry just typical of this ghastly new money breed? Exaggerated public school accent, absolutely minted and with property deals coming out of every orifice, yet completely lacking in culture.

He loathed his obsession with profit and today it came leaking out of every pore. The mere hint he would consider ripping out his beautiful walled gardens to make way for more money-making development had angered him beyond belief. James needed no further proof. Peregrine Hampton had exposed himself for the demon he really was.

So maybe he had offered to restore their home. But only James knew the sacrifices expected of him would be unbearable.

II

As Perry cruised out of Aldwyck, the blur of forest faded into the distance. Rowena sat very still, so triumphant she was almost purring.

"Well, what an interesting visit," Perry said with a smirk. "They've whittled down their staff and it's unlikely they'll be opening the hotel for a while. Let's face it, darling, the man is broke!"

"So it seems," Rowena drawled, allowing her head to roll back against the headrest. "Lovely meal though... They've got some talented chefs! I don't suppose you remembered to ask that Avalon girl to put our names on their mailing list did you?"

"No, I'm afraid I forgot," Perry muttered. "I'll mention it when I see him next week, but you've got to admire their spirit. They're desperate to claw in any income they can."

"He seemed very passionate about his vegetable garden," Rowena laughed. "James lives in another world! Sweet man though, you can't malign his

73

character."

"Soft hearted old fool, more like," Perry crowed, keen to join in her sniping. "I can't wait to get the lawyers involved. I've got a feeling this will be a pushover!"

"I wouldn't bank on it," Ben intervened from the back seat. "He seems very resistant to change. This might not be as easy as you think..."

"The biggest trouble with James Barton-Wells is he's generous to a fault," Perry snorted. "He might be stuck in his ways but he'll do anything to save his home. Admit it, Ben, he needs us!"

Steering his car along the darkening stretch of road, he could not resist wallowing in the fantasy of it. To think that Rowena's dream of becoming the new proprietor of Westbourne House now hung on the brink of reality.

III

By the time Monday arrived, the entire county was gripped by frost. It encrusted the grounds in a silver veneer and iced over the windows.

James had been settled in his office for some time, engrossed in a number of tasks. Included on the list was Avalon's impending sixteenth birthday; a special meal out had been arranged with friends in London, and they had agreed to take her back to their house for a party. That pleased him no end. It would do her good to get away, after which time Christmas would be imminent.

The next phone call on his list however, was the one he was dreading.

"James," Perry murmured.

Already James could hear the satisfaction tucked into his deep voice.

"Good morning, Perry," he greeted him. "I trust you are well."

"Couldn't be better!" Perry exclaimed. "Now, let's get down to business shall we. Have you contacted your solicitor?"

"No, Perry," James sighed, "in fact, before you say another word, I think it's only fair to inform you I have decided *not* to go ahead with this partnership."

A stunned silence bit the atmosphere, leaving James on edge.

"You what?" Perry finally responded, his voice lowering to a growl.

"Please don't take this badly," James urged. "I just cannot bring myself to accept your offer. This is a huge investment and puts me under too much obligation. I am sorry!"

"I don't believe I'm hearing this," Perry retorted. "I am trying to rescue your home here. How else are you going to raise that sort of money? Have you had a better offer?"

"N-not at all," James faltered, "but this is my ancestral home. What you are proposing is a huge gamble. It would be a gamble between friends, yet I hardly know you! What is more, I feel we are two very different people and our ideas will clash. It won't work, Perry and if you are truly honest to yourself, I suspect you know this too."

"I learned enough to fathom out you're haemorrhaging masses of cash into useless projects!" Perry thundered. "Take that walled garden! And those guest rooms were enormous! You could double the capacity with a little forward planning. You are sitting on a gold mine yet too blinkered and stuck in your old fashioned ways to see it!"

"Well, thank you, Perry," James said with humour. "Obviously, you think I'm some silly, romantic old fool, but do you know I am proud of my role in this village. Westbourne House is as much a part of our community as the church and the pub. Your vision to turn it into some heartless corporation disturbed me. So I'm sorry but the deal is off."

"You are making a very big mistake, James," Perry continued to rant. "Not many people turn down my offers and I warn you, you are going to *regret* this decision."

"Really?" James frowned. "Well, that sounds a little like a threat to me. In fact, while the gloves are off, I may as well confess someone warned me not to have dealings with you…"

"And who would that be?"

"It doesn't matter," James snapped. "I was prepared to give you the benefit of the doubt. It is perhaps unfortunate that our meeting confirmed everything I feared."

Waves of fury resonated as Perry kept ranting. Convinced James could *never afford the restoration*, he even had the effrontery to pour scorn over Avalon's supper parties.

"Oh yes, I'd almost forgotten about Avalon," James massaged into the conversation, "and she won't be seeing your son again either, not since I've discovered how much he frightens her! I never wanted to fall out. I appreciate everything you did, as well as your generous offer to fund the restoration, but that's the trouble, it was too generous! I couldn't help wondering what your real motive was."

Perry exhaled loudly. "I told you! My only motive was to develop your hotel for the corporate market! With my connections it would have worked!"

"Westbourne House is not that type of establishment," James argued, "and never will be. People love my hotel for its old-fashioned charm. Besides that, I doubt if I could handle the pressure."

"Bit of a lightweight really, aren't you," Perry sniffed. "Didn't I say your only role would be to look after the house and estate?"

"But under your management," James finished.

"Of course! You didn't think I was prepared to shell out that sort of money without some sort of return did you?"

"No," James admitted. "But let's not fall out over this, Perry. At the very least, you have saved yourself a considerable sum."

"You will never manage this alone!" Perry kept sneering. "Your house will decay into ruins and I'll be watching on the sidelines when it does!"

James gripped the telephone, shocked by his malice.

"Well, I'm sorry you feel that way," he finished coldly, "but nonetheless, we will make a go of it. Should we fail, I guess it will end up on the market. You may get to acquire it, Perry, and at a greatly reduced cost, given its condition..." and with no desire to tolerate any further vitriol, he dropped the receiver, almost breathless.

IV

"Bloody man!" Perry roared, slamming down the telephone.

Tugging at his tie, enraged, he saw his carefully compiled dossier of notes practically mocking him. Perry grasped hold of it, hurling it across the room. It hit the wall with a thud, sending a shower of paperwork flying into the air.

"Bugger it!"

He turned to see Rowena hovering, eyes cool as they bore into him.

She raised a pencil-thin eyebrow. "Turned you down did he?"

Her eyes never left him, the sound of her heels clicking across the hardwood floor a moment of pure torture. Perry released a sigh but he had broken out in a cold sweat.

"Did he give a reason?"

"Oh yes," Perry muttered, his voice sharpening to a hiss. "Someone warned him not to have any dealings with us! Must be that gypsy slut who lives in the caravan!"

"Perry, you don't know that," Rowena argued.

"Who else could it be?" Perry spat. "He's known that girl for years." He shook his head, worked up beyond reason. "She's like those bitches at Greenham Common! Always stirring up trouble! Wasn't it just a few weeks ago James was coming round to our idea?"

"Oh, will you shut up!" Rowena shouted. "I doubt if that girl even remembers you and I am so sick of your obsession with the past! If this is anyone's fault, it's yours!"

"How can you say that?" Perry spluttered. "I did everything I could!"

"Apart from nearly giving the game away, blathering on about your plans for development. I knew it was a mistake to air your opinions about those gardens!"

"Even you couldn't hide your contempt for those gardens," Perry protested.

"James is no fool," Rowena said, "and he probably saw right through you.

All you are really interested in is his land, am I right? Whereas I *loved* that house!"

"I know," Perry sighed, "and I swear to you, my love, I will get it for you! Maybe not quite as quickly as we hoped but we are still in with a chance!"

"I don't see how," Rowena taunted. "Not without the partnership."

"There are other ways," he said. "I tried the soft approach but if James won't play ball..." He broke off, weighing up his options. "First, I'll contact the building firm Edward recommended. I want them to delay the rebuild of the staircase. James cannot reopen the hotel until it's finished and will continue to lose income. Eventually, we will make him bankrupt."

A spark of greed lit Rowena's eyes.

"Next, I need to talk to Ben... Something happened between him and Avalon."

"Oh dear," Rowena lamented. "Well, it doesn't surprise me. You know what Ben can be like when he develops these little obsessions..."

"That's hardly the point," Perry's voice ebbed, "but we are not going to give up."

"Well, good luck," Rowena finished snidely. "Because right now, I'm off to the West End. I need a new coat! I almost froze to death wandering around their estate the other day."

Perry watched her go, his hate-fuelled ambition consuming him. But no sooner did he hear the front door slam, he picked up the telephone.

"Ben," he said softly. "Would you come down here please, I want a word with you."

Ben had no idea why his father had summoned him. Bruised by Avalon's rejection, he had escaped his home, to enjoy a night's entertainment in the hub of the city.

Nathan had ferried him to a number of futuristic looking wine bars before moving on to one of the sleazier night clubs in Soho. There he had picked up a girl of about seventeen. Leaving Nathan to his own devices, he had booked a hotel and after snorting a few lines of cocaine, indulged in a night of wild sex. With pale skin and a mass of shaggy brown curls, she reminded him of Avalon. Satisfied to lose himself in his own dark fantasies, whilst possessing her young body, Ben guessed his parents were none too pleased when it emerged he had been out all night.

With a cocky smile he sauntered into the hallway.

Yet it took one glance at Perry's thunderous expression to knock the smirk off his face.

"Is something wrong?" he began.

Perry lowered his eyes. "James Barton-Wells has declined our partnership," he said. "Ben, what happened between you and Avalon?"

Ben felt an immediate prick of fear. "Nothing," his voice echoed down the hallway.

"Don't lie, Ben," Perry drawled, the volume in his voice rising. "Tell me what you did."

He turned, grey eyes blazing. Ben recoiled without even realising it.

"I kissed her," he spluttered, forcing himself to stay calm. "Father, I swear that is all that happened!"

"James said you frightened her," Perry accused.

Ben gave a twisted smile. "It's not my fault she's so sensitive and I'll hedge a bet this had nothing to do with James's decision. Now was there anything else you wanted to talk to me about?"

"There was actually," Perry muttered, and even Ben recognised the calculating edge in his tone. "As things stand, we cannot turn back the clock. But there is a chance we can use this regrettable situation to our advantage. Come with me."

Ben followed him into his office and Perry closed the door. The first thing Ben noticed was the paperwork scattered across the floor. Obviously, James's withdrawal from the partnership had sent his father into an insane rage.

"Sit down," Perry ordered, waving him towards one of his deep leather chairs.

Ben did as he was told, curious to wonder why his father was involving him.

"As I was saying, James Barton-Wells has pulled out! I am not sure how much this had to do with a malicious rumour, or whether he came to the decision on his own. But he was a fool to turn us down and for that, we are going to make him pay!"

"Why are you so desperate to get your hands on the house?" Ben quizzed.

"Your mother wants it," Perry snapped. "She has always dreamed of owning a house in the country and I promised I would find a way of acquiring it."

"Why Westbourne House?" Ben pressed. "Can't you find another?"

"Do you really want to know why this house is special?" Perry sighed. "First, it is within a commutable distance from London; second, I'm convinced we can turn it into a profitable business venture, which will be an exciting new challenge for Rowena. And last, Westbourne House has fallen into disrepair. I know damn well James can't afford it, in which case, we should be able to acquire it cheaply, without having to take out another mortgage."

"So why not wait until he puts it on the market?" Ben said with a shrug.

"What? You think I'd be the only bidder?" Perry said. "No, Ben. We have to find a way of acquiring it, before things reach that stage. The truth is, James will do his utmost to save it, so his children can inherit it. But he's getting old and not in the best of health..."

Ben leaned forward in his chair, hankering to know where this was leading.

Perry fixed him with a long, steely gaze. "It is essential we keep an eye on them, so when the time comes, and they appear to be struggling, we will be ready to pounce."

"You want me to spy on them?" Ben whispered with undisguised glee.

"Oh, I want you to do more than that," Perry added. "Tell me, Ben. How much do you know about fear tactics? Have you ever wondered how some people in this world rule by terror?"

Ben stared at him, his mind exploding with intrigue.

"A long time ago, I found myself in an awkward situation; a time when I was involved in politics. Some troublesome little harpy turned up, making the most damning allegations! But in those days London was controlled by a criminal faction. A colleague of mine had connections with a man who was greatly feared."

"You mean some sort of gangster?" Ben frowned.

"Yes," Perry finished with satisfaction. "His name was Dominic Theakston. He knew ways of inspiring such terror, he could make people disappear just like that!" He gave a snap of his fingers as if to press the point.

Ben shifted in his chair. He had heard the name, most likely from Nathan, who had mixed with some seriously dodgy types in his time.

"It worked for me, Ben," Perry gloated. "Whatever was said, it succeeded in driving that little madam out of London and she never returned! But you must be wondering where this is leading, which brings us back to the Barton-Wells girl. She is frightened of you, am I right?"

"Yeah," Ben nodded. "You've got that right. Even when I tried to kiss her, she struggled like a wild cat. I confess, I would have enjoyed seducing her..."

"So work on her fear!" Perry's voice rose ominously. "Visit the village occasionally and make sure she sees you. Find ways of making her even more *frightened*; so scared, in fact, she may consider moving out of Aldwyck altogether."

"It would be my pleasure," Ben whispered, thrilled by the suggestion.

Chapter Nine

I

The weather remained exceptionally cold throughout December as temperatures continued to dip. Despite the chill, Avalon enjoyed her sixteenth birthday celebration in the home of their oldest friends, the Fortescues. Eager to escape the inherent problems of Westbourne House, James had been horrified to discover the door handles of his Jaguar frozen solid. But with the help of his staff, (along with several buckets of warm water), he eventually managed to thaw them, relieved to reach London before dusk.

Reunited with their friends in an exquisite restaurant, they had revelled in their celebration dinner with champagne. Then, as formerly arranged, the Fortescues took Avalon back to their house, to party with friends from her old school, as well as their son, George.

Her last recollection was of a typical adolescent boy, several inches shorter and plagued with spots. William secretly referred to him as 'Wing Nut' due to his unfortunate sticking out ears. One year on however, George had grown several inches taller. His spots had cleared up to reveal a smooth, dewy complexion, his hair beautifully cut in a modern 80s style; short and spiky on top with the sides left a little longer to hide his protuberant ears.

Chatting with him at dinner had been fun.

Yet the party at their house was even more effervescent, dancing to 'Wham' and the 'Pet Shop Boys,' getting tipsy on punch... Sometime later they had ultimately tumbled into bed where Avalon had lost her virginity. It started in the usual innocent way of teenagers, a frenzy of kissing. Clumsily pulling off her embroidered tunic, George delighted her further by caressing her breasts and kissing her nipples. She made no attempt to stop him; not even when he slipped a hand inside her knickers. Gradually he manoeuvred himself on top of her, but as their union reached its blissful climax, they were giggling so much, it only lasted a few seconds.

Avalon sensed her awakening from childhood to womanhood, delighted the transition had been so nice. Somewhere in the darkness of her mind, though, hung the fear of what it *could have been like* had she succumbed to Ben...

Her return to Westbourne House brought the memories swirling back like snowflakes. She felt a shiver of cold as the woods took shape in the distance, remembering the savage way he had kissed her. He had shown no tenderness - more a desire to dominate and control...

Avalon shoved the thought aside, pleased to be home. Wandering through the door, she pulled off her scarf and fake fur hat, throwing them onto the coat stand. Her thoughts had already drifted back to George, thinking how nice it would be to see him again, especially as his family were due to stay with them in the New Year. This had become something of a tradition.

Racing upstairs, she paused outside her father's office, unnerved to hear him rowing with someone on the telephone.

"It's not bloody good enough! You said it would take four weeks to rebuild that staircase! How on earth are we supposed to manage with the hotel being closed for all this time?"

Avalon pressed her eyes shut, horrified to be caught up in the turmoil of their restoration again. He must have been talking to the building company.

"This is your last warning! I want that staircase rebuilt by the beginning of January. I have guests staying in the New Year and if you continue to delay this job for any longer, I will not be using your company for the bulk of the restoration. Do I make myself clear?"

Avalon felt the touch of a smile, proud to hear her father making a stand.

Though little did she know that at some point, Perry would learn of this conversation.

II

A week later and with Christmas approaching, Avalon hummed softly to herself as she and William began to decorate the eight-foot Norwegian spruce tree that had been delivered.

William, home for the holidays, was looking forward to three weeks off school, hoping there would be snow, so they could go sledging. Right now, though, nothing pleased him more than to see his sister looking happier, a renewed sparkle to her eyes as she pulled the glittering ropes of tinsel from an old tea chest. How much this had to do with being shot of that repulsive Ben Hampton, he couldn't say. There had been something inherently creepy about him from day one, although he did not dare express his true thoughts, especially with negotiations concerning the house underway.

"Heard from 'Wing Nut' lately?" he smiled, lining up the Christmas tree baubles.

"Don't call him that," Avalon whispered. "But seeing as you ask, yes. I've had a letter! He can't wait to see me and the whole family are looking forward to spending the New Year with us."

"Sweet," William murmured, plucking another gold bauble from the box. "I'm really happy for you and don't worry... Dad says that if the staircase isn't finished, he'll leave the door unlocked between the guest rooms. He didn't think we'd need so much privacy, seeing as we're friends..." He gave a cheeky wink. "Handy for you and George, if you want to spend some 'quality time' together."

"I don't know what on earth you mean!" Avalon gasped, her cheeks flaring crimson.

Mercifully, and as if to save further embarrassment, Bryony breezed into reception carrying a parcel. Pausing by the tree, she gazed at its feathery branches with a nod.

"What a beautiful tree," she complimented. "It'll look even better when you two have decorated it and don't forget to put the fairy lights on first."

"Of course not," Avalon smiled as she continued to haul great swathes of tinsel from the box. "What have you got there?"

"A parcel's arrived," Bryony muttered. "Here, take it. It's addressed to you."

The parcel felt light. Long and conical in shape, it was wrapped in layers of brown paper, Avalon's name written in block capitals with a black felt marker.

"Well, aren't you going to open it?" William pressed.

Avalon rose to her feet with a frown. Darting from reception to escape his scrutiny, she couldn't help feeling a little mystified. There was no way the parcel could have been sent by George. For a start, she would have recognised the handwriting.

Wandering into the library, she bit her lip, unable to contain her curiosity. She tore back the enveloping paper where a bouquet of roses was revealed.

Except they were dead.

Avalon stared at the blackened stems in horror, petals so grey and withered they crumbled to the floor like ashes. A sudden chill crawled over her. *Who on earth would send her a bunch of dead and decaying roses?* It didn't make sense. Furthermore, it was sick!

Then a scrawl of writing caught her eye on the inner wrapper:

Cold and dead, just like you.

Avalon dropped the parcel with a shriek.

Seconds later, William burst into the room.

Frozen in the doorway, his mouth fell open. "Avalon, what is it?"

"Oh my God!" she whimpered, backing away from the debris.

William took another step. His eyes wandered from the parcel to the shower of dead petals scattered over the carpet. Crouching down to retrieve it, he recoiled in horror.

"Ugh!" he breathed. "How disgusting! Who the hell sent you those?"

Avalon shivered. Deep down, she already suspected who the sender was.

An image of Ben's and his obsessive stare tore into her memory. Yet, how could she tell him? She could hardly believe it herself...

Charlie felt an unexpected tug of nerves. Steering his car through the ornamental gate posts, he observed the tree-lined drive stretched ahead of him. His own children, along with Eleanor and Elijah, were packed into the car and since the weather had turned colder, they were snuggled into thick winter coats.

A month had passed since their momentous meeting in Rosebrook.

Eleanor had promised she would take them to see Westbourne House, hankering to introduce James to Charlie. Today seemed an ideal opportunity. They were about to face their first Christmas without Anna.

Outwardly, Charlie had coped well, though the grief struck deep.

Even today, he was suffering flashbacks of her funeral. Swept into the past, he remembered the wake, a day he had at last drowned his sorrows. After two large glasses of red wine, the alcohol had numbed his senses, dragging him out of the sinking marsh of desolation he had been immersed in.

There were times his gaze had inevitably drifted towards Eleanor. She had made herself scarce at the crematorium but attended the wake. Head swimming, everything had turned surreal. The melody of voices shifted and echoed, yet the only one that stood out had been *hers*. Husky and doleful, it rose above the others.

Charlie would never forget the scattering of words Anna had whispered.

"Stick with Eleanor. She's been good to us..."

He couldn't deny he needed her. She was the only person who had gone out of her way to help them and for that reason, he was not going to push her away; more for the sake of Margaret, whose friendship with Elijah continued to flourish. He cherished her companionship and the special bond the three of them had shared once...

Feeling the jab of her stare, he captured her eye in the driver mirror.

"Just keep going until you reach the end of the drive."

As the house loomed closer, he felt a lump in his throat. Nothing could enchant him more than the sheer scale of its beauty; solid walls the colour of ripe peaches, the delicate stonework around each window. Even more captivating was its symmetry. Each wing was perfectly balanced, the central façade distinguishable by a triangular stone pediment.

"Bloody hell!" he gasped aloud. "It's magnificent!" Already he had started pointing. "See that little dome in the centre of the roof, kids? That's a *cupola* and typical of the renaissance style of the late 1700's, which I'm guessing is around the time this house was built, right?"

"I would say that was about right," Eleanor replied.

"The windows are beautiful," he kept enthusing, "and look at all those chimney stacks!"

Andrew shot Eleanor a furtive glance. "He's always like this," he muttered.

"This is a historic house, Andrew!" Charlie exclaimed with a chuckle. "How can I not be ecstatic? Is there any more you can tell me about the restoration, Eleanor?"

"Well, I told you about the survey," she said darkly. "Poor James... I'm sure he mentioned some deep inner rot which has affected the timbers."

"Hmm," Charlie remarked, flicking a glance at the house again. "Deterioration of the inner framework is not unusual in period properties."

He pulled up, the doors flying open simultaneously as everyone jumped out. Eleanor and her son showed no hesitation as they headed in the direction of the house.

"Come on then!" she hollered to the others. "He won't bite!"

"Who lives here, Dad?" Margaret whispered, sidling up to him. "Is he someone rich?"

"I'm not sure," Charlie smiled back. "They're friends of Eleanor's..."

On first impression, the house was effervescent with activity compared to the last visit. Hoards of smartly dressed people meandered between restaurant and bar. Eleanor smiled, enchanted by the decorations, the sparkling garlands dripping with fir cones and silver baubles. The tree Avalon and William had decorated now twinkled with lights, and they were reflected in the ornaments dangling from the branches.

"Eleanor!" a girl's voice echoed from the other side of reception.

All heads turned as Avalon emerged from the crowd. Wrapped in a knee-length, cable knit sweater dress in cherry red, she looked gorgeous, her river of bronze curls tumbling over her shoulders. Andrew stopped dead, unable to take his eyes off her.

"Avalon," Eleanor beamed, embracing her. "It's good to see you. Seems busy today!"

They were hosting a special Christmas dinner for the Rosebrook Conservation Society, Avalon explained. Her gaze wandered towards Elijah. From where Charlie stood, the way they greeted each other suggested an enduring friendship. Avalon poked the rim of his trilby.

"Love your hat."

"Jake wore a trilby once," Eleanor reminisced. "It reminds me of him. Anyway, I've brought my friends along with me today."

The smile on Avalon's face lingered as she introduced them.

"This is Charlie, the building specialist I told your father about. He runs his own business, along with his son, Andrew..."

As Andrew shuffled on his feet like a schoolboy, Charlie glanced away.

"And this is my daughter, Margaret," he added.

Margaret's face stretched into a wide smile as her eyes locked with Avalon's.

Yet Eleanor was aware of more people, just as Elliot's face materialised within the mass. Capturing her gaze with a smile, the subtle upward flick of his eyes implied they were getting overwhelmed.

"Look, I won't hold you up," she said. "I can see you've got a lot on, but is James around? I'd love to introduce him to Charlie."

The smile dropped from Avalon's face. "Dad's not been well," she sighed. "He's had another one of his dizzy turns. Albany insisted he take at least two days rest..."

Eleanor felt deflated, a mixture of disappointment and sorrow. "I've been worried about your dad. Didn't he have some tests done?"

She saw the anxiety flit across Avalon's expression.

"He's okay. He's just had a lot on his mind recently... such a shame. He would have liked to have met your friends."

"Eleanor told me about the house," Charlie broke into the conversation.

Avalon looked at him sadly. "It's about to undergo a massive restoration."

"So, what's happened with this *partnership*?" Eleanor pressed.

"It's all off, thank God!" Avalon breathed. "Dad saw right through those people in the end!"

Eleanor nodded, relieved James had taken their warnings seriously. But with no time to elaborate, Avalon finished the conversation on a positive note.

"We're going to try to rescue the house ourselves somehow, but we'll start by auctioning off some of our stuff. Promise you'll come back though... Maybe after Christmas?"

"Damn," Eleanor muttered, as they ambled back down the steps.

"Never mind," Charlie reassured her. "We can still wander around the grounds. What a delightful young lady!"

"She's like a princess," Margaret piped up softly.

Regrettably, this was the one innocent comment that drew out Andrew's surliness. Wildly jealous that *Elijah* of all people could be so openly affectionate, he hurled him a look of contempt.

"What's so special about *you* then?" he sneered.

"Avalon and I have known each other for ages!" Elijah protested, cheeks reddening.

"Doesn't give you the right to drool over her!" Andrew kept sniping.

"Pack it in, Andrew!" Charlie shouted. "Don't you dare be so rude! It's not Eli's fault you were acting like a buffoon in there..."

"Was not!" Andrew argued, stomping across the grass.

******

85

As Charlie observed his son, he couldn't help but feel saddened by the change in him. It took him back to the dreaded era he was telling Eleanor about, the day Dick dissolved his company.

He had failed to find another job. Forced to live on a measly allowance, whilst scouring the boards at the Job Centre, he faced an unbelievable shortage, other than for unskilled labourers. He had hoped these jobs would be more suited to Andrew. Yet no firm seemed willing to take him on until he had completed his apprenticeship.

Unfortunately, it didn't take long for the frustration of being unemployed, coupled with a lack of things to do, to transform Andrew into a foul-tempered, moody teenager. Charlie had no choice other than to sign him up for a 'Youth Training Scheme,' a government initiative spurned by the Brixton riots of 1981 when unemployment spiralled to over two million. There was only one drawback; his wages amounted to little more than the dole.

But a month later the bailiffs had come.

The nightmare of having to watch the violation of their modest home was nothing compared to the reaction of his family. Anna had unlocked the door, no doubt chilled by the silence that greeted her. It took one glance inside the lounge for the three of them to freeze. Squares of space devoid of dust betrayed the absence of the items which had occupied them.

"Where's the fucking TV gone?" Andrew bellowed.

Just one look was enough to cause Anna to back, trembling, into the far wall. She almost fell against it. But the memory of her face would cling to his mind forever, like a condemned prisoner about to face execution.

Next came the horror of explaining the worse news.

In two days time, they would be evicted.

"We'll have to go to the DHSS," Anna mumbled.

Charlie could clearly recall that day. Dawn broke to reveal a low sun. It lit up the strips of cloud until they shot across the sky like flames. But with a heavy heart, he revealed the truth to his children; the sooner they started packing, the better. As the house had been rented fully furnished, they didn't actually have much other than their personal possessions. Most of their electrical goods had been seized by the bailiffs.

The worst however, was yet to come; their move into temporary housing.

Placed in a shabby apartment block, their accommodation teetered on the rough edge of town. They would receive full housing benefit and an allowance sufficient to support their needs. Anna's part time job (working in a local bakery) had to be taken into account and they scored additional points on the basis that Andrew was on a YTS.

Yet it was really down to Charlie finding a decent job in the construction industry to dig them out of the appalling hole they had fallen into. So he kept looking...

Watching Andrew now, he felt his heart lurch. What had happened to that happy-go-lucky boy he remembered? Heavily into his music, with a love of the bands like 'Echo and the Bunnymen,' Andrew bounded effortlessly through life, following their image; dark hair gelled into spikes, a long tweed overcoat more suited to older men... but what had extinguished his twinkle?

Even Margaret gaped after him in dismay.

Why Andrew had to be so vile on a pleasant day like this came as something of a disappointment. Yet her eyes followed his path, snapping Charlie out of his reverie.

"Look, Dad," she called. "Look at the lovely gardens!"

Even in their dormant state, they were breath-taking. Stepping up their pace, they were stirred by their magnificence; the ornamental fountain with its pattern of box hedging, the tall urns where points of white cyclamens seemed to glow against the ivy spilling over the edges.

The adults watched in admiration as Elijah and Margaret went charging ahead.

"Bloody hell," Charlie murmured for the second time that day. "Oh Eleanor, Anna would have loved it here..."

"I know," she sighed. "Just think. If you can help James out in some way, you could bring the kids over any time."

"It's a wonderful idea," Charlie sighed, pushing his hands into his coat pockets, "but I won't build my hopes up..."

They wandered a little further. The kids were scattered in all directions by now, as the paths extended into open parkland. Pausing in the shadow of a cedar tree, they gazed back at the house, observing it from a different angle.

"Can you see anything wrong from this side?" Eleanor probed.

Charlie squinted to get a better look. Sure enough, the weak sunlight had illuminated a jagged scar carving its way down the outer wall, forcing it apart in places.

"Oh yes," he said ominously. "See that crack running down the wall? It needs underpinning before it can be fixed... and do you know something else? He should get rid of that ivy. It has a habit of working its way into the masonry, causing more damage."

As his eyes travelled over the outer shell though, more faults began to reveal themselves.

Charlie sighed. "Some of the windows are in a pretty bad state, too."

He shot a glance towards Andrew, lingering a few metres behind.

"Their style is quite intricate. These are not standard frames. Each one will have to be rebuilt, which is something we can definitely help your friend with."

"Good," Eleanor said, catching his eye again. "You see, there is another advantage to this partnership going by the wayside. James will be looking to save money."

Chapter Ten

Avalon shivered as she wandered along the cobbled pavements of Aldwyck, despite the warmth of her overcoat. Absorbed in memories of their New Year's celebration with the Fortescues in residence, she was missing the effervescent mood. Ever since their return to London, though, the house seemed somewhat desolate. George, as well as her brother, had returned to their respective private schools, but she cherished their light-hearted chatter.

At least the new staircase was reinstated. The builders had obviously taken her father's ultimatum seriously, fearing he would end the contract.

So finally, they were allowed to re-open the hotel.

Avalon sighed, absorbed in her own reminiscences; the cosy evenings by a log fire, playing charades and sipping ginger wine... The food, too, was unforgettable. Gathered together in their restaurant with staff, they had enjoyed a festive feast of roast goose and an array of vegetable dishes, from Dauphinoise Potatoes to a tangy casserole made from red cabbage, all harvested from their walled gardens. The Fortescue family were delighted by the efforts of head chef, Angelo, coupled with Bryony's exquisite desserts.

With few opportunities for Avalon and George to be alone, she recalled one mild evening when they had stolen themselves away, before settling down in the Orangerie. Clinging to each other in the darkness, their kisses grew more passionate, until they could no longer resist making love again. But on this occasion, it was exquisite; a contrast to the drunken fling on Avalon's birthday.

Plunging her hands into her coat pockets, she felt the touch of a smile. The nightmare of the dead flowers and Ben Hampton were all but forgotten... Yet just as she found herself wandering past the 'Olde House at Home,' she jammed to an abrupt halt. For there in the pub car park, gleaming under the pale winter sun, lurked a car that looked disturbingly familiar; a silver Mercedes sports. Her mouth ran dry as she glanced at the number plate: BH21. There was no mistaking the same car Ben's sinister, leather-clad chauffeur had driven on the night of their date.

Avalon shuddered again. Lowering her eyes, she spun on her heel, then walked in the opposite direction. Hurrying across the village green, she focused her attention on the cottages, but even their charm could not expel the sudden chill in her veins.

Ben Hampton was in the village.

Darting inside the post office, she felt safer, then remembered she needed postage stamps. She wandered into the queue, where several people smiled at her, yet she hardly recognised them. Other matters crowded her mind.

Just before Christmas, she had received a birthday card from her mother. Tucked inside was a £50 cheque, alongside a newsy letter. Avril no longer lived in the South of France, having recently moved to America. William had scoffed at that; his theory being *she must have hooked up with some Texan oil billionaire*. Avalon really didn't care. She felt quite touched her mother had contacted her and wanted to write her a thank you letter. The queue shuffled slowly forwards. Older customers liked to chat, though Avalon was in no hurry.

"Good afternoon, Miss Barton-Wells," beamed the wife of the postmaster. "I'm glad you called by. What can I do for you?"

"I'd like an airmail envelope please," Avalon answered, "and a dozen first class stamps."

"Right you are," the woman muttered. She gently tore a square of stamps off a sheet. "I've got a parcel for you too... We were going to drop it off, but you might as well take it now."

A small padded parcel was poked through the window. Avalon froze, reluctant to touch it at first but it looked to be the size of a cricket ball. She glanced over her shoulder, aware the queue had grown a little longer. With little choice other than to accept it, she scooped it up with one hand, paid for her items and left.

Exposed to the cold again, she stared at the package. Already, she had a bad feeling about it. Her name and address was printed on a label, suggesting it might have been sent by a mail order firm. Unable to contain her curiosity, she prized open the seal, feeling inside, until at last her hand closed around something hard.

But as the mysterious object was revealed, she could not halt the gasp bursting from her lips. Staring down at a rabbit's skull, she was taunted by its hollow eye sockets. Its muzzle reminded her of claws, the upper and lower jaws grinning eerily. She released a sob, hit with a flash of memory. A similar object on a woodland path, Ben had mindlessly kicked it away. She pressed her eyes shut but it was no use. The macabre image stained the canvas of her mind like an ink blot.

Giddy with fear, she started walking again, her feet ferrying her back in the direction of the pub. But just before she reached it, a blast of music cut the atmosphere. She had never imagined the nightmare could get much worse, but there was something very haunting about the powerful electronic beat and robotic voices, the spine-chilling chords of a synthesiser...

Avalon glanced up. And in precisely the same moment, the silver Mercedes crawled past. Already, she had spotted Nathan hunched over the wheel, eyes narrow as he smirked at her. But her gaze was drawn to Ben slouched in the passenger seat, one arm dangling from an open window. He leaned out to stare at her and as their eyes locked, the expression on his face was satanic.

Avalon did not know how she managed to get home. Yet by the time the fog in her mind had cleared, she had almost reached the front steps.

Those last moments in the village had been awful.

Frozen on the spot, she could only pray no one had witnessed her fear.

The instant she slipped through the ornamental gate posts, though, she gave way to tears, sobbing her way up the driveway, until she had finally reached her home. Only now did she pause, reluctant to step inside. Anyone who saw her would know she had been crying.

Cautiously turning the knob, to make as little sound as possible, she poked her head around the door. The wooden coat rack stood just feet away, her father's tweed jacket dangling. Avalon sneaked across and feeling into the pocket for his hip flask, tiptoed back outside. She knew she would have to face him at some point but needed time to think; a chance to analyse this ominous sequence of events.

Lost in her thoughts, she started striding across the grounds, where the fated woodlands lured her. The landscape was white with frost. Behind the mist rose the ghostly silhouettes of trees, most distinctive of all, the cedars. Their feathery branches opened out as if to embrace her and Avalon breathed deeply. Clouds of breath swirled into strange shapes and as she headed towards the forest, the memories started to rise up again.

But this time she did not suppress them...

She remembered the exact path she and Ben had walked; his kiss, the violent flare in his eyes as she tried to fight him. Avalon bit her lip, seeing the familiar woodland trail. The rabbit's skull was still there, half submerged in thick grass.

So it hadn't been this one, though clearly this was what he wanted her to think.

Avalon unscrewed the hip flask and took a swig, soothed by the brandy as it warmed her chest. She did not venture further, but as she pondered over the facts, they fused into a chilling truth. There was no question in her mind that Ben had posted that skull. What disturbed her most was the difficulty in proving it. He was clever using a label. All the postmark revealed was an ambiguous sorting office in London, nothing to track the ghoulish package back to him.

As for the dead flowers, the parcel had been handwritten. But only now did she wish she had kept the packaging, instead of dumping it in a rubbish bin.

Dead roses and now a skull.

Death seemed to be a common theme embedded in the mystery parcels. The way Ben had materialised in the village, though, seemed even more disturbing; the terrifying way he had ogled her, that spine chilling music...

Finally she understood the concept of stalking, recalling a magazine article she had read.

Why do people stalk?

The answers had been there, the notion that people who stalked possessed *a desire to control; people who were obsessive - or lonely.*

Avalon pressed her eyes shut, Rowena's words flooding back to her.

"He is so very shy, you see and lonely..."

The truth was staring her in the face. Two parcels added to his presence in the village; this was Ben's way of trying to control *her* by driving her insane with fear. Avalon swallowed. Taking another swig from the flask, she felt a sudden urge to talk to her father now.

Perhaps they should go to the police.

Regrettably, the absence of proof would be a problem. She had destroyed the flowers and what was there to suggest the origin of the skull arose from Ben's twisted imagination? She had never told anyone about their walk. As for seeing him in the village, so what? Visiting Aldwyck was not a crime, no more than his choice of music.

With a swell of sadness, she felt the tears bubble again and with the air turning colder, noticed she was shaking. She so badly wanted to tell someone - but what would be the point? If Ben was lurking around Aldwyck, she could just as easily stay away. Deprived of the opportunity to torment her, maybe he would get bored with his nasty psychological games.

II

One week later Ben was feeling frustrated.

He had taken several more trips to Aldwyck, where the marked absence of Avalon was really starting to bite. Ruthless in his quest, he decided to try a different tactic.

The next time he ventured into the village, he did so alone. Easing his Harley Davidson into the pub car park, he ambled inside. The landlord was a striking man, whose rosy face and warm smile projected a certain charm. Though as Ben stepped up to the bar, he couldn't help but notice his eyes adopting a searching quality.

"Haven't I seen you before?" he dropped out casually. "I recognise you."

"I've only been here twice," Ben snapped. "Didn't think anyone would even notice. Now could I have a tonic water please?"

Boris offered him a polite nod.

Unbeknown to Ben, it wasn't really *him* the locals had 'noticed,' as opposed to the dangerous looking brute who had accompanied him. Unnerved by his black leather clothing and chilling stare, some began to wonder whether he was some type of *Hell's Angel*.

Ben however, appeared to be alone today, donning similar bikers' leathers.

Maybe they were just a pair of motorcycle enthusiasts.

With another furtive glance, Boris poured his drink and set it down on the bar.

This youth looked relatively harmless; but with pale, pointed features and a cap of ruffled fair hair, he betrayed a hint of awkwardness.

"Are you new to the area?" Boris persisted.

"Just passing through," Ben shrugged. "My parents were thinking of moving here. Do you know the village well?"

"Do I?" Boris laughed. "I've lived here all my life, son!"

Ben forced a smile, his eyes zooming in on him. "In that case, could you tell me a bit about Westbourne House and the owner. Mr Barton-Wells, isn't it?"

"Huh!" a loud voice grunted from behind him.

Ben spun around, faced by a giant of a man hunched on a bar stool. With a large face and a florid flush to his complexion, he appeared to be observing him.

"James is very well respected in this village!" Boris barked at him. "He knows everyone who's ever lived here and he's a pillar of the community!"

"Well, not all of us agree," the other man barked back, "especially with his liberal views towards those damned gypsy people!"

"Oh, don't start that again, Herbert," Boris said through gritted teeth, "and if you're about to pick on young Eleanor, you might as well leave right now."

The man let out a snort. "I wasn't talking about your darling Eleanor. I was talking about the other rabble he allows on his land."

"Are you referring to the new age travellers?" Ben drawled, enjoying their banter. "My father did mention them. He was disgusted... lovely village like Aldwyck."

"Hear, hear," Herbert gloated portentously. "See, there *are* people who agree with me, Boris! James Barton-Wells has let the whole village down."

"Rubbish!" Boris spat. Braced behind the bar, he started furiously drying up glasses.

"Can you tell me anything about the house?" Ben pressed, eager to divert the conversation away from the travellers. "Isn't it undergoing some restoration?"

"How do you know that?" Boris muttered.

"My father is a property developer," Ben said. "Has dealings with all sorts of building firms. It's rumoured *a country house hotel around here* is in need of vital repair work and has temporarily closed down..."

"Yeah, don't I know it," a female voice rose darkly from a nearby table. Ben turned towards the source, spotting a scruffy looking girl. She too, appeared to be watching him. "Lost me bleeding job I did, and without a lot of notice..."

"You used to work there?" Ben murmured.

"Yeah, as a chambermaid," she continued to broadcast.

He observed her with interest. Fixing him with heavily made up eyes, she had a thin fox-like face, surrounded by a mass of spiky black hair. He tapped his wallet on the bar.

"Can I get you something to drink?" he offered.

"Okay, I'll have a vodka and lime," the girl smirked.

For now, Ben ignored the other people milling around the bar. His attention was focussed on this girl who he sensed held the key to everything. He kept his questions benign to begin with, in case anyone was listening, curious to know what the rooms were like, how expensive they were...

"My mother's dying to spend a weekend there."

By the time she had downed her first drink, the pub was turning busier. Ben bought a second round, drawing his head closer.

"Tell me about the staff," he whispered. "Who do you like the best?"

"Elliot," the girl sniggered, eyes glittering. "He's the butler. Spent his whole life as a bachelor, or so I've been told. Funny, I often wondered if he was gay."

"And the residents?" Ben probed. "Have you ever met the family?"

"Sure," she divulged. "James Barton-Wells and his daughter run that place. He's got a boy too. William. Nice kid, he is, used to make us laugh..."

"What about the daughter," Ben snapped. "What's she like?"

"Avalon?" The girl sneered, taking another swallow of her drink.

Straight away, Ben spotted the contempt flickering across her face. He raised an eyebrow.

"Little Miss Perfect! All she's got to worry about is making herself look pretty and smiling at the guests. She ain't got a clue what real work is. I was the one who had to clean her room. Didn't help that she had all that ivy growing over her window which she keeps open half the time!"

"Which room?" Ben kept delving. "What part of the house?"

"Second floor," the girl muttered carelessly, "corner where the ivy grows thickest."

Ben almost shivered. Already, he was visualising the house again with its bank of gleaming ivy. Yes, he could distinctly remember which corner it was clustered around...

A heavy darkness cloaked the secluded grounds that night. Settled in the lounge with her father, Avalon felt more relaxed. She had eventually confided in Bryony, since she already knew about the dead roses. In a moment of despair, she had also told her about the skull, never forgetting Ben's presence in the village.

James fumbled around his pocket for his hip flask. Only as he shook it, did he discover it almost empty, glancing at her with suspicion. Avalon shrugged, insisting she had just borrowed it whilst walking in the grounds, simply because it was chilly...

What she didn't want to confess was the real reason she had craved its effects. But of course, he forgave her and as the evening progressed, they found themselves discussing more pressing matters.

Which part of the restoration to tackle next?

Poring over the survey, they arrived at the same conclusion. The next essential phase was the roof. The cold snap had receded, but with milder weather forecast came an increasing threat of rain. James didn't dare put it off, given the likelihood of more water leaking in and spreading further dampness.

This however, was the most expensive part of the restoration. With an original estimate of £100,000, it was time to consider pooling their assets. Sell some antiques. He left Avalon with the promise there would soon be an auction at Sotheby's. It would make a pleasant day out for the two of them, especially if they returned with enough cash.

Avalon spent the rest of the evening in her bedroom, uplifted by the hope they might yet save their home. Switching on her portable TV, she craved some light-hearted entertainment, happy to watch a weekly chat show hosted by Terry Wogan.

By the time the programme ended, she tried to watch the news but it was heavy with politics... With a lengthy yawn, she turned it off, snuggling up in bed with a book. She spent the next half hour reading, until her eyelids became heavy, then switched off her bedside lamp.

The house lapsed into a peaceful silence. Avalon closed her eyes, conscious of the tick of her bedside clock. She could hear a gentle thud of footsteps, guessing it to be Elliot doing his last rounds. After that came the usual creaks and groans from deep within the old house as every so often the timbers nudged. From somewhere outside, rose the haunting cry of a bird. Avalon's thoughts began to wander before a creeping tiredness overcame her.

She was hovering on the brink of sleep when a new sound registered.

Her eyes sprang open. Seeing the dark outline of the wall opposite, she couldn't define what it was at first; a soft, crisp scattering that reminded her of sand hitting a window pane.

She heard it again, wondering if it was rain - a blast of hailstones maybe. Yet there was no wind outside and the weather, though chilly, had been unusually calm.

Avalon sat up in bed, head cocked, listening. The next time, she flinched. Sitting bolt upright, she switched on her lamp, a sudden fear worming its way into her. It sounded for all the world as if someone had flung a handful of earth at the window.

With a nervous swallow, she crept out of bed and tip-toed to the window. Her hands shook as they gripped the curtains. Yanking them apart, she hoped to catch a glimpse of whoever was out there, except she saw no one. Without thinking, she unlatched the window. An icy draft poured into her room, the emptiness of the grounds almost taunting. The only movement resonated from the trees, a flutter of shadows dancing on the lawn.

Then a bright flare materialised on the edge of the far lawn.

Avalon frowned. She wanted to shout *who's out there...* Yet the next sound not only took her by surprise, but turned her icy with shock.

Undoubtedly, this sounded familiar; a pulse of electronic music rising from some hidden place in the grounds. Loud enough to be audible, without waking up the entire household, it sent a shimmy of dread through her. Captured in the powerful beam aimed at her window, she knew who was out there - recognised the same music from that awful day in the village when Ben had driven past. She could picture him now, with his evil-eyed stare.

Avalon slammed the window shut and closed the curtains, desperate to shut it out...

Except she couldn't.

The music had tunnelled deep, torturing her with memories.

Lurching towards the door, she grabbed her dressing gown. Her hands shook, her breath exhaled in shuddering gasps. But no way was she was going to drop off to sleep with the knowledge that Ben Hampton was lurking outside.

She stepped silently from her bedroom and crept downstairs. Her feet ferried her to the lounge, where the first thing she noticed was a blueish gleam of moonlight beyond the patio doors. Fearful someone was watching her, she sneaked across the floor to close the curtains.

Convinced she was concealed, she felt the breath slowly leave her body. She sank into a chair. Yet she couldn't shake off that all pervading sense of being stalked. Curling into a ball, she drew her knees right up to her chest. For several seconds she listened to the steady tick of their antique bracket clock... until another sound pierced her senses.

An echo of footsteps rose outside in the corridor.

They were drawing closer, slow and methodical as if designed to be menacing. Avalon braced herself, heart pounding.

He couldn't be in the house, surely?

She drew in her breath, about to scream, before a figure loomed in the doorway.

Avalon blinked. Dressed in pyjamas and a flannel checked dressing gown, it was none other than their butler.

"Elliot!" she gasped, lowering her feet to the floor. "Thank God!"

He stepped into the room with a frown.

"Avalon... whoever did you think it was? Is something the matter?"

She froze, as if the mere mention of Ben's name would draw his demonic presence into their home. "Did you hear the music outside?"

"Music?" Elliot echoed. The frown on his face deepened.

"Yes," Avalon shivered, "someone was out there. I saw a flashlight! There was music coming from somewhere, creepy, synthesiser music. Whoever it was, they must have a ghetto blaster."

"I'm not quite sure what a *ghetto blaster* is," Elliot faltered.

"It's a massive cassette player with speakers," Avalon tried to explain. "Haven't you ever seen the Lenny Henry Show?"

Elliot chuckled lightly. "Forgive me for being a little out of touch, but I can't say I have. Do you think someone may still be out there? Would you like me to check?"

"No!" Avalon blurted. "Leave it, Elliot. It might not be safe..." Her gaze shifted towards the patio doors again.

"Look, why don't I make us a night cap," Elliot said. "We can keep each other company for a while. Would you like some hot chocolate?"

"Oh, yes please," Avalon sighed, sinking into the cushions.

He was only gone a few minutes but returned with a tray bearing two mugs and a jug. A warm fragrance of chocolate coiled into the lounge. Balanced on the edge stood a half bottle of whisky. Avalon sat, observing the lightness of his hands as he poured the cocoa, topping each mug with a tot of whisky.

"Might help you sleep a little better," he added with a conspiratorial wink.

"So, why couldn't you sleep?" Avalon quizzed.

A dragging silence followed, until finally he spoke.

"Like James, I too, feel concerned about the future of this house. Your father is certain he can raise the money over time. But in order to meet the cost of the restoration, he may have to take out a loan. I probably shouldn't be telling you this..."

"But I thought we were going to sell off some antiques," Avalon interrupted.

"Yes, that would be a first step," Elliot said, "but I'm not sure you will raise more than a few thousand. As you know, it will cost considerably more than that to restore this house. I think some form of loan will be inevitable."

"It doesn't matter," Avalon snapped, sipping her chocolate. "Sooner that, than deal with those vile Hamptons…"

As she looked up, their eyes met. The doting expression on his face brought reassurance.

She had to tell him.

"It was Ben in the grounds," she spluttered. "I'm certain of it!"

"Ben Hampton?" Elliot breathed. "How can you be sure?"

Avalon paused. Unsure how to explain it, she dropped her head into her hands.

"I just know! I haven't told anyone except Bryony - but - but - that music I heard… It was *his* music. I heard it in the village the other week. He drove past me, practically hanging out of the window, leering. That creepy henchman was driving, but the music playing in his car was the same…"

Elliot gaped at her in disbelief.

"It terrified me, Elliot. I don't know why, but it just did!"

Letting go of her tension, she felt her shoulders drop several inches.

"Avalon, this is very disturbing," Elliot muttered. "It sounds to me as if he is using some nasty psychological tactics to frighten you…"

"So, what am I supposed to do?" Her voice wavered, the tears gradually surfacing.

"I think you should talk to the police," he said gravely. "Ask if this sort of behaviour could be classified as stalking. And you should definitely tell your father… If that boy has been sneaking around the grounds at the dead of night, he is trespassing."

"But I didn't actually *see him*," she added weakly, "and Dad's got enough on his mind."

Elliot shook his head, the contours in his face tight. "In that case, try to put it out of your mind. Don't let him get to you. I'll tell you this much, my dear. I never did like those Hamptons. The effect they had on your father, especially the day he collapsed… I've long suspected they might have been plotting something."

"I wish he'd never had anything to do with them," Avalon shuddered.

In a small way Elliot was right. She would have to tell her father at some point. It just didn't seem fair to do it now, not when he had so many other worries burdening his mind.

Chapter Eleven

I

Avalon was not the only one thinking about Westbourne House.

Elijah too, had been reflecting...

That trip with the Baileys seemed a long time ago and now they had slipped into January.

Yet the anniversary of Anna's death had brought a melancholy atmosphere into their home. The last time they visited, his mother had cooked Sunday lunch. As soon as they stepped through the door though, he knew something was wrong; the way Charlie looked up, his face torn with anguish... and there in his hands lay the newspaper, listing her obituary.

The kids too had been silent and withdrawn. Andrew had never quite been the same since losing his mother, but added to his occasional bouts of temper, he had started smoking.

"I can't believe it's been a year," Charlie shivered.

Eleanor poured a glass of wine. As she lowered a comforting hand to his shoulder, Elijah caught the stab of Andrew's stare. She so much wanted to comfort him. But those silent waves of suspicion emanating from his kids were impossible to ignore.

Elijah had problems of his own, though. He had survived the first term of his second year without drawing much attention. Then without warning, came a fresh wave of bullying. It started in the aftermath of some TV coverage about the new age traveller movement; people he found himself being compared to.

He had tried explaining it to Margaret. "It's bad enough they call me a gypsy but suddenly we're *crusties*, like those people the police arrested at Stonehenge!"

"Crusties?" Margaret frowned.

"New age travellers," Elijah snapped. "D'you remember the Battle of the Beanfield?"

A riot known as the 'Battle of the Beanfield' had erupted in the previous June. A large convoy had been heading to Stonehenge before police stormed their vehicles, methodically smashing windows and beating people over the heads with truncheons. Elijah was curious, wondering if they could really be classified as *new age travellers,* since they too, lived in a caravan.

Eleanor laughed it off, reassuring him that they were nothing like them.

Margaret however, was another issue.

Her new primary school happened to be on the same site as his secondary. Mornings they were seen chatting together had not gone unnoticed, but ultimately resulted in this latest spate of ribbing. With a small and wiry frame, he lacked the strength to stand up to his enemies. There was one in particular; Gary Boswell, a lardy lump of a boy with a waxy face and small, mean eyes like black currants. As a rival resident in Aldwyck, he knew they lived in a caravan. Boastful of his father, who held a senior rank in the local police force, he wielded an air of superiority.

Even now, Elijah could hear his sneering words: *"Who's your girlfriend, Gyppo? Is she one of those pikeys who live in that field?"*

Still he refused to rise, his mother forever warning him to control his temper, so teachers had no excuse to malign him. Regrettably, half the teachers were so prejudiced, it didn't matter how well he behaved. But Gary, desperate for an excuse to needle him, began spreading rumours that *Margaret's family had to be crusties, to mix with the likes of him.*

It finally drove him to breaking point and before he could stop himself, Elijah had rounded on him, telling him to *shut his fat face.*

He did himself no favours. Come lunch time, Boswell and his gang had him trapped inside the boys' changing rooms. They tripped him up, booted him in the backside and after hauling him to his feet, proceeded to work him over with their fists. The attack left Elijah bruised and burning with humiliation, though fearful to tell anyone of his ordeal.

Craving the sanctuary of his home, he returned to the caravan, dismayed to find it empty.

It was down to his kindly neighbours, the Harpers, to explain; Eleanor had been called to the hospital to work an emergency shift. They were happy for him to stay with them until she returned, but Tom had clocked the anguish on his young face, guessing something was up.

Eventually, he coaxed the truth out of him. Furthermore he offered to drive Elijah to school next morning, to save him further torment.

"You can't bottle this up, young man," he advised sagely as they drew up to the school gates. "Have a word with the headmaster. Just tell him what happened."

"I can't!" Elijah spluttered. "They'll kill me!"

"If you don't report it, they'll keep picking on you," Tom argued.

Elijah let the breath stream slowly from his lungs. The thought of being back in that classroom filled him with dread, more so, given the sadness afflicting Margaret's family. It would be impossible to control his emotions if Boswell started slandering Margaret again. He fidgeted in his seat. Nibbling his lip, he could feel an ache in his ribs, not to mention the bruise on his right buttock. As Tom pulled up outside the door, he took another gulp of air.

"Go on then, run along!" Tom smiled. "Let's hope you have a better day."

Elijah felt numb. Pausing by the school doors, he was reluctant to go in. Hoards of pupils rushed past him, sending the doors swinging back and forth like pendulums. But conscious of Tom's car on the periphery, he slipped through the doors. At first he froze, submerged in the mass of kids swarming around him. But it took one sound ringing above the commotion to make him flinch; none other than the hectoring voice of Gary Boswell.

Before he could stop himself, he had spun on his heel and belted back through the doors. Running down the driveway in the direction of the exit, he was oblivious to the shocked face of one of his teachers. He didn't stop though, his stick-thin legs pounding along the path like pistons.

As the soft green edge of the park materialised, only then did he stop. Straight away, Elijah knew where he wanted to go. Without further hesitation, he bought a bunch of chrysanthemums from the nearest florist, then headed in the direction of the graveyard.

This was the place in which Anna had been laid to rest. He found the cemetery easily, comforted by the yews, whose overhead fan of branches felt protective, grass like cushions beneath his feet. Drawing himself towards a familiar marble stone, a tear rolled down his cheek.

To hell with school. He couldn't remember much about Anna's death, but he would never forget Margaret's fear, the day they stopped by in Aldwyck...

There was little anyone could do to bring Anna back, but plenty of ways they could comfort the bereaved. Plucking the flowers from their wrapping, Elijah poked them carefully into the vase at the foot of the headstone, fuelled by a sudden defiance.

II

No sooner had Eleanor returned to the caravan, she felt duty bound to call in at the Harpers. She wanted to thank them for looking after Elijah. Though before she had even reached the door, Marilyn confronted her, white faced.

There had been an angry phone call from Elijah's school, demanding to know of his whereabouts.

Eleanor was stunned. Never in his life had her son played truant.

With some reluctance, Tom divulged a little about the bullying. "He did seem quite scared..."

By the time Elijah ambled casually into the field though, Eleanor was furious.

"Where the hell have you been?" she shrieked.

"I went to visit Anna's grave," he told her. "Don't be cross."

Eleanor sighed, touched by his compassion for the Baileys. Yet in no way did it compensate for the way the school might react over an entire day's absence.

"I couldn't face school," he blurted, "and I'm sick of being picked on."

"So why haven't you said anything to the teachers?" Eleanor gasped.

"The teachers don't give a shit about me," he muttered to himself.

Eleanor flinched, shocked her twelve year old son would use such language. "Eli, this isn't like you! What on earth is going on?"

Elijah blinked, fighting the next layer of tears bubbling. Today had been the first time he had fled from that school and if it was up to him, he would never go back.

"I just wanted to lose myself," he spluttered, "get as far away as possible, where no one would know me, so I jumped on a train. I ended up in Bromley..."

Next thing he knew, she had yanked him around to face her, eyes blazing with fury.

"You did what?" she hissed. "What if something had happened to you?"

"Like what?" Elijah shouted. Picking up on her constant over-protective fear, he was beginning to feel irritated. "I got on a train, Mum! Kids do it all the time, I'm not a baby!"

"Oh, if only you knew," Eleanor choked, releasing him.

The anger in her eyes dissolved into misery and she looked haunted.

"Why are you so worried something will happen to me?" Elijah pressed. "Has this got anything to do with my dad?" He could see her guard rising; the same steely resolve that always held her back. "Why won't you tell me?"

"Sweetheart," Eleanor sighed, cupping her hands around his shoulders. "I swear I will tell you, one day, but all the while you're so young, I need to protect you. This was the last thing your father begged of me..."

"My father," Elijah said numbly. "His name was Jake Jansen and he played in a rock band... but you have never told me how he died."

"I know and I'm sorry," he heard her sigh, "but the truth is very painful. Please try not to think about it any more..."

And Elijah sensed her heartache.

Even the Harpers could tell how devastated she was. The fact that Elijah had gone gallivanting off on his own was a serious worry in itself, but topped with the harrowing tale of the bullying... Her resolve was beginning to crack; so much so, Tom urged her to leave her son in their company for just a little longer and grab a well-earned drink in the pub.

Boris looked up from the bar, engrossed in pouring pints. One glance at her frozen features brought him to an abrupt halt.

102

"Eleanor, love, is something the matter?"

"It's okay, Boris, finish serving your customers," she muttered. "I'll tell you in a minute."

She gave her head a brisk shake, wishing she could untangle the thoughts chasing around her mind, Charlie's enduring grief, Elijah's troubles... Closing her eyes, she rolled her head to stretch out the tension in her neck, her softly-wound dreadlocks glistening.

From another corner of the bar, a man was watching her. Young, slim with pale blonde hair, his eyes latched onto her like lasers.

"So what's the news?" Boris sighed, leaning heavily against the bar. "Drink?"

"Half a cider please," Eleanor began to say. "No, make it a pint, I feel a bit crap. A very dear friend of mine passed away last year, leaving a husband and two kids. It was the anniversary of her death this weekend..."

Eleanor never did tell Charlie how appalled she and Elijah were when they had visited their home. While Anna had made every attempt to liven it up - from colourful hand-made curtains to woollen throw-overs, disguising the worn furniture - nothing could hide the reality; a cold, dank flat set in a cheerless apartment block, without even a gas fire to radiate a glow of warmth. The heating was electric. Overriding everything, the air was befouled by a damp, fetid smell, which was gradually been replaced by paraffin fumes. One of Charlie's friends had leant them a heater. It helped ward off the chill but had worsened their condensation problem.

With windows beaded with moisture, rivulets dripping down the panes, spreading pools on the sills, Anna fell gravely ill a few weeks later.

As her mind lapsed into the past however, she knew there were many more factors than the cold and damp affecting Anna.

She had been depressed.

Armed with one of her home-baked Christmas cakes, Eleanor had also brought her some candles, to add a little cheer to the winter evenings.

But such was a day when a peculiar twist of fate dredged up memories of another life. Finding herself face to face with an attractive black woman with a teenage girl, she had no concept how this might affect the future.

"Eleanor?" the woman grinned. "Hey, what you doing here, babe?"

Eleanor remembered Della from her old life in London.

Yet she had bumped into her many years before that...

There had been an even stranger encounter, a day she risked a visit to the park in Poplar: 1975. Their chance meeting flung her right back to the day she had been dumped in a brothel. Della had been a prostitute then, her eyes filled with contempt, as if to remind her of her escape.

How could Eleanor forgive herself?

Only when Della's eyes fell to her two-year old, had she let go of her bitterness. She was dying to know what had happened to her since that fateful day, even more shocked when Eleanor told her...

"So how come you're living in Bromley?" Eleanor gasped, pushing aside the memory.

Thankfully, Della had given up prostitution. Her mother had passed on and with a teenage daughter to bring up, she had abandoned her digs in London for the more pleasing suburb of Bromley. They had lived there for seven years.

Eleanor was compelled to ask her if she knew the Bailey family.

Oddly enough, as soon she described them, Della had known exactly who she was referring to. She had already sussed that *they didn't belong here.* Furthermore, she knew Anna was being taunted by some menacing girl gang, who had a habit of congregating by the lifts.

Huddled together in the foyer, Eleanor made a final plea.

"Can you do something for me, Della? Keep an eye on Anna and her daughter? I'm worried about them, see..."

Her worries were not unfounded.

In the weeks that followed, Anna possessed a pale, wan look, that her makeup did little to disguise. Her eyes harboured a haunted look; an element of fear which had been absent before. But she would never forget how Anna had turned to her, the magnetic tug of friendship like a knife in her heart as their eyes connected. *As if she knew...*

"She had a weak heart, Boris. That's the reason she didn't survive."

They had visited the family in the new year. But as Eleanor sat shivering in their flat, she had finally voiced her opinion. Anna had a severe case of bronchitis.

"Charlie did everything in his power. Got her to see a doctor, made sure she took her medicines and kept her warm. He was trying to build up his own business..."

She could clearly remember the day he had left some postcards in Aldwyck.

The day the kids had skated on the ice. Even then, he seemed fearful of chasing too much business in Bromley, filled with a nagging sense someone would ruin him.

Only now did Eleanor guess the identity of that person, but shelved the thought for now...

How could they forget the night Anna had died? That around 5.00, he had arrived at the flat to discover she'd been rushed into hospital? Della had called an ambulance on Eleanor's instructions and yet still they were unable to save her.

"It wasn't his fault," Eleanor finished softly.

Taking a deep gulp of cider, she shakily lowered her glass.

Immersed in grief for his beloved Anna, it was hardly surprising Charlie looked so broken.

And it wasn't just Anna's unexpected death troubling her, but the bullying. To think it had driven her son to skip school... Eleanor kept talking, until a tear escaped her eye. Boris topped up her glass, gently covering her hand with his own.

Then eventually, the story moved on to the Barton-Wells family.

"Have you seen James lately? Or Avalon?"

The young fair haired man in the shadows stiffened.

"I haven't actually," Boris said. "Not for a couple of weeks. Why do you ask?"

"We visited them before Christmas," Eleanor replied, drawing her head close. "James wasn't well. This restoration is really stressing him out, but we did have a word with Avalon."

"And how was she?" Boris pressed.

"She looked beautiful," Eleanor smiled tenderly. "They had a function on."

"Really?" Boris smiled back. "Well, that's good. You do know they had to close the hotel."

"Hmm," Eleanor sighed. "Must be hard for them right now. Though she did mention they were thinking of auctioning some antiques to raise funds..."

Out of the blue, the fair haired man abandoned his corner and sidled up close. Eleanor turned. She couldn't dispel the instantaneous chill she felt from the bore of his pale blue eyes.

"Ah, hello again, Sir," Boris's voice broke through the tension. "What can I get for you?"

"I'll have a gin and tonic please," drawled the voice of Ben Hampton. His eyes swivelled back to Eleanor. "Did I hear you say you knew Avalon?"

Eleanor gripped the handle of her glass, fighting an urge to inch away. "I've known Avalon since she was a kid," she said huskily. "Why do you ask?"

"It doesn't matter," Ben said, averting his eyes.

Except as far as Eleanor was concerned *it did matter*. She had observed the exchange between this man and the landlord. It implied he had visited before. But right now he appeared to be fishing for information, *spying almost,* and it had something to do with the Barton-Wells family.

"So, they're definitely going ahead with the restoration," he kept digging. "Oh, don't look so suspicious, darling, it's common knowledge."

Eleanor suppressed a shudder. "I prefer not to talk about James's affairs behind his back!" she snapped and drained her glass.

"Can I get you another drink?" he smiled at her.

"No, thank you," she said curtly.

Boris gave a shrug, momentarily disappearing to fetch some ice.

No sooner had he gone though, the man's eyes were raking over her in a way she found unpleasant. For some reason, Eleanor was reminded of those hateful hooray-henries who had tormented her all those years ago.

"Love the uniform," he murmured with a leer. "Are you really a nurse? You can come and play *doctors and nurses* with me, any time you like…"

"Oh, fuck off, you pervert!" she hissed, banging her glass down on the bar top.

Boris reappeared. Frozen in disbelief, he let out a spurt of laughter.

"I should warn you, son, young Eleanor here is a feisty one!"

"How dare you speak to me like that!" Ben hissed.

In the blink of an eye, his voice had changed. Eleanor caught the intense hatred in his expression but even more terrifying were his eyes; flaring with a look of evil, bordering on insanity.

"Then stop hassling me!" she shrieked. "I've got enough problems as it is, without having to put up with your smutty remarks!"

The atmosphere inside the pub buckled into silence. People paused mid conversation, turning to stare. With a sharp breath, Ben raised his palms in mock defeat.

"Okay," he whispered. "I gather my affections are not wanted."

He forced a twisted smile. Picking up the gin and tonic Boris had poured, he knocked it back in one, slapped a five pound note on the bar, then promptly left the pub.

III

The moment Ben stepped into the crisp night air, he grabbed for his cigarettes and lit one. Inhaling the smoke deeply, he felt his heart soar.

At last, he had gleaned some news for his father.

So they were still clawing in some revenue by hosting private functions, but now it seemed James was considering auctioning some of their valuables.

He knew damn well this morsel of information would enrage him.

Though at the same time, he was convinced he had just met the one deadly adversary his father never stopped talking about.

Eleanor.

This had to be the same woman.

Ben scoured his mind, recalling everything his father had voiced; *some troublesome little harpy.* Allowing himself a smile, he took another drag of his cigarette. Somehow, he had expected some *feminist,* one of those butch, rebellious types his parents despised. Yet the woman in the pub had been a beauty. Visualising her now, he savoured the seductive swell of her lips. Felt the allure of her honey coloured eyes. In fact, the stirring of lust he experienced excelled anything he had felt before, even for Avalon... Of even greater significance though, was the impression she was close to the Barton-Wells family and that in itself made her all the more fascinating.

Chapter Twelve

I

In the aftermath of Ben's intrusion, Eleanor chose not to linger. Boris couldn't resist telling her he had visited the pub on more than one occasion, where his obsession with Westbourne House had not gone unnoticed...

By the time morning arrived though, Eleanor felt choked. She couldn't deny she was nervous when Marilyn drove them to the school.

Elijah looked pale and frightened as they escorted him through the doors, the prospect of facing his form teacher even more daunting. Eleanor had dressed smartly, her dreadlocks tied back. She hoped it might banish some of the prejudice - though the faces of both the school secretary and Elijah's form teacher looked distinctly stony as they crept into the office.

Eleanor tried to explain a little about Margaret's family. How an innocent friendship could evoke such nastiness from Elijah's classmates seemed cruel, given their circumstances. His impulsive dash to put flowers on Anna's grave might be forgivable, but if only he had told them...

Elijah's form teacher, Mr Robinson, was not entirely satisfied with his reasons for playing truant, giving Eleanor no choice but to explain the reality; he was being bullied.

At first the man looked uncomfortable.

"Sad though it seems," he said crisply, "children always pick on those they consider to be different. Elijah's lifestyle does him no favours."

Eleanor was flabbergasted. "But there's nothing wrong with our lifestyle," she protested, "and we're not gypsies! If it wasn't for the fact our home had wheels, would it make a difference? Most people think he's a great kid."

When Elijah returned to his classroom, the oppressive silence hung like fog.

Something had been said.

Shuffling towards the area where Gary Boswell sat, he fired him a look of defiance. How he would react if he overheard even the slightest slur towards Margaret didn't bear thinking about... And at the same time, Gary's eyes narrowed, implying their quarrel was far from over.

II

"I can't bear the thought of him being so unhappy," Eleanor whimpered to Marilyn, when they had eventually driven away from the school.

Reluctant to leave her son, she nevertheless felt indebted to Tom and Marilyn for all the help they had given her. The feeling spiralled from the moment they crossed the boundary into Aldwyck and hit with an urge to visit Westbourne House, she offered to treat her to a coffee.

Marilyn on the other hand, was busy with other engagements, but didn't mind taking a detour to save her the walk.

Eleanor was delighted to see James. His statuesque face had lost its hollowness, the trace of a smile uplifting, as she swept over to him.

"Eleanor," he murmured. "What an absolute pleasure!"

Engaging in light-hearted conversation for a few minutes, he was curious to learn about the friends she had brought on her last visit.

This prompted her to explain a little about Charlie's plight.

"Poor man," James muttered. "I know what he's going through.... I lost my first wife and I know damn well you don't heal overnight."

A moment later Avalon joined them.

"We were talking about the Baileys," Eleanor enlightened her, although it seemed inevitable the restoration would slip into the conversation.

Leaving Elliot in charge, James steered them towards the back of the house, where the privacy of their living room seemed more appropriate. Eleanor felt a rush of pleasure. Surveying the pastel colour scheme, her gaze wandered to the views beyond the patio doors.

They had only just settled when James started speaking again. "I suspect Avalon's already told you, but we are doing this on our own now. I chose not to go along with that partnership, especially after your warnings..."

"Charlie's warnings," Eleanor corrected him.

"Let's just say, I was a little more wary," James sighed. "Perry showed his true colours in the end. Then, as soon as I told him the deal was off, he turned quite nasty."

Eleanor stared at him, shocked. "So what's happening now?"

"We need to get the roof fixed," he added. "It's full of leaks, which will obviously lead to more dampness. The surveyors agree. I don't think I can put this off for any longer."

"But we're going to an auction soon," Avalon intervened, "just like I said."

"I see," Eleanor muttered.

Distracted by memories, she was launched right back to the Olde House at Home; that creepy young man who had materialised.

"Avalon, I feel I must warn you, but there was someone in the pub last night, asking questions... Questions about you and the house."

With a frown, Avalon glanced at her father.

"Go on," James said. "What sort of questions and can you describe this person?"

This time it was Eleanor who frowned as she scoured her mind for details. That first cider had gone to her head, leaving her slightly befuddled.

"He asked me how I knew *you*... whether you were still going ahead with the restoration. He was a young man, fair-haired..."

Avalon turned ashen, spoon rattling in her saucer as she placed her cup down.

"Ben!" she breathed. "That sounds like Ben Hampton!"

"So it would seem," James nodded. "I wonder what that little bastard's playing at."

"Boris said he's called in a few times," Eleanor added. "He is very curious to know what's happening with your house. It's not the first time he's been quizzing the locals."

"Oh, Dad!" Avalon started whimpering. "I should have told you b-but Ben *has* been sneaking around the village! I saw him! So did Bryony..."

"Don't get upset, love," James soothed her.

"But who is this man?" Eleanor pressed. "Why are you so scared of him?"

"He's evil," Avalon shivered, her arms snaking around themselves in fear. "This is the man I was dating if you remember - b-but he's been hanging around ever since I ended it. I'm sure he is doing it to frighten me!"

"I knew there was something nasty about him," Eleanor muttered.

"That whole family is corrupt," James snapped. Draining his cup, he slammed it down on the table with a force of anger which surprised them both. "But I will not tolerate that obnoxious boy skulking around the village, scaring my daughter!"

"James, if this man is stalking her, you should go to the police," Eleanor suggested.

"No!" Avalon gasped. "It'll only make things worse... but I've been hiding myself away for a few weeks, to avoid him."

"You cannot let him control your life!" James berated her. "This worries me. It brings me right back to what I was saying. The reaction I got when I didn't want to go ahead with the partnership..." He shook his head. "That man was unbelievably hostile, Eleanor. He even told me, '*I would regret my decision.*'"

"But that sounds like a threat," she breathed.

Only now did she remember the other warnings Charlie had divulged.

Hampton is not a man to cross... he can be very dangerous...

III
February 1986

It was in fact, many weeks before Charlie and James would come into contact. Yet James pushed ahead with his plans, charged with a bullish determination.

Elliot watched them depart before the first light of dawn penetrated the darkness; James's black Jaguar perched by the steps like a crow, a shimmer of moonlight reflected in the door panels. As James and Avalon tucked themselves into their seats, they were ready to make the journey to the auction house. To the rear lingered a hired removal van, packed to the gunnels with antiques. Tea chests filled with silverware fought for space amongst solid wood furniture, ceramics and paintings layered with bubble wrap.

With a wrench of the heart, James decided it was time to part with their most treasured possessions, including an 18 carat gold pocket watch that had belonged to his father. Of even greater sentimental value was his grandmother's platinum engagement ring. With a dazzling circular cut diamond, this ring could be worth thousands.

She would turn in her grave.

Uttering a silent prayer, he hoped his actions would be forgivable. He was after all, only doing this to save their ancestral home...

Several hours later, Elliot witnessed their return.

Dusk had fallen, plunging the grounds into darkness again and a light rain swept across the windscreen. Avalon was first to slide out of the car. She looked radiant, Elliot thought, eyes sparkling as she raced up the steps, into reception.

"We did it, Elliot," she announced. "We managed to sell everything!"

"Well done, my dear," Elliot smiled, reaching across to take her coat.

James, on the other hand, looked exhausted.

"How are you feeling, James? Are you happy with the result?"

"Words fail me," James said with a thin smile. He shrugged off his jacket, now beaded with a film of raindrops. "It's hard to explain... but it felt quite sad to see some of our prized family heirlooms go under the hammer, though we did manage to raise over sixty grand."

As they clustered around one of the tables in the lounge, Bryony also joined them. She had only just managed to grab a break from preparing a set of beautiful desserts for tonight's dinner menu. But with the success of the auction resonating, it was time to discuss their next venture: a fund-raising ball.

James seemed incredibly passionate about the event he had in mind; a formal black tie dinner dance with a 'Glen Miller' style jazz band.

Another gleam lit up Avalon's eyes. "We were thinking about April. The grounds are at their best when all the spring flowers are out, especially the tulips!"

The only part of the discussion that dampened her enthusiasm was the mention of having some posters printed. There was a small printing shop tucked at the back of the village book store.

Avalon peered up warily from beneath her eyebrows. "Aldwyck," she faltered, "aren't there some better printers in Rosebrook?"

James exhaled a sigh. "You're worried about seeing that Hampton boy, aren't you? You can't hide yourself away forever, Sweetheart."

It was impossible to ignore the furtive glances between Elliot and Bryony.

"Then why don't I go with her?" Bryony proposed.

Concentrating on the next stage of the restoration, James once again found himself drawn into heavy discussions, not only with Booth Chartered Surveyors, but the firm of restoration specialists assigned to carry out the work. Fast approaching the end of February, the weather was moving towards a spell of heavy rainfall; a nagging reminder he couldn't afford to delay matters.

The one thing James had not anticipated however, was that the original estimate might change; that in the months since the surveyors had prepared their *initial* estimate, costs would go spiralling upwards. The conversation threw him into turmoil. But as his fear rose, so did his urgency to get the work underway, while he could afford it. Thus, without hesitation, he handed over nearly all the proceeds from their auction.

On the same morning as the scaffolding was erected on the west facing side of the house, Perry Hampton was hidden in the heart of his London residence. He had been poring over a number of proposals when the ring of his phone interrupted him.

"You asked me to update you about any developments concerning Westbourne house," drawled the voice of Edward Booth.

"Do go on," Perry coaxed him. "Given up yet have they?"

"Far from it," Edward announced. "James is pressing ahead with the roof."

"You what?" Perry gasped, rearing up in his seat.

"Th-they've obviously raised some cash. I don't know how... but yesterday I was informed that Mr Barton-Wells handed over a cheque for £59,000 to get the work started."

"Did your firm hike up the costs as I instructed?" Perry barked.

"Yes," Edward replied. "They've increased their original estimate by *twenty thousand* on the basis that building materials have soared in cost. Yet it still hasn't deterred him."

Perry's mood blackened. But as he tunnelled through his mind to recover what he had learned recently, the answer hit him in a flash.

"There were rumours of an auction..." he whispered. "That's it. They've been hocking their valuables."

A wave of intense hatred seized him, but like a shark drawn to blood, every drip of information brought out the predator in him. Overriding everything was that crucial conversation he had shared with his son. News he had crossed paths with the Chapman girl.

Perry shuddered. Despite James's fragility, he was putting up one hell of a good fight and although such news infuriated him, it also stimulated him.

His victory would be all the more sweet.

But the true extent of his Machiavellianism was yet to be unleashed. The instant the conversation ended, Perry scooped up his Filofax. He ordered his housekeeper to bring a jug of fresh coffee, flipping through the pages until he had found his media contacts. Reaching for his phone again, he was hoping to catch the editor of 'Country House,' a prestigious monthly magazine.

"Heard the news about Westbourne House?" he gloated.

As he continued to plant an idea *the whole property was falling into ruins,* he knew he had the man's attention - before shamelessly condemning the roof.

"Imagine the disruption! Hammers pounding away, workmen, scaffolding... Won't be much fun for those hoping to get a relaxing break, eh? And you should see the state of those bedrooms! You'd be lucky if the roof didn't cave in over your head!"

"Are you proposing I run an article?" his companion appeased him. "Do you not think the owner might be a little put out?"

"A couple of columns will do the trick - enough to get the stories rolling - and if any other publication picks the lead up, they can print what they like. The state of Westbourne House is no lie, though, I assure you!"

Winding down that conversation, Perry felt no remorse. He was revelling in it.

This left one more person to talk to.

Ambling into the hallway, he caught sight of his face in one of the many gilt-framed mirrors. Eyes narrowing, he allowed his mind to drift back to another time; imagining himself as a younger man. His appearance had changed very little in twelve years. He had been just as charismatic with his square-jawed face, his grey eyes emitting a chill. His thick hair had been more blonde than white, the lines around his eyes less pronounced.

But as he studied his reflection, he could no longer push back the memory of a most compelling conversation with Ben.

"You never told me she was a looker..."

He was referring to Eleanor of course. No one could deny her beauty, those tense few seconds at the press conference when she had sailed towards their table; gracefully slim, the sweep of her collar bones shadowed against her flawless skin. The blaze in her eyes was a moment of pure torture. Yet he wasn't really acknowledging her beauty, only her power to destroy him.

And now his son had met her.

He did mention she was a nurse. Couldn't resist remarking *how sexy* she looked in that uniform, propped against the bar, casually discussing the fate of

Westbourne House. Such obsession and desire, Perry reflected, so typical of his son... Yet his festering anger at her rejection drew a smirk to his lips.

It would do no harm for Ben to despise her too.

Settled in their lounge, he pinned Ben with his intense stare.

"How long has it been since you've seen Avalon?" he began.

Ben averted his eyes. "I told you. She's hardly ever in the village, which hasn't given me much opportunity to approach her..."

"Then I suggest you find one!" Perry said. "The builders are about to start the rebuild of their roof, so I want you to find out more!"

Ben started pacing, heels clicking on the polished wood floor.

"Look," he protested. "I can't keep visiting that pub! People are getting suspicious, especially since that gypsy friend of yours humiliated me there!"

"She is no friend of mine, Ben," Perry hissed and grabbing his cup, downed his fourth cup of coffee. "If you bump into her again, ignore her. All I want from you is to keep an eye on those Barton-Wells people!"

"Why do you hate that woman?" Ben taunted, unfazed by his father's outburst.

Perry seemed incensed. Nostrils flaring, he snorted like a horse let loose in a field.

"Is this the girl you drove out of London?" he kept probing. "That 'troublesome little harpy' you hired the notorious Dominic Theakston to deal with?"

"What's it to you?" Perry snapped.

"I'm curious," Ben kept pressing. "Why is she such a threat?"

"I have no wish to dredge up the past, Ben," Perry answered guardedly. "But let's just say, there was a debate, one that concerned *me*. A rumour proliferated by her drug dealer boyfriend, who ultimately ended up dead! I did not appreciate the things they were insinuating..."

"So?" Ben smiled.

"This woman harbours a vendetta," Perry said. "But we're digressing. Forget about the Chapman girl and concentrate on Avalon!"

"But the villagers are on to me," Ben argued. "They're wary of my interest in Westbourne House and as for sending any more parcels, it's too risky..."

"Then why not pay her a visit?" Perry suggested. "How many weeks has it been since we toured the house? You could walk around the gardens, have a coffee! It's all open to the public, James made no secret of that!"

"Okay," Ben relented, unable to think of any reason to refuse.

"Just make sure you have a good look around," Perry finished, lowering his coffee cup, "and speak to that dear girl, Avalon. Something to remind her that we are still around and we are not about to disappear..."

Avalon felt tense, knowing the house would be busy. James had been summoned to a meeting with the surveyors and builders. She knew the discussion was crucial, as outraged as her father they had dared to inflate their prices. As Elliot warned though, on the night she had heard Ben's music resonating, *some form of loan would be inevitable...*

Snapping her eyes shut, she dispelled the memory. There had been no further sightings of Ben since Eleanor's report, yet the feeling of persecution had not vanished.

Today both her father *and* Elliot had left her in charge, entrusting her to look after a party of senior ranking military officers and their wives, who had booked a regimental lunch.

Catching sight of one of their posters, the words 'Springtime Ball at Westbourne House' triggered a smile. Printed in a fine loopy script, the design was undeniably stylish with its hand-drawn illustration of a waltzing couple. Avalon pushed her way through the door and wandered outside, pausing above the steps. A windy day, the trees were disturbed by violent gusts, sending the last of the autumn leaves somersaulting over the lawn.

Despite the angry weather, she released a shiver, still thinking about the ball. Seeing the cars of their guests pouring into the parking area, she watched the first couple advance towards the entrance. As she took another tentative step out to greet them, her hair flew around her face in tendrils, completely out of control.

"Good morning, my dear!" the man greeted her. "Name's Brigadier Paget. I see you're having some work done." He added a conspiratorial wink.

"That's right," she found herself nodding. No one could miss the scaffolding pinned to the west wing. "But it won't affect your lunch, though, I promise. Come in."

Stepping aside, she took another sweeping glance over the car park.

Then, on the periphery of her vision, a movement caught her eye. A lone figure lingered in the middle distance. Tall, statuesque, wrapped in a long black overcoat, the flash of his white-blonde hair was unmistakable. Avalon froze, hit with a powerful jab of recognition.

Except more and more cars were arriving. Heart sinking, she knew she had to attend to them and without allowing Ben's proximity to unhinge her.

A cold smile crept its way onto Ben's face. With his car hidden in the trees by the farmhouse, he had been surveying the house for some time, just waiting for James's Jaguar to emerge. Unbeknown to anyone, he had prior knowledge of his meeting; a discussion concerning the spiralling costs of the restoration.

The sight of his butler accompanying him was a bonus. He felt his excitement soar.

Thus, with no wish to delay his visit, he had stepped from the car to make his way to the house on foot. He was a little taken aback when a succession of cars began crawling up the drive. Their very make and models suggested wealthy people. Counting at least half a dozen, he guessed they were attending some function...

But finally, he saw Avalon. Keeping very still, he could hear the sound of car doors slamming, a mumble of voices, followed by a gale of laughter. Even from a distance, he detected the swing of the solid oak door opening, as each and every guest was admitted.

More cars rolled past. The next time he glanced up, Avalon had stepped aside, yet her body had turned rigid. Sensing her scrutiny, he observed her face, her mouth hanging open, her mane of golden-brown ringlets flung wildly around her shoulders by the wind.

Ben strode the last fifty or so yards up the driveway. By the time he reached the steps, at least another six people had arrived. Following them inside, he smuggled himself into the bar, now submerged in their celebration. His eyes flickered over the women, beautifully turned out in dress suits and cashmere twin-sets. Jewelled brooches sparkled under the light of a chandelier, though the men intrigued him even more. Going by their ties and regimental badges, it did not take long to realise this was some sort of military reunion.

"Can I help you, Sir?"

Ben spun around, glaring at the boy waiter who had approached him.

"I understand you serve coffee," he snapped.

"Yes, that's right," the boy answered politely, "if you'd care to choose a table, I'll bring you some over. Sorry we're so busy. We've got a private function on."

"I was only after a coffee," Ben drawled. He took a deep breath then stared into the boy's eyes. "Is there a chance Avalon could serve me? I'd like a few words..."

Hidden behind the reception desk as guests kept arriving, Avalon had so far managed to suppress any lingering thoughts of Ben Hampton. She had no idea he was lurking in the bar, until their fresh-faced young waiter sidled up to her.

"I'm busy," she hissed under her breath. "What does he think he's doing here at a time like this anyway? Tell him to go away!"

"I'm not sure I can do that," he mumbled, cheeks turning pink. "He seemed quite - um - persistent."

"Then he'll have to wait," Avalon responded, her voice unintentionally curt. "I'm sorry, Ross, I can't abandon our guests. We should feel honoured to be

116

hosting this function..."

Glancing up, she watched with regret as the boy backed away, disheartened. *But what else could she say?*

She forced a smile, wary of her thumping heart, as the reality of the situation took root. As each new guest introduced themselves - Major this - Colonel that - the names barely registered. Her hands had adopted a tremor as one final senior ranking army officer reached out to her.

"G-good day, Sir. Would you care to go through to the bar for pre-dinner drinks. There will also be a wine list with your meal..."

"In that case, I think I'll wait, thank you," the man smiled pleasantly.

She watched his back as he wandered into the lounge. Avalon swallowed, her head swimming in a strange way. Her eyes stared blankly into the lounge, absorbing the sea of faces as they swayed and bobbed, trying not to look too hard at any one of them.

Then suddenly Ben loomed in the doorway.

"Avalon," he greeted her softly.

"I can't talk to you right now!" she whimpered.

Staggering away from the bar, she had no desire to go in, especially as he was barring the entrance. With a sob, she fled to the restaurant. *This was turning into a nightmare.*

Yet she had to pull herself together. Today was such an important function and she would not allow Ben's creeping approach to ruin it.

As she wandered towards the kitchens, she hoped to catch Bryony, but the activity appeared equally frantic. Bryony was immersed in a task that required all her concentration. Having prepared a mousse, swirled into layers of vanilla, milk and dark chocolate, each dessert required individual decoration - a cap of cream, a spiral of tuille biscuit... Observing the speed and grace of her movements, Avalon did not dare disturb her.

The waiting staff were advancing and with the clock ticking like a time bomb, lunch was imminent. Avalon backed into the wall to give them space, reluctant to leave the sanctuary of the kitchen.

Back inside the lounge, Ben felt his mood plummet. Already these people irritated him with their loud braying voices. They were indeed an assembly of high ranking officers from her Majesty's Armed Forces. Not that he cared... The purpose of his visit was to make small talk with Avalon. He had forgotten how much she stirred his desire, from that one fleeting glimpse.

Gradually, the knots of people began to disperse, until the bar lay empty. Hearing their receding voices, Ben gritted his teeth. *He still hadn't been served coffee.* Unused to being ignored, he spun away from the window, recalling the second reason he was here; his father had specifically asked him to look around.

Ambling from the bar and into reception, he followed the corridor to the rear. Seconds later, he had rediscovered the library, a sight that made him smile as he recalled his father's admiration; his love of its masculine grandeur. Eyes wandering, a poster then caught his eye.

With the publicity of their 'Springtime Ball' revealed, Ben couldn't resist a smirk. Shooting a glance over his shoulder, he carefully unpicked the blue-tac before folding up the poster and tucking it into his coat pocket. There was no question how much his parents would be intrigued by this latest fund-raising venture. Yet at the same time, he wanted to study the outside of the building. Like Brigadier Paget, he couldn't fail to notice those scaffolding poles. He had just started to make his way back through reception when to his utter delight, he came face to face with Avalon.

She froze a second time. He saw the colour drain from her face before she spun on her heel and headed towards the lounge, momentarily slipping out of reach again.

"Avalon, please!" he shouted after her.

"What do you want?" he heard her squeak.

"I only visited for a coffee," he answered coolly, "I've been dying to see you. I'm sorry. I didn't realise you were so busy, but is it possible we could have a few words?"

Avalon refused to move.

Ben on the other hand, lowered himself into one of their plush sofas and patted the spot right next to him.

Still she remained frozen. "I have nothing to say to you."

"Why?" Ben murmured. "What is your problem, Avalon?"

"How can you say that?" she gasped. "After everything you've done!"

"Done?" Peering up from beneath his brows, he gave a twisted smile. "Look, I apologise for trying it on with you in that forest. It was stupid of me but..."

"I-I'm not talking about the kiss," Avalon shivered, pressing her eyes shut. "You sent me roses, Ben. Dead ones! Th-the next parcel had a skull in it! And what about the music you were playing outside my window? And I know it was you. Vangelis was it? The same creepy, electronic music you were playing in your car when I saw you in the village..."

"I don't know what you're talking about," he sneered. "Music? You must have been imagining things. It wasn't Vangelis I was playing in my car anyway, it was Kraftwerk."

She curled her arms around her body, eyes glassy as the first slick of tears shone across their surface.

"It doesn't matter!" she exploded, backing away from him. "I-I just want you to go!"

Eyes anchored to her face, he savoured her fear. He barely noticed the flutter of a shadow in reception but as Avalon's last words reverberated, Bryony emerged in the doorway.

"I think this has gone far enough, Mr Hampton!"

Avalon whirled around. "Bryony!" she gasped. "I tried to catch you earlier but - but..."

Even from a distance, she must have heard the bubble of tears in her voice.

"It's okay, Avalon, you have nothing to fear." She stared into Ben's taunting eyes. "You heard what Miss Barton-Wells said. So will you leave this house right now!"

"You can't force me," Ben retorted. His eyes shot back to Avalon. "Westbourne House is open to the public and so are the gardens. Your father said so himself!"

A chilling silence fell, but in those final tense seconds, Avalon had been inching her way towards Bryony. Ben shifted his gaze, recognising the disdainful, dark haired woman as one of the chefs.

"This is harassment," Bryony added in a voice of stone, "and if you do not leave the premises, I am calling the police..."

With little choice but to comply, Ben levered himself out of his seat. But before he left, he remembered Perry's instructions, pausing to draw level with Avalon.

"You may have won this time, darling," he whispered in her ear, "but I swear to you, I am never going to go away..."

He saw her flinch as he completed his path to the door. Turning one last time, he stared back at Avalon and blew her a kiss.

Before the day ended however, it was Perry who wallowed in the greatest satisfaction.

His friend and confidante, Edward Booth, had fed him every morsel of information concerning Westbourne House. *So, James was haggling over the costs...* He had nailed the building company down to a final figure - in writing - and with the added clause *there was to be no further increase*. But that final figure stood at £275,000. Even if James sold every stick of furniture in his home, Perry was convinced he would never raise it.

Finally, he smoothed out the creases of the poster his son had filched from their library.

A 'Springtime Ball at Westbourne House' at £100 per head.

Unable to shift his smile, he was impressed. All this effort on James's part seemed only destined to unleash the more vindictive side of his nature. And Perry knew precisely what he had to do, as a calculating three-fold plan took root inside his mind.

Chapter Thirteen

I

The next time Eleanor visited, Charlie was in a considerably brighter mood. Inspired by an improvement in the weather, he had revisited one of his first design projects; a bespoke conservatory he had built shortly after Anna died...

Their lives had been so miserable - the mugging in Rosebrook the final straw. He and Andrew had done their utmost to track down the perpetrator but it had all been in vain. By the time they returned to the pavement though, he recalled some hippie-like character, crouched next to Anna.

He had to confess, it was the dreadlocks that made him suspicious.

Yet in the moment she whisked her head around, he caught his breath, seeing her features for the first time - sharp cheekbones, a lovely mouth with full lips soft as marshmallows - something in her eyes had jolted him. Huge and startled, they gave her a look of vulnerability, a clear golden brown that reminded him of whisky, *or honey*, he would later reflect.

That day not only sparked an enduring family friendship, but a turning point in their lives. It was a memory that brought such hope... because he had never forgotten his pessimism.

Had Hampton ruined his chances of getting employment?

A peculiar chill crawled down his arms, despite the glow of sunshine.

The events of that weekend had revived his spirits. So much so, it encouraged him to return to one of the first companies he had submitted his CV to. For nothing could have prepared him for the disdainful response he'd received when following up his enquiry...

"If we had any job opportunities, they would be advertised in the local newspaper!"

The receptionist had been employed by a firm he had worked for, one he thought had taken a shine to him. So why had her attitude been so frosty?

On the next occasion however, she could not have been more amiable.

"Tania," he challenged her, "six weeks ago, I sent in my CV on the off chance you had a vacancy. I followed it up with a phone call. Spoke to you in person..."

The confused look in her eye had initially startled him.

"Did you?"

"Yes," Charlie snapped, "and do you know what? You treated me like shit off your shoe! Why, Tania? Whatever did I do to deserve that?"

He clocked the hurt in her eyes, then a glitter of tears. Yet she had no idea what he was talking about.

"What, you don't remember a CV and a prospective job application from Charles Bailey? It might even be on file somewhere!"

"Oh no," Tania breathed. "You couldn't be *that* Charles Bailey? I never knew..."

"Well, how many other 'Charles Baileys' do you know?" he gasped in disbelief.

"I've only ever known you as *Charlie*," she said in a small, apologetic voice. "The awful thing is, our MD told us under no circumstances should we consider you..."

Charlie felt the room spin slightly.

Tania inched her head closer. "I shouldn't be telling you this, but there are rumours going around that you're unreliable. That no building company would touch you with a barge pole..."

The pound of his fist on the desk made her flinch. "That's bollocks!" he snarled. "I've never had any complaints about the standard of my work and you know it!"

"I'm sorry," she started to sob. "I only did what I was told."

Charlie, being the man he was, couldn't bear to see her in tears. Pulling out a hankie, he spent the next few minutes consoling her. Yet her story had turned him cold.

Despite his simmering fury, they had at least parted as friends.

Furthermore, she had made a suggestion. "Why not request a reference from Oakwood Construction and discredit these rumours?"

And as if to make amends, she had even managed to track down Christopher Farrin, his former project manager...

"The trail eventually led to Croydon," he sighed.

Charlie met Eleanor's eye. He had never fully explained his reasons for suggesting *Hampton could be dangerous*... but in the light of her concern for the Barton-Wells family, she needed to know the full story.

"Christopher was taken on by a new construction firm. I went to see him."

Yes, he was instantly put at ease by his cordial greeting, although Christopher had been appalled to learn of *his* circumstances. Almost out of pity, he had taken him down the road for a pint - then updated him on the fate of their former MD. Convalescing in a spa town in Derbyshire, Dick Harrison had suffered a serious heart attack.

"Poor sod," Charlie whispered. "Hampton not only destroyed his business, I don't think he ever bounced back..."

The news shocked him to the core and it hadn't taken long for the conversation to drift back to his own situation. He didn't hold back. Grateful for an opportunity to offload to his former manager, all that pent up frustration had found an escape route.

It seemed some of the larger construction companies were black-listing him; that someone was rolling out the most venomous lies... Finally, he dropped the killer question, a concern that had been nagging him for weeks.

How much did he know about Peregrine Hampton? And did he have enough clout to destroy a man's career prospects?

Eleanor gaped at him in horror. "Seriously?"

"It would never surprise me," Charlie kept musing. "I told him about the time he approached me. That I would never work for a man like him and he didn't much like that..."

But of course, Christopher had denied it. Refused to believe *even Hampton would stoop so low.* Yet when Charlie considered confronting him, he did not miss the shadow of fear that passed across his face. He had begged him not to...

"The man is deadly! You cannot take on someone like him, Charlie, he'll chew you up and spit out the bones..."

He often wondered why he had said that. Perry Hampton had his fingers in a lot of pies and with much talk of the lucrative new housing projects being planned, perhaps Christopher's firm had been excluded. That being the case, was it possible that any building company employing Charlie would not be considered for these contracts either?

Money talked. No one would take the risk and it was enough to make him shudder. The one thing Christopher could not hide though, was the guilt coursing across his face. Maybe he was trying to throw Charlie off the scent, the reason he had chosen to help him.

So he was more than happy to write a reference but not only that. It so turned out, Christopher had something even better up his sleeve...

"He knew a couple in Rosebrook," Charlie said, a smile lifting his lips. "They were on the lookout for someone to build a porch for their lovely Georgian home."

Within a few days, his outlook began to improve. True to his word, Christopher's friends had commissioned him; the magnificent porch he constructed fully complimenting their home. The owners were so delighted that on the day they presented him with a cheque, they included an outstanding testimonial. Added to the reference Christopher had written, he found the confidence to advertise his services in the local paper.

It brought a glimmer of hope. From the very first advert in the Bromley Times, Charlie had been commissioned by a second home owner to repair a collapsed wall. It made good use of Andrew's bricklaying skills. Then a third enquiry arose; a couple seeking a specialist to design and construct a conservatory, a chance to practise his architectural skills.

Happy to handle the application, Charlie submitted a set of professional line drawings.

It was two weeks before Christmas when he discovered his future lay in founding his own business. And no one could have been more proud of him than Anna.

If only their story hadn't ended so tragically.

He never had taken any photographs. One year on however, and as the stranglehold of grief subsided, he looked forward to seeing his masterpiece.

Pleased to show off his portfolio to Eleanor and her son, Charlie had completed three more projects, including the garage conversion he was telling her about.

"I'm pleased you're busy," she commented.

Settled around the dining room table, she noticed Elijah had slipped away to join Margaret and Andrew on their faded sofa to watch 'Top of the Pops.' Charlie poured out two glasses of red wine. Lifting his glass, he swirled the ruby red contents and took a sip.

"Work has never been better. Next on the list is a single storey extension for another Granny flat. They're becoming popular... Hardly surprising when you consider the soaring house prices. It's cheaper to add an extension to a property than buy new."

"I'm so pleased for you, Charlie," Eleanor praised him.

"Better still, Andrew's only got another month before he finishes his YTS." He threw his son an encouraging smile. "He'll be qualified by the beginning of May."

From the corner of her eye, Eleanor observed him. Andrew was still a shadow of his former self, though right now he seemed content. Grinning at the TV set, he was enjoying his favourite comedy quartet, 'The Young Ones,' performing a charity rendition of 'Living Doll' with Cliff Richard. Margaret sat next to him giggling.

She turned back to Charlie. "So you'll be working together full time. When do you start the extension?"

"Ah, there's a problem," Charlie muttered. "A conversion like this requires planning permission but both sets of neighbours have objected..."

He released a sigh, attempting to explain the process; it would necessitate careful planning and design, as well as plumbing and pipe work. All the neighbours were concerned about was the noise and disruption.

"It seems so mean-spirited and they're such a nice family. The husband's mother is getting a little frail, but it's a wealthy neighbourhood and snobbish. They consider it an affront for anyone to alter their home."

"I hate to say it, Charlie," Eleanor said, "but it seems to be the way society is going. There isn't a lot of compassion these days..."

"You don't need to tell me that!" Charlie snorted. "I'm not saying Labour did things perfectly but there was a lot more camaraderie in the 70s!"

Eleanor shook her head, flicking her heavy locks over her shoulders. Yes, money did seem to corrupt people, for Aldwyck was changing too; Londoners selling their homes for a profit, moving into smaller villages and forcing up property prices. With more and more locals being pushed out, she recalled one couple in particular.

"Are you going to tell him about the Marshes?" Elijah piped up.

Eleanor smiled at him, guessing he was listening with half an ear.

"Remember those cottages on the green?" she said. "One came up for sale. A pair of newlyweds had set their hearts on it. Lived in the village all their lives they have and put an offer in. But they were gazumped by some stockbroker from London!" She felt a spark of fury. "They couldn't match the higher offer. They'll probably have to move out of Aldwyck."

"Bloody unfair," Charlie murmured. "Can't they rent?"

Eleanor shrugged. "There isn't a lot of rented property in Aldwyck. I guess the nearest place they could move to is Rosebrook."

Charlie sloshed more wine into her glass before topping up his own. A rich smell of savoury beef, herbs and onions was beginning to waft from the kitchen, signifying the proximity of dinner. Eleanor had made a cottage pie, assisted by Elijah and Margaret.

"So what about you, Charlie?" she added. "Didn't you say this place was about to go on the market soon? You were served notice to leave."

At first Charlie looked at her blankly. The heads of all three children turned.

"This is another problem," he divulged. "Property prices are rising here too."

It appeared the hapless newlyweds in Aldwyck were no exception. People from dozens of surrounding villages were being priced out of the market, which led to a soaring demand in towns like Rosebrook. Charlie had even toyed with the idea of taking out a mortgage. But the building societies were reluctant to agree to any form of a loan, until he could demonstrate at least two years of successful trading.

"We were lucky to get this house," he sighed, "but the average rent has shot up. The only solution would be to downsize - or move back to Bromley..." His head drooped. "I can't do it, Eleanor. The memories are too painful."

"I don't want to go back to Bromley!" Margaret whined.

"Of course you don't, love," Charlie replied.

It wasn't a bad town. In fact it was booming. Yet the kids longed to stay in Rosebrook, especially Margaret, who had settled into her new school.

"When are you coming over to Aldwyck next?" Eleanor broke in. "I've got loads to tell you about the Barton-Wells family, especially Avalon!" Her voice dropped to a whisper. "You know Hampton's son? He's been prowling around the village, virtually stalking her."

Charlie's eyes flashed. "I told you he was a nasty piece of work."

"I met him," Eleanor shivered. "He was in the pub, asking questions. There was something James said too, something that scared me..."

"What?" Charlie gasped. "You think they're plotting some sort of comeback?"

Eleanor gave a nod, reluctant to elaborate further...

"Listen," she added, her tone softening, "it's my birthday next Sunday. I'll be Thirty! Why don't you all come over and celebrate it with me?"

"Thirty?" Charlie beamed. "I'd never have guessed! What have you got in mind?"

"I was thinking maybe lunch in the pub?" she pondered. "You've never been to the Olde House at Home or met the locals. It'll take your mind off your worries and you never know... Maybe a solution will present itself."

II

On April 6th Eleanor awoke to brilliant sunshine. Stepping down from her caravan with Elijah, she breathed in the fragrance of hyacinths by her door. With a ringing chorus of birdsong dispensed from the treetops and a gentle breeze swaying the grass around her heels, Eleanor loved Spring. Thrown back to the time she was pregnant with Elijah, she recalled a similar day in the Merriman's garden, enjoying the subtle embrace of nature.

Elijah's feet were light as he fell into step beside her. At five foot tall, he was as slender as his father had been, his tousled brown hair gleaming with chestnut highlights. Turning to catch a glimpse of him, she sensed a tug in her heart; a sudden urge to protect him.

A few days earlier, the onset of Spring had attracted a new encampment of travellers. She had scrutinised their vehicles; a filthy Land Rover - an even shabbier caravan anchored to the tow bar - but their acid green painted camper van unnerved her. Parked clumsily to the side of the Land Rover, it was decorated with a motif which at first glance resembled toadstools. Caps like witches hats hovered above squiggly stems. Eleanor frowned, filled with a sense they depicted 'magic mushrooms.' A fast, heavy beat of rock music was heard pounding from the caravan. Yet the blinds were drawn, concealing the inhabitants.

Eleanor paused, dismayed to see a circle of blackened grass. A greying heap of ashes radiated a glow from last night's bonfire. She didn't mind travellers lighting fires, but preferred them to use a brazier. *Less of a fire risk.*

She had never encountered problems with the people who stayed here occasionally. The last encampment included a couple with a child, drawn to a more spiritual way of life. A sadder case involved a couple in their teens, evicted from their bedsit by some thuggish landlord. And she could never forget her own reasons for settling here... From the early 80s, when travellers had first started arriving, it gradually dawned on her that some chose to join the convoys when life offered them no better alternative. Many considered them to be anarchists. Yet they didn't always know *the truth* behind their circumstances; victims of a society that was turning ever more materialistic and harsh.

Something about these new arrivals however, had the hairs on the back of her neck prickling.

For no sooner had the door banged open, the frame of a young man was revealed. Eleanor flinched. His feral face was dark with stubble, mousy brown hair scraped into a ponytail. But most frightening were his eyes; pale, hooded, undeniably hostile.

"Yeah?" the youth snapped.

Ignoring his suspicion, she introduced herself. But as he leaned casually into the door frame, observing her, the chill in his eyes did not recede.

"Name's Fabian," he grunted. "Camper van's mine, which I share with me girlfriend, Sara. Me other mates live in the caravan. Bobbo and Eric, or *Scruffy* as we call him."

"I see," Eleanor responded, unsure how to proceed.

He turned and yelled into the caravan to summon his friends, then jumping down from the steps, strode right up to her. A bolt of fear speared her innards and she almost backed away. But the next youth appeared even grubbier; a beard and moustache concealing his features, his brown hair matted, hanging to his shoulders in rat's tails.

"Watch out, Scruffy," Fabian smirked. "We've got a visitor."

Bounding across to Fabian, the newcomer was about six foot tall and gangly. The breeze ferried across an unpleasant waft of body odour. Already Eleanor began to regret this encounter but nevertheless, attempted to engage with them, first by explaining the land was privately owned.

"His name is James Barton-Wells."

Both men responded with splutters of laughter. Although she cringed at Fabian's reaction to the ground rules she tried to lay down. *Treat the land with respect, don't leave rubbish and take care lighting bonfires.*

"Yeah, yeah, we'll bear it in mind," Fabian said. "Anything else?"

Suddenly, Eleanor did not appreciate the scorn in his tone.

"Actually, there is. This is a quiet village, so no loud parties..."

"We live to party, man!" Eric guffawed, thrusting a fist into the air.

"Then *please* try to keep the noise down," she begged. "Most of the villagers are nice people, but others are not so tolerant..."

"Is that so?" Fabian murmured in a voice laced with threat.

"Yes," Eleanor said. "I've lived here for twelve years and I know them well, but there is one more thing I need to say." She planted her hands on her hips, her expression stony. "I have a twelve year old son. He is a gentle, sensitive boy, so I do not want him exposed to any drunken behaviour or foul language and I might as well add, I am totally against the use of drugs!"

"Sex and drugs and rock and roll," Eric started to sing, rocking his body in rhythm.

"Do you understand?" Eleanor said, ignoring him totally.

Fabian did not reply immediately. Drawing himself up to his full height, he too parked both hands on his hips, mirroring her stance. Eleanor was chilled by the glare of his eyes, the heavy lids, which gave them an almost reptilian appearance.

"Listen, lady," he said in a low whisper. "We'll respect Mr James - so-and-so - what's his face - Wells - and won't upset no one. But you've got no right to tell us how to live our lives."

She could no longer ignore such menace, saddened her initial instinct was correct; there was nothing friendly about this bunch whatsoever.

Turning on her heel, she wandered away.

But she hadn't seen the way Fabian's eyes narrowed; nor the middle finger he jabbed into the air as she receded.

Flipping aside the memory, they arrived at the Olde House at Home. The pub was busier than usual, as more and more vehicles came pouring into the car park. Eleanor bit her lip, guiding Elijah towards one of the outside tables.

Moments later, she spotted the Baileys' orange Volvo as it crawled into a space.

"Happy birthday, Eleanor!" Margaret yelled, charging over. "We got you a present!"

"Yeah, happy birthday," Andrew added with a grin. "Let me buy you a drink while I'm flush. I cashed my giro yesterday!"

"That's very generous, Andrew," Eleanor beamed. Clutching the package, she coiled her other arm around Margaret's waist to stop her falling from the bench. "I'd like half a cider please. Eli, why don't you go and help him."

"It's alright, I'll go," Charlie's voice hummed into the air.

A shadow fell across the table, prompting her to twist her head around. He smiled warmly back at her, his tall frame blocking the sunlight.

Wandering through the door, Charlie gazed at the homely interior, loving the exposed brick walls and beams intersecting them. A giant hearth dominated one corner, hung with an assortment of copper kettles. As his eyes travelled further, he glimpsed a surround of high shelves cluttered with all sorts of paraphernalia; wicker baskets, dried flowers, even an old accordion. Charlie smiled. Amongst the hand-carved furniture, several barrels had been varnished to provide more tables.

A pleasant looking blonde man smiled from behind the bar. "Can I help you, Sir?"

"Two glasses of Seven-Up please," he responded, turning to Andrew. "Did you find out what Eleanor wanted?"

"Yeah, half a cider," Andrew mumbled, squeezing himself into the gap between his father and a large man nursing a pint.

"Did I hear you mention Eleanor?" the landlord asked.

"You certainly did," Charlie replied. "It's her birthday and she's invited my family over for lunch here. I gather you know her."

"I've known Eleanor for years," Boris mused. "Wonderful woman! So how do you know her? I'm guessing you're not from the village."

"No, we live in Rosebrook," Charlie said mournfully. "Eleanor helped my family get through one of the worst periods of our lives. Isn't that right, son?"

Boris paused, ice shovel suspended. "You're not the gentleman whose wife died, are you?" he asked softly.

"That's me," Charlie sighed, dropping his gaze.

Andrew turned rigid. Staring at the landlord with a hint of suspicion, he must have been wondering how he knew this.

"It's okay, son," the landlord added, "Eleanor was in here not long ago. Said it was a sad time of year. She mentioned a husband and two kids..."

"Eleanor's been good to us," Charlie nodded, casting a reassuring smile towards his son.

"I can imagine," Boris replied, filling another glass with cider. "Can't understand why she's still single! I'd snap her up myself if I wasn't married to my Sue." He glanced across at a plump, curly haired woman on the other side of the bar and winked. "Now what can I get for you two?"

"A bitter shandy and a pint of your finest ale please," Charlie answered.

He didn't miss the doting, faraway look that briefly shone in the man's eyes.

"Tell you what," Boris added, "seeing as it's Eleanor's birthday, you can have a nice bottle of wine with your lunch. On the house!"

By the time they stepped outside again, every table had been filled, leaving Charlie thankful Eleanor had managed to grab one. Gazing back at the pub, he observed the snowy white walls, divided with the same oak beams as on the inside. It was a lovely building, he reflected; one that had retained its 'olde-world' character.

"Open your present!" Margaret nagged, fidgeting restlessly.

Settling down the package, Eleanor picked apart the wrapping. Her fingers closed around a length of material, which felt luxuriously cool and soft. She extracted a scarf. Made from crushed velvet in squares of gold and bronze, it was threaded all over with sequins.

"I love it!" she raved. "It's beautiful! Thank you!"

"As soon as we saw it, we thought of you," Margaret added with glee.

Seconds later, Boris appeared, arms filled with menus.

"Here you go, folks!" he announced. "Didn't I hear you say you wanted some food? I've just told your friends you can have a bottle of wine on us. Happy birthday, Eleanor!"

"Thanks, Boris!" Eleanor gasped. "Go on, kids, take a look at the menu. Boris, do you remember when I last called in? This is Charlie and his kids..."

"It's okay, we've met," Boris grinned, sliding onto the bench next to her. "Charlie was telling me what a pillar of strength you've been... and speaking of your last visit, how could I forget?"

He threw a subtle glance at Elijah whilst he and Margaret scrutinised the menu.

"By the way," he muttered, lowering his voice. "You know that fair-haired bloke? The one who was quizzing you about Avalon before you told him to... well, you know."

"Go on," Eleanor whispered in intrigue.

"James called by," he said. "Asked me if I'd consider barring him."

"I think he's referring to the Hampton boy," Eleanor murmured to Charlie.

Boris nodded. "According to James, the man has been stalking her."

"Yes, I heard," Eleanor sighed, twisting the gorgeous scarf in her hands.

And suddenly they had everyone's attention, even the kids.

"There was another incident," Boris added darkly. "He sneaked into the house, when both James and Elliot were off site. Don't you think that's a bit creepy?"

Eleanor looped the scarf around her neck with a shiver. "Hmm. Thanks for updating me, Boris. Now come on folks, we need to order. What does everyone want?"

Everyone chose the Sunday roast, which came highly recommended.

Charlie however, kept pondering over that last conversation, not liking what he'd heard. He had only met Avalon once, a girl who struck him as sophisticated, but fragile, from every feminine gesture to the gentle way she spoke. But the notion of her being stalked by someone as evil as Ben Hampton left him cold... a raft of memories flooding back to him. The roar of a Harley Davidson resonated, followed by Anna's scream - that chilling sensation of fear, when Ben had showed up at the building site with his henchman. He had never wanted such dark thoughts to surface on a day like today, but how could they not? They symbolised a pivotal descent in his life.

Gradually his anxiety faded as people thronged in and out of the pub. Most seemed well acquainted with Eleanor and filled with a sense he was very much on *her territory*, he observed each and every one of them, while enjoying the flavour of his beer. He met the landlady, Sue, then a lovely looking young woman of Eleanor's age. She possessed a gentle heart-shaped face framed by golden-brown hair.

"Judy!" Eleanor squealed, leaping up from the bench to embrace her.

She was enthusing over some new job; a position that would entail her whole family moving from London to Rosebrook.

"That's where we live," Charlie intervened, draining his last drop of ale. "Sorry, I didn't mean to butt in... We're friends of Eleanor."

Judy perused him saucily. "Eleanor and I were at the same boarding school," she smiled. "That was, before she ran away to have young Eli here..."

"Judy," Eleanor breathed. "How can you say that? You know my father went missing. It wasn't exactly how I planned to spend my summer holidays."

"Sorry," Judy muttered, pressing her fingers over her mouth. "Did you ever hear any more news about your dad, Eleanor?"

"No," she sighed, "which reminds me. I need to make an appointment with my solicitor. He tried to contact me last week..."

Last of all, the strangest of exchanges took place and just as Boris was delivering a bottle of wine to their table. It involved the large man who had been dominating the bar. Only this time he was accompanied by a boy. The boy stared at their table, tugging the man's sleeve. Stockily built like his father, his eyes narrowed nastily.

"Oh look, it's Gyppo Jansen."

No sooner had Elijah turned his head, he whisked it away again. Eyes lowered, his face turned white as chalk. Charlie frowned, glancing at the boy. He gave an unpleasant snigger.

"Is there a problem, Eli?" he muttered.

With a shake of the head, Elijah shot him a look of undisguised terror. "Ssh, Charlie," he said in the lowest of whispers. "It's nothing, really..."

Charlie frowned. He recognised certain pecking orders, especially among children. Eleanor had already expressed some concern her son was being bullied - but now he felt certain he had witnessed it for himself. Elijah looked petrified, which left him no other choice other than to keep quiet - at least on this occasion.

130

Chapter Fourteen

I

The one scenario Charlie had never imagined could arise out of that day was that his family would move into Eleanor's caravan.

At first the idea seemed ludicrous, yet inevitable, given the thread of fate that continued to pull their families together. With a month's notice to leave their rented house in Rosebrook, his time was almost up. The only affordable accommodation had been snapped up, leaving a dragging waiting list.

Eleanor though, shored up by her usual sunny optimism, didn't see it as a problem.

"It'll only be a stop gap. Think of it as a holiday!"

Charlie's initial response was to protest. Eleanor's home easily accommodated two people, but he couldn't imagine how it would work out with the five of them.

The topic arose shortly after they had left the pub. It took every effort on both Charlie and Andrew's part to keep Eleanor upright, after an excess of wine left her staggering. Inside the caravan, Elijah had made coffee, while Eleanor drunkenly explained how the seating could be collapsed to make another double bed. She saw no reason why she couldn't sleep at one end, Charlie and Andrew the other, which left the bunk beds for Elijah and Margaret.

Still Charlie failed to grasp the feasibility of it - at least, not until the night they had finally agreed to stay over.

Never would he have believed that once the padded seats were flattened to function as a mattress, they would be so comfortable! Nor that he would lapse into a more peaceful sleep than he had enjoyed in months. At first it felt strange, the countryside so calm and empty of sound, apart from an occasional passing car or the hoot of an owl. He had woken up refreshed, if not a little disorientated. The approaching dawn was enlivened with a ringing chorus of birds, whilst the occasional moo of cows seemed to echo their surroundings.

"This is great!" Margaret reassured him. "Just like camping! I don't mind staying here for a while, Dad, it's gonna be fun!"

"It won't be for long," Eleanor continued to placate him. "Just think of it as temporary until you can find a new place..."

"But it seems like such an imposition," Charlie mumbled. "Think of the impact this will have on your life - and Eli's. I warn you right now, Andrew can be a moody sod! And what about other issues such as - er - privacy?"

"Charlie, there's a curtain across the bed and a concealed shower cubicle," Eleanor scolded him. "I work alternate shifts, so it's not as if I'll be around all the time anyway. Let's just give it a try. If it doesn't work out, you'll have to move into Bed and Breakfast or something..."

Eventually, he saw no reason to argue. Like she said, *this wasn't forever, more a transitory phase.* The caravan did at least provide a roof over their heads.

At times, it felt a little cramped. Their last house afforded them more space, but the initial anxiety wore off as the smell of cut grass, wood smoke and spring blossom filled their nostrils. Savouring the aroma of Eleanor's wonderful cooking, Margaret and Andrew were reluctant to admit how much they had missed having a mother figure to fuss over them - not to mention the joy of a home-cooked meal to come home to.

For the next few days, their lives were transformed. It was easy for the kids to snuggle up on the bed and watch television. Bringing the TV they had purchased in Rosebrook, they preferred it to Eleanor's clapped out old portable. From the other end of the caravan, Charlie and Eleanor often drifted into easy conversation. Other than that, Eleanor enjoyed reading, whilst Charlie was happy to spend time poring over his architecture manuals, forever finding ideas to implement into his own designs.

For it so happened, another piece of luck had rolled his way.

His latest client had been granted planning permission for their Granny flat extension, despite all objections. Charlie had to confess to feeling a little smug when the first pallets of bricks were deposited in the front yard - especially when a neighbour poked her head over the fence to complain. He was tempted to laugh. Her sharp, beaky face and pinched mouth further accentuated her scorn. In an attempt to curtail her fears though, he said he would keep disruption to a minimum; that all building work would take place within normal working hours; and that maybe one day, when she was too old to look after herself, she would be glad of a similar conversion, should her own children be so kind-hearted.

"That shut her up!" he was amused to tell Eleanor and the kids a little later.

For the first week, the five of them fell into a clumsy but somewhat easy harmony, much to Eleanor's delight. Some bickering did erupt between the boys, usually concerning their TV choice. Andrew preferred laddish comedies such as 'The Young Ones' and 'Spitting Image.' But on the few occasions Elijah wanted to watch a film or a nature programme, Andrew called him a sissy! Eleanor was forced to shrug it off. They were boys, they were bound to argue. It wasn't as if they were tearing each other's throats out.

During the day, hardly anyone was at home, which afforded them extra breathing space. The fact that Charlie worked in Rosebrook also had advantages; he was able to drive both children to school each morning. Andrew meanwhile, was determined to complete the last few weeks of his training scheme. Excited at the prospect of being a fully qualified joiner and brick layer, he would be working alongside his father soon. For three afternoons a week, he attended the technical college. Eleanor meanwhile, continued to work her shifts as a part time nurse, filling some of the empty hours whilst the others were out...

But she had not forgotten her conversation with Judy, nor the message to contact her solicitor. Stirred by a wave of intrigue, she arranged a trip to London.

II

A short tube journey brought Eleanor to an area of London known as Holborn and before she knew it, she was hit by a flood of memories. A long escalator ferried her slowly to the top of the station before a flash of daylight was revealed. Clutching her shoulder bag, she fought her way through the crushing knots of people all pushing their way towards the exit. Eleanor kept walking, keeping her head down. She didn't have to go far. An expanse of tall white office blocks swam into view, almost as soon as she had turned the first corner.

Seeing the blue sky reflected in hundreds of window panes, she was overcome by giddiness, the scene exactly as it appeared all those years ago... *Except on that occasion, she had been with Jake. The pressing matter of a legacy left by her father's boss, Sammie Maxwell, had been the one incentive that had drawn them here.*

Wasting no time, she hurried towards the office block where she knew her solicitor would be waiting. The firm had changed recently with the retirement of one of the partners. These days, it went under the name of 'Sharp, Bancroft and Blackmore.' John Sharp, the most senior partner, was in his fifties now, a man whose long, drooping face had barely changed. His greying blonde hair might have thinned slightly, but as he gazed at Eleanor through familiar soft brown eyes, his face conveyed a hint of anxiety.

"Please, take a seat, Eleanor," he began. "My secretary will bring some coffee. But how are you faring these days?"

Hidden in a small but nicely refurbished office, Eleanor felt her earlier tension melt. The subtle embossed pattern of creamy wallpaper blended pleasingly with the light ash furniture and sinking into a leather chair, she briefly described her circumstances.

"So, what is it you wanted to see me about?" she dropped into the conversation.

"Eleanor," John sighed, hands folded on his desk, "I might as well get straight to the point. Just over a week ago, someone broke into our office."

She raised her eyebrows. "You were burgled? Was anything stolen?"

She saw the light vanish from his eyes. "Nothing of value," he said, "but Eleanor... I have reason to believe that whoever came here was looking for your secret file."

Eleanor froze as soon as the words were out. "How do you know this?" she gasped.

"They forced open the filing cabinets," he continued gravely. "One of the drawers contained files of all our clients from A - D. Yet the only one missing was *yours*."

Her heart started thumping, an all pervading fear that her enemies were closing in on her. But why now? Why, after all these years, would the secret of Jake's murder be unearthed?

"At least there was nothing controversial in that file," John added. "Nothing other than details of the legacy left to you by Sammie... and an enduring wish to find your father. I took the liberty of moving your *secret* file to a secure bank vault some years ago and thank heavens I did!"

"But who could have done this?" she whispered.

John gazed up at her beneath furrowed brows. "I don't know. But I think we can assume that whoever took it has reason to be threatened by its contents! I have taken a copy for the purpose of this meeting, so I suggest you hold onto it. There seems no harm in keeping another copy somewhere, just as long as the original is safe. Here, take it..."

Without hesitation, she accepted the padded envelope. She didn't need to open it to know what was inside, picturing the sheath of pages written in her own hand. That chilling plot had culminated in Jake's murder. Yet the tunnel of secrecy furrowed deeper. Jake had been witness to something. He unwittingly held the key to a conspiracy so corrupt, it would send shock waves across the nation. As John implied, those responsible had much to fear. Even more momentous were the stories that emerged in the British press at the time; clippings which held little significance in isolation... but interwoven with Eleanor's story, would be damning enough to raise questions.

Eleanor gripped it tightly. This file was her insurance. It stopped the people behind Jake's murder from killing her too and she had felt moderately secure in this knowledge until now.

"Did you inform the police?"

"Of course," John reassured her. "Just because nothing of any monetary value was stolen, it doesn't mean a crime was not committed. Whoever the culprits were, they forced their way into our office and one of our client's files was stolen. Finger prints suggested a male whose hands may be larger than average. Unfortunately, they were wearing gloves."

"You don't suppose this had anything to do with Dominic Theakston, do you?" Eleanor shivered. Her skin crawled with goose pimples.

"I don't think so," John murmured. "In fact, you may be interested to know that Dominic Theakston moved out of London six years ago. It's rumoured he severed all links with organised crime, though one can never be sure."

"So where is he now?" she kept pressing, helpless to forget that Theakston had been the most terrifying character she had encountered.

John gave a sigh. "I've never told you this... but in the light of what happened to Sammie Maxwell, I remained somewhat vigilant with regards to the activities of Mr Theakston. Would you like to know what I discovered?"

Eleanor found herself nodding. This much feared crime boss was maybe the last person she wanted to think about, yet she could not contain her curiosity.

"Go on then," she urged him. "Tell me what became of that bastard! The last time I saw Theakston, he threatened to harm my baby son."

John frowned, lifting his coffee cup to his lips.

"He expanded his empire after you left London. Continued to operate in Whitechapel but gradually stretched his boundaries to Bethnal Green, even Soho. There was no shortage of illegal contraband, including hard drugs and firearms... but Theakston had his fingers in a lot of pies. Certain establishments were still in fear of him and paid protection money. He had already recruited some of the most vicious thugs in London, gradually taking on new territory with tactics of increasing intimidation and violence. What I find incredible though, is how someone like Theakston operated as such a professional criminal without conviction. Until it began to emerge some officers in the Metropolitan Police had close social ties with criminal gangs. They chose to sufficiently exercise their discretion in order to permit the continuation of such enterprise."

"I see," Eleanor said tightly. Already she could recall a particularly corrupt police officer; one who had played a significant role in Jake's death. "Please go on."

"It's no secret, Eleanor," John whispered, lowering his gaze. "There have always been links between Scotland Yard and organised crime. Those officers who chose to turn a blind eye received huge payoffs. But anyone who attempted to oppose it was swiftly dealt with. For a few years nothing changed much. That was, not until 1977..."

Eleanor tilted her head, captivated. "So what happened then?"

"There was an investigation," John smiled, "culminating in the 'Fall of Scotland Yard.' The scandal was exposed, which led to the dismissal of dozens of corrupt officers."

"Really?" Eleanor mused. "Tell me, was Inspector Hargreaves one of those officers?"

"He was," John nodded. "Sadly, they never uncovered his role in Jake's death but he was definitely 'removed' from the force. Lord knows what he's doing now but you must be wondering the significance of this. His dismissal from authority left Theakston vulnerable..."

He paused as if waiting for a reaction. Eleanor couldn't move, her eyes fixed on him.

"In 1979 a new police superintendent was brought in," John said, "specifically to deal with organised crime. There was wide speculation he had a vendetta against Theakston. His name was Barry Mason, his brother knifed in an alleyway not long after Theakston took on Sammie's empire but I'll tell you this, Eleanor. Barely a week went by when Theakston wasn't being investigated. With a noticeable drop in his criminal activities, his protection rackets died a death. But Mason was never actually able to pin anything on him. Theakston was clever, a master at covering his tracks. So much so, Mason tried to fit him up in the end!"

"Did he succeed?" Eleanor quizzed.

A smaller part of her could not resist imagining Theakston festering in jail.

"No," John confessed. "This was the era he *moved away* from organised crime. He invested his ill-gotten gains in setting up a gymnasium but in 1982, moved out of the capital altogether, severing all ties with his past. You see, Theakston's chickens finally came home to roost. Think of all the people he hurt... the families he threatened, the catalogue of ruined lives in the wake of his criminal reign, including yours..."

"And?" Eleanor prompted him.

"Everything came to a head when his own wife and child were kidnapped," he added coolly. "They weren't harmed... but let's just say Theakston got a wake up call! He's gone now, living it up in the country somewhere, so I gather. Though I would never underestimate him."

"Dominic Theakston, married," Eleanor pondered. "It seems hard to imagine, and as for being a father..." Strangely enough, she felt stunned by John's news.

"People do change, Eleanor," he muttered, "hence the reason I am convinced he played no part in this burglary. Yet what about the others who were involved? Is it not possible this could be connected to someone a little higher up the chain? Even you claimed that Theakston was merely Jake's assassin. But what about the people who commissioned that killing? Don't you think they would have even more to fear if ever the contents of your file were leaked?"

Eleanor lapsed into a strange, dreamlike trance, recalling the press conference. The folds of her innermost memories swung back like stage curtains, exposing a scene she would never forget.

Yes, there had been someone else...

The face of a mysterious blonde stranger momentarily flickered in her mind's eye.

"There was only one other man I named in my file," she murmured. "Councillor Whaley. I know he was involved, same as Hargreaves... but there *was* someone else, someone I never had a chance to identify."

"Are you certain about this?" John pressed, the frown on his face deepening.

"Yes!" Eleanor gasped, "except Theakston drove me out of London before I had a chance to find out who he was!" Gripping the file in both hands, suddenly she felt afraid.

That press conference had happened so long ago, but only now did she wish she could remember more of it, if just to summon up that final face...

III

The meeting lasted nearly two hours and in that time, they had briefly gone over the details of Eleanor's will. They also spoke of her father. No news had arisen to suggest Oliver Chapman was dead, which left a tiny ray of hope. Behind the scenes however, an inscrutable thread of evidence revealed that Ollie had been heading for Italy at the time of his disappearance. Picking up the thread, John had reason to believe he might still be out there.

By the time Eleanor retreated from the office, his disclosures had left her floundering.

On the one hand, she felt reassured by the news about Theakston. It meant her visits to London would no longer pose such peril.

But a burden of fear overwhelmed her, the file of notes heavy as it sagged in her shoulder bag. Only *she* understood the lethal power of those notes, the reason she didn't dare delay her departure. There were so many other things she would have liked to have done; a flying visit to the park for example, where the lure of Jake's memorial felt inviting. And she was yearning to talk to Luke Merriman, wondering if *he* would be able to recall the third man at the press conference. But all that would have to wait...

As she made her way across the London underground, Eleanor had no idea she was being followed. With twenty minutes to spare before her train, she slipped into a café in Waterloo Station to grab a cup of tea, unaware Nathan was still stalking her.

Abandoning his black leather garb in favour of a checked shirt and skin-tight jeans, he blended into the crowd quite easily. They guessed she would visit Holborn.

137

How fortunate, a security guard working in the same building had tipped him off.

Once in position, he had spotted her himself and just as she came wandering out of the office block; one that was very familiar by now.

He had been there before.

In truth, Perry had hired Nathan for many more reasons than to provide protection for his reckless son. Nathan's true value lay in his past, his links with the criminal underworld; the added advantage being he had even worked for Dominic Theakston.

In recent weeks however, Perry was starting to feel a little paranoid. It all started after Ben had accosted the Chapman girl in that pub. But it since transpired she was close to the Barton-Wells family. This was cause for concern, especially in the light of Perry's intentions. He wanted her out of the way, but only with the guarantee he was not about to land himself in the firing line. Such was the reason he had ordered Nathan to steal her file.

Though sadly, it didn't appear to be the one he was after.

He was still immersed in his thoughts, when Eleanor sailed out of the café in front of him. Wearing a long linen dress, she kept her jacket draped over one elbow. It revealed her muscular arms, her prominent tattoo. Nathan's eyes were drawn to her nose piercing, the silken dreadlocks as Ben had described.

Yes, Eleanor Chapman was quite an enigma, he thought to himself, his gaze travelling down the length of her body.

She momentarily glanced up, offering a surprisingly friendly smile.

Nathan, feeling he had no choice, found himself unwittingly smiling back.

But his eyes never left her, not until she had boarded her train. Only then did he turn away to begin his own journey back to Pimlico, knowing Perry would be awaiting him.

Chapter Fifteen

I

Andrew sensed times were changing. The country was changing, his whole life seemed to be changing and it was happening faster than he could adapt. But where the loss of employment left him vulnerable, the shock of losing his mother completely floored him; it had plunged him into an abyss where black clouds covered his days. First came the depression. Then came the bitterness and the anger. These days, he just felt lost...

The next pivotal crossroads occurred when he had returned to Eleanor's caravan to find it empty. He knew she was seeing her solicitor, he just didn't imagine it would take all day. To his further dismay, he fumbled around in his coat pockets to discover he had forgotten his key. Andrew bit back his fury. Frustrated at the thought of being marooned in this field until Elijah returned, he yanked out his cigarettes. Then a faint whiff of wood smoke hit his nostrils. Unable to stem his intrigue, he strolled a little further, his gaze drawn to a group of youths.

"What are you looking at?" someone hollered.

Andrew swallowed, clocking the dirty blonde dreadlocks and black clothes. Taking a drag of his cigarette, he cautiously approached their camp. Small lumps of wood sputtered and popped in the silence, two of them sat on logs around a campfire, the other two sprawled on a blanket.

"Hi," Andrew muttered. "Mind if I join you?"

"Yeah, if you want," rose a second voice. "Take a pew."

Switching his gaze, he met the pale eyes of Fabian. Instinct warned him there was something cocky about him, perched on his log, legs apart, his intense stare unwavering.

A girl of about eighteen sat close to him.

"What's your name?" she asked sweetly.

Andrew guessed she was his girlfriend; pretty and elf-like with long fair hair braided into shoestring plaits. Feeling slightly braver, he lowered himself onto a log.

"Andrew," he muttered, "my family's moved into Eleanor's caravan..."

"Yeah, we know," Fabian said, hurling a glance over his shoulder. "So what's it like bunking up with 'Miss Goody Goody?' Give you a hard time, does she?"

"Not really," Andrew shrugged. "Eleanor's cool. Why do you say that?"

"She never stops moaning, man!" drawled the fourth member of the group.
Andrew frowned, appalled by his dirty hair and clothes.

"No loud music, no parties, no fucking fun!"

"Oh come on, Scruffy, that's not true," the girl argued. "She asked you not to misbehave in front of her kid, right? I heard her!"

"You mean Elijah?" Andrew grinned, picking up their banter. "Yeah, I can imagine. She wraps that kid in cotton wool. So what are your names?"

With a smirk, Fabian levered his body upright. "Name's Fabian and this is me girl, Sara." He wound a possessive arm around her waist. "That's Bobbo and he's Eric. We call him Scruffy. So what about you, Andy, okay if I call you that?"

Andrew paused, eyes drawn to the embers. "I'm training to be a builder like my Dad. We got made redundant. Dad works for himself now and I'm finishing my YTS."

"YTS?" Bobbo snorted. "What, some firm hires you to work for 'em all day, so's you can pick up your giro? That's fucking slave labour, dude!"

Andrew shrugged. "I don't have much choice! What about you?"

"We don't do nothing!" Eric bragged, folding his gangly frame into a cross legged position. "We're rebels, fighting against an unjust society who don't give a shit about young people. There aren't no jobs out there anyway, man. Might as well just travel around and party like us!"

"Yeah, you're right about this country, it is shit!" Andrew grunted. "When Dad and I lost our jobs, we lost our home... ended up in a right shit hole!"

He sensed a shift in his mood. Kicking at the grass, he didn't want to continue down that road. Andrew liked to keep up the bravado, when in truth it felt like his world was breaking apart.

Fabian however, was still watching him. "Should have got yourselves a van then and taken to the road," he added softly. Then finally, his gaze flicked to Bobbo. "Skin up!"

Andrew said nothing, his heart swelling in pain. Inhaling deeply, he sucked in the fresh air, before a different smell permeated his senses. Andrew gaped at Bobbo. He appeared to be lighting a fudge-like substance, crumbling it into a king-sized cigarette paper.

"Is that dope?" he asked naively.

"Yeah," Bobbo said, his voice challenging.

Glancing up with a grin, he lit the joint, took a couple of deep drags and holding the smoke in his lungs, passed it to Fabian.

"Thanks mate," Fabian responded, puffing on the joint as if he owned it.

Time seemed to stand still, until he turned and offered it to Andrew. At first he froze.

His dad would go ape shit if he found out.

Yet making new friends was the one thing he needed more than anything right now...

"Thanks," he whispered, snatching the joint before he could stop himself.

He felt the bore of their eyes as he took one drag, then another. But seeing Scruffy fidgeting, he begrudgingly passed it on.

"So," Fabian sighed, invading his thoughts again. "You were holed up in some dump! So how come you're camping with her?" Once again, his eyes bounced towards Eleanor's caravan.

Grateful for a chance to offload, he told his story. The squalid flat in Bromley. The cold damp atmosphere that made his mother ill, before the advance of pneumonia wrenched her life away. The frustration of being broke; having no one to talk to except his little sister, who was a right pain in the arse and whose recent sulks were getting on his tits!

By the time he had finished ranting, his limbs and mind felt heavy. Yet before he knew it, a peculiar sensation soared inside him. *He felt high.*

"You know you can always come and talk to us," Sara's voice purred.

"Tell you what," Fabian said. "We usually have a bit of a session in the evening. You know, play music, chill out a bit. Come and join us if you want."

"Great!" Andrew replied, unable to wipe the grin from his face.

He had just spotted Elijah flickering into view with Margaret.

"Better put that spliff out, Scruffy," Fabian said coolly. "Looks like the kids are back..." He threw Andrew a last cutting smile. "I guess we'll see you around then."

By the time Eleanor arrived home, she was delighted to find all three of them sitting around the table playing 'Trivial Pursuit.'

In the aftermath of smoking cannabis though, there was one thing Andrew was unprepared for; the paranoia he was about to experience, as soon as he looked at Elijah. His mysterious eyes burned into him like lasers. It was Margaret who suggested playing a board game.

"Science and nature for a triangle," Elijah said.

Several minutes later, Charlie turned up.

"Afternoon folks," he said, watching Eleanor as she switched on the kettle.

"Hi, Dad!" Margaret beamed. She picked out a card for Elijah. "Good day?"

"I suppose so," Charlie sighed, running his fingers through his hair. It was powdery with cement dust. "At least I *was* until that old bag next door stuck her miserable face in to have a go. I said I'd be there during working hours and I've hired a concrete mixer! She can't just expect it to stand idle, every time she comes home. I've only got it for two days."

"Don't let them get to you," Eleanor said and poured two mugs of tea.

"So how was your day?" Charlie asked her. "Did you see your solicitor?"

141

He detected a flinch in her shoulders, her actions slowing, as if concentrating too hard on an otherwise simple task.

"Yes, but I can't talk about that now," she said tightly.

Charlie had seen that look before, the shutters slamming down. Releasing a sigh, he sat himself down at the table where the kids were playing their board game.

"Okay, so who's winning?"

"Eli, of course!" Margaret said in her teasing tone. "Andrew's brain's gone on strike!"

"Shut up!" Andrew snapped. "You're not doing so well yourself, smart-arse!"

"Let's not fight, kids," Eleanor sighed, placing Charlie's mug down.

"So, what are you up to now?" he grinned, dismissing her earlier secrecy.

"Getting dinner of course," she replied in a monotone.

Charlie frowned, troubled by her mood; the only reason she would ever be this tight-lipped was because Elijah was in the room.

"Look," he murmured, "why don't we wander down to the pub later, just the two of us? The kids seem happy to amuse themselves. What do you think?"

"I'd like that very much," Eleanor relented. Closing her eyes, she rolled back her head to ease the tension from her shoulders.

"You're going out?" Andrew muttered.

"Mmm," Charlie said, "you don't mind, do you?"

"No," Andrew said with the ghost of a grin. "Can I go out too? See some mates?"

"Okay, but promise not to be late," Eleanor answered for him. "I don't want these two left on their own for long, especially after dark. Is that reasonable?"

"Sure," Andrew answered. He could barely conceal his glee.

"We'll go after dinner then," Eleanor finished.

Turning away again, she picked up her bag and locked it in an overhead cupboard.

II

It was almost 8:00 when they left. Dusk edged its way into the sky, layering the landscape with indigo and reducing the trees to silhouettes. The air had turned colder but Eleanor kept her dress on. Filled with a desire to look pretty next to Charlie, she slipped on a jacket and scooping up the lovely scarf they had bought her, she slung it around her neck.

"Well, this *is* a treat," she enthused as they ambled along the country lane.

"I think it will do us good," Charlie smiled, "give the kids some breathing space. I can't believe we've been here nearly a week and it's gone so fast." He turned, his gaze warm. "I really appreciate you putting us up, Eleanor. With a bit of luck, there'll be some places up for rent soon. The paper comes out tomorrow…"

The white walls of the pub gleamed in the dwindling light. Tonight it wasn't so crowded, just the usual band of regulars. From the corner of her eye, Eleanor spotted Herbert Baxter, hunched by the hearth like a toad. His eyes turned frosty, in the instant he glanced up. She also recognised the stocky dark-haired man propped on a stool reading a newspaper, unsure why he unnerved her.

"Eleanor!" Boris grinned, sashaying up to the bar. "What can I get for you both?"

"I'd like a pint of your excellent beer," Charlie said, returning his smile, "and half a cider for the lady. I'm so smitten by your pub, I couldn't stay away!"

Boris grabbed a heavy beer glass and chuckled. "Thanks! Oh, and perhaps I should warn you, our Eleanor here usually drinks pints!"

The stocky man looked up coolly.

"Boris!" Eleanor breathed. "A half will do very nicely, thank you, Charlie."

"Go and grab a seat," he whispered, sensing the silent scrutiny of the other man.

The seconds ticked by as Boris poured the drinks. Charlie and the dark haired stranger exchanged glances. The man let out a sniff and flipped the page of his newspaper.

"Do I know you?" Charlie said.

"Don't think so," he snapped.

"Hang on," Charlie muttered, keeping his eyes fixed ahead. "I remember now. There seemed to be some hostility aimed at Eleanor's son. Didn't I overhear your boy call him some name? What was it now… 'Gyppo Jansen'. I didn't think that was very nice."

"They *are* gypsies," the man sneered, keeping his voice low.

"No," Charlie argued. "They just happen to live in a caravan. Why should it matter? Eleanor's turned that place into a delightful home…"

"Think what you like," the man grunted, flinging back another sheet of his paper.

Boris cleared his throat loudly. "Let's not get into an argument now," he warned. "I'm guessing Eleanor only came here for a quiet drink and she doesn't get out much."

"No," Charlie sighed, gazing over to where she was sitting.

Observing her lovely profile, he was reminded of a Roman statue. She had removed her jacket, slender arms like bronze in the glow of soft light. Yet he didn't fail to miss the paunchy man resting by the fireplace, his face sour as he hurled another glare in her direction. Charlie felt tense, picking up an onslaught

143

of prejudice that was starting to annoy him. Boris caught his eye.

"Quite lovely isn't she," he whispered. "Don't worry, Charlie. Most people here adore her and I hope you don't mind me asking... but are you two together?"

Charlie laughed lightly. "Just friends. We became close when my wife was alive."

"I see," Boris pondered. "Well, I know I wouldn't let such an opportunity pass me by. That will be £2.50 please."

"Everything okay?" Eleanor asked. "Who were you talking to at the bar? Do you know him?" She took a long and thirsty swig from her glass.

"Enough to know he's a pompous arse," Charlie muttered under his breath. "Anyway, the less said, the better. Now are you going to tell me about your day or what?"

The smile dropped from her face. "Oh, Charlie..." she sighed.

With some difficulty, she spluttered pieces of her story; *of Jake, the innocent witness, killed to protect a secret.* Except the secret had never quite died with him...

"So let me get this right," Charlie breathed, "you wrote it all down?"

Eleanor nodded numbly.

Fighting his discomfort, he shifted in his chair.

"Is the file still safe?" he pressed.

"It is now," Eleanor began to explain, "the reason my solicitor wanted to see me. Someone attempted to steal it..."

"Shh," Charlie hushed her.

He flashed a warning glance, just as Boris sauntered around the bar. A second round of drinks gleamed in the shadows, which seemed destined for their table.

"Tell me later," his voice grazed against her ear.

As Charlie guessed, Boris had briefly escaped from the bar. Lowering his tray on their table, he slid himself into the chair next to him.

"Mind if I join you for a minute?" he muttered. "There's something I need to talk to you about. These are on the house, by the way."

"Thanks, Boris," Eleanor gasped, pulling her lips into a smile. "So what's up?"

"It's about that lot camped in your field," Boris cautioned. "I've had to bar them. They're an unruly bunch. Their language is foul, one of them stinks like a pig and I bet you any money they're on drugs!"

Eleanor glanced at Charlie in panic.

"The only reason I'm telling you," Boris continued, nudging his head closer, "is because *you know who* over there is rallying up a campaign to have them

144

evicted from the village."

But already Herbert Baxter had heaved himself from his stool. Scowling at Eleanor directly, he was ready to launch a personal attack, now advancing towards their table.

"Well!" he snorted. "We've had to put up with some rabble but as for this latest bunch..."

"Look, Mr Baxter," Eleanor retorted, "this may come as a surprise but I agree! I'll be as glad to be shot of them as you."

He seemed to deflate a little. "Is that so? Well, maybe if people like *you* didn't encourage them, we wouldn't have to tolerate them at all!"

"That's not fair, Herbert!" Boris shouted, rearing up in his seat.

From another side of the room, the dark haired man looked up with intrigue. Closing his newspaper, he too, began to advance towards their table.

"I have never encouraged anyone," Eleanor said, a look of hurt glittering in her eyes.

"So what have *you* done about them?" Herbert barked.

"Told them to respect our village," she insisted. "I have my own son to think about. I've already warned them about rowdy behaviour and drugs."

"Have you now?" Herbert relented and with a sigh, sagged into a chair.

"Why are you being so foul to Eleanor?" Charlie intervened. "She's just admitted those travellers are a problem. It sounds to me like you're trying to make her a scapegoat!"

"If she is on our side, I apologise," Herbert muttered. "I can't help it. I'm old fashioned. It angers me to see how much society has degenerated."

"It's okay, Mr Baxter," Eleanor said, "and I'm sorry if my caravan offends people."

For the next few seconds, nobody spoke.

Then a deep voice barged into the silence. "Did I hear mention of drugs?"

Eleanor whirled around, staring into the menacing dark eyes of the man towering behind her. Charlie too raised his eyes, unable to hold back his outrage.

"What's it got to do with you?"

Boris leapt to his feet. "We were just discussing those hippies, Sir, the ones I recently barred. Now, I really think this conversation has run its course, don't you?"

"Ah, but it's just got interesting," the other man smiled. "The fact is, if there's even the slightest suspicion those people are on drugs, they're breaking the law, which means my force has good reason to investigate. We could start by searching their vehicles."

"Your force," Charlie echoed in dread, "you're a policeman?"

"A police inspector actually," the man added.

Eleanor stared at the man, then back at Charlie.

Boris on the other hand, squirmed. He had clearly overheard Charlie's accusations, concerning those taunts towards Elijah.

"Allow me to introduce Inspector Ian Boswell, folks," he babbled. "Now does anyone want another drink, seeing as I'm heading back to the bar?"

"We're fine with these, thanks," Charlie said.

Raising his glass, he averted his eyes from Boswell, whose look of smug satisfaction left him uneasy.

"You okay, love?"

Eleanor, half way through her second glass, simply nodded.

"I suppose so," she replied. "Sorry, Charlie... I wasn't expecting quite so much drama and to think, I was really looking forward to telling you about my day."

"You still can," Charlie smiled, "though maybe not here. Let's stay for one more round then shall we go for a little stroll somewhere?"

By the time they ventured into the cool limpid darkness, they were both a little tipsy. Charlie followed Eleanor as she crept through the back of the pub, into the beer garden. It was surrounded by flower beds, clumps of daffodils barely visible in the shadow of a low stone wall. A small gate led to a footpath, bringing them into an expanse of farmland and forests.

For several minutes they wandered in silence. With the air so still, even the slightest sound seemed amplified - from the hollow crunch of their feet on the path, to the breeze rattling the tree tops. They could just about detect the movement of animals as an occasional cow or sheep plodded across the ground, munching grass. Eventually they came to a five-bar wooden gate.

Ignoring the gate, Eleanor turned onto a bridleway. The ground was lumpy, rutted with hollows from the passage of horses' hooves. Yet the grass under their shoes felt soft.

Gradually she started talking again, relaying the saga of her file.

A thickening cape of trees closed around them.

"I might even show it to you," she whispered. "I've got my own copy now... but at least the original is safe."

"Why do you suppose someone tried to steal it?" Charlie dared himself to ask.

He saw the freeze of her shoulders, the way her head became very still.

"There is only one reason anyone would want my file, Charlie," she shivered. "Someone out there is scared. It makes me wonder if some new evidence has turned up... but I'm worried what this means for me and Elijah."

Hands clasped in fear, she shot glances in all directions, as if fearing some presence.

Charlie touched her shoulder. "Eleanor..." he began, but the flinch of her muscles startled him. "Hey, don't be scared."

"You don't know what it was like, Charlie," her voice rose huskily. "One day, when I've explained a bit more, only then you'll understand."

The broadleaf woods were getting thicker and before they knew it, they had entered the forests surrounding Westbourne House. From that point the conversation flowed more easily, inspiring Charlie to reveal what he had discovered. Taking an instant dislike to the stocky man at the bar, he suspected it was his son who was bullying Elijah.

"What chance has the poor kid got if the father is prejudiced?" he added.

Eleanor agreed. She would have words with Elijah to coax the truth out of him. She knew he was frightened but had refused to name the boys who had attacked him.

With her last words withering, she stopped and peered into the distance. An outline of hills was faintly illuminated under a glittering sheet of stars.

"We must go back to Westbourne House," she murmured. There was something hidden in her tone that suggested a frown. "I so much want you to meet James..."

"Then let's go tomorrow," Charlie offered. "I could even knock off work early."

"On second thoughts, maybe leave it until after the weekend," she relented. "They've got a big function this Saturday... a ball to raise funds for their restoration."

As the path dipped and rose, drawing them deeper into the trees, Charlie's hand slid towards Eleanor's; just a brush of the fingertips to begin with, until gradually they became entwined. It was a silent, secret gesture where neither spoke, a warm current passing between them.

At the end of the forest, the trees parted, revealing a wide track. They could have turned and wandered down to the road, but instead chose to cross it. Climbing over a stile, they were drawn into another patch of woodland, still holding hands. With little need for words, they savoured the intimacy of the moment. But as the trees started to thin again, the towering canopy of an oak tree seemed to beckon them.

Eleanor paused and gazed at Charlie. The moonlight enhanced his striking features; the high cheekbones, the shapely curve of his mouth. He was a handsome man, his eyes so dark and soulful. Already she could sense the warmth in them as he clung to her stare.

Taking a deep breath, she felt a rise of anticipation as he moved closer. His fingers slid under her jawbone, tilting her head and yet still he seemed hesitant.

Oh, how he longed to kiss those lips. So plump and velvety, they had always reminded him of marshmallows...

He could no longer hold back. Lowering his mouth, he savoured their sweetness.

Before they knew it though, they had shuffled right up against the oak tree. It felt like a dream, a passion they yearned to grasp before it had a chance to slip away. Eleanor wound her arms around his back, pulling him harder against her body.

His hand slid under her jacket without preamble, closing around her breast.

Charlie smiled, loving the swell of warm flesh in his hand. Her breasts might not be so voluptuous as Anna's, in fact they were small by comparison. Yet he relished their roundness, caressing each one in turn and to his further delight, she made no attempt to fight him.

Unsure quite how they had got there, they found themselves sinking into the grass.

Charlie slipped off his overcoat and spread it on the ground. Seizing Eleanor's hands, he rolled her onto her back. They knew what they wanted. Eleanor wriggled on the ground, pulling up her dress. *As if he needed further encouragement.* Kneeling over her, he slid his hand into the valley of her thighs, seeking the core of her womanhood.

She carefully unzipped his jeans, his erection springing upwards, before the barrier broke between them. Surging together in union, their coupling was as sweet as it was intense; a feeling they had been denied for too long.

Panting on the grass in the aftermath, it was Charlie who broke the silence.

"Eleanor," he spluttered. "I'm so sorry! I couldn't help myself!"

"What are you on about?" she whispered. "That was amazing! If it wasn't for the fact we had to get back to the kids..." She propped herself up on one elbow.

"You don't think it's too soon?" he mumbled, fastening up his flies. "It doesn't seem that long ago s-since Anna..."

"Ssh," Eleanor interrupted him. "You mustn't feel guilty. What does time matter anyway? We've both lost someone we loved, so don't you think we deserve a little pleasure?"

III

Tumbling into the caravan at about 10:00, Andrew meanwhile, had spent the last two hours in the company of the new age travellers. From the moment he set foot inside their caravan, they seemed intent on getting hammered. Passing a couple of joints around, Fabian tossed a can of beer into his lap. He slurped it down thirstily to the sound of 'Hawkwind' blasting from the speakers.

At times they subjected him to heavy topics, from militant left-wing politics to their own exploits, bumming around Britain, joining the various hippie convoys. The subject inevitably led to Stonehenge and the 'Battle of the Beanfield.' Andrew felt unnerved by their description of the police, who were said to have stormed in like some sort of militia.

Before the evening ended though, Fabian extracted a silver tin, concealing his *personal stash*; the resin black and oily as tar, its fragrance intense, but strong. And just before he left, he swore he could get him *anything he wanted*. With his face masked in shadow, his pale eyes shone like orbs; a surreal moment when Andrew truly believed he had found a kindred spirit.

Back inside Eleanor's caravan, the atmosphere was very different.

Elijah and Margaret were sprawled across the bed on their stomachs, watching TV with a bowl of crisps balanced between them. Without a word, Andrew rammed his hand into the bowl and grabbed a load, stuffing them into his mouth.

"Hey, slow down," Elijah berated him. "What's the matter with you?"

"I'm starving," Andrew managed to mumble.

Next he started rummaging through the bread-bin. Helping himself to two thick slices, he made himself a peanut butter sandwich. Finally satisfied, he lowered himself onto the edge of the bed, staring glazed-eyed at the screen as he wolfed down his sandwich.

"Good time?" Elijah quizzed. "What are the travellers like?"

"How do you know I went to see them?" Andrew said furtively.

"We saw you," Margaret smiled. "It's okay. We won't tell Eleanor."

"She's a bit wary of them," Elijah added somewhat defensively. "Did you have fun?"

"Yeah, they're okay," Andrew chuckled. "Lazy bastards, though! They don't work or nothing but we had a good laugh..."

Elijah and Margaret exchanged amused glances. The interior of the caravan ran silent again as all three of them stared at the television, listening to the gentle hum of voices emanating from the set. It was a programme about the Green Movement; the thinning of the ozone layer believed to have been caused by man-made chemicals such as CFC gases. Elijah found it quite enlightening, since they had studied a similar project at school.

"What's this shit you're watching?" Andrew then grunted.

"It's not shit!" Elijah snapped. "Scientists think the hole in the ozone layer's caused by aerosol cans..."

"That's bollocks!" Andrew scoffed and lifting his buttock in the air, broke wind loudly. "That'll put a hole in the ozone layer!" He just about managed to force the words out before he collapsed onto his back, shaking with laughter at his own joke.

Margaret looked horrified.

"Andrew!" she breathed, hauling herself up onto her elbows.

Elijah looked incensed. Then, as if refusing to be outclassed, rolled over onto his back, cocked his leg and also let rip. Andrew exploded into even fiercer paroxysms of laughter.

"Eli!" Margaret squealed. "Not you as well!"

Both boys completely corpsed, unable to control themselves. It could have been a turning point, a ripple in time where they almost bonded. Except in the splinter of time Andrew turned, Elijah noticed his eyes. They looked peculiar; heavy lidded and bloodshot.

"What's wrong with your eyes?" he whispered. "Have you been smoking wacky baccy?"

The cocky smile fell from Andrew's face. "Don't be fucking stupid, Eli."

Seconds later, the caravan door flew open.

Andrew leapt from the bed as if electrocuted. Although no sooner did he realise it was his father and Eleanor, he collapsed back down.

It was difficult to ascertain who, out of the three of them, looked more guilty.

"Nice evening?" Elijah said, rolling back over to watch his programme.

"Very nice," Charlie muttered, switching the kettle on. "What were you lot laughing about? It sounded as if there was a party in here and we were missing all the fun."

"Oh, I wouldn't say that," Eleanor murmured, pausing as she turned to lock the door.

It didn't seem long before Andrew lapsed into a deep sleep. Fully clothed, curled up in a foetal position, he looked so peaceful, Charlie didn't have the heart to wake him. Covering him with a blanket, he tucked it around his shoulders. He felt a rush of love, sensing his inner torment. He had long suspected Andrew was still hurting; that no amount of cosseting could ever make up for his mother's absence.

Margaret and Elijah quietly changed into their pyjamas before slipping into the bunk beds. Within minutes, the interior of the caravan lapsed into an ambience of calm. The only sounds were the children's breathing, combined with Andrew's gentle snores. Eleanor lit a few candles, extinguishing the main light, then poured them a tot of whisky each.

Their hands joined across the table.

"So where do we go from here?" she said.

"We need to take things slowly," Charlie whispered. He glanced over to the beds with a sigh. "Look, I want us to be together. It feels like destiny and much as I've tried to fight it, I think I'm falling in love with you..."

"Same here," Eleanor sighed. "I didn't want to jump in too soon out of respect for Anna."

"How do you think the kids will handle it?" he challenged.

"I don't think Eli will mind," she murmured. "He'll be delighted. What about your two?"

Charlie shrugged. "I can't imagine Margaret will have issues, but Andrew I'm not so sure about. We'll have to be discreet... He's still cut up about his mum, like there's something bubbling below the surface. Something bitter, angry, and it worries me."

She sipped her whisky. "Maybe things will be easier when you've found a place of your own. It will help him settle. But we can still carry on seeing each other..."

The hint of something mischievous rose in her voice as she said it.

Staring into the deep golden pools of her eyes, Charlie felt a knot of emotion. A tiny part of him was afraid to let go of Anna. Yet as Eleanor's beauty filled his vision, it occurred to him how long he had fought his attraction. Even the words of Boris echoed inside his head:

I know I wouldn't let such an opportunity pass me by.

Thinking back to the scene in the forest, that spontaneous burst of passion... it had consumed them like a fire. He knew with little doubt, he would be a fool to let her go.

His grip on her hands strengthened as he stroked his thumbs over her knuckles. "Then why don't you and I meet for lunch, tomorrow," he found himself murmuring. "Maybe slip back here for a little while..."

"Why not?" Eleanor nodded, eyes huge with longing as she squeezed his hands in return.

Chapter Sixteen

I

Eleanor and Charlie were not the only ones moving forward with their lives. In another corner of the county, James had finally decided to tackle the Hamptons about Ben's behaviour.

"James!" Rowena crowed down the telephone. "To what do I owe this pleasure?"

"This is not a social call, Rowena," James responded.

She let out a sniff. "You're not inviting us to your ball then?"

The sarcasm in her voice was not lost on him, leading to a brief but uncomfortable pause.

"How did you know about the ball?"

"News travels fast, James," Rowena said guardedly.

At first, he was tempted to laugh! Here was a family who had sneered at his walled gardens and referred to him as a 'lightweight.' Yet those humiliating taunts were nothing, compared to the malevolence of Perry's words. The threat, he would *regret his decision,* still hurt.

"No, Rowena," he announced, his tone turning colder. "In fact, I never want any of you to set foot on my property again! Especially your son!"

"What?" Rowena gasped.

James could no longer contain his anger. "Ben has been stalking Avalon! He tried to kiss her in the woods and she ended their relationship. But as for this relentless campaign to frighten her... I am telling you this has got to stop!"

"I have no idea what you are talking about," Rowena lashed back in fury.

"Haven't you?" James breathed. "Ever since you visited, your son has been snooping around the village, interrogating the locals about her! Worse, he's been sneaking up on her, throwing stones at her bedroom window at night and playing spine-chilling music in the grounds. Then last week, he had the audacity to turn up at the house when I was out!"

"What if he did?" Rowena retorted. "The house is open to the public, is it not?"

"Ben is trying to unhinge her!" James ranted. "And if he goes anywhere near her again, I shall inform the police. Do you understand?"

"So that's it, is it?" she snapped without even the hint of an apology. "This is the only reason for your call?"

"I'm afraid so," James sighed, sensing her dismay. "I'm sorry but it's over,

Rowena. I chose *not* to go along with your partnership and you will just have to live with my decision. But please, let's have no more unpleasantness..." He was astounded to hear a click as the phone went dead, leaving his last words dangling in silence.

II

Just a short distance away, all five residents in Eleanor's caravan gradually shrugged themselves into action. Eleanor brushed Margaret's dark blonde hair while Andrew stomped around the caravan, moaning about the crumpled state of his clothes. Charlie smiled as he sipped his coffee. Already dressed and shaved, he was ready to tackle work with a renewed spring in his step. Elijah, in his school uniform, hovered by the door.

No sooner had everyone departed, Eleanor found herself drifting. The breeze was cool, the grass sparkling with dew. Breathing deeply, she drank in the crisp air. Euphoric from the events of last night, she could hardly wait to meet Charlie later... She hadn't realised how far she had wandered though, until the travellers' vehicles loomed into view and there, hunched on a log like a gnome, Fabian puffed away on a roll up. She risked another few steps.

"What do you want?" he said, his voice soft and clipped.

She met his icy stare with a shiver. Even Elijah had taken to calling him *Crocodile Eyes*.

"I hear you got yourselves barred from the pub. Didn't I warn you this was a quiet village?"

"Now listen, lady," Fabian hissed, "you told us not to throw no loud parties or smoke ganja in front of your boy!"

"Elijah is not stupid," she said, "and neither are the locals. They've long suspected you take drugs and want you out of the village..."

A particularly unpleasant laugh tore out of him. "Oh, do they now?"

Eleanor released a sigh. She had never wanted to make enemies of these people, a tiny part of her fearing the imminent threat this could yield for Elijah.

Fabian rose to his feet, wild hair loose as it spiralled around his shoulders. "We ain't going nowhere," he added, "and if we wanna smoke the odd spliff then it's none of your fucking business. So, tell that to all them stuck up bastards in the village!"

Three hours later, their clash was long forgotten as she lay naked under the bedcovers in Charlie's arms, warm from the afterglow of lovemaking.

They had taken things slower this time, exploring and caressing each other. Eleanor found herself marvelling at the strength of Charlie's body; his muscular limbs, the tautness of his smooth skin. Savouring his scent, she buried her face in his chest hair, her hands running over his shoulders again, savouring every contour.

"You are one very sexy woman, Eleanor Chapman," he murmured.

He stretched out his body in ecstasy as she continued to caress him.

"It's been a long time," she whispered back. "Over two years."

"Really?" Charlie grinned. "I can hardly believe that."

"I'm no slut, Charlie," she added. "I've been saving myself for the right man..."

Charlie rolled over onto his side and propped himself up on one elbow. Pulling back the covers, he gazed lovingly down at her body. "I promise I won't disappoint then."

Moments later, he rolled on top of her again, driving eagerly in and out of her, as if he knew this was how she wanted it.

Having had few lovers in her life, Eleanor could remember a time with Jake once, an explosion of passion that arose out of fear. She tried to push the memory away, but it kept haunting her, a day they should have made their escape and a meticulously planned ambush had prevented it. Sadly, it was too late for regrets, everything associated with those memories confined to the past. *Or were they?* One final legacy existed, apart from their beautiful son; her secret file and even that was under threat.

But as she journeyed towards another climax, she found herself reliving their walk in the forest, recalling Charlie's words. *"Hey, don't be scared..."*

Smiling to herself, she sensed a new era unfolding. Being part of a family was something Eleanor craved, not only for her own sake, but for Elijah. If Charlie could find an affordable house to rent, then maybe all their prayers would be answered...

There was just one shadow on the horizon; the fate of the Barton-Wells family and the predatory family still stalking them. But with the weekend approaching and the Springtime Ball imminent, their long awaited discussion lingered just to the other side...

III

In fact, nothing brought the tranquil village of Aldwyck to life quite like the build-up to the Springtime Ball. The weather remained dry, much to Avalon's delight, the gardens exploding with colour. Banks of tulips had sprung into bloom, from the palest pinks to the most regal of reds and purples. The photographs would be stunning.

Even Boris sensed the celebratory mood, the Olde House at Home even livelier. Locals poured in from every corner to toast the event; perhaps hoping for a glimpse of someone rich or famous as dozens of luxurious cars swept through the village.

Not one of them could have known that Perry was surveying the scene from the top of a hill; Rowena smarting with fury to be excluded from such an event.

His predatory eyes honed in on every passing car from behind his binoculars - he was counting, extrapolating the number of guests, while mentally calculating the revenue James would make from this enterprise.

But as the dazzling event ensued, even Charlie had something to rejoice.

Aggrieved by the shortage of affordable rented accommodation in the paper, he had registered his details with a letting agency. A recently modernised town house had become available, subject to some last minute repairs. If he was happy to sign the letting agreement and put down a deposit, his family could take up residence as early as next week.

"I'm afraid you'll have to put up with us for a few more days, love," he explained to Eleanor. "Are you sure you don't mind?"

Naturally, she had no problem and to his greater surprise, neither did the children. They had adapted amazingly well to village life, happy to make the most of this brief but enjoyable respite from suburbia.

Having discovered the buzz of smoking weed, Andrew knew he would miss Fabian and his gang, but he wasn't really thinking straight... Such was his disenchantment, he had decided to skive off college for the day. Any excuse to get high and lose himself. He couldn't face yawning his way through English literature, unable to understand what relevance the literary works of Shakespeare had with bricklaying, not to mention the tutor, who was a right boring old fart!

Two days earlier, he had scored drugs for the first time. Beckoned into Fabian's camper van, he was intrigued to see him dig into his pocket, extracting a lump of the same fudge-like substance they had smoked on their first encounter. Just before he left though, he had inadvertently let it slip that Elijah might have sussed what they were up to, that first evening. He didn't miss the sinister scowl darkening Fabian's face but let it go, oblivious of what it could lead to.

The caravan predictably lay empty. With a sly grin, he made a mug of tea, then got straight to work, laying out the Rizlas as Fabian had taught him, sprinkling in the softened cannabis resin and tobacco... For a few minutes, he puffed away joyfully.

But as the world began to turn dreamy, a movement caught his eye.

Andrew shot up and gaped out of the window. He thought he was imagining things but was that the chestnut head of Elijah he saw shooting into the trees?

"Get him!" he heard someone holler.

A blur of black streaked across the field. *Bobbo?*

Next to appear was Fabian.

With a sense of unease, Andrew struggled to his feet and out of the caravan. It looked as if Elijah was in some sort of trouble, but undeniably the travellers, *his friends,* who were chasing him.

Elijah lost all sense of direction as he stumbled into the trees. The spidery branches got in the way. Wrenching them aside, he forced his way deeper into the labyrinth, his pursuers gaining ground. To his spiralling fear, they were closing in on him, blocking his escape. Recognising the trees encircling their side of the field, he hurtled towards them... before an invisible foot shot out of nowhere, tripping him. With a sob, Elijah clawed the ground, devastated.

Who could have sneaked up on him like that?

Twisting his head, he was even more shocked to see Andrew. The others had caught up too, *Crocodile Eyes* glowering down at him.

"Nice one, Andy," he smirked.

"What's he done?" Andrew shrugged, an undeniable shadow of guilt crossing his face.

"Grassed us up to the pigs," Fabian said. "Our van got busted last night! Good job most of our stash was buried somewhere secret..."

"It's not true!" Elijah whimpered. "I swear, I've never said anything about drugs!"

"Liar!" Fabian hissed. "Your mum's done nothing but nag us since we got here. So let's have no more bullshit. We know it was you."

In response to a nod from Fabian, the others hauled him to his feet.

"What are you doing?" Andrew spluttered. He could barely look at him.

"Time he learnt a lesson," Bobbo grinned. "Come along, *Elijah*, let's see you sample our goodies. Can't knock it 'til you've tried it!"

Andrew let out a nervous snigger. "Aw, c'mon guys! Why don't you let me sort this out?"

"Forget it," Fabian said. "Consider it a rite of passage."

Helpless to fight, Elijah found himself being marched towards their encampment. A sense of fear consumed him, never mind the fury of Andrew's betrayal. By the time they forced him onto one of their upright logs, he was shaking. The embers of their fire still glowed. Elijah stared down hypnotised, as 'Scruffy' prodded it with a stick to get the flames flickering.

Crocodile Eyes hunkered down right next to him and shrugging off his tatty rucksack, dropped it to the ground. He dug out a can of beer.

"There you go," he sniggered, ripping back the ring pull.

"I don't want it," Elijah shivered.

"Drink it!" Fabian ordered.

A can of 'Tenants Super' was thrust into his hand, one of the strongest beers on the market. Andrew looked horrified. Yet Elijah had no choice. He could sense their eyes digging into him like blades, egging him on. Clutching the can, he took a swig and almost choked. With a sense of utter desolation, he tried passing it to Bobbo.

"It's all yours, kid!" Bobbo taunted. "Drink up!"

Elijah took another swig. But it fizzed in his oesophagus, precipitating a belch.

"It's disgusting!" he shuddered, screwing his eyes shut. "I can't drink any more..."

"Stop being a wimp," Fabian sneered, "or we'll pour it down your throat."

Elijah fought tears as he continued to drain the can. Used to being victimised, he knew when he was beaten. The circle of youths fell silent as he continued to gulp from the can. *They were an unsavoury looking bunch.* Yet there was no way he had grassed on them.

Taking a last gulp of beer, he found it impossible to swallow. It burst from his lips like a water hydrant, drenching their fire. The embers sizzled.

"Hey, that's enough, guys," Andrew pleaded, lowering himself onto the one remaining log. His eyes slid towards Bobbo. Having laid out the cigarette papers in preparation for a joint, he was piling in the resin. "Oh no, you're not serious!"

"Chill out, Andy," Fabian smiled. "It's just one of life's little lessons!"

Bobbo lit the joint, taking a draw of smoke. Elijah watched him fearfully, the beer churning in his stomach. He met Bobbo's eye as he handed it to him.

"Please!" he sobbed, struggling in his seat. "I didn't snitch on you, I swear..."

"Yes, you did," Fabian muttered. "We know it was you. That pig as good as said so and he knows you live on this site."

"It's not true," he whispered.

A cruel look swept across Fabian's face. "Smoke it!"

Andrew fidgeted in his chair as Elijah took a puff.

"You didn't take it in," Fabian jeered, pushing it towards his mouth again.

Elijah exhaled an angry sigh. Snatching the joint from his fingers, he took another puff, only this time, he held the smoke down. At first he felt nothing before a certain defiance took over him. The gang watched in intrigue as he took one drag after the other... until the smoke caught in his throat eventually, sending him into a coughing fit, and he dropped the spliff on the ground.

Fabian scooped it up and paused, letting the tension fill the atmosphere. He smiled nastily.

"There! Wasn't too bad was it, kid?" he said and hauled himself to his feet.

Elijah could not speak, the clouds inside his head swelling. He gazed at the embers of the fire pit without expression. The minutes ticked by slowly.

"You okay, kid?" Eric leered at him.

"He's up there with the fairies," Bobbo laughed, "look at his face!"

Elijah blinked, confused as to why they were staring at him. As he struggled to his feet, head spinning, only Fabian now obstructed him.

"Let me take him home," Andrew pleaded, "before Eleanor gets back..."

Before anyone could react however, Elijah's face turned ashen. Andrew watched in horror as he stumbled to his knees.

"Eli, are you okay?"

"Uh oh," Bobbo muttered, a moment too late. "White one!"

Elijah retched. Clamping a hand over his mouth, he lurched forwards, then vomited all over Fabian's trainers.

Andrew lowered himself to his side. "Eli," he gasped. "Oh shit!"

The other two were laughing their heads off. Fabian on the other hand looked furious.

"Come on, I've got to get him home," Andrew begged. "I'm sure he's learned his lesson!"

"He better have," Fabian finished in a low, hate filled voice.

With a whimper of fear, Elijah stared up at him and nodded, while Andrew helped him to his feet. Pale as a ghost, he was still fighting nausea, though for now his ordeal was over.

Andrew practically shoved him inside the caravan and without wasting a second, grabbed a washing up bowl. Elijah swayed where he stood, only to be violently sick again. Andrew clasped his shuddering shoulders to keep him upright. His body convulsed several times until he was sure the worst of it had passed.

"Did you really grass them up?" he then whispered.

Elijah gaped at him, lips falling apart as if to say something but the words never made it... Before they knew it, the door banged open where Eleanor materialised like lightning.

"What the hell is going on?" she shouted, dropping two carrier bags.

Margaret followed her inside, having agreed to go shopping with her. Eleanor surveyed the scene in horror before her eyes fell to the bowl. The contents swirled in a foaming yellow pool.

"I-I-I'm sorry, Mum..." Elijah spluttered.

Yet as soon as he spoke, she must have detected the smoke on his breath. Next she studied his eyes; the heavy lids, his glazed expression.

"No!" she gasped with a sob. "Not drugs as well! Oh Eli, how could you?"

Andrew tried to explain but it came out all wrong. Pacing from one side of the caravan to the other, he felt cornered. But in the instant Elijah glared at him, the guilt must have shown on his face, leaving no question he was hiding something.

"I want the truth!" Eleanor thundered. "First, I'm appalled you would even mix with those people but to allow my son to end up in this state..."

The atmosphere inside the caravan blackened, the argument building to a crescendo. But without warning, the door swung open again, only this time it was Charlie. Everyone froze as he took in the scene; Margaret cringing in one corner - Elijah huddled on the bed, white faced - Andrew and Eleanor glaring at each other like two fighters in a boxing ring.

"What's going on?" Charlie gasped.

"Why don't you ask your son?" Eleanor snarled, her voice shaking with anger.

"Andrew's been hanging out with the travellers," Margaret bleated, "and Eli's drunk."

Andrew turned and shot her a look of pure loathing. "You stay out of it!"

"Great!" Charlie retorted curtly. "I knew this wouldn't work. In fact, the sooner we get ourselves out of here and into a bigger place, the better..."

A sob tore from Eleanor's throat and backing towards the door, she staggered outside.

"Eleanor!" Charlie yelped, but a moment too late...

In the end he went looking for her.

Stunned by her hasty departure, Charlie had doggedly squeezed the truth out of the boys. But as the air turned chilly, his anxiety started to gnaw. A peculiar sixth sense lured him up the path and into the forest... and there she was, huddled up against an oak tree, the very place they had made love.

He tiptoed gently towards her. "Eleanor, love," he whispered.

"You're still here then," she sobbed. "I thought you were desperate to move out..."

"I never said that," Charlie interrupted.

Clasping her hands, he leant in to kiss her but she twisted her face away.

"You never let me finish," he pressed. "When I mentioned moving into a bigger place, I meant for the *five of us*."

He watched the anger drain from her face, a tear coursing down her cheek. With a sad smile, he stroked it away tenderly.

"Didn't you say Andrew would have a problem with that?" she gulped.

"Andrew doesn't have much choice," Charlie said. "I want us to be together. Why do you think I came looking for you?"

"How's Eli?" she whispered fearfully.

"Eli is fine," Charlie replied. "A bit upset you buggered off like that, but no harm done. Andrew told me everything. He's actually quite shocked by what happened..."

With her arms hugged around her knees, her bottom lip started trembling.

"What is it, love?"

"Do you know one of the last things Jake begged me before he was shot?" she whimpered. "He urged me to keep our child safe. Hid me under the floorboards to protect me..." She released another sob. "Sometimes I think I'm failing! That I can't do it!"

"Rubbish," Charlie protested. "You're a great mum, anyone can see that."

"But he's as much of a victim as I am! How can I protect him? First, the bullying and now this! I never wanted him to be exposed to drugs..."

"So give me a chance to explain," Charlie persisted. "Because both things are connected. Did you know those hippies were raided by the police last night?"

He had spoken to the girlfriend, after the rest of that sorry bunch had skedaddled. She too seemed convinced Elijah had ratted on them. Something had been said, something that implied there were others on the site who had it in for them.

"Fabian thought the pig was talking about Eleanor... but insisted it was the kid."

Charlie shook his head, reeling. He had sensed something strange the previous day; pulling up at the school gates, watching the kids part company - Margaret running across to her primary school, burnished blonde locks flying - Elijah wandering ahead, where a trio of boys were lingering... He saw none other than Gary Boswell and his gang, the police inspector's son.

Charlie could not forget the way they hung back, as if they could not wait for Elijah to reach them. But according to Elijah, Gary had been interrogating him about the travellers. He had already picked up the impression they were a rowdy lot and *always high on drugs*.

Elijah in his innocence had agreed: *"Yeah, that pretty much sums them up."*

Regrettably, such an admission had been leaked to the boy's father. With Elijah's name fixed in everyone's minds, Sara confessed that *even Andrew had warned Fabian Eli he had sussed they were dope smokers...* words destined to add another spark to the imminent fire - and sure enough, the police had busted their vans that same evening...

"So that's how the rumour started," Charlie finished, "but it gets worse. According to this lady, it appears *Inspector Boswell* dropped him in it..."

"But that's outrageous," Eleanor breathed.

"I know," Charlie said. "So now will you come back to the caravan?"

Slipping his hand into hers, he was gratified to feel the squeeze of her fingers. Eleanor gave a shudder. The news had understandably left her dazed.

"I guess we've got a lot to discuss," she said as they wandered back through the woods.

"Yes," Charlie sighed, "but irrespective of whether Eli grassed them up or not, those yobs had no right to do what they did. You don't force beer and drugs onto a twelve year old."

"No," Eleanor spat, "and as for that Fabian, I could kick his scrawny arse!"

Charlie picked up his pace. "But you don't want a war on your hands. Surely, the best thing you could do is to get them out of the village, which is what everyone here seems to want."

"But the field doesn't belong to me, it belongs to James."

"Then James has the power to evict them," Charlie smiled.

"Of course," Eleanor nodded. "So let's speak to him. In fact, let's go tomorrow, all of us, kids too. Didn't I promise we'd take another trip to Westbourne House soon?"

"You certainly did," Charlie said, pausing as they reached the road.

"Then what are we waiting for?" she whispered.

She offered him a kiss laced with such tenderness, he felt as if his heart would burst. There was no question she needed his protection; that despite the waves of persecution rising, they would continue their quest as lovers.

Chapter Seventeen

Departing the following morning, Eleanor could barely contain her excitement. It seemed such a long time ago she had told Charlie about the restoration.

No sooner had he eased his car into the parking area, Elijah and Margaret jumped out and started racing towards the house. With the sky streaked with ribbons of silver cloud, it looked magnificent, taking Charlie's breath away. Straight away he found himself studying the windows again, their delicate frames and mullions.

By the time they reached the entrance the children had rushed inside, Elijah skidding to a halt, just as Avalon appeared in reception.

"Eli!" she greeted him heartily. "Oh, and hello you... Margaret, isn't it?"

Their footsteps echoed eerily on the ceramic floor tiles. Turning to greet them, Avalon offered her warmest smile. There was no denying how much happier she looked.

"How was the ball?" Eleanor asked.

"Amazing!" she gasped. "Can you believe we had over a hundred and fifty guests?"

Closing her eyes, she took a deep breath, absorbed in a flurry of memories; how the gardens had been at their most splendid, filled with beautifully dressed people. The afternoon had remained dry and as the ladies wandered in the grounds, she had never seen such a stunning array of ball gowns. Her own dress, made from a blue watermark taffeta had fitted perfectly, moulding itself to her figure. Also on this night she had captured the eye of Hugh Bambridge, a dishy young British polo player with whom she had danced for most of the night. Before the event ended, he had asked for her phone number. Hugh lived in the neighbouring county of Surrey and with plenty of time to devote to her, when he wasn't training on the polo pitch, it was the exhilaration of dating him that had put the glow back into her cheeks.

"There might even be a feature in 'Tatler' next month," she kept chirping.

By the time James appeared at the foot of the stairs, his eyes captured Eleanor's with a twinkle.

"Haven't stopped talking about it yet, then?"

Charlie and Margaret spun around and for one fleeting second, the six of them silently observed one another.

"Oh, come on, Dad!" Avalon protested. "You have got to admit, it was our best event ever! This is Charlie, by the way, and his daughter, Margaret."

"What a pleasure it is to meet you at last," James said.

As the two men shook hands, Charlie smiled. There seemed little need for words. A wave of camaraderie loomed between them, a sense they had finally found each other.

But when James went on to discuss the restoration, Charlie couldn't resist studying the inner architecture; from the exposed stone walls stretching to the first floor, to the exquisite wooden mouldings on the staircases. As Eleanor described, there appeared to be little evidence of decay, irrespective of the sum required to restore it.

"I hear you had a survey done," Charlie faltered. "I did notice a serious crack in the outer wall."

"Ah, yes," James sighed, "though I warn you, the damage goes deeper. Have you noticed the work we're having done on the roof? That started in February. Rain water's been leaking into the house for years, spreading dampness, which is no doubt how the decay started. Incidentally, I'm so sorry I wasn't around the last time you visited."

"There is no need to apologise," Charlie shrugged. "We said we'd come back."

James nodded. "Then let's wander through to the library and have coffee."

Charlie allowed himself to be guided into a warm, softly lit room. Elegantly furnished and surrounded by bookshelves, it possessed an ambience that felt comforting. The next person to appear was Elliot, his silver tray dispensing a cloud of fragrant coffee.

No sooner were the introductions complete, Charlie drank in the beauty of his surroundings. Eyes drifting to the windows, he observed the stonework, the craftsmanship in their construction. The grounds were clearly visible behind the heavy panes. Yet it was the panes his gaze was drawn to; the flaking paint and worn putty.

"How old is this place?" he murmured aloud.

"Over two-hundred years," James announced. "It's been in my family for five generations. Rotten luck that all the wear and tear of the last two centuries should fall on my shoulders!"

As a bubble of conversation rose up again, Charlie frowned. Feeling restless, he wanted to examine the room more closely. A smell of beeswax polish filled his nostrils. It mingled pleasantly with the underlying scent of leather, before he was drawn towards the bookcases. The shelves were packed with books. But as his eyes wandered, they stopped dead, honing in on a suspicious trail of dust. Fine as talcum powder, it was a sight that wrenched his gaze upwards again and there he saw it; a set of minute bore holes peppering the underside of the shelf.

"You've got woodworm," he stated bluntly.

The room fell silent. Lowering his coffee cup, James rose to his feet, as if curious to examine what Charlie had stumbled across.

"I do believe you may be right, Charlie," he said. "The original survey did report evidence of a wood boring beetle in the building's main structure..."

"How long ago was this?" Charlie demanded, turning to meet his eye. "I mean, when did you have the survey done?"

"October last year," James said in a resigned tone. "Why do you ask?"

Charlie was struggling to find the right words. "Is there any chance you can remember the type of infestation they identified? Was it deathwatch beetle?"

"I think so," Avalon intervened. "Is it serious?"

"Oh yes," Charlie said darkly, gazing up at the shelf again. "The damage caused is extensive, because they tunnel right through to the centre of the wood. You need to get this treated..." He paused, backing away from the book shelves. "In fact, why haven't these restoration experts addressed this? It should have taken priority over everything!"

"This gentleman has a good point, James," Elliot said, also rising. "Though at the time, we were desperate to get the staircase fixed, so we could re-open the hotel."

"And we agreed the next priority would be the roof," James added. "I guess it got overlooked."

Charlie shook his head. "You have got to call in a remedial expert before the problem gets any worse or spreads to other areas of the house... that is, if it hasn't done so already." He was beginning to sound quite bossy but felt duty-bound to warn him. "I could even recommend a reputable company."

James looked at him, a smile gradually smoothing away the furrows of anxiety. "Thank you," he muttered. "Eleanor said all along I should talk to you. I'm sorry it took so long, which reminds me of something else I wanted to ask. I understand you've had dealings with *Mr Hampton*..."

Charlie froze, a familiar black cloud rolling into his mind.

"Yes," he shuddered. "I don't like to be reminded... but for the benefit of this meeting, I'll tell you my story. Did Eleanor explain any of it to you?"

"Not all of it," James pondered. "But seeing as the weather's holding, why don't we take a stroll in the grounds? You can confide in me. That is, if you can bear to..."

It had been many months since Charlie had voiced the heartbreaking events that brought such devastation to his life. How could he forget the instrumental part Perry Hampton might have played? Something about James's soothing, easy going manner encouraged him.

"It started on the building site. That hooligan of a son nearly ran my daughter over on his bloody motorbike! But do you know, I don't remember hearing much of an apology. The outcome could have been tragic... Margaret was in tears!"

"Unbelievable," James muttered to himself.

The fury bit deeper, as he went on to describe Perry's reckless housing scheme, his failure to follow proper planning procedures. And he could hardly bear to divulge the aftermath of losing his job, never mind the confrontation when Ben had turned up with Nathan. The intimidating way they had approached him still left him cold.

But the fear on Avalon's face was unmissable.

"I never did like that henchman of his," she whimpered. "They're both evil."

"And can you believe Hampton had the effrontery to turn up, too?" Charlie spluttered. "He tried to headhunt me for his own company, but I told him to shove it..." He pressed his eyes shut in dread, the memory still torturing him. "Even Anna said I shouldn't have spoken to him like that but I was just so angry!"

Persevering with his story, they continued their way along the beautifully maintained garden paths.

"How come you had such trouble finding another job?" Avalon asked him.

Charlie paused again as the memories came charging back... *you are a fool! Have you any idea who you're dealing with here?* There had been something undeniably threatening about the way Perry had ended that conversation.

"Someone started spreading rumours about me, maligning my skills as a builder. I'm certain Hampton was behind it! I guessed he was powerful, even then, and couldn't think of anyone else I could have made an enemy of..."

He would never forget the horror on Christopher Farrin's face either.

A deeper part of him had always suspected he was hiding something. But what would any of these larger construction companies gain by blocking his prospective job applications, unless their own profit-making potential had in some way been compromised?

"Even my old project manager warned me the man was deadly."

He knew he had their attention now, their footsteps slowing.

"I'm certain he set out to destroy me," he shuddered as his story drew to a close. "Although it was impossible to prove at the time."

James listened without interruption. His immediate gut feeling was that Charlie could hardly blame himself for his family's misfortune. But as Avalon trailed along beside them, Eleanor and the children skipping ahead in the direction of the walled gardens, he contemplated the facts.

Charlie's story brought a chill to his blood. So much so, it didn't take long for his own memories of Perry to resurface. They took him right back to the

165

night of the dinner party. Reeling in the aftermath of that dreadful survey, James was so humbled by their hospitality, never mind the offer to save his home, it was too tempting to refuse. Looking back though, they would have destroyed *him* in the end. Even the horror of Ben's stalking bore testimony to the evil they were capable of... James shivered, curling a protective arm around Avalon's shoulder.

How lucky they had been to escape that partnership.

"So, what happens now?" Charlie piped up.

"The only problem I'm faced with is how we will manage this restoration without the funds, and this is the one hold he may still have over me."

"You seem to be managing okay so far," Charlie reassured him. "You've had a staircase rebuilt and those builders are working on the roof! What's more, you've raised some extra revenue from the ball. My advice is to get the woodworm treated and fast. I'm certain I can find a decent firm and at a reasonable cost."

"That's very good of you, Charlie," James sighed, "but what about the other repairs?"

"Well, you've got *me*," he announced boldly. "Wasn't this the whole point of our meeting?"

James turned to him, the darkness in his mind lifting at last. Perry's chilling words, *you are going to regret this decision,* became a distant echo.

"Does this mean you're offering to help us?" Avalon said wistfully.

"It would be an honour," Charlie smiled. "For starters, how would you like me to repair your windows? I couldn't help noticing some of them were in a pretty sorry state."

"You're right," James muttered. "The survey listed sixteen in need of replacement, and at an estimated cost of £20,000."

"£20,000?" Charlie baulked. "How much per window? I could rebuild every one of those for less than half what you've been quoted - and my son can help too."

"I'd be more than happy to hire you, Charlie," James pledged, before turning towards the walled gardens. "When do you think you can start?"

Charlie lowered his eyes. He had only very briefly mentioned their living situation; that they would be around until the following weekend, but then what?

Before the meeting closed, James knew what he had to do. Already he felt indebted to Charlie, shuddering to wonder what would have arisen out of Perry's partnership deal, had it not been for his early warnings.

Ushering them a little further, they slipped into the walled gardens. He clocked Charlie's expression. His eyes were everywhere, swivelling to the orchards, lacy with blossom, the intersecting paths enclosing the vegetable plots. Rows of newly planted seedlings thrived in regimental rows; a line of bell-shaped terracotta pots concealing the growing crowns of rhubarb. On the other side of the path towered the remains of last year's onions, balls of soft mauve petals that resembled lollipops.

"This is absolutely beautiful," Charlie murmured, gazing ahead.

Following his gaze, where the Orangerie nestled between the glass houses, James and Avalon exchanged smiles.

"Let's go inside," James insisted.

They wandered into the flint structure, the interior warm and sunny, furnished with cane furniture. A small music centre stood in one corner and a large potted lemon tree in another. One by one, everyone chose a seat. James waited a few seconds until they were all sitting comfortably.

"So, how would you feel about coming to live here?" he sprung on them. "All of you! Eleanor and Elijah too. What do you say?"

Charlie was speechless. Yet James remained firm in his conviction; it presented a solution to all their problems. He was even happy for Charlie to continue with his own building projects, whilst employed as his personal foreman.

"This is very good of you," Charlie gasped, "but this place is exquisite! What sort of rent were you thinking of charging?"

"I wasn't thinking of charging you *any* rent," James said. "I see this as a way of helping each other and with the added advantage of thwarting those odious Hamptons."

Eleanor's face lit up into a bright smile, having never expected such an outcome.

To work here would be a dream *but to live here?*

"I don't know what to say," Charlie floundered, his voice breaking with emotion. "Are you sure this won't be an intrusion on your own lives?"

"Listen, Charlie," James said. "The hotel is barely attracting any guests, especially with all this building work! So don't worry. There are lots of empty rooms and plenty of space."

"Oh, Charlie!" Eleanor whispered. The first glitter of tears swam across her eyes. "This is an answer to *all* our prayers... I can hardly believe it."

James gave a dismissive wave of his hand. "Eleanor, I would have invited you and Eli to stay here years ago if my wife hadn't created a fuss! We all know your life has not been without tragedy and it's no coincidence Charlie ended up homeless, thanks to that vile *Peregrine Hampton*. But if he can help me restore my home, the least I can do is offer you accommodation!"

"Perry swore we would never succeed in rescuing our home," Avalon added excitedly. "So let's prove him wrong."

Eleanor, on the other hand, was gripped by an unexpected knot of anxiety. For some unknown reason she was thinking about Jake again; the mystery surrounding his murder.

What was it about those last words that left her chilled?

Somewhere lurked a memory, an indistinct thread she couldn't quite grasp. The same feeling had plagued her on the day she heard of the attempt to steal her file... but for now she suppressed it. They had too much to rejoice.

Chapter Eighteen

I

If there was one thing James was right about, *Eleanor's life had not been without tragedy.*

Yet on the advent of moving to Westbourne House, she was troubled by a different dilemma: Elijah was beginning to fall prey to the same type of people who had victimised her in the past.

Such thoughts fuelled her with a renewed sense of purpose as they marched towards the Olde House at Home. For in the light of their good fortune, they had booked a table for lunch.

Boris greeted them warmly.

"Hello, folks," he beamed. "Good to see you again. What can I get for you?"

"Just an orange juice and lemonade for me, please," Eleanor said, flashing a smile.

Straight away, she had recognised Ian Boswell whose family dominated the largest table. There was no mistaking that cropped dark hair, nor the shirt straining across his broad back. A smartly dressed woman sat next to him who she guessed to be his wife. In fact, there was no denying the family's affluence. Even the children's clothes looked brand new, including expensive looking trainers. She noted a girl and two boys. The eldest bore a striking resemblance to his father.

Eleanor's smile faded. A day earlier she had visited the library where for the first time ever, she had used their electronic magnifying machine to search the newspaper archives on Microfiche. But whilst foraging for information on Inspector Hargreaves, she had instead stumbled across a most interesting article concerning *P.C. Ian Boswell* from 1979.

She watched as the older boy hauled himself to his feet, nudging his father, badgering him for change. With a look of irritation, Boswell fished into his pocket for some coins.

Eleanor blinked and dragging herself out of her reverie, she met Charlie's eye.

"Listen, kids, why don't you go and choose a table," he murmured.

Lowering a protective hand on Elijah's shoulder, he too, had spotted the Boswell boy, his splinter-like eyes zooming in on him.

With a gulp, Elijah slipped away and as Charlie's children followed, he turned back to Boris.

"We'd like to order some food, please," he added, bracing his shoulders. "Is it okay if we sit in the restaurant today?"

"Of course," Boris replied.

As soon as the kids disappeared however, his expression turned serious.

"Eleanor, I wouldn't go picking a fight with *you know who* if I were you. You must have heard... The police paid those travellers a visit last week."

"Yes, we know," Charlie muttered. With the Boswell boy loitering by the fruit machine, he chose his next words carefully. "But there was an incident shortly after and it affected Elijah. I think it's high time our friend over there knew about it."

Boris gave a nod, though his eyes didn't shed their anxiety. Eleanor felt a stab of irritation. Boris, like many others in the village, seemed almost scared of this family, not helped by Boswell's status as a police officer. Her eyes fell to the stockily built boy engrossed in the fruit machine.

He glanced up suddenly, as if sensing her scrutiny.

"What are you looking at?" he grunted rudely.

Placing her drink on the bar, Eleanor wandered a few steps closer. She cocked her head to one side. "Sorry, were you talking to me? Because if you were, I don't think much of your manners."

"You're Jansen's mum, aren't you?" the boy snapped at her.

"Elijah Jansen is my son, yes," Eleanor answered. "I hear you've been giving him a hard time."

The boy's eyes narrowed nastily. He was an evil looking child, she mused.

"Is that what he told you?" he jeered.

Eleanor shook her head. "He didn't need to. When I asked if he knew anyone at school by the name of *Boswell*, he turned white as a sheet. I know he's being bullied. I've seen the bruises..."

Gary flinched, a red flush flooding into his bloated cheeks. "It's not just me," he whispered. "All the boys hate him. *He's a gypsy.*"

This time Eleanor flinched as she drank in his appearance - fat face, lumpy frame... her own son, slender as a wire by comparison.

"Elijah is not a gypsy," she said icily, drawing her head close, "and what gives *you* the right to be so superior? You're as fat as a pig."

Gary turned redder than a tomato. "Dad!" he roared across the lounge. "Dad!"

"What now?" the man snapped, turning briskly.

Gibbering with rage, Gary was pointing at Eleanor; a sight that prompted Ian to erupt from his seat and shoving his chair to one side, he crossed the room in three strides. Boris, busying himself with the task of wiping the bar, kept his eyes down.

"She says I'm fat!" Gary bellowed, his finger still jabbing at Eleanor.

"So what are you going to do, arrest me?" Eleanor taunted.

A look of outrage flared Ian's nostrils. "Well, I can't say I've ever really taken to your lot," he snorted, "but is this true? Have you just insulted my son?"

"What if I did?" Eleanor drawled, clocking Charlie's return. "I mean, look at him! What do you feed him on, a diet of crisps and doughnuts? I'd be ashamed of my Eli if he was that size."

Ian Boswell turned puce with anger. "How dare you," he growled. "What sort of woman are you to humiliate a twelve-year-old?"

"And what sort of man are *you* to set up a twelve-year-old as a police informant?" Charlie accused.

Boswell spun around, the flush in his complexion darkening. The atmosphere prickled with tension as the two men looked daggers at each other.

"Sit down, Gary," Ian said curtly. "I'll deal with this." He waited for his son to be seated, his eyes glinting like flints. "What did you just say?"

"You heard," Charlie said. "The night you busted the travellers' camp, you left the impression it was Eleanor's son who grassed them up."

Ian gave a shrug. "I may have let something slip. Obviously the boy knew they were on drugs and if he passed that information on to my Gary, then surely it was my duty to act on it."

"You didn't have to implicate him," Eleanor hissed. "As if your son doesn't make his life miserable enough at school and now the travellers have started victimising him!"

"So what do you expect me to do?" Ian sneered, folding his arms across his broad chest. "It's not my job to sort out disputes among travellers' communities."

Eleanor turned rigid, appalled by such disdain. "Well, here's what *I'm* going to do. First thing on Monday, I'll be speaking to the school about your son's disgraceful bullying, and as for you! It's time I made a formal complaint to the police authorities about *your* conduct?"

"Really?" Ian sneered. "I can't imagine some *brief mention* as to where I got my information from is likely to be taken seriously."

"I disagree." Eleanor said. "You see, inflicting your prejudice on me is one thing, but if you're going to start persecuting my son, I consider that to be very serious. But then you are prejudiced aren't you? You still pick on minority groups, same as you did in 1979."

The impact of her words hit hard. Ian Boswell froze, the flush on his face dissolving.

"I don't know what you're talking about."

"Yes, you do," Eleanor challenged. "You were nearly suspended once for police brutality. You and a colleague decided to pick on a group of black youths

171

in Brixton and one of them was punched; a boy of just fifteen, Inspector Boswell."

"That's enough," Ian spat. "That business happened a long time ago…"

"But you weren't suspended," Eleanor kept goading him, "you got off the hook. So this time, I'll see to it you don't get off so lightly."

"Alright, I am sorry if I implicated your boy," Ian said through gritted teeth. "I did not purposefully mean to cause trouble but if an offence was committed, I will investigate…"

"It's a bit late for that," Charlie intervened. "But what about the bullying? At the very least, just tell your son to stop picking on Elijah."

"Alright, I'll talk to Gary," Ian said, "if you refrain from issuing a complaint."

They could see he was seething, the threat to his reputation a serious worry.

"I think that would be a good compromise," Charlie said in a tone that implied he wasn't off the hook. "Just don't underestimate us, Mr Boswell. We will take this further if we have to, though I personally hope it doesn't come to that."

II

That Sunday heralded their final overnight stay in the caravan. Eleanor could not help but revel in their victory against Boswell, the second time in her life she had stood up against injustice and it felt good; although her next confrontation would involve the travellers.

Charlie couldn't be present. For both he and Andrew were needed in Rosebrook, collecting the last few possessions Christopher Farrin had stored in his garage for them.

Eleanor however, was not alone. On this occasion, James stood by her, if for no other reason than to establish his authority as the landowner.

Peering out of the window, she trembled at the sight of Fabian's hideous camper van and its emblem of magic mushrooms. With their vehicles scattered untidily around the field, the constant passage of tyres had carved muddy grooves into the grass.

"Right!" she said through clenched teeth. "Let's get this over with."

Elijah too, lingered. Eleanor did not want him to miss out on this showdown, hoping it would be a first lesson in standing up for himself.

Wasting no time, the three of them strolled over the field.

Fabian emerged from his camper van. Loping across the grass, his eyes latched on to Eleanor, as pale and reptilian as ever. Then at last, he registered James's presence.

"This is James Barton-Wells," Eleanor announced. "The gentleman who

172

owns this field."

"That's right," James added, keeping his voice light, "and now I want you off it."

Fabian's expression darkened, hands closed into fists as they dangled by his sides.

"Did *she* put you up to this?"

"Not only Eleanor," James snapped. "Practically every resident in the village."

"You can't force us to leave!" Fabian shouted.

"I'm hoping I won't have to," James said acidly. "You can go peacefully, otherwise you leave me no choice than to have your vehicles forcibly towed off my land."

"My land!" Fabian imitated in a phoney, upper-class accent. "Why you - you stuck up, toffee nosed old wanker!"

James laughed. "Oh, you can call me all the names you like. Foul language doesn't bother me! It's your attitude I despise."

In the background, the others had begun to emerge; silent grey figures who slipped into view like shadows. But despite their growing numbers, James did not move.

"I thought you were supposed to be cool about travellers!" Fabian bellowed.

"I've been very tolerant until now," James argued, "but as for you lot! You've just jumped on the bandwagon. You see the hippie movement as an excuse not to work, draw your dole money and treat life as one big party! Well this party is well and truly over!"

"This is down to you, isn't it, you bitch!" Fabian hissed.

For all the while he was creeping closer, Eleanor braced herself. Conscious of Elijah pinned by her side, rigid with fear, she narrowed her eyes.

"I've put up with you for long enough, you piece of shit," she said. "I tried to be reasonable but you crossed the line, the day you turned on my boy!"

She saw a shift in his character. He looked furtive, eyes flitting sideways as if hoping for some backup, until eventually Sara joined them.

"It was only a bit of fun," he sniffed. "We made him try some beer and a spliff! So what? He shouldn't have grassed us up!"

Eleanor opened her mouth to protest but James touched her arm.

"Why not let your son explain?" he urged. "Go on, Eli."

"When I said I didn't snitch, I-I was telling the truth," Elijah blurted. "The police inspector's son... he - he was the one who set me up. He's always had it in for me..."

The tremor in his voice made Eleanor's heart squeeze.

"You heard what he said," she added, "and we've confronted the police inspector. So how dare you stand there and blame him, considering you didn't even get your facts right. Putting him through that ordeal was the last straw. Now piss off, the lot of you!"

Sara's mouth had fallen open. Fabian on the other hand, fidgeted with a roll-up. For those last few seconds, he had degenerated into a stumbling mess and couldn't even look at her.

"We're real sorry, kid," Eleanor thought she heard Sara murmur.

"It's too late for that now," James said, "so just leave! Otherwise, one of our farmers is waiting by the trees in a heavy duty tractor, ready to tow your vans out of our village!"

"Okay! Okay!" Fabian shouted, backing away, having clearly lost the battle.

Eleanor did not move. Glancing at Elijah, she caught a little grin on his face and it filled her with pride. Reminded of her pledge to Jake, *she would die for this child if she had to*.

III

In the wake of the new age travellers' eviction, everyone expressed relief. Aldwyck would lapse back into the peaceful haven it was renowned for, the consensus being there had been something inherently rotten about them from the outset...

Compelled to forget them, Eleanor found herself being guided up an elegant staircase towards the bedrooms. When James had confided in her about the state of his home, she had never imagined it would unite them like this. But the very notion of moving into this beautiful house was a dream. Overwhelmed by the sheer size, never mind the opulence of the rooms, she felt her excitement soar, as Avalon showed her the guest accommodation.

At the same time she could not quite shake off some lingering sense of anxiety. It had started in the Orangerie. Something had been said that sent her mind spinning into the past.

Then without warning, she was plagued by a nightmare...

She saw Elijah running through the woods until the scene changed - those same woods enclosed by black railings, the trees thinning to reveal the planes of a park. The park too, started to dissolve, the sky turning blacker as a railway tunnel loomed ahead. Sobbing with fear, she knew of the danger that hid there. Elijah turned and waved, just as a shadowy figure stepped from the tunnel mouth. A moment later he had vanished. Eleanor tried to scream but the sound never left her lips.

In a flash, the scene had changed again; a beautiful lounge, a boardroom table, a pair of men in dark suits hunched like crows around the perimeter.

"Where is he? Where is my son - what have you done to him?" Eleanor started howling.

174

One of the men turned but she couldn't quite make out his features. All she could discern was his stocky build. A head of thick blonde hair surrounded the outline of his face. Yet she could feel his smile, even behind the mask of shadow...

"You and Charlie could always take the master suite," Avalon said.

Eleanor blinked, jolted back to the present. It took one glance at Avalon's glittering eyes to understand the nature of that remark. She felt her cheeks turn warm.

"I-I'm not sure," she faltered, lowering her eyes. "This is your best room and it's huge."

Avalon giggled. "It's okay, I can tell you two are together. It's the way he looks at you! And you seem so happy."

"Is it really that obvious?" Eleanor sighed. "Look, please don't say anything. Charlie's a little sensitive about how his kids might react, see, especially Andrew."

Avalon gave a subtle nod. "Okay. I can keep a secret."

"Are you seeing anyone?" Eleanor piped up, as she unlocked the door of the next room.

"I'm still seeing Hugh," Avalon said dreamily, "that is, when he's not touring the world playing polo. He's so dishy, you know; lovely smile, floppy dark hair, an almost permanent suntan..."

Eleanor picked up the waves of devotion in her voice. "Sounds gorgeous," she mused. "I'm really pleased for you. So, no more hassle from that other gentleman?"

"Ben?" Avalon shuddered. "No, thank God! Dad spoke to his family."

"Good," Eleanor nodded as the corridor rolled out in front of them.

Their conversation faded as Avalon unmasked the last few rooms.

Eleanor could barely take it in, immersed in surroundings more luxurious than she could imagine; beautiful fabrics and rugs, the subtle lighting that enhanced the rich colours and sumptuous beds. In the end however, she was drawn to the smallest of six rooms arranged around the central section. Not only did it overlook the village, but she loved its cosiness.

With gleaming floorboards partially covered by a Turkish rug, it reminded her of the Merriman's lounge and not only that. It lay closest to the attic rooms where she knew the children had been offered a room each. Best of all though, there was a four-poster bed. Eleanor had always dreamt of sleeping in one of these, caught up in her own fantasy world of the passionate nights she would spend here with Charlie.

The only one slightly unhinged by the move was Andrew. The quality of their accommodation had never really mattered to him. It was a sense of

175

belonging. Even Eleanor's caravan had been adequate, where meeting the new age travellers lured him to new avenues of fun... Yet the day they were evicted brought a sense of emptiness once again.

The news they were moving to Westbourne House should have thrilled him, but the sheer vastness of the estate felt unnerving. *It would be like living in a castle.* For no matter how idyllic, Aldwyck was remote. His friends lived in Rosebrook, including boys he had met on his work placements. Furthermore, Andrew had been allying himself with the more laid-back hippie types, secretly hoping they would be dope smokers. He recognised the signs from the transitory days he had mixed with the travellers; a preference for smoking roll ups, a less than immaculate dress sense. Praying he would stumble across a new source of cannabis, he had never wanted to admit how disheartened he was by Fabian's departure.

Now here he was, on the verge of moving into this exquisite country hotel, resigned to endure the company of none other than his annoying little sister - and Elijah.

Elijah already got on his nerves, but the business with the travellers had exacerbated it. Looking back, he hadn't come to any harm. Most mates of his age would consider a beer and a spliff more of a prize than a punishment. Yet Eleanor's incessant cosseting didn't help.

No wonder the kid was turning into a right softie!

Another issue was money. Just days from completing his YTS, he had banked a giro every week. But from what his father insinuated, they were only working here for board and lodgings.

Maybe he could find himself a part time job...

All these musings were swimming around his head when Charlie led him up to the attic. But it was the first sight of this snug retreat that finally put a smile onto his face. With a sloping ceiling criss-crossed with beams and a high dormer window, his room enjoyed magnificent views. Eleanor had already made up the futon bed with his favourite pac-man quilt cover, their old portable TV set installed on top of a chest of drawers.

"What do you think?" Charlie chuckled from behind him.

"Cool," Andrew said, though his voice felt drained of enthusiasm.

Charlie let out a sigh. "Is something wrong, Andrew?"

"It's nothing," he shrugged. "I'm just a bit worried about cash. I mean, I'm gonna enjoy working for James and that... but I still need some money of my own."

"Fair enough," Charlie agreed. "If we work together on my private jobs, I'll give you a cut of the profits. We've got that extension to finish for starters."

Andrew muttered his thanks. Yet something about his father's smug face irked him, reminding him of another issue; his relationship with Eleanor.

How could he miss the subtle signs? The adoring glances, the way he touched her and held her coat open for her? But the final straw arose from a sniggered comment 'Scruffy' had made, who swore blind *the old man was shagging her*. Spotting Charlie sneaking back to the field on more than one occasion, the subtle jostling of her caravan spoke volumes.

Andrew shuddered. The very thought of it tore his inner wounds like barbed wire.

"So which room are *you* taking?" he said, his voice heavy with sarcasm.

"There are some nice rooms in the central section."

"*Rooms*," Andrew echoed, eyes narrowing. "One room or two?"

Charlie lowered his eyes but there was no mistaking that furtive look.

"I see," he added icily. "So it's true. Eleanor's your *girlfriend* now, is she?"

"Ssh!" Charlie breathed. "But you can't deny she's been good to us!"

Andrew's lips tightened, a fusion of anger and hurt consuming him.

"What's your problem, Andrew?" Charlie snapped. "You're a man yourself."

"What about Mum?" he hissed. "I thought you loved her!"

"I will never love anyone as much as I did Anna," Charlie protested. "She was my soul mate and no one can ever replace her. But you can't expect me to spend the rest of my life on my own."

Andrew gritted his teeth. "How could you bunk up with another woman so soon after her funeral?"

"It's been over a year, Andrew," Charlie pointed out softly, "and nothing will bring her back. Now pull yourself together will you, please? We've finally landed on our feet here!"

Turning away, Andrew collapsed on his futon. Hearing that final confession bore out his worst fear, a revelation that left him crucified.

Chapter Nineteen

I

For the first few days, they all felt disorientated. After the close confines of Eleanor's caravan, they had been spirited away into a whole new world. Westbourne House gave a sense they were living in a luxury hotel. Though it didn't seem long before they tumbled into an easy harmony.

Eleanor had feared the possibility of personality clashes.

Yet James's estate offered a haven of such space and freedom, that at times they hardly saw one another. The expansive grounds offered limitless opportunities for the children to explore, the surrounding woods ideal for climbing trees and playing hide and seek.

Out of respect for the Barton-Wells family, they kept themselves discreet. Yet eating meals in the downstairs restaurant, they were bonding with other members of staff.

Mesmerised by the variety of food prepared by Angelo and Bryony, Eleanor was quick to offer assistance. Shopping for supplies or gathering vegetables and herbs from the walled gardens, she felt happiest chopping and preparing ingredients for whatever masterpiece they had in mind. Everything they ate was fresh and beautifully prepared, and when the restaurant was busy, Eleanor felt it only fair to take responsibility for the children's meals, which they were happy to enjoy on trays, tucked in the cosy confines of their attic rooms.

For those first few weeks, Margaret really began to flourish, especially under the wing of Bryony, who adored the company of a little girl to assist her. Enthralled by the array of pretty cakes and desserts, Margaret marvelled in adding the finishing touches.

Shortly after moving in, she had also celebrated her eleventh birthday.

Charlie had collected her from school, to take her to the cinema with her friends. Back at Westbourne House meanwhile, the entire household had arranged a surprise party; a picnic in the grounds, including an incredible cake constructed in the shape of a fairy tale castle. With festoons of pink and white icing, silver piping and edible jewel-like sweets, not only did it take Margaret's breath away but moved her to tears.

Throughout this joyful occasion, James had insisted on opening a bottle of vintage champagne. Raising their glasses, they paid a special tribute to Anna.

Oh, how she would have rejoiced in this event, wherever her gentle spirit lay.

Charlie had also begun to bond with the staff, Elliot in particular.

Elliot liked to confide in him, especially over the events following the Hamptons' first visit. James's collapse, then the arrival of that survey had left him vulnerable. But once ensnared in their house for an evening, anyone could see how easily he might have been swayed by their partnership, a time he was at his lowest ebb.

Charlie however, seemed confident that with his expertise, their worries would soon be over. He had scrutinised the building survey and whilst it contained nothing unusual, especially in the context of a house of this ripe old age, there were a few areas that concerned him.

He had touched base with Christopher Farrin, who recommended a reputable firm to deal with the woodworm. But as the re-construction of the roof timbers took place, a discreet team of period property specialists were carefully examining other areas, to reveal the true status.

II

As May approached however, the one thing James could never have predicted was an alarming shortage of hotel bookings. This was the one time of year Westbourne House came alive; rambling paths enriched with a riot of Spring flowers, the mature trees verdant with new leaves.

Avalon had been yearning for an opportunity to get her hands on the latest 'Tatler' magazine. Given the prospect it contained photos of their magnificent Springtime ball, the publicity would give them a boost. It was a good excuse to take a trip to Rosebrook by bus and Eleanor agreed to accompany her. With Elijah's thirteenth birthday just around the corner, she was looking forward to shopping for presents.

The sun beamed down warmly as they made their way along the high street but Eleanor was still thinking about Elijah. He seemed a lot happier. The splendour of his surroundings had lifted his spirits, his eyes finally shedding that tortured look. His school life too, had improved since her conversation with Ian Boswell, and she was ecstatic to hear he had excelled in his art class; his tutor of the opinion he possessed a rare talent for a boy so young.

Ambling into WH Smiths, Avalon made a beeline for 'Tatler.'

Eleanor observed it briefly, wowed by the cover shot of a model poised in a skimpy white outfit, photographed by the notorious David Bailey. But as Avalon dipped into the contents, she heard a gasp. It was only a small selection of photos, yet enough to reveal the splendour of their estate. More photos displayed the guests, the loveliest of which had been taken in the grounds; an assembly of young women in pastel ball gowns gathered against a backdrop of stunning countryside.

Eleanor gave a smile before her gaze drifted towards the homes and gardens section.

At first, she thought she was imagining things when a sudden chill swept over her. It appeared that 'Tatler' was not the only glossy periodical that featured Westbourne House.

Eleanor swallowed. Risking another glance at the publication, 'Country House,' there was no mistaking one of the cover articles.

'Could This Highly Acclaimed Historic House Be On The Road To Ruin?'

Plucking it from the rack before Avalon saw it, she suppressed a shiver.

"Do you mind if we look at the art materials?" she said quickly.

"Of course not," Avalon replied. "Is everything okay?"

Eleanor paused, torn in the dilemma of whether to say anything. Yet how could she bring herself to expose what she had seen, in the wake of Avalon's euphoria?

"This is rubbish!" Charlie spluttered. "It gives the impression the house is on the brink of collapse!" Lounging across their four-poster bed, he stabbed a finger at the text: *"'Anyone hoping to escape for a quiet country break will be sadly disenchanted when they discover the deterioration...'* The rooms are nowhere near as bad as they make out!"

"I know," Eleanor mumbled. Emptying her shopping bag, she was admiring the box of Derwent fine art pencils and sketch pads she had bought for her son.

"We can't keep this from James a moment longer," he added gently.

He ran his hand down the curve of her spine. They were secretly hoping to spend some quality time together before the kids returned, but with the devastating impact of this article, any romantic aspirations would have to wait.

"He'll be shattered when he reads this," Eleanor said. "Poor James! He's trying so desperately hard to keep on top of things. The last thing he needs is bad publicity."

Slipping her gifts back into her bag, she rolled off the bed.

Charlie caught her in his arms, gazed into her eyes and kissed her lips. "Let me do the talking, love. There's something I want to say that might reassure him."

His hand slid into hers as they descended the stairs. Wandering into reception, they spotted James in the bar. He was surrounded by a mountain of paperwork, a pot of tea on the table in front of him.

"Hello," he greeted them warmly, "I hear you had a nice time shopping with my daughter..." Yet his words petered out. "Is something the matter?"

Charlie slumped into the chair next to him. "I hate to break this to you, James, but it was during their shopping trip, Eleanor saw this..."

With a frown, James took the magazine, the pages folded back on themselves, exposing the article. Eleanor and Charlie braced themselves as his eyes flitted over the print. Shock and outrage flashed in his expression as the horror of the article sank in. A small inset picture depicted the house in a particularly grim light. Taken from an angle where the scaffolding was most visible, a thunderous dark sky boiled in the background, portraying an air of utmost desolation and doom.

"This is slanderous," James gasped, slamming the magazine down onto the table. "It might even explain why we've had so few bookings this month!"

"I know," Charlie responded in a voice drained of optimism.

"What appalls me is the insinuation that my house cannot be saved!" James kept ranting. "That the building works are likely to continue for the whole summer..."

He broke off suddenly, his gaze drawn to Eleanor. Her eyes glittered with sorrow.

"I think this article was deliberately meant to be scare mongering," she added.

"Well, obviously," James shuddered, "and I think we can guess who's behind it! I bet you any money Hampton's got connections with this magazine."

"Any chance you could sue?" Charlie sighed.

James became very still before he eventually voiced his own fears.

One of their last guests had been a journalist. Furthermore, he had expressed a preference for the 'Violet Suite,' esteemed for its delicate pastel colour scheme. Yet this room bore terrible cracks around its badly warped window frame. James had adamantly tried to put him off, but not before revealing the damage, to convince him.

"How else would they know about the state of that window?" he lamented. "He must have leaked all those defects to the editor..."

Other memories pained him. They included a call from a second journalist, the publication he couldn't even remember; an invitation to comment on recent allegations that '*Westbourne House was in desperate need of renovation*' but regrettably, he had declined.

"James, don't despair," Eleanor soothed. "There must be a way of disputing this story. You've got Charlie now, who is convinced your house can be saved."

"It's the truth, James," Charlie added, "and I'm happy to speak up for you. But this leads me to my next point, something I can't wait to tell you. The state of your house may not actually be as bad as you think..."

Charlie knew he had his attention as he raced through his explanation. The current phase of dry rot was not as serious as the survey had made out and whilst spores had been identified in some areas of the house, the problem was not prolific.

Any unaffected timbers could be treated with chemicals, thus preventing the further spread of spores before they reached the fungal stage.

"Are you saying it might not be necessary to replace the underlying timbers?" James whispered in hope.

"That's exactly what I am saying," Charlie persisted. "Right now, we need to concentrate on preventative measures. Deathwatch beetle favours damp conditions. So the problems with damp must be addressed. But unless the timbers have reached a critical stage of decay, there is no immediate need to replace them..."

There was a heavy silence as James digested this.

Then his face adopted a sudden wily look. "Tell you what. Let's forget about this pitiful article for now and concentrate on what is important. I invited you here for a reason, Charlie. So I'd like to hear your opinion with regards to my roof."

"Okay," Charlie nodded, "I'll look into it. But let's get the damp experts in to investigate my suspicions. Because there's something very fishy about this article and I can assure you, there is no way this house is on the *road to ruin*."

James nodded in agreement, though anxiety clung to his expression.

At the same time, Charlie gazed at Eleanor. He was thinking about Perry Hampton again; wondering to what extent this man continued to weave his deadly web all around them.

Chapter Twenty

One week later James had stopped agonising over the article, of a mind to concentrate on more important matters, such as the lavish party about to take place.

The prestigious event commemorated the sixtieth birthday of Geoffrey Ascombe, a well-known TV presenter and journalist. Having been acquainted for years, James was further uplifted when Geoffrey (whose media contacts included a prominent writer for the Times) assured him he would do everything in his power to include a complimentary feature in their travel supplement.

With his spirits boosted, he was looking forward to seeing William too, whose timely release from school coincided nicely with Elijah's birthday. For not only did he inject an aura of joy into the household, but perked up Avalon. She too, had finally seen the damning feature in 'Country House,' which in the aftermath of their publicity in 'Tatler,' hit her like a slap in the face.

But with all that unpleasantness behind them for now, they were eager to plan a celebration for Elijah; a surprise party in the Orangerie.

James summoned his children to join him in the lounge, mainly to update William about the restoration. He seemed to have grown at least an inch taller, his youthful face conveying a new maturity. But first, he told him about Charlie.

"He's a professional builder and very knowledgeable. His son, too, has completed his training, so I've invited them to move in. They're going to manage the whole project."

"That's brilliant news, Dad!" William reacted. "How did you find him?"

James felt it necessary to relay some of Charlie's past. Plagued by a suspicion Perry Hampton had set out to destroy *his life*, he saw their alliance not only as a blessing, but their best chance of pulling off this restoration successfully.

"He's also a close friend of Eleanor's," James added, "and you'll be pleased to know that she and Elijah are staying here too."

William was ecstatic. He hadn't seen Elijah for ages, thrilled by the notion of having other youngsters in residence to hang out with.

"I can't wait to meet them all," William enthused, "but I've been thinking... Maybe I should drop out of private school. It would save you thousands in fees."

James, whilst touched by his son's sensitivity, would not hear of it though.

Adamant the next four terms had been paid for up front, he had no wish to sacrifice his son's education.

"You leave me to worry about funds," he finished with his usual practised smile.

With a boisterous celebration in full swing in the downstairs of the house, William and Avalon sneaked through the walled gardens towards the Orangerie with a box of balloons and streamers.

Eleanor had purposefully kept Elijah out of the way; first by taking a trip to the caravan to collect a few extra belongings, before hiding themselves upstairs with Margaret to open his presents.

By 5:00 the Orangerie was transformed. Masses of balloons, fastened to the doors in bunches, bounced and swayed in the breeze. William briefly disappeared, only to return wheeling a trolley laden with a lavish buffet. It included two chilled bottles of 'Pink Lady,' a sparkling pear cider, low in alcohol, but enough to allow them a celebratory tipple. Elijah was overwhelmed.

"Wow, you guys!" he gasped.

Margaret and William had been leading him up the path, blind-folded, when they sprang the surprise. Andrew, already sprawled in a chair, nibbling crisps, was accompanied by Avalon.

"Happy birthday, Eli!" she smiled at him.

Settling themselves into cosy bamboo chairs, they stumbled into easy conversation. Elijah was delighted with his presents, especially the art materials from his mother. These would inspire him to seriously take up sketching. But he was just as thrilled with the stylish trainers and jeans the Baileys had treated him to. These had been the kids' idea. A number of secret mutterings had resulted in the consensus that Eli needed better dress sense, which in turn, might endear him to his peers if he just looked a bit more cool! Finally, Avalon whisked out a parcel from under her chair; David Attenborough's book, 'Life on Earth.' The photo of a luminous green frog on the cover with bulging eyes made everyone laugh.

Andrew, who had knocked off work early, started boasting about the window frames they had been working on. Hidden away in the yard, where one of the empty garages served as a workshop, he was proud of the intricate craftsmanship in each frame. William, who had met them earlier, was intrigued. In fact, Andrew had taken a real shine to him. Using a lathe, Charlie explained how once the wood was cut into lengths, each section would be shaped and mitred to create a perfect join. And not only was William impressed but kept them entertained, possessing the type of wit that had Andrew in stitches.

Eventually the sun started to sink below the walls, drawing long shadows across the gardens.

For the first hour, they had got to know each other better, before William's eyes drifted towards the music centre.

"Did anyone think to bring any tapes along?"

"There's one already in there!" Elijah pointed out.

Without a second thought, he flipped the power switch and pressed play.

Yet the music pulsing from the speakers was nothing like they expected. Avalon froze. A familiar electronic beat pierced the silence. Then came the eerie synthesiser chords...

"Turn it off, turn it off!" she started yelling.

Springing to his feet, Elijah hit the stop button.

"What is it?" he gasped.

"Sounds a bit like Kraftwerk," William said numbly.

"I know that!" Avalon cried. "But it's Ben's music! That horrible, creepy racket I heard in the grounds, one night, when he was trying to scare me!"

"What?" William breathed in horror.

To everyone's shock, she wilted into a flood of tears. Andrew placed a comforting hand on her shoulder, Elijah quick to haul another chair over.

"Don't cry, Avalon," he mumbled. "I-I'm so sorry. I didn't know what it was..."

"He must have been here and left his tape in the machine," Avalon shivered. "No one's used the Orangerie for months!"

Gulping back her tears, she didn't want to say any more. Ben's last whispered words were still haunting her: *I am never going to go away.*

"You're convinced this was Ben's doing?" William pressed.

From the other side of the room, Margaret and Andrew exchanged fearful glances.

Elijah on the other hand, looked confused. "What's the big deal with the music then?"

Avalon had no choice but to tell them; from the sighting of Ben's car in the village, right up to the day he had materialised inside the house. Talking quickly, even the horror of relating it injected the fear back into her mind.

"Who is this psycho?" Elijah frowned.

"Ben Hampton," William spat. "Haven't you heard about those people Dad nearly went into partnership with? Ben was their son. He always did give us the creeps..."

Margaret, having said very little, leaned forwards to catch Elijah's eye.

"The man on the motorbike," she whispered breathlessly. "He nearly ran me over at the building site! Don't you remember me telling you?"

Elijah's mind wandered.

185

Winter 1985, a day they had skated across a frozen pond; the year Margaret's mother had fallen gravely ill...

Thinking back, he could picture her shivering, whilst relating her story of some demonic motorcyclist who had shot out of nowhere.

But something else had gone wrong, something that wrenched away her father and brother's jobs. Somehow, they were never able to escape from that situation...

Yes, he could clearly remember now.

"What a bastard!" he snapped, pulling his thoughts back to the present.

Whoever *Ben Hampton* was, he had frightened Margaret and now Avalon. The fear on her face lingered, a sight that drew him towards the music centre before he yanked out the cassette.

"Let's not talk about him," Avalon sighed as she quaffed back her drink. "Like William says, he is evil... and right now he's spoiling our party, so bugger Ben Hampton!"

"I'd rather not," William smirked, words that sent Andrew into a fit of giggles.

With laughter drawn back into their conversation, William rose, resolute on popping back to the house to find some 'seriously good party sounds.'

Seizing the opportunity to smoke a crafty joint, Andrew dragged himself out of his chair with the excuse he needed a pee.

By the time the party got going again, they started tucking into the food. William tapped his foot to the energetic sound of 'Divine.' Avalon opened a second bottle of Pink Lady, raising her glass for a toast.

"Elijah Jansen!" William bellowed. "In celebration of your teen birthday!"

Catching his eye, Margaret smiled. "Why is your name Jansen?" she asked him.

"That's his dad's name, stupid," Andrew mumbled through a mouthful of chicken.

"It's true," Elijah said. "My dad was a musician. Jake Jansen. Mum told me he came from Holland and played in a rock band."

"Cool," William remarked, tapping the side of his chair to the beat. "Was he famous?"

Elijah frowned. Thinking about the day on the ice again, he had shared his innermost secrets with Margaret. *He died before he was born but there was some mystery surrounding his death.*

"Anyone heard of 'Free Spirit?'" he mused. "Mum's got a recording somewhere."

"But did you ever find out how he died?" Avalon asked in sympathy.

"No, but he died young," Elijah murmured, his eyes wandering into the distance.

His gaze was drawn to the flowers spilling onto the path, the fading daylight capturing their luminescence. Yet he wasn't sure what to say. The sparkling pink fizz had gone to his head.

"Well, I reckon that's even more cool," Andrew indulged him, mellowed by his earlier smoke behind the walls. "They say all the best rock stars die young. Take Jim Morrison and Marc Bolan. They both died in their twenties. I wonder if it was drugs or alcohol..."

Elijah turned. Gaping at him in sudden horror, he wondered if this could be the reason his mother was so cagey. It would explain a lot, especially her antipathy towards drugs.

"Oh, come on," Avalon argued. "You can't jump to that sort of conclusion..."

"I don't know how he died," Elijah blurted. "Mum's never explained."

It seemed obvious he needed to tell them a little more about his mother's youth; her father, Oliver, employed by one of London's notorious gangsters, then forced to go on the run.

"You're kidding," William whispered in intrigue.

"I'm not," Elijah said, guessing it sounded a little like make-believe. "I'm really not."

Even Andrew gazed at him in awe.

"We sort of sussed you were a bit different," he teased. "I've seen a photo of Eleanor's old man. He married some coloured bird... looks a bit like Diana Ross."

"She was a singer at Sammie's nightclub," Elijah nodded. "Sammie was a legend! Look him up in the library if you don't believe me."

"It's okay, Eli, I believe you," Margaret soothed and gazed deep into his eyes.

"Hmm," Elijah murmured. "Well, I guess I'll find out the truth about my dad one day." He raised his glass in the air. "To my absent father. To Jake!"

With a burst of confidence, he then rose from his chair and grabbing Margaret's hands started pulling her to her feet.

"C'mon, let's dance," he urged. "This is supposed to be a party!"

"You're pissed!" Andrew sniggered, also rising. He captured Avalon's eye. "Wanna dance? We can't be outclassed by these kids."

"Sure," Avalon agreed and slipping into a light embrace, they began to sway around the room. "We should go clubbing in Rosebrook one evening. I hardly ever go out. How about the next time Hugh visits, which is in a couple of weeks time?"

The party ended on a high note. No sooner had William swapped the cassette for a chart compilation, they were bopping to the sound of Five Star's

'System Addict.' Elijah was enchanted to dance with Avalon, whilst Margaret took a turn with William.

Blushing sweetly, she lowered her eyelashes. Her soft brown eyes glittered with the appeal of a small puppy. For as much as she adored Elijah and cherished his friendship, William was quite simply the most gorgeous looking boy she had clasped eyes on - and there was definitely something different about the way she felt towards him.

II

The party wound down when dusk started to creep in. It cloaked the grounds with an indigo veil, leaving the paths illuminated by the stars.

Warmed by new bonds of friendship, the kids reluctantly parted company. William and Avalon joined their father in the downstairs living room, eager to hear how *his* social event had panned out. The others made their way up to their living quarters. And there, Elijah spotted Eleanor. She was sprawled out on their four-poster bed, reading a magazine, while Charlie lingered in the restaurant with Elliot.

"Eli!" she gasped. "How did it go?"

Still in high spirits, he began enthusing about his birthday. *The best ever.* Delighted with his gifts, he told her about the party, touched by the efforts the Barton-Wells family had gone to.

At the back of his mind however, lurked the troubling issue of his father. It was during that fleeting conversation, Andrew had imparted an idea...

He stared into his mother's eyes. "Do you remember Margaret's birthday? We raised a glass to Anna, so I did the same. I raised a glass to *my* father. To *Jake*."

"Sweet," Eleanor said. "He'd be so proud of his son. A teenager no less."

He didn't miss the shadow of sadness passing across her face.

"What happened to him, Mum?" he whispered. "How come he died before I was born?"

"Oh, Eli," she murmured. She stroked his cheek, though already he could see her guard rising.

"He was a rock musician, wasn't he?" he pressed. "I always imagined him to be - a little like - like Jim Morrison from 'The Doors.' Was his death down to drugs or something? Like, did he die from an overdose?"

"No!" Eleanor gasped, recoiling in alarm. "Certainly not! Whatever made you say that?"

Elijah shrugged. "I thought that's how lots of rock stars went..."

"Sweetheart, your daddy did not die from drugs," Eleanor whimpered. "Jake, as the name of his band implied, was a *free spirit*. But he had a pure heart..."

"So why won't you tell me?" he kept grilling her. "You promised me you would, especially when I got older. I'm thirteen now. Isn't it about time I knew the truth?"

Eleanor froze, eyes drifting towards the corner cupboard. Locked away inside, she could picture her secret file, a journal that would explain the whole story.

At times, she was tempted to show it to Charlie but something held her back; her fear of the people she had named in there. *The harm they could do to her son.* A tiny part of her even toyed with the idea of giving it to Elijah. Let him discover the secrets for himself...

Yet suddenly she was thinking about those names again. Inspector Hargreaves; possibly no longer a threat since he had been ousted from the police force, but what of the other two?

Where was the local politician, Robin Whaley; a man whose calculating scheme had lured them to a dark place where Jake had finally met his killers? He had been a local councillor back then. How much further up the ladders of power might he have escalated?

And what of the cold-blooded killer, Dominic Theakston? He had ruled the East End by fear. Could she really bring herself to utter his name?

Eleanor closed her eyes where the railway tunnel loomed; her worst nightmare, the place he had her trapped. That final vision of his cruel face would stay with her forever, never to forget his words: *Cause me any more grief and I could snatch hold of that son of yours... I could make him suffer in ways you couldn't even imagine and make you watch!*

A finger of cold shimmied over her as she opened her eyes; and there, in front of her, lingered her son in all his innocence... She turned her head away with a sob.

"I'm sorry, Eli," she spluttered, "but I still can't tell you! It will put you in too much danger, you have to trust me on this."

"He was murdered, wasn't he?" Elijah whispered, sinking into her arms.

For those next few seconds, she clung to him.

"You got that bit right," she finally confessed, her voice so soft it was barely audible, "I wish I could tell you, but you're all I've got left. I can't risk losing you too, please understand that."

III

Before the May Bank Holiday ended, Charlie braced himself to look inside the roof. The western section had only just been completed, new scaffolding soon to be erected right across the front of the house. James had narrowly managed to postpone this, for fear the unsightly poles would destroy its ambience on the day of Geoffrey's party.

The builders, however, were scheduled to return the next day.

Once inside the cool confines of the attic, Charlie switched on his torch. He observed the rafters and tie beams, which had taken nearly three months to assemble.

Moving along the length of the roof, he entered the eastern section.

With a sinking heart, he discovered the surveyor's findings were no exaggeration. Tell-tale pock marks bore evidence of an enduring beetle infestation, while in some places the wood had deteriorated. Grasping one of the beams and squeezing it, he felt a crumbling, sponge-like texture that horrified him. There was no mistaking these timbers were beyond repair, leaving James no choice but to replace them.

As Charlie crept his way along the platform, he mentally rehearsed what to tell him.

The roof was barely half finished.

Yet if these builders continued at the same dawdling pace, it would unlikely be completed before September. Even Charlie realised the detrimental effect this would have on the hotel business, which had already suffered a decline.

He shook his head.

James simply could not afford to wait that long.

"It's ridiculous!" he heard himself ranting. "I've never known such laxity! My former employers would have completed the work in half that time!"

James sighed, having opted for the privacy of his office for this meeting. "I hear what you're saying, Charlie, but the truth is I had no idea how long this project would take. The company had me in a tight spot. I paid them sixty grand up front, which is too much money to write off!"

Charlie stopped pacing, sensing his gullibility. James gazed at him in despair.

"I'm not suggesting you *write it off*," he said in a gentler tone. "But why not let me speak to them. At the very least, I might be able to chivvy them along a bit."

"I'd appreciate that," James replied. "In fact, I should have known better than to put my faith in this company. The signs were there when they rebuilt one of the staircases..."

Charlie listened with mounting dismay as he explained. Maybe James's ultimatum had forced them to complete the job, though he was foolish to give them a second chance.

It left him wondering whether to use the same tactic.

190

"Except we're not going to give them a third chance are we?" James snapped.

"No," Charlie said coldly, "you are finally starting to cotton on, James. So say, we issue them with another warning? Then terminate their contract and be done with it."

"And then what?" James frowned.

"Andrew can start plastering the bedrooms," he continued, "then at least Avalon can redecorate, which I know she is keen to do - especially with the hotel being so quiet."

"Is this going to cost much?" James enquired with raised eyebrows.

"Andrew is a skilled plasterer," he placated him, "so any costs will be minimal. I know there isn't much left out of the ten grand you raised from the ball, but on the plus side, the house has been treated for dry rot and deathwatch beetle..."

There was, however, the outstanding balance for the roof.

"Another sixty grand," James shuddered. "Be honest, was the rebuild really necessary?"

"The condition of the roof was no lie," Charlie said, "but I still have my doubts about the embedded timbers in the main house..."

"Do go on," James muttered.

"I-I spoke to the remedial experts," he faltered, "who confirmed my suspicions."

Already he had started pacing again, drawing to a pause by the window.

"It's to do with those Chartered surveyors, the ones who did the original survey. I don't think they're trustworthy."

"Whatever do you mean?" James gasped.

Charlie turned to face him. "The extent of deterioration in their report is way out, the reason I consulted these specialists. I wanted to show them the survey and get a second opinion."

"Fine," James nodded. "Much as I want to save my home, I have to know the truth."

Yet new lines of worry rippled his forehead.

What Charlie didn't know was that at the back of his mind, a devastating ribbon of thought was unwinding. It took him right back to the day he had read that building survey.

How could he have forgotten? Edward Booth Chartered Surveyors: a company recommended by none other than Perry Hampton.

Straight away James felt a chill spear his veins. He recalled Perry's benign phone call; sensing his power, even from a distance, like a cold mist rolling in from the sea.

Chapter Twenty-One

I

Charlie was in the yard, working on the window frames, when the tell tale clang of scaffolding poles echoed in the distance. Working faster, he was keen to finish shaping one of the tenon joints which allowed each section to slot together.

The moment he was finished, he set down his tools and brushing the sawdust from his hands, made his way to the front of the house. A clean white van bearing the name 'Heritage Building and Restoration' loomed into view. Charlie squinted into the distance. He had also spotted the scaffolding truck but for now he ignored it. He was more interested in the small work force chatting away in the background. A more senior man lounged by the steps, smoking a cigarette.

"Yes?" he barked, hauling himself away from the parapet.

"Are you responsible for the work on the roof?" Charlie challenged him.

A sneer crossed the man's face. "Is there a problem?"

"I'm afraid so," Charlie said, fighting to keep his temper. "Would you mind explaining why this rebuild is taking so long? You've been working on it since February."

"What business is it of yours?" the man growled, an angry flush darkening his face.

"James Barton-Wells has taken me on as his foreman," Charlie replied stonily, "and put me in charge of the restoration. Now will you kindly answer my question?"

"Ten weeks is nothing for a roof of these proportions," the man scoffed.

"Rubbish!" Charlie spouted. "I've been in the building trade for over twenty years! All you've done is dismantle a few rotting beams and replace them with new ones…"

"We are a small, specialist workforce," the other man hissed, taking a menacing step towards him. "Old properties require certain expertise."

The men lingering by the van had gradually been wandering closer. Charlie turned, wary of their scrutiny. Yet what incensed him more were the little smirks flickering on their faces.

"Then why aren't you working up there now?" he thundered.

"The scaffolding isn't ready," one of the men argued.

Charlie was having none of it. "You can access the roof through the loft hatch! That's how I got in yesterday..." He left his words hanging, dismayed by their lack of regard.

Eventually he shook his head, knowing there was only one way to get through to them.

"Look, I may as well inform you the property owner wants this roof finished by June! But if it's too much for you to handle, we'll just terminate your contract."

"You can't do that!" the other man snarled.

"I can't," Charlie said icily, "but James can and those are his conditions! Do you think you can meet them, or would you like me to source some extra labour for you?"

"We prefer to use our own labourers," the man said through clenched teeth. "We don't need your help. We are quite capable of managing this on our own!"

"Good," Charlie nodded. "In that case, I suggest you pull your fingers out of your arseholes and get on with it!"

The other man's eyes blazed.

"Oh, and one more thing," he added, turning away. "I am a little surprised you're using brand new materials for the re-tiling. This is a natural slate roof tile and perfectly salvageable. So perhaps you could bear that in mind, since James is working on a tight budget."

Before the day ended, James received a phone call from Vic Mills, MD of Heritage Building and Restoration. Enraged by Charlie's intervention, he seemed adamant the roof had taken *no more time than expected for a property of this size*.

But James stood his ground. His foreman was a highly experienced professional and unless they were willing to meet his deadline, he reiterated Charlie's threat.

By the end of the conversation, they had reached an agreement. Fearful of losing this highly lucrative contract, Vic would endeavour to have the roof finished in June. But in doing so, he imposed a condition of his own, demanding a further instalment of 25% in advance.

"That's £30,000, Charlie," James said, as they wandered through the grounds together that evening. "I don't have it!"

"But you must have known you would need to take out a loan at some point," Charlie said. "How else were you going to pay for this? The roof will realistically cost you another sixty grand and there are other parts of the house that need work."

News however, travelled fast. And the MD of Heritage Building and Restoration was not the only one to be perturbed by this situation...

II

In the time it took for Vic to track down Edward Booth, he was fuming.

To think that James'd had the tenacity to employ his own foreman.

Edward, on the other hand, was flung into a state of complete panic.

Up until this pivotal point, both companies were relying upon the fact that James was at their mercy. Having meekly consented to everything they suggested, he seemed determined to save his home at any cost, even when they had hiked up the fees.

Thus, with no choice but to accept his deposit, they continued working; but at the same idle pace, leaving the rest of the house to decay. Edward had secretly hoped the woodworm infestation would spread, gnawing deep into the underlying timbers like a cancer. Given the probability the inner core would become so weak and unstable, James would be forced into permanently closing the hotel and putting the house up for sale.

Yet today's unfolding drama was something no one had anticipated.

Edward had broken out into a cold sweat, dreading having to relay this to Perry.

"Well, this is intriguing, isn't it?" Perry mused next morning over a coffee.

They decided to hold a meeting in the secret confines of his house; a site where no one could overhear their plans to cripple James's property.

Edward squirmed uncomfortably in his chair. "I'm surprised you're not more concerned. According to James Barton-Wells, this man is something of a building expert! Not only is he muscling in on the restoration, but called in a firm of specialists to deal with the woodworm and the damp. This is extremely worrying, Perry. If they expose the truth behind the survey, my company could be sued!"

Perry shrugged. "So the damage to the embedded timbers may not be as bad as you diagnosed," he sniffed. "So what? If any accusations are levelled against your company, you need only say you were erring on the side of caution and that due to the presence of deathwatch beetle, some timber replacement was advisable. There is nothing illegal about that."

"Apart from suggesting work that wasn't necessary," Edward argued, "work that is *expensive* and can no longer be addressed, now this gentleman is interfering! The situation does not bode well, Perry. Despite your tactics, James is managing this restoration on his own. Does that not bother you in the slightest?"

"You have no idea what I have up my sleeve," Perry said softly. "You leave James Barton-Wells to me."

Lowering his coffee cup, he felt a flutter of palpitations. This in turn brought a rush of giddiness when in truth, he was buzzing. James was putting up such a valiant fight, one Perry knew he could never win, despite his efforts.

The next time he looked at Edward though, his expression hardened. Edward shifted nervously in his chair again.

"So, he's found himself a building expert," he muttered. "I don't suppose you could find out who could you?"

"I've already discovered who he is," Edward drawled, "or rather Vic did when he spoke to James. His name is Charles Bailey. I gather he used to work for Dick Harrison's firm."

Perry turned rigid, teeth bared. "Did you say Charles Bailey?" he whispered.

"You know him?" Edward frowned.

"Oh, I know Charles Bailey," Perry snapped. "I tried to get him to work for *me* once but as you know, Edward, no-one defies me and gets away with it..."

Perry broke off, his thoughts leaping into the past.

For all these months, he imagined Charles would be long gone. How perplexing *he of all people* would be the one adversary to come slithering out of the woodwork.

"What an interesting piece of news," he pondered. "So how did Charles Bailey come into contact with James, I wonder?"

"Does it matter?" Edward sniped. "More to the point, how do you intend to deal with him?"

"Same as I deal with anyone who stands in my way," Perry finished. He gave a smile. "Thank you for bringing this to my attention and if there are any repercussions with regards to the survey, you can be certain I will back you in your defence."

"I appreciate that, Sir," Edward answered silkily, offering a small, sycophantic bow.

Rowena returned home from an extravagant lunch with friends to find him wandering alone in the garden. Straight away, she suspected something troubled him. It was reflected in every slow step; the intense loathing that simmered in his eyes.

Eventually, she got him talking, the entire story tumbling out.

More revelations had emerged from a series of phone calls, the last of which involved the man who had come into direct contact with Charlie. Perry wanted him to spy for him; take photographs and uncover as much information about the man's activities as possible.

His mood changed abruptly though, when he recalled that last tale.

He released a chuckle. "Can you imagine? Charles Bailey bollocking one of our own men?"

Tucked in an idyllic surround of topiary, Rowena poured him a glass of wine.

"Shouldn't you be taking this a little more seriously?" she snapped. "This isn't funny, Perry!"

"Oh, but it is," he muttered. Accepting the glass, he tapped it against her own. "Have you ever heard the expression *keeping your friends close, but your enemies closer?*" He pursed his lips. "Well, right now, all my enemies are congregated in one place, which is exactly where I want them to be..."

Rowena glanced at him coolly. "Won't this affect your game plan?"

"Not at all," Perry replied, throwing her a smile. "In fact, if you think about it, my dear, this game is about to get a whole lot more interesting."

III

"Good news, folks!" James beamed not long after the post arrived. "We've finally got ourselves a lender!"

It had been an agonising week. He was convinced he must have approached every bank and building society in the land, thinking *surely one would agree to a loan.* To his deepening dismay though, their response left him floundering; their concern not only the sum he wanted to borrow, but the dwindling income from his hotel business. Unless James could turn this around in some way, it seemed no finance company was prepared to take the risk.

With an ugly web of scaffolding stretched right across its facade, the house had become less appealing to all who visited. This was despite a glowing article in the Times arranged by Geoffrey Ascombe. But just at the point where James began to panic, this letter had thrown him a life line... and from none other than a financial investment company he had approached two days ago. Attracted to their mail shot, James had made a first tentative approach, never to forget how uplifted he felt when they agreed they might be able to help him.

Today's letter had just confirmed this.

"This is excellent news, James," Elliot responded.

He too, had resigned himself to accept the possibility that if James couldn't find a financial backer, there was little chance of saving his property.

Charlie was ecstatic and about to impart some even better news. The team of damp specialists, who had carefully reassessed the property, had confirmed their findings. Just as they suspected, the embedded timbers within the core of the house were structurally sound. They would remain so for many years, especially now they had been treated.

Such news, though it lifted James's heart, left a bitter aftertaste.

"Why do you imagine the surveyors reported such dilapidations?" he spluttered. "They insisted the worst affected timbers would need cutting out and replacing!"

"That building survey was a scam," Charlie said darkly, "purposefully designed to pressurise you into spending more money than you had to! I bet this is what Hampton was banking on. Did he, per chance, have anything to do with this firm?"

"I'm afraid so," James sighed. "He did after all, recommend them, and as for that building company hiking up their costs... I've a good mind to take the lot of them to court!"

"I wouldn't give them the satisfaction," Elliot advised gently. "Is it really wise to stir things? Particularly if it involves those Hamptons? A court case could be very stressful for you."

"Elliot is right," Charlie nodded. "So let's just concentrate on what really needs doing."

"Which is?" James probed.

"The windows will be finished by June and hopefully the roof. So let's keep quiet about that survey. If they know we're onto them, they might sabotage that too."

James caught the flash in his eyes as he said it, knowing that 'Heritage Building and Restoration' were soon to receive their marching orders. Here was another company embroiled in Perry's web of deceit... and James could not wait to be shot of them.

Before the month ended, Charlie confided his fears to his son. Andrew was very much involved in the restoration now and deserved to know the truth - especially on the advent of his eighteenth birthday. Charlie had never really shared his suspicions concerning Perry Hampton. Andrew needed to know the type of enemy he was; the manner by which he operated.

But right now, Andrew was thinking about Avalon. Stirred by her beauty, he couldn't deny he felt a little awkward in her company. What's more, she was dating some eligible toff. Engaged in the glamorous world of polo, Hugh was a player he could never compete with, given his humble status as a builder's labourer.

These thoughts came to him on the evening of his birthday. He splashed on Kouros aftershave, a gift from Eleanor. He had dropped plenty of hints it was his favourite. The best treat of all however, came from the Barton-Wells family. They had kindly offered to treat *him*, along with a few friends, to an all inclusive night's clubbing in Rosebrook. Determined to impress, he was busy preening himself in the luxurious bedroom his father shared with Eleanor. At least it had a full length mirror. Admiring his reflection, he thought he looked quite fetching in his brand new jeans with a fashionable white silk shirt flowing loose on the outside.

Avalon too, seemed excited. The event fell on a weekend her boyfriend

197

happened to be around. Meeting Hugh Bambridge however, left Andrew feeling even more awkward; decked out like Tom Cruise in a burnt leather flying jacket, his dark hair windswept, his complexion tanned the colour of olive wood, which enhanced his perfect white teeth...

Andrew was nonetheless determined to enjoy his big birthday night, having invited along a couple of his better behaved friends. Matthew was a fellow dope smoker yet retained an adequately neat appearance; Mike, a close friend from Bromley.

No sooner had Elliot dropped them off in Rosebrook, Andrew, accompanied by Avalon and Hugh, headed for a wine bar. This flashy, noisy establishment boasted 'Happy Hour' between five and 7:00pm, time to enjoy their 'half price' cocktails. At first the conversation seemed forced. Until Avalon, as if sensing Andrew's shyness, launched into the subject of their house restoration.

"Andrew's been re-plastering the guest rooms!" her voice rang cheerfully around the table. "I can't wait to start decorating them!"

"What colours do you like?" Andrew quizzed, feeling his earlier tension slip away.

"I like the new subtle shades," she mused. "White with a hint of some other colour."

"You can create any colour you like now," Matthew added boldly. Lounging in a chair in a black vest and combat trousers far too big for him, he had combed his long hair into a ponytail.

Avalon squeezed Hugh's hand and beamed at him. For the next hour the conversation flowed a little easier and after a second round of cocktails, they were beginning to feel merry.

Eventually, they abandoned the wine bar in search of Tiffany's.

The club hid in one of the backstreets; an imposing block with rusticated walls painted coal black. Two heavily built bouncers guarded the doorway, scrutinising the queue snaking towards the entrance. So before they reached the doors, Andrew and Matthew slipped into an alleyway for a quick spliff, knowing they wouldn't get another chance.

By the time Andrew loped into the club, he was enjoying himself. Head spinning, he collapsed into a horseshoe of leather seating and surveyed the party scene unravelling around him.

Avalon had never been inside a nightclub yet seemed mesmerised by the decor. Pillars studded with mirror tiles reflected the disco lights, the crowd swelling as hoards of young people poured onto the dance floor. But with a solid wall of music thumping around them, they had little choice but to dance. Any further conversation was impossible...

Andrew completely lost himself as he gyrated on the dance floor with his friends. But as the evening peaked, so did the temperature until eventually the slow numbers came on; music that drew several couples onto the dance floor, Avalon and Hugh among them. Clinging to each other for a last dance, a fog of cigarette smoke swirled overhead, infused with the glow of the disco lights.

Come midnight, it was a relief to step into the cooling night air.

Andrew waved goodbye to his friends and no sooner had they parted company, he led the way along the pavement in search of a taxi. But with hoards of revellers spilling out onto the streets, the town was becoming rowdier.

Suddenly, Avalon found herself witnessing an uglier side of youth culture. Girls rendered worse for wear staggered along in high heels, cackling with laughter. But more threatening were the gangs of boys bellowing lewd comments. Eyes fixed ahead, Avalon fought hard to ignore them yet there seemed to be no escape... Without warning, one of them hauled down his trousers, bent over and flashed a set of hairy male buttocks. She clutched Hugh's arm in horror.

"I want to go home!" she whimpered, twisting her head away.

"It's okay," Hugh soothed her. "The taxi rank's over there, look."

Head reeling as she hurried towards it, Avalon had never imagined Rosebrook would feel so menacing. Unlit shop fronts stood several feet back, disguising the shadows of anyone hidden there. Drawing to a pause, she was out of breath, praying a taxi would turn up soon.

But the raucousness had not receded, still resonating in their wake. Then before she knew it, a procession of footsteps arose out of the darkness, gradually advancing towards them.

"Hello, Avalon," a voice echoed.

Avalon whirled around, recognising that cold, clipped voice. Before she could grasp the reality, Ben sauntered into the glow of streetlight. He was accompanied by Nathan; a terrifying figure in tight leather trousers and coat buttoned up to his throat. His face gleamed, as hard and hostile as ever. But with her gaze unavoidably shifting to Ben, Avalon felt her throat run dry. She glimpsed a suit under his long beige raincoat and his pale eyes shone like orbs.

"What are *you* doing here?" she hissed, her grip on Hugh's arm tightening.

"Enjoying a night out, same as you," Ben drawled. His eyes bounced from her to Andrew.

"Is everything okay, sweetheart?" Hugh muttered.

His voice sounded unnaturally loud, almost fated to draw Ben's attention.

Avalon pressed her eyes shut. "It's nothing..."

Teetering back a few steps, she shook her head, helpless to know what to say.

"I thought you lived in London!" she blurted, daring herself to look at Ben again.

"So we fancied a change of scenery," Ben smirked. "Isn't that right, Nathan? A chance to sample the *local* nightlife and see what it has to offer!"

His choice of words turned her cold.

"You never imagined a 'city boy' like me would take to this place," he added, "well maybe you were wrong..."

"What are you talking about?" Avalon gasped in panic. "You can't still be thinking of moving here, surely? Not now the partnership is off!"

"Who says it's off?" Ben taunted, extracting a cigarette from a box and lighting it.

She spun to Andrew, who looked stunned. Hugh encircled her in his arms yet for once even he seemed lost for words.

"Who are they, Avalon?" Andrew mumbled.

"It's Ben Hampton," she whispered, "and his minder..."

Andrew frowned, his eyes pinned on Ben.

Recalling his father's warnings just days ago, suddenly he did remember him.

That fateful day on the building site took shape in his mind. *The unexpected arrival of the bosses; of Perry Hampton.* Only now did he recall the leather clad youth tearing into the field on a motorbike... a bike that had almost collided with his sister. He had witnessed the scene from his elevated position on a scaffolding platform yet had definitely seen Ben's face. His white blonde hair distinguished him, his finely honed features giving him an almost angelic appearance.

Right now though, Ben's behaviour struck him as predatory. It brought flashbacks of the conversation they had shared in the Orangerie on the evening of Elijah's birthday.

"C'mon, let's go home," he said curtly, just as a taxi cruised into the curb.

Without waiting for an answer, he wrenched the back door open. Nudging Avalon and Hugh inside, he fought to avoid Ben's unwavering stare, whilst clambering in behind them.

"They're still around!" Avalon shivered to Eleanor the next morning over breakfast.

She had briefly described their night out, disturbed by the way it had ended.

"Do you know the last thing Ben said to me? *He was never going to go away.*"

At first Eleanor said nothing but it took one glance at Avalon's face to decipher the fear in her expression.

"Don't let him get to you," she whispered. "Are you worried he may be stalking you again?"

Avalon shook her head, not in denial but dismay. How alarming that Ben could just show up like that and more than a coincidence surely? Was it possible he had followed her? Or perhaps it was as he suggested; a chance visit to Rosebrook to sample the night life. But as for that chilling reference to Rosebrook being *local*...

She let out a sob. "It's more than that, it's all the other things! That awful magazine article, the business with the survey... Stuff that's happening in the outside world we don't know about and I'm sure Dad senses it too. Ben even suggested the partnership wasn't over!"

Eleanor let out a sigh. "He's obviously playing out some sick, twisted fantasy, Avalon. Now stop this, please. We can't give up now, not when we've got this far. Think about everything we have achieved. The windows, the rooms upstairs..."

"Ben is a very deluded young man!" James's voice chimed from behind them.

Avalon jumped. "Dad!" she whispered in shock. "I had no idea you - you..."

James ran a gentle hand over the back of her hair.

"As Eleanor says, we are well on the way to rescuing our home without them," he finished softly. "The Hamptons will just have to find some other mansion to turn into a corporate venue. But I can assure you it will not be ours."

Chapter Twenty-Two

I
June - August 1986

It seemed impossible to imagine Avalon's fears might not be unfounded. That before the summer ended, the full extent of the Hamptons' evil would bear terrible consequences.

It began shortly after the roof rebuild had reached completion. Next came James's unwavering decision to terminate all dealings with 'Heritage Building and Restoration.' But as Eleanor continued to absorb herself in the splendour of his estate, she was oblivious to the unravelling spool of events about to completely shatter their destiny.

As spring turned to summer, they saw a gradual change in their surroundings, the best bluebells of May radiating a vivid purple haze. Weeks later, the spikes of foxgloves peaked alongside banks of intense blue delphiniums. Come June, even the roses were revealing their beauty, a time when Eleanor had almost forgotten the troubles of the past.

Charlie too, was immersed in his various building assignments, honoured to be in control of the restoration. They did not flaunt their love for each other, conscious of Andrew's feelings. In some ways he was still crucified by their developing relationship. Yet having a new man in her life brought Eleanor such exquisite happiness, she no longer felt so haunted by the pain of Jake's death. He was never absent. A deeper part of her sensed his presence; whether it was the sound of his uplifting music or the beauty emanated in the world all around her.

Having temporarily left Rosebrook hospital, she missed her nursing job, though for the time being, felt her true calling lay here at Westbourne House. She continued to assist in the kitchens and the gardens. Tending to her vegetable patch, she was occasionally joined by other locals. And as the days grew shorter, she loved nothing more than the early mornings; the sun hovering low in the sky as birds enriched the ambience with their chorus.

Such appreciation inspired her to assist in the maintenance of James's formal gardens too, knowing he would struggle to employ extra contractors. Clipping, pruning and weeding flower beds proved just as therapeutic and she was turning into something of a gardening expert.

But as the house loomed on the other side of the walls, her thoughts drifted towards the restoration. She knew from Charlie that James had borrowed

£150,000, a considerable amount of which had been spent.

His overriding concern was they needed to work fast if they intended to draw in any tourist trade for the remaining summer months. All the while the weather remained pleasant, it attracted the usual crowds of tourists to admire the gardens and book the restaurant for lunch or cream teas.

Yet by the end of June, an unrelenting shortage of hotel bookings triggered anxiety - until it emerged Westbourne House had been the subject of further bad publicity. Where the first damaging article sewed the seeds as to whether James's property could be saved, it had since been broadcast that he had abruptly laid off his workforce.

Further rumours left the public speculating as to whether Westbourne House had run into money problems, its owner approaching bankruptcy... It took a considerable effort on James's part to reassure them the articles painted a much gloomier picture than the reality. The restoration of Westbourne House was in fact, coming along nicely and by Autumn would be complete.

Regrettably however, no one could predict the darkening cloud on the horizon; the eye of a storm about to turn James's life into the worst nightmare he would live through.

II

The first ruinous affair arose in July with the arrival of a letter from the Inland Revenue.

How strange they suddenly wanted to probe into James's finances.

Somehow, the profits from the auction in February had been exposed, as well as their Springtime Ball. But his initial anxiety descended to despair when they demanded to know why he had not declared this income - convinced he was deliberately misrepresenting the true state of his finances to reduce his tax liability.

"These were my family possessions," James protested bitterly. "How can it be so wrong to auction a few antiques, items that already belonged to us?"

What emerged though, was that any profits James made from the auction would be subject to Capital gains tax at 18%; that unless he was an *antiques dealer* he would be liable for this amount, or otherwise face a fine for tax avoidance.

It seemed hard to imagine how he would pay this, given the drastic fall in business and added to the pressure of his loan repayments, such disclosures left James floundering.

Struggling to sustain an income and with his finances thrown into turmoil, everyone witnessed a change in him and none so much as Avalon. She had never seen her father in such a dark place, a situation that inspired her to suggest taking meals together in the restaurant. Maybe the additional companionship of the staff, Charlie and Eleanor would gee him up a little.

On some occasions, Eleanor snuggled the children into their attic rooms, specifically if the conversation revolved around money. Added to the fear of what would happen to the hotel, should business not pick up, she sensed the malaise. It hung blackly around the edges of their world like scorch marks, withering away any optimism James had felt during those early summer weeks.

But of even greater concern was his health, which appeared to be on the decline again.

James had suffered two further blackouts, the last occurring on a rainy day. He stood before the patio window, staring gloomily across the gardens. Then without warning, his knees buckled and he crumpled to the floor. Avalon screamed for Elliot, who had in turn, got into contact with his doctor.

Albany Price could no longer deny he was worried.

On another occasion, James was admitted to hospital. But as he lay there, a ghost of his former self, it sadly dawned on them that summer was fading fast. Almost an entire year had passed since this fateful restoration business had come to light. Shocked by the condition it had reduced him to, Avalon couldn't help wondering if a quick sale might have been a better solution. At least it would save him from all this stress.

III

James battled to save his home nevertheless and before the end of August, Charlie had drafted in a team of floor specialists from London. Their undertakings created more upheaval than expected, as one by one, each section of timber flooring was reconstructed, along with the installation of a damp-proof membrane at plinth level.

Charlie knew the damage to the outer wall was potentially caused by the movement of water beneath the earth. Unfortunately, it meant having to close the hotel for another two weeks, whilst the work was underway. Yet it was reassuring to know that any future problems would be minimised. He found himself explaining this to James as he lay convalescing at home.

"Your house is almost restored," he updated him, "the hotel rooms re-plastered and decorated... and the new floors will ensure you suffer no more problems with rising damp. It is only the cracks in the outer walls that need attention. We are so very nearly there."

"I'm so grateful to you, Charlie," James muttered weakly.

He turned his gaze to Eleanor. With a slight chill creeping into the air and the gradual approach of autumn, she had draped a soft woollen blanket over him to keep him warm.

"So what about *you*, James?" she asked him. "Has your doctor said anything about the cause of these blackouts?"

James offered her a wan smile. "I'm afraid so... but can you promise that what I am about to tell you goes no further?"

"Of course," Eleanor mumbled. "What is it, James?"

His voice turned grave as he explained. At first, the blood tests had revealed nothing life threatening. But as more time elapsed, Albany's latest diagnosis confirmed his fears; the giddy spells and the blackouts appeared to be a succession of mini strokes.

"Transient ischemic attacks..." Eleanor gulped.

Charlie shot her a glance, shocked to see her eyes well up with tears.

She leant closer to James, clasping his hand. "I've come across them before. They could be the early warning signs of a future stroke. What else did he say?"

"Much as you've described," James replied, squeezing her hand in response. "The risk of a stroke increases dramatically in the days after one of these. Although they are only minor, they can still cause neurological damage, especially to the arteries supplying oxygen to the brain. This is the reason they are becoming more frequent. It makes sense... the dizziness, the fact I'm becoming more clumsy. I suppose I should think myself lucky I haven't ended up paralysed in some way, although I have experienced some numbness in my right arm..."

Charlie threw him a look of horror before his eyes flickered back to Eleanor. He saw the torment distort her features. She was fighting tears.

"Isn't there any medication he could give you?" he shot back wildly.

"Aspirin apparently," James chuckled. "If all else fails, Albany can prescribe some anti-clotting drugs and as a last resort, vascular surgery... but it carries a risk."

"Who else knows?" Eleanor choked. "Have you told Avalon?"

James shook his head.

He felt a little better, having drawn them into his confidence. Yet he could no longer deny how close he sensed his mortality. It lurked on the fringe of his world like a shadow.

"Please don't mention this," he begged. "I don't want to frighten her, but there is something very important I need to say. I fear I may be dying, Eleanor, and have a favour to ask. In the event of my death, would you take care of her? Her and William?"

Eleanor let out a sob. Unable to hold back her tears, she clamped her hand over her mouth before they came tumbling down her cheeks.

"You know I will," she gasped, seizing James's other hand. "I will always be there for them, not just for the immediate future but for as long as they need me. You looked after *me*. I never did discover what happened to my own dad yet you more or less stepped into his shoes."

"Thank you," James sighed, relaxing into the embrace of his sofa. "Your words bring me more comfort than you know. I could always contact their mother but she never really took to the children. Very cold woman... You, on the other hand, are an angel."

"Stop it!" Eleanor whimpered. "You can't be dying, James! We've only just managed to save your home!"

"I know," James smiled, running his thumbs tenderly over the backs of her hands, "and I dearly wanted to save it, so my children could inherit it. If I can achieve that much then I will die a happy man, I promise you."

Eleanor left the lounge completely devoid of spirit. Dragging her way up the stairs to their bedroom however, she came face to face with Elijah.

He could tell she had been crying, curious to know what was wrong. Fighting to divert her sorrow away from James, she instead began to reminisce about her own father.

"It would have been his birthday last week." She forced a smile. "August 16th! Just imagine, he would be in his late 50s by now..."

"When did you last see him?" Elijah frowned.

"When I was sixteen," Eleanor told him.

Same age as Avalon is now.

Closing her eyes, she would never forget the day her father had told her to pack her bags, before ushering her into a taxi to visit Sammie. Her father's boss looked close to retirement in those days, his whole empire crumbling under the threat of Dominic Theakston. This rival gang leader had sworn revenge on her father for the fatal shooting of his partner. Only on Sammie's insistence, had Oliver Chapman fled from London. But Eleanor had never seen him again.

"My life changed dramatically," she continued sadly. "I was dumped in a brothel! Do you know what that is? I met my friend, Della, there..."

Elijah turned red, a signal that suggested he knew exactly the type of place it was.

"It's okay, I was never a prostitute," she reassured him. "I escaped! That was the day I met *your* father, Jake. We ran away together..."

"I see," Elijah said numbly, staring at the floor. "I'd love to meet my Grandpa," he added almost as an afterthought. "I told the others he was a gangster."

His casual remark brought a smile to her lips.

Though thinking back, Elijah had given her much to smile about lately. Inspired to make good use of his new art materials, he had taken up sketching in the grounds of Westbourne House. Capturing every detail, he produced some outstanding drawings of the building.

Some of them even rivalled Charlie's.

Except the one memory that gripped Eleanor's heart, was catching him secretly sketching Avalon. She had been resting on a stone bench, reading. Yet his sense of proportion was incredible. Depicting her face with unbelievable accuracy, he had been focusing on her hair, his skilful shading accentuating the shine of every ringlet.

IV

Strangely enough, Eleanor was reminded of that beautiful drawing a few days later.

Stumbling across Avalon slumped in the Orangerie, she had been about to harvest the last of the courgettes, when a heart-wrenching volley of sobs resonated just meters away.

She knows, Eleanor thought, sliding through the door to comfort her. *There was no denying Avalon would be torn apart by the news of her father's declining health.*

"I'm going to miss him so much!" she blubbered, her hazel eyes spilling over again.

Eleanor swallowed. "Yes. I-it's going to be very hard, but we have to find a way to cope..."

"But he was two timing me!" Avalon shrieked.

At first Eleanor looked at her agape. Until it suddenly dawned on her she was referring to her boyfriend, Hugh; and so the story unravelled...

Determined to welcome him home after an overseas tour with his polo team, she had taken an unannounced train journey to his house in Surrey - mortified to find him with another girl, a pretty blonde dressed in nothing more than a short, silk dressing gown.

"I'm so sorry, Avalon," Eleanor mumbled uncomfortably.

For the rest of the day, Avalon was distraught.

This unexpected turn of events however, triggered an impromptu visit to the 'Olde House at Home.' Sympathetic of Avalon's heartache, it was Andrew who suggested they should go out for the evening to cheer her up.

Charlie, impressed by his son's chivalry, escorted them, since Avalon was still underage.

Lost in their thoughts, they wandered along the village path, past cottages smothered in roses and honeysuckle. Clusters of late summer flowers tumbled over low stone walls, yet an icy nip pierced the air as the sun sank lower.

Since the decline in his health, Charlie endeavoured to spend as much time

207

with James as possible and he in turn, had kept him well informed over the state of his affairs. With funds squeezed almost to breaking point, it would be hard for him to meet his loan repayments. Interest rates were soaring, leaving Charlie tense with fear.

Already a high risk loan, missing even one payment would likely incur a penalty.

James's friend, Cyril Fortescue, had tried to help, having convinced the MD of some blue-chip computer company to book his sublime country hotel for an annual board meeting. But even a potential £2,500's worth of business would not save him, especially with a hefty tax bill looming like a curse. The situation broke Charlie's heart.

Forcing aside his worries, they stepped inside the pub. It was noticeably busier in the summer months as tourists from all corners of England flocked here. Andrew shot towards the bar and eager to impress, ordered a bottle of wine and a pint of Charlie's favourite ale.

"How are things?" Boris greeted him warmly.

Andrew swallowed, as if unsure what to say, but then no one could ignore the melancholy atmosphere stifling Westbourne House.

"Okay," he muttered, settling the wine glasses on a tray.

"I hear you've been battling to save Westbourne House all summer," Boris coaxed him.

Sensing his unease, Charlie sauntered up to the bar.

"We've nearly finished," he added. "*Battling* being the operative word! It's not been without problems, no thanks to those unscrupulous sods James had dealings with from the outset..."

Boris looked baffled, which in some way encouraged Charlie to spit out the whole story. He felt no shame exposing the deception behind the original survey; nor the foul play enforced by their recommended building firm.

"Can you imagine what state the house would be in now if we hadn't sussed them out?"

His words trailed off as Eleanor drifted up to the bar with Avalon. Avalon looked pale. Her lovely face harboured a deep sadness, a pink flush around her eyes betraying the tears she had shed. Boris's gaze slid towards Eleanor.

"Let's sort you out with somewhere to sit, folks," he sighed.

With Boris's help, they rounded up some more stools and arranged them around an upturned barrel. It was close enough to the bar to allow Boris to join their conversation, in between serving customers. Andrew poured out three glasses of wine.

"Cheers!" he grinned, tapping Avalon's glass.

She forced a smile. "Thanks, Andrew... and sorry to be such a misery. It's not just Hugh. I'm worried about Dad. He hasn't been himself lately. Does anyone know what's going on?"

"Your dad's a bit worried about this loan, Avalon," Charlie said quickly. He threw a quick, but warning glance at Eleanor.

For the next hour, the conversation kept flowing. Charlie tried to maintain a cheerful banter but it was difficult, given everything Avalon's family had suffered. The subject of bad publicity reared its ugly head, as did the issue of the tax investigation. They had endured so many pitfalls.

Andrew slipped outside for a smoke. Avalon, reaching the end of her second glass, was getting a little tipsy, which at least put some colour back into her cheeks. But as the crowds began to thin out, Boris pulled off his apron and hauling up another stool, joined their assembly.

"I don't know what you're all worried about!" he said, having caught the gist of their earlier discussion. "This part of the country is booming and in a couple of months time, the London orbital road will be open."

The brand new motorway known as the M25 had been built throughout the early 80s. Its gradual construction had ensued in stages, resulting in an extensive road which encircled the whole of London, affording easier access to all other parts of the country.

"Yes, well that's not necessarily going to be great for us," Eleanor snorted. "For starters, it'll make Aldwyck even more commutable for Londoners! As if we haven't had enough of these city types moving in and pushing up house prices."

"But there's an up side," Charlie argued. "What if this motorway has a positive effect on Westbourne House? Make it more accessible, which is bound to boost trade."

"Maybe," Avalon said softly, "but I do worry about the village. Dad never wanted Westbourne House to be too commercial. He wanted to keep its historic character. We've all noticed the nature of the village has started to change recently."

"This is exactly my point," Eleanor said, thumping her fist on the table top. "Local people are being driven out! Take the Marsh couple for example. They lost their dream cottage..."

"Oh yes, I remember you telling me," Charlie muttered, draining his glass. "Didn't you say they were gazumped by some stockbroker from London?"

There followed a heavy drag of silence as they digested his words.

"Stockbroker?" Avalon echoed, glancing at Boris.

Boris, never one to hide his emotions, froze abruptly.

"What is is, Boris?" Eleanor whispered.

"Oh, Christ," he muttered in a low voice. "You are not going to like this."

Avalon turned white. "It's *him* isn't it?" she croaked.

Hadn't Ben said he was training to be a stockbroker? Ben, who had taunted her several weeks ago with the hint he was sampling their local nightlife?

Her eyes remained fixed on Boris, as she waited to hear the worst.

"I never wanted to tell you this," he said with a shiver, "but if you're referring to that young fair-haired chap who used to hang around, then yes. He turned out to be the buyer."

Like a prisoner condemned to death, Avalon lowered her head.

"Who are you talking about?" Andrew blurted naively.

"Not the Hampton boy?" Eleanor gasped.

"Sneaky little bastard!" Charlie hissed through clenched teeth.

They all turned as if joined by a single thread, unable to ignore the horror on Avalon's face.

"I-I need another drink," she gasped, her voice shaking, "because if Ben Hampton really is moving to Aldwyck... I don't want to live here any more!"

Chapter Twenty-Three

I
September 1986

Everything changed that evening. And whilst Avalon fought hard to conceal her emotions, it was impossible to ignore the state of terror she had been reduced to.

One by one, each member of the household noticed a bleakness in her mood. Yet not one of them dared to divulge her latest findings to James.

James was facing an agonising dilemma of his own. Everything they had worked so desperately hard for was slipping further and further from his reach. The restoration of Westbourne House had been accomplished, but due to a severe shortage of funds, he had defaulted on his last loan repayment. The final blow was a penalty imposed by the finance company, who had hiked up the interest on the outstanding balance.

"I can't take much more," he announced to Charlie one morning.

Propped up in his four-poster bed, he had suffered another minor attack in the last week. He might not have collapsed... but was consumed by a wave of such intense giddiness, Elliot had helped him upstairs before getting straight on the phone to Albany.

When James awoke the next day, he was left with a lingering stiffness down one side. It made walking difficult; so much so, he was resigned to using a walking stick.

Now overriding everything, came this harrowing letter.

"This is outrageous!" Charlie thundered. "They can't do this to you!"

"Under the agreement I signed, I'm afraid they can," James said weakly. "It was written in the small print. I was so grateful for this loan though, I overlooked it..."

Charlie banged the letter down on the bedside table. "Is there nothing we can do to help?"

"You have helped me enough already, Charlie," James said in earnest. "You saved my home. I can never thank you enough for that, but I think we have to accept the inevitable; that despite our best efforts, I may have to consider putting Westbourne House on the market. At least it should fetch a good price now..."

Charlie stared at him in alarm, wishing he could dream up something positive to say. Bitterness clawed his heart. *It wasn't fair.* This honourable man

211

had battled so hard to save his ancestral home; a man who lay in the grip of infirmity, the threat of mortality dangling... and here he was being victimised. How typical of the authorities to react like this, first the tax man who had squeezed him for every last penny, and now some faceless corporation, who seemed even more unscrupulous, reeling away any last thread of hope.

Charlie shook his head. "James, you can't give up!" he heard himself cry.

"I'm not giving up, Charlie," James protested. "I just cannot see another way forward. I'll have to contact the lenders tomorrow... see if there are any other options."

In an ultimate stroke of irony, it was *the lenders* who proposed a rescue deal, thus freeing James from the rising quagmire of debt he had sunk into. But with compound interest spiralling from 11% to 17%, his debts were likely to accumulate faster than he could repay them. Finding a potential buyer could be a long drawn out process. And in all that time, the debts would continue to mushroom, creeping towards the worst possible scenario. *His house would be repossessed.*

It now seemed this company was tossing him a lifeline.

Allied to a real estate company, they were willing to purchase the property at its current market value: £1.2 million, minus the estate agency fee and any outstanding balance owed.

What surprised James even more was the reaction he got from his children.

At first William was shocked. "What about George's dad?" he gasped. "Didn't he get you a booking recently? Why can't you just ask *him* to lend you the money?"

"People of our class do not borrow money from each other," James said shamefully.

There was no use fighting. Even they could see how the debts were crippling him, unable to bear the impact this was having, given his progressively frail condition. But no sooner had Avalon explained to her brother about the loan situation, he very quickly came around.

"Okay, Dad," he relented. "You can't hold on forever. It looks as if we might lose our house anyway if these loan sharks carry out their threat."

James smiled at that. *Loan sharks.* His son always did have a good way with words.

"You may well be right, " he responded with a sigh. "But are you sure you don't mind? This is after all your ancestral home..."

Avalon shook her head wildly, the tears welling.

The truth was she felt tortured by the concept of Ben Hampton taking up residence.

But in the aftermath of that fateful pub conversation, all she could think about was his evil seeping into the village, her life turning into a nightmare. She would never feel safe here again.

"Much as I love this house, you've been offered a good price," she concluded. "It's more than enough to afford a new home. So why are we killing ourselves trying to cling on to it?"

With his heart sinking into his chest, James ultimately signed over the deeds.

A couple of days later, and firm in the conviction he had done the right thing, he summoned Charlie and Eleanor into the lounge to join him. Elliot, who was subject to every confidence, was also present. He poured them a glass of sherry each.

"Well, folks," James began, "as you know, I have been forced to make a heartbreaking decision. I hope you understand... I had very little choice in the end."

Eleanor was fighting tears. "James, we are so sorry. Aldwyck will never be the same without you. Are you absolutely sure there was nothing more we could have done?"

James gave a resigned sigh. "Oh, Eleanor, I wish there was! I appreciate how nice it would have been to re-launch the hotel; indulge in a grand opening. Yet I no longer have time on my side. The children fully support me in my decision and we've loved having you here. But I'm afraid our time has come to move on..."

"Who was the buyer?" Charlie questioned.

"Ah, I thought you might ask that," James said. He forced a mirthless smile. "It was some *real estate firm* allied to the finance company. Seemed the best way really. A quick sale without complications..."

Charlie frowned. "What, the company who arranged the loan? They've proposed to buy Westbourne House?"

Thoughts of that outrageous letter came back to him; the drastic change in James's loan agreement. In fact, it was more than odd. *Such actions struck him as downright unethical.*

"They would have repossessed the house anyway, Charlie, the way things were going," James added with his usual lion-hearted stoicism.

"But who is this company?" Charlie pressed. "Do you have a copy of the sale agreement?"

"Indeed I do," James answered. "Elliot, would you be so kind as to look in the top drawer of that sideboard. I think that's where I kept it."

He looked so fragile, Charlie thought, clocking his ghostly pallor.

Seconds later, Elliot returned from the sideboard, clutching a thick white envelope.

"Thank you," James murmured. Extracting a sheaf of papers, he passed them to Charlie. "A company known as 'Falcon Finance.'"

Charlie scanned the document, which clearly listed the terms agreed between both parties. With the ownership of Westbourne House signed over to the company, a sum of £900,000 had already been transferred into James's bank account.

Yet his eyes were drawn to something else; an indistinct logo that looked disturbingly familiar. Tilting the paper towards the light, he spotted it again, subliminal like a watermark. The shape of a falcon's head registered; the hunch of its wings, the cruel curve of its beak, so sinister and predatory. Charlie felt a shiver of cold sweep over him like a shroud, knowing exactly where he had seen it before.

"Charlie, what is it?" Eleanor said softly.

"Nothing," Charlie snapped, handing the document back to James. "I-I was just a little surprised, that's all. This isn't something I've ever come across..."

II

In the end, Charlie could not bring himself to tell James for fear of what the shocking truth behind that sale agreement might do to him...

James on the other hand, drifted around the house in silent oblivion, having resigned himself to the task of making an inventory.

On this particular Sunday however, he found himself reminiscing. He recalled the day of the tea party and his unexpected collapse. It seemed strange how almost an entire year had passed since that ominous day.

William would be turning fifteen in a few days time. With a sense of desolation, James realised how much his son had loved having other youngsters to mix with throughout the summer.

Dismayed to be returning to boarding school, William looked more like a teenager now. His limbs had become long and supple, his face less child-like, as new signs of maturity emerged. James could hear the crack of a cricket ball echoing from somewhere in the grounds, knowing his son, Margaret and Elijah were engrossed in a game.

Being a typical Sunday, everyone moved around the house in their familiar circles. Charlie would be relaxing in the bar with a coffee by now, immersed in his favourite newspaper. It wouldn't be long before he and Eleanor would be engaged in some lively debate. He imagined Avalon would be there too; Andrew most likely in bed, enjoying his Sunday lie-in.

Drawn to the restaurant, he joined Bryony and Angelo. They were discussing today's menu; Angelo pondering over the best dish he could create from the lovely piece of beef the catering suppliers had dropped off and at a greatly reduced price, since it needed to be used today.

Bryony suggested a French *boeuf bourguignon*.

"Or how about a steak and ale casserole?" James smiled with a conspiratorial wink. "We could ask Boris to supply a flagon of that beer Charlie likes."

Turning towards the kitchens, Bryony was about to reply... except the smile froze on her face. Her eyes moved to the subtle gleam of a car. Momentarily captured in the sunlight, it appeared to be crawling towards the house.

"Looks like we've got visitors," she announced.

Craning his head to get a better view, James limped up to the window.

But as the car drew closer, the make and model quickly registered; this was none other than the pale biscuit coloured Mercedes Benz he knew only too well.

"Good Lord," he choked, backing away from the window.

"Who is it?" Bryony reacted sharply.

An icy chill rolled down his spine. "It's the Hamptons," James said. "What the hell do they think they are doing here?"

The horror in his mind intensified, his eyes widening.

"The children! Where's Elliot?"

"I'm here!" Elliot's voice called from the doorway. "James, I feel I must warn you but..."

"I know!" James barked, whirling around to face him. "I've seen them! Could you round up the kids and get them inside, please. Quickly!"

Without a moment's hesitation, Elliot fled from the doorway.

The car meanwhile, continued to advance. Bryony and James stared at each other whilst Angelo hovered in the background, arms folded across his chest. He shook his head.

"Why do they come now, Meester Barton-Wells?" he muttered in his thick Italian accent.

"I have no idea," James shuddered.

Chapter Twenty-Four

I

William was braced on the lawn where they had set up some cricket stumps. With a few stumbling steps, he lobbed the ball to Elijah who whacked it high in the air. The ball whistled over several bushes before rolling into the distance. But before Margaret had a chance to run off and retrieve it, Elliot came jogging down the path.

"William!" he hollered. "Your father wants you all back inside, now!"

"What for?" William retorted in a manner that sounded quite petulant.

Elijah on the other hand, dropped the bat on the grass. He read the fear in Elliot's eyes.

"Let's just do as he says," he snapped and tugging Margaret's sleeve, began to run towards the house.

Elliot had just about succeeded in herding them across to the steps when without warning, the Mercedes swerved into the same spot. Parked in a clumsy, lop-sided fashion, the car's passenger door flew open. All four of them froze, watching in dread as Ben stepped from the car. His cold eyes danced from each one of them in turn, narrowing cruelly when they met William's. He took little notice of Elijah. But as his eyes fell to Margaret, they lingered.

She let out a frightened gasp, gripping William's arm.

Ben offered her a twisted smile. "Well, hello again, little one," he murmured.

"I think we should go inside," a woman's voice chimed from behind.

All heads turned to Rowena, a tall, forbidding figure in her tailored grey dress suit and full length black boots. Margaret let out another gasp. Struck by the glare of her aqua-marine eyes, she was reminded for all the world of some evil cartoon character.

"Go on up, kids," Elliot urged, ushering them towards the steps.

As they sped to the top without delay, Elliot hauled the door open. He was woefully aware of the driver door opening, where only Perry could be lurking.

Racing into reception, they found James awaiting them. He stood still as a statue, walking stick gripped in one hand, as if mentally preparing himself for a confrontation.

William paused. "What's going on, Dad?" he said.

"I wish I knew," James muttered, "but for now, I think we had all better assemble in the bar. For whatever reason that man is here, I know it is not going

216

to be pleasant."

Elijah darted through the lounge with Margaret, quick to reach the sofa where their parents were seated. Charlie looked up. Dropping his newspaper, he instantly recognised the shock on their young faces. But before another word was spoken, Elliot stumbled across.

"The Hamptons are here," he whispered. "James has no idea what this is about yet, but if you wanted to make yourselves scarce…"

"It's okay, we'll stay!" Eleanor insisted.

Charlie turned rigid as he watched the scene unfurl. There was something quite shocking about the way James limped into the bar, assisted by William. Every footstep seemed painful.

Looming in his wake, Ben was next to appear. Charlie caught a glimpse of white blonde hair, a terrifying vision dressed in black. Ben's eyes scanned the area as if looking for someone. Avalon, who had been crouched behind the bar, collecting cups, let out a terrified whimper. Although the creeping approach of Perry had the greatest impact of all.

His solid frame reared in the doorway.

At first Charlie couldn't move. Anchored to the sofa with his arm slung casually around Eleanor's shoulder, he detected an instant change in her. Her muscles jerked as if she had been electrocuted, but as for the expression on her face… it had morphed into a mask of pure terror.

The seconds passed quickly as Perry turned to close the door, trapping them all inside.

But in precisely the same instant, Eleanor had flown to her feet and grasping Elijah's hand, shot away from the table.

Moving towards the darkest corner of the lounge, she backed into the folds of the long velvet drapes to conceal herself. Her dark clothes and long dark hair merged into the shadows, her golden eyes shining like orbs as she held her son tightly in front of her.

Yet even from a distance, Charlie could see she was shaking.

With Perry Hampton standing in the centre of the room, gazing at each person in turn, his wife and son positioned themselves on both sides.

Together they formed a menacing trio.

Their eyes raked over the residents and for that moment no one really knew how to begin.

As Eleanor stared at Perry though, there was little doubt in her mind where she had seen him before. His thick hair appeared to be more white than blonde, eyes pale as frost glaring out of a familiar florid face. She closed her eyes, assailed by memories. They took her right back to 1973, to that devastating press conference where she had vowed to make one last stand against her enemies.

In her mind's eye lingered the beautiful lounge of the Grosvenor Hotel; the two men in dinner suits sat around that table and the heated discussion, which had finally brought her face to face with this mysterious man. It happened moments before she had uttered those fateful words:

'All I know is that his friend, Andries, spoke the truth when he told you Jake witnessed something. Just follow the clues!'

And never in her life would she forget the crazed reaction the man had exhibited. She could visualise him now, tearing at his collar and tie as if choking, his face turning purple.

Wasn't it always her intention to find out who he was?

Yet regrettably time had run out. The revelations of that press conference had unleashed the truly intimidating power of Dominic Theakston, whose threats had driven her away before she had a chance to discover more.

Eleanor shrank deeper into the shadows, feeling the chill of fear in her veins. Sensing the fragility of her son, she hugged him tight against her body. His small, thin frame felt warm against her chest, the bones of his shoulder blades jutting beneath his T-shirt. They remained very still but as her eyes continued to drink in the image of Perry Hampton, words of that conversation from thirteen years ago echoed in her head like a tape recording…

Seeing this man now brought everything back to her with a sudden clarity. Eleanor knew without any doubt this had to be the man who had organised Jake's murder all those years ago.

For several more minutes she was rooted to the spot. Desperate not to draw attention to herself, she pressed her eyes shut, filled with a sense that past and present had just collided.

II

"Well, hello, James," Perry said smugly. "What a pleasure it is to see you again. Obviously you weren't expecting us, but I have something to tell you."

"Perry," James replied, determined not to betray his anxiety. "What is this about?"

"First, I wanted to see the house again," Perry continued. "We thought about breaking this to you gently but there seems no point beating around the bush. So you might as well hear it straight. I am the one who's just bought it!"

James stood very still, unable to believe the words resonating in the air. He gripped his stick tighter, knuckles whitening.

"That can't be true," William whispered, twisting his head around to stare at him.

Avalon too, had sidled out from the bar. Circling around to her father's side as if to protect him, she was shaking her head in disbelief.

"You're lying," she gasped, "Dad would never sell our house to you!"

"Wrong!" Perry continued to goad them. "Is it not true that last week you signed an agreement, transferring the deeds of your house to one of the partners of a financial investment company? A company by the name of Falcon Finance?"

"Yes, I did," James admitted warily.

A cruel smile slid across Perry's face. "Oh dear," he muttered. "Did it never occur to you that Falcon Finance was my company?"

Avalon and William gaped at each other as the truth locked into place.

"I see," James sighed, bracing himself to face him. "What can I say? Obviously you have played a very clever game, Perry, though I won't deny I cottoned on to your shenanigans. It started with those surveyors didn't it? You thought you had me conned, but we saw through them in the end. Was this per chance another company of yours?"

Perry gave a dismissive shrug. "No, but Edward and I have known each other for years. Whatever work he recommended was only intended for preventative measures. But you may as well face facts, the place *was* riddled with deathwatch beetle. It was only a matter of time before the infestation would spread to other parts of the house."

From another corner of the room, Charlie shuddered with rage.

"So what about those so-called *restoration specialists*?" James added coldly. "I suppose their grossly inflated costs were another part of your scheme were they? I mean, good God, I've heard of *raising the roof* but in this case it was by thousands!"

Perry laughed. "I like your humour, James, and I must say, you're taking this remarkably well! But I make no apologies for my long-term plan to take over your establishment. I offered to bail you out and you rejected my proposal."

James shook his head sadly. "You are unbelievable, Perry," he sighed.

"Was it you who stirred up the bad publicity?" Avalon accused.

"Why not?" Perry smiled. "Surely you must have known I would have media contacts, my dear, and that article was no exaggeration. As far as I recall, the state of those bedrooms was appalling. I felt it was only fair the public should be warned…"

"You absolute pig!" Avalon sobbed.

As James curled his arm around his daughter, Perry laughed again. Even more torturous were the smirks creeping onto the faces of both Ben and Rowena. In the light of such revelations, this seemed particularly cruel.

"Like I say, you should have played ball," Perry kept tormenting him. "It was my dream to find a property like this and I spotted an opportunity, not just to rescue your home, but to maximise its business potential. You have no idea how dismayed I was when you turned me down."

"It would never have worked!" James thundered. "All you cared about was profit! You had no respect for its character, our Victorian walled gardens you seemed so determined to build over!"

"Perry never said that," Rowena sniffed. "Even I respected your love of those gardens. But the one thing we could never understand was how a magnificent property like yours could be so freely available to any member of the public."

"This house is part of our national heritage," James protested. "You would have ruined it!"

"Rubbish!" Perry snapped as if tiring of the argument. "You never gave us a chance. You shied away from my proposition, the instant someone warned you not to have dealings with me. That hurt, James! I do not take kindly to being maligned, so I decided to make you bankrupt! I knew you would never manage this restoration alone and I was right!"

"No actually, you were wrong," Charlie's voice clanged into the room.

Rising from his chair, Charlie could no longer bear the sight of James wilting against the bar whilst this puce-faced bully kept chipping away at him.

Perry turned sharply, eyes glittering with recognition.

"James did manage this restoration," Charlie continued. "Everything went perfectly to plan, the day he got rid of those overpriced cowboys you conned him into hiring!"

"Charles Bailey!" Perry snarled, sauntering a few steps closer. "And yes, your interference with this project *was* finally brought to my attention!"

"So?" Charlie snapped. "Why shouldn't I offer to help James? You bankrupted my last employer. I needed the work, same as James needed a builder, someone who wasn't going to rip him off royal!" He faced him directly, his face hardening with anger.

"Well, it so happens, you did a fine job," Perry whispered icily. "Do you not remember the day I spoke to you? Did I not say I recognised your skills as a professional architect and foreman... that I specifically wanted you working for me?"

Charlie narrowed his eyes, knowing what was coming.

"It appears I got my wish. I was the one who ultimately wanted this house restored. So how ironic that you, of all people, took the job on, not to mention the money you've saved me! I thank you for that, Charles."

"I did it for James, not you," Charlie hissed, feeling the clench of his own fists.

If it wasn't for the fact that the children were in the room, he would have hit him.

But Perry stared deep into his eyes. "Very commendable of you," he smiled, "and this may come as a surprise but I would still be willing to employ you - and for considerably more than *board and lodgings*. I hear your craftsmanship has been exceptional."

"What?" Charlie spluttered, unsure he had even heard him right. "How can you say that after the malicious rumours you were spreading? And it was you wasn't it? How else was it possible that no building company in Bromley wanted to employ me?"

"You have no proof of anything that may or may not have been said, Mr Bailey," Perry whispered in a voice so soft, it was barely audible. "But whatever misfortune you've suffered in the past, it is *your future* you need to consider."

Charlie turned cold as the words pierced his heart. There was so much more he wanted to say; the memory of their ruined lives, of Anna's death... they spun around his mind with a force that turned him dizzy, leaving any unspoken words trapped.

With a last mocking smile, Perry turned back to James.

Charlie stared at Eleanor, concealed in the folds of the drapes. Her expression reflected nothing but shock. She hadn't moved since the conflict had started, her son too, imprisoned in the grip of her arms. His eyes filled with panic as they momentarily clashed with Charlie's.

Perry meanwhile, continued to strut around the bar. He clearly relished his power, as he paused in front of James again.

"Anyway, moving on. The crux of the matter is that I am the new owner of Westbourne House, which brings me to my next point. I'm afraid your family will have to move out, James. I will, of course, allow you a reasonable amount of time to find a new home but you have a considerable sum of money at your disposal, so I suggest you start looking! I am not prepared to wait forever!"

"You are despicable, Perry," James spluttered, turning ashen. "I have lived in this house all my life and you cannot deny this sale was forced on me. We've barely had time to get our heads around this. Yet here you are, ordering us out of our home before I've even had a chance to get an inventory together. Couldn't you have at least spared us this indignity?"

"I don't have time for compassion," Perry sneered. "So I'll spell it out to you in black and white. You have exactly one month to remove yourselves and your belongings from this house. I am not going to evict you... but should you remain here for longer than the time I have specified, then you will be charged, as would any other paying guest."

James shook his head in disbelief. "You expect me to pay to stay in my own hotel?"

Perry smiled, his eyes resuming their chill. "It's not yours any more, James."

"Maybe not," he said, "but there is no question the means by which you acquired this property were utterly immoral, and I assure you I will be taking legal action."

"Oh, please!" Perry laughed. "You wouldn't stand a chance against my lawyers! You were the one who ultimately signed the deeds over, which means you haven't got a leg to stand on."

Avalon detected the sag in her father's stance and suddenly it was too much.

"Stop it!" she screamed. "How can you do this to him? Can't you see how frail he is?"

"Avalon, sweetheart, don't rise," James protested. "Don't give him the satisfaction."

"But this is an outrage!" she kept babbling. "How dare these people stand here and laugh at us! Isn't it bad enough they've taken our home?"

This time it was Ben's turn to intervene.

"Avalon," he murmured silkily, "you had every opportunity to keep your home. My parents offered you a most generous partnership deal and for such a small sacrifice. As for me, all I ever wanted was a relationship with you... Just think, we might even have been married."

"Are you crazy?" Avalon gasped. "We were completely incompatible!"

"So you say," Ben said, taking slow steps towards her. "The truth is you've got no one else to blame but yourself, Avalon, and now your family are paying the price."

"Shut up!" she shrieked, spinning away from the bar. "I never liked you anyway! Even less so when you started harassing me. Now stay away from me, you revolting creep!"

The atmosphere prickled with tension. Nobody moved, not even Perry or Rowena. James and William exchanged horrified glances, whilst Avalon, who had long recognised the sadistic flare in Ben's eyes, was reminded of the day in the forest.

"I said stay away! Don't you dare come another step closer!"

"Or you'll do what?" Ben added with a leer.

"Avalon, calm down, please," James whimpered weakly in the background.

But what happened next came as a shock to everyone. Without warning, Avalon drew back her fist and with a howl of rage, delivered a punch into Ben's face. She had thrown so much force into it, he staggered back with a gasp. His hand flew to his cheek.

"You bitch," he hissed at her.

The flame was ignited.

222

For in all the while she had been inching away, she wasn't paying attention to where she was going. Backing into the far wall, she felt the coolness of the stone rear up to meet her. Ben's face twisted with hatred.

From another corner of the room, Elijah absorbed the scene, until he could no longer stand by and watch. Witnessing the terror Avalon was being put through, he wriggled out of his mother's embrace. Eleanor let out a gasp but it was too late.

Elijah had shot into the gap between the two young adults.

"Leave her alone!" he protested angrily.

Ben's eyes slithered over him as if he was worthless. "And who the fuck are you?" he spat.

William was next to dash across to the spot, in a gallant attempt to defend him.

"Don't you talk to my friend like that!" he shouted.

Turning his attention to William, Ben released a chuckle. "Shut up you little pip squeak," he muttered in a dangerous tone, "before I smash that pretty face of yours..."

A ripple of shock filtered among the residents and Margaret started to cry. But hearing that unwarranted threat towards William was enough to send James berserk.

"Enough!" he roared, forcing himself forwards. "How dare you terrify my daughter, then have the cheek to threaten my son!"

No one could ignore the flush in his face as he took one jolting step after another.

"Whether you people own this house or not, you have no right to intimidate us and if you do not leave *right now*, I shall call the police!"

His words were cut short as the door banged open, the newcomer none other than Andrew. Hair uncombed and messy, his face shadowed with stubble, he looked as if he had just stumbled out of bed.

Surveying the scene, he fired Ben a look of malevolence. "What the hell is going on?"

Ben turned, a hint of recognition crossing his face as Andrew strode across to the spot where they were standing.

"Get away from her, you sick bastard!"

"So who are you, her boyfriend?" Ben's voice lashed back. "Likes a bit of rough does she? So where's the posh one?" He spun back to Avalon. "Or is Avalon such a slag, she's got to have two blokes on the go?"

Shoving Elijah aside brutally, he took his final few steps. But Avalon lashed out a second time, the strike of her nails sharp as they tore down the side of his neck. Ben let out a yelp.

223

"I told you to stay away from me!" she whimpered.

At last she leapt away from the wall. Charlie, who was comforting Margaret, just about managed to catch her as she fell sobbing into his arms.

Ben, on the other hand, glared at her in shock. His hand flew to his neck, where long streaks of blood stood vividly against the whiteness of his skin.

"It's alright, Avalon, you're safe," Charlie murmured.

"She's crazy!" Rowena shrieked. "Ben, get back here, right now!"

"I think it's time you left," James added coldly. "There's been enough violence."

"The only violence I've seen came from *your* daughter!" Rowena cried, her eyes focussed on Ben now. "Look what she's done to him..."

"Serves him right!" Charlie retaliated. "We all knew about the stalking! We even heard about the cottage he bought, which was obviously designed to unhinge her! In fact, everyone's just about had a belly full of Ben's nasty little mind games!"

"Cottage?" he heard James mumble from behind him. "What cottage?"

But Charlie never had a chance to reply.

Ben spun around in outrage, when a movement caught his eye.

His eyes locked with Eleanor's.

Hidden in the corner, almost camouflaged in the shadow of the drapes, she stared dazedly back at him and her golden eyes widened.

"Well I never," Ben said icily. "It's the gypsy slut!"

Perry followed his gaze and there was a sudden shift in the atmosphere as he spotted her too. Barely discernible but unforgettable, she had materialised like a ghost.

III

As Perry sauntered towards her, the recognition on his face was unmissable. Such a vision instantly brought back memories of the 1973 press conference.

Eleanor pressed her eyes shut, powerless to hold them back.

All she had ever wanted was the truth. Jake had not been murdered for drugs, the stories smeared across the tabloids nothing but a smoke screen designed to cover up the real reason he was killed. But Eleanor held the key. Jake had been present on the day an eminent politician had been blown up in a car bomb explosion. He had told her about the blonde-haired stranger seen lurking in the lane. Whoever was responsible was at risk of being exposed. So a powerful group of men plotted to get rid of Jake and tragically, they had succeeded.

That press conference was Eleanor's one chance to explain there was something far more sinister behind Jake's killing than the lies perpetuated in the papers. Convinced it would entice the very people who had conspired to murder him, she had been spot on. Inspector Hargreaves had attended and so had Councillor Whaley... but he was accompanied by this enigmatic stranger, the same man whose pale grey eyes were searing into her now. He had said very little at the conference, until the moment Eleanor had appeared.

"You," Perry breathed, "I might have guessed it would be you..."

"What are you talking about?" she shuddered.

"Somebody warned James not to have dealings with me," he said, taking one step at a time.

She felt the grip of fear as he positioned himself in front of her.

"You leave her out of this!" Charlie shouted. "If you really want to know who warned James against this so-called partnership, it was me!"

Perry tilted his head to observe him. "Is that so? Well, you should have known better than to do that, Charles Bailey." With a look of undisguised hatred, he turned back to Eleanor. "We have met, though, haven't we?"

"Yes," she found the courage to say. "For months I've been hearing the name, Hampton... I just never realised it was *you*."

A sob caught in her throat. Despite all efforts to conceal herself, he had finally rooted her out. Then another thought started to unravel itself; the issue of her secret file.

"Did you know I lived in Aldwyck?"

She broke off again, struck with another memory; *somebody had attempted to steal it.*

"Oh yes," Perry said in a voice of ice. "Fortunately, my son kept me very well informed about your little chat in that pub. Furthermore, we are going to be neighbours soon, so we'll be able to keep an eye on you." He took another menacing step.

Stationed only inches away, he tucked his fore-finger under her chin, tilting her head upwards.

"Don't touch me!" she spat.

"Why not?" he muttered evilly. He tickled her chin. "Just don't ever dare cross me again, *Eleanor*. You've already seen what I can do."

She twisted away with a shudder, a gulf of silence left hanging.

The next time Perry turned to face everyone, however, his expression turned demonic.

"I have nothing more to say," he finished with a hiss. "You all know the score... So I suggest you start packing. I'll be back in a month!"

Chapter Twenty-Five

I

"Eleanor, what the hell was all that about?" Charlie gasped.

Moving upstairs to their bedroom, the impact of that showdown had finally sunk in. Eleanor was shaking all over as she clung to him.

"What is your connection with that man? I can't believe you knew him, after everything we've talked about."

"That's just it," Eleanor whimpered. "I didn't even know who this *Peregrine Hampton* was until today. Honestly, Charlie, I had no idea."

"Ssh," he whispered, kissing her trembling lips. "Don't be upset. You have met him before though, haven't you? I could tell. Not so much from your reaction but from *his*."

"Oh, Charlie," she shivered.

From the instant Perry materialised though, Charlie had known something was wrong, confused as to why she had tried to hide from him.

She flinched to a volley of raised voices coming from above. Swiftly remembering that his kids were up there with Elijah, Charlie surveyed her with suspicion.

"Has this got something to do with Eli's father?" he said. "C'mon Eleanor, you know you can confide in me…"

"I will," Eleanor whispered, "but now is not the time. Can we talk about this later? Somewhere more private where we won't be overheard. I want James to be present too, see."

The opportunity did not arise until later in the evening.

As soon as Eleanor had composed herself, they gathered up the kids, suggesting a stroll in the grounds. Elijah was not blind though, as curious as the others to know why Perry had turned on her like that. But Eleanor wouldn't have known where to start.

"Let's not talk about it, Eli," she sighed. "Let's just enjoy this place while we still can."

Gazing across the lawns, they noticed the trees had begun to change colour. They had lived here for almost six months, Charlie reflected, where nothing brought a greater sense of pleasure than assisting James with the renovation. Yet what had it all been for?

Not a single one of them stood to benefit apart from those despicable

Hamptons.

Anger bit painfully into his heart. Turning around however, to observe the house from a distance, he forced his bitterness aside.

It had not been in vain. He had kept a journal, chronicling every phase of the restoration.

With his portfolio embellished with some of the most pleasing photographs he could hope for, he would take several more before they left. To his further delight, Elijah had offered him some of his own sketches too, having captured the finer details of the architecture.

But as the sunlight faded, they finally congregated in the restaurant for dinner.

Devouring the mouth-watering steak and ale casserole Angelo had cooked, it was not long before the conversation turned sombre.

"We can't let them get away with this," William snarled. "They're evil, the lot of them!"

"James, is there nothing you can do?" Eleanor added.

"Well, I spoke to Inspector Boswell," he said. "Perry may think *I don't have a leg to stand on,* but I can still bring charges against his family for intimidation." He swilled his wine around his glass, his expression one of steely contemplation. "I'll be talking to Geoffrey Ascombe too. Those articles in the press were slanderous and deliberately intended to harm my business. I should certainly have good grounds to sue! But as for the rest... There is very little I can prove really. At the end of the day, Perry warned me *I would regret my decision* and now he's won."

Eleanor and Charlie exchanged a glance. But with little they could say to contest that point, not one of them could have anticipated the sheer cunning behind Perry's strategy.

"I never imagined he could be so ruthless," Avalon whispered as if to echo their musings.

Eleanor turned cold. For the story she was about to impart to James would eclipse everything they had ever known about him.

II

All five youngsters disappeared upstairs, piling into William's bedroom to watch a video. Bryony, sensing they needed a little cheering up, had made them popcorn.

By the time the grandfather clock struck 8:00, Eleanor and Charlie made their way into James's lounge. Tolling through the corridor, every chime sounded eerie. They found James by the patio doors, gazing over the grounds before the darkness crept in. Elliot poured them a glass of wine each and closing the door, left them in private.

"Well, I have to say I am absolutely stunned that you and Perry Hampton knew each other," James began. "I didn't notice you were there, hiding! But there was a lot going on..." He gazed at her in sympathy. "Eleanor, where have you seen that man before and does this have any bearing upon your past?"

"It does," Eleanor shivered. "I only ever met him once. A press conference in 1973..."

She broke off, struck by the memory of a dream just before they had moved here; *a dream that portrayed a beautiful lounge, a boardroom table and men in dark suits. One of them had turned but she couldn't make out his face.*

"It happened at the Grosvenor Hotel in London," she continued. "Various people attended to discuss the mystery surrounding Jake's murder... and that man was among them."

Charlie shot her an anxious frown. "One of the first things you told me was that you suspected the men behind it were powerful," he started to intervene.

"That's right," Eleanor nodded, "but before I go any further, I need to explain some of the things that happened before this event, if you can just bear with me..."

She took a gulp of wine, a ripple of fear running through her as she reached inside her shoulder bag. Both men watched in silent apprehension as she extracted a sheaf of papers.

"Is this your secret file?" Charlie asked.

"Yes, Charlie," Eleanor said. "This is the file where Jake's story is hidden. I wish I could let you read it... except I've named people who are dangerous and that could have repercussions for my son. I'll start by explaining the reason Jake was killed."

She closed her eyes, gripping the papers tightly.

"I met Jake in 1972. He'd been abducted by a criminal gang. Held prisoner in a basement. But I overheard a conversation that told me one thing; he was going to be *dispatched* that night."

"It was a contract killing?" Charlie gasped in disbelief.

"Yes," Eleanor replied. "We escaped... but not before this gang chased us half way across London. Jake and I lived in hiding. We knew they were looking for us but I'm digressing. Jake told me everything that led to his capture."

Carefully leafing through the papers, she selected a single news clipping: *Bomb Tragedy Claims the Life of a British MP.*

"Do you remember this?" She dangled the cutting. "In July 1972, Labour MP, Albert Enfield, was killed in a car bomb explosion, along with several others. Here..." She passed it to James.

He swooped forwards to peer closer. "Dear God, I remember! A callous attack sanctioned by the IRA. We all knew Enfield had enemies but..."

"It was not the IRA," Eleanor interrupted.

James's frown deepened.

"Tell me what you know about Albert Enfield," she added in a gentler tone.

"Hmm," James muttered, "he certainly ruffled a few feathers. People considered the current prime minister, Ted Heath, to have let them down by failing to negotiate better wages. Enfield's popularity grew. It was rumoured he might even be the next prime minister but the higher echelons of society didn't like that. Some seemed determined to stop him."

"Why?" Eleanor demanded, curious to hear James's stance.

"I-I'm not absolutely sure," James struggled to answer. "Let's just say his policies didn't suit everyone. Some thought him to be a communist, planning all sorts of reforms. He promised better pay and conditions, but there was widespread speculation he would impose crippling taxes on the wealthy... re-allocate property considered too large for the inhabitants. Take this place for example."

"Westbourne House is a hotel!" Charlie disputed. "Surely you don't believe his government was about to make some claim on it do you? That would be an outrage!"

"The rumours were enough to make men like me a little nervous, Charlie," James said. "We were led to believe this man could start a revolution! That Britain would end up like the Soviet Union... under Stalin."

"That is absolute rubbish!" Charlie scoffed. "Sorry to dispute you, James, but the British had no reason to spark a revolution and I don't believe they would."

"That's what Bernard James said," Eleanor murmured dreamily, "the social worker who tried to help us. He couldn't understand why anyone would want to kill Albert either. But somebody did and Jake was there when it happened."

The two men froze, James's eyes still glued to the news clipping.

"The bomb explosion took place outside a country hotel in Surrey," she added, "a remote place where Albert was celebrating his 40th birthday party. Jake's band had been hired for the entertainment."

Her hands shook as she stared at her notes. Glancing towards the door, to be absolutely sure no one was listening, she began to dictate them.

"Jake saw someone parked in the lane directly opposite the minibus hired to take Mr Enfield's party home. But someone was lying underneath, tampering with it. He thought it was a mechanic. The man parked in the lane however seemed to be watching. His car was a shiny black Daimler. Jake didn't really get a proper look at his face but described him as stocky with blonde hair and dark glasses. He only left the party to collect an amp from their camper van..."

She broke off, jarred by the intensity of James's stare. His eyes pierced into her.

229

"At the end of the party, Jake watched Mr Enfield and his group step aboard the minibus. It drove a few yards down the road then exploded in a ball of flames. Jake wonders if the men he saw in the lane were responsible. He was so shocked, he told the police everything..."

"Jake was a witness," Charlie commented.

"Jake was the *only* witness," Eleanor echoed, "and this is where the plot thickens. A police officer singled him out; a man who seemed determined to hear Jake's evidence. He invited him to Scotland yard and interviewed him himself."

"Just him?" Charlie pressed.

"Yes," Eleanor said. "But he detained Jake for longer than necessary; forced him to repeat his statement over and over... and by the time he left, there was this van hanging around. And the next thing he knew, he'd been captured."

"They set a trap," Charlie muttered in disbelief, "and the police officer was in on it?"

"I guess so," Eleanor mumbled, biting back her anguish. "In fact, I might as well tell you Jake's enemies went to extraordinary lengths to end his life. That same officer handled the murder enquiry. It was a conspiracy they were determined to cover up. So they made out that Jake was a *drug dealer*; his shooting the result of some 'gang related feud.' I was the only person who knew the truth and this was the purpose of the press conference."

"Which is where you bumped into Mr Hampton," James concluded. "So where does he fit in? I didn't want to interrupt back then, but this man Jake described... stocky, blonde hair, expensive car. It actually sounds a bit like him."

"This is where my story becomes more interesting," Eleanor said, finally giving way to a wry smile. Bundling up her notes, she stuffed them back into the envelope. "It was the Merriman family who organised the press conference. One of the sons knew a journalist from NME and *he* managed to contact Jake's manager. The music press handled the story from an entirely different angle, see. I was hiding when the guests arrived and they included Mr Hampton. But at one point, I could no longer stomach their lies, so I confronted them." She shook her head. "I have never seen anyone lose control like he did!"

"But why do you think he reacted like that?" Charlie frowned.

"There is only one explanation," Eleanor said shakily. "Those men in there *were* Jake's killers, my suspicions confirmed when I saw this man! But I was scared, Charlie. I warned them about my file... that if anything happened to *me*, the contents would be leaked." She gripped the envelope in her hand, shaking it.

"You told me someone tried to steal it," Charlie whispered in dread.

"Exactly!" Eleanor reiterated.

James turned pale. "Eleanor," he breathed, "are you saying that the man responsible for the contract on Jake's life could have been Perry?"

"I don't know," she faltered, "but given his reaction at that press conference... it's the reason I tried to hide earlier."

"Jesus," Charlie whispered under his breath. "How come you've never told anyone? If this is the man who conspired to kill Jake, is it not possible he might be the man he saw by the minibus?"

"I have no proof of that, Charlie," Eleanor argued, "and you know why I kept quiet. They threatened my son. And if they could harm him *then,* they could still do so *now.*"

"Who made these threats?" Charlie pressed. "Was this down to Hampton, too?"

"They hired a man," Eleanor said, "a very dangerous man. Someone I would never dare cross, even after all this time. I couldn't bear the thought of Eli being hurt, which is the reason I left London..." She raised her head. "Yet Hampton *knew* we were living in Aldwyck. Like you say, there was an attempt to steal my file, which suggests we're in danger again." She shook her head. "Hampton's son was the one who spotted me. He remembered me from the pub..."

"So what are we to do?" James prompted her. "These are evil people, Eleanor, and they have got to be stopped."

"I agree," she nodded, "but how can we fight them?"

"Well, you might like to know I contacted Perry," James soothed. "I chose not to mention this over dinner, but I warned him to stay away from us and away from you! I wanted to make him *aware* that I'd contacted the police; and that any further intimidation would give them good grounds to prosecute."

"Are you sure that was wise?" Charlie breathed.

"I don't see why not," James said, "and as for that cottage, Perry only bought it so that his foul son could keep him up to date with everything. They obviously achieved their goal a little quicker, so they've decided to rent it instead."

"I see," Eleanor murmured.

She felt a surge of bitterness; the overwhelming thought of what James had been through to save his home... Yet that last vision of Perry's demonic face lingered, pushing her towards a decision.

"James, I won't deny I am frightened. But you're right, he has got to be stopped." She spoke coldly, a sudden hatred pounding through her veins. "I had no idea who he was when I met him at that press conference, but I do now... so the first thing I'll do is add his name to my file. If it's possible to gather more evidence, I will! I'll do it for you, James and for you, Charlie, but most of all, I owe it to Jake."

"Be careful, Eleanor," James responded. "You mustn't put yourself at risk."

"I won't," Eleanor reassured him.

"Don't forget she's got me to protect her," Charlie added. "She's not on her own, not like the first time..."

"I appreciate that, Charlie," James said weakly, "but I wouldn't want you to take on someone like Perry Hampton and *regret it*... like I did."

Eleanor turned to him, her anger spiking again. "Maybe he's the one who'll regret his decision," she said. "He should never have chosen Aldwyck to play his nasty games."

"No," James sighed, "and I'm sorry how this has ended. I feel a fool for allowing that man to manipulate me, which brings me to the next regrettable part of this discussion." He stared at them both, his face drained of hope. "Obviously, you won't be able to live here for much longer."

"Don't worry about us," Charlie intervened. "We can always find a house in Rosebrook. We'll start looking tomorrow."

"Charlie's right, James," Eleanor added gently. "I'm with Avalon on this. I don't feel safe in Aldwyck any more."

"Fair enough," James sighed, draining his last few drops of wine.

He smiled thinly, fighting to keep his composure, the impact of this day finally taking its toll. "Don't forget we have a month. I'll be contacting the estate agent myself tomorrow."

Eleanor felt a sudden heartfelt affection. "James, we will never forget these last months! They've been the best days of our lives. But before we leave, there is one more thing I have to say. Everything we discussed must remain a secret. That until we have *proof* against Perry, we must never speak of it..."

"Of course," James replied in earnest.

No one seemed to notice the glitter in his eyes but for some reason, he could not stop thinking about Albert Enfield. Such a whirlwind of thoughts threw him right back to 1972.

Something was troubling him; something yet to be realised.

PART TWO
The Face of Evil

Chapter Twenty-Six

I

As they set out next morning, the clouds rolled back to release a spreading pool of sunshine. It brightened the lawns, drawing the moisture from the grass in threads of white mist.

With heavy hearts, they wandered down the magnificent stone steps, anxious of the day ahead. There seemed little point in delaying their house hunting. The Hamptons were due to return in a month and would take exquisite pleasure in evicting them.

Andrew clasped James by the hand.

"I hope you find a way to get your house back," he said with conviction. "Those bastards don't deserve it."

"Well, thank you, Andrew," James replied warmly, squeezing his hand in return, "and good luck with your house hunting. I hope you find something."

Charlie was mulling over Andrew's words as he cruised down the driveway.

For days he had been brooding over the legality of what Hampton had done. How could this company, *Falcon Finance*, force James to the brink of bankruptcy, before swooping in with a seemingly altruistic offer? It was immoral.

The interior of the car fell silent and as he drove out of Aldwyck, everyone tried not to look too hard at the idyllic surroundings that had been their home for the last six months. Given the secrets they had shared last night though, it was unlikely Eleanor would want to set foot inside the village again. Such thoughts left him choked with unease.

Gradually they arrived in Rosebrook, where a familiar high street presented itself. Charlie was lucky to find a space by the public park, Andrew opening the back door, hopping out, before he had even switched off the engine.

"Mind if I go and see Matt?" he muttered furtively.

"Later," Charlie snapped. "We came here to look for accommodation, remember?"

Eleanor was next to step from the car, followed by the two children but their eyes were down. Anyone could see how traumatised they were from the sheer savagery of yesterday's conflict. Margaret had never forgotten the Hamptons from their altercation on the building site, Charlie reflected, and yet the nightmare lingered on.

"Where do we start?" Eleanor asked, falling into step beside him.

"I could go back to the letting agency," he replied. He threw her a wistful smile. "They did, after all, find us a house once before... What do you think?"

"I was thinking about visiting the Community Centre," Eleanor said. "There's a Citizens Advice Bureau and they're bound to keep an accommodation list. Neither of us are in full time employment, so we might be entitled to some help."

"Oh, don't worry about that," Charlie sighed. "I managed to keep hold of my savings from the last two jobs... you know, before I worked for James."

"But there's another reason I want to visit," Eleanor said, sliding her head close to whisper. "It's like Andrew says; I can't believe James lost his home to that monster. It's left me wondering if he's got any recourse."

"You must have read my mind," Charlie muttered back softly. "It would do no harm to ask. Do you want to meet up later?"

II

Drawn to the heart of Rosebrook, they paused by the war memorial opposite the Town Hall. It seemed a good place to rendezvous. Charlie had already spotted the letting agency.

As the shops petered out, Eleanor continued past the bus station with Elijah. Just to the other side was a street shaded by horse chestnut trees. Crossing the street, she saw the Community Centre; an imposing two storey block constructed in mud brown brick.

No sooner had they entered, they paused on the threshold. The bustle of activity inside was overwhelming, from groups of youths painting scenery, to a hall filled with elderly people. Some chatted over cups of tea, whilst others played cards. Reading the signs on the wall, Eleanor realised the Community Centre was home to several organisations, including the 'Citizens Advice Bureau' and 'Women's Royal Voluntary Service.' But as they lingered inside the hall, her eyes drifted to the cafeteria, managed by a team of older ladies.

The scene struck her as familiar. It reminded her of Toynbee Hall, an establishment she and Jake had turned to, when they were desperate for help.

Stirred by the memory, she glanced at Elijah, never to forget she had been pregnant at the time.

Determined to escape London, hindered by the evil men hunting them, it was at Toynbee Hall she had met Bernard James, a benevolent social worker who had stuck his neck out to help them.

"What now?" Elijah said dazedly.

"I'm not sure," Eleanor mused. "I saw a sign for the CAB but let's find someone to ask."

Inching her way across the hall, sensing curious glances from some of the older folk, she saw another set of doors and a corridor beyond. Without knowing why she found herself mysteriously drawn towards it, when a man swept into view. Gracefully slim with greying hair, he paused at the foot of the staircase.

For a second they just surveyed one another.

"Can I help you?"

"Um - yes," Eleanor faltered. "We're looking for accommodation in Rosebrook. I'm out of work right now, so I'm also after advice..."

"You've come to the right place then," he replied. "Follow me. We can have a little chat in my office."

As Eleanor followed him upstairs, she felt comforted by his presence. Despite his silver hair, he possessed the face of a man considerably younger. His delicate brows hovered above the gentlest of blue eyes, an animated smile tilting his features.

"Sorry, I should have introduced meself," he muttered. Eleanor picked up the hint of an Irish accent. "My name's Peter Summerville."

Eleanor found herself smiling back.

Moving with the fluid grace of a teenager, he swung around and crossed the room to pull a chair out. In fact, he so much reminded her of Jake.

"It's nice to meet you, Peter," she blurted. "I'm Eleanor Chapman and this is my son, Elijah. What is it you do here exactly?"

"I'm general manager," Peter responded warmly, "involved in a little bit of everything really. I look after the volunteers... it's their hard work that keeps the wheels rolling. We also run an Information Centre. May I ask what brought you here?"

Eleanor hesitated. She saw the smile slip from his face, leaving only empathy in its wake.

"My son and I have lived in a caravan for the last thirteen years," she began. "That was until very recently."

Before she knew it, she was telling him about Charlie; his role in overseeing the restoration of Westbourne House...

"Westbourne House?" Peter echoed, cocking an eyebrow. "How lovely! Do I take it you've had to leave then?"

"I'm afraid so," Eleanor said, her voice starting to break a little. "The owner was forced to sell it and now the buyers want us out."

"Do go on," he prompted her.

"James is such a good man," she added with a sob.

Elijah fidgeted in his chair but it was Peter who reached out. The concern in his eyes coaxed the truth out, no matter how painful. He did not interrupt as she galloped through their story; from the details of the restoration, to the agonising slump in business that forced James to secure a loan... but her revelations about

236

the people who had bankrupted him brought out the true force of her sentiments. An escaping tear rolled down her cheek.

"They were determined to get their hands on the house at any cost! Sorry to offload. I haven't told anyone how I really feel and as for poor James..."

"Such a terrible thing," Peter muttered, as much to himself as to her. "I'm so sorry, and for your friend, too. I fear there are some wicked people in this world. Please don't cry."

Passing her a tissue, he shot a glance at Elijah and winked.

"I wouldn't worry," he tried to reassure her. "He'll find himself a lovely new home, so he will! But what about you? What exactly are *you* looking for?"

"Maybe we can rent somewhere," Elijah piped up shyly.

"We keep a list of rented accommodation in the Information Centre," Peter nodded. "Come with me. I'll see what I can find."

Eleanor couldn't help but feel touched by his concern as he led them back towards the hub of the Community Centre. He never ran out of chatter; as curious to know about Elijah, who was delighted to tell him about his sketching. Yet only as they hovered on the edge of the hall, did Eleanor discover something even more astonishing.

"Hectic here, isn't it?" Peter laughed. "I don't suppose you've seen anything like it!"

"Oh, but I have," Eleanor mused. "It reminds me of somewhere I visited with Eli's dad... a place in London known as Toynbee Hall."

Peter's eyes lit up in awe. "Toynbee Hall? That's where I did me training in the 70s! East London was desperately poor in them days..."

"The 70s," Eleanor pondered. "What year? Did you know Bernard James?"

His eyes turned misty as if the words had enticed some memory. "Bernard James," he whispered. "That man was both my mentor and my saviour. Oh Eleanor, you have no idea..." A lump rippled in his throat.

"How did you meet him?" Eleanor pressed.

"It's a long story," Peter said. "I was sixteen, a runaway living rough on the streets of London. If it hadn't been for Bernard, I would have surely died..."

"I-I'm so sorry," Eleanor whispered.

"But he took me to hospital," Peter continued. "I know I shouldn't be telling you this, but I started working at Toynbee Hall as a volunteer. He taught me everything I know and so I followed in his footsteps. He's the reason I'm here!"

Eleanor felt a groundswell of compassion. "He took care of me too," she said. "Thank goodness there are men like Bernard in this world..."

As their eyes locked, he seemed to gaze right into her soul, bringing back that earlier sense of camaraderie. *Was it possible their paths had crossed?*

"I've had an idea," he announced. "Did you say you were a single parent?"

"Yes," Eleanor frowned, wondering where this was leading.

"And there are five of you?" he persisted. "It's just that... one of the almshouses has recently become vacant. Why don't you come and take a look?"

Turning away from the hall, they reversed through the corridor towards a fire exit. Once outside, Eleanor found herself gazing across the same side street they had passed earlier. The screen of horse chestnuts concealed a row of terraced houses. She couldn't help thinking how pretty they looked, painted in pastel colours, their wide front windows gazing out over a small strip of lawn.

"What's an almshouse?" Elijah quizzed.

"Traditionally, almshouses were to help the poor," Peter answered, "mainly old folk who wanted to stay in the community but retain a bit of independence. This is charitable housing, which we administer from here. But the rules have changed recently, more so with the rise in *sheltered accommodation* for the elderly. The association has started renting them out to low income families, regardless of age."

"We're not exactly poor," Eleanor said. "We wouldn't qualify for one of these, surely?"

Peter flashed her a secretive smile. "You would if I was to whisper a few words in the right ears. The one thing you have in your favour is your local connections. All those years living in Aldwyck will be an advantage and you say your Charlie is out of work? I think you have a strong case. The rent is low too, about half what you would pay elsewhere in Rosebrook."

He felt into his jacket pocket, extracting an ample set of keys.

Eleanor watched numbly. She didn't want to build her hopes up. Yet the moment they stepped inside the house, she knew her prayers had been answered. Her first impression was of a large light room, the windows stripped of curtains, allowing the sunlight to pour in. The room was unfurnished but Eleanor could see its potential; the decor a little shabby but a good sized kitchen, bathroom and one more undefined room, which could be a dining room or even an extra bedroom.

Three small bedrooms awaited them at the top of the stairs. Eleanor adored the low, sloping ceilings, the dormer windows reminding her of the cottages in Aldwyck. They would definitely have to invest some of Charlie's savings in furniture but given a little work, this place could be turned into a haven.

"How much is the rent?" she asked Peter eagerly.

"£75 a week," Peter grinned. "So what do you think?"

"I think it's great, Mum!" Elijah answered for her.

At first Eleanor said nothing. Captured in a choke-hold of emotion, she had never imagined such kindness in the aftermath of the Hamptons' visit.

"I'd love to take you up on your offer," she whispered huskily, "as long as you can clear it with the association. I don't know what Charlie'll say but I'm sure he'll be delighted."

It was almost 12:00 noon when they returned to the communal hall. Then just as they were escorted in the direction of the front door, a deep voice resonated from the hallway.

"Ah, Peter!"

Peter spun around, seeing another man emerge from his office.

He didn't seem to notice Eleanor at first, though she found herself studying *him*. Taller than Peter, he was formally dressed. A crucifix glinted below his neckline, his brown hair peppered with grey. Yet something disturbingly familiar about his blue eyes struck her. Eleanor picked through her memory, wondering where she had seen him... Until finally, he clocked her presence, his eyes widening with recognition.

"Heavens above," he gasped, fingers creeping towards his crucifix.

"What is it, Reggie?" Peter frowned.

"Reggie," Eleanor echoed. "Reginald Magnus?"

Bernard's assistant. She had never felt entirely comfortable in his presence, even when he had gone out of his way to fulfil Bernard's wishes - escorting her and Jake to the hidden, underground bed-sit, that was destined to be their last sanctuary.

"I remember you," the man murmured, "you were in some sort of danger..." A look of horror clouded his face as his eyes fell to Elijah. "Is this your son?"

"Yes, Mr Magnus," Eleanor said cautiously.

Turning to Peter, she smiled, filled with an overwhelming desire to end this conversation before Elijah became suspicious.

"Small world, isn't it? But right now, we need to get going. It's time to meet the others but we'll be back, I promise. Thanks for all your help."

"It's no problem," Peter faltered.

Frozen on the spot, he watched as they pushed their way through the doors, then turned and gaped at Reginald.

"What was all that about? You've already met this lady?"

"Oh yes," Reginald shivered. "I remember her well, as I remember the father of her son."

"So what happened to him?" Peter kept pressing.

Reginald lowered his head. "He was murdered," he finished darkly.

III

"I don't believe it," Charlie spluttered, staring at the almshouse thirty minutes later. "You clever girl! How did you manage to wangle it?"

There had been a definite slump in his posture when she returned to the war

239

memorial. But with a limited choice of accommodation, apart from one ex-council house stuck in a concrete jungle, the only other choice was some ramshackle house split into flats. It needed extensive renovation.

Heart fit to burst, Eleanor could not wait to tell him about the almshouse.

At first, Charlie seemed sceptical, more so when she dragged them to the Community Centre. Something about its drab outer shell disheartened him. Yet the feeling quickly dissolved.

Uplifted by the volunteers and the bustling atmosphere embracing them, Charlie was as pleased to meet Peter as Eleanor. Revisiting the almshouse had thrilled him, though on this occasion they were accompanied by Reginald.

For some reason, his presence unnerved Eleanor. She didn't like the way he stared at her, picking up waves of disapproval.

Charlie, on the other hand, had impressed him. Quick to express concern over a spreading stain of damp on the Community Centre ceiling, he feared it might collapse. Reginald had made some forlorn comment about waiting for council funding - until Charlie insisted the work was so vital, he was of a mind to fix it himself as a favour to them.

Already they were excited at the prospect of moving into the almshouse. Conveniently situated on the edge of town, it was perfect for the youngsters. In fact, this could be a brand new start for all of them.

Yet she could not suppress her fear for James. She had so little to show from her visit to the CAB, other than a leaflet explaining how to consult a Financial Ombudsman. Eleanor hoped she might inspire them to begin their own house search; wondering if there was a chance that they too, would consider Rosebrook. For she had never forgotten her pledge to protect James's children, especially in the light of their recent turmoil.

Chapter Twenty-Seven

I

On the advent of moving to Rosebrook, a fitting celebration took place in honour of William's birthday. He wished for nothing more than a cosy dinner party, accompanied by the Baileys, who he had grown to love like a second family.

Everyone seemed subdued, though. The Hamptons had breathed a baleful air into the household and it hung in the corridors like a poison. His father looked more frail than ever; a shadow of his former self, shuffling around with his walking stick. Avalon too, harboured a tortured look.

A party was what everyone needed to cheer them up, William thought. Strolling into the restaurant, he relished the thought of the exquisite food being prepared, the promise they would drink champagne later. The table had been beautifully laid out with candles, brass holders gleaming, a vase in the centre filled with the loveliest roses from his father's garden.

"So, you're moving into the almshouse tomorrow?" he smiled at Elijah.

He had been the first to wander into the restaurant with Margaret, whilst Elliot hovered in the background, polishing wine glasses.

"Are you excited?"

"I am," Elijah enthused. "Nothing'll ever be the same as living here, but I'm glad we've found somewhere else."

"I'll never forget Westbourne House," Margaret added dreamily. "We're gonna miss you..."

She bit back the sentence, before saying any more, a flush of colour springing to her face. There was no denying William looked good in a black dinner suit as he moved around the table, lighting candles. Beautifully cut, it emphasised his height and slenderness.

Margaret lowered her eyes, as if embarrassed to be caught staring.

"By the way, this is for you," Elijah said.

Momentarily breaking the tension, he slid a parcel into William's hands. Without hesitation, he tore the wrapping off.

"Oh cool!" he gasped. "I've been after this for yonks!"

It was a copy of 'The Complete Naff Guide,' a tongue-in-cheek journal published in the early 80s.

Next to appear was Avalon, demure in a simple black party dress, her hair loose around her shoulders. She smiled gently, though no one could ignore the lingering sadness in her eyes.

"Cheer up, Sis!" William called out, holding up the book. "Look what I've got! Now sit down and have a glass of wine. This is supposed to be a party."

"I'm fine, really," Avalon sighed, easing herself into a chair.

The room plunged into silence but everyone seemed to be looking at her.

"No one could blame you for being upset," Elliot eventually broke in. "That Hampton fellow has got a lot to answer for..."

"I've always been scared of Ben," Avalon shuddered, "but last Sunday, I saw a really nasty side to him. I dread to think what would have happened if you two hadn't muscled in."

"It was nothing," Elijah shrugged. "You did pretty well to sock him in the face!"

"That's the trouble," Avalon added. "It's not like he's going to forget, is it?"

Elijah and Margaret looked at each other in alarm.

"Don't dwell on it!" William snapped, moving across to the drinks cabinet.

"But he said such horrible things," Margaret gulped, "not just to Avalon, but to you! Why does he hate you so much?"

"Oh, I don't know," William shrugged. "I don't s'pose he's ever forgiven me for jumping on his precious motorbike and taking off on it!"

Before anyone had a chance to respond, Andrew came sauntering in. Wafting Kouros aftershave, he was dressed to impress in a richly coloured paisley shirt and black jeans.

"You're not talking about that nutcase again are you?" he snorted.

"Avalon's still a bit shaken," Elijah jumped in defensively.

Eleanor and Charlie must have overheard them. They paused on the threshold, perhaps wondering if they would ever set eyes on the restaurant again, once Perry had taken up residence.

"Have you heard any more from them?" Eleanor asked.

"Not since Sunday," Avalon said, "and I hope we never do."

"Evil people," Elliot grunted as he flitted around the table, pouring drinks. "James spoke to his friends, you know, the Fortescues. Cyril was appalled. Insisted he should sue. Even *he* would have lent him some money, if he'd just confided in him."

"Hmm," William muttered, joining their circle. "That's what I suggested. Anyway, let's just relax and enjoy our party. Dad will be down in a minute."

"I should go up and help him," Elliot added. "He's a little unsteady on his feet now, especially when tackling those stairs... I won't deny I'm worried."

As Elliot vanished, so William took his place. Scooping up the tea towel, he took over the polishing of glasses, until eventually the conversation shifted to their own situation.

A month hardly seemed like any time at all to find a new home.

242

Although Avalon did confess they had found a pleasing country house in Surrey to view.

"The gardens are gorgeous, which will be nice for Dad," she said with a smile.

As if on cue, James appeared in the doorway with Elliot. Gazing across fondly, he hobbled into the room and like William, was dressed formally in a black dinner suit. He looked unquestionably smart, Eleanor thought, though its sombre shade emphasised his pallor.

Unable to hold back, she swept across the room to embrace him.

"James," she whispered.

He was fading fast, she could sense it, having long recognised the signs in her nursing career. The expression on his face seemed beyond sadness; more *a look of defeat,* which left her uneasy. As she kissed his cheek, his skin felt soft and dry, a little like old leather.

"And how is my lovely Eleanor?" James murmured. He touched the back of her head. "Looking beautiful as ever, even with the Rastafarian dreadlocks!"

"Dad!" Avalon gasped in shock.

Eleanor laughed lightly. "Do you know, James, I've been seriously thinking about getting them cut, but I feel as if they've become a part of me."

"Always be true to yourself," James murmured, staring deep into her eyes. "God only knows there are enough charlatans in this world." Drawing his head close, he whispered in her ear. "We need to talk, but later... There is something important I need to tell you."

At last they took their seats. Despite the fact it was his birthday, William proved to be an excellent host by assisting Elliot in serving the drinks. No sooner had he poured a glass of chilled white wine for Eleanor, he immediately began quizzing them about their new home again.

"Come on, spill the beans!" he grinned at Elijah. "What is this almshouse like?"

"Nice," Elijah blurted, sensing Andrew had been about to butt in. "It's got three attic bedrooms and a lounge. There's even a fourth room downstairs, but Andrew bagged it for himself."

"Seemed the best idea to me," Andrew shrugged, "then I don't have to share with you! At least I'm not going to disturb anyone if I get home late."

Charlie raised his eyebrows.

"Elijah's right, though," he then mused, addressing the whole group now. "Traditionally almshouses were for the poor, but this is a family-sized house and perfect for us. Give us a couple of weeks and we'll have that place turned into a palace!"

"It needs redecorating," Eleanor chipped in. "Margaret's going to help me make some curtains and cushions too, aren't you, love?"

As Margaret nodded joyfully, pleased to be included, Avalon flashed them a smile.

"Tell you what," she said, "we've got masses of paint left from the guest rooms we decorated. There are some lovely shades, Eleanor. Why don't you take some?"

"That's very kind," Eleanor smiled back.

"It's nothing!" James blustered. "Which reminds me of something else I wanted to ask you. Is the house furnished, Charlie?" A twinkle leapt in his eye as he said it.

"Not fully," Charlie replied, "but I've sourced a beautiful second hand dining table..."

"Well, before you buy anything else," James added, "let me know what you need. Because if there is anything in this place you could make use of, I'd like you to take it."

"I can't do that!" Charlie spluttered. "The furniture here is exquisite, far too good for us!"

"Rubbish!" James barked. "Don't be so humble. I've finished my inventory and we've decided which items we're keeping. Anything with a yellow sticker on it is going to be auctioned, so at least take a look. If it doesn't go, it means those ghastly Hamptons will get their hands on it, and if I'm honest, I'd sooner dump it!"

A ripple of laughter arose around the table, scattering away any lingering tension.

Finally everyone started to relax, the wine taking effect. Within minutes, Bryony and Angelo emerged from the kitchen, bearing trays laden with food. This splendid feast included the light and golden quiches they were reputed for, a hand-raised pork pie and a side of salmon nestling on a bed of watercress leaves. There were bowls of salad, mixed canapés, as well as platters of cold meats, pickles and cheeses.

As the last tray was lowered onto the table, both chefs joined the party. But before William had a chance to rise, Elliot placed a gentle hand upon his shoulder.

"Allow me to serve the drinks," he smiled. "Relax, William, this is your birthday."

"Thanks, Elliot," William smiled in gratitude, "and thanks to Angelo and Bryony for preparing this lovely grub! Cheers everyone!"

"Happy birthday, son," James announced, "and congratulations to our friends here, for their success in finding a new home. Well done, folks!"

There followed a simultaneous clink of glasses but as Eleanor turned to

James, she seemed unable to drag her eyes away. Observing his gentle statuesque face, she felt especially close to him tonight; not only for everything he had done to help her, but the companionship they had shared.

"So, I hear *you're* going to view a house tomorrow," she prompted him.

"Yes," James said, "a lovely stone-built manor house over Surrey way..."

"Have you ever thought of moving to Rosebrook?" Eleanor cut in. The words popped out before she could stop them. "Think about it, James. We can stay in close contact, which'd be great for the kids. There are some really beautiful properties in town and while they may be out of our financial reach, they're certainly not out of yours! I know you love the countryside but face facts, you're not getting any younger..." She broke off, afraid to voice her real fears.

"There is another advantage," Charlie intervened. "I appreciate you feel you may have *lost* Westbourne House, but you can still keep an eye on it. Any alterations the Hamptons make will require planning permission. It's a historic building, James!"

"That's not a bad idea, Dad," Avalon whispered, caught up in a spiral of hope.

James hovered by the table, as if digesting this. "Maybe you're right," he admitted. "We can still take a look at this place in Surrey, but we won't rush into a decision yet. In the meantime, do tuck in, folks. There's enough food to feed an army and I'm ravenous!"

II

It turned out to be an uplifting evening. Everyone moved around the restaurant in overlapping circles, savouring the wondrous fare. Occasionally pausing to top their plates up, they tumbled into easy banter; circulating, swapping chairs and helping themselves to more wine.

In one corner, Angelo was chuckling at something Charlie said. In another, Eleanor conversed with Bryony over interior design and Avalon had joined them.

The kids harped on endlessly about their schools. Andrew in particular, admitted he had never been much of an academic but was curious to know about life at private school.

Elijah leaned back in his chair and sipped his coke. Compelled to go along with Andrew, he had never much liked school either. Yet he was listening with half an ear to Avalon's conversation.

Interior design was becoming a popular subject and to Elijah, the ambience of his home had always been special. He had grown to love the caravan, simply because his mother made it so beautiful. But guessing she would work the same

245

magic on the almshouse, he had a few ideas of his own...

Before darkness fell, the youngsters melted into the grounds where they were last seen chasing each other around the trees. James insisted they were to be back indoors by 9.00. William's birthday cake was waiting to be unveiled, along with chilled champagne to round off the party.

For the time being though, he made sure the adults were tucked comfortably inside the library. Elliot joined them, wheeling in a trolley of fine wines and liquors.

Charlie must have known James had something to discuss with Eleanor, watching warily as the two of them left the room.

Once concealed in their family lounge, James switched on a table lamp. Requesting Eleanor close the curtains, he limped towards the sofa, before easing himself into it.

A mist of secrecy surrounded them.

"Eleanor," he began, "what I have to tell you is of crucial importance."

"Is this about your health, James?" she whispered.

"No. Though despite all the pills I'm on, I am still suffering from giddy spells. This is why I wanted to talk to you sooner rather than later..."

She leaned closer to meet his gaze, her expression one of steely resolve.

"This is to do with the secret you divulged the other day," he continued in a low voice. "That business with the car bomb. Ever since hearing your story, something's been troubling me. So I did a little digging. All my life, I've kept a diary, but I was curious to know what I'd written in 1972 and then I remembered something." He closed his eyes.

"Go on," Eleanor murmured.

"It seems your Jake was not the only person who may have seen Perry Hampton that day."

Eleanor froze.

"It came to me, the instant I read one of my old diary entries," James shivered. "A few days after the atrocity, a friend came to visit me. Her name was Evelyn Webster. She and her husband had booked a room to celebrate their wedding anniversary. So Avril and I invited them to join us for a discreet supper. We were discussing the news. Evelyn was engaged in politics, you see. She regularly attended Westminster and spoke of some *political advisor* she knew; someone she had dated at university. I even jotted down his name..." He shook his head as the memories bombarded him. "She clearly remembered bumping into him at a service station in Surrey."

He felt a creeping chill as he relived the scene; a conversation that had suddenly taken on a whole new meaning...

"I was surprised to see him out in the sticks!"

Evelyn's eyes had been alight with intrigue, her features distinct in the candlelight. Stealing a glance in the mirror, she patted her dark hair, elegant in its chignon.

"I may look a little older but Perry hasn't changed! Same powerful presence and thick blonde hair... a little red in the face perhaps but then he always was. But I was amazed to bump into him so far from London."

"What exactly is the relevance of all this?" her husband complained.

"It was a few miles away from that village, Basil!" she snapped in irritation. "The one where that dreadful car bomb went off! He pulled up at the service station in that lovely Daimler of his... But even more curious was a man in overalls jumping out of the back!"

At this point, she had seized James's attention, his hands unsteady as he poured the wine. It slopped onto the table cloth, leaving a spreading red stain. Avril tutted.

"This is what confused me," Evelyn continued, "some chap with a beard. Hardly the sort of company Perry would keep. I wandered across to say 'hello' but he seemed shocked to see me. And when I asked him who the man was, he insisted he was just some hitch hiker..."

"Didn't you ought to mention this to the police?" James recalled asking her.

"I can't!" she spluttered. "Perry's a friend! Apparently, he was visiting his mistress that day and begged me not to say anything."

"I was talking about the hitch hiker," James said darkly. "Don't you think this sounds a little suspicious? What if this 'person' had something to do with that car bomb?"

She had turned very pale, her smooth fingers twisting around her wine glass. "Do you know it never even occurred to me. You're right, James - maybe I should speak to him..."

"And did she?" Eleanor intervened.

Her voice became distant, lost in a nebulous cloud of memories.

"I can't be sure," James sighed, shaking himself out of his reverie. "Obviously the name *Perry* meant nothing to me at the time, but everything seems so different now. It never occurred to me *this friend* she spoke of might actually be involved. I mean, even if Evelyn had gone to the police, her story would carry very little weight. She bumped into a friend who just happened to pick up some hitchhiker. So what? But marry it up with what Jake saw..."

"Oh my God," Eleanor whispered. She appeared almost trancelike.

"I know," James said. "Perry must have been desperate to silence *the only other witness*, before his evidence went public. Or Evelyn would have put two and two together."

247

"James, I cannot thank you enough for sharing this," Eleanor said numbly, "and you're right. It all makes sense now - so what do you think I should do?"

"You could start by finding Evelyn," James insisted. "She might still be involved in politics but I'm certain she will verify what I've just told you."

He saw the horror seep into her face. "But what if word gets back to Perry?" She gave a subtle shake of the head. "James... I think we may have to bide our time. Perry is on to me! He knows I'm a threat and this could have terrible repercussions."

"Alright," James placated her. "I understand the fear of reprisal, especially for Elijah."

"And I don't think Perry operates alone," she shivered. "I bet there are others out there, eager to do his bidding..."

"In that case, the next best thing you could do is record our conversation in that file of yours," James added sagely.

"I will," Eleanor murmured.

"Good girl," James nodded with the first flicker of a smile. "I'll even give you that page from my diary. You said you needed evidence. Maybe this will help you to seek the justice you've always wanted."

Tears glittered in her eyes. "Thank you, James," she said, "but let's just get our lives back on track. We can sort all this later, as soon as we're more settled. I promise."

Slowly she rose to her feet.

"We should go and join the others," James said, reaching for his stick.

As he levered himself off the sofa, Eleanor swooped in to help him. Pausing to face each other, they joined hands.

"*Please* consider the possibility of moving to Rosebrook," her voice rose huskily. "We're worried about you. Even more so, after what those Hamptons did..."

"There, there, don't go agonising about them," James smiled. "We'll survive."

"I said I'd look out for your children," she added. "Charlie will pass on our telephone number... and we'd love to take you up on your offer of furniture! You've been so very kind to us."

"Oh, stop it!" James blustered, "I'll be getting all emotional in a minute."

Hooking his arm through hers, they gradually made their way back to the library.

Yet Eleanor paused.

"You said you were selling everything, but what about your land? Are you selling that too? In which case, should I move my caravan?"

James released a gentle laugh. "Oh no! The house might be sold but I have no intention of selling my land. The surrounding woods and farmland remain in my ownership for now. When the children inherit it, they can do what they like, but in some small way, I hope they'll hang on to it. All the while the land is private, it means that someone like Perry Hampton cannot develop it and this will be my last legacy to seal our family connection here. Consider it payback."

Eleanor smiled at that. For despite Perry's scheming, James was not about to disappear.

Chapter Twenty-Eight

I

On the same day as the Baileys moved into the almshouse, Peter Summerville found himself mulling over Charlie's concerns about the ceiling. Delving into the filing cabinet for the paperwork, he felt a stab of irritation. It had been many weeks since he had written to the Council.

He stared at the original estimate addressed to *Councillor Swan*, his hand levitating above the telephone. But filled with an urge to get the matter resolved quickly, he slid the paperwork into an envelope. It took just minutes to reach the council headquarters by foot.

Once inside the building, a long flight of stairs guided him up to the planning department. He wandered into reception to find it empty, so with nothing better to do than wait, he lowered himself into a chair.

His thoughts settled on the Baileys, having rarely met a family so virtuous. There was no denying it had awakened a sense of fulfilment in him, but something about Eleanor's plight stirred him. He would never forget the pain hidden in the depths of those golden eyes. Yet that critical mention of *Bernard* plucked an even deeper chord. Her life, like his, had been torn apart; an intuition proved correct, as soon as Reginald let slip about her boyfriend's murder.

So Peter had fought tooth and nail to reserve the almshouse for them.

Sure enough, he had met resistance, surprisingly as much from Reginald as anyone. But fortunately, Charlie's offer to mend the ceiling had swayed him. Peter closed his eyes where once again the face of Eleanor sprang to mind, bringing light to his personal darkness. Unlike Reginald, he could see past the dreadlocks and nose piercing, inspired by her inner goodness...

"Can I help you?" a voice echoed from the doorway.

Peter glanced up to see a man hovering. Dressed in a suit, he possessed pale, smooth features, a slightly down-turned but shapely mouth, matched by evenly spaced blue eyes.

"I hope so," Peter replied. "I'm chasing up an application for a grant made several weeks ago. It's for some urgent repairs to the Community Centre. I wrote to Councillor Swan..."

"Ah, I'm afraid Councillor Swan has been unwell for some time," the man said softly. "Perhaps I could look into this on your behalf. Come through."

Peter rose to his feet, somewhat unnerved by this professional dark-haired stranger. "I-I'm sorry to hear about Councillor Swan," he faltered. "You - you haven't told me *your* name."

The man gazed deep into his eyes. "My name is Robin Whaley," he smiled silkily.

He led Peter into a large open plan office. Alongside a gentle bustle of activity, various telephone conversations hummed in the air. As if sensing the need for privacy, Robin guided him into a room which was clearly *his* office. He summoned a secretary to bring some coffee and source whatever documents she could find on Rosebrook Community Centre.

"I really appreciate your help," Peter resumed. "I've brought the paperwork with me as it happens. Here, you might want to take a look..."

Sliding himself into his plush executive chair, Robin immediately began scanning the document. The application had been made in August. Yet it was almost October. The ageing sash windows rattled in the wind, drawing in chilly draughts, which in turn evoked complaints from the older, arthritic visitors. To make matters worse, a gradual increase in rainfall had culminated in water leaking in, the ceiling saturated, from where it dripped to the floor in puddles.

"Winter's coming," Peter pressed. "The wet floor is proving to be a hazard..."

He then went on to explain Charlie's proposal. He had after all, agreed to do the work as a favour, a professional builder no less. All they wanted from the council was to supply the materials although at first, Robin seemed skeptical.

"He just wants to get the job done before the whole lot caves in! I realise the council has a tight budget but the materials will only cost about two hundred pounds."

Before Robin had a chance to respond, a tap on the door caught his attention. He rose to open it to find his secretary lingering, bearing a file and two coffees.

"Thank you," Robin muttered before closing it again.

Stealing a glance inside the file, he digested the contents.

"You're right," he eventually relented, "on the grander scale of council expenditure, this sum seems quite paltry. In which case, I am going to agree to it with immediate effect."

Peter sat very still, coffee cup suspended. Given the bureaucracy councils were renowned for, he could hardly believe he was hearing this.

"All it needs is a signature," Robin smiled in earnest. "In the meantime, tell your friend to go ahead. We just need an invoice for the materials from the builder's merchant."

"Are you serious?" Peter frowned.

"Peter, this council has kept you waiting for long enough," Robin reassured him. "I see no point in delaying the matter any further. Please accept my decision as a goodwill gesture."

Peter was so choked with gratitude, he couldn't finish his coffee. Rising shakily, he felt an overwhelming urge to return to the Community Centre before he changed his mind.

He threw Robin his sunniest of smiles. "I am so pleased to have met you, Mr Whaley. Perhaps you'd like to come over and see the work when it's finished - visit our Community Centre."

"It'd be a pleasure, Peter," Robin replied, "and consider me an ally."

Just before he left, Robin scrawled his signature on the application form then led him towards the photocopier. He paused by a rack of leaflets. Peter's eyes were drawn to it where one stood out in particular: *Council Customer Care Award*.

"Ah, that's a new incentive scheme issued by the personnel department," Robin dropped out casually. "If any member of the public feels they've received exemplary service from a council employee, they can nominate them for an award."

Without hesitation, Peter pulled out one of the leaflets and pocketed it.

"I cannot think of anyone I'd sooner nominate than you, Mr Whaley..." He threw him a boyish grin. "Thanks again for agreeing to our repairs."

II

Later that evening, Robin found himself basking in triumph.

Such an opportunity to schmooze another naive member of the public not only came as second nature but left an intoxicating sense of power. But there had been something quite alluring about Peter; easy going, passionate and easy to manipulate. Peter had no idea his application had already been approved. Robin had gleaned that little gem of information, as soon as he peaked inside the file. It was perhaps unfortunate that due to Councillor Swan's illness, he had never received the letter. But what a pleasure it was to oblige his request, leaving that young man stammering with gratitude.

It had taken Robin ten years to claw his way up the ladders of authority, securing himself an influential position in the planning department. He might even make the grade of *senior planning officer* if things continued to run smoothly. Thus, a few nominations for the 'Customer Care Award' would go a long way to securing his promotion.

Just as he relished that thought, the telephone rang.

"Hello, Robin," a familiar voice purred from the ear piece.

"Perry!" Robin gasped with pleasure. "How are things?"

"I've got some rather good news," Perry began to gloat. "It looks as if we'll be moving down your way after all. You are now speaking to the new owner of Westbourne House."

"Perry, what marvellous news!" Robin gushed. "However did you manage it? You left me with the impression the current owner had declined your partnership..."

"And much to his regret," Perry said icily, "but you know me, Robin. Once I set my heart on something, I never back down."

Robin listened with growing wonderment, as Perry exposed the sheer ruthlessness behind his campaign.

The seeds had been planted from the day he had arranged the survey. For a while, James had been governed by it, allowing Perry a delicious degree of control. Yet James had thwarted him, the one spark guaranteed to ignite a more malicious side of his nature. He felt no shame in setting out to ruin James financially. He knew about the auction and the fundraising ball; doubtful James would declare any of this additional income to the Inland Revenue.

So Perry had shamelessly leaked it, knowing the tax man would catch up with him.

The second part of his plan involved destroying the reputation of his idyllic hotel. And that first first derogatory article in 'Country House' precipitated the process very nicely.

"James was a fool to think he could outsmart me," Perry sneered down the telephone.

He was in his element, relishing the waves of pleasure rolling over him.

But James's decision to recruit his old adversary, Charles Bailey, had been a foolish one; a pivotal day in which Perry had feared he could gain the upper hand. Edward's survey would be challenged; the restoration might succeed, despite his clever machinations.

"That's why I had to make him bankrupt," he added pompously, "my final game plan to ensure he took out a loan with *my* company!"

It wasn't difficult. Perry enjoyed the advantage of having a few spies working for him; the MD of 'Heritage Building and Restoration' for example. Hence, no sooner had he discovered James was *desperate to secure a loan*, the delivery of one of his special fliers had been critical.

But it took just one default on the repayments to engender a harsh penalty and to his ultimate victory, James had caved in.

"What a very well-thought out plan," Robin indulged him.

Perry allowed himself a smile, conscious there were darker elements to his strategy. Yet he had no desire to divulge Ben's role; even though he had excelled in his long term plan to unhinge the Barton-Wells girl. Such a concept however, led him to the next inevitable part of the discussion. For his momentary hubris was overshadowed by something more worrying: *Eleanor Chapman.*

"It seems Miss Chapman has a habit of hiding in the background," he finished.

"You had no joy locating that file of hers?" Robin asked.

Perry paused, thinking about her solicitor in Holborn. It seemed such an obvious place and yet Nathan had found no sign of it.

"No, which puts me in something of a dilemma. I feel exposed. In fact, we both have reason to be worried, given the *stories* she may have recorded..."

He felt a sudden shiver. There was no doubt Eleanor must have realised the extent of his villainy by now. *'Someone had Jake killed to protect a secret...'* Her words cut deep.

The burning question was how much had Jake Jansen actually told her?

He had only one fleeting memory of the auburn haired youth who had delivered his statement to Inspector Hargreaves. And it turned him cold.

"She cannot prove anything," Robin drawled.

"We don't know that!" Perry kept ranting. "She is the only person who knows the truth and that bothers me! What a pity we couldn't have just dealt with her, same as her pitiful boyfriend! Yet that file of hers is our biggest problem!"

"So, what do you intend to do, Perry?" Robin pressed. "Have you said anything to her?"

"I warned her never to *cross me again*," he snapped, "but somehow it didn't seem enough."

Before he had a chance to say more however, Robin broke the deadlock.

"There is one way we can guarantee her silence... through fear of anything happening to her son."

"Oh yes," Perry uttered darkly, "do you know I had almost forgotten about him."

He felt a surge of malevolence. Reliving that scene in the bar, he recalled the wiry chestnut-haired boy who had flown across the room to Avalon's defence. Perry felt the smile creep back onto his face. William had referred to him as *his friend* but of course, that was before he knew of Eleanor's presence. This had to be the boy to whom Robin referred.

"How much do you know about him?" he probed.

"He must be thirteen," Robin said, "and no doubt attends Rosebrook Comprehensive. Maybe you have the advantage, Perry. After all, they'll be living on your doorstep soon."

"That's right," Perry finished. "In which case, I suggest we wait for an opportunity. There is bound to be a time when that boy is on his own. I'll make sure Nathan is around and then I promise you, Eleanor Chapman will receive another warning..."

III

Ironically, less than half a mile away from Robin, Elijah was making himself at home in the almshouse, for within the course of a week the place was transformed.

Hauling up the rough orange sitting room carpet, Charlie had hired a sanding machine to smooth down the floorboards. Andrew, assisted by Elijah, applied several coats of varnish and with the exposed boards gleaming, Eleanor chose an oriental rug from Westbourne House. Its decorative blue border enhanced the golden-brown wood. But nothing added more glamour than the classic Chesterfield suite James had donated from his library. The glossy leather exuded a heady fragrance, which would forever evoke memories. In keeping with the theme, Charlie constructed a bookcase, which Andrew varnished the same shade as the floorboards. Thus, with an abundance of natural wood, their home was gradually developing character.

Concentrating on soft furnishings inspired Eleanor to browse the stalls of Rosebrook Market. Rolls of fabric in every colour and texture lay stacked beneath green and white striped canopies. But with the predominant colours leaning towards blues, golds and earthy browns, she sought Elijah's opinion. Eventually they agreed on a glazed cotton chintz, whose mottled stripes captured every shade and Eleanor purchased several yards of it.

For the next few days, she and Margaret set about the task of making some full length drapes for the lounge, matching tie backs and an abundance of scatter cushions.

Margaret, who had developed a flair for Home Economics, was delighted to help with the cutting, the pinning of hems, and tacking on frills and piping. Eleanor in turn, sewed them with incredible speed and dexterity, using her old Singer sewing machine.

But throughout these darkening evenings, she described the years she was employed as an out worker when Elijah had been a toddler. The old textile factory, which had long closed down, routinely employed young mothers for the job of sewing garments together.

"Every week, a van delivered pieces of fabric to Aldwyck by the sack load," she explained joyfully. "By the time it returned, those sacks were filled with hand finished garments."

Just the mere mention of Aldwyck however, tugged Margaret's curiosity.

"I miss the village," she murmured. "I wonder what's gonna happen to William's family."

Eleanor bit her lip, reminded of the emotional farewell they had shared on

255

his birthday. James seemed almost a ghost of his former self, as if the very life essence had been drained out of him.

"I don't know, sweetheart," she said, her attention drawn to Margaret's questioning brown eyes. "They have been house-hunting. But I think they want to make the most of the time they've got left..." Even as she said it, her eyes drank in the exquisite furniture James had given them. It brought a heaviness to her heart.

By the time the curtains were hung though, Elijah had painted the walls in shades of cream and soft honey gold from Avalon's left over paint collection. Together, they had created a delightful room, complimented by beautiful furnishings.

Elijah meanwhile, continued to absorb himself in decorating upstairs, applying various shades to each bedroom; a feminine peach for Margaret, a cool mint green for himself and a subtle mushroom shade for the adults.

Andrew, for the sake of being awkward, chose to decorate his own room. But after snubbing Avalon's colours as too 'girlie,' he was ecstatic when Charlie delivered the futon he had grown to love from the attic of Westbourne House. Eleanor even joked what a treat it would be if he could pick up their four poster bed. If only it was possible to get it up the stairs!

"When can we invite them round?" she found herself fantasising one evening.

Snuggled up in their solid pine bed, they had enjoyed a particularly blissful session of love-making. Margaret and Elijah were at a nearby youth club, which offered a range of activities. Andrew meanwhile, worked for three evenings a week in a wine bar.

"They've got a lot on their plate, love," Charlie's voice fluttered against her ear. "I said I'd go round tomorrow and help James shift more furniture. He's putting it into storage for now. Do you know it's less than two weeks before they have to leave?"

Eleanor closed her eyes, recalling her latest conversation with Elliot. James's family had been invited to stay in London with the Fortescues for a while.

It will take the pressure off having to move so soon, he had told her in confidence.

"Well, let's at least invite them for afternoon tea," she added wistfully. Rolling over, she couldn't resist stroking his chest. "And what about Peter? We should ask him round for a meal! He's been so good to us."

"You're just looking for an excuse to throw a dinner party," Charlie teased. "Okay, so how about Saturday? I suppose we should invite Reggie and his wife, too..."

256

Eleanor stiffened. She could no longer deny how apprehensive Reginald made her feel. The couple lived in a house on one of the coveted new housing estates near the Community Centre; Peter just across the road in a flat situated above the fish and chip shop.

But with everyone on site, all Charlie wanted to do was to blend in. Admiring Peter for his role, managing a busy community centre, neither could he deny the respect he felt for the Magnus couple. Employed in a more specialist capacity as drug and alcohol counsellors, their role was to offer advice, as well as addiction therapy.

"Oh, come on, love," Charlie muttered, giving her shoulder an affectionate squeeze. "At least they went along with Peter's recommendation and let us rent this house."

"I'm worried about what they think of me," Eleanor sighed. "If Reggie believes everything he reads, he might think I'm going to start pushing drugs in the community."

Charlie's face tightened. Having already divulged the propaganda surrounding Jake's murder, she had shown him the news clippings from her file, as she gradually leaked its secrets...

"Then you need to come clean about those press stories," he sighed. "Especially if Reggie was around. Why not dig out the article by NME? It challenges those lies."

"Maybe," Eleanor whispered.

Yes, the ultimate result of the press conference; a skilfully worded piece in which Jake had been revered for his musical talent.

Despite Charlie's assurances however, she had no desire to be drawn down past avenues, especially in front of Peter. Rising from the bed, she exhaled a sigh.

"Look, if you think we should invite them, fine! On the plus side, they have got a daughter who's Margaret's age and I'll cook something extra special to prove how civilised we are!"

Stimulated by Charlie's passion, the dinner party took place as agreed.

The kids consumed a simple microwave meal, while Eleanor concentrated her efforts on a delectable menu for the adults. Andrew, who planned to go out socialising after his shift, wouldn't be home until late.

"Something smells nice," Elijah muttered.

"Dauphinoise potatoes," Eleanor said as a rich garlic fragrance wafted across the kitchen. "Angelo's recipe. And I've made chicken and white wine casserole. Don't worry, I'll save you some," she added, clocking the look of longing clinging to their faces.

With everything under control, which included a luscious black cherry

257

cheesecake left to chill in the fridge, Eleanor dashed upstairs to get ready. She selected a dress made from dark blue velvet, the sleeves long enough to hide her tattoo. Conscious of the woolly dreadlocks trailing down her back, she found a chiffon scarf to tie them back with, looping the ends into a bow.

With some reluctance, she also removed her nose-stud.

However she presented herself, she would never quite meet the approval of Hilary Magnus; a small, neat woman whose formal attire left her feeling outlandish. But when the doorbell rang and Margaret leapt up to answer, she was dismayed they were the first to arrive. She was hoping to exchange a few light-hearted words with Peter before they stifled the atmosphere with their icy formality. Charlie however, stood proud as they ambled into the front room.

"Oh my!" Hilary exclaimed in surprise. "This is nice!"

From her concealed position at the foot of the stairs, Eleanor struggled not to laugh.

"What a magnificent suite," Reginald added, "however did you manage to get your hands on one of these?"

Drawing them into the lounge, Charlie explained the origin of the suite. Their eyes were everywhere, devouring the walnut coffee table with its intricate mouldings. The glass fronted cabinet was of similar design; exclusive furniture they knew they couldn't afford.

"I hope we have a chance to introduce you to James soon," Eleanor said, taking her first tentative steps into the room.

Hilary's head whirled around, eyes flickering over her before they rose to meet her gaze.

"Eleanor!" she greeted her in a smug, clipped voice. "You look smart... and what's cooking? It smells divine."

"It's a surprise," Eleanor said, while from another corner, she felt the stab of Reginald's blue eyes. "Sit down, Reggie. Would you like a glass of wine?"

"Thank you, but I don't drink," Reginald answered. "Do you have lemonade?"

"Of course," Eleanor said sweetly, escaping into the kitchen.

Moments later, she heard the ring of the doorbell again, her mood soaring as a familiar Irish lilt piped into the lounge. A heavy darkness had descended, allowing her to catch a glimpse of her reflection in the window; pleased she had made the extra effort to look pretty.

The evening flew by quicker than expected. Everyone had been most complimentary about her cooking and none so much as Peter. Even in the company of the Magnus couple, she was amazed how much they found to talk about. Although she fought to avoid any twists in the conversation that would inevitably swerve her towards her past.

Out of sympathy for the Barton-Wells family, she instead told them about the restoration. Reginald seemed curious to know why James had lost the battle.

Eleanor caught Charlie's eye. They would have to mention Perry at some point, except she didn't want to talk about him right now; a man who had stepped out of one horrific chapter in her life, only to reappear in another without warning.

She felt the touch of a shiver. *Bumping into Reggie the next day had been almost as shocking.*

"I'll spare you the details," she said. "Let's just say James fell prey to an unscrupulous loan shark and then his health started to deteriorate."

"We managed to restore his house," Charlie added, "but the last few months were hell for him." He turned to Eleanor, his smile reassuring.

"Poor man," Hilary simpered. "I cannot imagine what it's like to lose your home..." She broke off, scraping the last flecks of cheesecake from her plate. "What a lovely place to live though. I gather you used to live in a caravan, Eleanor."

"I didn't have much choice," Eleanor said tightly, lowering her gaze.

"Eleanor had a very tough start in life," Peter rolled into the discussion. "Though it seems incredible we found protection in the same man. Bernard James."

"The social worker in East London?" Charlie picked up.

"That's right," Eleanor mumbled, sensing the agony of her past rearing up at last. Having strenuously avoided Reggie's eye, her gaze now drifted towards him. "You worked with him too, Reggie. Can you tell me what became of him. Is he still around?"

"Regrettably, no," Reggie answered tonelessly. "His wife died from chronic heart failure and Bernard followed shortly after..."

"Not Edna!" Eleanor gasped. "She was such a lovely lady."

Reginald lowered his eyes. "She was indeed. Have you heard the phrase *to die of a broken heart?* Such was the case with Bernard."

"I'm so sorry," Eleanor whispered, fighting tears.

Charlie covered her hand with his own.

"This couple really looked after me, Charlie..."

Reginald tensed visibly, as if she had disclosed something he had never wanted to be reminded of. But Eleanor was still watching him, bracing herself for her defence.

"Then why did you leave London?" he probed. "Bernard could never understand that. He hoped you would stay in touch."

Eleanor took a deep breath. "I had a baby to protect. Bernard tried so hard to help me b-but I had enemies. I feared so much for Elijah's safety and still do!"

"Seriously?" Peter spluttered. "Was there nothing anyone could do?"

259

She looked at Charlie, whose expression turned grave.

"It's okay, Peter," she choked. "You found us a place to live and in a safe community, which is all that matters - especially for the kids."

Peter smiled with such tenderness, Charlie too, was inspired to add a few words.

"This almshouse is a gift from the Gods and I know we're going to be happy here!" He tapped glasses. "In fact, Eleanor and I wanted to know what *we* could offer in terms of voluntary work. What are your plans? You see, I get the feeling there is something on your mind, Peter..."

With the Magnus couple exchanging glances, the conversation about to take a completely different turn, nothing more was said of Eleanor's past for the remainder of the evening.

The room plunged into silence, the candles flickering. They threw odd shadows around the room as Peter sat and fiddled with his napkin. His eyes were downcast. Eleanor studied his face; the sombre expression and spikes of his eye lashes. Slowly, she rose and searched for a tape, guessing it would lighten the mood.

"You're right, Charlie," Peter murmured. "I have an idea - although it's more of a - a - vision really." He raised his eyes. At the same time, a fast drumbeat began pulsating into the room, diffusing some of the tension.

"Oh Peter, I know you mean well," Hilary drawled, helping herself to a drop more wine, "but the council would never agree to it..."

"Agree to what?" Eleanor interrupted.

Peter drew his head close in a manner that seemed furtive. "It's about the Community Centre," he muttered. "Let's be honest, folks, it's ugly! It's a characterless square lump and the brickwork is truly horrible. What I want you to imagine, Charlie, is a building we can be proud of. Something magnificent. The problem is, the council see it as no more than a drop in centre for lonely old people. Yet it could be so much more, if only the building looked more appealing. I think it would improve the whole town."

"It's a pipe dream, Peter," Reginald sighed.

"Not necessarily," Charlie protested. "I think it's a great idea! Why don't you put your recommendation in writing, Peter, and present it to the council?"

"Because they need to visualise it," Peter elaborated, his eyes pinned on Charlie. "It has to be presented as a plan, including drawings... and I'm no architect."

"Ah," Charlie smiled, "now I see what you're getting at." He threw an amused glance at Eleanor. "I expect she told you, did she? That I'm an architect?"

"I might have mentioned something," Eleanor said, feeling a glow of colour in her face.

"So you're asking me to do some drawings?" Charlie echoed, unable to contain his glee. "Designs for a new building? It would be my pleasure!"

Reginald squirmed in his seat. From Hilary's pursed lips, even she appeared to exhibit disapproval. Yet Eleanor was ecstatic, impressed how quickly Charlie had embraced Peter's proposal and in the face of so much cynicism.

"Well, I like the idea," she taunted, "and what a challenge for Charlie! Just imagine! Official designer of a new Community Centre. I'd be so proud..."

"Hmm, well I wouldn't get too excited, young lady," Reginald murmured. "You haven't dealt with Rosebrook Council and I warn you they can be difficult. Like Peter says they've shown precious little interest in us over the years. I can't see them changing overnight."

"They've just approved the repair for your ceiling," Charlie argued.

"You can hardly compare a ceiling to a brand new building," Reginald protested.

"Oh, come on," Eleanor said teasingly. "Peter only asked him to do some drawings. We won't get too excited but Charlie would love the opportunity to design something."

"Is that one of yours?" Reginald questioned, his gaze wandering towards a pencil sketch on the wall. "It's very good... what a lovely looking house."

"Actually my son did that," Eleanor couldn't resist boasting. "That's one of his best drawings of Westbourne House."

"He told me about his sketching," Peter added in amazement. "You must be so proud and I must ask you, what is this music?"

With the tracks turning progressively softer, the energetic rock tempo had died away, giving way to a beautiful ballad. Perfectly balanced by the haunting notes of a male vocalist, it flowed gently from the speakers.

"Free Spirit," Eleanor told him, her voice a whisper. "Jake's band. This is their one and only recording..."

"Beautiful," Peter sighed, closing his eyes. "And please ask young Eli to get down here. I have got to congratulate him on that drawing."

There was no denying the success of the evening. Despite the aloofness Eleanor detected in the Magnus couple, she felt sure *some* social ties had been established.

From the moment the children had appeared, they brought an extra sparkle to the room. Hilary seemed particularly affectionate towards Margaret and could not wait to introduce their daughter, Holly. Reginald meanwhile, quizzed Elijah about his art.

On the final day of September though, Eleanor found herself in deep thought. A watery sunshine cast a glow over the horse chestnut trees, illuminating the leaves like flames. It had been two weeks since that terrible showdown in James's bar, yet to think how much had happened; from their initial meeting with Peter, to the painful wrench of having to leave...

At least they had been rewarded with a new home and for a short while, Eleanor could almost forget the turmoil overshadowing their lives.

But no one had any clue how the week was going to end. Her mind was never far from Westbourne House. Braced by the window, she watched, mesmerised, as the leaves fluttered over the grass - when the ring of the telephone pierced the silence. Eleanor tensed, fearful to answer it. She let it ring a few times, before anxiously grabbing the handset. At first it sounded like heavy breathing, until she just about discerned the sound of a girl sobbing.

"Eleanor.... is-is that you?"

"Avalon?" Eleanor gasped, her hand tightening on the receiver. "Avalon, slow down. Tell me what's wrong."

"It's Dad!" Avalon kept blubbering. "There - there's been an accident! He - he f-fell down the stairs! I-I don't know what to do, but he-he's out cold..."

"Call an ambulance," Eleanor said quickly, "and ask Elliot to contact his doctor. We'll be there as soon as we can..."

Chapter Twenty-Nine

I

Watching from the lounge, Charlie froze. Eleanor's face had turned ashen.

"What is it?" he gasped.

"It's James," she whispered. "We need to get over to the house right away..."

As she spluttered out the details, he could barely take it in.

"Get in the car," he ordered quietly, knowing it was down to him to explain to the kids.

The next person he had to face was Elijah, still glowing from the praise he had been showered with last night. Charlie so much wanted to confide in him. Yet the happy shine in his eyes made it impossible.

"Look after the house, mate," he murmured, giving him a gentle pat on the shoulder. "There's something going on at Westbourne House, so your mum and I have to leave you. Sorry, but it's urgent..." and before Elijah had a chance to dig for more details, he was gone.

Jumping into the car, Charlie sped towards Aldwyck. But before they even reached the village, an ambulance shot past in the opposite direction, a blur of flashing blue lights.

"Oh my God, Charlie!" Eleanor whimpered. "What if we're too late?"

He kept driving regardless, face rigid as he braced himself for the worst.

Waiting in reception, Elliot faced them, his expression a mask of dread. The accident had descended into chaos, leaving Avalon so inconsolable that she too, had left with the ambulance, accompanying James to the hospital. Eleanor stared ahead with a shiver. No one could ignore the blanket crumpled at the foot of the doomed staircase.

"Elliot, can you bear to tell us what happened?"

"He-he just froze at the top of the stairs," Elliot bleated. "I wasn't even sure what was wrong and then he tumbled. It happened so fast... he bashed his head on the newel post." He met Eleanor's eye, the fear in his expression growing. "I felt for a pulse but there was none! That's when Avalon phoned you."

"You mean the accident was fatal?" Charlie breathed in horror.

"I'm so sorry," Elliot finished, "if only I had reached him sooner..."

Hearing the wobble in his voice, Eleanor rushed over to embrace him.

"Elliot, none of this is your fault," she mumbled tearfully. "It must have been another stroke. They might yet be able to resuscitate him."

She feared they were wasted words, her dearest friend caught in the grip of death long before they reached the casualty department. It was the suddenness that hit so harshly. No one was prepared. Eleanor always imagined James would suffer a slow decline as each stroke gradually weakened him. But on this occasion the stroke had been a major one, the consequential blow to his head triggering a brain haemorrhage.

Eleanor, as well as Charlie, felt chilled to the core as the doctor took time to explain this. His words were laced with empathy, in so much as *the end had been swift*. No sooner had James collapsed, he would have plunged into a well of oblivion, his life snuffed out like a candle with little time to reflect or to suffer.

"He always said he'd live at Westbourne House until he died," Eleanor's voice echoed.

For James's children, however, the impact was unimaginable.

By the time they caught up with Avalon, she was paralysed with shock, face white, apart from the tear trails on her cheeks. They had only just lost their home but to lose their father on top seemed a particularly cruel twist of fate.

William on the other hand, was back at boarding school. After driving there the previous week, the family had shared an emotional farewell. It seemed impossible to envisage that in a few short days, their father would be torn from their lives forever.

"H-how will we-we ever manage without him?" Avalon struggled to say.

"Avalon, we are so sorry," Eleanor tried to comfort her. She was fighting tears of her own. "I loved him too, you know, but this is dreadful for you. Have you spoken to William?"

"Not yet," Avalon sobbed. "Elliot said he-he'd drive over and collect him. He needs to come home..." Fresh tears had distorted her voice.

And Eleanor held her in her arms as she wept bitterly.

II

Eventually William did return home, while Charlie was condemned to share the terrible news with the other children. As the days drifted by, he excelled in his duty to comfort the bereaved. Forced to bury his own emotions however, he pressed ahead with the job of saving the Community Centre ceiling, despite the desolation surrounding them.

October came with little warning, as did the threat of rain.

But when a deeply moving funeral took place the following Friday, dark clouds rolled across the sky, as if to reflect the melancholy atmosphere.

Nearly every person in Aldwyck was gathered along the pavement. The crowd stood motionless as two majestic black horses clomped their way through the village, ebony plumes swaying. Tears brimmed in Eleanor's eyes as they were drawn towards the carriage. Intricate in design, its gilt framed edges and decorative glass surrounded James's coffin. But it felt unbearable to imagine him lying there, in the silent wilderness of death.

The service took place in Aldwyck's church on the other side of the brook. Avalon and William were hovering outside. Even from a distance, Eleanor could see that William was fighting tears. Immaculate in a black suit, his face appeared pale and composed, but every so often she caught the tremor in his lips, his eyes glazed with shock. Avalon fidgeted by his side, a pillar of despair in her long, black coat. Her hair was tightly coiled up with pins, barely visible beneath the rim of her pillbox hat. Despite the diaphanous veil concealing her face though, anyone could see that she was crumbling inside. The damp air rang with her sobs as the coffin bearers, Elliot and William among them, carried James into the church.

An eerie silence prevailed as the service began. Eleanor cherished the presence of her own family; Charlie to her right, Margaret and Elijah tucked together, heads bowed and finally Andrew, whose silent tears had not gone unnoticed.

William and Avalon were so torn apart by grief, neither could face narrating the eulogy they had prepared. Thus, it was Eleanor who bestowed them this honour. With much tribute paid to James's life-long quest to maintain Westbourne House, not one person could deny he had been an integral part of the village. Aldwyck would never be the same without him.

By the time they stepped outside, the sky pressed down heavily, a spray of rain cascading from the clouds. For Eleanor, this was the saddest funeral she had attended. She slid an arm around Avalon's shaking shoulders, while Margaret and Elijah did their best to console William.

A crowd of mourners huddled beneath a spreading bouquet of umbrellas, watching in silence as the coffin was lowered into the ground. Avalon swept back her veil, cheeks wet from crying as she walked bravely forwards. Pausing by the graveside, she stretched her face towards the sky. The branches of a Monterey Cypress tree hovered above like a dark and comforting cloud. It reminded them of the cedar tree peering over the walled gardens, but for a few seconds she just stared at it, as if sensing her father's spirit before the first shovel of earth landed.

As the church yard began to empty, a silent river of people traipsed their way towards the Olde House at Home. Boris had closed the pub to the general public in honour of a wake for James.

The villagers of Aldwyck swelled in their ranks, alongside his close friends and allies. The Fortescues had driven down from London, as had the recently retired TV presenter, Geoffrey Ascombe. Doctor Albany Price lingered among them. Devastated by this dreadful turn of events, he was one of the few people who had known about James's declining health. But Charlie and his family stuck close to his children, as did Elliot.

The pub throbbed with movement as people circulated; pausing to offer their condolences before discreetly ambling away to give them space.

"You knew he was ill, didn't you?" Avalon whispered as the crowds began to thin at last.

Elliot and Charlie exchanged glances.

"Avalon, we always suspected there was something wrong with your father," Elliot said softly, "ever since his collapse at that tea party. Perhaps you could explain, Albany..."

The doctor briefly relayed his fears. The weight loss James suffered, coupled with his fatigue, could have been early signs of cancer. Until it eventually emerged such factors were symptomatic of his anxiety about the house. He explained the blackouts - a series of mini strokes, which had not only weakened him but resulted in some paralysis.

"It grieves me to say this, but that last stroke was a serious one," he finished morosely.

"I see," Avalon mumbled, her tearful gaze drifting to Elliot.

"I'm sorry, Avalon," Elliot said in earnest, "but James didn't want you to worry..."

"He'll be very sadly missed," Boris chipped in from the other side of the bar. "To think, I only saw him last Thursday. He called in for a chat."

There was a darkness in his tone that compelled them to turn and stare.

"Did he tell you about the house?" Eleanor quizzed him.

"Damn right," Boris snapped, his tone completely out of character. "We knew the house had been sold, but that was before James mentioned those bastards who swindled him out of it! Just who the hell do they think they are?"

"The Hamptons?" Charlie snorted. "Well, it doesn't seem that long ago we were talking about their son! The night you mentioned the cottage on the green, remember?"

"Oh God, not him," Boris shuddered, flicking a nervous glance towards Avalon. "That would explain a lot. I gather they're renting it to the Marsh couple now. Though from what James told me, I bet it's some *brown-nosed* gesture to endear himself to the villagers."

"Obviously," Charlie muttered, "and I don't wish to sully the atmosphere by talking about them but it's high time everyone had some inkling of what those Hamptons are really like."

He turned towards William and Avalon who stared at him intensely. Despite their ghostly pallor, their eyes betrayed a glitter as if urging him to continue.

"Tell him how that evil old monster really got his hands on our house," William said.

"Remember the bad publicity?" Charlie sighed. "It was down to him apparently."

It took several minutes to enlighten them, first by describing some of the nastier tactics Perry had used; not only the malicious magazine articles, but the campaign of terror his son had subjected Avalon to.

"Perry Hampton was determined to get his hands on the house using whatever means possible," Elliot added bitterly.

The gears of the conversation turned swiftly, as they each related their stories. Those who listened had already begun to challenge the morality of it, amidst wide speculation as to whether there was scope for legal action.

Eleanor on the other hand, was floundering. What was it about this debate that disturbed her so? There was hardly anyone in the pub who had *not* been touched by Perry's wickedness, herself included. Yet as all the recent communications with James came back to haunt her, she could hear the echo of his words:

"These are very evil people, Eleanor and they have got to be stopped."

Hadn't she promised she would find a way, as she had sworn to seek justice for Jake? Staring at her hand, she saw his engagement ring encircling her finger. The stones of golden amber and green tourmaline glowed eerily in the shadows as if to serve an uncanny reminder of her pledge: *Elijah and I will find others like us... and together we will create a society where everyone will be able to live in safety.*

As Eleanor raised her eyes, the party were still engrossed in their debate, deliberating over how they could fight someone like Perry. She wondered if she alone held that power.

Only a few remained now, including their own assembly. But before anyone had a chance to say more, she spotted Herbert Baxter shuffling towards them.

"I know your dad and I never saw eye to eye," he told the children, "but he was a fine man. He contributed more to this village than I gave him credit for."

With his head bowed, cloth cap clutched in his large hands, even Eleanor felt a little sympathy.

"Thanks, Mr Baxter," William mumbled.

"It's what's going to happen to these kids we're worried about," Boris said tightly. "You do know they're about to lose their home? Westbourne House has been sold."

"I did know, yes," Herbert sighed. "Shocking business! Is there no way you could involve a solicitor to keep your house?"

"Unlikely," Charlie answered him. "Not now Hampton's the legal owner."

"Who is this man?" Herbert thundered. "Some big shot from the city, I suppose!"

"You met his son," Boris replied. "Young, fair haired chap, remember?"

"How could I forget?" Herbert sniffed. "Forever interrogating me about Westbourne House, the arrogant little bastard!" He staggered slightly, obviously a little drunk as he collapsed onto a stool. "What are they planning to do with the house?"

"He wants to tap into the corporate market," Avalon said with contempt. "They even scoffed at Dad's walled gardens. I bet he wants to put some ghastly building in there!"

"He can't do that!" Herbert bellowed. "Those are traditional Victorian kitchen gardens!"

"In truth, we can't be sure what they're going to do," Charlie tried to placate him, "but it's like Avalon says... If they intend to attract the corporate sector, Perry will likely make changes."

"In that case, I'll make a promise to you kids!" Herbert barked. "I'm going to keep a very close eye on Westbourne House and if there is even a hint those people are trying to ruin it, I'll be straight on to the council. Do you hear? I'll do it out of respect for your father!"

"Th-that's very good of you, Sir," Avalon mumbled.

A tear plummeted down her cheek, reminding Eleanor of her own pledge.

They needed to forge a strong community.

"And what about you?" she whispered, touching Avalon's hand. "Have you thought any more about moving? It's just - you don't have very long now..."

Avalon's eyes swam with tears again, causing William to stare in panic.

"How can we even think about leaving our ancestral home at a time like this?" he gasped. "We've only just lost our father!"

"I know that," Eleanor whispered, "and I'm sorry to bring it up."

"But we've got no money!" Avalon croaked. "What about the will? It could be months before Dad's assets are passed onto us. "

"It seems we have a lot to discuss," Elliot sighed. "Supposing we go back to the house. *All of us*," he added, shooting glances at not only Boris and Albany, but Herbert too.

"Only if you're sure," Boris faltered.

"Yes, I'm sure," Elliot confirmed. "These two youngsters need all the support we can give them. Furthermore, this could be your last chance to take a good look at the estate and on the advent of those Hamptons moving here, I suggest you make the most of it."

Chapter Thirty

I

By the time they got home the weather had not improved. The horse chestnut trees swished in the wind, hurling showers of wet leaves across Charlie's windscreen.

"It seems so unfair," he heard himself mutter. "There is no way those kids will find a new home before the month is up."

"D'you reckon the Hamptons will kick 'em out?" Andrew shouted from the back.

"I wouldn't put anything past them," Eleanor answered darkly, "Maybe Elliot should just talk to them..."

For the past two hours, they had drifted around the bar at Westbourne House in a state of shock as the reality sank in. Perry had a lot to answer for. It left them wondering how anyone could instigate such a ruthless campaign against a dying man. But the discovery that James had not been entirely honest about William's school fees came as a further blow, as disclosed in a recent letter. They had been settled for one more term, although William refused to return.

"I've only got six more weeks anyway," he protested. "But we have got to sort out our living arrangements... a-and Avalon needs me!"

Next, they were forced to discuss the legal matters of settling James's estate. As Elliot explained though, the first step was applying for a grant of probate, a process that could take several weeks, if not months. With Perry's deadline looming, Charlie and Eleanor, along with the remaining skeleton staff pledged to do everything in their power to help them.

Elijah too, sensed the distress they were going through, and seeing their beautiful house again had been agonising.

Closing the curtains to shut out the gloom, the world seemed a desolate place now James was no longer a part of it; a man he had grown to love as much as anyone. He switched on one of the pretty table lamps, the effect soothing, inspiring him to light some candles.

Settling down with his sketchpad, he idly flipped back the pages, hit with a flood of emotion as his drawings were unveiled. They portrayed the sheer magnificence of Westbourne House from a distance, as well as the close-up architectural detail.

Tears burned his eyes and as he ran his fingers over the lines of pencil, he imagined the coolness of the stone. At the same time, a more spiritual side of him clung to the hope that the Barton-Wells children might yet be able to keep their home.

II

From a distance Peter kept an eye on them, especially Eleanor. Her heartache dragged her down like a millstone. He knew about the funeral and of the highly esteemed gentleman she had idolised. Yet despite their inner turmoil, they had thrown themselves into voluntary work.

He and Reginald were delighted with their new ceiling and not only that. Charlie seemed eager to carry out any maintenance jobs they required. Eleanor not only helped out in the Community Centre, but was passionate about doing something about their ramshackle gardens. Unable to suppress her enthusiasm, Peter had naturally agreed to it.

Pleased to find two people dedicated to improving the Community Centre, he found himself thinking about the Council again. He could no longer deny having grown increasingly frustrated by their lack of interest. But where Reginald and his wife seemed resigned to their negativity, Peter was determined to fight it. That first spark of hope had been ignited by Robin Whaley, who seemed openly supportive... It left him wondering if he dared approach him with his wider ambition to renovate the entire building.

"Have you thought any more about those drawings, Charlie?"

Such dreams inevitably drew him to the almshouse.

"Of course," Charlie answered.

He glanced at his son, sprawled on the sofa. Andrew was flipping through the latest 'Smash Hits' magazine while Elijah lingered silently at the table, sketching away in pencil.

"I've been looking at the style of the town," Charlie continued. "For whatever I design, it needs to be in keeping with its character. Here, take a look..."

Unrolling a sheet of paper, he positioned it carefully across the table so as not to disturb Elijah. It revealed the outlines of a building; a classic archway flanked by tall windows to draw in the light. These were offset by smaller, mullioned windows above.

"Imagine the lower half in a more pleasing style of brickwork," he said, "leaving the top level rendered in concrete."

Finally, he had added a long sloping roof to increase the building's height.

"It looks splendid," Peter muttered. "Is it likely to be expensive?"

"It won't be cheap," Charlie said. "A brand new building of these proportions is unlikely to fall below six figures... unless there's a way of adapting the existing structure. What do you think, Andrew?"

270

"Dunno," Andrew grunted, engrossed in his magazine.

"Can't you come up with any suggestions," Charlie snapped, "considering the months you spent working on the restoration?"

"Yeah, as a labourer," Andrew snorted. "You're the architect."

Charlie's lips tightened. "Forget it! Just thought you'd show a bit more interest, that's all!"

He hauled his chair around to face Peter again.

Andrew icily ignored him, snapping the pages of his magazine as if to make a point. Elijah meanwhile, took no notice. His pencil swept over his sketchpad in long straight lines.

"What's that you're drawing, Eli?" Peter quizzed him. "Can I see?"

As Elijah peered up furtively, Charlie frowned. The square, squat building was not only recognisable, he had captured its austerity in the brickwork.

"The Community Centre!" Peter laughed. "You've got it down to a T, it looks hideous!"

Elijah smiled, his eyes sliding towards Charlie's drawing - when an image of Westbourne House leapt out of nowhere. *It was the mullioned windows.* Yet as he studied the fine lines Charlie had etched with such precision, his imagination started to run wild.

"Charlie," he muttered, "can I have a piece of tracing paper?"

"Okay," Charlie faltered. Reaching down to his briefcase, he pulled out a sheet of the same translucent paper he used for his own plans. "What's on your mind?"

"Just an idea," Elijah replied and taking the sheet, he positioned it over his sketch.

How was it possible to create a building in keeping with the town, but on a tight budget?

With their banter flowing around the table, Elijah absorbed himself in his vision. Filled with an unstoppable urge, he began sketching again, the outlines of the Community Centre forming a blueprint...

Before he knew it though, he was adding extra panes to the windows, then a light ornamental surround. Focussing on his memories of Westbourne House, he sketched a parapet along the edge of the flat roof. He was even tempted to carve grooves into the corners, mirroring the same rusticated stonework. Oddly enough, the result possessed an instant aesthetic beauty but for additional finesse, he sketched pillars above the steps; a classic design where the walls were smooth, stripped bare of that gruesome brick work.

Snapping out of his trance, he stared mesmerised. He had turned the Community Centre into a small-scale version of Westbourne House.

"Dear Lord!' Peter breathed.

271

With Andrew now absent and Eleanor tucked away in the kitchen, Elijah proudly presented his masterpiece. Charlie followed Peter's gaze.

"That is amazing," he spluttered, stabbing a finger at the drawing. "He's only gone and visualised it from a completely different angle!"

Dipping inside his briefcase, he extracted a bundle of papers that illustrated various techniques in architecture.

"You like it?" Elijah mumbled, feeling a warmth spread through his heart.

"The building you've drawn is lovely," Peter enthused, "but whether the council can run to something like this... Charlie, you said a new building would be expensive."

"Yes, I know," Charlie replied. His eyes sparkled. "But this design doesn't really constitute a *new building*. The existing brick can be rendered over with concrete, rusticated grooves scored into the material before it dries. Specialist work but not impossible!"

"And the windows?" Peter asked.

Charlie shuffled through his papers to find the section on window styling. "So we build new sashes," he continued, "but sturdier and with more mullions to divide them. We could even apply a decorative surround - but with concrete mouldings instead of stone..." He paused for a second, beaming. "Eli, this is brilliant! Whatever gave you the idea?"

Cheeks burning, Elijah shrugged. "I was thinking about Westbourne House and the picture just came to me. Are you saying this might work?"

"Yes," Charlie nodded. "You've discovered a way we can transform the building without replacing it."

"Your son is a genius, Miss Chapman!" Peter called to Eleanor. "We've been tearing our hair out here, and Elijah has come up with a solution. Look!"

Suddenly they were all crowded around the table. Elijah shrunk into himself, bashful of the attention. But as the heat in his face cooled, he couldn't hold back his smile.

"Very well done," Eleanor whispered in his ear.

"Can I borrow this?" Peter grinned. "I want to run it past the council."

"Okay," Elijah whispered. He felt a shiver of delight.

"So what colour would we paint it?" Charlie contemplated. "Maybe add a little colour, using crayons... present it as an artist's impression."

"I think it should be the colour of butter," Elijah mused, "a golden yellow..."

Closing his eyes, he was captured in his fantasy. What if his design really could be turned into a reality? It would be like bringing a piece of Westbourne House to Rosebrook; not only as a tribute to James but as a fitting monument for his children.

It might even give them an incentive to move here.

III

The following morning, Peter could barely contain his excitement. To his greater surprise, Robin Whaley was not only pleased to hear from him but intrigued to discover what his plans were. Thinking the matter was *a little too complex to discuss over the telephone,* Peter invited him to visit the Community Centre in person.

As the hour crept near, he found himself clock watching. The knock on the door made his heart leap. Robin had shown up on time.

"It's good to see you," he said quickly, "has anyone offered you a drink?"

"It's okay, Peter," Robin replied, lowering himself into a chair, "I had tea before I left."

Once again his appearance was impeccable; his dark suit spotlessly clean and not a speck of dust. With his hands folded on the desktop, Peter couldn't help noticing how smooth they were, the nails beautifully manicured. He gazed into his cool blue eyes.

"So, what's your opinion of this building?" he began. "And please, be honest."

"Well, it's not the most attractive site," Robin drawled. "What exactly is it you do here?"

Peter wasn't sure what it was about the man's tone that put him on edge but it forced him to justify his role. The Community Centre was primarily a place for the elderly to drop in for a bit of company. Yet it accommodated a number of professional organisations; the Information Centre, Citizens Advice Bureau... never to forget their essential counselling service for those suffering from addiction problems.

"If we can help turn people's lives around, then surely this town will be a better place for all its citizens," he concluded.

Robin gave a sniff. "I admire your work, Peter, though intrigued to hear how you think you can renovate this building."

Peter swallowed, sensing his opportunity. "What if I was to tell you the same gentleman who fixed our ceiling happens to be an architect. Yesterday we came up with a drawing that illustrates exactly how the building could be remodelled..."

Robin's stare did not waver. "Do go on," he murmured.

Reaching into his folder, Peter plucked out Elijah's sketch. As Charlie proposed, he had traced over it, using a fine precision marker, so that it resembled an ink drawing. Soft veils of creamy yellow had been carefully applied to some of the wall areas.

For a moment Robin studied it, his features softening. "What a lovely drawing. An architect, you say? Interesting. I see exactly how the design

273

mirrors the existing building structure. This man is clearly a good lateral thinker and I admire such vision."

"Do you think it's in keeping with the town's character?" Peter kept probing.

"Most definitely," Robin said, finally giving way to a smile. "It suits our town far better than the monstrosity we're sitting in now. Sorry. I don't mean to be rude..."

Peter finally let go of his tension and laughed heartily.

"How easy would it be to turn this vision into reality?" Robin asked. Enraptured by the drawing, he could barely take his eyes off it.

"Charlie reckons everything here is possible," Peter said. "It involves applying some sort of cladding to the outer walls and rebuilding the windows. But the cost could be kept within five figures. Do you think the council would agree to such an investment?"

"Possibly," Robin muttered. His eyes locked with Peter's in a way that was almost hypnotic. "It strikes me you are a visionary, Peter, same as me - and that you and I are going to work very well together..."

As he lowered the drawing, Peter felt the lightest brush of his fingertips as they briefly skimmed past his hand.

"Tell me about the man behind the drawing," he continued. "We could use someone like this in our planning department."

"Who, Charlie?" Peter mumbled, almost dumbstruck. "Well, maybe I should let you in on a little secret. Charlie didn't actually do this sketch. It was drawn by his stepson."

"Really?" Robin pressed. "And how old is he?"

"Thirteen," Peter confessed. "Charlie and I were merely discussing the idea and with no prompting, he just came up with it. Wonderful, isn't it?"

Robin's penetrating blue eyes continued to hold his gaze. "I won't deny I'm impressed. It would be good to meet him... as well as his father."

"Stepfather," Peter corrected him. "His real father is no longer alive."

It took a few more minutes for the conversation to wind down. But before it reached a conclusion, Robin proposed a second meeting.

Finally, he asked for a photocopy of Elijah's sketch.

Peter escorted Robin back through the double doors. No sooner had they reached the foot of the steps though, he broke off mid-sentence.

"Well, speak of the devil!" he piped up. "Eli! Over here, quickly!"

Robin followed his gaze, his eyes honing in on an adolescent boy loping across the road.

Faltering on the pavement, he glanced up nervously.

"C'mon, don't be shy," Peter called. "I'd like you to meet someone."

Robin observed the boy as he wandered closer - his wiry frame, his shining cap of chestnut hair, the fluid loose-limbed grace with which he moved...

Could this be the artist to whom Peter had referred?

"Eli, this is Mr Whaley," Peter grinned. "Robin works for the council. He's been admiring your drawing."

"Oh, thanks," Elijah muttered, peering up beneath slim, dark brows.

"It's a splendid design, young man," Robin smiled indulgently. "I am impressed. You should come and visit the council planning department. With this level of skill, they might even want to employ you one day."

Elijah blushed, eyes lowered. Robin knew he should be returning to the council yet there was something intriguing about this boy.

"Where do you go to school?" he persisted, keen to get him talking, to look at him.

"Rosebrook Comp, Sir," Elijah answered and finally he raised his head.

The boy had an exquisite face; his eyes glittered in a myriad of colours, long and appealing with sweeping lashes. For a second, Robin couldn't drag his eyes away, struck with a flash of familiarity he could not quite put his finger on.

"Seriously, Eli, your drawing is wonderful!" Peter reassured him. "Mr Whaley is going to run it past the council!"

"Really?" Elijah gasped and with a smile of unconcealed delight, he reached out to shake his hand.

Robin found himself reciprocating, feeling the delicate bones as their hands joined.

Then a car backfired in the high street, compelling Elijah to glance around.

As soon as he turned sideways, Robin studied his profile; the straightness of his forehead, the shallow nose bridge, the way his chin ended in a small point. What he saw jolted him but he could no longer ignore that chilling resemblance to someone from the past.

"What did you say your name was?" he muttered.

"Elijah, Sir," he piped up. "Elijah Jansen."

"Jansen..." Robin echoed. He turned rigid, dropping his hand as if scalded.

"Are you alright, Robin?" Peter laughed airily. "You look as if you've seen a ghost."

"Did you know my father?" Elijah intervened.

Lost for words, Robin stumbled back a step. "I-I'm not sure. I don't think so..."

"Why don't you run along now." Peter winked at Elijah, "and I'll let you know if any decision is made with regards to your drawing."

With a polite nod, Elijah turned and disappeared behind the other side of the Community Centre. Peter guessed he would return to the almshouse.

"Well, that was an interesting meeting," Robin muttered. "Thank you... and for introducing me to the boy."

Peter could not ignore the tension lingering in his expression. He fiddled with his tie.

"I meant what I said, though... I'll show his sketch to the Head of Planning. But if this is to be classed as an official planning application, we also require front and side elevations. Do you think your architect friend could supply those?"

"I'm sure he could," Peter nodded.

There was something very different about Robin's demeanour. His blue eyes seemed cold and strangely distant.

"Tell me about his family," he probed. "Didn't you say they'd just moved into one of the almshouses?"

"Yes, that's correct," Peter replied. "Charlie has a son of his own, also in the building trade, and a daughter of about eleven..."

"You mentioned Elijah was his stepson," Robin broke in. "Does he have a mother?"

"Oh, yes," Peter sighed. His face melted into an adoring smile. "She is a lovely young woman. She's even started helping out in the gardens here. Her name is Eleanor."

"I see," Robin said softly.

Despite the arctic chill in his eyes, he gave a mirthless smile, a sight that left Peter uneasy.

"Mum!" Elijah chirped, as he shot through the back door. "Is Charlie around?"

Eleanor frowned, turning to him. "Not at the moment," she replied. "Why?"

"Peter's just showed my drawing to some guy from the council," he told her. "He was dead impressed. Said it was great!"

An expression of undisguised joy spread across her face. It seemed a long time since he had seen her look so happy, filled with a sense his drawing had put a smile back into the world.

She ran her hands down the sides of his arms. "Eli, that's wonderful news!"

"He seemed nice..." Elijah started to say but broke off. He couldn't shake off the man's strange reaction the moment he had revealed his name.

"Go on," Eleanor coaxed him. "What else were you going to say?"

Elijah shrugged. "It's nothing... He just went a bit weird when I told him my name. Even Peter said he looked as if he'd seen a ghost. I asked him if he knew my father."

The smile on Eleanor's face faded. "And did he?"

"He didn't say," Elijah mumbled, "but surely there are some people who remember him."

276

"Oh, I'm certain there are," Eleanor said darkly. "Jake was an unforgettable person and you are starting to look more and more like him every day... Anyway, what else did this man say about your drawing? Because I can tell you now, Peter is ecstatic."

"I like Peter," Elijah grinned. "Just imagine if Charlie did get the job of doing up the Community Centre. Wouldn't that be so cool? Especially if it turned out like my drawing and here's another bit of news... Mr Whaley says he's gonna run it past the council."

Her reaction was not quite how he expected.

"Whaley?" she echoed. "Not *Robin* Whaley?"

It was as if all the light had been extinguished from her eyes, a look he had seen before.

"What is it, Mum?" he dared himself to ask. "Do you know him?"

"Did," Eleanor said with a cool smile. "So he works for the council now does he? Interesting." Gradually, she met his eye, her expression tender again. "Oh, Eli, you must be thrilled. Forget I said that. I'm so very, very happy for you..."

Elijah said nothing more. He could almost imagine the cogs in her mind turning; a past he had so little knowledge of. Her reaction in that brief transit of time was almost as strange as that of the council officer. But suddenly, Elijah had experienced enough strangeness for one day.

More than anything, he was dying to call William and Avalon; hear how they were faring. He could not wait to tell them about his sketch either, inspired by Westbourne House. Its fabled beauty had reached out to him when he needed it, but there was no mistaking he had moulded its architectural beauty onto the shell of the Community Centre with them in mind.

Chapter Thirty-One

I

Elijah was not the only one thinking about the Barton-Wells children.

It was inevitable Perry too, would hear of their father's death as soon as the announcement hit the papers. News of his deeply moving funeral had followed. The Hamptons, meanwhile, exercised sufficient tact to keep their distance. Any further contact with the family would do them no favours at such an emotive time.

Yet Perry's stone-hearted ambition stalled any compassion he should have felt.

His concern was the effect this would have on his own plans. He knew damn well his deadline for the family to leave had been unreasonable, but what did he care? In the end, he felt little but contempt for them and given the sum he had invested, was hungering to relaunch the hotel.

Unfortunately, James's unforeseen death had complicated matters. Even Rowena, in a rare moment of sympathy, warned it would be insensitive to move in so soon after the tragedy.

To make matters worse though, he had received a heart-felt plea from the butler, urging him to allow the children more time. Out of sheer frustration, he eventually arranged a meeting in London between the lawyers serving both parties.

"First, you have my condolences," he began silkily. "News of James's death has come as something of a shock. I understand he suffered a major stroke."

"I'm afraid so," James's solicitor answered in an undeniably cool tone. "A major stroke, which culminated in a tragic fall. The children are devastated."

"Of course," Perry simpered. He lowered his eyes. "In fact, it is the children I am here to talk about. Will you update me on their situation please?"

Frank Winterton let out a sniff.

A shrewd and professional man in his fifties, he had served as James's solicitor for years. Even he found it hard to be civil towards this cold, calculating man, who he had since discovered was solely responsible for his client's financial ruin. He could not deny his surprise to hear that James had sold his ancestral home - though a decision he supported, especially when the debts had been spiralling out of control. A speedy sale to the company known as 'Falcon Finance' seemed like a reasonable solution at the time. But like James, Frank was woefully oblivious to the truth of who really hid behind that company.

"They are still living at home," he informed Perry, "I do not envisage they have much choice. Furthermore, William has been forced to drop out of private school. Their situation is a little delicate right now."

"I am aware of that," Perry said tightly, "but I would still like some indication as to how long they intend to stay there."

Frank raised his head, staring at him with incredulity.

"I don't wish to come across as unsympathetic," Perry continued in the same steel-tipped voice, "but surely you are aware they cannot stay there indefinitely. Westbourne House belongs to me now. So, I was wondering if there was anything I could do to facilitate their move."

"They have nowhere else to go, Sir," Frank snapped.

"Don't they have a mother?" Perry pressed.

"Their mother lives in America," Frank sighed. "We are trying to trace her. But I assure you the staff are doing everything they can to shift the furniture. So I beg you to be lenient. These children are deeply traumatised by the unforeseen loss of their father..."

Perry shifted in his chair, his own lawyer braced next to him. There was a murmur of disquiet before Frank spoke again.

"There is of course another problem. The children do not yet have access to their father's funds. This is the reason the butler contacted you. We are awaiting the grant of probate."

"But how long will that take?" Perry shot back at him.

"James's will was not complicated," Frank replied in earnest. "Realistically, it should take no longer than three months..."

"Three months?" Perry murmured in a low voice. "Well, I can't wait that long."

Seeing the mask slip, Frank stiffened his stance. Perry's solicitor had said very little but in response to his rising displeasure, he finally intervened.

"Has anyone been appointed to act as power of attorney?" he demanded.

"Regrettably no," Frank replied.

"But there has to be some way to resolve this," the other man continued. "Surely, there are assets other than the proceeds of the house sale..."

"There are!" Frank barked. "But not enough to buy them a house."

An angry flush had crept into Perry's complexion now.

"It seems there are few options open to me then," he finished. "Though please be aware, I am particularly keen to re-launch the hotel. All this time is costing me money."

Frank shook his head in disbelief. "The children are in mourning, Sir. You cannot put a deadline on grief, particularly where children are concerned. Have you no heart?"

279

"You underestimate me," Perry added. "I am not about to throw them out. But I must warn you that whilst I am prepared to allow the designated time to dissolve James's estate, I urge you not to prolong the process. Because if I discover you are purposefully dragging your heels, there will be repercussions."

Frank's face tightened, his contempt rendering him speechless.

II

With James's assets entangled in a legal process that Perry was well aware could take months, there was only one way he was likely to resolve this. No sooner had he parted company from his solicitor, he jumped into his car and peeled himself away from the capital.

It was time to visit Westbourne House in person.

Jaw clenched in readiness for conflict, he marched up the steps and grasped the door handle, dismayed to discover it locked. Fearing his journey might be wasted, Perry hammered on the wood. But a few seconds later, he was rewarded by the sound of footsteps.

At first Elliot froze. "Mr Hampton..." he started to protest.

Pushing his way in, Perry held up a restraining hand. "Don't worry, Elliot, I have no intention of causing distress. I just want a quiet word with the children. Are they at home?"

"Of course," Elliot faltered, "but I warn you they are very distressed. In the light of what's happened, they might not take too kindly to your visit."

"Well, this cannot wait," Perry snapped. "I realise I'm probably the last person they wish to see, but it is essential I speak with them alone."

"Fair enough," Elliot relented, desolation hanging in his voice.

Perry strode through reception, heels echoing in the sepulchral silence. Drawn to the staircase, he saw Avalon huddled on the steps. The poor girl looked haunted, her face ashen. Raising her head, she glared at him through eyes swollen from crying. Yet they blazed with hatred.

"What do you want?" she snarled through gritted teeth. "Come to gloat?"

"Not at all," Perry said softly. "I came to offer my condolences. What happened to your father has genuinely shocked me... despite our differences, he was a good man."

Avalon staggered to her feet. "This is your fault!" she started sobbing. "His health was already suffering! But what you did completely destroyed him!"

"Avalon, my dear, I cannot be held responsible for your father's death," Perry consoled her. "I gather he suffered a stroke. It could have happened any time..."

"You broke his heart!" she kept whimpering. "All he ever wanted was to save our ancestral home so we could inherit it. When you took that away from him, he lost the will to live..."

"Avalon's right!" a different voice chimed from the other side of the hall.

Perry whirled around, shocked to see her brother. Positioned half way down the opposite staircase, he stood as still as a statue.

"Hello, William," Perry greeted him.

William's almond-shaped eyes burned into him, the contours of his face so sharp, he looked as if he had lost weight.

"Why are you here?" he demanded.

Perry flinched, shocked by the razor edge in his voice. It served as a harsh reminder this was no longer a child he was dealing with.

"It's time I paid you a visit," he said benignly. "I appreciate this has come as a terrible blow and I am genuinely sorry about the way things turned out..."

"Like hell you are!" Avalon shouted, forcing him to spin around again. "Dad didn't want to go into partnership with you! Why couldn't you just accept that? He moved heaven and earth to save this place. You had no right to purposely ruin him!"

Strutting away from the stairs, she advanced with growing menace. From the opposite side, William too, had completed his descent and together they circled him like tigers.

"You made him bankrupt," William hissed, sidling closer.

"That's right," Avalon added. "Dad died in this house... right here, at the bottom of these stairs as it happens. I hope he comes back and *haunts you*."

Perry felt a momentary giddiness, before a rolling wave of fury replaced it. "That's enough, Avalon, I will not be spoken to like that! How dare you! I came to offer my sympathy!"

He was satisfied to see her stagger back, almost tumbling into the newel post.

"Is everything alright, Avalon?" Elliot called. He had been lingering by the door.

"A small misunderstanding," Perry barked, "but everything's okay..." He shot an icy stare at William who had not yet backed off. "Isn't that right, William?"

"You're evil," he protested. "Why should we back down?"

Unprepared for such insubordination, Perry puffed himself up like a toad. "I think you should hear what I have to say before you display such insolence! Now let's go into the bar shall we?"

With a furious sigh, William flounced in the direction of the bar. Perry could have smiled, sensing he had gained the upper hand at last. Elliot held the bar door open, not daring to intervene as Avalon meekly followed her brother.

"You want us out, don't you," William snapped, dropping himself into a chair.

281

"All in good time," Perry said, lowering himself into the chair opposite. "I am not about to evict you. Even I realise that would be cruel under the circumstances. Now if you please, Elliot, I would like some coffee."

Without waiting for an answer, Perry turned back to the children.

"I am here to re-address the terms of our agreement. So tell me about your house search. Have you found anywhere?"

"Not yet," William said crisply. "Dad died only two weeks after your last visit."

"I see," Perry muttered. "What about the furniture? I hear the staff have been helping you to shift some of it."

"That's right," Avalon nodded, "but only into storage. Charlie's been helping us too." Her tone had resumed its acidity, leaving Perry no doubt she had only mentioned Charlie to rile him.

"I thought the place looked emptier," he sneered and allowed his eyes to wander. He saw a distinct bareness to the edges, devoid of the luxurious sofas formerly occupying them.

"Anyway, moving on," he pressed, "there is still a lot to move, especially from the guest accommodation, so supposing I offer you a deal?"

"There's no need," Avalon retorted. "We don't want you to have anything of ours. You've already taken the house…"

"Is that so?" Perry sniped back. "Well, perhaps you might consider what you are going to live on for the next few months, before you make such flippant remarks!"

He watched with growing satisfaction as tears sprung to her eyes.

"Everything our dad put into this place meant so much to us," she croaked.

"Harsh though it seems," Perry reprimanded her, "now is hardly the time to hang on to things for sentimental value! Now do you want to hear my offer or not?"

"Don't let him upset you, Avalon," William sighed. "What is it you were going to say, Mr Hampton?"

Perry looked at him with begrudging respect; *a model of the English public school*.

As Elliot returned with a tray of fresh coffee, Perry observed the faultless manner of his deportment as he set the cups carefully down.

"Thank you, Elliot," he said. "In fact, while I am here, I wish to speak to all the staff. Would you care to round them up for me?"

Elliot looked fearful. Even the children exchanged glances before he cast his steely gaze back to William.

"Now, where were we? Oh yes, your furniture… My wife was rather fond of that bamboo set in the Orangerie, so I am prepared to offer you two thousand pounds for it."

The two of them gaped at each other.

"We can't," Avalon breathed. "Dad chose that furniture. What if we want to keep it?"

"We all know that's impractical," Perry intervened, pulling out his chequebook. "Better it remains where it is..." and refusing to listen to further protests, he scribbled out a cheque.

"We don't want your money!" Avalon gasped.

"Just take it!" Perry snapped, tiring of their obstinacy.

William looked horrified, reluctant to accept it, until Perry lost his patience.

Grabbing his hand, he pressed the cheque into his palm. "This will help with your living expenses..." and refusing to break eye contact, he rehearsed his next words, hoping he had sufficiently crushed their defences. "This leads me onto another matter: your father's hotel, which I assume is now closed."

His words trailed off just as Elliot returned, accompanied by Bryony and Angelo. Perry allowed himself a smile. *The timing could not be better.*

"Sit down, please," he insisted, helping himself to a second cup of coffee. "You must be wondering why I've summoned you. Well, the hotel will be reopened at some point but under *my* management. I must therefore ask if you wish to continue working here."

Angelo threw him a look of contempt, his Latin temperament boiling over.

"Angelo, isn't it?" Perry goaded him. "I understand you are head chef."

"I will not work for you, *Meester Hampton,*" he growled in his strongest Italian accent, "and eef I ever have to cook for your family again, I swear I will put poison in your food!"

William was struggling not to laugh. Perry scowled, before turning back to the chefs.

"So be it," he sniffed, "now what about you, Bryony? I gather you have a reputation as a fine Pâtisserie chef. Will you be staying on?"

She gaped at him in anguish, hands knotted together in her apron. Yet Perry's eyes bore into her like lasers, demanding an answer.

"Out of loyalty for James, I don't think it's right," she said miserably. "What your family did was unforgivable... So no! I'm sorry, but I can't!"

"Don't be," Perry said, lounging back in his chair. "It is no problem. I can always recruit new staff. You two on the other hand, had better start looking for another job."

William watched carefully, drinking in the scene. Aware of Avalon's fidgeting, he saw the panic in her eyes.

"So, Elliot," Perry muttered, his tone filled with mockery, "what is *your* decision?"

Elliot faltered. He must have picked up William's fear yet still he hesitated.

"What can I say?" he said. "Like the others, I feel a certain loyalty towards James. On the other hand, Westbourne House has been my life! I don't think I could bear being parted from it just yet. Is it possible I can think about it?"

Perry gave a curt nod. "Alright! But don't take too long. I want a firm decision soon."

Lowering his coffee cup to the table, he let out a sigh. With the seconds ticking painfully, William sensed he held the whip hand, his entire household dangling on a thread.

"Now, going back to you two," he addressed them. "In the light of the fact you are in mourning, I'm prepared to be lenient. I will allow you to live here for three more months. That should give you sufficient time to get over your father's death and for the grant of probate to come through, thereby freeing up his assets. Does that sound reasonable?"

William gave a nod. "Okay," he said softly. "That seems fair."

"Elliot, you too, may stay," he added. Turning to the chefs however, his eyes resumed their chill. "But you two can pack your things and clear off!"

Avalon let out a gasp. "You can't do that!"

"Yes, I can," Perry said nastily. "I gave them a chance and they threw it back in my face. Like it or not, Westbourne House belongs to me now, so I'm under no obligation to accommodate them. Be grateful you still have your butler."

Avalon shook her head, her tears rolling. "I'm so sorry!" she bleated to Bryony.

"It's okay, love," Bryony soothed her, "Angelo and I have already talked about this. But we intend to pursue our careers together now, in London."

No sooner had they vanished, Avalon glared at Perry. Slouched in his chair, one arm draped over the rest, he surveyed them coolly.

"How could you do that to them?" she gasped. "You bastard..."

"Be careful, Avalon," Perry berated her. "I've said you can stay here but I can always withdraw that offer..." with those words dangling, he was savouring his power, a feeling he clearly wanted to reinforce. "Whilst I realise you two are not my responsibility, I will do whatever it takes to help you back on your feet. So, I suggest you continue your house search and as soon as you find what you're looking for, let me know. I will even arrange a short term loan as a deposit."

It seemed obvious the conversation had reached its conclusion as he rose to his feet.

"What? You think we'd risk another one of *your* loans?" William spluttered.

"It's your choice, William," Perry finished, "I will leave you to ponder..."

"Maybe we should talk things over with Charlie then," Avalon taunted, "and Eleanor."

Perry paused. A raft of emotions swept across his face, before he turned to

284

her once more. "You have until the end of January to find a new home," he finished, "but I promise I will return. Maybe I'll bring Ben next time... I'm sure he'll be delighted to see you again, Avalon."

Terror flashed in her eyes as he left them to dwell on that final chilling prospect.

Chapter Thirty-Two

I

Charlie and Eleanor were not the first to hear of Perry's forceful intrusion. A select group had gathered in the Olde House at Home to ponder over the ramifications. That the children were not about to be evicted came as something of a relief; while the sacking of the chefs left them reeling. Eleanor could only guess the calculating motive behind Perry's actions. In the absence of Angelo and Bryony, it would be impossible to open the restaurant and they would miss the delicious cuisine they were accustomed to. But in true Hampton style, this was his way of unhinging them.

Thank God they still had Elliot to look after them.

Conversely, she could see exactly why Perry had dangled his £2,000 cheque like a carrot and as for the suggestion of a loan... it was as if he wanted to exert some control over them.

She found herself explaining this to Elijah and Margaret, as they tended to the weeds around the Community centre.

"When are you going to see them again?" Elijah asked. "And can we come?"

"I don't see why not," Eleanor replied. "There's nothing to stop us jumping on a bus. But if we leave it until Sunday, Charlie can drive us..."

Charlie had not lost sight of their vision to revamp the Community Centre. But even with professional front and side elevations drawn, it would be a while before the Council discussed it. In the meantime, he had begun to advertise his building services again, the rent for the almshouse sufficiently low to allow them a good standard of living.

Above all, Eleanor adored having a family to look after. In the last few weeks their lives had become ever more integrated with the Community Centre and this in turn, brought a ray of sunshine back into her world.

If only James hadn't died... and although the pain had started to recede, she missed him terribly. It was her deep feelings of love for James that compelled her to travel back to Aldwyck occasionally; not only to comfort his children, but to cherish her memories of him.

Margaret turned and looked at her. "Dad's teaching you to drive, isn't he?"

"Yes, he is," Eleanor smiled. "It's about time I learned."

"That'd be great," Elijah muttered. The muscles in his slender arms danced as he kept digging at the weeds.

Once these flower beds were cleared, Eleanor wanted to plant bulbs in them; dainty snowdrops for January, followed by crocuses in lilac and gold. Come April, there would be banks of daffodils; then tulips in as many shades as the varieties seen around Westbourne House... It seemed uncanny how that place had inspired them all. Her son's outstanding sketches had started it and now her personal goal was to turn this outdoor space into as much a replica of James's formal gardens as possible. She was also toying with the idea of installing some ornamental urns, her mind crowded with visions of cyclamens and tumbling ivy.

Even Margaret had delighted her with her idea to plant a herb garden. In her child's mind, she imagined neat bushes of rosemary and sage, tall terracotta pots packed with thyme. Between them they had so many ideas, pleased to be part of a community.

Eleanor clung to the hope that the Barton-Wells children too, would establish their home here, despite their yearning to spend as much time as they had left in their old home. Thinking back to Perry's visit, she felt a shiver of cold. His threatening presence still lurked. Yet her son's chance meeting with Robin Whaley had brought another dark cloud rolling into her world.

How could she forget Robin Whaley? Smooth, silver-tongued, disturbingly convincing, a man who had pretended to be their ally, yet spun a web of deceit. She could picture him now, lounging at the boardroom table where the press conference had taken place, his eyes taunting, in the aftermath of his lies. Obviously Peter thought very highly of him. He had even nominated him for a customer care award. So how could she tell him? How could she bring herself to expose the evil that hid beneath his charm? Because deep down, she knew it was only a matter of days before their paths became entwined.

II

Unbeknown to Eleanor, the man who stoked her innermost fear was also thinking about her. Striding his way towards the Community Centre, accompanied by two colleagues and an elected ward councillor, he knew he should be concentrating on Peter's vision; his plan to turn this repellent lump of a building into something more pleasing. But his mind drifted into the past.

It was the first sight of the boy that disturbed him, that chilling and unforgettable resemblance to his father, Jake Jansen.

Swerving around the corner, he was blinded by a flash of sunlight. Robin blinked but in that second of darkness Jake was there, just as he remembered him leaving the police station; those same bouncing steps as he had observed in his son, auburn ponytail swaying...

Robin swallowed. He didn't want to think about the transit van tucked in the

287

shadows, nor the thugs waiting to pounce on him. *Young Jake had no hope of fighting them. Hovering nearby, watching, he saw them bundle him into the van, shocked but intrigued by what he was involved in.*

He had never imagined what it would feel like to arrange the killing of another human being but the assignment had drawn him to new avenues of power. The man behind it had known he was as corruptible as the police inspector, Norman Hargreaves. And together they had conspired to get rid of the one 'witness' whose evidence could have plunged their futures into jeopardy.

Robin shivered, never able to forget that fateful second encounter. Approaching Jake in person, in Holborn, had left a deep and lasting impression; a meeting that led to a betrayal... and although he wasn't actually Jake's killer, he had devised a scheme so cunning, it would guarantee the end result. But how regrettable, his girlfriend, *Eleanor*, had known it too.

Eyes narrowed, he scanned the boundaries of the Community Centre, looking for her.

"You're quiet, Robin," his line manager, Terry Griffiths, muttered. "Not nervous are you?"

"Not at all," Robin said, holding the door open. "I've already seen the potential of Peter Summerville's plan. I just hope we can convince the others."

And so they proceeded to one of the upstairs meeting rooms. Peter could barely curb his enthusiasm it seemed, though sadly Charlie could not be present, due to work pressures. He had nevertheless left Peter with a sheaf of notes. These allowed him to explain the concept behind the renovation but with none other than Reginald Magnus to champion him.

"Mr Whaley," Reggie spluttered, freezing to a standstill.

"Hello again, Reginald," Robin greeted him coolly. "How are things?"

The pristine cut of Robin's suit could not be more of a contrast to the roll-neck sweater and faded cords he wore beneath his ageing tweed jacket. Reggie lowered his eyes.

"You two know each other?" Peter piped up.

"Did," Reginald chuckled to himself. "Many years ago, *Councillor Whaley* governed a ward in East London..."

"Really?" Peter said, frowning. "Such a small world."

Neither man had a chance to reflect before the tide changed and they were swept into a debate as to whether Peter's idea was even feasible.

As they pored over Charlie's drawings, their voices droned on.

Robin began to feel frustrated, dismayed by the negativity dispensed from the outset.

"I don't need to point it out," he intervened, "but this building as it stands

288

does Rosebrook no favours. We are all familiar with the predominant style of architecture, our Town Hall being a fine example."

"These plans resemble something like a financial institution," Councillor Montgomery scoffed. He squinted to get a better look. "Doesn't this all seem *over the top* for a community centre?"

"Why do you say that?" Peter gasped, as if sensing the snub towards his organisation.

"I think what Peter's trying to say," Robin sighed, "is that whatever purpose this building serves is irrelevant. It will add a pleasing aspect to this side of town."

Refusing to be discouraged, Peter passed around copies of Elijah's sketch.

This time, the noises were at least a little more encouraging; though as Robin glanced at the drawing, he found his thoughts wrenched back to its creator. There was no mistaking the boy was talented. But with the memory of his father looming, he experienced the same chill as earlier.

Unable to relax, he rose to his feet and began to pace around the room. Sensing Peter's scrutiny, he flashed a smile.

"What does everyone think?" he couldn't resist the urge to badger them.

Councillor Montgomery gave a shrug. "No one can deny this is a most pleasing interpretation but how do you propose to turn such a grotesque building, if you'll pardon my phrase, into something remotely similar... and at what cost?"

Referring to Charlie's notes, Peter explained the process. Filled with hope, Robin knew this proposal would go a long way to enhancing the charm of Rosebrook.

If only they could see it.

Yet still they argued, which in turn left him demoralised.

In an attempt to stop pacing, he paused by the window. His eyes fell across an expanse of lawn rolling towards a conifer hedge. Then suddenly, a lone gardener caught his attention.

Straight away, he felt the tension grip his shoulders. That person appeared to be a girl.

She's even started helping out in the gardens here...

Peter had, of course, been referring to Eleanor.

Robin raised his hand to the Venetian blind, deft fingers prising them open to get a better look. Yet in precisely the same instant, the girl turned, as if detecting his scrutiny.

He stood back, letting the dividers ping shut. And already his heart was thumping.

Before the meeting ended, Robin knew he had won the support of his line manager. The other two were reluctant to show such commitment until the costs had been estimated. They did, however, agree to a second meeting, which in itself was encouraging. If the final figure fell below the £75k mark, Peter might be in with a chance; although it would involve some effort on his part to generate a proportion of the funds.

This proposition left Peter elated, Robin cheered by his incessant chatter. But as his colleagues turned to the exit, he chose not to join them. Driven by an unwavering desire to take a walk in the gardens, he craved a little fresh air.

No sooner was he alone though, his thoughts returned to Eleanor. *From that very first glance, he had known it was her.* Robin recognised her not from her looks but the way she moved; the graceful slide of her shoulders as she reached for the wheelbarrow, the subtle twist of her waist... Eleanor had always possessed a feminine grace that reminded him of a swan.

The memory took him back to their encounter in Holborn, before the unforgettable night of the press conference.

As he strolled into the garden, he found the absence of people reassuring. She appeared to be packing up now. Removing her gloves, she nudged the wheelbarrow to one side, where it could no longer obstruct the public. Nothing but a leafy path separated the lawn from the tree-lined avenue where the almshouses lay; the very opportunity Robin was waiting for.

He stepped out in front of her, blocking her way.

Eleanor took one glance at his face and gasped. He studied her closely; taking in her wild hair wound in dreadlocks and the glittering stud in her nose. Last, his eyes searched her face. In all these years Eleanor had not changed. Her face might be leaner yet she possessed the very features that stopped men in their tracks; skin as flawless as that of a magazine cover girl, her golden eyes wide with recognition.

"Eleanor Chapman," he murmured in a voice of hate.

"Hello again, Mr Whaley," she faltered.

She seemed visibly startled yet made no attempt to rush past him. Robin drew himself back a step, a sneer creeping onto his face.

"Well, look at the state of you," he drawled, his eyes raking over her.

"There is no need to be rude, Mr Whaley," Eleanor retorted.

Eleanor on the other hand, had quickly realised Robin Whaley was as loathsome as he had ever been. She observed his immaculate pin stripe suit with a shudder. His hair might have been a little greyer but his blue eyes seemed frostier than even she recalled.

"What are you doing here?" he demanded.

"I live here," Eleanor hissed. "If it's any of your business..."

His jaw tightened. "Didn't we make it clear *we did not want you around?*"

his voice lashed back. "Didn't the warning sink in?"

Eleanor flinched. "That was thirteen years ago, Mr Whaley and you were a councillor in East London..."

"Situations change, Eleanor," he added softly.

"So?" Eleanor challenged him. "At the end of the day, you wanted me out of London. So I left. Nobody told me where I was supposed to end up living."

Robin smiled though it did nothing to thaw the chill in his eyes. "Eleanor, I have always known where you were living... and if you want my advice, I suggest you crawl back to that hovel in Aldwyck. This is my battleground now and you're not going to last five minutes on it."

"Are you threatening me, Mr Whaley?" she questioned.

It took the fearful pitch of her voice to draw the attention of two passers-by. They paused to stare. Robin's eyes narrowed.

"Because if you are," she added, dropping her voice to a whisper, "it won't add much credibility to this *customer care award* Peter's nominated you for will it? And I know you work for the council. You met my son the other week."

"That's right," Robin murmured. "A charming boy if I may say so. Does it not bother you that I know who he is now?" His smile faded. "Perhaps you should be a little more concerned..."

She backed away, her expression hardening. "Mr Whaley, I have a new partner in my life and a whole community behind me. So I'm telling you now, I am not going anywhere. If anything, *you're the one* who should be scared." She felt a first flicker of triumph, her voice dropping even lower. "I haven't forgotten, you know. I haven't forgotten what you did."

"I have no idea what you're talking about," Robin sighed, "you have nothing on me."

"Really?" Eleanor taunted. "You may not have killed Jake but conspiring to have someone murdered is still a crime. I will never forget the lies you told Bernard James; nor the lies you told at that press conference."

Conscious she was teetering on dangerous ground, she considered his veiled threat somewhat hollow. Whaley had never risen to the position of power she feared. He had aspired to little more than a council worker. Inspector Hargreaves had been ousted from the police force, which left only Theakston. Yet several months back, her solicitor had revealed that even he had severed all links with organised crime and left London.

Was it possible Whaley was the only one of them left?

"Be careful what you say, Eleanor," he whispered evilly.

"Or what?" she threw back at him. "Because just for the record, I have never voiced my suspicions about Jake's murder. But like you say, situations can change..."

His eyes sparked with hatred. "You have no idea who may be hanging

291

around," he added, "nor who I'm still in contact with. So I suggest you keep quiet... and stay out of my way, especially if you want to carry on living here."

With a sideways flick of his head, he shot a warning glance towards the almshouses.

Eleanor swallowed. Desperate for the sanctuary of her home now, neither could she disregard the *professional relationship* he shared with Peter, wondering how much influence he really did have in this town.

III

"She's here, Perry!" Robin's voice thundered down the telephone. "The Chapman woman has moved to Rosebrook!"

"Is that so?" Perry responded. "Well, thank you for letting me know. I thought the caravan seemed empty..."

Back in his London residence, he hadn't forgotten those last taunting words from Avalon; the hint that he and Eleanor shared a past.

"You went round there?" Robin gasped.

"Only to press home a warning," Perry said. He took another drag from his cigar, his mind whirling. "I was in the village anyway, visiting the Barton-Wells children. Did you know their father died? An unforeseen and regrettable accident. I'll have to postpone my move to Westbourne House now, for another three months."

"I see," Robin drawled in a tone of nonchalance.

"Now what are you really worried about, Robin?" Perry whispered. "Has she threatened you in some way?"

"She said I had reason to be scared," Robin answered. "To be honest, I think we all do."

"Is that so?" Perry muttered, feeling the malice slip into his tone. "Well, it sounds as if this young lady is becoming a little cocky. It's time we taught her a lesson."

"Whatever do you mean?" Robin faltered, betraying the first note of anxiety.

"You know exactly what I mean," Perry sneered. "Do you know her address?"

"Yes," Robin said. "She lives in one of the almshouses near the Community Centre. Managed to worm her way in with the manager, Peter Summerville, who I've just discovered may be useful. But I digress... He spoke of an architect by the name of Charlie, the man she is now living with."

"Charles Bailey," Perry muttered to himself. "I suppose, I should have guessed..."

Stabbing his cigar into an ashtray, he watched the embers glow from its tip. With his enemies closing in on all sides now, *first the Barton-Wells pair and now Charles Bailey,* he experienced a swell of hatred.

"And what about the boy? Have you had an opportunity to meet Eleanor's son?"

"Elijah," Robin said dreamily. "His name is Elijah… and yes, I've met him."

"Then what are you waiting for?" Perry said. "You remember our last conversation. If it's no longer possible for my security guard to corner him, perhaps *you* can!"

"What?" Robin breathed. "I can't do that! Have you any idea of the effect this could have on my career? What you're suggesting is unthinkable."

"Talk to him then," Perry snapped. "Lure him to a place where Nathan can find him."

"Perry, you are being unreasonable," Robin argued. "I cannot be involved in the abduction of a thirteen-year-old boy!"

"So tell me where he lives!" Perry kept hounding him. "That boy is our only insurance, Robin, so I suggest you play ball! What exactly is your problem?"

"It's complicated," Robin argued. "I haven't yet explained Peter's role, but he was the one who introduced us…"

"Are you sure you haven't gone soft?" Perry taunted. "That boy's father posed a serious threat, as did the woman! Don't tell me you feel any compassion towards their bastard son!"

He could sense Robin's tension mounting by the second.

"If this is your only solution then it can't happen in Rosebrook. It would have been better if Eleanor had stayed in Aldwyck…"

"Then the next best thing would be to get her thrown out of that almshouse!" Perry fired back at him. "Use your skills, Robin. Do whatever it takes to turn *this Peter* against her."

"Have I ever failed you?" Robin whispered. "Though I warn you, Peter holds her in very high esteem. It seems the whole family has been working with the Community Centre…"

"That woman has spent the last thirteen years living as a gypsy," Perry growled. "She mixes with hippies and does not belong in society! So maybe consider *that* supposition, the next time you converse with this colleague of yours."

"There is someone else," Robin revealed. "His name is Reginald Magnus. He, too, is aware of Eleanor's shady past. But if I cannot persuade Peter then perhaps he can. As you rightly say, she's been an outcast for the last thirteen years, so let's make sure it stays that way."

Chapter Thirty-Three

I

How Eleanor managed to suppress her fears amazed her. There was no mistaking her clash with Robin Whaley left her feeling persecuted. Everything associated with him was painful, a vicious reminder of all the heartache she had suffered in the wake of Jake's death. There was only one way to conquer such anxiety; by focussing on everything good in life.

Yet as she immersed herself in the Community Centre, she sensed something different about the atmosphere - a prickle of tension - and it seemed to emanate from the Magnus couple. Hilary seemed distant. Something in her eyes mirrored suspicion. At other times she noticed Reginald staring at her, the disdain on his face turning her cold. Eleanor kept her head down and refusing to buckle, found her sanctuary in the gardens.

True to her word, she had sourced four urns, each adorned with an intricate pattern of leaves on the plinth. Avalon insisted she would rather give them up for the benefit of the community than allow the Hamptons to keep them.

With her newly planted bulbs buried deep under the soil, she had covered them with pink cyclamens and winter pansies in soft purples. With the borders stripped of weeds, only a few remaining shrubs filled the gaps. Adding hardy bushes of sage and rosemary to inaugurate Margaret's herb garden, she had been gradually working her way around the perimeter.

But at first, she was oblivious to the men lingering on the edge of the lawn.

By the time Peter caught up with Robin again, they were approaching the end of November. Boosted by his support to renovate the Community Centre, he couldn't resist showing him the gardens. He was curious to gauge his reaction.

"You do know the council manages the gardens around town," Robin said cautiously. "It maintains a level of consistency."

"Are you not happy with what we've accomplished here?" Peter muttered.

"I can't fault it," Robin replied, his eyes scanning the area. "But self-governing an area of public green space is not something we encourage... I don't wish to appear mean-spirited."

"Why does it matter?" Peter said in a tiny voice. "The garden's been neglected."

In the distance he saw Eleanor, silhouetted behind a film of mist. She appeared to be working on the overgrown shrubs, pruning them.

"The council wouldn't expect you to carry out *all* maintenance," Robin persisted, following his gaze. "I'd like to think you can turn to me from now on..."

As the discussion ensued, Eleanor shimmied into view, neither man detecting her proximity until she sailed across the lawn in front of them. With a sack-full of clippings hoisted over one shoulder like a workman, her appearance could not be more Bohemian; from grubby dungarees to the dreadlocks swaying around her shoulders.

Robin's words ebbed into the silence. "The Chapman girl," he murmured as if thinking out loud, "hmm - I thought so..."

Peter turned to him sharply. "You know her?" he whispered beneath his breath.

Dropping the sack on the path, she began to attack the shrubs closest to the building, where the spiny branches crawled over the paving slabs.

"Eleanor Chapman and I go way back," Robin whispered back, "though I feel I must warn you, she will bring nothing but trouble..."

"I can't believe you said that," Peter chuckled, "she is a delightful young lady."

"You're aware of her past?" Robin mocked, turning to him.

Peter was shocked by the iciness in his eyes.

"Is this about her boyfriend?" he faltered. "I-I heard he was murdered."

Robin let out a sigh. "Peter, I hate to tell you, but Miss Chapman came from a violent criminal background. Her father worked for a notorious crime boss and is even rumoured to have killed a man. It is no secret both she and her young man got on the wrong side of some gang. The fact he ended up dead is regrettable, but it's widely reported that drugs were involved..."

"Even I know London was a violent place in the 70s," Peter protested. "But ever since she's moved here, she's done nothing but help out."

"She's trying to worm her way into your heart, Peter," Robin's voice dripped.

Eleanor picked up her sack. Peter felt his heart quicken, praying she hadn't overheard their conversation, though just as she drew level, her enchanting smile lifted the tension.

"Peter," she purred, "got a visitor?"

As she turned to Robin, their eyes locked; he nevertheless offered a cool smile in return.

"Miss Chapman," he drawled. "Good morning to you."

She held his gaze, then continued along the path to the door. A strained silence prevailed. Robin fiddled with his tie, waiting to hear it close.

"How long have you known her, Peter?" he sighed, resuming his icy stare.

"Do you know anything about the hippie lifestyle she's been immersed in for the last thirteen years?"

Peter shrugged. "She lived in a caravan. So what?"

"She turned that field into a camp for new age travellers," Robin sneered, "and one particularly disgraceful bunch offended the whole village. I hear they were raided for drugs... Miss Chapman was seen rowing with a police officer shortly afterwards. Wherever she goes she creates anarchy."

Peter felt a flood of sadness, staring over the gardens. Her beautifully planted urns stood out proudly against the neatly cleared paths and flower beds.

"Eleanor is a good person!" he persisted. "She and her partner have done so much here!"

The contempt in Robin's expression didn't waver. "Peter, I am only trying to help... but if you persist in letting *that woman* infiltrate your community, I'm not sure I can support you."

"I can't believe you said that!" Peter gasped.

"Then let me put this another way," he said more gently. He lowered a caressing hand onto his arm. "If I can't convince you, talk to your colleague, Mr Magnus. He remembers her too... and has good reason to be wary."

The conversation left Peter stunned. Barely able to concentrate on his duties, he drifted around the Community Centre in a daze, until eventually Reginald cornered him.

At first, he wondered if the council had gone against his wishes to have the building renovated. It would never surprise him.

But only when they retreated into Reggie's office did he spill out his troubles.

"Calm down, Peter," Reginald said. "I've been meaning to talk to you about Eleanor..."

"Why do you think he said such dreadful things?" Peter whispered.

Reginald tensed. As he stared out of the window, Peter couldn't see his face.

"We know so little about her," he sighed, "and you cannot ignore the rumours... I never wanted to tell you this, but there is wide speculation her boyfriend's murder had something to do with drugs. No secret she had connections with the criminal world..."

Reggie closed his eyes.

Only he knew it wasn't prejudice that lay at the heart of his diffidence, but guilt. He should have spoken out sooner. *If only Robin hadn't got to him first.* But it didn't take long for Robin to remind him of the time he caught him swigging gin from a bottle, hidden in Bernard's stationary cupboard. The memory filled him with shame.

Like Bernard though, Reginald had sensed a purity in the polite young

Dutchman known as Jake Jansen. Bernard had refuted all allegations about drugs, adamant he was innocent. But in the weeks after Jake's murder, tales of *drug dealing* and *organised crime* flooded the media. With his career hanging on the brink of ruin and Robin's accusing looks, it seemed so much easier to keep his head down and go with the consensus: *Eleanor did not belong here.*

"What does Hilary say?" Peter demanded, shaking him out of his reverie.

Reginald shook his head. It seemed only natural he would discuss his suspicions with his wife, whose bigotry towards Eleanor merely confirmed what people wanted to believe.

"Neither of us can deny she is somewhat hippie-like," his voice echoed. "That awful Rastafarian hair! Hilary told me some of the old folk were a little scared of her."

"That's ridiculous," Peter spluttered. "You sound as prejudiced as Robin! Next, you'll be telling me she's about to turn this place into a hippie commune!"

Reggie's reply died on his lips as the door burst open and Hilary strutted in.

"What are you talking about, boys?" her voice chimed into the void.

"Er - n-nothing," Peter stammered.

"But Peter," she smiled, as he inched towards the door. "There's been a phone call from Councillor Montgomery."

Peter sighed. "I suppose that means the renovation's off, does it?"

"Far from it," Hilary argued. "He wants you to attend a meeting at the council chambers. Charlie too! He supports your scheme, but the final decision rests with the planning committee."

"Great," Peter said with a grin. "I'll let Charlie know."

The magnetic pull of the almshouse had never been stronger. Peter made his excuses and slipped away. Yet in the moment Eleanor materialised, he felt the breath catch in his throat. Warmed by her golden eyes, he couldn't bring himself to accept the things he had heard.

Wandering into the lounge, he was further astounded to see Holly Magnus with Margaret, sprawled on the sofa, watching 'the Raggy Dolls.' Holly was a pretty child. She possessed the same neat features as her mother; a dainty upturned nose, blonde hair and pursed lips. But her eyes gleamed the same bright blue as Reggie's.

Charlie was slouched in an armchair, feet up, reading a newspaper.

"Everything okay, Peter?"

"Of course," Peter muttered. "I've got some news. How would you feel about attending a council meeting to present our building design to a planning committee?"

"I'd be delighted," Charlie grinned. "Do you think they'll pass it?"

"Possibly," Peter said. Seeing as the girls were taking up most of the sofa space, he lowered himself onto a dining chair. "Where's Eli, by the way?"

"Cricket practice," Charlie replied, just as Eleanor returned with a pot of fresh tea. "Can you believe he's been selected to play in the school's under-fifteen team? I guess all the practice with William during the school holidays paid off."

"William?" Peter queried.

"William Barton-Wells," Margaret said dreamily.

"The boy you fancy!" Holly teased.

Peter watched in amusement as a flush of colour swept into Margaret's cheeks.

"No, I don't," she mumbled beneath her breath. "I just think he's nice, that's all." She glanced at Charlie. "When can we see them, Dad? It's Avalon's birthday soon?"

Peter said nothing. Sipping his tea, he let the conversation float over his head. He guessed they were referring to the children from Westbourne House. To his eternal regret, he never did get a chance to meet their father.

"Why don't we go over and cheer her up," Margaret insisted. "Have a party!"

Eleanor gazed across with an expression of profound sorrow.

"Their mother will be there, sweetheart," her voice broke in huskily.

"The authorities have traced James's ex-wife," Charlie added, "and it's great that she's flying back to visit them. But I'm not sure we'll be welcome."

"She never took much of a liking to me, see," Eleanor added. "Probably thought I was trying to steal her lovely rich husband. Though much as I loved James, I saw him as more of a father figure."

Peter shifted in his chair. "Do you not have parents of your own, Eleanor?"

A heavy silence dragged the atmosphere. Even the two girls turned and stared, their attention momentarily distracted from the television.

Eleanor frowned. "My mum was killed in a car crash when I was little," she faltered. "As for my dad... That's another story. He went missing when I was sixteen."

"Is it true what Eli said?" Margaret blurted. "He worked for a gangster in London?"

The tension in the room solidified as Holly gaped at her open-mouthed. Peter too turned rigid; the shock of Robin's slur coming back to him. Eleanor nodded intuitively.

"Of course," she said bitterly, "you've been talking to Robin Whaley."

Charlie, who had been watching them, sat up in his chair. "Girls," he intervened, glancing at the clock. "Won't Holly's folks be expecting her home?"

298

"Oh yeah, it's five-o-clock," Holly said, sliding down from the sofa. "Is it okay if Margaret walks back with me? I wanted to show her my rabbits..."

Lost in a stream of chatter, their voices trailed outside the door long after Charlie had closed it. No sooner had they left though, he lowered himself opposite Peter.

"Okay, what's all this about?" he probed. "Why are you suddenly so keen to know about Eleanor's past?"

"Charlie, I feel I must warn you, there's a bit of gossip flying around," he said miserably. "I don't mean to pry. I just wanted to know if there was any truth in it."

"That my father was a gangster?" Eleanor choked. She wiped a tear from her face. "Yes, it's true! Dad worked for Sammie Maxwell, a notorious crime boss. Not that I knew much about it at the time, because he packed me off to boarding school!"

"Eleanor, I never meant to upset you," Peter spluttered. "I stuck up for you. But there were other things. Things about drugs and new age travellers..."

"If you're referring to those scumbags in Aldwyck," Charlie thundered, "it was Eleanor who got them slung out - and as for drugs! I do not know anyone more anti-drugs than she is!"

"Charlie, I believe you," Peter insisted, "it's just that... Reggie needs to hear this too."

"Reggie!" Eleanor gasped. "I thought he seemed off with me. You spoke to him?"

"I had to," Peter shuddered. "He and Hilary see themselves as some sort of moral crusaders, so I wanted to know if we could refute these rumours..."

He lowered his eyes, battling with the idea of whether to mention the story surrounding Jake's murder, but Charlie interrupted him mid-stream.

"This is crap!" he exploded. "Sounds like these people are twisting things!" Turning to Eleanor, his eyes darkened. "Who is this *Robin Whaley* anyway?"

"He's the planning officer, supporting our ideas, Charlie," Peter said, "and this is what I don't understand. What has he got against you, Eleanor?"

"Peter, I have my own suspicions concerning Mr Whaley," she murmured, "but I don't wish to voice them. Let's just say he has reason to be nervous. He doesn't want me around..."

Peter turned cold, recalling the day Robin had met Elijah, but pushed the thought aside.

II

Charlie could not dismiss that conversation. There was something quite fishy about Robin Whaley stirring up all this bad feeling and his fears were not unfounded.

Eleanor finally confessed to him she had mentioned him in her file - that he had turned up at the press conference as an ally of Perry's.

"But how was he involved?" he kept pressing.

"He spun a web of lies," Eleanor shivered. "Just be wary of him, Charlie... He is a manipulative man and whatever else happens, we have to live in this town."

In the end, Charlie was compelled to bury his suspicions.

As Peter escorted him to the council headquarters, he was as keen to involve Elijah. Luckily the school could not be more obliging, proud of his artistic influence. Elijah's schooldays had in fact, improved vastly, since his brief interlude as a Westbourne House resident, which had elevated him from his lowly 'gypsy' status. Ever since moving to Rosebrook though, he was beginning to socialise with kids around town. It had sent his confidence spiralling.

The only downside was Andrew's jealousy. Infuriated by Elijah's design skills, he was convinced he was trying to upstage him. To his disgust, Charlie even discovered one of his drawings screwed up in the wastepaper basket. An explosive row had followed, Elijah quick to diffuse it. Knowing Peter kept the original in a filing cabinet, he insisted it was only a photocopy. But in the days leading up to the council meeting, Andrew's sourness did not improve. It left a nasty atmosphere that took even Charlie by surprise, thankful his hours working in the wine bar kept him away from the almshouse - and he did appear to have a steady girlfriend.

Charlie shook these thoughts from his head as they paused on the edge of the council chamber. Given the decision rested with a group of elected councillors, he felt his tension rise.

Enthroned in high-backed chairs, they spent a considerable time chewing over the details.

The case for renovating the building was presented by Head of Planning, Terry Griffiths, while Robin Whaley and Councillor Montgomery sat in silent anticipation, having seconded the proposal. As they scrutinised Elijah's sketch, alongside the drawings Charlie had submitted, all he could do was cling to the hope their proposal would be accepted.

There were a few mumbled questions - a moment of nail-biting silence... Then finally, they cast their vote.

At first it felt like a dream. With the committee almost unanimous in their support, Elijah let out a gasp. An affectionate chuckle rippled through the chamber and only then did the truth sink in.

Their building design had been given the go ahead.

Peter felt more overjoyed than anyone. Gazing across at Robin, he threw him a smile laced with gratitude. Robin offered him a nod. Yet there was a gleam in his eye; something cold and authoritarian that implied he held the upper hand.

Peter turned away, unsure why it unnerved him.

Forced to bury his anxiety, he joined the group revelling outside the council office. Charlie stood among them, proud to be the instigator of such an ambitious scheme, while the small, almost ethereal figure of Elijah hung close to him.

Robin sidled up behind him. "Congratulations," he murmured.

Elijah whirled around. He seemed overwhelmed to be at the centre of attention, amongst these powerful suited men. But unable to contain his nerves, he reached up and whispered something to Charlie, before peeling himself away from the group. Charlie, who seemed anxious to accompany him, bade the men farewell.

"So," Robin's voice drawled in Peter's ear. "He's the architect..."

Peter turned, not missing the smugness in his voice. "That's correct, Robin. His name is Charlie and I swear he will work wonders in this town."

"Good," Robin smiled, "and I'm sorry if I offended you the other day. I am happy to support your ideas, especially for the benefit of Rosebrook."

Peter nodded, hit by that same prickle of unease as Robin fell into step beside him.

"Mind if I join you for a while?" he added.

"Not at all," Peter said. There seemed no sense in arguing. "But the Community Centre is about to close soon... Is that a problem?"

For some reason, Robin said nothing.

By the time they approached the Community Centre it was almost dark. Robin paused by the steps and stared up at the building; perhaps imagining the smooth golden walls about to transform the dull brickwork into something beautiful.

"Shall we go inside?" he said. "I bet you can't wait to share the news with the others."

As they made their way into the hall, a scattering of people shuffled towards the exit. The kitchen was closed, Emily Cuthbert, a stout lady in her seventies, already locking the serving hatch.

"If you lot are after a cup of tea you've left it too late," she announced grumpily.

"No worries," Peter smiled, "I'm sure we'll survive. Have you seen Reginald?"

"I'm right here," his deep voice boomed from behind them.

Peter whirled around, further taken aback to see Hilary by his side.

"Peter," she said sweetly, "and Mr Whaley! How did it go?"

"Great!" Peter chirped. "The council not only approved our building design, they agreed to nearly all the funding. The only condition is we have to raise five thousand ourselves to prove our commitment. But that doesn't seem unreasonable, does it?"

"Not at all," Reginald smiled. "Well done! You must be delighted and sorry if I seemed sceptical. I never imagined the council would agree to it."

"Ah, but we have Robin to thank for that," Peter added with pleasure.

Turning to acknowledge him, there was no mistaking the authority he exuded. Perched on the edge of the circle, he pinned him with his cool smile.

"It was nothing," Robin said silkily, "although it might be an idea to go through some of the finer details. Shall we sit down?"

With no argument, Reginald pulled out a flimsy plastic chair from one of the tables. Robin followed his lead, though Peter felt it would be more discreet to move to an upstairs office. Just as the thought hit him, the kitchen door swung open and Eleanor materialised. Peter froze, aware of the imperious, dark suited figure of Robin sat next to him.

"Okay, so - so when would be a good time to start the project?" he stammered quickly.

"That very much depends on you, Peter," Robin replied.

Peter shivered, not liking the snide undertone creeping into his voice. He was all too aware of Eleanor moving silently in the background. She slipped off her apron.

"Oh, you mean the funding?" he said, desperate to divert attention.

"I wasn't talking about funding," Robin murmured, "right now, I am more concerned about the people you choose to have working here."

He broke off, his glance sliding towards Eleanor.

"Reginald," he hissed under his breath. "What is *she* still doing here after everything we discussed?"

"Can we not talk about this another time?" Peter whispered, feeling his cheeks burn.

"Peter," Robin shot back at him. "The council made a huge commitment to this organisation today. All I want in return is a little compliance on your part."

"The council agreed to renovate the building," Peter protested. "It's not up to them to dictate who can or cannot be recruited as voluntary workers."

"The council will support your organisation all the while it proliferates good causes," Robin retorted, "but they will not support those whose intent is to create anarchy."

"This is crazy," Peter breathed, fighting hard to hang onto his composure. "If it wasn't for the creative talent of her son, we wouldn't even be here."

In those last tense seconds, Eleanor had been drifting towards the exit, each step bringing her closer and closer to the suppressed whispers darting around the table. Peter closed his eyes, dreading the moment she would pass them.

Trust Reggie to choose a table so close to the door.

His fears were not without cause. The instant she paused by their table, Robin raised his head and the atmosphere turned to ice.

"What's going on?" Eleanor demanded.

"Your son's design for the building has been approved, Eleanor," Peter muttered, although he could no longer disguise his anxiety.

"Well, that's good news isn't it?" Eleanor bristled. Her eyes bounced from each of them in turn. "So why the long faces?"

"Eleanor, I'm afraid there's been some dispute as to the suitability of your role here," Reginald answered. Shifting nervously in his chair, he looked a little sheepish.

Hilary on the other hand, suppressed a smirk.

"Is this down to *him*?" Eleanor spat, glowering at Robin.

Robin's scornful expression did not change as he leaned back in his chair to survey her. "You can't deny your link with the criminal underworld," he said, "nor that for the past few years, you have lived as a diddicoy! I don't think you belong here."

"I'm sick of this," Peter spluttered. "You can't do this to her."

"Peter, we have to do what is right for the Community Centre," Reginald said pompously.

"So give her a chance!" Peter snapped. "Eleanor does a lot more to help out than you realise. I've got no reason to question her suitability…"

"There's more to it than that," Reginald sighed. "The more troubling issue is whether or not her late boyfriend had any involvement with drugs, as was reported by the police. Surely you understand our concerns, given our role here is to cure people of drug addiction!"

Eleanor shook her head in disbelief. "That was a pack of lies!" she gasped.

Her gaze was drawn to Robin. He retained a polished composure, smooth hands folded on the table top. Only the hate-infused glint of his eyes reflected his true sentiment.

"Didn't Bernard explain anything?"

"Why are we doubting her?" Peter said. "Bernard was a good judge of character."

"Yes," Eleanor whimpered, "and I'll show you an article that contests all those lies. An article from a press conference with NME. You remember, don't you, Mr Whaley? You were there!"

A stony silence descended. Yet Robin had not finished. Face white with fury, he rose to face Eleanor directly.

"You have no proof of anything!" he spouted with undisguised malice.

"Neither have you!" Eleanor hissed. "You lied to Bernard! In fact, everything you ever said was a lie from the very first day I saw you!"

"The first time I saw *you*, Miss Chapman, was in a brothel in Poplar, remember?" Robin whispered evilly. "Is that a lie?"

Eleanor could not speak, staring in stunned bewilderment as he turned to address the whole group.

"That's not true..." she started to mumble.

"Do you deny I saw you in that brothel?" Robin's voice lashed back at her.

"N-no, but..."

Suddenly it was all too much for Hilary. "I've heard enough," she spluttered, enraged.

"Hang on," Peter gasped, "won't you even let her speak now?"

"It seems this woman is associated with everything sordid in our world," Hilary sneered. "Criminals, anarchists... but prostitution?" She surveyed Eleanor with disgust. "Unless you can prove otherwise, I do not want to see your face in here again."

"He's twisting things!" Eleanor sobbed. "I was never a prostitute..."

Unable to suppress her tears for another second, she turned from the table and fled.

III

Peter wasted no time. Chasing Eleanor back to the almshouse, he seemed determined to restore some peace after the rumpus Robin had created. First he ordered fish and chips from the shop beneath his cosy bachelor pad. Then, after uncorking a magnum of sparkling wine (which he was saving for a special occasion), insisted on celebrating for Elijah's sake.

The poor boy looked crestfallen to see her in tears and at a time they should have been rejoicing in the afterglow of the council meeting.

It took every ounce of Peter's inner calm to massage away their despair. The only burden left was how they would tackle Robin's blatant persecution of Eleanor.

As a consequence, she set off to London the next day.

Initially, she felt an urge to talk to her solicitor to re-iterate her discoveries about Perry.

Given the turmoil in her life however, there was only one person she could confide in about Whaley - and that person was Rosemary Merriman.

Pressing herself into a train seat, she watched the familiar lines of trees flit past the window.

That showdown with Robin had resurrected horrible memories of the press conference. In truth, she had never quite got over James's death but much as she wanted to focus on his children's welfare... this new storm of conflict had side-tracked her.

By Friday however, people were starting to miss her.

Emily Cuthbert was heard loudly complaining there weren't enough hands in the kitchen. Dirty cups piled up by the serving hatch faster than anyone could clear them. Only in her absence, did people start to realise that Eleanor did the work of three people.

Next came the disgruntled murmurs from the elderly folk who visited the centre. They admitted to missing her company. For however busy she was, Eleanor always had time for people. Whether it was to let them offload their problems or talk about their health complaints, she would find reassuring words to console them. Furthermore, the hall was becoming untidy. Few people ever really noticed that Eleanor was continually wiping tables and stacking unused chairs. Potted plants wilted from a lack of water. Even the little vases of flowers she had added so lovingly to the table tops could not survive another day.

"Has Eleanor left?" Hilary asked on the one occasion Charlie poked his head through the door.

"Would you blame her?" he retorted savagely, "after the disgraceful way you and *your friend* from the council insulted her?"

Hilary's eyes flashed. "I was hoping we could sort out that unfortunate business."

"I see," Charlie answered. "Well, if you must know, Eleanor is catching up with an old friend... someone more than willing to vouch for her!"

Eleanor meanwhile, stuck to her plans. It was good to catch up with John Sharp, secure in the knowledge her newly updated file had been hidden in the same bank vault as before.

But nothing brought more solace than revisiting the park, where she had installed her tribute to Jake. To discover the tiny green stone still present, even after all these years, brought a sense of joy to her aching heart.

The park however, had changed. Towering blocks of flats formed an imposing backdrop, the area of green space receding as the spread of urban development closed in. The mature trees she remembered had been felled. This left a naked expanse of lawn, devoid of the paths she and Jake had raced down on the momentous day they had met. Yet she chose not to dwell.

Continuing north to reach Rosemary's home, she stayed for the next two nights.

Rosemary, now in her fifties, looked older than Eleanor had imagined; her hair completely white, cropped in a shorter style. Such maturity was enhanced by the lines etched in her face from many summers spent abroad. Naturally, she hankered to know how Elijah was, though horrified to hear of James's death. So she prompted Eleanor to pour her heart out; from her blossoming relationship with Charlie to her clash with Perry. Coming face to face with the mystery man at the press conference was shocking in itself, until she described her encounters with Robin Whaley...

"Be careful, Eleanor," Rosemary warned. "I've long suspected he is dangerous. I figured that out from what Joshua told me. How could I forget how much he spooked him?"

She was referring to the night her youngest son, Joshua, had infiltrated the press conference. He had aroused Councillor Whaley's suspicion without question; even her elder son, Luke, sensed something predatory about him. Rosemary had always been intuitive when it came to human nature and the thought of him being anywhere near Eleanor's son made her shudder.

Sadly, it was shortly after the press conference that Dominic Theakston had delivered his deadly threats, driving Eleanor from their home.

"I'll never forget the day we took you to Aldwyck," Rosemary kept reminiscing, "and even on that journey, Joshua feared we were being followed?"

"He never said," Eleanor frowned.

Rosemary shrugged. "Only later did he mention a black Hackney Carriage tailing us. Luke remembers the same car loitering by the park when you made your final visit... But the synchronicity of it made Joshua anxious. He jacked in his job soon after and spent the next few years travelling."

"Oh my God!" Eleanor breathed. "I always imagined Joshua being the sort of boy who would go off globetrotting anyway."

"I know," Rosemary confessed, "he just didn't want to hang around. But Joshua's been back in London for nearly a year now. He works in the music industry and wants to be a journalist. As for Luke; he's finally opened up a wine shop in Forest Haven. If there's one good thing that's come out of Mrs Thatcher's government, it's this 'Enterprise Allowance Scheme,' designed to help people like my son set up their own businesses."

Nothing could have delighted Eleanor more. Rosemary's daughter, Alison, meanwhile, was living in the US, an aspiring actress who had played her first role in a major film. Such companionship made Eleanor smile. Rosemary was gifted with the same ability to reach into people's hearts as Peter and this alone, brought her back to her own predicament.

"What am I going to do?" she pressed. "Whaley despises me. My reputation is ruined and we might even lose the almshouse if he continues spreading his poison..."

Rosemary's eyes glittered. "Why not look up your old friend, Della? You said she remembered you... Let her tell your story."

Come Saturday, Eleanor cherished the tranquillity of Rosemary's home for a few more hours before reluctantly setting off again; except this time she took a detour to Bromley.

It wasn't difficult to find the ugly block of flats where she had bumped into Della all those years ago, amazed to discover her old friend still living there.

IV

Face blanched, no one could be more surprised than Hilary, when Peter rapped on her office door, accompanied by Eleanor and her friend.

"You may not like the type o' woman I am or what I've had to do for a living," Della began coldly, "but there's no way this girl was a prostitute!"

"Is this true?" Reginald intervened, shuffling from one foot to another.

"I wouldn't o' travelled all the way from Bromley if I weren't tellin' the truth, Mister!" Della shouted. "Either of you heard of sex trafficking? Eleanor was dumped in that place against her will. Didn't sell her body to no one! Just for the record, she hit me over the head with a vodka bottle to escape. Do you wanna know why?"

"I'm not sure I do," Hilary said stiffly.

"Some guy turned up to be her first," Della persisted, eyes blazing. "Real nasty man! And when she escaped, he sent his guys round..." Wrenching up her sleeve, she exposed a deep scar trailing down the length of her arm. "Did this to me!"

Hilary closed her eyes. "Reggie, I've heard enough," she whispered.

"Have you now?" Peter muttered softly.

He had taken an instant shine to Della, amused to see the Magnus couple squirm.

"But what made *you* turn to prostitution?" Hilary could not resist the urge to ask.

Della chuckled. "Let me tell you something, lady. When my Ma came to England in the 1950's, she broke her back in an accident an' got disabled. Couldn't look after me no more and I was put in a care home. Trouble is, there's bad men in them places too. Abused me when I was eleven! By the time I was fifteen, I felt like nothing! Going on the game weren't no different!"

Eleanor's blood ran cold. Yet she was watching Hilary's face, the disdain in her expression fading, before her eyes widened.

"What's the matter, Hilary?" she taunted. "Does it upset you to know what a sick society we live in? And Reggie... you counsel people for drug addiction. Don't either of you wonder *why* people end up in that state in the first place?"

"Of course," Hilary said tightly. "The only thing that troubles me now is

307

why Robin Whaley brought this up? Why is he so against you, Eleanor?"

"Because I know he's a two-faced, lying bastard," Eleanor hissed. "He may come across as sincere... but I know from first hand experience he is not!"

Peter shook his head in bewilderment. "Yet he's been so supportive of our renovation."

"I know," Eleanor said, "and as a planning officer, maybe he's trying to do what's best for the town. But I warn you, be careful. Whatever Whaley does, always question his motives."

An interlude of silence followed as her words sank in. Reginald sighed heavily.

"Let's say no more about this," he mumbled. "I want no more unpleasantness. Eleanor, I apologise for having doubted you."

"So what about Mr Whaley?" Hilary broke in. "Shouldn't someone have a word with him? At the end of the day, we have got to get along..."

"I'll speak to him," Peter pledged.

Eleanor smiled, impressed by the steel in his tone.

"Well, that was an eye-opener," Peter said as they wandered across to the almshouse. "It's good to meet you, Della. I told you the Magnus's were prejudiced. It does them good to face up to some of the rottenness in this world, especially in our care system..."

Eleanor did not miss the shadow passing over his face.

She bit her lip, wondering what had gone wrong in his own life; that hint Bernard had discovered him as a homeless runaway on the brink of death...

As they settled inside their home however, the conversation inevitably centred around Della. Very little had changed in her life. She was still working at a local supermarket; still living in the same squalid block of flats and worried about her sixteen year old daughter, Lara, who had ultimately got herself recruited into some fearsome gang.

Eleanor wondered if it was the same lot who had terrorised Anna.

"She's only gone and got pregnant... you can see how she's gonna end up. Single Ma like me! I wish I could get her away from that dump, away from all them bad kids."

"Apply for a council house," Peter insisted. "There might be some available in Rosebrook."

"Peter, that's a great idea," Eleanor gasped. "Oh Della, please say you'll think about it."

"Okay," Della grinned. "There ain't nothing to keep us in that shit hole in Bromley."

She left before dusk but not before Peter had unearthed as many leaflets as he could find with regards to applying for a council tenancy.

With the darkness creeping in, Eleanor luxuriated in their lounge with an overpowering sense of relief. The curtains were drawn, a shroud of candlelight cloaking the walls. As the fear in her mind receded, she felt indebted to Della. *They were not about to lose the almshouse.* Finally, she could concentrate on getting their lives back on track, her thoughts drifting towards the Barton-Wells children.

"We should phone them," she said, "find out if their mother's still around. If not, let's pay them a visit tomorrow. I'll drive..."

"What's going to happen at Christmas?" Margaret piped up. "They'll be on their own! Wouldn't it be nice if we could go and spend it with them?"

Eleanor threw her an indulgent smile. She had been dismayed to miss Avalon's birthday.

"It's a lovely idea," she sighed, "but we can't. Don't forget the house belongs to Perry Hampton now. If he found out he'd be furious! He might even throw them out!"

Eventually, she spoke to Elliot.

Perry had paid them another visit and in the light of Avril being present, it was not a pleasant encounter. Soon to return to America, she had even invited the children to live with her. Yet both had declined. Conscious of the clock running faster, they wanted to savour every moment they had left in their old home.

Thus, on the following Sunday, they visited. Eleanor took the wheel under Charlie's supervision but couldn't deny being nervous. Carefully rolling up the driveway, she felt her heart lurch, as the familiar mansion took shape on the skyline.

Once inside the house though, she swallowed back her tears, hit by a sense of melancholy. The house had become emptier as each beautiful piece of furniture was removed. Ornamental rugs, paintings and tapestries had also started to vanish, its character fading away.

Eleanor brought up the subject of Christmas. The idea of inviting them to Rosebrook floated on the edge of her tongue; although nothing pleased her more than to hear they had been invited to stay with the Fortescues in London. They had done little more about house-hunting, but at least Elliot was granted power of attorney. It enabled him to recruit a housekeeper, a part time governess for William. But no one could ignore the creeping approach of Perry's deadline.

Secretly Eleanor was dreading it.

Avalon and William however, were not the only ones embarking on a trip to London.

In another hidden corner of Rosebrook, Robin stood in the lounge of his elegant townhouse, sipping a glass of port. He had decided to spend Christmas with his own family, or what little was left of it. His estranged father was dead, his older brothers despised him and their mother, who was becoming progressively more frail, could barely remember him.

But he revelled in the love of his sister, Jennifer, the one family member who had ever shown him affection - now married with teenage children. Robin had also developed a tender rapport with his niece, Naomi. Naomi was one of the few relatives gifted with the same intellect as himself and whose blossoming academic achievement he swore to nurture. Robin himself had no children. He had only ever married once and the relationship had been a disaster.

What aggravated him most though, was his latest encounter with Peter. Saddened by his prejudice towards Eleanor, oh how he relished imparting the news; *she had managed to clear her name, even in the eyes of the Magnus couple and would remain in their community for the unforeseeable.* That final taunt hit him like a slap in the face. Robin knocked back his port, slamming the glass down on the table. He had failed in his duty to appease Perry, which in turn brought a spiralling wave of hate.

Deep in his heart, he feared there was only one solution.

Time to bring in the big guns and track down Theakston.

Chapter Thirty-Four

I

January 1987

Robin's search drew him to a town named Swanley. It lay within a commutable distance from London and conveniently just seven miles to the east of Rosebrook.

Staring in wonderment, he noted the houses on the approach road... from snowy white walls and bay windows, to the lines of crisp hedge guarding the front gardens. With all the hallmarks of a town inhabited by wealthy upper middle classes, how a man like Dominic Theakston could end up here seemed bizarre.

Eventually his journey brought him into the town centre, lined with smart shops and trendy restaurants. Theakston's enterprise lay on the outer fringe; a splendid health and fitness club known as Atlas Leisure. Robin smiled. Here was a man who had risen from a violent criminal background; a much feared gang leader who had conquered the notorious Sammie Maxwell. He had ruled the East End with his own gang, men reputed to be the most brutal thugs in London. Robin also knew the man had been a professional contract killer.

Parking his car in a side street, he experienced a frisson of fear. He couldn't deny he felt uneasy, now wondering if Dominic had changed. According to rumour, he had progressed from organised crime to evolve into a formidable business tycoon. Yet he would never forget the man he was in the 70s; a terrifying character whose lean face and slanted dark eyes conveyed a sadistic nature. Even the way he moved reminded people of a tiger.

Finally, Robin located the French restaurant he had booked. With creamy walls adorned with a shroud of Virginia creeper, its scarlet blaze reminded him of blood.

Shooting a furtive glance over his shoulder, he slipped through the door. He recognised Dominic instantly. Lurking in the dimly lit corner farthest from the door, his face was masked in shadow. Robin felt his heart quicken as he approached the table. Dominic raised his head, offering him a cold smile. His face was broader than Robin remembered, a distinct clench to his jaw. With his eyes softened by fine lines, he possessed a maturity that enhanced his looks; his dark blonde hair shorter, his powerful frame less bulky.

"Robin Whaley," Dominic drawled, as he lowered himself into the chair opposite.

311

As Robin extended his hand, the other man grasped it with his left, a powerful gangland handshake that practically crushed his bones.

"It was good of you to come," Robin began, "it's been years..." He broke off, his throat dry as dust. "I was about to order a Stella. Can I get you the same?"

"Nah!" Dominic replied. "Don't drink beer. Like to keep myself in shape, see, 'specially in my field of work." He patted his iron-hard abdomen as if to press the point. "Tell you what though, seeing as it's been a while, I'll stretch to a glass of white wine."

Robin raised an eyebrow. "I never imagined you to be a wine drinker..."

Dominic leaned forward, his eyes sharp as flints. "Look! Just because I'm an ex-con, doesn't mean I'm a lout," he whispered dangerously.

"I wasn't implying anything of the sort," Robin said, summoning a waiter. "Do you have a preference? I'm a red wine drinker myself, but I expect they do a lovely white Bordeaux."

"I'd sooner have Frascati," Dominic snapped. "Anyway, how are things? Hear you're some big shot at Rosebrook Council. What's it you wanted to talk to me about?"

"Many things," Robin smiled, "but tell me about yourself first. Why did you leave London?"

Dominic shrugged. "Things got a bit heated. I had to keep me head down but life was sweet... I was running all sorts of cartels, besides Sammie's protection rackets. I spread me wings. Found new avenues, 'specially 'round Bethnal Green and Soho. You know the sort of thing..."

"Go on," Robin pressed, his intrigue spiralling.

"You know the kind of stuff people crave, Robin," Dominic said, lowering his voice. "Strip joints, swingers clubs, porn... Depends where you get your kicks. I liked taking risks, 'specially when it came to shifting contraband. At the lower end of the spectrum it was fags and booze; a little higher up the scale, drugs and firearms."

"What about *hired violence?*" Robin whispered, drawing his head even closer. "Did you ever take on any further contracts?"

Dominic's eyes betrayed a flash. "Not since the last," he said. "Even running a protection racket involves violence, as you know, which is how I met my lovely wife. Her daddy owned a nightclub. Brash bastard! Expensive suits, fancy roller, magnet to every toe rag trying to make a fast buck! His club was raided on a regular basis but one night, those fuckers trussed up his girl. Threatened to do some nasty things, unless the ol' man gave 'em the combination to his safe. Made off with several grand they did... and that's when he approached me."

312

Dominic smiled to himself. He'd demanded £100 a week from Donald Appleby, twice what he charged others in that business, but the man was desperate. The next time those scumbags broke into his club, Dominic's men were on standby. Subjected to an attack of extreme brutality, every one of them had been hospitalised. One even died.

The smaller gangs left Donald alone after that. No sooner did Dominic start paying regular visits to his club though, it was fated he would be attracted to his daughter, Crystal. Mesmerised by her looks, which combined long, shimmering hair and glossy skin, he was most taken in by her eyes; huge, thickly lashed and such a lovely shade of blue, they reminded him of an Aegean sea. Working as a fashion model, she not only possessed a fabulous figure but was dynamite in bed! In fact, the adrenalin charge he got from all his criminal wheeler-dealing was nothing compared to her.

So one morning, he dreamily asked her to marry him.

Dominic closed his eyes without thinking. Looking back, life had been great. Beautiful wife, nice house, lucrative deals seeping out of every nook and cranny... right up until Hargreaves was slung out of 'the yard' on the discovery he had been liaising with professional criminals such as himself and taking back-handers.

In 1979 things got heavy. With Hargreaves ousted, Dominic knew he had to tread carefully, quick to wind down the protection rackets. More covert operations such as his drug cartel continued, but at a very underground level. What Dominic hadn't been counting on was that someone like Barry Mason would weasel his way into the police force, with a view to capping the lid on organised crime. Yet he knew from day one that bastard had it in for him.

Randomly arrested for just about every crime going down in the city, hardly a week went by when he wasn't flung into a police cell on some pretext or another. He even joked *they might as well install his name plaque on the cell door.*

But Mason wasn't laughing. It was no secret his brother had been knifed in an alleyway during the turf war on 'Sammie's Patch.' The perpetrator could have been anyone, but as gang leader, Mason held Dominic personally responsible.

Even Mason went too far one night though; bribing some destitute drug dealer to falsely implicate him in a cocaine smuggling operation that had nothing to do with him. The arrest took place just as Crystal went into labour with their first child. He was about to rush her into hospital when they practically bashed his door down. Despite all protests, he was forced to endure yet another long night in a police cell, when he should have been by her side. Dominic felt murderous. Sure, he was no angel, but they had nothing on him! It seemed Mason was determined to fit him up, exploiting his powers to goad others into lying.

That night everything changed.

First, he became a father. No sooner had he been released, he was over to the hospital like a shot where Crystal joyfully presented him with a baby son.

Next, he recruited his own solicitor to bring a lawsuit against Mason for harassment.

And finally, he severed all ties with organised crime, handed the reins over to his partner, Dan Levy, and laundered his entire fortune in setting up his East London gym.

"So, you gave it all up?" Robin breathed. "No more dealings with organised crime?"

"Yeah, that's right," Dominic grinned, just as the waiter brought their drinks over.

They waited until he disappeared before resuming their conversation, though Robin's eyes had adopted a penetrating quality.

"What?" Dominic demanded curtly.

Robin released a sigh. "Somebody has resurfaced," he muttered, flipping open the menu, "but I'll talk about that in a moment... Now what are you ordering?"

"Not sure I wanna order anything," Dominic snapped, sipping his wine, "'specially not this poncy French shit! Why didn't you let me choose the restaurant? There's a really nice New York Italian just up the road, at least we could have had pizza..."

"Oh come now, Dominic, stop acting like a pleb," Robin said gently, tapping his glass. "It's been years since we've had a catch up and I wanted to choose somewhere special..."

"Special for you maybe but not for me," Dominic grunted, "and I'm not a pleb! Drawn out lunches are not my thing, okay? I grab snacks on the move. I'm a busy man, not like you laid-back council workers who nearly always seem to be on holiday!" He glowered at the menu. "What's that?" he added, pointing to the *Salade Niçoise*.

"A combination of tuna, eggs, olives, anchovies, salad leaves..." Robin started to say.

"That'll do," Dominic said, snapping the menu shut, "and I'll have chips with it. Get us a bottle of Perrier and that's £12.85 I owe you! I ain't letting you pay."

"You added that up quick," Robin trotted out before he could stop himself.

Dominic let out a loud laugh. "You don't know anything about me, do you?" he sneered. "I might have come from a shitty background but I'm not thick! Top of my class, I was!"

314

"I never doubted your intelligence," Robin placated him. "Maybe we've got more in common than you think. I was top of my class too. And it may surprise you to learn I also hailed from a rough background. So you left school at sixteen, am I right?"

"Wrong!" Dominic spat. "Fourteen! I was mixed up in the gang life."

"I see," Robin sighed, "though you still haven't told me why you left London. What brought you to Swanley?"

Dominic gave a shrug. "Getting out of crime did me no favours, Robin. People thought I'd gone soft when all I wanted to do was to settle down with me family and run a proper legit business. Gym was doing all right. Made a mint I did and that's when the worst happened. Crystal was kidnapped, along with me boy, Anton. Fucking bastards demanded half a mil. Well, even I couldn't raise that sort of money... The pigs weren't a lot of help either."

"What did you do?" Robin spluttered.

"Got the boys involved," Dominic said, his voice lowering to a barely audible whisper. "Still had me contacts. Dan Levy and a few choice heavies. Managed to trace the address where they were held captive..."

He broke off, unable to continue. He didn't want to think about what Dan and his boys had done to those kidnappers in the aftermath of rescuing his family; the cans of petrol used to torch the place while the perpetrators lay trapped inside. Dominic smirked. It still didn't do anyone much good to get on the wrong side of him. But that nightmare had been a wake-up call. Worst, it had left Crystal traumatised and scared for the kid. She had been desperate to move away from London and hide somewhere out in the countryside.

"Swanley seemed a good choice," Dominic finished, just as the waiter sidled up to their table. "Near enough to London to scoot back if I chose, but remote enough to enjoy a nice quiet life. East London Gym's under new management now, though I've still got a share in it. I set up a new club, right here, which is doing even better! Hit the market just at the right time I did..."

As the waiter took their order, Dominic could not help but revel in his good fortune.

Traditionally, weight-training was a male dominated market. He'd got into it himself, whilst serving a couple of years in jail. By the early 80s however, a revolutionary health and fitness boom had attracted the *female* market, when Jane Fonda's workouts swept the nation. With a second club launched in 1983, women in lycra and leg warmers came flocking to the place in droves. Being a successful businessman brought back all the buzz that had been absent since turning his back on organised crime. Though sadly, his marriage had gone downhill, embroiling him in a messy divorce. He fired Robin a long and searching stare.

"Anyway," he drawled, "enough about the past. What's the real reason you asked to meet me? C'mon, spill the beans. You said someone's resurfaced. Who?"

"Do you remember Eleanor Chapman?" Robin taunted.

Dominic froze, as Robin expected, that lingering look of pleasure sliding right off his face.

"How could I forget? Thought we'd got shot of that girl, once and for all. You saying she's back?"

"I'm afraid so," Robin replied, folding his hands on the table. "Just moved to Rosebrook and she's been worming her way in with the Community Centre."

"Really?" Dominic said. "So what's the problem? Don't tell me she's stirring things."

Robin planned his next words carefully. "She's said enough to raise people's suspicions, especially Peter Summerville, the manager. I warned him not to trust her, along with the Magnus couple. *Reginald* Magnus... he already knew about her boyfriend's murder."

"Has she mentioned my name?" Dominic snapped.

Robin watched with pleasure as his hand coiled into a fist.

"Not yet," he kept goading, "but it's only a matter of time. She's living with another man now. One cannot imagine what she might have told him. Finally, there's the issue of her secret file. Not one of us knows what is written, but I'm certain we are all mentioned..." He shook his head. "This is not a good situation, Dominic. Mr Hampton is particularly concerned."

"Then surely it's up to *Mr Hampton* to deal with it," Dominic snarled. "What do you expect me to do? This ain't got nothing to do with me no more, I don't even live in Rosebrook..."

"From what you've been telling me, it seems there are plenty of people who hold a grudge against you," Robin coolly reminded him. "Doesn't the thought of that woman living so close bother you in the slightest?"

Dominic gave a sniff. "Like I say, it's not my problem. She knows it'd be a bad idea to cross me again, but to throw the ball back in your court, Robin, what have *you* done?"

"I've spoken to her," Robin whispered. "Told her she had no place in our town."

Lifting his head, Dominic gave a smile that carved deep dimples into the sides of his mouth. "Tell you to *fuck off*, did she?" he taunted.

Robin looked uncomfortable. "She didn't quite use those words, but my plan to get her removed from the town failed. Mr Hampton wants her driven out, preferably back to that caravan in Aldwyck, so I'll get straight to the point... She needs another scare, Dominic."

"You're asking me to threaten her again?" he said coldly. "Didn't I just

316

explain, I've turned me back on organised crime."

Robin felt a surge of panic. "It has to be you," he insisted. "You're the only one she is genuinely scared of. Mr Hampton *will* deal with her personally, as soon as she's out of Rosebrook..."

"And I'm telling you, I ain't interested," Dominic retorted. "I'm in the middle of a divorce. I don't need this shit! I even sold the family home to give my wife a generous settlement, but she's a vindictive cow and wants to take my kids! She'll use my criminal past as a lever if she has to, which means I've got to keep my nose clean, and I ain't about to screw up my chances for the sake of your paranoia, so forget it!"

Even the waiter exposed a look of fear as he flitted towards their table. After despatching the plates containing Dominic's salad, along with a Coq au Vin for Robin, a warm garlic fragrance permeated the air, momentarily snapping the tightrope tension.

"That looks superb," Robin said, flashing the man a smile. "Thank you."

Dominic said nothing. Shrugging himself out of his jacket, he slung it over his chair. His black polo shirt revealed lean arms, corded with hard, shapely muscles. Robin observed a shimmer of golden hairs; the curling fronds of a tattoo around his forearm. Although they did not quite conceal the pattern of scars lurking beneath.

"It's just a warning, Dominic," he added softly.

The man grabbed his fork, attacking the island of tuna on his plate.

"You don't need to repeat your threat, just remind her of it. Ask her if she remembers what you said last time..."

"Dunno," Dominic mumbled between mouthfuls. "What if she goes to the cops?"

"She won't," Robin reassured him, "not if she cares about her son, who incidentally I have met. D'you know he looks very much like his father."

Dominic froze again, raising his gaze from beneath furrowed eyebrows. Robin could sense his fury. *He did not like to be reminded of the killing of Jake Jansen.*

"Eleanor Chapman will do anything to protect him," his voice tolled. "You don't have to say much. All that needs to happen is for Eleanor to see your face... to understand the threat that still hangs in the balance."

"Right," Dominic said curtly, "and what if I don't want to see her?"

"Maybe you should," Robin smiled. He had never forgotten how he lusted after Eleanor in the old days, when his gang had spread themselves all over London, looking for her. "Aren't you curious to see how she's changed?"

"Why should I be curious?" Dominic probed, "and has she changed?"

"Is she still attractive?" Robin's voice mocked. "Oh yes! But not as you remember. A little more - wild and rebellious - which may prove something of a challenge for you."

Dominic exhaled a sigh and banged down his fork.

"What exactly is it you want me to do?"

"Just approach her," Robin purred, feeling his tension lift. "There's an open day at the Community Centre in February. She'll be hanging around... All you need do is whisper a few choice words in her ear. Would that be possible?"

"I'll think about it," Dominic answered.

II

For twenty minutes they continued their lunch in a cocoon of light hearted conversation. Robin was surprised to notice Dominic had left half his food. But in the short interlude, when he briefly disappeared to the Gents, Robin took the liberty of topping up his wine glass. His mood seemed to shift from one extreme to another; cocky and humorous one minute, until a darker more sullen side spiralled up like a storm. Robin knew the man had never really liked him much. Only their collaboration in Jake's murder connected them.

Yet all the same, Dominic fascinated him. Intrigued to tunnel deeper into his past, he couldn't help wondering what had happened to turn him into the ruthless gangster he was renowned for. He had already let slip he was a high flyer.

By the time Dominic returned, he seemed more in tune with his surroundings. As he rested his elbow on the table however, Robin's eyes honed in on his arm again, squinting to locate those scars. Like metal studs punched into leather, they hid under the ink of his tattoo.

"What happened to your arm?" he whispered, reaching over to turn it.

With a look of fury, Dominic wrenched it away. "Take your hands off me," he spat.

"Sorry," Robin said gently. "They're cigarette burns aren't they? Did your father do that?"

Dominic gave a harsh laugh. "Never even knew who me dad was," he joked. "My mum lost the man she loved in the war. Turned to gin! Ended up in some slum tenement shit hole in the north of London! Place was full of girls like her... unmarried, most of them on the game, string of snotty-nosed kids. The name 'Theakston' came from our landlord 'cos he was shafting her an' all."

"I didn't realise," Robin muttered in embarrassment.

"Doesn't matter," Dominic smirked. "I know he wasn't my father. He was a short, fat, ugly little bastard. Me real father would have been tall! Looks wise, I took after me mum. Her name was Belle and she was a nice-looking woman; blonde hair, blue eyes, lovely smile..."

"So modest!" Robin teased. "But you haven't answered my question."

"What this?" Dominic challenged, now unashamedly flaunting his forearm. "Let me tell you something, Robin, when you grow up in a neighbourhood like mine with no proper family to speak of, you get into the gang life. It was the only way us kids found a sense of belonging, see. Me and me half brothers practically grew up on the streets. Our gang was family and we looked out for each other. But when I was seventeen, I got on the wrong side of a real nasty gang leader called Li-liang Lee. Half Chinese he was, ran one of the torture gangs in the sixties. One night I was snatched and dragged to their gaff, where they subjected me to the worst night of my life."

"They tortured you?" Robin gasped in horror.

His dark eyes seared into him. "Yeah! Battered me with metal bars - busted half me bones... They screwed my right hand into a vice and that was the worst..." He flexed his right hand and tried to wriggle it but the thumb and outer fingers wouldn't move. "Crushed me hand. Imagine what that felt like. I screamed so loud, one of 'em had to wrap his arm around my face to shut me up and that's when they started burning me with their fags..."

Robin squirmed in his chair. "Jesus," he spluttered, wishing he had never asked. "Was there nothing you could do?"

"Nothing!" Dominic replied in low hiss. "It just went on and on until I passed out. Lucky one of me own gang members found me, otherwise who knows where I'd be now? I spent a long time in hospital recovering from them injuries and I swore revenge, but someone else got the bastard."

Robin stared at him, mesmerised. He had actually turned quite cold.

"It's not something I broadcast," Dominic added, "so keep it to yourself."

"Of course," Robin reflected. "Seventeen though... it must have affected you badly."

"Yeah," Dominic growled. "Went right off the rails after that, I did. Took out every gang who crossed me, then finally did a stretch for manslaughter. But the day I walked out of prison, no one dared touch me. I was full of hate. Had no problem tackling Maxwell. Hargreaves encouraged it and you know the rest... In fact, it's taken me a long time to break away from that life and now you and your buddies are trying to drag me right back into it."

"That's not true," Robin retorted, fearing he may have pushed him too far.

Shocked by the mercurial dive in Dominic's mood again, he knew it was time to leave.

Dominic was desperate to walk back to his health club.

Robin, fearing it was too soon to end their discussion though, suggested driving him. Guided towards his sleek silver Audi, Dominic slid his tall frame into the seat.

"I'm sorry about your hand," he tried placating him. "It's paralysed, isn't it?"

"One of my many war wounds," Dominic echoed. "I'm no stranger to violence, even if I did spend the last years dishing it out rather than being on the receiving end."

"No one is trying to lure you back into crime, I swear," Robin pledged, "but the Chapman girl will create ripples. Out of the three of us, I fear you have the most to lose..."

He knew he was purposefully trying to manipulate him yet couldn't bear the thought of the meeting ending without *some* reassurance he would approach her.

"Anyway, how come you're getting divorced? I thought you loved your wife."

"Still do," Dominic sighed, "just couldn't stay faithful. Can't help myself where women are concerned. They're my biggest weakness and the trouble is I'm surrounded by them. You should see some of our aerobics instructors... gorgeous! Amazing figures!"

"Right," Robin muttered, leaving the path open for him to elaborate.

"First time I had an affair, Crystal forgave me. But she went right off sex after our daughter was born. Could hardly blame me when I strayed a second time."

"I don't have a lot to do with women," Robin said. "Parasites for the most part. At least my divorce was mutual, we both knew it wasn't working..."

He broke off, not wanting to think about his ex-wife, Theresa; the only girl he thought he could ever fall in love with. Yet the longer the marriage went on, the more he ended up hating her.

"So, what do you get up to?" Dominic probed. "What gives you a buzz?"

"I play golf," Robin smiled. "I like classical music, the theatre... and I enjoy my job. I have goals for Rosebrook. I broke away from mainstream politics, so I'd like to think I can make my mark on at least one town, and preferably without someone like Eleanor Chapman in the way..."

"I wasn't asking about your work," Dominic kept pushing, ignoring the issue of Eleanor. "Where do you get your kicks? Any girlfriends? Or do you prefer the ladies of the night?"

Robin stiffened, knuckles white as they tightened on the steering wheel. "I told you, I don't have a lot to do with women these days..."

"Really?" Dominic taunted, just as they were pulling into the business and retail park. "Well, you must have some secret desires. Don't tell me you're a poofter."

"We're not all like you, Dominic!" Robin snapped. "Just because I don't chase after anything in a skirt, it doesn't mean I am gay."

Dominic let his head roll back against the chair rest. He was tempted to wind him up even more, by asking him the real reason he had resigned from politics, given his success as an elected councillor. But like his predecessor, Sammie Maxwell, Dominic had developed a habit of digging into people's *personal* lives, especially those trying to claw their way to power. *How could he forget the rumours that linked Whaley's name to a string of teenage rent boys?* Dominic smiled, of a mind to keep that little gem to himself for now.

They stopped outside his health club; a smart building in light golden brick.

"Right," Dominic said, unsnapping his seat belt, "this is my gym! I'd invite you in but I've got a lot of catching up to do, seeing as I've been off site for a couple of hours."

"Impressive," Robin said, staring up in wonder. Steps led up to a smoked glass frontage. It reflected a scattering of white clouds suspended in the sky. "What's the nature of your work?"

"I'm a fully trained fitness instructor now," Dominic replied with relish. "Offer one-to-one personal coaching, which is getting popular, especially with the yuppies! The old gym is still doing well too, and at the end of the month, I'm opening up a wine bar in Swanley."

"I'm glad you've turned your life around," Robin said, "and look - please consider visiting Rosebrook. Who knows, there could even be business opportunities for you there... What do you think? Can I count on your support?"

Dominic paused. Fishing into his jacket, he pulled out a business card, before slipping it through the car window. "I said I'd think about it. Call me..." and without another word, he turned on his heel, jogged up the steps, leaving the other man gaping after him.

III

Dominic charged up to the top floor before anyone had a chance to distract him. Slipping into his private dressing room, he slammed the door shut, his heart hammering.

Back in the restaurant he had nearly lost the plot. A sneaky line of coke snorted in the 'Gents' had lifted his mood, until Robin had dragged him straight back down again by dredging up the demons of his past. He had always considered Whaley an ingratiating little shit and he hadn't changed one bit! In fact, there was only one person who got under his skin more... and that was Eleanor Chapman.

Lowering himself into his chair, he closed his eyes. He hoped he would never again have to be reminded of that fateful summer in 1972; a year he had risen to power. Hand-picked by Inspector Hargreaves to get rid of the hapless witness known as Jake Jansen, his gang had successfully captured him. For 48 hours they had him right where they wanted him; concealed in a secret underground cell, in readiness for his execution.

Yet the plan had disintegrated into chaos when the Chapman girl found him.

Dominic clenched his fists, feeling the bite of his fingernails. There was no denying he had hunted the girl for his own pleasure, except it took months to track down Jake. Then, on the night they had finally dealt with him, she had been hiding under the floorboards. He felt a shudder of cold, never able to forget *Eleanor* had instigated his arrest. And on the evening of the press conference she had unashamedly named him as *Jake's killer*, right in front of a bunch of sodding journalists!

Dominic blew out a sigh. It seemed obvious Whaley would never let this go, especially now Eleanor had re-appeared in their lives. *Whaley who had ordered him to threaten her; Whaley, whose hateful words had hedged around the sadistic abuse of her son.*

Such a concept brought him out in a cold sweat but was it wise to stir things?

On the other hand, could he stand back and run the risk of Eleanor shooting off her big mouth again? Something about Whaley's words had provoked him; *aren't you curious to see how much she's changed?* And a piece of him did, that tiny tug of temptation which might actually draw him to Rosebrook. It would all very much depend on how he was feeling on the day.

Chapter Thirty-Five

Avalon's footsteps slowed as she wandered around the edge of the grounds. The surrounding woods loomed in a silver cloud as an enduring frost clung to the branches. The air was silent, apart from her ragged breathing. Drifting a little further, she was dismayed to see the state of the gardens; from the shrivelled rose heads, whose petals had long abandoned them, to the tangle of shrubs left to wither.

Her return from London had left her deflated. Both the house and grounds conveyed a bleakness, filling her with a sense it was time to move on. Before the festivities of Christmas, they were too crippled with grief. So much so, they dared not venture far from its boundaries, fearing it would augur the first stage of letting go.

That short break in London had broken the spell. Spending Christmas with the Fortescues had revived them, bringing back the embrace of companionship that had been missing from their lives for too long. Avalon had wondered if George would try to rekindle their romance. Yet he seemed distant and awkward, unsure what to say to her in her grieving state. He had instead taken to entertaining William, with whom he bonded more easily. Avalon didn't mind though. She actually found more comfort in the company of George's parents - the cosy evenings spent by the fireside, reminiscing about her father - days out, exploring London, its splendid museums and art galleries.

But ever since their return to Westbourne House, she had begun to realise the importance of *closure*. With her father gone, there was nothing else to keep them here other than memories. Long walks around the grounds had brought a calmness to her mind, allowing her to focus on what really needed to be done. So, they had concentrated their efforts on packing the rest of their belongings, either to go into storage or to sell at the auction house. The gentle passage of a brand new year had also inspired a spate of house hunting.

Although even that had not been without problems.

Avalon flinched, torn out of her daydream by the sound of a car engine. As the familiar beige Mercedes crawled into view, her heart sank. She had no choice but to drag herself away from the gardens and face him. Only as she reached the steps however, was she hit with a sudden fear. On closer observation, *there appeared to be two men in the car.*

Turning her head, she sped up the steps and into the house.

"He's here," she bristled to Elliot as he moved forward to take her coat, "and I'm sure he's brought his son with him!"

William hovered anxiously, until the door creaked open. For a second he froze, glowering at Perry with as much contempt as he dared. Yet in the instant Ben materialised, it was too much for him. Turning to flee into the library, he slammed the door.

"Hello again, Perry," Avalon said, deliberately ignoring Ben.

"Avalon," he responded smoothly. "Now how is your house search going?"

Avalon lowered her gaze. "Not as well as we hoped..." she started telling him.

The intimidating swell in his posture caused her to falter. Until eventually, she was forced to explain.

There was a house that had caught their interest; a listed property nestling in a substantial plot of land. Full of character, with flint walls and a thatched roof, it had been a much sought after property. Though maybe the reason they had lost it to a higher bidder.

Charlie had been quick to placate her, though, seeing it as a blessing in disguise. The roof would require a re-thatch every 20 years, which for a property of such proportions would incur high maintenance costs.

Their second choice of property had suited them better. Hugging the edge of Rosebrook, it seemed destined to draw them closer to their friends. The property itself, a Tudor mansion with decorative half-timbering, was surrounded by an idyllic garden. The asking price of £250,000 was well within their reach, so once again they had put in an offer. Unfortunately the vendors were caught up in a long property chain and this in turn, had delayed matters.

But the more she attempted to justify their situation, the more Perry's face seemed to darken. Ben hovered in the background. She sensed the prick of his eyes as he surveyed her, his look of undisguised hatred.

"Your time is almost up, young lady," Perry finished icily. "I have been more than patient but I am not prepared to wait forever."

"Has anyone been granted power of attorney?" Ben's voice chimed, as if he could no longer bear to be excluded.

Adamant in her refusal to look at him, Avalon locked eyes with Perry.

"Elliot has been appointed," she snapped. "Obviously it is our duty to maintain the upkeep of the estate, all the while we are living here..."

Ben smiled nastily. "You're just going to hang this out for as long as you can, aren't you?" he muttered almost to himself.

Finally Avalon hurled him a glare. "We're doing as much as we can!" she rounded on them. "It's just a couple more weeks, Perry, then I swear we will be gone for good!"

"Really?" Perry murmured in sarcasm. "Well, as long as you understand that by the end of this month, I am perfectly within my rights to evict you."

Avalon bit her lip, fighting to regain control. Up until now she had handled herself well.

"If that's what it comes to, so be it," she challenged him and with a last look of scorn, she turned on her heel, racing into the library to join her brother.

At last the two men left but not before turning the thumbscrews on Elliot.

Pressurised into making a decision as to whether to continue working for them, he felt the safest option was to agree - having secretly conspired with the children. In all eventualities, there was nothing to stop him from leaving as soon as the Hamptons took up residence.

Yet as Perry cruised down the driveway with the shadow of Westbourne House in his wing mirror, the conversation was about to take a sinister turn.

"So, it seems they're not quite ready to leave," Perry sighed. "Pity. Though I still think we should give them the benefit of the doubt; allow them to stay a little longer... perhaps right up until the middle of February. What do you think?"

Ben sighed, restless as he fidgeted in the passenger seat.

"And then are you going to evict them?" he demanded.

"No. I'm not going to evict them," Perry replied, as he steered his car back towards the main road. Pausing by the gates, he flashed him a smile. "You are!"

Chapter Thirty-Six

I

Oblivious to the undercurrent of whisperings, Eleanor had barely stopped thinking about the wonderful Christmas they had shared with Charlie's family. Their visit to London had been just as enjoyable, Margaret and Elijah mesmerised by the window displays in the West End. With the streets hugged by tall Regency buildings, the lights had been spectacular.

On this memorable day, they had also caught up with the Barton-Wells children.

Unsure what to buy them for Christmas, Eleanor had stumbled across a fetching silk and wool scarf from 'Tie Rack' for William. For Avalon, she chose a glossy hard back book, compiled by the Laura Ashley design house. Its pages were filled with inspirational photos. She knew Avalon would cherish it, even more so when they found a new home. Both seemed more cheerful, which Eleanor put down to the fact they had been well looked after by the Fortescue family.

January passed by uneventfully and as the community slowly began to shrug itself out of hibernation, the weather turned colder, painting feathery swirls of frost on the windows.

For Charlie, it served a cruel reminder of the incredibly harsh winter before Anna had died. A tide of sadness swept over him. But pushing aside painful memories, he channelled his energy into helping Avalon and William with their house search. Losing that thatched property was not a disaster, since the Tudor style house had more in its favour.

He prayed the transaction would be successful, particularly in the aftermath of Perry's visit. If there was one aspect of his life though, that never failed to uplift him, it was his flourishing relationship with Eleanor. Delighted that she had passed her driving test, he had snapped up a second hand mini from the local paper; a perfect set of wheels for running around town.

Yes, life definitely seemed to be improving.

With the revamp of the Community Centre ahead, work too, was profitable and he had a ravishing young woman to share his life with. The thought she had almost been banished from the community brought crashing waves of anger. But resolute in his pledge to protect her, Charlie knew that whatever life threw at them, he would do anything to keep her by his side.

February 1987

Eleanor meanwhile, found herself completely swept up in preparations for the Community Centre open day. Mercifully the weather looked promising. The icy temperatures had receded, giving rise to a spate of mild, dry days. Even the flower beds had erupted with a scattering of her crocuses.

With the increasing likelihood the festivities would spill into the grounds, she spent the first hour hacking back thistles and a few unsightly brambles sneaking their way over the fence. Pleased with her efforts, she removed her gardening gloves. She was hoping to slip through the door of the Community Centre unnoticed, but almost collided with Hilary.

Hilary stared at her in dismay. Eleanor knew she looked a mess, her denim dungarees grubby, her locks tumbling around her shoulders. In a recent trip to the hairdresser she had enquired if they could *unravel* her dreadlocks but unfortunately her hair had become too matted. The only way to get rid of them was to have them lopped off. Yet she had never quite forgiven Hilary's prejudice and for the sake of being bloody-minded, desisted for a little longer.

"Eleanor," Hilary snapped, "you do realise the town's dignitaries are attending, including the Mayor! Can't you at least attempt to look civilised?"

"That's unkind, Hilary," Reggie's voice rang out from behind her.

Eleanor glanced at him and their eyes locked. She couldn't fail to notice how smart he looked; his jacket newer, his silver-streaked hair swept neatly back from his forehead.

"It's okay, Reggie," she purred. "The gardens needed a tidy up. I was going to shower and change before the event got off to a start, so I promise I won't embarrass you..."

Her smile lingered. Added to her maintenance work, Eleanor had organised a competition for the children, to create a miniature garden inside a shoe box. The entries were waiting to be arranged on trestle tables at the rear of the garden.

What Eleanor didn't know was that Hilary was determined *Holly* would win this contest. She had spent hours foraging through their loft for the model trees and hedges bought for her dolls' house, and had even purchased some alpine grit to create a path and rockery.

Hilary hovered by the door, no doubt hoping she would disappear.

But Eleanor wandered defiantly past. Sashaying over to the bakery stall, she stopped for a chat with Emily Cuthbert, who was busily displaying the cakes people had donated.

"Eleanor, is there any chance you could pop home and fetch your cake?" she started nagging. "I wanted to put the best ones out first."

"You're flattering me," Eleanor smiled, "but I do need to sort out my shoe box gardens."

As if on cue, Elijah sidled up to the stall, hungrily eyeing up the cakes.

"Would you like me to go?" he volunteered.

"It's okay," Eleanor said, "I need to get back and change before *Mrs Goody-two-shoes* over there gives me any more stick for looking a mess."

"Eleanor, it would be really helpful if your son could bring it," Emily fussed, hands twisting the front of her frilly apron. "If he wouldn't mind..."

Before Eleanor had a chance to argue, Elijah gave them a thumbs up and sped across the hall in a flash. The two women gave each other a conspiratorial smile.

"He's a good boy, your Eli," Emily whispered.

Elijah thought nothing of it. He knew exactly where Eleanor's cake was, picturing its buttery golden-brown icing studded with walnuts. Flitting towards their home, he was excited about the open day. An enlarged print of his drawing nestled in a display cabinet, inside the main hall. Letting himself into the house however, he was disturbed by the bang of a door.

Then Andrew stumbled out of his bedroom.

He looked rough; unshaven and sallow with dark circles under his eyes. Yet if only Elijah had known the reason - that intent on getting high, Andrew and his friend, Matthew, had experimented with magic mushrooms - that he had enjoyed the effects to begin with before his mood went hurtling downhill. Never once had he anticipated this would turn into a bad trip and that *Elijah* was the last person he wanted to clap eyes on right now.

"Hi, Andrew," Elijah said in his innocence. "Heavy night?"

"Sod off, you little bastard," Andrew snarled.

"What's up?" Elijah frowned. "I only popped in to fetch Mum's cake. Aren't you coming to the open day?"

"Later!" Andrew snapped. "Right now, I wanna bit of peace and quiet but seeing as you're here, you can make me a sandwich!"

"Make it yourself, you lazy git," Elijah snorted, turning to make his way to the kitchen.

Surging forwards, Andrew grasped the collar of his T-shirt and yanked him back.

"What did you say?"

Almost choking, Elijah struggled out of his grip. Yet the way Andrew glowered at him was terrifying.

"What the hell is wrong with you?" he couldn't stop himself from spluttering.

"You, that's what!" Andrew spat. "Crawling around Peter with your stupid drawings and bloody building design... any excuse to show off! You make me sick!"

"That's not fair," Elijah gasped. "You knew I loved sketching when we were living at Westbourne House. Charlie opened my eyes when he restored that place..."

"Yeah, and you're forever sucking up to him too!" Andrew ranted. He took another menacing step forwards. "I bet you wish he'd rather have *you* as a son!"

"That is crap!" Elijah whispered in shock. "Stop being such a prat..."

His words were cut off as Andrew clawed the front of his T-shirt and rammed him against the kitchen wall. To his increasing horror, he raised a fist.

"Please!" he whimpered, shielding his face with his arm.

Andrew's fist trembled, an undercurrent of aggression building. In fact, it took a crescendo of voices outside to snap him out of his frenzy. He lowered his fist, but not before flinging Elijah against the wall in a fit of anger.

"Just get out," he finished huskily, "and don't you dare go crying to *mummy* or I really will deck you one, do you hear?"

Without another word, Elijah scuttled into the kitchen to retrieve his mother's coffee and walnut cake, relieved to hear Andrew's receding footsteps as he stumbled towards the bathroom.

By the time he returned to the Community Centre though, an expanding crowd of people had started to congregate, Mrs Cuthbert too engrossed in conversation to notice him.

Placing his mother's cake on the table, he drifted away in a trance. The shock of Andrew's attack had left him shaken; that all too familiar sense of being the underdog... So he tried focusing on other things; the jumble of second-hand books and piles of bric-a-brac, a stall set up by the Women's Institute (of which Hilary was a member), displaying preserves in hand-decorated jars.

But as the hoards condensed, he searched madly for his mother. It took Charlie to put his mind at rest, disclosing she had only popped home to change.

The almshouse meanwhile, lay in a raft of silence as Andrew slept in peaceful oblivion.

Eleanor crept upstairs to take a shower. Then slipping into their cosy bedroom, she hauled a rectangular box from under the bed. With a sigh of pleasure, she opened the lid. A sweet papery fragrance wafted upwards and pulling back the folds of tissue, she uncovered an exquisite dress Charlie had bought her for Christmas. Spun from downy cotton, it was decorated with a pattern of pink and white roses; delicate and feminine with thin shoulder straps, yet maybe a little too chilly to wear on its own... Eleanor found a black T-shirt to wear underneath. The material swayed heavily around her ankles as she pushed her feet into dainty ankle boots.

Next she tidied her hair and face, palm-rolling her dreadlocks in conditioning wax to add shine. After pinning them back with combs, so they tumbled in a cascade down her back, she wandered across the garden to mingle, feeling considerably more glamourous.

Charlie stood back, unable to conceal his pleasure as she approached him.

III

As morning slipped into early afternoon, Peter strode over to join them. He was accompanied by two councillors, including the Mayor, distinguishable by a thick gold chain roped around his shoulders. Eleanor was honoured to show them around the gardens as well as present her competition. An enchanting array of shoe boxes had been arranged on a horseshoe of trestles tables. Each revealed a tiny garden and to her delight, the Mayor seemed happy to judge them.

For the interim, she bathed in a glow of happiness, proud to be participating in the event.

Robin Whaley on the other hand, found it hard to conceal his loathing. The Mayor of Rosebrook clasped Eleanor's hands. Yet despite her hippie dreadlocks and that ghastly tattoo on her arm, people seemed to adore her.

It did not seem long though, before he felt the jab of her golden eyes.

He turned away sharply and with no desire to be caught staring, immersed himself in conversation with a stray councillor, one who just happened to wander into his vicinity.

But as the minutes ticked by, his eyes were unwittingly lured in her direction again. The sun had crept out from behind a cloud, flooding the grounds with sunshine. He found himself gazing at Charlie, the dark haired man Peter had introduced. Then, as the small assembly broke apart, Charlie leaned in and kissed Eleanor on the lips. Robin glanced at his watch, incensed to see it was almost 2:30. The day was galloping by at an alarming rate yet there was still no sign of Dominic.

Hit with a stab of anxiety, he strolled back towards the Community Centre, now wondering if he was loitering inside the hall somewhere.

"Robin!" Peter exclaimed, throwing a radiant smile. "Good of you to come! Have you seen the stalls? We've had a deluge of local artisans, it's like a mini craft fair in there."

"Marvellous," Robin replied in a tone that didn't quite disguise his apathy. "I'm glad to support an event that draws visitors to the town. You've done a fine job, Peter."

"Thank you," Peter faltered, as if unsure how to proceed. "Did you invite anyone?"

"I did," Robin smiled, "except he hasn't turned up yet. When he does, you'll be the first to know... In the meantime, can we forget our little dispute? I can see how serious you are about raising funds for the renovation."

"Sure," Peter said. "I hope we can put our differences behind us."

As if to serve an untimely reminder, Elijah flitted across the grass with two younger girls in tow. The watery sunshine illuminated the chestnut shine of his hair and Robin caught his breath.

"In case you didn't know, Eleanor still lives here," Peter added as if reading his mind. "She's not a bad person, Robin. She's run a great little competition for the kids. You should see it..."

"I'd be delighted to," Robin said through gritted teeth, "but first let me see if my guest has arrived. Please excuse me."

Snaking his way through the crowds, Robin launched into a frantic search of Dominic. It soon emerged however, he wasn't in the hall either. With a sense of defeat, he bought a cup of tea before settling himself down at one of the tables. The shifting mass of people bobbed around him, captivated by the stalls. There came a point when he felt obliged to join them, although the multitude of crafts held no appeal whatsoever.

Another torturous hour passed. To kill time, he even bought a slice of cake, until he was finally accosted by Hilary. She had a sickly smile stapled to her face.

"Mr Whaley! How good of you to attend. We weren't expecting to see much more of you after that altercation with Peter..."

"Oh, that's in the past," Robin placated her. "Now tell me about your role here today."

"Just helping out," Hilary beamed, swinging her hand towards the Women's Institute stand, "and explaining a little more about the work we do... If you hang around for the speeches at 4:00, I'm giving a short spiel about our work on drugs counselling."

Robin fought an urge to laugh. He wondered how that would go down with *Dominic*, having so shamelessly boasted about his former drug cartel. Yet as time elapsed, he decided he quite enjoyed conversing with Hilary; sincere, straight-laced, not a hint of flirtatiousness... In fact, he had only just started to relax when she broke off mid-stream.

Her eyes shot towards the entrance. "Now who in the world could this be?"

Following her gaze, any last lingering doubt was blown from Robin's mind as a tall, menacing figure sauntered into the hall. How uncanny that Dominic's presence created such a ripple, the crowds peeling apart to let him through. He radiated an aura of power. Even his clothes looked expensive, from the tailored cut of his sports jacket to the sleek black cords that enhanced his physique. Eyes scanning the hall behind dark glasses, they rested on Robin.

A faint smile lifted the corners of his mouth.

"You know him?" Hilary whispered under her breath.

"Dominic," Robin murmured, rising to shake his hand. "How good of you to come. Hilary, allow me to introduce you to Dominic Theakston, a successful entrepreneur from Swanley."

"Delighted to meet you," Hilary smiled.

Five minutes later, Robin was rushing him towards the rear of the building.

"You took your time," he hissed. "The event finishes at five!"

"Turned up, didn't I?" Dominic taunted. "You never mentioned a time..."

"Well, thank God you're here now," Robin whispered. "Last time I saw the Chapman girl, she was hanging around at the end of the garden and at some point, she needs to see you..."

"Let me play this my way," Dominic said brusquely. "Why do you think I wore the shades? I know exactly the right time to approach people *and* spring an element of surprise. But first you can introduce me to this Peter. I like to know who's turf I'm playing on."

It didn't take long to track him down, alerted to his effervescent passion as he loitered on the lawn. He was still raving about the building design and the funds he hoped to generate...

Then, from another side of the garden, Andrew strolled into view.

Lingering on one of the paths, Elijah froze, before shuffling towards the spot where Peter was standing. Robin smiled.

This could not have turned out better.

Ushering Dominic towards the same spot, he joined their assembly.

"Excuse me, folks, but would you mind if I introduced someone?" he broke in. "Peter, I'd like you to meet an old associate of mine..."

At first, Peter looked bewildered by the stranger drawn into their circle; a man who appeared respectable yet moved in a manner that seemed restless.

As his eyes scrutinised his surroundings though, Robin was all too aware of Elijah. He had started to inch away, as if he detected some threat.

"It's okay, Eli, don't go," Peter intervened. He flashed Dominic a smile. "Name's Peter Summerville, I'm general manager here."

"Nice to meet you," Dominic murmured, his eyes flickering to the boy by his side.

"And this young man is Elijah," Robin announced. "Elijah Jansen... the artist responsible for the new building design."

"Seriously?" Dominic responded. "Well - this is a surprise."

For several seconds, he pinned him with his stare.

"Thank you," Elijah muttered.

Glancing from one man to another, a sweep of colour filled his cheeks. Dominic smirked.

"So, what brings you here?" Peter asked. Speaking directly to Dominic, he lowered a protective hand on Elijah's shoulder.

"Who me?" Dominic shrugged. "I'm in the leisure business. Run me own gym."

Peter frowned. Taking a nervous gulp, he would have said more, Robin was sure of it, until the chime of a spoon pierced the hubbub.

With people pouring into the garden, the speeches were about to begin. Hilary and Reginald took their positions along the back wall where several more volunteers had congregated.

Robin momentarily vanished, only to return in a flash.

"I've seen her," he whispered to Dominic. "She's at the far end of the garden, engrossed in some competition."

Watching the crowds as they continued to migrate from the area, Robin knew that within a few more seconds it would be deserted.

Eleanor remained rooted to the spot, watching the crowds thin out. Drifting away like sheep, they were drawn towards a mass of people, now gathering to hear the speeches.

But for a moment she cherished the solitude. What a joy to gaze over these miniature gardens again, charmed by the efforts the children had gone to. Little balls of coloured tissue paper had been screwed up to resemble flowerbeds; carpets of green felt inside walls of Leggo. Holly Magnus had excelled herself and hers was by far the best entry. Eleanor smiled. The Mayor had already indicated this was the winner. It might even inspire Hilary to be a little more civil to her.

Eleanor breathed deeply, feeling a chill in the air. With the sun starting to recede, long shadows stretched across the ground, the light bleeding away. Though gradually she sensed another presence and from the corner of her eye, noticed a man sauntering towards her. She felt the hairs on the back of her neck prickle, unsure what it was about him that unnerved her. Tall, outwardly respectable, he drew to a pause right in front of her table, hands folded behind his back, lenses dark, despite the dimming sunlight.

She had been about to speak when a soft, chilling voice broke the silence.

"Hello again, Eleanor."

The sound of his voice startled her; one she didn't quite have time to recall before he slowly removed his sunglasses. But the impact of those slanted dark eyes made her gasp. It had been fourteen years since she had clapped eyes on

Dominic Theakston, a face she would never forget. Fingers of ice crept over her skin as he gave the hint of a smile.

Eleanor swallowed, her first instinct to dive through the gap between the trestle tables and escape. As if predicting her move though, Dominic took a side step, blocking her path. Easing himself through the gap to join her, he had her trapped inside the enclosure.

The silence between them swelled before she finally found her voice.

"What do you want?"

"Just dropped by for a chat," Dominic said. "So... you came back then?"

"This is not London," Eleanor replied.

"Near enough!" he snapped. "Enough to make *somebody* nervous. I hope you haven't been making a nuisance of yourself..."

"I haven't said a word," Eleanor hissed at him.

"Good," Dominic said, yet there was an ominous ring to his voice. "Best make sure it stays that way. You're looking good by the way. How are you?"

"Fine," Eleanor mumbled, forcing herself to look at him.

He wandered closer, circling around to her side. With his warm fingers closing around her upper arm, her heart began to pound.

"Nice tattoo," he drawled, pressing his thumb over the surface. He allowed his fingers to trail down her arm. "Good muscle tone too. Do you work out? I'm in the gym business myself now, you know. Got me own club over in Swanley..."

"Don't touch me," she gasped, wrenching her arm away.

Eleanor grit her teeth, having prayed she would never have to face this hateful man again, not to forget the hell he had put her through. There was no mistaking the ripple of threat lurking under the surface. That he was being so friendly and polite seemed even more sinister.

"What's the matter, love?" he said. "Still scared? Well, perhaps you should be."

Eleanor whirled around, conscious of her thick locks as they swung around her shoulders.

He smiled icily. "And how is your son, Eleanor? Elijah, isn't it? Met him a few minutes ago. Your friend, Peter, introduced us. Nice looking boy..."

Eleanor recoiled, the impact of that chilling reference to her son enough to send her charging back through the gap in the tables. Catching her hip on the edge, she nevertheless succeeded and desperate to escape Theakston, she sped across the lawn.

Her only mission now was to melt into the crowd before he had a chance to catch her up. She glanced madly in search of Elijah. Yet all she could hear was Hilary in the background, droning on about their drug rehabilitation program. She barely took in a word. *Elijah had to be here somewhere.* With her deadliest enemy lurking in the grounds, nothing else mattered.

Elijah was buried inside the crowd, still frantically trying to avoid Andrew. His dark eyes narrowed as soon as he spotted him, his muscular arms hanging by his sides.

Yet at the same time, Elijah focussed on Hilary's speech.

"… the effects of drugs are one of the biggest threats to society," her voice chimed.

Elijah blinked, remembering the cold, almost psychotic behaviour he had observed in those horrible new age travellers.

"We need to be more intellectually aware, especially family members..."

Elijah stood very still, allowing her words to permeate.

"Do any of you know someone who might be addicted?" she continued to bleat. "Do they suffer from mood swings? Are they constantly hankering for more money?"

Her words fused into a chilling reality, even before his eyes were drawn back to Andrew. Elijah watched in fear as he drew a forefinger across his throat, a silent threat that had him backing away from the crowd.

As Eleanor spotted him too, she felt a tiny leap of hope. If only Dominic hadn't wandered back into view, merging with the mob of people in precisely the same moment Elijah squeezed his way out. She wanted to scream, watching with mounting dread as Dominic paused. Gazing down in amusement, he reached down to ruffle the boy's hair. She saw Elijah smile unsuspectingly back, a scene that seemed almost surreal in its horror.

Just when she thought the situation couldn't get worse though, she caught sight of Robin Whaley again. Lingering on the edge of the crowd, he too had witnessed the exchange. His eyes met hers, icy with threat, leaving little doubt who had invited Theakston here today.

A pulse drummed in her ears. *She had to get away from this place.*

Staggering in the direction of the almshouse, she felt drained. But she had barely reached the path when Hilary breezed in front of her.

"Eleanor!" she crowed. "I've just heard! The Mayor tells me Holly won the miniature garden competition and I just wanted to say thank you."

"Great," Eleanor said tightly. Her eyes flitted in search of an escape route.

"Look, I know we don't always see eye to eye," Hilary added sweetly, "but I do appreciate what you've done here today..."

"Thanks, Hilary," she replied, flashing a smile, "and I'm sorry but I have to go. If you see Eli, could you tell him to get back to the almshouse immediately. It's important."

"Of course," Eleanor heard her murmur as she hurried away down the path.

Collapsing onto her bed, she could not stop shaking. The most sensible thing would be to tell Charlie - or Peter - except past experience had proved that messing with someone like Theakston would bring terrible consequences. Hit with despair, she saw only one solution: to get away from Rosebrook to the only bolt hole she had left, her caravan.

Eleanor grabbed a hold-all and began cramming it with clothes. Packing enough to tide her over for a few days, she headed towards Eli's room. As the door swung open, the interior of his room with its peppermint walls and overcrowded shelves brought a lump to her throat. But gulping back her misery, she snatched his school uniform from its hanger, then found another bag to shovel some of his belongings into.

Eventually she crept downstairs, relieved to discover the house still empty. How she would explain her actions to Charlie was another matter... Tears squeezed from her eyes. She had no choice but to leave a note. *But what the hell was she going to tell him?* However hard she tried to encrypt her reasons for leaving, it was bound to incur some risk.

"My dearest Charlie, Eli and I need to get away but I'll phone when I can. Love you xx"

Slipping from the house, still in her lovely dress, she felt a millstone of sadness. What a perfect day this should have been. Yet once again her enemies had surfaced. It jarred her to think of Elijah's safety being compromised, especially when he sauntered into view at last.

Waving frantically, she beckoned him towards the car.

"Eli!" she gasped. "Over here... get in the car, quickly!"

To her relief, he didn't argue. Waiting for him to slide into the passenger seat, she started the engine, her breath trapped in her throat.

Chapter Thirty-Seven

I

They continued the journey in silence at first. The town faded from view, until eventually the wooded roads began to swallow them. Elijah glanced at his mother. There was something stiff about her posture; her face tight with some undefined but troubling emotion.

"Where are we going?" he dared to ask.

"Aldwyck," she replied. "Something's happened. We have to go back to the caravan..."

"What?" Elijah shouted. "But what about the others?"

"Charlie and the kids are quite safe," Eleanor said. "Unfortunately, we no longer are. I'm sorry, Eli, but I don't think we can stay..."

Elijah collapsed back into his car seat. He was already wrestling with the idea of whether to tell her about Andrew. Yet something else must have happened, something that eclipsed everything.

The minutes flashed by. Before he knew it, the familiar sights of the village began to emerge, from the first row of shops to the sprawling green. He winced as he spotted a group of boys gambolling around on the grass, recognising Gary Boswell. Not only had he grown taller but bulkier since turning fourteen. The sight filled him with despair; a fear his short-lived confrontation with Andrew was nothing, compared to what these boys had subjected him to. Pressing his eyes shut, he dreaded the possibility of the bullying starting up again; more so if he plummeted back down to his inferior status as *Gyppo Jansen*.

Eleanor pulled up sharply and leapt from the car. Fumbling in her handbag for her caravan keys, she glanced back at him.

"Well, come on!" she ordered him. "Let's drop our bags off, then we'll go next door and visit Marilyn. See if we can scrounge a cup of tea..."

With a furious sigh, he flung the car door open and dragged himself from his seat. For several minutes he stood fuming, refusing to go inside. Eleanor hauled both bags from the boot of her car then carried them indoors. But no sooner did she reappear in the doorway, he angrily turned and faced her.

"I don't want to live here any more!" he snapped.

"Eli, please don't be unreasonable," Eleanor begged. "There's a reason for this, I swear."

The slam of a door jolted them and Eleanor whirled around. Tottering out of the farmhouse, Marilyn joined them as they stood by the enclosure of trees.

337

"I thought it was you," she remarked. "How's Rosebrook?"

"We've just had to leave," Eleanor said bitterly.

Mood blackening, Elijah kicked at the stones on the ground.

"Is it possible we could come inside for a chat?"

"Of course," Marilyn kept frowning and turned back towards the farmhouse.

Following her into a hallway, they slid into the lounge. The embers glowing in the fireplace immediately wrapped them in warmth.

"Sit down. I'll make a pot of tea and you can tell me everything."

Still Elijah chose not to say anything as she temporarily disappeared into the kitchen. Only after some coaxing from Eleanor, did he crash down onto the sofa next to her. He knew he was behaving like a surly teenager, but for once he didn't care.

"Now what's this all about?" Marilyn sighed, as soon as they were settled with cups of freshly brewed tea. She peered at Eleanor with a look of concern. "Don't tell me you and that lovely man of yours have quarrelled?"

"This has got nothing to do with Charlie," Eleanor shivered. She curled her arms around herself, despite the warmth. "Marilyn, do you remember the time when I had to leave London?"

"Hmm, that was a long time ago," Marilyn mumbled. "Didn't someone threaten you?"

"Yes," Eleanor said. "That's exactly what happened. Except it wasn't me they threatened. It was Eli!"

Turning to him now, she could no longer hide the panic in her eyes. Elijah stiffened, sufficiently numbed to listen, despite his persisting fury.

"This is why I fear for your safety! In 1973, the men responsible for your father's death caught up with me and one of them threatened to harm you. We tried to expose the truth, see; me and Rosemary's family. One night, we came too close. So one of those men put the frighteners on me. We ran away. You were just a baby, Eli, I had no choice!" Her lips started trembling. "Today that same man showed up at the Community Centre and he reminded me of that threat..."

"But I don't want to spend my life hiding!" Elijah yelled. "Why can't we go to the police?"

Even Marilyn was shaking her head, her face creased with worry. "Rosemary told me about this man. Wasn't he some sort of gangster? Your mother's right, Eli, you're safer keeping your head down." She fixed her gaze on Eleanor. "We should talk to Rosemary... and while we're at it, why not use the phone to contact your Charlie?"

"I don't know what to say to him," Eleanor choked, finally giving way to tears.

Elijah said nothing, too clammed up with frustration to indulge her in any sympathy. *She had kept too many secrets from him.* Another sigh burst out, before he hauled himself to his feet.

"Eli, what are you doing?" Marilyn gasped. "Sit down!"

"I'm sorry, Aunt Marilyn," he said in a cold, curt voice, "but I've had enough. I really loved our house in Rosebrook. I had friends, people who cared about me... people like Peter!"

"I know, sweetheart and I loved it there too..." Eleanor whimpered.

"Then why can't we stay?" he ranted. "This is so ridiculous! My father was dead before I was even born! It's not as if we've done anything wrong!"

"Because some people are too powerful!" Eleanor sobbed. "Our presence in Rosebrook has angered someone and they've used every underhand tactic to get us out. This is what happened before. I can't risk it, Eli, I can't bear the thought of anything happening to you."

Glancing from one woman to the other, he felt a crumbling sense of defeat. Yet as he scoured his mind, he tried to remember who he had met today, including the tall stranger with the sunglasses... until one obvious candidate stood out.

"Mr Whaley!" he breathed. Straight away he saw Marilyn flinch. "He's always acted a bit weird around me. He even called you a prostitute. Holly told me!"

"Eli, that's enough!" Eleanor gasped.

"So tell me the truth!" he shouted. "Was it him? Did Whaley kill my father?"

"No," Eleanor sighed. "Not *kill*. If it's any consolation, I'd be surprised if that limp-wristed little creep could swat a fly! You've got it all wrong, Eli!"

"Fine!" he spluttered in exasperation. "I'm off then!"

Before either of them could stop him, he turned and ran into the hallway.

"Where are you going?" Eleanor squealed after him.

"A walk," he replied and before anyone could stop him, he was swept into the deepening dusk where the cold air practically swallowed him.

Head down, he pelted across the road. The gates of Westbourne House beckoned and with a quick backward glance, he slipped through the entrance, the shadow of the trees concealing him. He could still hear his mother calling, until eventually the sound receded. Perhaps Marilyn had coaxed her away and they might just leave him alone for a while...

Creeping away from the gateposts, he jogged up the driveway. The thought of seeing William and Avalon was the only thing that could cheer him up. But as the air rushed into his lungs, his legs pounding up the driveway, it took this wild expenditure of energy to finally work off his rage. Leaping up the steps, taking two at a time, he thumped on the door.

"Eli!" William shrieked. He moved forwards to peer outside. "On your own?"

"Yes," Elijah spluttered. "I had to come! Got loads to tell you!"

No sooner had William closed the door, the two of them wandered into the hallway.

The barrenness of the house shocked him, so eerily silent it reminded him of a church. The bar, as well as the restaurant, were completely stripped of furniture. But as their footsteps slowed, William divulged that nearly everything they were keeping was in storage now and only the guest rooms remained fully furnished. With the help of James's solicitor though, they had begrudgingly thrashed out a deal with Perry; he had consented to offer an extra ten grand for it.

This twist in the conversation inspired him to mention the visit.

"Yeah, the old bastard's been back," William whispered, just as they reached the lounge.

Once inside, Elijah spotted Avalon slouched over her father's writing desk, immersed in the interior design book Eleanor had bought for her. She glanced up.

"Hello, Eli!" she gasped, rising to her feet. "What a nice surprise."

A smile tilted her lovely features yet Elijah could not ignore that prevailing sad look. As they gravitated towards their suite, still a prominent feature, he sank into a chair.

"He's not having our best suite, though," William said, continuing the thread of conversation. He patted the arm of the settee. "We spend lots of time in here now."

"I don't blame you," Elijah remarked.

His eyes drifted around the lounge, pausing at the patio doors and to the darkening grounds beyond. Mindful of his mother's fears, he bit back his anxiety, diverting his attention to the side tables. The tidy stack of books and needlepoint kit were undoubtedly Avalon's; the other table piled high with a clutter of magazines, William's audio cassettes and Sony Walkman. A TV and video recorder nestled in an elaborate walnut surround. *Obviously they were keeping themselves entertained in the absence of their father.* Struck by how traumatic their lives had been, he momentarily forgot his own troubles.

"We're keeping all the furniture in this room," William added boldly. "It'll remind us of Dad. Apart from the furniture in our bedrooms, that's it!"

"Right," Elijah pondered, dazed by the finality of it. "So what were you going to tell me about old Hampton? You say he's been back?"

"Yes," Avalon sighed, "and on one of those visits he brought Ben..." Recounting the experience, her smile fell. But she couldn't resist mentioning William's escape to the library.

"Why would I want to speak to him?" William snapped. "Tosser!"

"The fact is, Eli, they're trying to force us out," Avalon said. "We were given until the end of January, but our house search hasn't gone well."

"But I thought you found somewhere," Elijah argued. "Charlie told us…"

"We did," Avalon interrupted, "and it's not as if we're trying to delay this. William and I are ready to move on but…" She broke off, clutching the lovely interior design book in both hands. "The sale fell through."

"The owners took the house off the market," William added. "Sod's law isn't it and now we're back to square one."

"So what are you going to do?" Elijah mumbled. "What if the Hamptons come back? Worse, what if they throw you out?"

"Let's cross that bridge when we come to it," William said curtly. "We'll just have to rent somewhere for now. Elliot will explain. He's agreed to stay on, to keep the peace."

For a few more minutes, they filled him in on everything else that had been happening; the clandestine visits from Bryony and Angelo. This was Bryony's idea. Concerned for their well-being and determined to defy Perry, they had spent a good few hours in the kitchen, rustling up their favourite dishes and filling the freezer up. Avalon was so touched, she had unashamedly offered them £200 each from the money Perry had paid them. The villagers checked up on them too; people like Boris and Sue from the pub, Marilyn Harper and even the corpulent farmer, Herbert Baxter.

"The grant of probate's nearly through," William finished. "So at least we'll have some money to play with. We're gunning for next weekend and if the old monster does turn up to evict us, we'll just have to doss down at your place."

With those words Elijah turned rigid.

William, who had been watching him, tilted his head to one side. "Anyway, enough about them. You haven't told us the reason you're back…"

Elijah stammered out his news in stages; his fight with Andrew, right up to the moment Eleanor had bundled him into her car and charged back to Aldwyck.

"I can't believe Andrew would behave like that!" Avalon gasped.

"Andrew's the least of my worries," Elijah said. "It's this business with Mum I'm worried about. She thinks we're in danger. Someone threatened her years ago and it's got something to do with the men who killed my father."

William stared at him in shock.

"Eli," Avalon whispered, "are you saying these people are still around?"

"I guess they must be," Elijah shivered.

William squirmed in his chair, risking a glance towards Avalon. "Eli - Avalon and I have been thinking…" he faltered, "have you ever wondered if

341

there's some history between your mum and Perry Hampton?"

"Why do you say that?" Elijah frowned.

William shifted in his seat again. "Because of the way he turned on her! That day they came here, remember? It was scary... and he said something I will never forget. He-he told her *never to cross him again*. What do you suppose he meant by that?"

Elijah felt a flicker of fear. "I don't know," he whispered, "as usual, she wouldn't talk about it. But you're right, he was horrible! And there's been lots of bad stuff going on ever since..."

"Don't you think you should call her?" Avalon nagged. "She'll be worried about you."

"Let her worry," Elijah sulked, his anger foaming to the surface again. "I'm sick of all her secrets. She's so bloody tight-lipped. Maybe if she'd been straight with me, I wouldn't be so pissed off..." He let out a sigh, picturing the caravan on the edge of that cold, stark field. "Look, is there any chance I could kip here tonight? I'm sorry! I can't face spending another night in that caravan. It's small, it's cramped and our old TV set is rubbish!"

"Absolutely," William grinned. "That'd be cool."

"On one condition," Avalon added sternly, "you have got to let me phone Marilyn and tell her you're here. Sorry, Eli, but you can't go missing all night. Eleanor will go insane and that's not fair. I know what it's like to feel scared."

Avalon was desperate to make her call. Six warning chimes from the grandfather clock told her Elijah had been with them for almost an hour.

By the time she got through to Marilyn however, Eleanor was no longer around. She had gone in search of Elijah, though she swore to pass on a message. As the darkness intensified, the air became chilly. Elliot lit a fire in the grate and leaving the youngsters contentedly settled in the lounge with pizzas, he ventured out into the night for a swift half down the pub. He wanted to check if anyone else had seen Eleanor, so that he, too, could reassure her.

But it wasn't long before the ring of the telephone pierced the silence. Exchanging glances, the three of them slipped into reception. Avalon knew the telephone was on answer-phone, so she let it ring, right up until the recording mechanism kicked in.

"Hello? Is anybody at home, please pick up..."

Hearing the first tearful notes of Eleanor's voice, she flicked a switch to keep the speaker on.

"Eleanor, it's Avalon! Calm down. Eli's here. You've got nothing to worry about."

"I know," she resounded huskily, "Marilyn told me - b-but I need to say a few words to you first... How are things?"

"Not bad," Avalon said. "William and I are coping okay. We're lucky we've still got Elliot. But never mind us, what was it you wanted to talk to me about?"

"Eli doesn't understand the danger we're in," she confided.

From the other side of the desk, the boys gaped in horror.

Avalon pressed a finger to her lips. "Go on," she urged, "I'm listening."

"He's got no idea what his father and I had to live through in London. I don't suppose you do either. We were being hunted, Avalon, by men more dangerous than you could imagine. Jake and I had no one to turn to. We couldn't even trust the police..."

Elijah's mouth dropped open, as if he couldn't believe what he was hearing.

"I've never told Eli this," she whispered, "he was just a child. He would have kept asking questions... and they might have come after us again. I've often wondered if these people were keeping an eye on us, yet I was too scared to cross them..."

Avalon turned cold. *That expression again.*

"For years, I lived in fear of what they might do to him," her voice echoed from the speaker, "and this is the reason I kept quiet."

"So what did they threaten to do?" Avalon coaxed her gently. "Can you tell me?"

"Avalon, the gang leader they hired to put the frighteners on me was one of the most evil men in London. He swore that if I ever spoke a word of what I knew, they'd snatch my son. He more or less implied they would torture him. So is it any wonder that when - this - this - same person showed up today, I could forget that threat? He more or less repeated it!"

"But isn't there anyone you can talk to?" Avalon gasped. "What about Charlie?"

"I dare not put anyone else at risk," Eleanor croaked, "so please keep this secret."

"Okay," Avalon mumbled, "just one last thing. Eli wants to stay the night. Is that okay?"

"Of course," Eleanor sighed. The pain in her voice finally softened to relief. "At least I know he's safe. Could I have a word please? Is he there?"

After a long, tense pause, Avalon switched the speaker off before turning to the boys. She passed the phone to Elijah, who had turned as white as the ceramic floor tiles.

"Mum," he muttered quickly. "Don't worry, I'm fine. Everyone is looking after me."

"Eli!" Eleanor breathed. "I could kill you for running off like that!"

"Okay, I'm sorry," Elijah soothed her. "I never meant to go storming off but I didn't like the way we left. It was too sudden! Don't mind if I spend the night here, do you?"

"Not at all," Eleanor whispered adoringly. "It will do you kids good to spend some time together. Ring me in the morning and whatever you think of me, I do love you."

"I know," Elijah whispered, "same back."

By the time he lowered the handset, his hands were shaking. William lowered a comforting hand on his shoulder.

"Bloody hell," he breathed. "Your dad must have pissed off some seriously bad people."

"I could hardly take it in," Elijah said dazedly. "I had no idea..."

"It's obvious your mum's just trying to protect you," Avalon reinforced. "Face it, Eli, we've been hounded by some horrible people. Now let's finish our pizzas, they'll be getting cold. I'll find us a film to watch. It might take our minds off all this other stuff."

II

When Sunday dawned, the tranquility of Eleanor's surroundings startled her at first.

Telephoning Westbourne House for an update, she was happy for Elijah to stay until late afternoon. A weak, watery sunshine had emerged above the treetops. It drenched the countryside in a river of golden light, enticing the three of them outside, and with an urge to explore the woods, William had offered to take them to his den for a picnic.

Eleanor returned to her caravan, reassured to imagine her son and the Barton-Wells kids having some fun together.

No sooner had she settled down with a cup of coffee however, when she jumped to a pounding on the door. Dazedly unlocking it, she was shocked to see Charlie looming, dark eyes blazing.

"Can I come in?" His voice was so tight and cold, she recoiled.

"Charlie!" she gasped. "I meant to phone you..."

"What the hell is going on?" he snapped and shoving her aside, barged his way into the caravan. "One minute we were having a lovely day... next thing, you'd packed your bags and buggered off!"

"Sit down, Charlie," Eleanor said in a tone that lacked resilience, "and I'm sorry. I know I should have hung around a little longer to explain, but..."

"Damn right you should!" he raged. "I thought you loved me!"

"I do," Eleanor tried to placate him.

"Then why leave?" His voice shook her with its intensity. "Why give up all we've got?"

"We've been threatened again," she whimpered. "There are people who want me *out of town* and they've reiterated their threat towards Eli! I thought you, of all people, would understand."

Still his anger did not abate - not even when she collapsed, trembling at the table, hands unsteady as she clasped her mug, sending drops of coffee slopping over the surface.

"So who threatened you?" he demanded.

"I can't tell you," Eleanor said, at which point he lost his temper.

"For fuck's sake!" he roared, thumping the work surface by the sink. "Not this again! When are you going to start confiding in me? We've known each other for over two years and if you *still* can't trust me, then maybe we should call it a day! I'll get on with running my life and you can spend the rest of yours hiding in this bloody caravan!"

Eleanor stared at him in disbelief. Her bottom lip wobbled, her eyes swimming with tears and as the strangle-hold of misery took root, she broke down sobbing.

At the sound of such anguish, Charlie knew he had handled this badly. Despite his inner hurt, he should have demonstrated how deeply he cared for her; not blown his top. Edging himself closer, he gathered her into his arms and for several seconds, allowed her to weep.

"I'm sorry," she spluttered, ripping a tissue from a box to blow her nose. "I don't know how to explain this. I wish I could tell you but I can't! The memories are too upsetting!"

"Ssh, my love," Charlie whispered, stroking a tear from her face. "Don't cry. I shouldn't have shouted at you but we were so happy in the almshouse. What went wrong?"

"My enemies caught up with me," Eleanor whispered. "I left Rosebrook for precisely the same reason I left London. You already know someone threatened to harm my son. Well yesterday, the man who issued that threat reared his head again..."

Pausing to chew over this awful revelation, he crushed her against his chest.

"Sweetheart, how old were you? Seventeen? You had no one to protect you, Eli just a baby!"

He felt the tension slowly drain from her body.

"Think how vulnerable you were. Yet everything's different now, you've got me and whatever else happens, I'll protect you."

He stroked the back of her hair and as his words ebbed away, he was gripped by a sudden impulse, lowering his mouth to her ear.

"I'll protect you from the hooded claw, keep the vampires from your door..."

The next time she raised her head, the ghost of a smile played around her lips.

345

"Remember that song? 'Frankie goes to Hollywood.' We played it when you came over to our flat at Christmas..." He started singing softly. "*When the chips are down, I'll be around - with my undying, death-defying love for you...*"

Eleanor started to cry again, limbs quaking beneath this sudden deluge of tenderness.

"Charlie, I don't want to lose you," she blubbered. "I love you so much."

"Well, that's lucky," Charlie said and kissing her lips, he stole a quick glance around the caravan. "Where is Eli, by the way?"

"Westbourne House," she mumbled. "He was so cross with me, he ran off. But he's okay. He's up there enjoying himself with William and Avalon."

"I see," Charlie smiled and sliding his hand inside her bra, began caressing her breast. He felt the quickening of her breath, before their lips came together in a tentative but searching kiss. "In that case, let me remind you of one of the best reasons we should stay together."

He tugged her gently to her feet and closed the curtains, nudging her towards the bed. In the moment they collapsed on top of it, he began to remove her clothes. His own clothes too, were hastily discarded. They were still kissing hungrily as he rolled up next to her. Hauling over the duvet to ward off the cold, they sank below the covers and began to make exquisite love.

They did not rush. Charlie stroked her from her shoulders to the soles of her feet, savouring her curves and the essence of her skin. She clasped the sides of his face, kissing as if afraid to let go. It was possibly one of the sweetest sessions they had known; a release of intense emotion, boosted by that wild and uninhibited freedom of knowing there was no one around to hear them.

Eleanor melted into his arms, her face resting in the warmth of his shoulder. Her breathing slowed and for the next half hour they relaxed together in silence.

But Charlie became restless. Nothing had been resolved. Thinking of her plight, he could not imagine what it had been like for her in 1973; a fragile seventeen-year-old with a baby, cast out into a cruel world. Her enemies might have been powerful yet they were cowardly and corrupt. The concept of their inhumanity gnawed deep.

"Look," he whispered. "Why don't we move? We can live in the Outer Hebrides of Scotland for all I care, I just want us to be together!"

"It won't be fair on the kids," Eleanor argued. "Eli and Margaret seem so settled in their school, not to forget Andrew. His job, his friends, his girlfriend..."

"Andrew will make new friends wherever we go," Charlie placated her.

"And you?" she sighed, rearing up from beneath the covers. Propping her chin on one hand, she ran her fingers over his chest. "You've made such a success of your business... and what about Peter's Community Centre revamp?

It will never succeed without you!"

"Why not?" he grinned. "He can find another builder but maybe not at such a discount."

"Then we'll be letting him down too," Eleanor said, biting her lip, "and Eli. He can't wait to see the result of his design. It'll break his heart. And another thing, we can't abandon James's children! They need us more than ever now..."

"So, we have to tackle this another way," Charlie insisted. "Why don't you just tell me who threatened you."

The caravan fell silent again and Eleanor's breathing began to deepen. Charlie felt content just lying there, listening to the sound, a smile glued to his face. It sounded as if she was drifting off to sleep. He, on the other hand, was wide awake, the gears in his mind still turning.

"Look," he whispered, kneading her shoulder, "sorry to keep on, but can't you just inform the police about this guy who keeps threatening you? There must be some way we can fight him."

"Oh, Charlie," Eleanor murmured, her voice dreamy, "you can't fight a man like Dominic Theakston..."

Charlie flinched and Eleanor's eyes flew open. He felt her stiffen beside him.

"Theakston?" he gasped. "Dominic Theakston?"

"I never meant to say that," she blurted, springing into an upright position. "Just forget I did."

Except Charlie was gaping at her in disbelief.

"Don't tell me you know him!"

"Not personally," Charlie breathed, "but I know *of* him! He's an extremely hard-nosed businessman. One of the companies I worked for in London did a job for him once."

Something had transpired in 1981; his employers drafted in to carry out some remedial work on a gym in East London. The owner had a reputation for being a shady character, until it gradually emerged that another firm had started the refurbishment.

"Their work wasn't up to scratch. The flooring not strong enough to support the weight of the gym equipment. But when the firm was called back to fix the problem, they demanded more money. Theakston refused to pay them a penny until the floor was reinforced. So the company took him to court..."

"Did they have any joy?" Eleanor mumbled.

"No," Charlie finished. "Theakston turned up with some shit hot lawyer and accused them of shoddy workmanship. They accepted an out of court settlement, but fifty percent of the agreed fee. It was my firm who completed the job."

"I see," Eleanor said numbly.

"And this is who threatened you?" Charlie spluttered. "What did he actually say?"

Eleanor shivered, hands gripping the duvet. "I-I'm not sure. Though you're right about one thing; he *was* a shady character. He was a thug, Charlie, and he ruled the East End by fear. The first time he threatened me, he-he had me trapped inside a railway tunnel..." She pressed her eyes shut in agony. "He said some horrible things a-and yesterday he reminded me of them."

Wriggling from the bed, she started to get dressed. *But what had he said? Was it possible she had been so petrified, the memory had been distorted?*

"He made some reference to me *coming back*. Then asked after my son..."

"Well, that doesn't sound much like a threat to me," Charlie argued.

"I know, but somewhere along the lines, he said *I should be scared,*" Eleanor rebounded. "You could say it was a veiled threat."

"Or a clever play on words," Charlie muttered. "What did he say the first time?"

Her eyes slid furtively towards him as she buttoned up her top.

"He gave me one warning; if I ever breathed a word of what I knew about Jake's murder, he would snatch my son - make him suffer unimaginable pain and make me watch. Then he told me to get out of London - for good."

As she lowered her eyes the fear lingered. She had omitted the parts where Theakston had pressed a knife against her cheek; punched her in the face before slamming her up against the tunnel wall with his hand around her throat. *He had even threatened to torch the Merriman's home.*

"Hmm," Charlie pondered, winding his arms around his knees. "Well, I personally think that's a monstrous thing to say to a young girl... and he lives in Rosebrook?"

"Not Rosebrook," Eleanor shuddered, "though he did say he owned a gym in Swanley."

"Right," Charlie said, a snarl creeping into his voice, "in that case, I might go over there and have a little word with him..."

"Charlie, no!" Eleanor shrieked, leaping from the bed. "Didn't I just explain how dangerous he was? Take on someone like Theakston, you could end up seriously hurt..." *Or even dead*, a small part of her wanted to shout.

"Oh, come on!" Charlie snorted. "This is a business man we're talking about! How do you think his clientele would react if word got out he was going around, threatening peoples' kids? Do you know what I think? It's bullshit! As for those terrible things he said in the past, didn't you say he was deliberately hired to frighten you?"

"Yes," Eleanor said weakly, "but he was already an enemy..." She turned away, wondering just how much she dared tell him. "You know my dad was mixed up in organised crime? His boss, Sammie, was Theakston's rival. Dad shot one of Theakston's top men and he swore revenge. Truth is, he's the reason my dad disappeared…"

She broke off quickly. No way could she bring herself to divulge the worst secret; *that Theakston had been Jake's killer.* The threat to her son, the feud between her father seemed more than enough to satisfy Charlie's curiosity.

"Charlie, please don't go looking for him," she begged. "He's a nasty man."

"Eleanor, I want you to come home," he protested. "I want the five of us to carry on living in Rosebrook, but without this threat hanging over us. So how real is it?"

"Charlie, please…" Eleanor whimpered, snatching for his hands.

But he pressed a finger over her lips to hush her. "Listen, I don't want to lose you. One day, I'd even like to think we'll get married. So let me speak to him. See if I can find out where the land lies…" He displayed a boyish grin. "And I'll try not to get my legs broken."

Chapter Thirty-Eight

I

Two days later, Charlie found himself in Swanley, observing the same landscaped business park that Robin Whaley had visited. Yet despite Eleanor's warnings, he did not feel afraid in the slightest. As 9:00 approached, he guessed Theakston was on his way. He had telephoned 'Atlas Leisure' beforehand but for now, gazed at the striking building, sipping coffee from a flask.

Within minutes, a midnight blue '5 series' BMW swept into one of the reserved parking spots. Charlie's eyes narrowed as they zoomed in on the number plate; *DT100. So this hard-nosed businessman was a wealthy bastard.* But was he really prepared to destroy his reputation for the sake of some past vendetta with Eleanor?

He watched, as a tall figure in a black tracksuit slid from the driver side door. Charlie screwed the lid onto his flask, anxious to sneak his way into reception before him. As luck would have it, Theakston was fumbling around in the boot, before hauling out a massive holdall.

Charlie wasted no time. He jogged up the steps and was through the doors within seconds.

The blonde stationed behind the desk smiled up at him. Her flawless face reminded him of a supermodel. In fact, the whole place radiated splendour, tastefully refurbished with a fresh, cool decor. Charlie felt alien to this stimulating world of health and fitness but pausing by the desk, he waited for the doors behind him to open again.

"Is it possible to have a word with the manager?" he announced somewhat loudly. "Dominic Theakston..."

The figure behind him froze.

At the same time the woman glanced up, eyes flickering past his shoulder. "I'm sorry, but do you have an appointment?" she asked him sweetly.

"I'm afraid not," Charlie confessed, "though I do need to talk to him about a fairly serious personal matter. Just tell him it concerns a lady by the name of Eleanor Chapman..."

The atmosphere around them seemed to darken. Already his heart was pounding.

"It's okay, Melanie, I'll handle this," a male voice pulsed through the air.

Charlie whirled around, coming face to face with Dominic. Nothing could have prepared him for his overbearing presence; a man who stood only a couple of inches taller yet towered over him in a way that seemed intimidating, every muscle braced.

"Seems I'm the man you want," he whispered. "Who are you and what's this about?"

Charlie felt the heat of his slanted dark eyes, determined to stand his ground. "I'm sorry, but this is something I prefer to discuss in private. My name is Charlie Bailey..."

"Lucky I've got thirty minutes to spare," Dominic cut in coldly, "but that's all. I'm busy! Got appointments to keep, clients to see."

"I understand," Charlie said, holding his blistering stare.

With a flick of the head, Dominic moved from the desk, beckoning him to follow. Gazing in awe, Charlie found himself led across a marble-effect floor, past all sorts of contraptions strung with weights and pulleys. He experienced a first tingle of nerves, especially when his escort coaxed him inside a room, the interior masked in shadow. Dominic waited for him to step over the threshold and closed the door. He flicked a switch, a discreet meeting room unveiled under a flare of spot lights.

"Take a pew," he snapped. "My receptionist'll bring us some coffee in a sec. Now what's this about? Eleanor Chapman, eh? Can't deny I'm curious."

"How do you know her?" Charlie quizzed, testing the water.

Dominic dropped himself into the opposite chair and lounged back, folding an ankle over his knee as if to flaunt his designer trainers.

"Eleanor Chapman and I go way back," he murmured in a monotone, "always been a thorn in my side, that one."

"I got the impression you were a thorn in hers," Charlie retorted. "So I'll get straight to the point, Mr Theakston..."

"Dominic," he interrupted. "Mind if I call you Charlie?"

Charlie gave a shrug. "Look, I may as well tell you Eleanor and I are an item. I'm a builder by trade. We've only just recently settled in Rosebrook where we live together. At least we were until Saturday... She's left."

"Is that so?" Dominic said. He smiled mockingly. "Well, I hope you haven't called me away from my work to discuss your domestic problems! Like I say, I'm a busy man..."

"Far from it," Charlie reacted coolly, "but I do need to discuss the reason she left. I believe you threatened her in some way; that whatever you said had the effect of scaring her away. So maybe you can understand why I'm not happy."

Dominic's eyes narrowed. "Is that what she told you?" he said. "Funny - 'cos as far as I can recall, I just said 'hello' to her."

"You threatened her before though, didn't you?" Charlie pressed. "1973, not long after she'd had her baby. She said you drove her out of London..."

351

"That was different!" Dominic snarled, uncoiling himself like a snake.

They were momentarily distracted by a tap on the door, before the ravishing girl from reception breezed in to deliver a jug of filter coffee. No sooner had she left however, Dominic slanted his body forwards.

"Now you listen to me," his voice grated, "things were different in them days. There was stuff going on... and your Eleanor pissed off some powerful people. According to my sources, she and her hippie friends staged some media event. How they managed to get those big shots in one room to discuss the murder of her fella was a minor miracle. But how she ended up in a face off with one of 'em in particular... Those men were shitting bricks!"

Charlie nodded to himself, wondering if he meant Perry. "So, they hired you to put the frighteners on her."

Dominic pulled back slightly, though his dark eyes seared into him. "What else did she tell you? Anything?"

"No," Charlie said, "Eleanor is very secretive about her past. It's only very recently she even spoke of her boyfriend's murder... unless there's anything *you* can tell me?"

Charlie knew he was stumbling on perilous ground yet it was a risk worth taking. Convinced this man knew a hell of a lot more than he was letting on, he observed him carefully. He poured the coffee into mugs, his right hand unsteady.

"Do you know why he was killed?" Charlie added lightly.

Dominic shook his head. "Far as I know he witnessed something. Ended up in the wrong place at the wrong time. Someone wanted to silence him and that's all I'm saying."

Charlie frowned, surprised he had so glibly confessed what he already knew. Yet there was a glint in his eye that chilled him. It was time to change the subject.

"Okay," he nodded, "well, that's another story but the whole point of me coming here was for Eleanor's sake, so I'll get straight to the point. Did your threat involve her son?"

An electric pause followed. Dominic sat paralysed and suddenly he looked furtive.

"Look," he sighed, "threatening Eleanor's kid was not my idea, okay? But that's what I did in them days. It's what people hired me for."

"And what about now?" Charlie pressed. "You see, Eleanor and I have got a lot going for us. It's taken a long time for her to find happiness. Yet there are people out there intent on wrecking her life. So I must ask you... are you one of those people?"

"Charlie, you're trying to pin me to the wall here!" Dominic said through clenched teeth. "So let me tell you something. This may come as a surprise but

I've got kids of me own. What's more, I'm in the middle of a fucking divorce. I could lose all access to them kids if my wife had her way! So any mention of my shady past ain't gonna do me no favours, which is why I don't want someone like your Eleanor stirring up shit!"

"Threatening her child won't get you much sympathy in court then," Charlie said brutally.

Dominic glared at him. "Threatening *me* now, are you?" he shot back.

"Not at all," Charlie said. "I just want some reassurance that Eleanor's son is not in danger. Why did you tell her *she should be scared*?"

Dominic shrugged. "It's not me she needs to be scared of."

Charlie felt the fear roll over him again, as the sinister notion of *Perry* arose.

"Does this mean you'll leave her alone?" he pressed him.

Dominic quaffed back the last of his coffee. "I won't cause her no bother, so long as she don't cause me any."

"She won't," Charlie said. "I just want her back home. Do you have a problem with that?"

Dominic smirked, slamming his cup down. "Charlie, you have my blessing. Why not just marry the girl? If you really wanna know what I think, you're a lucky bastard! Eleanor's a beauty. I know I wouldn't kick her out of bed."

There was something of a leer in his voice, which Charlie did not like yet he chose not to rise. "I'll tell her that then, shall I?" he kept grilling. "Because just for the record, I gather you were her enemy once... or rather, her father's."

"Who, Ollie?" Dominic taunted. "Well, fancy you dredging him up! Heard from the ol' man lately, has she?"

Charlie froze, unsure whether he had heard right. "Do you know what happened to him?"

"Nah!" Dominic smiled, "'cept for one thing. Last I heard of Ollie Chapman, he was a 'house guest' of Signor Gennaro Ponti in Italy." His eyes narrowed slyly. "Not a nice place to be..."

"Who's he?" Charlie whispered.

"Never you mind," Dominic shot back, "it's in the past. All you need to understand is that your Eleanor needs to be careful. Tell her not to go dredging up the past or it'll come back and bite!"

Charlie felt a chill. Though it seemed he had not quite finished.

"And as for that boy of hers, *Elijah*. It's not me he needs to worry about."

Charlie sat very still. Saw him glance at his watch, guessing his time was up.

"Okay, well I'm glad we had this chat," he finished, "and I'm sorry if I caught you on the hop. Thanks for being so honest. I won't bother you any more."

Dominic rose to his feet and to Charlie's greater surprise, extended his hand.

"Not a problem, Charlie," he replied. "Been an interesting discussion."

353

II

Charlie left the building and Dominic watched him go.

He knew from Robin that Eleanor had scarpered and his triumph had been insufferable.

How he longed to see the look on Whaley's face though, as soon as he realised she had someone like Charlie to fight her corner. It would give his game plan a whole new take.

With a sigh, he turned from the smoked-glass frontage and wandered back towards the gym. As for Eleanor... he couldn't drive her out of his mind. She *had* changed since the last time. He had recognised the signs of maturity, her face thinner, her profile sharper; but her honey-coloured eyes were just as mesmerising. He had to confess he quite liked those dreadlocks. They gave her a somewhat wild look, which reminded him a little of himself at that age.

Yet the encounter had unleashed a riot of emotions. He would never forget the day he had issued his ultimatum; it was the only way to get her out of London.

Returning home the previous Saturday, he had let himself into his luxurious apartment in a daze, hands unsteady as he poured a glass of wine. At times like this, he craved a cigarette, despite having given up years ago. At least he had a romantic evening with his new girlfriend, Pippa, to look forward to; except he couldn't relax, not with Eleanor rattling around in his head.

Seeing her again had dredged up everything sordid in his past; the contract to find Jake, the relentless stalking and the killing... never to forget that irrepressible stir of desire.

It had taken a lot of effort on Pippa's part to drag him out of his reverie; massaging the rock-hard tension from his shoulders, followed by some sensational bedroom activity...

Dominic felt a smile creep onto his face, despite his inner turmoil.

But his looming court battle was never far from his mind, which drew him right back to the dilemma he was stuck in now.

Whaley was ecstatic Eleanor had left Rosebrook. Yet he could not quite shift that tiny seed of fear he had implanted: *what if she talked?*

Funnily enough, he'd quite taken to Charlie. It felt good to reassure him he intended no harm towards her boy. Maybe if he kept Charlie on side, she wouldn't pose such a threat.

On the other hand, how could he be sure?

Dominic shuddered, knowing there was only one solution and that despite their camaraderie, *Charlie* needed to watch his back now.

Chapter Thirty-Nine

I

Unbeknown to Eleanor, this was the very scenario she dreaded. She had never been happy about Charlie's idea of confronting Theakston, for fear he would throw himself into the firing line.

Regardless of her worries though, Charlie seemed confident. He explained the situation with the divorce; the threat of Dominic losing access to his own kids, which was a powerful enough incentive. She already knew Dominic had extracted himself from the criminal world, but whatever Charlie said she could never quite shake off that ever-present slick of fear.

"Men like him don't change," she shivered.

"But how can you be sure?" Charlie argued. "He said he's got no problem with you living in Rosebrook. That it's not *him* you need to be scared of..."

"So who do you imagine he did mean?" Eleanor couldn't help wondering. "Perry?"

"I imagine so," Charlie consoled her, "which is another reason you should come home."

He had almost managed to persuade her had it not been for one final factor. Determined to stay in the village a little longer, for the sake of the Barton-Wells children, Eleanor was pained to hear their house sale had fallen through. The notion of Perry evicting them was even more terrifying and despite their complacency, she felt a powerful urge to be around for them.

"What happens now then?" Charlie pressed, as they journeyed to Westbourne House. "Didn't we ought to get them fixed up with some rented accommodation?"

"That seems the best idea," Eleanor murmured.

Her eyes danced around the building, checking for any cars that would indicate the Hamptons' presence. Luckily, the place looked desolate and hurrying towards the door, she was relieved to see Elliot, hoping he would pluck up the courage to speak to Perry again.

But this was the start of a conversation Elliot felt better undertaking in private.

Leaving Charlie to reassure the kids that whatever else happened he would arrange something temporary, everyone agreed that come Friday, they would leave their ancestral home forever...

Explaining the situation with Perry however, Elliot was shocked by the force of his acrimony.

"They have outstayed their welcome for nearly two weeks," he barked down the telephone. "They're purposely delaying their move and I want them out!"

"It is not their fault the house sale fell through," Elliot protested, "but we are aiming to get them moved into rented accommodation before the weekend..."

From the other end of the phone, Perry was fuming. With nearly a million pounds worth of assets tied up in Westbourne House, he had hoped to re-open the hotel by the end of January. Only the lingering presence of James's children inhibited him.

"They could have done that weeks ago!" he kept ranting. "What about those friends in London? And they have a mother in America..." He broke off with a shudder, tempted to add that there might even be spare capacity in the *Bailey household*.

"Mr Hampton, we are doing everything we can," Elliot confronted him, "which brings me to my next point..."

Perry listened in stony silence. Elliot's mother had been admitted to hospital. Filled with a suspicion she was terminally ill, he feared he could be called away at short notice...

"I hope you're not about to do a runner," Perry responded icily. "You have my sympathy, Elliot, and I'm sorry to hear of your predicament. However, once the Barton-Wells children have left, I expect you to be in residence to welcome myself and Rowena."

"How can you expect me to abandon my family at a time like this?" Elliot gasped, devastated.

"I don't expect you to *abandon them*," Perry hissed. "I just want some guarantee you will return. The employment contract you signed is legally binding and if you choose to defy me, I swear I will make life very unpleasant for you..."

He awaited a response but there was none. The frozen lull of silence seemed loud.

"Just see to it, those children are gone," he finished. "I want no more excuses..." He didn't even mention the threat of eviction; it dangled on the edge of that last ominous sentence.

II

Elijah meanwhile, was thrilled at the prospect of returning to Rosebrook, especially with William and Avalon in tow. Alone with his thoughts, he leapt off the bus, recalling the latest encounter with Gary Boswell. He was dying to know if they had moved back into their caravan, no doubt revelling in the prospect of picking on him again... But as Elijah explained, their brief stay in Aldwyck was a stop gap to spend some quality time with the Barton-Wells kids.

With that satisfying thought, he began to amble his way home.

At least Charlie had found them a nice, fully-furnished apartment to move into, the last of their furniture to be shifted into storage. It was the perfect solution. Elijah had also begun to wonder which school William would go to. The independent day school would probably be his first choice. *But how cool would it be if William enrolled at the same school he and Margaret attended?*

Lost in his dreams, he meandered along the road verge, where the gates of Westbourne House lingered. He had almost reached the caravan when a muddy Land Rover pulled sharply into the roadside. Elijah glanced up, just as the driver leaned out of the window.

"'Scuse us, kid, d'you live 'ere?"

Elijah studied the man who had spoken; unshaven, donning an army-style pullover and woolly hat, which didn't quite conceal his dirty-blonde hair.

"Yes, I do," he replied in his innocence. "Why?"

"Don't 'spose you know a farmer round 'ere called 'erbert Baxter, do ya?"

Elijah nodded, hit with the impression this man was also a farmer.

Next thing he knew, he was pressed for directions to the farm. Elijah frowned. Eager to be of help, he pointed in the direction he had just walked from, describing the concealed farm track he had passed. Banked by thick forests, it climbed uphill to an expanse of farmland, eventually leading to the farm itself. The man craned his neck as if struggling to hear. Elijah stepped closer to the window, engrossed in his spiel, before a sudden crash of boots made him jolt.

Breaking off mid sentence, he whirled around.

The second man towered over him, tall and powerfully built. With the lower half of his face concealed by a scarf and eyes hidden behind black shades, the gist of danger loomed, but a moment too late. The man seized his arm, yanking him towards the back of the Land Rover.

"Just get in the back, kid," a voice whispered in his ear.

"Let go of my arm," Elijah croaked, his fear so intense it drained the volume from his voice.

"I'll break it unless you do as I say," his attacker snarled. "Now get in!"

Elijah knew he had to think quickly. Waiting until the man had forced him right up against the lip of the rear door, he tilted his body sideways to climb in. With his captor braced directly behind him though, he planned his next move carefully. In the instant the grip on his arm slackened, he rammed back his elbow, delivering a blow into the man's groin.

A bellow of pain erupted as he tore himself from his grasp. Desperate to escape now, he surged across the road in the direction of the track he had described, then dived into the woodland.

Elijah kept running, wary of footsteps hammering in his wake. To his soaring dread, they had followed him into the forest. Struck with a feeling his whole life had been building up to this moment, he ran faster than he had ever done before.

Shards of memory punched into his mind: the times he had sped across the school field to escape Boswell's gang; the pursuit of the new age travellers when he had pelted towards the caravan *(and would have made it if bloody Andrew hadn't tripped him.)* Yet tucked among those memories lurked a deeper fear; and it had a lot to do with the ever-present cocoon of his mother's protection. Recalling her whispers to Avalon, everything made chilling sense... except it was too late now.

He was about to be snatched, as her enemies had threatened all those years ago.

Driven by this thought, he prayed he had the advantage. With his slim frame, he moved quickly, darting through the trees with the same agility his father had done years before him. It put him yards ahead of his pursuers as they crashed their way through the undergrowth.

Yet his triumph was short lived, as a shout registered.

Elijah panicked, fearing his burgundy school blazer stood out against the forest like a beacon. Burning from the heat of exertion, he took a moment to pause and remove it. But the delay cost him dearly. He glimpsed the two men within a second. They came pounding through the woods and to his horror they were gaining ground.

Elijah took off again, entering the woodland clearing where the bridle way passed through. The ground was lumpy and uneven but he could not let it deter him. Skipping across the clearing, he saw an area where the trees parted and a style beyond.

This in turn, brought him to the aforementioned farm track.

Vaulting over the stile, he stumbled a few yards, until a rustle of vegetation seized his attention. The men had also reached the stile. Refusing to give in, Elijah leapt into the neighbouring forest to the right side of the track. Here the trees were thinner, the branches spidery, affording him less cover. None-the-less, the expanse of woodland ahead he recognised; it encircled the grounds of Westbourne House and if he kept heading north he would reach it.

Finally he had made it. Drawn into the forest bordering James's land, he observed the landscape through the gaps in the trees, before another thought flashed up.

He remembered William's den.

Elijah did not look back. He could tell the men were still pursuing him from the unrelenting thud of their boots. But with a final burst of energy, he charged up the path in search of an ancient oak tree. It reared up suddenly, as did the glitter of William's school prefect badge pinned in the bark. Then at last he saw the den; a deep woodland hollow concealed under a canopy of bushes.

Elijah threw himself to the ground and parting the bushes, rolled inside.

He heard his pursuers stumble up to the same spot but their footsteps slowed. They seemed disorientated, feet dragging the earth, twigs snapping as they turned in circles. Elijah closed his eyes, his heart thumping. They were so very close even the slightest movement would betray him.

"Where the fuck's 'e gone?" he heard the first man panting.

Elijah recognised the Cockney accent from earlier.

"He's got to be around here somewhere!" the other man growled. "Come out, you little cunt! We're gonna find you wherever you're hiding!"

Elijah turned cold, aware of them foraging around, pushing apart the bushes, shaking trees as if they expected him to be hiding in one. Moving from one side of the wood to the other, their footsteps began to recede - until regrettably, they shuffled back. His eyes widened in horror as a pair of boots took shape through the concealing foliage at the mouth of the den. Holding his breath, he felt the air seep from his lungs when they retreated. They seemed reluctant to abandon their search, rooting through the undergrowth until at last they moved on to scour another area of forest.

Yet still he dared not move, not even when the sky began to darken. The temperature plummeted and robbed of his blazer, he started to shiver.

It was close to an hour before he crept from his hiding place where to his relief, the men had long gone. Elijah tiptoed through the darkening forest, inching himself as close to the edge as he dared. The grounds of Westbourne house yawned out before him and he saw a glimmer of light shining in the windows. Like a moth to a flame, he was nearly tempted to run there... but to do so involved crossing the open parkland. If those men were still around, he would be exposed.

Thus he hid himself within the confines of the forest, circling the perimeter until it joined the main driveway. If he made it to the gates, the caravan would be within easy reach.

He was so very nearly home.

Sidling up to the gate posts, he saw the caravan, *his sanctuary*. He shot across the road without delay, one final dash to freedom before he shakily stepped inside.

"Eli!" Eleanor gasped, spinning around.

She was hovering by the stove, stirring a saucepan. It infused their home with a savoury aroma laced with herbs, but as her eyes met his, her expression turned to dread. Elijah guessed he looked awful, his hair a tousled mess, littered with dried leaves and twigs. In the aftermath of his ordeal, his breathing rose in

359

slow laboured gasps and he was also missing his school blazer.

"Eli, what's wrong?" she begged. "Marilyn said she had a call to say you were at Westbourne House…"

"That's not true," Elijah choked, the misery welling inside him like a dam.

She scooped him up into her arms where for a few seconds, he could not stop trembling.

"What on earth has happened?" Eleanor kept murmuring, squeezing him tight.

And he told her everything.

A heavy darkness cloaked the village but Eleanor kept her curtains shut.

At times like this, she was glad of the metal screens shielding their windows, that extra layer of security as she attempted to console her son. The shadows were soft, the smouldering wood burner embracing them in a haze of warmth.

But everything Elijah had reported chilled her to the core. She was even toying with the idea of whether to knock on Marilyn's door, phone the police or at the very least, Charlie. More than anything, she was anxious to know more about this 'gentleman' who had lied about Eli being at Westbourne House. Only the force of her fear held her back though, as if an all pervading sense of danger lurked in the village. There was no telling those men might not still be skulking around and for that reason alone, she could not force herself to step outside.

Frozen in turmoil, how could she ignore the fact that a few days earlier, she had come face to face with Dominic Theakston? *Charlie seemed convinced he meant no harm, but was it possible the bastard was lying?* That Theakston had put her through a terrifying ordeal once before made him the most obvious suspect. And neither could she dismiss Elijah's description of the men, one of them tall and powerfully built. Yet he recalled a tanned complexion and close-cropped dark hair. So if Theakston wasn't involved, that left only one other possibility.

What if someone else was stalking them? Someone even more dangerous, her thoughts inevitably drawn to Perry Hampton…

III

Eleanor had no idea how accurate her suspicions were.

Several miles north in Pimlico, Perry was pacing around on the polished wood floor of his London mansion. He sucked heavily on a cigar, his face engorged with fury. The two men, Nathan included, hovered in front of him.

"You fucking idiots!" he hissed. "How could you let him get away? We had a perfect opportunity to snatch that boy and you cocked it up!"

"We did our best, Perry," Nathan said coldly, "and I'm sorry, but that kid was slippery as an eel. You're not the one who had an elbow rammed into your bollocks!"

"You should have been more vigilant then," Perry snapped. "I expect they will have gone to the police by now!"

"Don't worry, Mr 'Ampton," the other man placated him, "the Land Rover's stashed away in the East End and I swear no one saw us. That village is right out in the sticks."

"I see," Perry fumed. "Well, let's hope his mother assumes *Dominic Theakston* is behind this then you might just avoid arrest!"

Nathan clenched his fists, a muscle flickering in his jaw.

He despised failure as much as Perry but what else could they do? They had combed the woods for what seemed like an eternity and by the time darkness fell, they had no chance of capturing him. He remembered his cursory glance across the grounds towards the house, hoping a shadow would appear... then another thought struck him.

"We thought he'd go sneaking across to Westbourne House," he muttered, a snarl creeping into his tone, "and you might as well know there were a lot of lights on in there!"

"Really?" Perry whispered. "Does this imply the Barton-Wells pair are still in residence? I specifically told that butler I wanted them out!"

"Yeah, well I got the impression the place was very much lived in," Nathan taunted.

Perry stopped pacing and sank himself into a chair. For now, his anger seemed to have dissipated yet at times like this, Nathan knew he was at his most dangerous. The fact that they had failed in their mission to abduct Elijah Jansen had enraged him; but if the Barton-Wells kids were still proving to be defiant...

"I think we had better check this out," Perry muttered, "because if they haven't left by now..."

He trailed off, allowing his words to linger. The next time he met Nathan's eye, the atmosphere turned to ice.

"Fetch my son," he added coldly. "It's time we taught those brats a lesson... and see to it they receive a proper scare."

Chapter Forty

I

By the time Ben rode his Harley Davidson up the driveway of Westbourne house he was smiling. He couldn't deny having dreamed of this moment, a secret part of him hoping Avalon would delay her departure. But she always had been an arrogant bitch. If they had taken his father's warning seriously, they would have left by now. He surged ahead, fully intent on making them pay and with Nathan clinging to his rear, they swerved right.

The silhouette of Westbourne House stood against an oppressive black sky. Ben's eyes narrowed. It seemed a very long time since they had visited, yet he could clearly remember the layout. His malevolent stare swept across the lawn, tracing the outline of box hedging. He was visualising the yard where the vehicles were parked; the very place he was rolling towards right now.

With a noticeable absence of cars since the staff had left, he was further gratified to see James's black Jaguar missing. So, it would appear his father had been correct; the butler might not be around. Stepping away from their bikes, he felt a thrill charge through his veins.

This could not have turned out more perfect.

Leading Nathan through the yard, they reached the back of the house. The grounds lay under a canopy of darkness, where they froze by the patio doors. With a soft light shining behind the curtains, Ben sensed they were in there. He could hear a murmur of voices and music echoing from a TV set. Turning to Nathan, he placed a finger to his lips and pointed towards the doors. Nathan gave a curt nod, knowing what had to be done.

Ben was almost tingling, watching with pleasure as Nathan extracted a small hammer. His fingers crept to his neck, where the scars Avalon had left seemed to goad him. Nathan bashed one of the glass panes before sliding a gloved hand through the aperture. It took no time at all to wrench the handle up and with a brutal shove, he forced the door open.

As they marched inside the lounge, Avalon gave a shriek. *Yes, it was just as Ben imagined; there they were, lounging on their fancy sofa, watching a film.*

With a smirk, Nathan reached down and switched off the set. He drank in the interior, his eyes drifting. William leapt from the sofa. For a few seconds no one spoke, the shock on their young faces so pronounced, Ben wished he could capture it on a polaroid.

"Hello, kids," he murmured softly.

"What are you doing here?" Avalon screamed. "Get out!"

Ben stared deeply into her eyes. "More to the point, what are *you* doing here?" he taunted. "You were supposed to have left by now."

"We're leaving in the morning," William said, forcing a calmer tone.

"Is that so?" Ben sneered. He swung his arm in a wide circular arc. "Then how come this lounge is still furnished?"

William faltered, the fear in his expression growing as he glanced from one man to the other. Ben let out a chuckle.

"You've got no intention of moving out and to think my father gave you all this time."

"This is the last furniture to be moved!" William protested. "Honestly! It's just this and our stuff upstairs... Everything else is staying!"

Ben listened to his bleating voice with amusement. "Oh yeah, I gather my father paid you a few grand for it," he laughed, "but hey! Seeing as we're here, let's party! Where's the booze?"

From her corner of the sofa, Avalon squeezed herself into a ball. Her mind battled to find a solution but what could they do? They had released Elliot from his duties to visit his mother, and about to move out anyway. *If only Elliot was here now, though.* She surveyed their intruders, formidable in their black motorcycle leathers; at Nathan, whose powerful frame dwarfed her brother. With the patio doors closed, trapping them inside, there seemed to be no escape.

Avalon closed her eyes. "There isn't any booze," her voice shuddered.

Spinning away from the sofa, Ben strode towards the sideboard and immediately began searching the cupboards. A second door revealed a few gleaming decanters.

"Liar!" he accused.

Yanking out a bottle of ruby port, he unscrewed the stopper and took a swig. William and Avalon exchanged horrified glances, neither sure how to react.

Finally, William found the courage to speak. "Look, maybe we should go now, okay? Leave you to it! Just as long as we can come back tomorrow and pick up the rest of our stuff..."

"You needn't go just yet," Ben said, nailing him with his stare. He took a second swig from the decanter. "Find us some glasses! I didn't drive all the way here for nothing, you little kill-joy. I've had a snort of cocaine and I'm in a party mood." He turned to Avalon.

She watched, paralysed, as Ben strolled towards the settee. William meekly picked out glasses from a china cabinet, while on the other side of the room, Nathan stalked the perimeter, surveying the contents as if clocking their worth. A violent energy radiated from every muscle in the way he moved. Then, to her

363

rising horror, Ben lowered himself down next to her. Sliding his hand into her thick hair, he started separating the ringlets, the brush of his fingers sending shivers over her.

"Why are you really here, Ben?" she heard herself whisper.

"Why do you think?" he drawled. "We've got some unfinished business. Only this time, I'm not going to let myself be punched in the face... or clawed."

With a gasp, she pulled away yet he retained his hold on her hair.

"Ben, stop this!" she whimpered. "Your father wouldn't be very proud if he saw the way you were behaving right now!"

"My father's not here!" Ben retorted. "I can do what I like!"

She kicked out wildly but within a few strides, Nathan had crossed the room. With a cruel smile, he reached over the back of the sofa and grabbed her wrists, tugging them above her head to pin her down. Avalon screamed, writhing and fighting, but of course, he was way too strong.

Ben's eyes slid over her body, inspecting her brushed cotton shirt and clinging black leggings. Then seizing the fabric with both hands, he tore viciously downwards. As he stared at her breasts swelling from the lacy cups of her bra, she clocked the glitter in his eyes. He reached down to grab one, squeezing it hard.

"Get your hands off me," she sobbed, "or I swear I'll press charges for assault..."

She broke off as Nathan's grip tightened and to her increasing shock, he leaned right over the back of the sofa, pressing his face up close.

"Shut up, you bitch," he snarled. "Go on, Ben, go for it! It's high time you taught this little hell cat a lesson!" His narrow eyes skewered into hers, the expression on his face satanic.

"Patience, my friend," Ben smiled back, "you know I like to take things slowly..." His eyes emitted a flare as they swung back to Avalon. "He's right, though. You've had this coming to you for a very long time, my darling and I won't deny I am absolutely dying to fuck you. But let's not rush things... Are you a virgin?"

"No," Avalon told him defiantly. "I've had two boyfriends since I went out with you and I slept with them both!"

"Pity," Ben murmured, stroking her cheek, "I had hoped to be your first. Still, we've got plenty of time to savour the delights of you yet..."

From the other side of the room, William could barely look. Eyes lowered, he plucked a lead crystal goblet from the cabinet and then another. Creeping towards the sofa, he started to position them onto a side table. Yet the closer he drew, he felt a wave of loathing.

William paused, hand tight around the stem of one of the goblets. His eyes honed in on the back of Ben's sleek blonde head before he slowly raised it. The glass in his hand trembled yet he was a fraction too late. Nathan had spotted him. Releasing his grasp on Avalon, he swung around the settee and snatched his wrist. One vicious twist forced him to drop the glass. It tumbled to the carpet and smashed. But as he gaped up in terror, Nathan drew back his hand and struck him hard across the face, sending him sprawling to the floor. Avalon gave a cry of shock.

"Silly boy," Nathan sneered as he lay cowering on the carpet.

Next it was Ben's turn to whip his head around.

"He nearly got you then, mate," Nathan taunted. "One more second and he would have smashed your head in!"

"Right," Ben whispered. "In that case, maybe it's *this one* who needs teaching a lesson."

His eyes raked over him in a particularly nasty way as he struggled to his knees. William gulped back his fear, rigid with shock, his nose bleeding.

"Here," Nathan muttered, pulling out a handkerchief. "I don't believe we've met. I'm Nathan, by the way, Ben's security guard. William, isn't it?"

William nodded, accepting the handkerchief. He started dabbing at his nose to stem the flow of blood then felt the grip of Nathan's fist on his arm. Too stunned to struggle, he was hauled to his feet. Ben did not move, one arm slung around Avalon's shoulder. Nathan dragged him back towards the table where he had been positioning the glasses.

"Now pour us a drink!" he growled. "Try another trick like that again and I'll cripple you, do you hear me?"

"Yes," William mumbled.

"Leave him alone!" Avalon squeaked as the scene unfolded.

"Be quiet, Avalon," Ben snapped.

The icy edge to his tone she recognised, fearful her protective display towards her brother was about to unleash his true evil. Ben seemed to be revelling in it, waiting for William to pour the port. He squeezed Avalon's thigh, pinning him with his stare.

"Are *you* a virgin?"

William looked up anxiously. "Uh huh," he nodded.

He removed the handkerchief from his face, where his nose had finally stopped bleeding.

"What?" he snapped. "I-I never had much opportunity to meet girls... I went to a boys' school."

Clouds of tension gathered and all the while their eyes seemed to feast on him.

"So what about boys?" Ben said with a smirk.

William betrayed a flush, his eyes flickering back to Nathan. There was something unnervingly intrusive about the question.

"Absolutely no way," he whispered in outrage.

"Oh, come on, we know what goes on in boys' public schools," Ben jeered. "I went to one myself before I was expelled. Are you saying none of your peers ever tried to seduce you?"

His eyes narrowed dangerously and Nathan glanced back at him with a wink. The exchange left Avalon chilled, wondering whether something secret had been planned, especially when Nathan lowered a caressing hand to William's shoulder.

"What do you think?" Ben muttered. "Pretty little thing, isn't he?"

William flinched as the grip of Nathan's hand tightened. His hands shook as he lowered the decanter but no one could ignore the predatory way Nathan was leering at him.

"Take him," Ben ordered. "Give him a taste of what he's been missing!"

"No!" Avalon shrieked. "You can't!"

William tried to fight, but his efforts were fruitless as Nathan wrestled him towards the sofa. His legs kicked out madly, his face blanched with terror.

"Let him go!" Avalon screamed just as Ben twisted around to face her again. Only this time he held her arms, forcing them behind her back. Pulling her tight against his body now, he had her locked in position. His breath blew hot against the back of her neck as the excitement inside him bubbled.

"Please! Not my brother!"

"Oh yes, you really love your brother, don't you, Avalon?" Ben said viciously. "But don't worry, my sweet, you can watch."

She gaped in disbelief as Nathan managed to throw William across the sofa arm; powerless to do a thing all the while she was trapped in Ben's grip. With a sneer, Nathan yanked at his clothing. William let out a sob, his eyes stretched wide as they momentarily met her own.

"Don't hurt him!" Avalon howled. "I swear I'll go to the police. You could go to prison for this..."

The sound of Ben's laughter in her ears was like thunder. "The police will never believe you! There are no witnesses and they'll assume you made it all up to get back at my family!"

She was aware of William's helpless struggle; of Nathan fumbling in his pocket. Catching the gleam of lust in his eye, she started sobbing.

"Your turn next, darling," Ben hissed into her ear. "Soon as Nathan's done with your brother here, we're taking you upstairs to one of the bedrooms... and in case you hadn't realised, Nathan and I are both going to have you... *maybe together*."

She gave a whimper of terror as Nathan unbuckled his belt. Screwing her eyes shut, she could blot out the sight but not the sound; a nightmare that would haunt her forever as the pitch of her brother's scream tore the silence.

Avalon felt sick. It might not have gone on for long, yet those awful minutes seemed like an eternity. *If only she had been the victim on this occasion.* Anything to be spared the horror of witnessing this heartless assault on her brother, hearing his sobs of pain.

When he eventually fell silent, Avalon feared he had passed out. He crumpled to the carpet like a rag doll, leaving a smudge of blood on the sofa. But for the interlude she couldn't stop crying, helpless to banish the invasion of Ben's laughter.

Struggling from his embrace, she lowered herself to the floor next to William. His eyes were pressed shut, his face so pale it harboured an eerie pearlescent sheen. Yet she sensed the shadow of Ben looming. Grabbing her by the hair again, he forced her head back to look at him. But his twisted smile turned her stomach. Already she had some notion of what they planned to do to her, before he reached into his jacket, extracting a set of gleaming metal handcuffs.

"Let's take a tour of the house," he gloated to Nathan. "They've got four-poster beds upstairs." He dangled the handcuffs in front of Avalon's eyes.

As they temporarily left the room, Avalon froze, her eyes flitting madly before William wriggled into an upright position.

"William," Avalon whimpered. "Oh my God..."

He was still unnaturally pale, his pupils dilated, making his eyes look black. Yet somehow he found the strength to speak.

"We should get out of here while we can."

"Are y- you sure you're okay?" she gasped.

He stole a glance at the door. With the impending return of their assailants, they guessed this terrible night was far from over.

"Let's just go," he spluttered, "come on..."

Tip-toeing to the patio door, Avalon unlocked it. She stepped into the cold winter night and shuddered. It was fortuitous they were wearing shoes but her shirt hung in tatters, exposing her to the icy chill. Fearful of being discovered missing, they quickened their pace and within a few steps, reached the walled gardens.

"In here," Avalon whispered, "c'mon, before they see us..."

As they slipped through the gate, the intersecting paths gleamed under the darkness. Yet they clung to the walls, praying the shadows would disguise them.

Avalon felt a tug in her heart as she gazed across at the orchards. *This was possibly the last time she would ever see them.* At the same time though, she

367

was conscious of William inching painfully along beside her, heartbroken to imagine their time here could end so brutally.

Then an eerie rush of movement emanated from the woods beyond. The trees swished, followed by a rumble of hooves. Avalon tensed, imagining some deer herd making their way across the valley. The sound barely registered however, before another took its place.

A loud bang erupted from the house, which could only signify one thing; the patio doors had been flung open. With her grip on her brother's hand tightening, she moved faster, flitting past the Orangerie, wary of footsteps pounding across the lawn. It seemed obvious those men were heading this way now, advancing closer and closer to the walled gardens.

Sure enough two figures appeared, silhouetted against the gateway.

Avalon pressed her finger to her lips, pointing to the far wall. Moving with extreme stealth, they edged themselves into the corner that concealed an exit. Avalon reached out and felt for the wall disguised by ivy. Grappling at the edge, she was reminded of the climbing rose which added to its cover, but ignoring the prick of thorns, coaxed herself and William into the gap. The mass of ivy and roses on the facing wall gave the illusion the sections were joined, yet it took the greatest of effort to stand still.

The beam of a flashlight flickered. Avalon tensed as the circle of light danced along the wall, veering close to their hiding place. Pressing herself harder against the brickwork, she prayed it wouldn't pick out their shadows.

"Where are you, my little beauties," she heard Ben's voice hiss just metres away.

She could hear them breathing. A pungent smell of leather wafted into the air, mingled with traces of aftershave and sweat. Her heart pounded. For one awful moment, she sensed their escape was fruitless. *They were going to find them...*

But to her relief they swung right, moving in the opposite direction.

Avalon held her breath, watching the torch beam bounce up the path. With their footsteps receding, she was sure she heard one of them mutter something: *some commotion in the woods.* A thunderous charge of hooves had risen up again. For several more minutes, she did not dare move, until eventually William glanced at her.

"We should get away now," he breathed. "We can't stay here."

Avalon nodded before they crept through the parallel walls. Skirting around the other side of the garden, they rushed into the yard. William stopped dead. For there right in front of him, loomed Ben's Harley Davidson. Without another thought, he drifted towards it, allowing his hand to trail over the leather seat. With its key still dangling from the ignition, Avalon felt a leap of hope.

"Can you remember how to ride it?" she whispered.

"I think so," William replied. He eased himself carefully up onto the saddle.

Avalon helped him. She stroked his back tenderly, feeling a wave of despair, but they couldn't afford to waste time. No sooner had she hauled herself up onto the pillion, William turned the key. She flinched as the engine roared to life, splitting the air like thunder.

William pushed down the gear pedal with his foot and closed his eyes.

One down and four up.

The scene in London was coming back to him and revving the engine, he released the clutch.

Avalon felt the icy wind slap her face as they surged out of the yard. They swerved diagonally across the grass to meet the driveway, certain they had escaped.

Yet at the back of their minds, arose a new fear. Their attackers had surely overheard the engine and there was another bike in the yard; and whilst William was confident he could *control* the bike, he was not an experienced rider.

The sight of Eleanor's caravan looked inviting, a faint glow in her window. William rolled the bike into the trees where they dismounted, then dropped it onto its side.

Eleanor heard the motorbike and froze. The horror of Elijah's near abduction still kicked at her thoughts, but next came a tap on the door. Glancing at her son, wary of him sleeping, she drew herself up to the door and pressed her ear against it.

"Who is it?" she hissed.

"Eleanor, open the door, please!" a girl's voice whimpered.

Recognising Avalon's voice, she unfastened the bolt and chain, unprepared for the sight that confronted her. Avalon's windswept hair tumbled wildly around her shoulders, her shirt torn apart as she stood shivering. As her eyes moved towards William though, she barely recognised him. His face harboured the look of someone possessed.

"Inside, quick," she whispered, grabbing Avalon's hand.

William followed. He glanced at her with the look of a frightened deer, arms curled guardedly around his torso. Eleanor closed the door. At first no one spoke, although she already suspected the worst from the state of Avalon's torn clothing.

"Take a seat, William, love," she murmured, offering the lightest brush of her hand.

He flinched as if her fingers were searing hot.

"What on earth's happened?"

Avalon let out a sob. "The Hamptons turned up," she gasped through trembling lips. "Ben a-and his minder! We only just got away…" The panic in

369

her eyes flared. "They m-might still be out there! W-what if they find the bike? It's how we escaped, Eleanor. We stole one of their bikes."

"So where is it now?" Eleanor whispered.

"We dropped it by the trees."

They stared at each other in bewilderment, while from the other end of the caravan, Elijah stirred. He hauled himself up in his bed, a look of sleepy curiosity on his face.

"What's going on?"

Eleanor shot him a glance, tempted to tell him to *go back to sleep*. Yet how could she when it seemed obvious his friends were in some sort of peril?

"I'm not sure," Eleanor said, "but it's got something to do with the Hamptons. What exactly did they do, Avalon?"

Avalon shook her head miserably. "They h-hurt William..."

Eleanor moved from the table and rifling behind the make-shift screen which concealed their clothes, she found a dark woollen top for her.

"Put this on," she snapped. "We need to hide that bike. Come on, quickly..."

With a glance towards her son, she beckoned him to join William.

"Look after him," she added. "We won't be long... and turn the light off."

"Okay," Elijah agreed, sidling over to the seating area.

Leaping outside, they rushed towards the trees. Ben's Harley Davidson lay in an abandoned heap. Yet despite the enveloping darkness, a tell-tale flash of chrome was illuminated in the headlight of every passing car.

Eleanor grasped the handlebars. Avalon quickly joined in and using every ounce of their strength, they managed to heave the bike upright. A hint of impending danger sharpened their minds. For Eleanor, it had never gone away. Yet despite Elijah's trauma, at least he hadn't been hurt and only now, as they rolled the bike into the field, did she turn to Avalon.

"Tell me the truth," she whispered gently. "Have you been raped?"

Avalon shook her head but she looked haunted. "No - n-not me..."

Eleanor frowned. "William... You don't mean?"

"Don't say anything," Avalon begged. "Not unless *he* tells you."

Eleanor swallowed back her shock as they dragged the bike to the field edge. The perimeter hedge concealed a ditch, the temptation to dump it too hard to resist. With one hard shove, they sent Ben's expensive bike sloshing into the mud, then moved stealthily back towards the trees.

They had barely made it though, before the roar of the other bike erupted. Its headlamp flared through the gates of Westbourne House, forcing them to drop to the ground. For several seconds it loitered. Avalon flinched with every belch of its engine.

To their mounting dread, the motorbike crept across the road and into the field, then proceeded to circle the caravan. Pinning themselves flat on the grass, they endured several petrifying seconds before it turned and surged out of the village.

"Thank God!" Eleanor spluttered, springing to her feet. "Now let's get back inside!"

II

Avalon collapsed at the table, where the boys rested in silence. She, on the other hand, was shaking all over. Eleanor lit a lantern. It cast a pool of soft light across the table, capturing their frightened faces. No one could ignore William's pallor, nor the pain evident in his eyes.

Eleanor felt a storm of emotions. Guessing he was in shock, she sifted through her cupboards for some brandy, at the same time wary of her son's presence. Clearly confused, Elijah was no doubt wondering what could have happened to reduce his friend to such a state.

All William admitted to him was that Ben's accomplice had backhanded him. She nevertheless tipped out two small measures.

"Drink this," she muttered softly. "It'll make you feel better."

She stroked his arm and this time he didn't tense up. Accepting the brandy, he knocked it back with a shudder. But as the protective surround of Eleanor's home registered, Avalon let go of her emotions and she started to cry.

No one spoke. Eleanor pushed the second brandy towards Avalon who gulped it down.

"What now?" she blubbered. "What the hell do we do? Elliot's away. We're too scared to go back... and we were supposed to be moving out in the morning!"

"I know, sweetheart," Eleanor soothed. "Charlie's coming over with a removal van. How we handle the Hamptons is another matter..."

Tears swam in Avalon's eyes again. Eleanor felt her anguish, unable to comprehend how they could be subjected to such cruelty on top of everything else they had suffered. She felt the bite of anger, despising the Hamptons for their vileness.

"What a terrible day," she shuddered. "I haven't even had a chance to tell you this - but - but Eli was nearly abducted."

"Abducted?" William whispered, drawn out of his trance.

"Two men tried to force him into a Land Rover," Eleanor continued, "then chased him through the woods. But Marilyn had a strange phone call saying he was at Westbourne House."

William and Avalon gaped at them wide-eyed.

"There's something evil going on in this village," she added, "and it all

371

seems to be connected with the Hamptons' arrival."

"We've got to do something about them," Avalon hissed.

"I know, love," Eleanor said, "but for now, we should try to get some rest. Avalon, you can sleep in my bed with me but what about you, William?"

Their eyes locked across the table. Although Eleanor guessed sleep would be the last thing on his mind, as he clung to her gaze.

Yawning, Elijah looked at him. "Take the other bunk if you like," he said softly.

Yet still, William said nothing.

The caravan fell still as Elijah drifted back to sleep. Even Avalon managed to doze off, her gentle snores infusing the silence.

But later in the night, Eleanor detected movement, conscious of William creeping across the floor. She had been awake for as long as he had, as the horrific events of the night kept churning. Fumbling his way to the bathroom, he closed the door. A thin sliver of light appeared under the door frame, followed by a sound of splashing water. She waited in silence but as soon as the door clicked open, urged him to join her at the table.

"How are you feeling?" she asked. "Look... I know what happened, William."

"I'm guessing Avalon told you," he mumbled.

"Not intentionally," Eleanor said. "She suggested it might be better coming from you."

William lowered his eyes. He couldn't look at her.

She took his hand. "Who did this, William?"

The story leaked out piece by piece. He could not bring himself to divulge the worst details, though Eleanor detected his horror. It emanated from the tremor in his voice.

By the time he had finished, his words left a lingering chill in the atmosphere.

"William, you have got to go to the police," Eleanor whispered.

He pulled away, shrinking into himself like a snail. "No way," he spluttered.

"William, those men committed a monstrous crime," she persisted. "You can't let them get away with it. People like them are dangerous."

"That's just it," William said. "They *will* get away with it. Ben seemed pretty sure of that..." He gave a shiver. "There were no witnesses. No one will ever believe us."

"Well, I believe you," she soothed, "and we need to get you to see a doctor."

William shook his head. "There's no need. I'll be fine."

Eleanor let out a sigh. "I'm a nurse, William and there's nothing to feel embarrassed about. Any traces could count as evidence..."

372

"There's no point," William hissed, lowering his eyes to conceal his shame. "If you really want to know, he used a condom."

Eleanor stared open-mouthed. "Oh, William... won't you at least let *me* talk to the police? I need to report this terrible business with Eli."

"No, Eleanor," William said firmly. The steely hardness in his eyes reminded her of James. "Hampton will have powerful lawyers. That man could get away with murder if he wanted."

Eleanor almost nodded, chilled by the truth in his words.

"They'll want to know why they singled *me* out instead of Avalon. Ben made some comment about being *pretty*... that this stuff goes on in boys' boarding schools. People will think I'm gay."

"Rubbish..." Eleanor started to protest but William had not quite finished.

"There's something else. He threatened me, Eleanor - r-right after h-he *hurt* me. He whispered something in my ear..." A tear trickled down his cheek.

Avalon had been present yet even she hadn't heard the vile words Nathan had hissed.

"If I breathe a word to the cops they'll do worse. Him and his friends... and that tonight's little session will seem like a picnic..."

The horror of it lurked even now.

"What if we lose?" he shivered. "We go to court and they walk free? I'd rather die! I'd sooner just forget this happened..." He broke off with a sob.

Eleanor turned cold. Hadn't she heard somewhere that rape victims blamed themselves? That although they feared retribution from their attackers, they experienced an even greater fear of being ridiculed by their friends?

"God, William, that is awful," she breathed, "and no one thinks you're gay. Those men are psychopaths. Imagine what they'd have done to Avalon if you hadn't got away?"

"Hmm," William nodded, "but I-I'm still not going to the police."

"Okay, I understand," Eleanor relented. "If you don't want to press charges, no one can force you. Though I still think you should get yourself examined."

William let out a sigh, his lips tight as he wiped the tear from his face. "Okay," he said. Then without warning, his grip on her hand tightened. "One more thing. Promise you won't tell anyone. Not Eli or Charlie. That everything that happened stays a secret and we never talk of it again."

"Alright," Eleanor agreed, "but one thing I will say is your sister was right about those Hamptons. We have got to do something about them before anyone else gets hurt."

William nodded again. It took just one fleeting mention of them to bring an icy chill back into the air, his grip on Eleanor's hand tight.

But he no longer wanted to dwell. He knew that given time, he would heal. He and Avalon would recover their lives... and as for Westbourne House; the battle was lost for now. This final atrocity could so easily tarnish the memory of their lives there but it would be an affront to their father

Yes, it would be so much more empowering to just banish the darkness Ben and his hateful accomplice had brought into their home tonight.

Chapter Forty-One

I

Come morning, Eleanor wasted no time. Leaving Elijah in the caravan to pack the few things they were taking with them, she found Avalon and William some clothes, then went next door to speak to Marilyn. By the time she had spluttered out the details of her son's ordeal though, Marilyn's face had turned ashen.

"But I thought it was Elliot," she breathed. "Softly spoken, cultured... it sounded so much like him! Oh Eleanor, I'm sorry."

"Don't be," Eleanor said tightly. "It's my fault, I should have checked."

She shook her head. Only one other voice could have matched Marilyn's description: *Perry's*. With no hesitation, she got straight on the phone to Charlie.

Hastily recounting each story, she didn't know how she kept her voice steady.

"Hey, slow down!" Charlie interrupted. "What else is wrong?"

"Ben Hampton turned up at Westbourne House with some thug of a henchman. Those kids were threatened horribly... and they're too scared to go back." Already she felt torn, wishing she could spit out the entire story. "What time can you get here? Avalon seemed to think Elliot would be back by mid-morning."

"You mean he's not there?" Charlie shuddered in horror.

"He had to go to London, remember?" Eleanor said. "His mother's in hospital..." She felt a sob catch her throat. "Oh Charlie, why didn't we think to get them out of there sooner?"

"Ssh," Charlie comforted her, "I'll be over as soon as I can. Now what about this business with Eli? Didn't you ought to phone the police?"

"That's next on my list," she finished sadly.

Twenty minutes later, a very different conversation took place.

"Who do you think *you are* to question my authority, Mr Bailey?" Perry demanded.

"They were ready to leave anyway!" Charlie thundered back at him. "You didn't have to send your deranged son round to threaten them!"

Perry's face hardened with outrage. Of all the people to turn up, the last person he expected to see was Charles Bailey, along with some youth who he presumed to be his son.

"Regardless of who I am," Charlie added coldly, "I'm here to collect the rest of their belongings and Elliot is on his way..."

Unbeknown to anyone, Perry had in fact been at Westbourne House since six-o-clock that morning, accompanied by Nathan - their goal to remove every last trace of their atrocious attack. Even now he quivered with rage. When Ben and Nathan had returned home, it was well past Midnight. Desperate to know where the land lay, he was unprepared for the state of his son. He recognised something wild in his expression, a look of manic fury, which made him nervous. Something had obviously not gone to plan.

But eventually the story crept out. *"You said they needed a proper scare."*

Except Perry could not quite dispel his disgust when he finally realised the truth; the disclosure his son had coerced Nathan into committing a most fiendish assault on the Barton-Wells boy. It was hardly a wonder they had escaped on his motorbike, Ben's one and only regret *he never did get his turn with Avalon...*

Unable to rein in his anger, Perry had turned on his son and blacked his eye. His role was to scare the kids into leaving, not embark on some depraved sexual orgy.

Only as a result of Nathan's reassurance, did he finally manage to calm down.

"He won't go to the police," Nathan said nastily. "I made sure of that!"

But Perry was not convinced. Driven by a power of vigilance, they had returned before dawn. Nathan had replaced the shattered pane in the patio door, before scrupulously cleaning up the broken glass on the carpet and the blood. The only remaining evidence was a tyre track carved diagonally across the lawn; *the mystery of Ben's missing bike another problem to be resolved.*

Right at this moment though, Perry had other things on his mind.

"Would you kindly step aside please?" Charlie's voice continued to goad him.

Then without warning, the rear door of his car swung open and the svelte figure of a boy emerged, the reddish gleam of his hair disturbingly familiar.

Perry glanced away, wary of Charlie observing him.

"What is that boy doing here?" he muttered guardedly.

"He asked if he could pay one last visit to the walled gardens," Charlie replied. "Do you have a problem with that?"

"I suppose not," Perry said, forcing a calmer tone.

"Couple of blokes tried to grab him yesterday," Charlie added, never once taking his eyes off his face. "Seems no one is safe in this world, not even a child..."

"I see," Perry snapped, refusing to buckle under the force of his stare. "Well, what can I say? I suppose we had better go inside."

Fumbling for the keys he had collected from the solicitor, he turned away. But the sight of Elijah unnerved him. Conscious of their ham-fisted attempt to capture him, he felt an urge to get Charles and his son into the house fast. Nathan lurked in reception. If that boy spotted him now, just one spark of recognition could plunge their entire futures into jeopardy.

At the back of his mind however, bloomed a whisper of hope; it seemed Charles knew precious little about the real atrocities committed. He had only mentioned the word *threaten*. But with emotions running on red-alert, he allowed them to pass through.

Charlie on the other hand, could express nothing but contempt for the way the Barton-Wells children had been treated. Ambling into reception, he was further appalled to see *that thug* lounging by the desk, donning motorcycle leathers. It threw him right back to their clash on the building site, only this time he was not going to be intimidated.

Pushing aside all thoughts of the Hamptons, as well as the glaring hostility of their security guard, he marched Andrew into the lounge where the last items of furniture were removed.

Twenty minutes later, he dropped Elijah back at the caravan and then Elliot turned up.

Horrified to discover the children had left, he never imagined Perry would carry out his threat. But he was even more distressed to learn he had sent his son to do it.

"I should never have left them," he mumbled to Charlie.

He looked pale and haggard, clearly encumbered with his own worries. In all eventualities however, Elliot possessed the stoicism to supervise the professional team of removal men who had accompanied him. Yet he could never quite escape the steely-eyed scrutiny of Perry, who seemed reluctant to let him out of his sight.

"It's alright, Elliot," Charlie muttered, "you're not to blame. The kids are safe now."

Hurling another glare at Perry, he felt his hatred rise. He could sense the power he wielded over them and none so much as this gentle, yet remarkable man, who had ultimately sealed a Devil's pact to remain here with James's children. All that mattered now was to get them securely re-homed in Rosebrook and be united as a group.

Though for poor Elliot, there was no such sanctuary.

Why couldn't I have just told him?
The question was stabbing at Eleanor's mind even now. Steering her car away from Elijah's school, they had not long left the police station.

Eleanor thought one phone call would be enough to lodge her report. But child abduction was a serious crime; a matter so unsettling, Inspector Boswell insisted she called in at the station, if not slightly critical she hadn't reported it on the day.

"Do you have any enemies, Miss Chapman?"

Buckling under the pressure of his stormy gaze, she had nibbled her lip as the perilous words teetered: *Perry's allies*. Yet she shooed them from her mind as quickly as they had fluttered in. It wasn't just Elijah she needed to protect, but William.

"Mr Boswell, we all have enemies," she responded. "The fact is, someone tried to snatch a child from the village. I thought you should be aware of that. You've got kids of your own."

Eventually he conceded that unless they could find clear evidence to identify Elijah's attackers, there was little they could do to bring charges. He had promised to start an investigation though - talk to Marilyn and Herbert Baxter, perhaps hoping *he* might know someone who matched Elijah's description. In the meantime, Eleanor urged him to keep the story out of the press, the fear of retribution never far from her mind.

Conscious of William braced in the back seat whilst Avalon sat trembling in the front, she scoured the hospital car park for a space. Only their fear spurred her on now, Avalon despising their attackers for what they had done to her brother.

It brought to mind a whispered conversation at sunrise, when they had flitted across the field to check on the motorbike. Lying at the bottom of a stagnant-smelling ditch, glistening with dew, it was the only sight that could rouse a smile in the aftermath of such terror.

Except Avalon had demanded to know why William was reluctant to press charges.

"I'd have gone to the police," she sniffed, brushing away a tear, "if it had been me..."

She had not heard Nathan's threat though... which in turn inspired Eleanor to explain the deep rooted fear William had exposed.

Avalon swore she would hide his secret but next came the problem of what to do with Ben's Harley Davidson. Avalon was of a mind to let it rust in the ditch; Eleanor, sensing its worth, wondering if there was a way they could hawk it on the black market. Yet they dared not loiter too long. With the sound of church bells tolling in the air like a warning and the Hamptons advancing, it was never more essential to get out of Aldwyck. So, no sooner had Charlie delivered Elijah back to the caravan, they had made their escape.

Once William was passed into the sympathetic care of one of her colleagues, they waited in silence. But only when they returned to the car, did she realise how deeply traumatising this had been for him. Charlie and Andrew were tied up with the move. This left only one person with the underlying compassion to aid his emotional recovery; a notion that inspired her to head for the Community Centre...

"What now?" Avalon shivered. "What's happening to the rest of our stuff?"

Eleanor sighed, frustrated by the time it was taking to get to the Community Centre. With dozens of cars clogging the high street, she had forgotten it was market day.

"Charlie will meet us later," she answered, "and as for your belongings, they're being packed into removal vans as we speak."

"But what about our personal things?" Avalon bleated. "Our clothes? We never had a chance to pack a suitcase!"

Eleanor picked up the sob in her voice. "Try not to worry," she placated her. "I imagine Elliot will have done that for you."

"Elliot!" Avalon gasped, covering her hand with her mouth. "We never even said good-bye to him!"

"It's alright, he's going to meet us too," Eleanor smiled as the traffic momentarily paused again. But turning from the wheel, she felt the smile drop from her face. "Poor man. Can you imagine what it will be like having to work for those evil people? He should get a copy of his contract, so we can check the legality of it..."

She swallowed, sensing the tension as it swirled inside the car. William fidgeted in the back seat, his eyes darting from one side of the street to the other. Lost for words, they continued the last leg of their journey in silence and by the time the bleak walls of the Community Centre loomed up, Eleanor had never been more pleased to see it.

"Where are we?" William said stiffly as she pulled into a parking spot.

"This is the Community Centre" Eleanor replied. "I'd like to introduce you to Peter. You'll feel a lot better once you've met him, I promise..."

No one argued as they tiptoed from the car. Eleanor coaxed them into the main hall where it felt strange to be back. Had it only been a week ago this room was packed with craft and cake stalls? She blinked, aware of James's children frozen by her side. One glance at their frightened faces betrayed their dark mood. So she hurried them over to the tea bar where Emily Cuthbert greeted them with a smile.

"Eleanor! Oh, I am so pleased to see you. Sit down."

Navigating Avalon and William to a table, they shared a few hushed words, Emily fussing over them like an old mother hen. Avalon forced a smile but William had completely withdrawn into himself again.

"Poor boy," Emily whispered. "Looks like he's seen a ghost. How about I bring you two a nice mug of hot chocolate?"

"You're very kind," Avalon mumbled, fighting tears.

"They've been forced out of their home," Eleanor said. "Any chance I could leave them in your care, while I go and find Peter?"

"Oh, he's upstairs in his office," Emily said, rolling her eyes, "in a meeting with that snotty man from the council. But I'm sure he won't mind being relieved..."

"I see," Eleanor snapped. *She meant Robin Whaley of course.*

II

Robin meanwhile, was still basking in his triumph, convinced Eleanor had gone for good. He had been a little anxious for the boy though, given Perry's plan to abduct him. Wary of their first bungling attempt, Robin knew he would never give up... But for now, he had other matters on his mind, delighted to be engaging with the divine Peter Summerville, who had finally agreed to discuss a building schedule. Engrossed in Charlie's plans, they were examining the proposed 'stonework' around the windows when a rap on the door jolted them.

Both men looked up as the door swung open. The last thing Robin expected however, was for Eleanor to burst in.

"Peter, I am sorry to interrupt..." she began.

"Eleanor," Peter smiled.

Stung by his expression of tenderness, Robin sprang to his feet.

"What are *you* doing here?" he spat at her.

"Peter, is it possible you could come downstairs?" Eleanor persisted. "There are two young people..."

"How dare you interrupt our meeting!" he ranted.

"Oh, just shut up will you?" Eleanor hissed with a force neither man expected. She exhaled a sigh, her eyes locking with Peter's again. "I've got two kids downstairs who have been through hell. I was just wondering if you could talk to them."

Peter looked stunned at first. Anchored to his desk, he seemed unsure how to respond.

"Robin, I'm so sorry," he then murmured, "but do you mind if I see what the problem is?"

Robin's face clenched as Peter headed towards the door. With no choice but to follow, they found themselves unwittingly wandering side by side. But the undercurrent of tension felt unbearable as they descended the stairs in silence. Every so often, they caught each other's eye. Cold blue clashed with deep gold, the atmosphere barbed with hate.

Returning to the hall, Eleanor soon forgot about Whaley, relieved to see the children where she had left them, nursing mugs of hot chocolate. Peter's footsteps slowed. Even Robin seemed unable to take his eyes off them and as Eleanor moved forwards, she captured Avalon's gaze.

"Peter," she began tenderly, "this is Avalon Barton-Wells and her brother. Do you remember me telling you about their father? He died not so long ago."

Avalon discharged a sob, fresh tears spilling down her cheeks. Eleanor stroked her hair in a manner almost destined to draw attention to her luxurious long curls.

"They've been evicted from their home. Put through a most harrowing ordeal... Is there any chance you might be able to help them?"

"You know I will," Peter whispered in earnest.

Robin lingered on the periphery, strangely moved by the scene. These were not the usual 'ragamuffins' who came in search of help. In fact, just from hearing their names, he knew who they were. He observed the girl, who seemed visibly shaken. Yet the boy intrigued him more. He hadn't uttered a word and even now, remained frozen.

Only as Peter approached him though, did he tentatively look up.

"And what's your name?" Peter asked him.

"William," the boy mumbled. He was ghostly pale, his expression one of anguish.

Robin studied his face, the ruffled golden-brown hair that framed it, and felt a rush of emotion that made his heart leap. As William shifted his gaze, he was dazzled by the impact of those almond shaped eyes, the same hazel brown as his sister's.

"How old are they?" he murmured without thinking.

"William is fifteen," Eleanor answered. "Avalon just turned seventeen."

"You're from Westbourne House aren't you?" Peter added. He lowered himself slightly to bring his eyes level with William's. "I guess you're feeling a little disorientated. Am I right in thinking you've got nowhere to stay tonight?"

"Charlie found them an apartment," Eleanor told him. "We were hoping to move them in later but I'm not so sure now; not after what's happened..." her words ebbed away.

A look of horror flashed across Avalon's face. "We'll be on our own?" she whimpered.

"It's okay, you're in safe hands," Peter smiled at her. "Though right now, I think you need more than a place to live... I think you need a little looking after."

Avalon smiled back, the tears in her eyes shining. "Can't we stay with you, Eleanor? I don't care if we sleep on the floor!"

"Well, maybe you won't have to," Peter grinned. "In fact, why don't we move to the Information Centre? It's a bit more comfy and quieter in there. I've got an idea..."

"Okay," William said, his voice a whisper.

As he struggled to his feet, Robin was still watching him. He sensed his torment. It was reflected in every step, stirring some deep inner pain he could not explain. There was no doubt in his mind they had been through something terrible; yet at the same time, could not deny that William Barton-Wells was simply the most beautiful boy he had ever set eyes on.

As they moved from the hall, Robin found himself following. Shrinking into themselves, heads down, they drifted through the doors of the Information Centre like shadows.

Robin slowed to a pause, subconsciously turning to Eleanor.

"What happened to them?" he couldn't resist asking.

She looked at him, startled. "They were forced out of their home by your *old acquaintance*, Perry Hampton. Unfortunately he sent his son. Let's just say things got a bit nasty."

Robin swallowed, fighting to find the right words.

"I'm sorry," he said gently.

They could see them through the glass door panel. Peter guided the children towards a sofa beneath the window. Yet for now, Robin remained outside in Eleanor's company, a situation which seemed uncanny.

"It was good of you to bring them," he conceded. "No one can argue you go out of your way to help others."

As Eleanor turned, her eyes pierced into him. "Nothing upsets me more than to see people treated badly," she reacted. "I promised their father I'd look out for them. But I wouldn't expect someone like you to understand..."

"That's not fair, Eleanor," he said softly. "Whatever you think of me, I do have a heart."

"I'm not disputing that," she retorted. "I could tell from the way you were looking at William..." She offered him a cool smile.

Robin froze, feeling his tension mount.

"No one can explain their motives," her voice hummed, "but what Perry Hampton did to that family was unforgivable."

The impasse lay suspended for a few seconds, until those final words hit home. The air became taut with malice again. The spell was broken.

"What are you really doing back in Rosebrook, Eleanor?" Robin whispered. "Didn't we make it clear you're not wanted around here?"

"Well, I'm back, so get used to it," she snapped. "I want to be with the man I love and the people I love. People like William and Avalon who need me right now! So tell that to your hired thug, Dominic Theakston... and as for you, Mr Whaley. Cause me any more trouble and I swear I will raise a complaint. Now back off and leave us alone!"

She shot him a final look of loathing and without awaiting a response, turned and swept into the Information Centre to join the others.

III

The encounter left Robin flabbergasted, so much so he could not stay silent.

"Perry, what did your son do to those kids last night?" he spluttered down the telephone.

Perry was taken aback. Having seen off the last of the removal vans, as well as those damned Baileys, he had returned to London triumphant.

"What do you know about it?" he growled.

"They turned up at the Community Centre," Robin enlightened him, "in the care of Eleanor Chapman. She knows you sent Ben round to evict them, so come on, what happened? We both know about your son's appetite for cruelty."

Perry felt a rise of fury, of a mind to let him rant. *So, it seemed evident they had stayed in her caravan overnight.* What was he supposed to do? He had ordered Ben to get rid of them; a plan that had been successful in its execution, since it was unlikely those kids would return...

"That's exactly my point," Robin sighed. "They're just kids, Perry."

"You dare criticise me?" Perry retorted. "What is that Chapman woman doing back in Rosebrook anyway? I told you to get rid of her! Failed again did you? Do I need to remind you how dangerous she is? The threat she poses for both of us?"

"Then why rock the boat?" Robin protested. "Why give her even more reason to hate you?"

Robin did not see the ice behind his smile. "You leave Eleanor Chapman to me and as for that other pair... I suspect I know where your real interests lie. They are after all, quite attractive aren't they, especially the boy." He was rewarded by a bombshell of silence. "Our enemies may be close but there are still ways to control them. Keep a close eye on Eleanor, because I *will* capture her son; and when that happens we can investigate that secret file of hers. But for now, we bide our time... maybe enlist the help of someone they trust. Are you with me so far, Robin?"

"Of course," he relented, reduced to his usual sycophantic self.

"Good," Perry said, "then why not continue ingratiating yourself with this *Peter Summerville*? And it would do no harm to befriend the Barton-Wells children either."

Robin released a sigh. "Perry, I should warn you Eleanor is very protective of them. Isn't it more likely she will turn them against me?"

"Use your charm, Robin," he kept pressing, "and stop whinging! Rowena

383

and I are moving into Westbourne House next week and I have some ideas I want to run past you. I could use your expertise with regards to planning permission."

"Perry, I would be delighted..." Robin kept fawning and by the time the call ended, Perry knew he had regained the upper hand.

Pushing aside Robin's worries, he had so many visions. He had long fantasised about the potential of Westbourne House, now hankering to turn his dreams into reality.

Chapter Forty-Two

I

For the immediate short-term future, William and Avalon had gleefully accepted an invitation to move in with Peter. His slightly haphazard flat above the Fish and Chip shop was not only quite spacious but stood a stone's throw away from the almshouses.

Eleanor could think of no better solution. For fear of isolation, they were reluctant to move into the apartment Charlie had found them. Yet the protective embrace of Peter's home and his kind nature would go a long way towards aiding their recovery.

"You'll love it!" Peter enthused. "So long as you don't mind the smell of chips. Or the potato-slicing machines thumping away at dawn!"

He was accustomed to having people to stay and happy to offer his home as a sanctuary.

Elijah meanwhile, agreed to say nothing about their eviction. Still a little shaken by his own ordeal, he suspected the Barton-Wells children had been through something far worse. Yet as he reacquainted himself with Margaret, he could barely suppress his delight to be home, of a mind to concentrate on more positive matters.

Right now, they were enjoying the sweet notes of her Top 40 single by 'Curiosity Killed the Cat.' Elijah smiled, having glimpsed Margaret swooning over the lead singer. *She thought he looked a bit like William.* Then Andrew strolled in.

Released from his duties, he had abandoned Charlie and Elliot, who were meeting the others. The moment he saw Elijah though, he stopped dead. Friction bit the atmosphere as the two of them just looked at each other.

But Andrew spoke first, fearful their sudden departure had been down to his own lousy behaviour. His arm fell to Elijah's shoulder.

"Okay, little Bro?" he said guardedly.

"Andrew," Elijah responded in a monotone.

Andrew frowned, unsure what seemed so different about him. Sensing a maturity that had never been there before, he grabbed him in a bear hug.

"Sorry about last week," he muttered. "I was a complete arse! You caught me at a bad time..."

"S'okay," Elijah said, patting his shoulder in response.

"You didn't say anything did you?" he whispered in his ear.

"About what?" Elijah grinned and stepping out of his embrace, their quarrel was forgotten.

<h1 style="text-align:center">II</h1>

No one saw the Barton-Wells children for the next few days, for as a result of Eleanor's insistence they needed time to adjust. At the same time, nothing had been resolved over her son's attempted capture. Charlie could understand her reluctance to tell anyone - the questions, the fear people would gossip... but it left behind the footprint of something ominous in their lives

Such a feeling inspired them to revisit Aldwyck, Elijah included. With a bullish sense of daring, this was Charlie's suggestion - if his intuition proved correct, chatting to the villagers might be helpful, especially if it threw a spotlight on his pursuers. As the familiar countryside began to unfold though, Eleanor started to fidget.

"I can't believe we're doing this," she whispered.

"We have to," Charlie snapped, firing a glance at Elijah's reflection in the driver mirror.

And as the journey ensued, Elijah finally began to talk about it.

Charlie listened in horror, his eyes fixed on the road as it dipped and twisted, drawing them deeper into the countryside. Its remoteness was startling, the vast fields, the tunnel of woodland so dark and threatening, it served a chilling reminder of how vulnerable Elijah had been.

Pulling into the pub car park, Charlie turned to him.

"I'll tell you something else," he muttered, "there wasn't half something shifty about old Hampton the next day."

"D'you reckon he had something to do with it?" Elijah said.

"I've been thinking the same," Eleanor sighed. "What if he's in the pub?"

"What if he is?" Charlie retorted. "We show our faces and stand up to him, now come on!"

Still she hesitated, before stepping gingerly through the door. Charlie strolled up to the bar where Boris and his wife seemed delighted to see them.

"Hello, folks," Boris grinned, hauling on the beer pump. "There's only a handful of us originals left, now James's kids have gone. Elliot told us. Do you know where they're living?"

"Rosebrook," Charlie answered, unable to hide the melancholy in his voice. "A friend of ours is putting them up for now. But they still haven't found a new home."

Boris paused. "What made them leave so suddenly?"

Charlie and Eleanor flashed each other a glance, unsure what to tell him.

"Hampton wanted them out," Eleanor disclosed. "He must have run out of patience but sent his son round there to evict them."

Boris shook his head, lips tight. "Poor kids. Everyone misses their dad, you know. This village won't be the same, not now that other lot have moved in. Typical Londoners! There's even talk of them digging up the walled gardens..."

"No!" Eleanor gasped. "Surely not!"

"Elliot leaked it," Boris whispered, "so don't say anything, it's supposed to be top secret."

"Bastards," Charlie hissed, "which reminds me, does anyone know where William's car is? He was asking about it the other day. I thought one of us could collect it for him."

"It's okay, Herbert Baxter's keeping it safe in one of his barns," Boris reassured him.

At the mention of Herbert Baxter, Elijah flinched, eyes drifting towards the one corner of the pub he tended to dominate. Sure enough, there he was, slouched in the shadows; and with a sharp flick of the head, Herbert appeared to beckon him.

"I suppose I should talk to him," Elijah muttered, inching away from the bar.

"A word, young man," Herbert prompted as he approached his table.

He stabbed a chubby finger towards the stool opposite.

"I had a visit from the police," he continued softly. "What's this I hear about some men trying to snatch you?"

Elijah blushed. "Th-they seemed to know you..."

"Thought they were friends of mine, did you?" he murmured accusingly.

"Not at all!" Elijah gasped.

A tiny smile danced around the corners of his mouth. "It's okay, son, I don't bite. I'd just like to hear your side of the story."

Elijah hastily described the scene by the roadside.

"He asked me if I knew *you* - asked for directions to your farm. I tried to explain b-but they were obviously trying to distract me..."

"Lucky you escaped," Herbert sniffed, stuffing tobacco into his pipe. He shook his head. "Bloody child molesters! Now you listen to me, boy, your mother and I might not see eye to eye but we are not enemies. Anyway, Boswell passed on your description..." He glanced around almost fearfully, before tilting his head a little closer. "Got me thinking about that young, fair-haired chap who started coming here. Always full of questions he was. Questions about James, about the house. Made a real point of trying to befriend me."

"Ben Hampton," Elijah mumbled.

"Mmm, and he eventually discovered my name," Herbert nodded, "but that's not the point. I remember some friend he used to drag along with at times. Looked like one of those Hells' Angels. Must have been over six foot tall, dark haired and built like a brick outhouse."

Elijah froze where he sat, his face rigid.

"Sound familiar?" Herbert muttered. His eyes glittered with conviction.

Elijah nodded. "I've never met Ben's bodyguard," he whispered, "but Charlie has a-and so have William and Avalon..." He broke off with a shudder.

"One last thing," Herbert finished. "Don't let on I told you this. Especially now those Hamptons have moved here. I don't want any repercussions... understand what I'm saying, boy?"

"Of course," Elijah nodded, sliding off his stool. "I won't say a word."

Backing away from the table, he returned to the bar. But the next time he stole a glance in Herbert's direction, the man was still watching him.

Elijah kept his head down. Aware of the excitable burr of voices, he was not really listening; at least not until the conversation drifted back to Ben.

"Incidentally," Charlie broke in, "I don't suppose you know anyone who can shift a Harley Davidson motorbike do you? You know, on the quiet?"

Boris almost stumbled against the bar. "Not Ben's bike?" he gasped. "Don't tell me you've nicked it. The Hamptons have banding accusations around, saying it's been stolen!"

"Really?" Eleanor said coolly. "Well, I don't suppose Ben told you William borrowed it, did he? It was the only way they could escape."

Boris shook his head, his expression troubled as he ran his fingers through his thinning blonde hair. "Be careful, Eleanor," he shivered.

"Boris is right, love," Charlie agreed. "Those Hamptons have screwed up enough lives... Imagine what they'd do if we tried to flog his son's precious motorbike."

Eleanor exhaled a sigh. "Okay, it's been dumped in the ditch at the end of our field. Maybe Herbert could tow it out with his tractor... but I imagine it's in a bit of a sorry state by now."

Despite everyone's dread of the Hamptons' arrival, they managed to laugh at that.

Before they left, it was a delight to see Elliot peeping around the door, his pale features instantly recognisable beneath his cap of snowy white hair.

"Hello there," he smiled. "Nice to see a familiar face." Gliding up to the bar with an order for Boris, he turned to Eleanor and Charlie. "How are the children?"

"Bearing up," Eleanor said softly. "Given time, I expect they'll be house hunting again soon. They're in good hands though... and miss you terribly."

"Tell them I miss them too," Elliot pleaded, "and if you can pass on their details, I would love to phone them." He drew his head close, his voice dropping to a whisper. "Things are not good at Westbourne House. Perry is already throwing his weight around..."

"How can you bear to work for such an ogre?" Charlie snorted.

"I have no choice," Elliot said. "Though Rowena can be quite charming. At least in my role as butler, I get to hear about their development plans."

"Oh yes," Charlie nodded. "Thanks for passing on that little nugget about the walled gardens."

"Hush!" Elliot gasped, flinching as if scalded.

"It's okay, we're not about to broadcast it," Eleanor soothed him.

He pressed his head even closer. "Be careful visiting Aldwyck. Perry is *on to you*. He knows the children hid at your place, on the night they were evicted."

Eleanor frowned, about to ask him how he knew this but he pressed a finger to his lips.

"We mustn't be seen talking. I've been ordered to have nothing more to do with you or Charlie otherwise..." His words broke off, the pallor in his face unmissable. "Let's just say, Perry is a very dangerous man to cross right now. We all have to be careful."

Charlie gaped at him in shock. "For God's sake, Elliot, we're friends!"

"I know," Elliot nodded. "It's just v-very hard for me at the moment. But how would you feel about meeting me in London? Come to my mother's home. She died by the way."

"Oh, I'm sorry..." Eleanor started to say but Elliot waved away her sympathy.

"Don't be. It's what she wanted. Just give me your phone number."

Charlie wasted no time and using an old petrol receipt, he scribbled down their details. Elliot thanked him before returning to the bar - collected a bottle of red wine for Perry, then swiftly disappeared from the pub.

"Like I say, Charlie, nothing is ever going to be the same," Boris said and by way of displacing his own worries, immediately grabbed a few glasses to polish. "But try not to fret about Elliot. He keeps us up to date with everything. He has to be discreet, though."

Nothing more was said as Charlie jotted down the same contact details on a notepad. But as Eleanor shuffled on her feet, her arm coiled protectively around her son's shoulder. That final disclosure that *Perry was in residence* was all she needed to hear, to feel his malice.

III

Elijah could not keep himself away from the Barton-Wells kids for any longer. Speeding across the road towards Peter's flat, next day, he glanced over his shoulder almost by instinct.

As soon as he stepped inside, Peter ushered him up a flight of stairs, into a large sunny lounge. It was filled with brightly coloured furniture, a set of flimsy DIY units almost sagging under the weight of his TV and stereo, the shelves crammed with books.

"Nice flat!" Elijah piped up, pulling off his coat as the stuffy warmth enveloped him.

No sooner did his voice resonate around the walls when William appeared.

"William!" Elijah greeted him warmly. "How have you been?"

"Fine," William replied. "It's great staying here."

Avalon was next to appear. She squeezed out a smile and for the first few minutes, they did nothing but enthuse over how well Peter had looked after them.

But eventually the conversation dwindled, Elijah wondering if it would be okay to take a short walk around town.

"C'mon," he coaxed them, "you can't hide yourselves away forever..."

Peter, reluctant to let them go, nevertheless appreciated their need for fresh air, as well as some privacy. Elijah guided them outside. Leading them away from the Community Centre, he took them somewhere he knew they would be safe; the public park, scattered with people and a favourite spot for dog walkers. Wandering along the paths, past ornamental benches shaded by horse chestnut trees, they could almost imagine being back in the grounds of Westbourne House... though it wasn't long before their conversation crept down darker avenues.

Elijah stole a glance at Avalon.

"What really happened that night?" he gulped. "Your shirt was all torn. Did Ben do anything to - to hurt you?"

Avalon shivered, gripping the collar of her coat as she walked. "It's okay, Eli. He didn't rape me if that's what you were thinking, though I suspect he would have done..."

"If we hadn't escaped," William interrupted. Elijah felt the sudden stab of his eyes. "So what about you?" he added curtly. "All that stuff about being snatched?"

While grateful for another chance to offload, reliving the story unleashed new elements of fear, given the secrets Eleanor had leaked to Avalon.

"Bloody lucky I found your den, William," he shuddered. "I might be dead by now! Unless they really were planning to put me through some gruesome form of torture!"

"Don't say that!" Avalon gasped.

"But what if he's right?" William hissed. "Do you remember what they looked like, Eli?"

"This is what I wanted to talk to you about," he said, his footsteps slowing.

"The driver was scruffy. He looked a bit like a farmer but the other one wore shades and a scarf to hide his face. He was tall... very brawny and muscly and he was also very strong."

Elijah stopped speaking, seeing the horror creep onto William's face.

"What colour hair?" he pressed.

"Brown," Elijah replied. "Short-cropped, dark hair. Spoke with a growl, London accent."

William froze again, his face rigid.

"William, that sounds a bit like Nathan," Avalon whispered.

Elijah threw another glance over his shoulder. He felt exposed, lingering on the footpath. having this conversation.

"C'mon, let's keep walking," he snapped. "Okay, so this *Nathan* character you mentioned... We're talking about Ben Hampton's body guard, right?"

"From what you've just said, I'm convinced," William shivered.

"That's what farmer Baxter said," Elijah nodded. "Ben used to be quite chummy with him but he remembered some scary guy who used to tag along..."

"He looks like a pervert!" William exploded. "Showy beard, all leather and studs... like one of those weirdos you see in porn mags. Oh shit, Eli!"

"But don't you see what this means?" Avalon said. "If those men are in any way connected to Ben, then Perry is involved! We talked about this, remember? The day you came to the house!"

Elijah spun around to face her. "How could I forget? All that stuff about Mums' past. That he warned her never to *cross him*..." He broke off abruptly.

Everything locked into place. Recalling the scene in James's bar, he could picture that sinister white-haired man again with his cruel slits for eyes. He had been at the house, rowing with Charlie, never to dismiss the way he glanced at him. Even Charlie said he had looked *shifty*.

They had reached a wooden bridge arching across a pond. Elijah paused, staring into the dark green depths. A circle of water lilies gleamed on the surface, the reflection of his shocked face staring back at him.

"Are you thinking what I'm thinking?" he whispered.

"Yes," Avalon's voice echoed. "We know someone threatened Eleanor. Even *you* said the men who murdered your father were still around. Two days later, someone tries to grab you, someone who sounds a lot like Nathan. It all fits, Eli."

Elijah glanced around again, wary of shadows creeping over the park. The screen of trees almost concealed them as they lingered on the bridge. But with a biting coldness wafting up from the water, he suddenly felt vulnerable.

"I don't think we should be talking about this here," he said, spinning towards the park again. "Let's go back to Peter's place..."

Almost without thinking, they linked arms, whilst traipsing across the open parkland. Plenty of people meandered nearby, walking and chatting, dogs chasing after balls... As they followed the path in silence though, it was as if a secret fellowship had been forged; something confirmed in William's next words.

"Let's make an oath," he murmured. "Let's find out what really happened to turn Perry against your mum. It sounds as if they were behind your abduction."

Elijah nodded, unnerved by the hatred glowing in his eyes.

"Okay," he whispered. "I agree."

William gripped his hand and turning to Avalon gave a sharp flick of the eyebrow. With a consensual nod, she folded her hand over theirs and the pact was sealed.

William couldn't sleep that night, conscious of Avalon in the opposite bed. Her breathing floated peacefully above the covers but their decision to share a room stemmed from her nightmares. William, being a light sleeper, was easily roused; quick to flit to her bedside to comfort her in the hope they wouldn't disturb Peter. What he didn't know was that Peter too, was something of an insomniac, yet fully aware of their turmoil.

A bedside lamp rested on the floor. With a sigh William reached down and flicked it on, illuminating his surroundings in a globe of soft light.

Sliding from his bed, he tip-toed into the lounge. A square of moonlight filtered through the curtains, enough to expose the shape of the furniture. He sank into the padded depths of the settee where the absence of light felt soothing. But it didn't seem long before a familiar, uneasy feeling crawled over him. Before he knew it, his mind was propelled right back to the night of their escape; the walled gardens, the beam of a torch flickering across the ground, a tremble of hooves in the distance. His heart started to pound, until without warning, the face of Nathan tore through the darkness. And Ben's sadistic smile flickered briefly.

With a sob, William leapt from the sofa and stumbled towards the floor lamp. The sight of Peter's living room replaced the terrifying visions, yet did nothing to vanquish his fear.

But as he stood there, chewing his fingernails, a sound of footsteps came padding down the hallway. Then Peter appeared in his dressing gown, a look of worry crossing his features.

"Oh, William," he muttered in his gentle Irish lilt. "Whatever is wrong?"

"Couldn't sleep," William muttered miserably.

With his arms coiled around his torso, he lowered himself back down onto the sofa.

Hunched in his thin cotton pyjamas, he started trembling. Peter knelt down and switched on the gas fire, before settling into an armchair.

"William, would you like to talk?" he urged. "I'm guessing you've been through hell... and I'm not just talking about losing your dad or your home. There's something else isn't there?"

William's face crumpled. "Can you promise you won't tell anyone?" he mumbled, unable to meet his eye.

"Of course," Peter nodded.

"I was - I-I was raped," William spluttered.

"Dear Lord!" Peter gasped.

As William cringed in his seat, fighting tears, a sense of desolation arose all around them. Peter froze, wrestling against the urge to sweep him into his arms and cuddle him.

"William, you have no reason to feel ashamed," he said. "I know what you're going through."

"How?" William shot back at him, yet still he stared rigidly at the floor.

"Because the same thing happened to me," Peter confided. "Perhaps it's time I told you a little about me own life... but I'd not long turned sixteen. I was brought up in an orphanage run by the Catholic church. Both me parents died in an accident..."

He knew he had William's attention as he slowly lifted his eyes.

"That place was like a monastery," he whispered. "One massive, sprawling set of buildings built around a Chapel. But the senior priest took an interest in me. I was a bit of a loner, you see. They always single out the quiet boys, since they're the least likely to tell. This man pretended to be my friend. He was kind, invited me to his office to help with my school work... On one of those evenings though, it was very dark and raining heavily. There was hardly anyone around when he ushered me inside. But once he got me up those stairs, he didn't lead me into his office... he pushed me into his bed chamber..."

As William stared at him avidly, his eyes widened in horror.

"What that man did to me I'll never forget! He abused me vilely and not just the once. It happened time and time again. He warned me never to tell! That I was a worthless piece of scum who no one would believe anyway..."

Breathing deeply, he gripped the arms of his chair with both hands. *The memory flared in his mind; the rain scattering itself against the mullioned window panes, the ornate wooden bed frame draped in luxurious silks and tapestries. An overhead chandelier lit up the room, the gilt framed mirror, a painting of the Holy Virgin Mary and Baby Jesus reflected in the glass. But the priest known as Father O'Brien, showed him no mercy; a powerful man who had threatened to do far worse if Peter breathed a word of his atrocities.*

"So what did you do?" William gasped, ashen-faced.

"Ran away," Peter said, "ended up on the streets of London, homeless. But a wonderful man saved me. Bernard James... it's thanks to him, I survived and that, William, is my story, the reason I sense your pain - but also my secret. So please keep it to yourself."

"Of course," William gasped, "and I'm sorry."

The silence swelled as the story sank in. But with little left to hide now, William gradually related his own experience.

"I was too scared to report him too," he shivered. "I can't tell you what he threatened b-but there is just one thing I have to ask. Does it change you in any way?"

Peter let out a chuckle. "You mean, am I homosexual? No, William! I live alone through choice. My life is my work and I probably haven't met the right girl yet..."

How could he explain to this naive young boy how his own trauma had left him damaged? His attacker had taken away more than his innocence; it had robbed him of any carnal desires. Peter adored women. Yet having fallen in love many times, every *relationship* had proved disastrous.

Swallowing back his pain, he gazed at the boy perched before him. There was no denying William's ordeal had been harrowing. Yet with enough emotional support, he would recover. He attempted to explain that given time, he would have no problem pursuing a happy life.

"You're going to be fine, William," he finished warmly. "It's *fighting the girls off* that'll be your problem. Good looking fellow like you..."

By the time William returned to bed, he seemed a lot more relaxed. The glowing warmth of the fire had put a bloom back into his cheeks, his eyelids heavy.

For Peter though, there was no escape as he reached for the Irish whisky. Counselling William brought a sense of fulfilment but had released his own demons; terrifying memories he hadn't thought about in years and as a consequence, he knew it would take a very long time to get back to sleep on this most turbulent of nights.

Chapter Forty-Three

I

"I'm glad he confided in you," Eleanor whispered. "I knew you'd be able to help him."

"It was no problem," Peter answered.

She observed him fondly. His chunky blue fisherman's knit woolly enhanced the smoothness of his skin. His silver hair, in dire need of cutting, flopped around his face as they walked.

A chilly day, sharp gusts of wind jostled them, banks of pearl-grey clouds racing each other across the sky. And as Eleanor drank in the Community Centre gardens, she noticed the shrubs shooting back to life. Wilting clumps of crocuses had long lost their petals, reminding her she needed to get back out here and plant something; primroses perhaps in jewel bright colours.

As their eyes met, Eleanor clung to Peter's gentle gaze.

"I've missed you," he sighed.

An instant camaraderie bloomed. Then lowering his gaze, Peter strolled a little further.

Eleanor followed numbly. "Peter, I've missed you too," she echoed. "It took just a few days in the caravan to realise how happy we were here. Eli was furious!"

"Then why did you go?" Peter asked.

"This is what I need to talk about," she mumbled, "so I'll get straight to the point. Going back to the open day, did Robin Whaley talk to you at some point? And did he introduce you to anyone? A man named Theakston?"

Peter gave a lop-sided frown. "Tall fellow, wearing sunglasses?" he mused. "Some business in health and fitness?"

"That would be the one," Eleanor nodded. "What was your first impression?"

"Not sure," Peter responded. "He did make me a little nervous. Maybe it was the dark glasses or the way he moved. He seemed restless... as if he was looking for someone."

"That 'someone' would have been me," Eleanor said in a tiny voice. "He's an enemy."

"How come?" Peter shot back, "and why did he come looking for you?"

Touching the green stone around her neck, she felt a sudden connection to Jake's soul. *How could she forget what Theakston had really done?* The thought of it turned her cold.

"He wanted to remind me of something said in the past. He met my son too, didn't he?"

"Yes," Peter recalled, pulling up sharply. "Eli was with me when Robin introduced us. He seemed to show a real interest in that boy. Could barely stop looking at him."

She gripped his arm. "Robin Whaley introduced *my son* to Dominic Theakston?"

"Well, I guess so," Peter frowned, "although not in any way threatening..."

"Right," Eleanor muttered. Hearing such disclosures, she let go of his arm, wondering what it was about Peter that reminded her of Jake. "Look, I'll keep this simple - once upon a time Theakston operated in the criminal world. Swear never to repeat this but he was employed to keep people like me under control..." She broke off, jarred by the shock flashing across his face.

"Eleanor, your secret is safe," he murmured. "Please go on."

"Jake's murder was a cover up. I know Whaley was involved but there was another man. One I met at a press conference in London, who I'm sure was behind it! It's only very recently I bumped into him..." She released a sob, jolted by memories. "Theakston was invited here to frighten me. This is exactly how it happened before!"

"But why?" Peter kept pressing. "Why do these people see you as a threat?"

"They're scared how much I know," she shivered. "They're even more worried about a file I compiled in 1972 but the story gets worse. Once back in my caravan, we didn't have the protection of your community any more..." and with no delay, she related Elijah's close encounter.

"Oh, dear God," Peter muttered under his breath.

"I have a suspicion the same people were responsible," she said. "That business at the open day... a deliberate ploy to isolate us. Make it easier for my enemies to snatch him!"

"So who is this man?" Peter pressed her.

Eleanor stared deep into his eyes. "Peregrine Hampton. He is rich, powerful and dangerous. You may as well know it's the same man who plotted against the Barton-Wells family and he sent his son to drive those poor kids from their home."

"Jesus," Peter mumbled uncomfortably. "Why are you telling me this?"

"It seems only fair," Eleanor said. "You need to know who our enemies are. I've kept too many secrets and it's left people vulnerable. Take Eli for example... What if he had been captured? Would any of us have known where to start looking?"

"Are you saying these people are still a threat then?" Peter kept fishing.

"Yes," Eleanor finished, "and Robin Whaley is an ally, a reason never to trust him."

Lost in his thoughts, Peter led her further and further towards the back of the garden, until they eventually reached the end. He threw her a furtive glance.

"Thanks for the warning," he said. "Now there is a small matter I'd like to confide in you. Come, take a look over here! There's something I want to show you."

Steering her up to the perimeter fence, he pulled back the leafy bushes. At first, she saw little more than a vast wasteland, before the old textile factory took shape. It was reduced to a framework of rusty girders that barely supported its corrugated metal shell. Shards of glass grinned from empty window frames, a skeleton left to rot.

"Charming isn't it?" Peter murmured, his voice heavy with sarcasm. "Like everything at this end of town."

"So what am I supposed to be looking at?" Eleanor queried.

"This land is up for sale," Peter disclosed. "Your mention of Mr Whaley reminded me. He told me the textile factory closed down more than nine years ago - but since the owner has finally agreed to sell up, the Council might be interested."

"What would they want it for?" Eleanor asked.

"This is what Robin was asking me," Peter smiled. "He wants me to come up with an idea. Well, don't laugh, but I have another vision... there's a severe lack of affordable housing here, thanks to Londoners driving up prices."

"Tell me about it!" Eleanor responded heartily.

"Furthermore, there's this government initiative that encourages tenants to purchase their council houses. But what will those people do if they move? They'll sell. I know I would! Make a nice little profit, which means a lot of council accommodation will drift into the private sector."

"You're worried there won't be enough social housing," she muttered. "So what's your idea? And I promise I won't laugh."

"I was thinking about a housing trust," Peter said in earnest, "for people on low incomes. Honest, working people who've been priced out of the property market."

Eleanor gazed at him in awe. "Peter, that's a wonderful idea! What inspired you?"

"I've been inspired by you, Eleanor," he confessed. "You brought an element of village life here; a close community where people look out for each other. William and Avalon have been entertaining me too. Telling me about Westbourne House, the gardens, the fruit picking, the traditional Christmas fairs..."

"It was all so quaint," Eleanor's voice wavered, "but those days will soon be over..."

Talk of Perry's plans to destroy such traditions had already started haunting her.

"Come now, don't get emotional," Peter said. "I told the kids I'm convinced they'll get their home back one day. In the meantime, why not concentrate on making our lives here as nice as possible."

"Did Mr Whaley embrace your idea?" she probed.

"He wants me to submit my recommendations. For despite everything else, that man has great ambition for this town. Imagine if he did persuade the council to purchase the land for development? It's not a bad thing, surely?"

She forced a smile, the cogs in her mind still turning. Peter was so trusting yet so naive. Could she bear to remind him of Robin's alliance with Perry again? *A property developer no less.*

II

Later that evening, Charlie sat gazing at her over a beautifully laid table. He had found a most intimate restaurant to have dinner. Tucked in a cobbled courtyard, its walls were painted a cool pastel green, a pair of bay trees in terracotta pots flanking the doorway.

He wanted it to be a surprise; even if it meant bribing the kids to stay at home. As an added incentive, he had invited William and Avalon over and ordered a Chinese takeaway.

Certain all five of them were enjoying themselves, he clasped Eleanor's hands. She looked so lovely, her face bathed in candlelight. It enhanced the golden glow of her eyes. She had just been relating Peter's suggestion about the land behind the Community Centre. Charlie listened in fascination. Peter had divulged that if his plan went ahead, he would ask none other than Charlie to mastermind the design.

"Don't get too excited," Eleanor warned. She took a sip of wine from a crystal cut glass. "I bet Whaley's got some other plan up his sleeve. I did warn Peter not to trust him."

"One can dream," Charlie murmured. He stroked her fingers. "So what about us, Eleanor? Is there any chance we can pick up our own lives?"

"I don't see why not," she answered, entwining her fingers into his own.

The waiter arrived with menus; a mixed cuisine, not dissimilar from Angelo's. Eleanor gave a sigh of pleasure, loving the little round tables with their deep red cloths; the romantic shimmer of candlelight, the vases filled with roses... But as soon as the waiter had taken their orders, they resumed their conversation.

"Wouldn't it be nice to settle down at last," Charlie added wistfully, "without the threat of Perry Hampton lurking? Do you think that might be possible?"

"I'd like to think so," Eleanor said. She bit her lip. "I didn't like the way Elliot said *he was on to me,* though. It suggests there's still danger. But let's not talk about that now."

She closed her eyes, breathing in the fragrance of the roses. The next time she opened them, Charlie was still gazing at her.

"This is a treat," she added, "I don't think anyone has ever wined and dined me in such a lovely restaurant. What's all this in aid of?"

"To celebrate being back together," Charlie whispered and feeling inside his jacket pocket, he extracted a tiny box, pushing it across the table. "Open it."

Eleanor could not curb her smile as she prized the lid open. Nor could she prevent the gasp that leapt from her lips at the sight of a ring winking up at her. Set in a band of yellow gold, a cluster of diamonds nestled at its heart in the shape of a flower. She stared at it as if hypnotised, every facet glinting rainbows of light.

"I'm asking you to marry me, Eleanor," Charlie added, taking her hand again.

"Oh, Charlie," she gulped hoarsely. "Are you sure we're not being too hasty?"

"It's been more than two years since I lost Anna," he sighed. "I will always love her but I can't hold a torch forever. What do you say?"

"Well *yes*, of course!" Eleanor laughed, plucking the ring from its box. She slowly turned it to savour its design. "This is so pretty!"

Rolling it towards her engagement finger, surprised Charlie hadn't thought to slip it on for her, she saw the reason why - her eyes drawn to the handcrafted ring Jake had bought from a street market in Forest Haven all those years ago. She had never taken it off. Tears burned her eyes even now, the pain of losing him striking a chord. Yet as Charlie said, they couldn't hold back forever. Life had to move on. Gently removing the ring, she slid Charlie's into its place. For now, she tucked Jake's ring into her purse, a keepsake she would forever cherish, alongside his stone pendant.

Leaning forward, she planted a kiss on Charlie's smiling mouth. "Thank you," she murmured, "I love you... I think we were destined to be together. So when shall we have our wedding?"

"How about summer?" Charlie replied. "Get the kids' birthdays out of the way and maybe we can organise something for June."

"June sounds perfect," Eleanor mused. "Maybe Midsummer's day. I'm so excited, Charlie, this is the best surprise ever."

Charlie chuckled. "Do you know one of the last things your old adversary, Dominic Theakston, said? *Just go and marry the girl...* I took his advice!"

"What?" Eleanor gasped.

The smile dropped from his face. "He seemed to have some idea where your father was, too. I'm sorry. I should have told you sooner, but I was so excited about bringing you home..."

"What did he say?" she mumbled, reaching for her wine.

"Tuscany," he revealed. "Said he was the *house guest* of some Italian guy. Gio, Gennaro... I can't quite remember. But when he said *guest*, I got the impression he meant prisoner. Maybe you need to talk to him, Eleanor."

"I'd sooner discuss it with my solicitor," she shuddered.

His words left her cold, the idea of talking to Theakston even more so.

How could she bring herself to face the man who had callously ended Jake's life? Even if he did hold some vital clue, it would never drive out her hatred for the detestable things he had done.

"Thanks for telling me." She gripped his hand, but this time in fear. "Just don't underestimate Dominic Theakston. Whatever you think, Charlie, he was invited to the open day to put the frighteners on me... and you've got no idea what he is capable of."

Chapter Forty-Four

I

Two days later they found themselves on a train bound for London. Nothing pleased Eleanor more than to travel in one of the newer 'Intercity' models, the crisp upholstered seats a comfortable alternative to the traditional three-seater bone-rattlers.

As the train pulled smoothly out of Rosebrook, Charlie and Eleanor stared at each other. Their hands linked across the table. Pushing aside her euphoria, she was anxious to visit her solicitor, although the purpose of today's journey was to join the Barton-Wells children.

With the contents of James's will about to be executed, a letter had arrived in a soft cream envelope, bearing the stamp of Frank Winterton. Since Elliot was listed as a beneficiary, he had begged Perry's consent to drive the children to London. What Perry didn't know however, was Eleanor too, was a beneficiary, presenting a perfect opportunity to meet up in secret.

On this occasion Eleanor decided she wanted to look her best. Smiling, she caught a glimpse of her reflection in the window as the train surged through a tunnel. Her hair, newly cut, finally free of the dreadlocks, bounced around her shoulders in waves and gleamed like pitch in the hazy spring sunshine. Having thrown on a black jacket, which clung to her slender figure, she wore the exquisite dress Charlie had bought her for Christmas with its flowing skirt and floral print.

She captured Charlie's eye again. Hopeful Peter would have escorted Margaret and Elijah to school by now, she had arranged for them to be collected by Hilary - though it had to be said the Magnus couple seemed more cordial towards her. Word of their engagement had spread through the community like wildfire, mostly from Margaret, who was bubbling over with excitement. Both she and Avalon were going to be bridesmaids and she could not wait to start looking at dresses.

Everyone was ecstatic. That was, everyone except Andrew.

Tortured by the loss of his mother still, he saw Charlie's engagement to Eleanor as the ultimate betrayal. Charlie prayed that given time, he would eventually come around. But right now, he had other things on his mind and looked forward to seeing Elliot.

For several minutes he was lost in his thoughts, oblivious to the train

401

slowing. It pulled into a small rural station. He thought nothing of the smartly dressed man, whose slow creeping footsteps brought him to a seat on the other side of the aisle. Tall, with glossy silver hair, he appeared to be surveying them.

"Chislehurst," Eleanor murmured, glancing at the sign on the platform. "Five more stops until Waterloo. Do you think we'll have time to whizz over to Holborn?"

"Maybe," Charlie said softly, "but I could murder a coffee first..."

Snapping open his briefcase, the man in the adjacent seat plucked out today's Financial Times and a mobile phone the size of a shoe. Charlie smirked. Mobile phones were relatively new on the market but growing in popularity among the business community. As the train picked up speed though, the man disappeared into another section of the train to make a call.

The one thing Charlie didn't realise was that *Edward Booth* had recognised him. He had no idea he had been photographed in the blissful summer months working at Westbourne House. Neither could he have known it was Edward who had shopped him to Perry; an unfortunate consequence of the row that had erupted with the manager of his unscrupulous building firm.

Charged with sudden acrimony, Edward felt duty bound to inform Perry. So he leaked his discovery; that the couple were heading towards London. Then no sooner had the train stopped in Elmstead Wood Station, Edward stepped off, vanishing as quickly as he had materialised.

The train proceeded to sail in a northerly direction, humming past rows of factories and cranes, before the distinctive skyline of towering office blocks rose hazily in the distance. But from the moment it was swallowed into a tunnel, transporting them to Waterloo Station, they were heedless of a Harley Davidson now weaving its way through London.

Hurtling towards the same location, Nathan had received his orders and was about to start tailing them.

II

With time on their hands, it was too early to start making their way to Frank Winterton's office in the Strand, just a stone's throw away from Covent Garden.

Wandering hand in hand, they followed the brightly-lit walkway to the escalator. This in turn plunged them into the hub of the station. Sunlight gleamed through the spectacular glass roof, triggering a sense of nostalgia. The station undulated with the movement of people, a ringing commotion of voices and footsteps echoing all around.

Seconds later, Eleanor recognised the café from her previous visit.

Sliding herself into a table, she breathed in the powerful aroma of coffee. Charlie eventually joined her, carrying two styrofoam cups. Customers wandered in and out, the tables emptying before they were gradually reclaimed by new visitors.

Eleanor took it all in as they relaxed in their seats. She loved people watching, unsure what it was about the man hovering around the station that caused her eyes to stop dead. She had seen him before, that hard chiselled face. Most memorable of all though, was his beard, a pencil thin line tracing the edge of his jaw. His eyes seemed to dart from one side of the station to the other.

"What's up?" Charlie muttered.

Eleanor dropped her gaze. "Charlie, don't look round, but there's a man hanging about who I recognise. It takes me right back to the time I saw my solicitor... I nearly bumped into him."

Slanting her body forwards to whisper, she felt the man's eyes hone in on her. She nevertheless tried to describe him: tall, muscular build, black jeans, leather motorcycle jacket... but in the second she began to elucidate the details of his face and beard, Charlie's eyes flared with horror.

"Sound familiar?" she murmured.

"I know damn well who he is," he hissed. "It's Nathan. Ben's bodyguard."

"Oh God," she spluttered. Her grip on his hands tightened, her eyes glued to the table top. "He must be following us. What if he was tailing me before? It was around the time when someone tried to steal my file. Oh shit, Charlie."

Every second ticked slowly as Eleanor released Charlie's hand to sip her coffee. The man's shape loomed on the shore of her vision before discreetly moving away.

The next time she raised her eyes, he was gone.

"I can't see him any more," she said quietly.

"Okay, so let's keep calm," Charlie whispered. "If he really is onto us, he's probably hanging around somewhere, just waiting to see where we go."

"So what now?" Eleanor said. "If we head for the Strand, he'll know we're meeting the others and that could be dangerous for Elliot, unless..."

Her mind wandered. *Perhaps a diversion to see her own solicitor wasn't such a bad idea.*

"Charlie, why don't we split up? You go on by taxi to Frank Winterton's office and let the others know the score. I'll scoot towards Holborn on the underground. He can't follow us both."

"Eleanor, no!" Charlie gasped. "I can't let you go off on your own, not with that thug hanging around. What if he decides to follow *you*?"

"That's just it," she smiled. "He is bound to follow me. I'll be a decoy. Have him running all over London and if I can lose him, I'll hop into a taxi and join you at the Strand."

Charlie shook his head, his features clenched tight with worry.

"I'm not likely to come to any harm," she reassured him. "Perry won't put his neck on the line all the while my file exists. They're just keeping tabs on me to see what we're up to."

With much resistance, Charlie finally agreed, though he was far from happy.

Her eyes clung to the back of his head as he marched towards the exit. By the time he reached the steps leading him out of the station and into the daylight, the crowd had folded around him, swallowing him from view.

Eleanor shivered. The scene felt horribly familiar, throwing her right back to the time she had been here with Jake. Acrid fear sharpened her senses; the notion that once again, a dangerous enemy was stalking her. Only this time, someone directly connected to Perry.

She wasted no time. Weaving her way through the knots of people, she headed for an escalator bound for the London underground. She needed to get herself onto the Northern Line and following the signs, eyes fixed rigidly ahead, she wondered if her pursuer was far behind.

Arriving at a second escalator, its steep descent plummeted her deeper into the bowels of the subway, the air turning ever more humid. As she stepped towards the platform, she could hear a train approaching. It delivered a rush of wind before it was spewed out of the tunnel. Without a moment to lose, Eleanor stepped aboard, the train destined for Embankment.

Scrutinising the overhead map, she came to a decision. As the train slowed, she surged towards the door and contrary to expectation, hopped back out onto the platform. Drifting along in search of an exit, she momentarily bobbed down as if to tie her shoelace. But at the same time, she flicked a backward glance and sure enough, he was there. He reared up further back, a head and shoulders above the swarming crowd, his brawny frame as distinctive as his sinister black clothing. Eleanor's heart took on a slow and powerful thump. Her theory had proved correct.

The crowds seemed to swell as people from all walks of life and different nationalities were thrown together en masse. Eleanor found herself swept up in the tide as it snaked through a gleaming blue tunnel. Ascending two flights of stairs, she came to a corridor where a choice of different passageways confronted her. If she was heading for Holborn, she would stay on the Northern Line, although she was no longer contemplating that option now.

There was no doubt Nathan had been watching her on her last visit; too much of a coincidence that he just happened to be in London. Her solicitor's office had been broken into. If someone had attempted to steal her secret file, that someone was probably still after it.

Eleanor quickened her pace. Revisiting Holborn felt too dangerous, especially with Perry keeping tabs on her. Such thoughts prompted her to follow the Circle Line, towards the West End.

Wary of the longer train ride ahead of her, she rifled through her handbag, extracting a compact to check her makeup, then subtly tilted the mirror. It took one flick of an eye to see Nathan standing a little further away. The glass captured his face, undeniably hostile as he glared across at her. Eleanor snapped the compact shut, extinguishing the image. For several more minutes, she sat still, noting each station. South Kensington. Gloucester Road. Kensington High Street... Eleanor made a sudden dash for the door and leapt out onto the platform.

Yet again she sensed his presence, a hunter in pursuit of his quarry. Eleanor sped up the metal staircase, crossing a bridge to reach the opposite side. Another train lingered temptingly on the eastbound platform; one destined to ferry her back in the direction she had just travelled from.

Driven by a force of sheer bravery, she flung herself aboard the train.

Nathan too, managed to squeeze himself through the doors, using a gloved hand to force them apart, just as they were about to slide shut.

Head down, he was rammed inside the aisle amidst a bunch of passengers. As the train began to move again, Eleanor's heart raced faster. With his face reflected in the grimy window pane, she saw the fury ground into his expression. Seconds later, they had returned to Gloucester Road. Eleanor knew she had almost reached a turning point. If she could throw him off now, there was a good chance she would make it to the Piccadilly Line, which connected to Covent Garden.

Her throat felt dry as she rose, the dark shape turning as predicted. Eleanor hung back from the door, waiting until the train paused. Only this time, she spun on her heel to face him.

Nathan froze. Their eyes clashed.

"Excuse me, sweetie, but are you getting off or what?" an effeminate male voice squeaked from behind.

Eleanor's eyes were drawn to a young punk rocker, a shock of spiky pink hair, black shades and various studs in his face and clothes. Nathan whirled around.

"Ooh, where have you been all my life!" the youth joked.

"Fuck off!" Nathan snarled.

Eleanor watched in sympathy as the young man retreated back towards the carriage. But the train had started to fill up again, Nathan trapped by her side as a tangle of new passengers closed in. She detected a look of insanity in him now.

"Nathan, is it?" she whispered in hatred.

She heard a sharp hiss of breath. "What's it to you?"

"I know you're following me."

The train lurched, propelling her forwards. She clung to the rail but it was impossible to avoid the midnight glint of his eyes. Eleanor gulped in the stale air.

"I know exactly who you are," she shuddered. "You tried to snatch my son... you dare follow me out of this station, I will call the cops."

"Dunno what you're on about, pet," Nathan said. He smiled evilly.

"Yes, you do," Eleanor persisted, "and I know what you did to William. You sick bastard. He's only fifteen. I wonder how all these people would react if I told them the man standing next to me was a paedophile?"

The look Nathan fired was murderous. A blade of fear ran through her as she stood her ground, waiting for the train to reach the next station.

"I mean it," she finished, before inching up to the door. "Now back off!"

Hopping from the train, she almost tripped as her feet struck the platform. But this time Nathan remained in situ, his eyes searing into her. People shuffled around him to disembark. The seconds dragged painfully, but as the train gradually set off, still he had not moved.

III

On the other side of the station, Eleanor flagged down a taxi, desperate to reach the Strand now, before Nathan had a chance of catching her up again. By the time she had fought her way through the revolving doors into Frank's office, her hands were shaking.

Next, she found herself shepherded into an elegant boardroom to join the others.

Charlie scooped her into his arms. "Eleanor, thank God!" he spluttered.

"I had to confront him!" she panted, clinging to him. "Nathan didn't dare follow me when I told him what I knew... I bet he's gone crawling back to Perry now, to warn him."

"Wasn't that a bit risky?" William reacted.

Eleanor turned, saddened to see him staring at her, so ashen-faced. He didn't want to be reminded of the man who had vilely abused him.

"What if he turns up here? Perry might have cottoned on that you're meeting us."

"William could well be right," Eleanor shivered, staring at Charlie in panic.

"Hush, now," Frank intervened. "Personally, I think it's unlikely, but to put your minds at rest, there is a way we can smuggle you out without being seen. James's car is in an underground car park, only accessible via a staircase in reception. Now please... sit down. I have some news which may cheer you up."

Eleanor was steered into a high-backed chair next to Charlie. Frank offered her a kindly smile over the tops of his half moon spectacles and with nearly all the beneficiaries gathered, he revealed the contents of James's will.

It came as no surprise he had left almost everything to his children. Yet from the proceeds of Westbourne House, he had requested a sum of £2,000 each to be paid to his faithful employees, Bryony and Angelo, in respect of their services. He must have guessed they would lose their jobs. But to everyone's delight, he had bequeathed his beautiful classic Jaguar to Elliot.

"Such a generous gift," Elliot muttered, stifling a sob. "I feel so honoured."

A smile spread across William's face, a sight that had been pitifully absent of late.

"Great news, Elliot," he said, having never forgotten their driving lessons around his father's estate.

Even more breathtaking was a legacy of £10,000 James had left to Eleanor; a disclosure that tore her emotions, especially when Frank read out the words James had dictated.

'Eleanor was one of the most loyal friends a man could wish for, quick to offer comfort when I needed it most. Even when our home was on the brink of ruin, it was against all odds that she found me a builder who could restore it...'

They listened with heavy hearts. *To think, they had ultimately saved it.* Eleanor bit her lip as she listened to Frank's oration; warmed by James's gratitude that she had pledged to watch over his children. Gazing at them now, she knew she would forever be their guardian.

"I'm so pleased for you, Eleanor," Avalon smiled. "Dad was right. You and Charlie have helped us so much over these months. I don't know what we'd have done without you."

"Thank you," Eleanor said, dabbing her eyes with a tissue. "When I was your age, I don't know what I'd have done without *him* either..." She tailed off, before her sentiments got the better of her.

James had been as much a father figure as she could hope for.

"We must now address the finer details of your father's estate," Frank declared, flipping back the cover of a large, leather bound ledger. Perusing the sheaf of papers written in spidery black ink, he gave a covert smirk.

"Would you like us to leave?" Charlie said, sensing the delicate matter of this topic.

Avalon shook her head, insisting they stay. There was something bright, almost feverish in her expression as if she knew what was coming.

"With regret, Westbourne House was sold," Frank continued, "along with the outbuildings and the immediate surrounding grounds. To be more specific, this included the gardens and open parkland, which extends to the boundary of the woods. However, it pleases me to inform you that the agreement made with Mr Hampton did not include your father's land..."

Charlie braced himself. "Are you saying the land belongs to William and

407

Avalon now?"

"I most certainly am," Frank agreed, "land which comprises 2,000 acres of forest and farmland, including the field next to the Harper's farmhouse." A light twinkled in his eyes. "James made no mention of this land when he made his final negotiations with the company, 'Falcon Finance' and I know I am speaking out of term here, but if Peregrine Hampton had not been so eager to get his greedy hands on James's property, he might have considered checking the fine print! He assumed the land would be included, but it is not."

Avalon gave a tiny grin. "It's ours," she quivered, turning to gaze at her brother, "which means he can't ruin it!"

Frank frowned. "Ruin it? Whatever do you mean?"

"Hampton's a property developer," Charlie said. "Imagine owning all that land. How long would it be before he started building on it?" He gave a chuckle of delight. "Excellent!"

"We thought you'd be pleased," Elliot added jovially, "and this is what the villagers were afraid of; that a man like Perry would destroy the character of Aldwyck."

"Well, I hope you can reassure them that's not going to happen," Eleanor said. "Though I confess, James did let me in on his little secret. This was his final legacy to secure his family ties with Aldwyck..." She beamed at Avalon. "And do you know, I'd love to see the look on Perry's face when he gets to hear about this."

They left the meeting euphoric. Perry had not quite won. Although the crawling apprehension that followed was unmistakable; the threat of another conflict.

But with so much to discuss, they had no wish to part company just yet. Elliot had booked a restaurant where they could enjoy a discreet lunch.

No one spoke as he led the way. A corridor from reception brought them to the deep underground car park Frank had spoken of. The air felt cool and musty, the darkness comforting, as Eleanor and Charlie scrambled into the back seats of the Jaguar.

"Tuck yourselves right down," Elliot warned. "You're not the only ones being watched. Like William says, you've already been sighted, so it may seem obvious we're colluding."

Like a scene in a thriller, they sat wedged in the footwells between the front and back seats and by the time Elliot surged from the car park, were completely hidden from view. He kept driving, waiting until he had covered sufficient distance from the solicitor's office, before turning to them.

"It's okay, you can relax now," he reassured them. "We haven't been followed."

Regrettably, time was short. Hurrying them into a small but charming Italian restaurant, they devoured a speedily prepared pasta dish, pan fried with seafood and basil.

"Okay, so what exactly is Perry planning for Westbourne House?" Eleanor pressed. "You mentioned something in the pub last week."

"I can hardly bear to tell you," Elliot said, "but he plans to build a conference centre in the style of a barn, fully equipped with audio visual facilities for companies to hold meetings."

"Why can't they do that in the main house?" Eleanor protested.

"He wants the house to be purely residential," Elliot replied, "and doesn't think the electrical supply will cope. The ballroom will be used for entertainment but I digress... He's proposing to put this new development on the site of the walled gardens."

"He can't do that!" Avalon gasped. "Dad knew he was planning something like this..."

Her voice, rising steadily in volume though, caused several heads to swivel.

"Shh, Avalon, calm down," Charlie muttered. "Elliot, is he planning to demolish the outer walls? If so, I doubt if he'll get permission. Those walls have stood for hundreds of years and they'll carry a listing. Maybe I could check this out with English Heritage."

"Really?" Elliot whispered, his eyebrows drawn in a frown. "Well, if he can't demolish the outer walls, is it not possible he might still build inside that area?"

"No," Charlie insisted. "It's a historic house. Victorian walled gardens are an important feature. It would be sacrilegious to alter their purpose. Even those glass houses might be listed."

"He'll just do it anyway," William snorted. "Since when did Perry Hampton let anything get in the way of his plans?"

"Planning law is very stringent, William," Charlie argued, "so he has got to apply to the council. If he carries out that work without consent, he could be prosecuted."

Avalon looked at him with hope. "Seriously?"

"Yes," Charlie smiled at her, "and to put your minds at rest, there will be a public consultation period. As soon as Perry submits his plans, anyone can object."

"I'm certain the whole village will object," Elliot muttered, flicking a glance at his watch. "Herbert Baxter will see to that."

"I want to be involved too," Avalon added. "This was our ancestral home."

"Avalon is right," Eleanor agreed, "we must all do our bit to protect Westbourne House, for James's sake," and feeling the force of Avalon's outrage, she raised her glass.

The meal ended swiftly. Wary of the time, Elliot began to chivvy along the children, insisting he would take them back to Rosebrook before facing Perry. If only they could spend more time together. But Elliot reassured them he would be taking several more trips to London. With a burning incentive to settle his late mother's estate, he left with the promise he would get a message to them.

Before they departed though, he gazed at Charlie and Eleanor with a tenderness that put the shine back into his eyes. "Enjoy the rest of your day in London," he finished warmly. "Oh, and congratulations on your engagement."

Chapter Forty-Five

I

That brief outburst of optimism was good while it lasted. Everyone seemed determined to rise up against Perry, especially Avalon, whose thirst for retribution radiated from her like sparks.

Eleanor, on the other hand, knew what a powerful enemy they were taking on. In the aftermath of being stalked across the underground, only she understood the real danger on the horizon.

Above all else though, they needed to pull together the threads of their shattered lives.

First was the issue of William's schooling. The education authorities took a dim view of the fact he had missed two terms. William swore that in the painful months after losing his father, he had continued his schoolwork with the help of a private tutor. But whilst the extenuating circumstances leading to his absence were accepted, he needed to undergo a series of tests.

What the authorities didn't realise was that William's public school tuition had given him an advantage. The tests confirmed he possessed a natural aptitude for learning and although his academic record had slipped in some subjects, he excelled in maths and foreign languages and had an excellent command of English.

Suddenly the future appeared rosy when he was invited to attend any school of his choosing. This included Rosebrook's Independent, which had won more awards for outstanding academic achievement than any other in the district.

All things considered however, William hadn't quite recovered from his emotional trauma and craving the security of friendship, astounded them by choosing Rosebrook Comprehensive.

Elijah and Margaret were ecstatic.

Now all he had to do was survive where Elijah turned out to be a good ally; especially when the rowdier kids started mimicking his public school accent. William had also learned the old adage of *keeping a stiff upper lip,* but despite the events which could so easily have damaged his life, he used his confidence, humour and irresistible charm to win them over.

In his elevated status as William's best friend, Elijah too, soared in popularity, both in class and on the cricket team into which William was recruited. Affectionately termed as 'Pikey and Posh Boy,' maybe their schooldays together would be a blessing.

With William's education back on track, the next task was finding a new home. Avalon cherished Peter's company but much as they drew strength from his guardianship, she was beginning to feel restless. On one cosy evening, whilst leafing through her beautiful Laura Ashley book, she became aware of the shell she had withdrawn into. So she contacted a few estate agents.

Rosebrook however, was fast earning the reputation of being a commuter town with house prices constantly spiralling. Pouncing on her naivety, one estate agent tried funnelling her towards the more exclusive dwellings on private estates. These not only threatened to gulp up a large percentage of their inheritance but seemed isolated.

It eventually took the kind heart of an older estate agent to steer her onto the right path; a man who had been acquainted with her father. The house he recommended was perfect and within walking distance of the Community Centre. Snowy-white walls slashed with dark beams gave it a Tudor appearance. An arch of pink and white roses surrounded the door but despite being smaller than any property they had looked at, Avalon could not help falling in love with it. With four generous-sized bedrooms and a sprawling lounge, it felt wonderfully spacious and light. Most endearing of all though, was the idyllic back garden, accessible via a gate.

Enclosed in pastel brick walls, it reminded her of Westbourne House with its sweeping perennial borders and patio. The fish pond below the rockery emanated a musical tinkle of water from its fountain and as she stood under the dappled shade of a weeping willow, the only other sound she heard was a chirping chorus of birds.

By the end of March and to everyone's delight, William and Avalon moved into their new home. With Charlie and Andrew's help, they managed to squeeze in their favourite possessions. A familiar ornamental rug covered the floorboards, their floral chintz suite taking pride of place in front of the hearth. Two Grecian urns flanked each side of the fire surround but the space above was devoted to a portrait of their ancestors. The misty faces of three generations (their father, just a baby) added an element of comfort to the atmosphere and although the sepia-toned picture possessed an eerie quality, it conveyed a feeling of someone watching over them.

III
April 1987

There came a day however, when Avalon backed away from the hearth, her vision blurring with tears. Whilst it felt reassuring to be settled, given the torment they had lived through, only now did the impact of it hit home.

William had been so brave. Peter's counselling had combatted his innermost fears, enabling his troubled mind to heal. Yet somehow, she had always known he would bounce back.

She, on the other hand, felt vulnerable. Wounded, angry, overwrought with the finality of her father's absence, she sensed a massive hole had been torn in her heart. They could never replace him. She could just about cope with the loss of their home. But like Eleanor, she was beginning to detect the prevailing danger. *Would she ever truly be safe from the Hamptons? Of Ben, whose act of violation had been the ultimate blow?* Avalon shuddered, powerless to drive out the insurmountable anguish that consumed her.

Dropping herself onto the sofa, she was relieved William was at school.

Yet she had to drag herself out of this rut. Find a job. Furthermore, she needed new friends. Westbourne House may have been idyllic but what a sheltered life she had led alongside her father, devoting themselves to its upkeep.

As if to add to her woes though, there had been news from Elliot. Perry was definitely pushing ahead with his planning application. An alarming orange notice had been spotted on the gates of Westbourne House and it took this final niggling thought to galvanise her into action.

Avalon rose to her feet and within minutes, found herself marching up Rosebrook High Street in search of the council headquarters.

Thrusting aside her anguish, she focussed on the high street, which she was finally beginning to see through new eyes. The pretty shops and restaurants loomed up one after the other, the characteristic brick paving adding colour to the pavements. She noticed trees planted between Victorian cast iron lamp posts; flowers blooming in every corner, from planters and hanging baskets, to a mass of shrubs cloaking one of the pubs.

Feeling her tension lift, the balls of her fists unfolded as her heart gradually began to steady itself. An elegant suit caught her eye in the window of 'Miss Selfridges,' bringing a smile to her lips. But if she was about to start job hunting, she would need some new clothes. Then eventually, the war memorial soared into view as did the honey coloured walls of Rosebrook Council.

Avalon bit her lip, unsure how to proceed. According to Charlie though, anyone could view the details of a planning application.

Guided upstairs to the right department, she asked a secretary to retrieve the file. But she did not have to wait long before a shadow emerged in the doorway.

"Well, hello," a voice echoed. "Miss Avalon Barton-Wells, isn't it?"

Avalon looked up, startled to meet the pale blue eyes of a man who looked familiar. Placing him in his forties, she sensed an air of sophistication about him from the cut of his dark suit.

"Do I-I know you?" she faltered.

"Not directly," he replied, "but I saw you on the day Miss Chapman brought you to the Community Centre. I don't suppose you remember me... How are things?"

"Um - better, thanks," Avalon mumbled, feeling her cheeks turn warm.

She had been too distraught to take much in, but only now did she recall the fleeting impression of a stranger in the background.

"I'm glad to hear it," the man smiled, lowering himself into a chair next to her. "My name is Robin Whaley and I'm one of the senior planning officers. I gather you're interested in some plans that have been submitted. I've brought you the file. But first, tell me a little about yourself. How are you faring in Rosebrook? And how is your brother?"

"William is okay," Avalon said. "He's just started school again and is coping very well. Though I suppose it's quite different from public school."

"I see," Robin murmured. "May I ask which school?"

"Oh, just the Comprehensive."

Robin frowned. "Surely a boy so well-educated could select any school, such as our very fine Independent."

"True," Avalon sighed, "but William will achieve good grades wherever he goes. Right now he needs friends to look out for him. Boys like Eli... that's Eleanor's son."

"Of course," Robin nodded, retaining a look of heart-felt tenderness. "I understand life has been hard for you. Are you still lodging with Peter?"

"Not any more," Avalon muttered, unnerved by his constant questioning. "We've bought a house of our own now... Anyway, about these plans. May I see them?"

"Here." Robin pressed his smile, placing a loose-leaf file right in front of her.

As Avalon glanced at it, she felt an initial stab of unease, before gingerly peeling back the cover. Yet it took one glance at the wording 'application to change the use of a fruit and vegetable garden...' to make her flinch. With a gulp, she closed her eyes.

"He's really serious about this then?"

"He wants to build a conference and training centre," Robin added.

Avalon shuddered. Staring at the application, she couldn't resist venting about the morality of it. *To think, her father had invested years to turn those gardens into something beautiful; walled gardens that had stood for centuries, one of the principal attractions that drew in tourists...*

"I'm not sure the applicant is even considering keeping Westbourne House open as a tourist attraction," Robin sighed, "though I am aware there is some strong public feeling..."

"Damn right there is," Avalon hissed. "Sorry. I'm very sensitive about this."

"I understand," Robin nodded. "Hard though it seems, though, traditions do change. If it's any consolation, the application will be treated with the utmost care and consideration."

"So who makes the decision?" Avalon said sharply, her eyes scanning the sheet.

"Usually a team of planning officers," Robin answered, "but if there is considerable opposition, the matter will be referred to a committee of elected councillors."

"And what if they pass it?" she pressed.

"You can appeal," Robin placated her. "If all else fails, the Secretary of State gets involved."

Avalon sat very still as she digested the facts.

"Mr Whaley," she said, "may I have a photocopy of this application and what can I do to stop it being passed? I'm sorry, but I have to fight this."

"Don't apologise," he murmured, "and call me *Robin*."

She felt the light brush of his fingers against her hand.

"First, I suggest you submit a letter of objection, clearly stating your reasons."

"Thank you," she said dazedly. "I'll do that."

"You might want to leave your address," he massaged into the conversation. "If there's any news, then you, as an interested party, will be notified."

He passed her a pen and wandering towards the door, mumbled a few words to the secretary to make a photocopy. But the next time she looked at him, she was close to tears.

"Mr - I mean, R-Robin," she said huskily, "is there a chance you'll support us on this?"

"There is," he nodded. "You understand I have to appear impartial, but you and your brother have nothing to fear. Consider me an ally."

As Robin watched her go, his smile lingered. What the Barton-Wells girl could never have known was he had made exactly the same pledge to Perry, but would do everything in his power to ensure permission was granted. It was simply a matter of dripping the right words into the right ears. Whilst Westbourne House was a historic building and everything should be done to preserve its character, did the traditions of a by-gone age really matter? He could not help but agree with Perry. A Victorian walled garden had no place in this modern age. The Hamptons had no desire to grow their own vegetables. Nor did they want a load of strangers turning up to tend to their own plots. It was practically medieval.

All Perry wanted was to develop the potential of Westbourne House for the corporate market and Robin saw no problem with that, especially if it attracted a more elite society into Rosebrook. He could not help but feel a little sorry for Avalon, though. He had so desperately wanted to appease her yet sensed her lack of reasoning; her obsession to cling to the past.

Waiting a few minutes until enough time had elapsed, he gazed at his notepad and at Avalon's address, scrawled in her beautiful handwriting. Returning to his office, he closed the door but with no wish to be interrupted, immediately dialled Perry's number.

Charlie's first reaction was to laugh. "This has got to be a joke! What sort of idiots does he take us for? He's planning to demolish these historic walls to make way for some hideous barn in brick and flint? It's incongruous with the style of architecture..." In his mind's eye, he could still picture the lovely building; the rosy hue of its legendary stone walls. "Thanks for getting a copy, Avalon. Who did you speak to by the way?"

"A senior planning officer," she said numbly. "His name was Robin Whaley."

Charlie and Peter exchanged glances.

"*Senior* planning officer?" Peter whispered. "He's been promoted then."

"Hmm," Charlie muttered, knowing the situation didn't auger well. "So, we've got six weeks to get as many people to write a letter of objection. Peter, is there anyone here who will vouch for us? I worked hard to save that beautiful house from ruin and I'll be damned if I'm going to let that bastard turn it into some sort of business park! He should have stayed in London!"

"I'll try," Peter faltered, glancing at the paperwork, "but it's just one building, Charlie. Do you honestly think anyone in Rosebrook will be that bothered?"

"Peter, a man like Perry Hampton will never stop at one," Charlie sighed. "If the council let this pass, he'll develop the whole estate. Avalon and I know this man and he is hateful!"

"Perry Hampton?" Peter echoed.

Judging by his frozen face, he knew exactly who the man was.

"Okay, I'll do whatever I can to rally up some protest. I've never been to Westbourne House but there are plenty o' folk here who have."

Avalon almost stumbled against him with relief. "Oh, thank you," she breathed, "and another thing... William and I feel indebted to you for taking us in. We never did pay you any rent."

Peter began to flap his hand in dismissal but Avalon halted him. "No, hear me out! You said you needed to raise £5,000 for the renovation of the Community Centre. How far have you got?"

The open day in February had generated around £3,500, but nothing could have shaken them more than Avalon's heroic gesture to stump up the difference.

"I can't accept that!" Peter gasped. "Avalon, I am sure your father would not have wanted you to squander your inheritance on tarting up our Community Centre."

"I'm not talking about my inheritance," Avalon argued. She flashed Charlie a secretive smile. "Perry gave us a cheque for £2,000 in exchange for some of our furniture. It wasn't long after Dad died. But we never wanted to accept his money! So I'd rather donate it to you."

Charlie laughed again. "Nice one, Avalon!"

Chapter Forty-Six

I

Incredible though it seemed, a staggering amount of people wrote letters. They included people like Mrs Emily Cuthbert, swept up in her own memories of summer outings with friends and the wonderful cream teas in the gardens. As a consequence, she started a campaign.

Even the Magnus's couldn't resist being involved and rallied up the support of their church.

Eleanor, whose heart still ached from her early mornings immersed in the beauty of James's walled gardens, put together a touching letter of her own; fearful a hallmark of England's past would be lost forever. Charlie's letter was more scathing, so much so, he even managed to persuade Andrew to scrawl a few lines of protest.

The Aldwyck locals were up in arms. Boris, much to Perry's fury, launched his own petition inside the Olde House at Home, considered to be the nucleus of the village.

But objection spread far and wide. Avalon, in honour of her father, felt obliged to contact his old friends: Dr Albany Price, retired journalist, Geoffrey Ascombe and ultimately Cyril Fortescue. In a fit of outrage, Cyril pounced on the National Heritage Society, of which he and James had been members. Thus, within a very short time, an invisible pressure group started swelling across the borders of London and Kent, and at first Perry knew nothing about it.

Avalon meanwhile, could no longer neglect the surplus of furniture from Westbourne House, still in storage. They had crammed all their favourite possessions into their new home, but the house offered less space. As Charlie rolled back the metal door of one of their storage units, her eyes fell upon a period chaise longue, which she longed to keep, but knew it was impossible.

"You'll just have to sell it," Charlie muttered in sympathy.

"But some of this stuff has been in our family for generations," she choked.

"In that case, why not contact a reputable antiques dealer?" Charlie suggested.

Avalon couldn't understand why she hadn't thought of it before, recalling the happy day of the auction she had attended with her father.

On that same evening, she draped herself in a deck chair, watching the sunset. A flurry of birds disturbed her before she spotted the golden eyes of a cat boring into her. Gazing back, she was struck by the beauty of its fur, tawny-brown shot through with silver tabby stripes. For some uncanny reason, the cat reminded her of her father. But such thoughts branched right back to the night of their escape; the volley of hooves in the woods, which had in all eventualities lured their attackers away. Was it possible some invisible power of nature had protected them?

Next day, she visited one of the larger antique valuation companies in Rosebrook. As official auctioneers for the borough, they hosted regular antiques fairs and weekly auctions. But as fate would have it, they also happened to have a job vacancy. Unable to resist, Avalon filled in an application form. The manager took an instant shine to her and having clocked her enthusiasm, was happy to take her on with immediate effect.

She returned home practically tingling. Stranger still, the mysterious cat she had locked eyes with sat perched under the rose arch as if to welcome her.

Before the week ended though, three incredible things had occurred. Avalon was in full time employment, the start of a career she was going to love. The stray cat, who William wanted to call 'Jim Beam,' moved in with them; and the next time she spoke to Charlie, he informed her the council had received an enormous stack of objection letters; so many in fact, the planning office had been forced to start a second file to cope with the deluge.

II

They revelled in their triumph, at least for a while but the feeling was short lived. Two weeks later, Avalon's worst nightmare materialised on her doorstep in the form of Perry Hampton.

"I had to come!" his deep voice boomed. "Avalon, we need to talk."

She stumbled against the door to shut it but with his palm rammed against the surface, he gave it a shove, then forced his way into her home. Backing into the hallway, Avalon stared in disbelief as he advanced step by step, and flinging the door closed again, he had trapped her inside.

"What do you think you're doing?" she whimpered.

"Calm down, Avalon," Perry snapped.

He had known he would catch her alone, for Robin Whaley had kept him well informed. *All those visits to the planning office; any opportunity to scrutinise his file, not to mention the objection letters that kept pouring in.* But how easily Robin had charmed her with his friendship. Perry knew about her job with the antiques dealer. He had also discovered they closed on Wednesday afternoons, granting her free time while her brother attended his crummy Comprehensive; and with the added advantage he stayed late for cricket practice.

If he played his cards right, he had at least an hour to work on her.

He fixed her with his cold smile. "Now, why don't we sit down," he insisted, waving an arm towards the lounge. "Come along, don't be scared. I mean you no harm."

With a furious snort, Avalon turned, Perry watching her as he followed. She lingered by the hearth where the ghostly faces of her ancestors stalled him. Gazing at the picture, he felt a finger of cold trail down his spine but lowered himself into an armchair without invitation.

"What do you want?" Avalon shivered.

"To see how you are," Perry said, "and to apologise for my son's behaviour. He was only supposed to evict you..."

"Evict us?" she echoed. "Those monsters broke into our home and *assaulted us*. Have you no idea what went on?"

"Regrettably, I do," Perry sighed, "and if it's any consolation, I dealt with Ben in a manner I saw fit..." He brandished his fist. "Let's just say, he's not looking so handsome right now."

With a look of horror, Avalon slid herself into the sofa. "William should have gone to the police," she mumbled. "As if what they did to him wasn't bad enough... They threatened to rape me too, you know - boasting about cocaine - and h-he had handcuffs. Your son is evil."

Perry exhaled a sigh. "I am aware of my son's flaws but how regrettable you had to find out for yourselves. You should have left when I asked and as for getting the law involved, I sincerely hope you don't. You are no match for people like us, my dear."

Avalon sat upright, her mouth dropping open. He observed her with triumph as a tear rolled down her cheek, sensing her anguish yet revelling in it.

"You have nothing to fear any more, though," he added. "Given Ben's career as a stockbroker, we left him in London. But it's not just him I want to talk to you about..."

"Then why are you here?" Avalon shot back at him. "Haven't you hurt us enough? I don't want you in my house, so please... just say what you have to say and go!"

"A rather nice house it is, too," Perry complimented, allowing his gaze to wander. He patted the arm of his chair. "Though a little suburban, I must say. I thought you would have aspired to something more upmarket..."

A look of shock flashed across her face. "How did you know our address?"

"I have my spies, Avalon," Perry smiled back at her.

"It's none of your business where we live," she raged, brushing the tear from her face. "So what, if we prefer somewhere smaller? Some place closer to a community..."

"Oh yes," Perry sneered. "It's all about *community* with you people, isn't it? Don't think I'm not aware of your little uprising."

"What are you talking about?" she gasped.

Perry surveyed her with amusement, gratified to have captured her attention at last.

"Has this got anything to do with Eleanor?"

"Ah, the lovely Eleanor," Perry drawled, nodding to himself. "I hear she's getting married. Yet I was most interested to read her letter with regards to my planning application. I understand there is a growing force of opposition against me."

"What?" Avalon spluttered. "So is that why you're here? You don't like the fact we're objecting and think you can just bully us?"

"Not at all," Perry smirked, "though I am a little surprised. All this effort to save a vegetable plot! And to think, Rosebrook is so desperately short of conference facilities..."

"It's not just about saving a vegetable plot!" Avalon rounded on him. "This is a historic feature! My father invested half his life designing those gardens and people travelled miles just to see them!"

"Well times change," Perry argued. "This whole county is changing, especially with the London Orbital road now open. You cannot cling onto the past forever..."

"In other words, write off a beautiful piece of our heritage!" Avalon protested. "This is a traditional country estate!"

Perry was impressed. He had never expected such passion. "I am aware of that. Why do you think I set my heart on it? Company directors would pay a fortune to visit such a lovely retreat but it needs facilities!"

"Then maybe you should have thought about that before you forced us out!" Avalon shouted. "And in honour of my father, I am not going to sit back and let you spoil it... So if that's why you came here, you are wasting your time!"

Fleeing from the room, she left him rooted to his chair. Regrettably though, there was so much more he needed to say to her... He breathed deeply, planning his next words. The sound of cups and glasses crashed from the kitchen. Then a cat strutted into the lounge. Pausing in front of him, it arched its back, fur rising in spikes, before gracefully leaping into an armchair.

The seconds passed slowly as it glared at him. Perry felt quite chilled.

"What are you still doing here?" Avalon gasped from the doorway. "Perry, I am not going to back down. Now would you kindly leave!"

"All in good time, Avalon," he said. "I'm willing to make a deal. But how would you feel if I withdrew my application, out of respect for your father?"

He could see he had taken the wind right out of her sails. Avalon staggered to a halt, water splashing over the rim of her glass. She looked disorientated.

"You'd do that?" she asked, lowering herself shakily back down onto the sofa.

"Yes," Perry nodded, "but not without some compromise. If I can't develop my conference suite on the site of these *historic walled gardens*, I'll have to consider an alternative, won't I?"

She said nothing at first; refusing to commit to anything until she had heard him out, and he respected her for that.

"Avalon," he continued. "It has come to my attention that I do not own the land attached to your late father's property."

"I know," she said numbly.

At last, he read the fear in her eyes as the tension stretched tightly between them.

"I suspect your father had the last laugh," he added. "But you and your brother now own the land, am I right?"

"Yes," Avalon faltered. "Our solicitor told us a few weeks ago. Why do you ask?"

Perry leaned forwards. "I'd like you to consider selling the land to me."

Hand trembling, she lowered her glass onto the side table.

"I will offer you a good price," he added silkily.

In the same instant, the cat crept its way silently onto the sofa before sinking into her lap. She ruffled his fur, the cogs in her mind turning... Yet still she didn't speak.

"Well?" he snapped, unable to bear the silence for any longer.

"So that's what you're after, my father's land?" Avalon mused. "Well, you can bugger off."

"But what would you and William want with it?" he frowned.

Avalon gave a shrug. "Protect it perhaps?" And reliving the scene in Frank's office, she recalled Eleanor's words. "This was my father's last legacy and you are not getting your hands on it."

"Oh come now, don't be silly," Perry argued. "That land is of no use to you. It will only tie up your assets... Yet if it was included in your father's estate, I would put it to good use."

"Develop it in other words!"

"Why do you even care?" Perry retorted. "Don't you even want to hear what I am prepared to offer you?"

"We're not interested in your money!" Avalon hissed. "If we were, we'd have spent the two grand you forced on us, but do you want to know where that money really went? I donated it! Put it towards the cost of renovating our Community Centre!"

"Then you are a fool!" Perry shouted, his resolve cracking at last.

Shaking with rage, he rose to his feet. Avalon, clocking the first flush of magenta in his complexion, caught her breath. Dreading the confrontation about to unfurl, she felt the barbs of Jim Beam's claws prickle her knees. He stared up at Perry and hissed. But settling him onto the floor to protect him, Avalon struggled to her feet.

"Your father stitched me up!" Perry snarled in her face. "All along, he led me to believe that land was included in the estate!"

"How dare you," Avalon breathed. "Nothing my father did came close to what you did to him! And as for Westbourne House... The house and land were two separate assets. Even our solicitor said you should have checked that out!"

"Avalon, I urge you to reconsider!"

She closed her eyes; anything to shut out his malevolent stare.

"My decision is made," she said in a voice of steel. "I will never *ever* forgive you for what you did to my father and will not be pressurised..."

"In that case, I will not withdraw my planning application," he spat.

"Sounds like your application is going to be refused anyway," she taunted.

Her bottom lip shook but for a moment she thought he was going to hit her.

"Oh, don't be so sure," Perry said. "I have influence in this town. Connections with certain people, not to mention very deadly people! You might want to consider that in future."

"Don't threaten me, Perry," Avalon shivered, backing away again. "My brother might be too frightened to go to the police, but I'm not! Now, I really think it's time you left."

She saw the purple flush recede, draining the colour from his face. Yet his expression struck a terror in her, reminding her of their oath; there was no denying they were the eyes of a killer.

"Foolish child!" he finished. "And you may as well forget your walled garden, because I will get permission. I will re-apply again and again, until I wear down the opposition, but as for you and your wretched brother... you've made yourselves a very bad enemy!"

Avalon said nothing. Watching him retreat, she waited for the door to slam. The sound boomed through the hallway, leaving an eerie echo; where even the benevolent gaze of her ancestors did nothing to thaw the chill in the air.

III

Perry did not disappear immediately. Hands stuffed into his coat pockets, he marched around the corner of a neighbouring side street, where his gleaming new black Mercedes awaited him, longer and sleeker than its predecessor.

He ran his hand over the door panel before climbing into the passenger seat.

Nathan glanced up from his newspaper and as he did so, Perry caught sight of his furious face reflected in his mirror shades. To begin with, he was speechless.

"Little bitch," he then growled. "No wait!" he added as Nathan reached down to turn the ignition key. "Not yet! Let's see if she leaves the house..."

His suspicions were not unfounded.

Five minutes later, Avalon shot down the opposite side of the street towards town, her face lowered, bronze ringlets swinging.

As their eyes followed her, Nathan smiled, running a hand over his clean shaven chin. Perry had ordered him to get rid of that distinctive beard, since the London Underground incident, convinced it made him stand out.

"Bastard!" Eleanor gasped.

Collapsing into her arms, Avalon started sobbing. Within minutes of Perry's exit, she had telephoned, before hurrying over to the almshouse.

But only now did his nasty words sink in. Margaret sat in silent horror as she spluttered out her story. Eleanor clung to her, fearfully reminded of herself at the same age.

"He's got no right to upset you after everything you've been through..."

"He's so cruel," Avalon whimpered, "especially when he doesn't get his own way. You should have seen him, Eleanor, it was horrible!"

"Oh, I can imagine exactly what he was like," Eleanor shuddered. An image of the boardroom table flickered in her mind; Perry's insane fury, his face turning purple...

With a sigh, she stroked a tendril of loose hair from Avalon's forehead - saw the deeply embedded gentleness in her that so reminded her of James.

"Don't let him get to you," she added. "I'll talk to Charlie. But right now, I know exactly what we can do to take your mind off all this... do you fancy going shopping? We'll look at dresses for the wedding, especially for my two bridesmaids."

"Yeah!" Margaret cheered and immediately sprang to her feet.

Avalon revealed the hint of a smile. "I'd love to, but maybe not in Rosebrook. I'm scared, Eleanor... what if Perry's still hanging around?"

"Let's go to Bromley then," Eleanor smiled back. "It's only fifteen minutes on the train."

Wasting no time, they hastily made their way to the station.

Regrettably, so immersed in their chatter they were, not one of them spotted a black Mercedes crawling into the car park as they raced towards the ticket office.

"Follow them!" Perry barked. "But try to keep out of sight. I'm going back to the planning office. You can meet me later at that pub by the war memorial..."

"Who's the other girl?" Nathan asked, eyes zooming in on the back of

Margaret's blonde head.

Perry followed his gaze. Recalling that momentous day on the building site with Charlie, he suddenly remembered the child... Younger then, of course. Yet she had also popped up in James's bar.

"Charles Bailey's daughter," he muttered. "You might want to bear that in mind, Nathan. We'll keep an eye on every single one of them now, especially that Barton-Wells pair."

Without another word, Nathan departed. Sauntering towards the edge of a railway bridge, he saw them loitering on the platform below. As they stepped onto the Bromley train, he was careful to stay hidden. Seconds before departure though, he slipped aboard himself, fortunate to grab a seat several carriages back.

The hour passed quickly. Flitting from shop to shop, they crossed the smart, paved pedestrian area where a huge 'British Home Stores' awaited them.

Oblivious to the transit of time and the predatory eyes pursuing them, they lost themselves in the bridal department. But Margaret could barely restrain herself. Sifting through rail after rail of gorgeous dresses, she found the choice of colours and styles overwhelming.

The dress Eleanor set her heart on was simple yet sophisticated. Cut from ivory lace, it featured an off-the-shoulder shawl neckline with a chiffon rosette at the bust. Breaking away from convention, she favoured its pencil skirt and lace trim; a close fitting style that hugged her waist and hips.

"You look beautiful," Avalon croaked, almost moved to tears again.

Eleanor swept from the changing rooms and gave an elaborate twirl.

"It doesn't quite hide my tattoo," she said, tugging down the enveloping chiffon.

"Why hide it?" Avalon frowned.

The band of red roses intertwined with barbed wire represented love and captivity. Two hearts completed the circle, one ripped apart...

"It's a part of who you are."

Eleanor smiled at that and with her wedding dress chosen, it was time to find something for the bridesmaids. Eventually they were drawn to a range of floating chiffon dresses with spaghetti straps. Margaret was the first to pluck one from the rail, loving its A-line skirt and draping tiers, almost a throwback to the 'Ra-Ra' style of the early 80s. They came in a choice of colours, so they settled on a blushing rose pink. Eleanor knew they had made the right choice; delighted by the way they complimented their girlish figures.

"I love it!" Margaret breezed, as Eleanor paid for them. "Pink and frills... I mean, it's like - it's got my name on it!"

With the sun sinking behind the buildings and the light turning hazy, they wandered towards the park behind the library. Following the curve of the path, where the surrounding trees seemed to swallow them, they settled on a park bench, gazing contentedly over the grounds. With twenty minutes to spare, they nibbled iced buns, a treat from a local bakers'.

For that moment, Avalon could almost have banished the nightmare of Perry's visit. Except she felt a strange, lingering fear.

Every few seconds meanwhile, Nathan's eyes drifted over the rim of his newspaper. Hovering near the back of the library, he had been unwilling to let them out of sight. It wasn't the most thrilling mission Perry had hired him for yet somehow, he must have known Avalon would go snivelling round to Eleanor.

Nathan gave a mirthless smile, puzzled by his obsession with the Chapman woman. He detected an underground vein of secrecy; a murky past that Perry seemed determined to hide, while at the same time, ecstatic to have discovered where she was living.

Chapter Forty-Seven

I

Perry's town house in Pimlico no longer basked in the luxury of silence. Sprawled on one of the big leather sofas with the sound of 'Twisted Sister' blasting from his expensive Bang and Olufsen stereo, Ben cherished his freedom. But the solitary life he led in Pimlico no longer mattered. He had hoards of friends in the city. Swallowed up in a new era of yuppiedom, they spent their days making money at the London Stock Exchange and evenings squandering it on Champagne at £100 a bottle.

For the last few weeks however, Ben hadn't touched a drop of alcohol, fuelled by determination to get his life under control.

The repercussions of their attack on the Barton-Wells pair had been a wake-up call. For not only had his father turned his fists on him but threatened to *disown him* unless he changed his ways. Ben had no choice. Furthermore, he was dating a really gorgeous blonde. Slender as a supermodel with sharp, feline features, Sasha was something of a hedonist and had a penchant for sampling new pleasures - her sexual appetites a little risqué, even by his standards. But as the daughter of a successful stockbroker who also happened to be his trade manager, this was a relationship he really didn't want to screw up. He had even shied away from cocaine recently, wary it brought out his sadistic side...

Yet it was that darker side that possessed him now. Bathed in the light of an overhead chandelier, he caught sight of his reflection; and like Narcissus by the pool, he felt a sudden power, a desire to relive that night at Westbourne House again.

No longer could he deny it was one of the most thrilling episodes in his life. His father might have thought he was sending them there to 'evict them,' yet he had been lusting for an excuse to get to Avalon. Her fear was the biggest turn on, the thrill of making her watch the remorseless abuse of her brother. Yet in all eventualities, their threats had sent them running - if only it hadn't been for the hijack of his motorbike. He had spent hours searching for it in the syrupy darkness, consumed by a dizzying rage. *How could those kids have vanished like that?*

At least the bike had been recovered - caked in oily black mud and slime, its chrome piping dented when they finally dredged it out of that ditch. Deep down, he suspected the Chapman woman's involvement and that in turn, evoked an even wilder surge of hatred.

427

The clang of the doorbell snapped him out of his reverie. Leaping into the hallway, he hauled the door open, startled by the sight of Nathan.

"Jesus!" he spluttered. "What the fuck have you done now? I hardly recognise you!"

"Yeah, well that's the whole idea," Nathan snapped, marching across the threshold. "Since your dad made me shave my beard off... thought I might as well lose the hair and all."

He patted his shaven head, as tanned and glossy as patent leather. Ben stood aside, gaping in awe as he sauntered into the lounge. Collapsing into one of the chairs, Nathan delved into his pocket, fishing out two wraps of cocaine.

"Here! Something to cheer you up!" He tossed one over to him.

Ben caught it before slipping it into his pocket. "Cheers, I'm having a break though. We can smoke this instead..." He plucked a joint from a silver tobacco tin. "I was just thinking about that *Eleanor,* so fill me in on your latest mission."

"What? Tailing them on some girls' shopping trip?" Nathan sneered. "That's not what I wanted to talk to you about. I had a visit from the cops..."

Ben listened in silence. It so transpired that Kent police had approached him about a disturbing incident in Aldwyck; the attempted capture of a thirteen year old. Two people had confirmed his resemblance to an outline description of the assailant.

Nathan's eyes narrowed, his face a mask of pure venom. "That bitch sussed me out... the reason your old man got me to change my looks."

"But what did my father want with that kid anyway?" Ben probed. "Why Eleanor's son?"

"I was hoping you'd tell me," Nathan growled. "I guess the kid must have talked."

"But he's never even met you," Ben argued.

"No," Nathan whispered dangerously, "but his friend, William Barton-Wells, has."

There was a lull of tense silence.

"We know the kids hid in her caravan, which is how your bike ended up in that ditch! But that's not all of it. One thing I *do know* is your dad's after some information she's got on file. He's hiding some secret... and that's why he's bricking it!"

Ben blew out a draught of smoke and handed the joint to Nathan. "How does she look these days? Last time I saw her, she was wild... Pierced nose, dreadlocks."

"Quite a stunner actually," Nathan smirked as if deliberately egging him on. "Dreadlocks are gone. Though I quite liked the idea of taking that one down when she had that hippie look. Remember what your dad used to say? The only reason new age travellers have dreadlocks is to protect their thin skulls from

428

police truncheons!"

Ben released a loud laugh. "Right on!"

He watched with growing pleasure as his partner sucked on the joint and as the drug released its mind altering effects, his thoughts became more lucid. There was so much more he wanted to discuss about *Eleanor*, his animosity flickering like a flame.

"You're right though," he drawled, "she's definitely got some dirt on my dad. Something that involves the notorious Dominic Theakston. Did you know he hired him to put the frighteners on her once? Actually drove her out of London."

Nathan raised his eyebrows. "No one bothered Theakston unless they were desperate..."

"You knew him too, didn't you?" Ben interrupted.

"Ran errands for him," Nathan smiled coldly. "Long time ago, mind. Kids like me were hired as pickpockets. And if I wasn't nicking stuff off folks, I was planting shit on 'em."

"Cool," Ben smiled, perusing him with respect. Nathan had always conveyed a sinister appearance but right now he looked lethal.

"Tell you what," Nathan continued, "there's a lot of opportunity if you know where to look. I'm talking about the criminal underworld. Ever been tempted?"

Ben fell silent, letting it sink in.

"... I wonder what became of Theakston. He hasn't been seen around London for years!"

"He runs a fitness club in Swanley," Ben disclosed.

Nathan froze, joint suspended mid air. "How do you know that?"

Ben let his head roll back, eyes drawn to the smoke swirling around the crystal facets of the chandelier. The effect was hypnotic. Yet he was recalling a day when that wimpish council officer, Robin Whaley, had visited; something shady that connected *all of them,* including Theakston.

"Dad used some friend to track him down," he murmured, "seems he turned his back on crime when the authorities came down heavy, then fucked off to Swanley to set up a new business!" Staring at him intensely now, he was caught in a rush of excitement. "I could join his gym!"

"Why the obsession?" Nathan quizzed.

"I'm curious," Ben said. "It goes right back to what you said about the criminal underworld. According to my father, Theakston ruled by fear. Maybe he could be our mentor... but the only way that's going to happen is if we get to know him better."

Nathan gave a patronising smile. "You don't want to mess with someone like Theakston, not you, Ben! Provoke him and he'd fucking kill you."

"Then why don't we both join?" Ben snapped. "Hire him as our personal fitness instructor..." A note of evilness curled into his tone. "Let's engage him in a bit of chit chat and get the low down on what *really* went on with my father."

Nathan nodded, eyes like chips of flint in the blurry light. Ben almost shivered.

"Okay, you're on," he agreed.

Ben grasped his hand. Putting the past behind him, he anticipated a brand new chapter in his life unfolding and could not wait to jump in.

II

Ben and Nathan were not the only ones speculating. With ominous ripples of threat resonating way beyond London, Charlie couldn't help wondering if they could ever resolve this terrible conflict between Eleanor and Perry Hampton.

News of him forcing his way into Avalon's home appalled him. *Those poor kids, after everything they had been through.* It was enough to inspire him to march into the nearest police station and divulge everything he knew about that man. So he decided to do some digging, based on the preliminary threads gleaned from Eleanor's file.

All Jake had witnessed was a man lurking in a lane; though shortly before a bomb blast, that had claimed the lives of six people, including the politician, Albert Enfield. This left one vital question tearing at the roots of his mind. *Why had Enfield been targeted?*

Lured to Rosebrook Library, Charlie decided to follow Eleanor's example. He relentlessly trawled through the newspaper archives stored on microfiche, looking for Enfield's political manifesto. To his greater delight, he found it.

"Charlie, what is all this?" Eleanor quizzed after the kids had gone to bed.

Sliding along the length of their sofa to snuggle closer, he unrolled a sheaf of papers. "In order to find the motive behind an assassination, it helps to know a bit about the victim."

Eleanor stared at the manifesto in disbelief. With the room swimming in candlelight, the atmosphere felt restful; perfect for dipping into the past.

"You should have been a detective," she smiled. "Where did you come across this?"

"Just read it," Charlie said, pouring them a glass of whisky each.

It took several minutes to absorb the contents. The era had been the 1970s. Labour were in favour of nationalisation, unlike their Conservative successors who in recent years, had done the exact opposite by selling off various sectors of industry and encouraging privatisation. Albert upheld the belief they should expand industrial development and exports; make the management of nationalised industries more responsible to the workers and re-negotiate the terms of the Common Market. What was wrong with that?

Eventually however, they stumbled across one clause that may have caused unrest. Enfield had campaigned for a *fundamental shift in the balance of power and wealth in favour of working people and their families*. His crusade to encourage a more caring society was no secret; nor that he was planning to instigate a wealth tax, but through a system that was sustainable and fair for all levels of income, without necessarily crippling the rich. Campaigning for higher wages, but through political reform, he pledged to overhaul the power of the trade unions and curtail the industrial strike action that had been the blight of the 1970s.

Charlie gave a sigh. "His vision was simple. He wanted to 'mould Britain into a proud nation where people, both as workers and consumers, would have more control over the forces that dominated their economic lives.' I don't see anything about sparking a revolution!" He shook his head. "Remember what James said? The widespread belief that Enfield was a *communist,* hell bent on seizing the assets of the rich? This manifesto proves that was rubbish! And Labour still won the election. They brought back Harold Wilson, whose manifesto wasn't that different. Yet all we saw were more strikes! For all Enfield's dreams, can you imagine he'd have had any more success in pulling this country back together?"

"We'll never know," Eleanor responded softly, "and we've got another election coming up. Neil Kinnock is in the front line. I wonder what changes we can expect if he gets elected."

"He won't," Charlie muttered sadly. "The consensus is that labour policies are old fashioned. They're ridiculed as the 'Loony Left' and people worry they'll put our defence strategy in jeopardy. Kinnock favours nuclear disarmament..."

"I saw something about that too," Eleanor gasped, scanning an accompanying news article. "Here it is. It claims that Enfield was a strong supporter of the 'NPT: The Non-Proliferation Treaty whose objective was to prevent the spread of nuclear weapons' and... 'to further the goal of achieving complete disarmament.'"

She stared at Charlie in alarm.

But Charlie shrugged. "So what?" he said, coiling his arm around her shoulder. "Dozens of politicians want nuclear disarmament. Do you know what I think? Those rumours James heard were part of a smear campaign. There is nothing in this manifesto to suggest England would be turned into a socialist state!" He stabbed a finger at the papers. "Someone wanted to stop him being elected and their campaign clearly failed. Enfield was on course to be Britain's next prime minister. Yet I see no reason why anyone would be so threatened by his policies to want him dead, can you?"

"Maybe their motive had nothing to do with politics..." Eleanor faltered.

"Exactly!" Charlie said, his voice lowering to a hiss. "I can't help wondering if Albert's politics were just a smoke screen; a means of justifying his death and blaming the IRA, when it is far more likely there was a *more personal* reason someone wanted rid of him."

Eleanor drained her whisky. Turning to Charlie, she observed the flicker of candlelight reflected in his intense dark eyes. "So what now?"

"Let's deliver this manifesto to your solicitor," he snapped. "It proves that Enfield wasn't a revolutionary... but begs the question what *was* he killed for? And why did those responsible go to such extraordinary lengths to get rid of an innocent by-stander like Jake?"

III

They managed to fix an appointment the next day but on this occasion, they drove, using Eleanor's mini. Charlie took the wheel. Writhing in the passenger seat, Eleanor was a tangle of nerves.

"I pray to God we're not being followed by that creep, Nathan," she shuddered.

"He can't be in a hundred places at once," Charlie argued.

Given Nathan had followed her on at least two occasions, there was never any question a visit to her solicitor could be risky. Yet there was no turning back. Trapped in the heart of London where the traffic was starting to thicken, Charlie forced himself to concentrate...

He had a lot on his mind. Thankful for an opportunity to take some time off work, they had never been busier. With house prices still on the increase, more and more people were opting to enlarge their properties. Yet adding a conservatory or an extension required planning permission. This in turn brought him into regular contact with Rosebrook Council - and Robin Whaley - but although Whaley treated him with respect, Charlie had long detected his underlying coolness.

Right now, they were crawling along in a thick mire of traffic, until they eventually arrived in Holborn. Here, they discovered a car park just yards from the towering white block where Eleanor's solicitor held his office.

It took little time before their meeting was in full flow. John's face drooped in a sombre manner, his brown eyes brimming with anxiety.

"Going back to your last communication," he said, "you suspected Peregrine Hampton might have been the man behind Jake's murder."

"Yes," Eleanor confirmed, "he was the blonde man who challenged me at the press conference."

"Is there a way we can prove it?" John urged. "Would anyone else remember him?"

"Alison and Joshua Merriman," Eleanor whispered, "and the reporters from NME. One of them took a photo..." A smile flickered over her face as she recalled Perry's outburst.

"Should we take our investigation to NME?" Charlie interjected. "There must be archives."

"It's worth a try," John smiled. Already he seemed to have taken a shine to Charlie in much the same way as he had to Jake.

"Luke will recognise him too," Eleanor added. "He served them wine... Robin Whaley accompanied him and he definitely referred to him as 'Perry.'"

Acquiring proof that Perry had attended the press conference would add substance to Eleanor's file. But a new dilemma had arisen; the issue of whether to trace the woman James had spoken of: Evelyn Webster. Eleanor froze, conscious they were about to uncover evidence that could uphold everything Jake had witnessed... *and possibly died for.*

"What if we do trace her?" she shivered. "Worse, what if Perry found out? This could have terrible consequences, John." The horror of Elijah's ordeal still loomed in her mind.

"We'll be very discreet," John assured her. "I added her name to your file as a precaution, along with James's diary..."

"Sweetheart," Charlie intervened, "according to James, this lady bumped into Hampton, just moments after Jake saw him. She even saw some stranger jump out of his car. It's a vital clue and we'd be fools to ignore it."

Eleanor felt petrified yet knew he was right. Evelyn was the only person who could unlock this entire conspiracy, but at what cost?

"If I agree to this, will you promise to be careful?" she urged him.

"I can recommend a good private detective," John nodded. "Let's just see if we can find her. It will do no harm and if we do... well, we'll cross that bridge when we come to it."

Time seemed to flip back on itself and as Eleanor closed her eyes, she inhaled the cool air infused with a familiar scent of furniture polish. Her fingers subconsciously crept towards Jake's pendant. Struck with memories of him sitting here right next to her, she remembered her oath: *I swear that one day, I will find out the truth...*

"Okay, let's do it," she relented.

She turned to Charlie, whose face appeared wistful.

But Jake was not the only person they had come here to talk about.

"I'm pleased we're in agreement," he said. "Only there's something else. This is about Eleanor's father. We've picked up some news."

"Yes," John replied. "It follows a lead I picked up myself some time ago.

But I didn't want to build up your hopes, Eleanor, not unless we could find him."

Eleanor stared at him dazedly. "Is he dead?"

"No," John retorted. "Not dead. About twelve years ago, he was found. Incarcerated but nevertheless alive, in Italy..."

The atmosphere seemed to darken all around them. It had started in 1972: the turf war, the riot on the docks where a man had been shot. *Giovanni Ponti, Theakston's right hand man.* His threat of revenge had ultimately forced Oliver into hiding. Yet after a brief trip back to London, he had vanished again, only this time destined for Tuscany.

As months drifted by, panic had set in, especially for the woman who was expecting him.

"Felicity Hargreaves," John said. "She promised to protect him as a favour to Sammie. Ollie was making his way to his villa... but he never arrived."

Two agonising years dragged by until Italian police had raided a rambling stone fortress; home to the notorious crime family ruled by Signor Gennaro Ponti. But only then, did they discover a man imprisoned in the basement.

"Hargreaves," Eleanor echoed. "Any relation to Inspector Norman Hargreaves?"

"Felicity was an ex-wife," John continued. "Turns out Hargreaves was a bit of a wife beater. Sammie only found out because he was a friend of her father's. It was *Sammie* who smuggled her out of the country. Installed her in his villa, where he knew she'd be safe."

Tears swum in Eleanor's eyes. "So, this man they found... was it my dad and was he harmed in any way?"

John felt a chill run over him, unsure how much to tell her.

From the report he had obtained, the man was mentally traumatised and suffering from amnesia. *He barely knew who he was any more.* And only by virtue of the fact Felicity had been searching for him, was it even suggested this might be Oliver Chapman.

"Against my better instincts, I spoke to Mr Theakston," John confessed, "but all he confirmed were these rumours... I'm sorry. I didn't want to have to tell you this."

He threw a surreptitious glance towards Charlie.

"Signor Gennaro Ponti fathered many children and Theakston's friend was one of them, but a son nevertheless. For an Italian crime family such as the Pontis, it was a matter of honour Gennaro would seek retribution."

"So where is Oliver now?" Charlie pressed, wary of Eleanor braced tearfully beside him.

"I'm afraid I don't know," John answered gravely. "He may still be in Italy with Felicity. Or he might have moved back to England, but living under a different name perhaps?"

"Why hasn't he come looking for me?" Eleanor whimpered. "It's been fifteen years!"

"Ssh, love," Charlie tried to soothe her. "You heard what John said. If he suffered amnesia, he might not even remember you - and don't forget you had to *disappear* yourself."

He raised his head, staring directly at John now.

"Is there any way you could trace him too?"

"Of course," John placated him. "I've been hoping to discover his whereabouts ever since I picked up this lead."

"Thank you, John," Eleanor sniffed, gulping back her tears, "and I'm sorry. I know I shouldn't be crying. This could be the best news ever."

No sooner had they left, Charlie grabbed hold of her hand and hurried her along the pavement. Unnerved by her earlier fears, he didn't want to run the risk of being seen.

Their next destination was Forest Haven to visit the Merrimans. Charlie had never met them yet Eleanor seemed desperate to see them, especially if Luke was around. Excited to share news of their engagement, she also wanted to invite them to the wedding.

Vacating the car park however, they thought nothing of the elegant Asian woman, poised on a park bench, wearing a dark blue suit.

John Sharp was not the only one to have considered hiring a private detective.

Riddled with paranoia, especially after Eleanor's accusations on the London underground, Perry was taking no chances. Earlier that day, he had received a notification that the couple were heading towards Holborn in Eleanor's mini. Quick to react, he had insisted she kept watch - clocking the time they left, noting with interest they had been in there for well over an hour - and that maybe Perry really did have good grounds to be worried.

Chapter Forty-Eight

I

The battle against Perry's planning application meanwhile, progressed with growing fervour. James's friend, Cyril Fortescue, proved to be a leading protagonist and using his influence to inveigle some of the most powerful players into their crusade, had won the support of a prominent cabinet minister.

At the same time, Charlie pushed ahead with his new building projects but in a recent clash with Robin Whaley, was incensed to hear a client's planning application had been refused. How ludicrous that to remove a section of wall, allowing vehicle access to the property, had been widely supported by residents; yet denied because one parish councillor insisted *it would disrupt the streetscape of the surrounding area.*

Charlie swallowed down his frustration. The family could still appeal. But if anything, the council's stance left him hopeful for Westbourne House, whose historic aesthetic balance was about to be 'disrupted' to a much greater degree. With two files bulging with letters of objection, no way could the council be so hypocritical as to allow Perry's plan to proceed now.

Avalon too, kept in regular contact with Robin, for despite Eleanor's warnings, he had promised to support her. Ultimately, they saw this as a relationship worth propagating, especially if she could glean some information about the land behind the Community Centre.

Robin had already let slip that two more parties were interested; news she passed to Charlie, who in turn leaked it to Peter.

Before the end of April, Margaret celebrated her twelfth birthday, then Elijah turned fourteen. Inspired by memories of their merrymaking at Westbourne House, Avalon and William had set their hearts on throwing a joint party in their home and invited several school friends.

Margaret and Elijah could think of no better celebration. They adored their new house, captivated by the garden and even more so by their resident cat, Jim Beam.

It was Margaret's love of animals that had Charlie buckling under an albatross of pressure, when Holly's cat gave birth to a litter of kittens.

Yet how could he refuse?

These innocent youngsters had been exposed to enough turmoil, so much so, he saw no harm in introducing a little gentleness into their lives.

Thus, by the end of May, two tabby kittens became the latest residents in the almshouse. Even Andrew revealed a softer side, seemingly taking more pleasure in the company of these young creatures than anyone.

But as Eleanor busied herself in organising their wedding, she sensed his inner conflict. Conscious she could never replace his real mum, she tried to placate him by offering to arrange a special birthday party just for him.

Andrew was quite touched, though adamant he would rather go clubbing with friends.

"Thanks, Eleanor!" he grinned. "But I'm cool! Just think, I'm legally allowed to do anything I want now, even vote. I'm gonna vote for the Monster Raving Loony Party!"

II
June 1987

One week before Charlie and Eleanor's wedding, Perry took a stroll around the grounds with Rowena. Following the path which led to the walled gardens, they were drawn towards the Orangerie. The dwindling sunlight spilled over the wall, illuminating the purple flower of a clematis. For a while they remained seated, enjoying a bottle of chilled wine.

Two momentous things had happened. First, the Conservatives had won the general election, granting Margaret Thatcher a third term of government. The news should have delighted him. Except their electoral victory had been overshadowed by a second disclosure: his planning application had been refused. Perry emitted a sigh.

"Oh come on, Perry," Rowena soothed him, "don't be cross. Let's cherish what we've got. For you have to admit this is quite charming..." She waved a heavily jewelled hand towards the walled garden, the intersecting paths enclosing strips of land, now lush with summer fruit.

"But I cannot believe the volume of opposition," Perry argued. "I mean the Secretary of State for God's sake! Nicholas bloody *NIMBY* Ridley!"

Rowena suppressed a smirk. Nicholas Ridley had been accredited with the phrase *not in my back yard* to malign those opposed to local building development.

"As for that blasted lot in the Olde House at Home," he kept thundering, "how dare they start a petition! I bet they'll object to everything we apply for now, especially that fat bastard, Herbert Baxter! He didn't even like James! Despised him for allowing those scumbag travellers to live in that field and I suppose they'll be back too, before long!"

This stung him more than anything. Not only were Avalon and William the rightful land owners, but seemed determined to hang on to it, by way of avenging their father. Crushed by defeat, he felt an ache in his chest, as if the swelling mass of hatred was gnawing a hole in his heart.

Rowena topped up his glass. "Perry, don't let them get to you. Shouldn't we be celebrating our victory in acquiring this house?" And a rare display of affection, she kissed his cheek. "I love you. I won't deny I feel a little sad for James. Wasn't it around this time they had their fundraising ball? Maybe we should throw a celebration of our own."

"Hmm, good idea," Perry said coolly. "It won't hurt to generate some publicity. Then maybe we can push ahead with our own plans..."

He took another sip of wine, allowing his gaze to wander and as the sun dipped behind a cedar tree, the carpet of shadow crept inwards. Perry could not help but feel utterly dismayed with Rosebrook Council. For despite Robin's clever intervention, even he could not fight such a barrage of opposition, wary of drawing suspicion among his own colleagues. But maybe they could enlist the help of a landscape gardener. The council might have refused him permission to demolish the *outer walls* but there was nothing to stop him restructuring the inside. Whatever ended up growing here, it would be preferable to rows of bloody cabbages!

"You're right, this is quite pleasant," he relented. "I even remember young Avalon saying it was a nice place to watch the sun set. And I've had an idea..."

The sky deepened to indigo blue and as the clouds puffed around the sun, they took on a delicate glow of pink. With the onset of dusk though, Perry rose and flicked a light switch. Two lanterns hung in glass canopies. Yet no sooner did they illuminate the interior, one of the bulbs started flickering. Then the light died rapidly, leaving their side steeped in shadow.

"Bollocks!" he hissed with undisguised fury.

Rowena rolled her eyes. "Perry, leave it," she sighed. "It doesn't matter."

"It bloody well does matter!" Perry ranted. "Sodding place with its archaic electrics! I bet you the whole lot needs rewiring and that's not all..."

Even the issue of a faulty light bulb was enough to enrage him, reminding him of another issue. Exactly one month after they had moved in, new cracks had appeared in the walls. Surveyors warned that due to the underground movement of water, the foundations were beginning to shift again. But this in turn, had led to a series of faults in the outer stonework.

Perry felt cursed. He had never admitted his deep rooted fear on hearing Avalon's wish; that *her father would come back and haunt him.*

"You worry too much," Rowena sighed. "Now drink your wine and calm down. There's a gorgeous sunset out there, so please don't spoil it. What were you going to say?"

Perry sank back into his chair. "I was thinking about all this space. Wouldn't it be put to better use if we turfed it over? Maybe turn it into a recreational green for putting and croquet."

"Perry, that is a wonderful idea," Rowena smiled.

With shadows falling into the contours of her vulpine face, she looked extraordinarily beautiful, her aquamarine eyes shining like gemstones. Perry could not help but smile back.

"You're right, let's turn this regrettable situation into a celebration," he gloated, tapping her glass. "We'll tear out these damned vegetable gardens whatever, though perhaps keep the orchards; if we employ the country bumpkins for another season to pick the fruit, it might even endear us to them a little. Then we'll eventually chop those down too."

For a moment they embraced the silence, mulling over Perry's idea. Yet after the effervescence of London, neither were used to such tranquility. Thus, it didn't take long before Rowena became restless, her eyes dancing across the Orangerie in search of entertainment.

"Let's put some music on," she suggested.

Reaching across to the old stereo, she noticed a cassette lodged in the tape deck.

Perry turned to her sharply, though. "Wait! If it was left by one of those Barton-Wells kids, it's probably some ghastly pop music..."

"Well, let's find out," Rowena argued, "and if so, I'll find something on the radio."

She pushed down the play button. Yet contrary to Perry's expectations, a folk song flowed from the speakers. With the atmosphere caressed by the sweet notes of a guitar, a lone male vocalist started singing.

"This is okay," she mused, closing her eyes.

Perry said nothing, refusing to be moved by the gentle music. But as he continued to glare across the gardens, his calculating mind was still working. Then without warning, the second bulb blew, discharging an explosion of energy. Rowena shrieked as the room was flung into darkness.

Perry shot to his feet.

"Shit!" he exploded. "That's it, we're going inside..." and in a final gesture of anger, he stabbed the stop button before extracting the cassette.

The deepening blue light was just sufficient to illuminate the wording on the label. Yet what Perry saw turned him cold.

"Free Spirit..." he spluttered.

The cassette dropped from his hand, hitting the floor with a clatter.

"Darling, whatever is it?" Rowena's voice echoed.

"This place *is* haunted," he whispered with a sob.

"What, you mean James?" she taunted. "Oh, stop this!"

"I'm not talking about James," Perry hissed. "I'm talking about *Jake Jansen!*"

Rowena flinched.

Pacing around the front of the Orangerie, Perry jabbed his finger at the cassette. "Free Spirit was his band! Spirit! The Chapman girl must have resurrected him when she was a resident!"

"Perry, you are being ridiculous," Rowena snapped.

Her voice swum in the rivers of his mind yet Perry felt quite giddy. There was only one time he had felt this threatened and it took him right back to 1972; a fragment of time in which Jake had spotted him in that lane. He could picture him now, sliding out from behind his camper van, the gleam of his auburn hair captured in the sunlight. He genuinely believed they had got rid of him, until the critical moment of that press conference... but Eleanor's face was next to flicker in his mind, taunting her secret file. If only he could get his hands on it, their mission to abduct her son yet another failure tearing at his thoughts.

"That tape was quite nice," Rowena's voice grated. "One of them must have forgotten it..."

"Or that bitch deliberately put it there to screw with my mind," Perry said. A sneer crept onto his face before he stamped on the cassette, smashing it to pieces. "Or maybe it was the boy! He visited the gardens before they left... little bastard!"

Yes, it had been the morning after they had tried to grab him - and to top it all, Eleanor had blatantly pointed the finger at Nathan.

The day the police had interviewed him could have sent him spiralling into panic. He knew she had visited her solicitor and now it seemed the locals were forming some sort of uprising.

"I promise you one thing," he snarled. "If ever that Chapman woman brings us any trouble, I will make her son wish he had never been born..."

Stars swirled in his vision and with his chest tightening, he took a few more stumbling steps. Rowena surged after him, shock filling her face as he clawed at his chest.

"Let's get you inside," she gasped, reaching for his arm, "quickly! You'd better have a lie down, I'll ask Elliot to call the doctor..."

A ribbon of tape fluttered in the breeze as the broken cassette lay in their wake.

Chapter Forty-Nine

I

The pavements of Rosebrook were gleaming with sunshine. Emily Cuthbert mopped her eyes as the glamorous couple swept from the Registry Office; Eleanor a vision of beauty in her ivory lace bridal dress, dark hair shimmering as it tumbled around her shoulders in waves.

Charlie stood by her side, gazing at her with heartfelt tenderness. Delirious with joy, he could remember the day he had married Anna, filled with a sense she was smiling down on them. Donning a suit in a deep slate grey, he too looked undeniably striking.

Clouds of confetti swirled, a fusillade of cameras capturing the moment; but with the ceremony complete, they were about to celebrate in one of Rosebrook's finest hotels. As the wedding procession snaked along the pavement, they were tailed by the bridesmaids, adorable in their rose pink dresses. At first glance they could have been sisters; Margaret with her dark blonde hair coiled up looking more grown up than ever. Her eyes twinkled as she glanced at Avalon. She too wore her hair up, so thick and luxurious, it was held into place with pins.

As they spilled into the hotel garden, the crowd fanned outwards, allowing them more space. A lawn rolled towards a rose arch, heavy with fragrant blooms. But the sweeping curves of the Perennial flower beds so much reminded them of James's gardens. Vibrant delphiniums and foxgloves intermingled with banks of roses in a profusion of shades. Eleanor felt a lump rise in her throat, moved by its splendour, before the wedding photographers swooped in.

With her eyes drifting towards the crowd, only then did certain faces register. Her old friend, Judy, looked radiant as she met her eye. Marilyn and Tom were accompanied by Rosemary Merriman and to her greater delight, she picked out the faces of her children. She saw friends of Charlie's in attendance, who she recognised from Anna's funeral; Christopher Farrin who he had chosen as best man. The Magnus couple too, lingered a short distance away, Peter keeping them company.

William and Elijah larked around in the gardens, chasing each other through the rose arch. Dressed in formal trousers, the same shade as Charlie's, they looked angelic in matching waistcoats buttoned tightly over their shirts. Andrew was donning the same outfit, but alerted by the sight of his father,

441

pressed two fingers to his lips and let out a loud whistle.

"Oi! Get over here, you two!"

As they sped, grinning, from the rose arch though, Eleanor's heart lurched. William looked so sophisticated; Elijah, an inch shorter, loping by his side. The photographers snapped away, arranging and rearranging them in groups, before calling people from the crowd to join them.

But no sooner was the photography over, Charlie and Eleanor faced each other. Running his hands down her bare arms, he tugged her towards him to plant another kiss on her lips.

"Thank God," he murmured under his breath. "Now we can all relax..."

A procession of waiting staff had begun circulating with trays of champagne. They tapped glasses, ready to mingle, where the first person to rush forwards to hug Eleanor was Judy. She was looking forward to rekindling their friendship. It would be like the old days, they reflected, recalling the moment they had first bumped into each other in Aldwyck.

"I knew you two would end up together," Judy whispered, as Charlie broke away with Christopher. "From the very first time I saw you in the pub, I could tell he adored you."

Drawing Christopher aside, Charlie had been hankering for a word in private. But having told him about the land behind the Community Centre, he was suspicious of Whaley's motives. Why involve the Council in its purchase, to serve the interests of the local community, when it was far more likely he had his own agenda?

He had asked Christopher to 'put some feelers out,' given his Masonic connections. And how ironic that Christopher had come into contact with the same councillor Perry had bribed to get approval for his housing development in Bromley.

"I just can't imagine the Council being interested," Charlie said as they sauntered towards the bar. "Even less so, to embrace some social housing project."

"Hmm," Christopher murmured. "You may well be right, Charlie. Two more parties *are* interested. Councillor Dean leaked something and you are not going to like it... but do I have your solemn promise this stays confidential?"

"Of course," Charlie nodded. He was about to order a couple of pints when a chorus of female voices rose up behind them.

"So, this is where you menfolk are hiding!" Christopher's wife, Penny, chortled.

Turning, Charlie was dismayed to see a group of ladies converging on them, including Hilary and the girls. With a wink, he guessed the conversation would have to be postponed.

442

"It'll keep," Christopher muttered. "Nab me later."

"Dad!" Margaret chirped, sidling through the crowd.

Patting her beautifully dressed hair, Charlie smiled indulgently.

"Isn't she lovely," he added, "and growing up so fast!"

"She definitely takes after Anna," one of the women muttered to Christopher's wife.

"Whose Anna?" Hilary blurted.

She saw a flinch in Charlie's shoulders as he stepped from the bar; waiting until he had moved out of earshot before turning to her new acquaintances.

"Anna was Charlie's first wife. I guess you wouldn't have known her."

"Wasn't Eleanor her nurse?" Penny intervened. "She was at the funeral. Now I don't mean to be unkind but I thought she seemed a little *bohemian*."

Hilary's eyes glittered like a bird of prey. "Ah, but Eleanor is anything but conventional," she said waspishly. "Those horrid dreadlocks! Thank goodness she got rid of them."

"Got in there a bit quick, didn't she?" the other woman smirked. "Charlie's a good catch..."

They didn't notice Margaret slip away with her head tucked between her shoulders.

By the time she escaped to the garden though, there were tears in her eyes. Fearful of smudging her mascara, she blinked them back, hating the turn in that conversation. Much as she missed her mother terribly, even Margaret had the sense to realise nothing would bring her back...

But how dare they be so mean towards Eleanor, who in the light of all their troubles, had turned their lives into something wonderful.

"What's up, Maggie?" a clipped, public school voice piped up behind her.

Margaret's heart galloped. Spinning around, she felt the tears in her eyes evaporate in the instant William materialised. He offered her some of his champagne.

"Oh, William," she sighed, "some of the women were being nasty about Eleanor. It upset me. I'm like - sad my mum died, but pleased Dad met someone else. Eleanor's lovely!"

William gave a shrug. "Women can be bitches, don't let them get to you. I know what happened to your mum, Andrew told me. He said the only reason he and Charlie lost their jobs was because of that pig, Perry Hampton, is that true?"

Margaret nodded. "Dad thinks he spoiled his chances of getting another job. That's why we ended up in that freezing cold flat..." Her words tailed off as Della shimmied into view in a floral summer dress, almost fated to resurrect the memory. "See that lady," she added. "She lived in the same block... called the ambulance when Mummy got ill."

An awkward silence bloomed. Margaret let out a hiccup, blushed the colour of her dress then handed the glass back to William. Yet his expression seemed sadly remote.

"So, what about you?" she asked, sensing his desolation. "You must miss your dad terribly. We all do! He was such a lovely man..."

"Thanks." William gave a tight smile. "But he was ill too, you know, the reason Avalon and I didn't put up much fight when he decided to sell the house. I know how badly he wanted to save it but we could see it was killing him."

Next, it was Elijah's turn to join them. "What are you two talking about?"

"Westbourne House amongst other stuff," William said. "I was just thinking about how hard my father tried to save it..." He trailed off, as if determined not to bring up the subject of the Hamptons again.

"I'm sorry," Elijah said. He accepted the champagne glass, taking a swig. "And I've been thinking about *my* father. I must ask Mum if we can make some more copies of his tape..." An impish smile flickered on his face. "I stuck the last of mine in your old cassette player."

II

As the afternoon raced on, Eleanor found it impossible to dodge the constant stream of people who kept diverting her. While Charlie's old friends all fought for a chance to get to know her better, there were others she yearned to talk to. With a lavish buffet scheduled for 6:00, her chances were slipping away. She had just spotted her son, hiding behind a bush with Margaret and William, sharing a glass of champagne. Their eyes danced furtively as they engaged in chatter, a sight that made her smile, until she noticed Holly Magnus hovering by the doorway. Her eyes honed in on them, narrowing with envy.

Eleanor frowned, before a gentle but familiar voice fluttered past her ear.

"And how is the blushing bride?"

"Elliot!" she gasped with undisguised pleasure.

To her further delight, he was accompanied by Bryony and Angelo, both grinning.

"I'm so pleased you made it. How did you manage to slip away? Don't tell me you're planning some sort of rebellion."

"Not at all," Elliot muttered. "I'm here of my own free will and his Lordship doesn't know."

"What, you mean he's fired you?" Eleanor whispered.

"I don't suppose you've heard, have you?" Elliot replied, drawing her aside. "Perry was rushed into hospital. He suffered a mild heart seizure. I'm not sure what brought it on, but I think it happened on the day his planning application was refused..."

His expression turned grave, despite the anguish Perry had put him through.

"I see," Eleanor said coolly. "Sounds like cardiac arrhythmia. He should reduce his stress levels and drink less coffee. Where is he now?"

"The doctor suggested rest," Elliot sighed. "So the two of them have gone to the South of France for a holiday..."

The words hung in the air as Eleanor digested this then finally his eyes betrayed a twinkle.

"Still, it's good news about the walled garden. You must be ecstatic!"

"We are," Eleanor smiled back. "Perry's got a friend in the planning department, see."

Elliot shook his head. "In that case, we must all be vigilant. I can tell you now, Perry has many plans up his sleeve and when councils want to pass something, they find a way. This 'friend' of his shouldn't be allowed to influence such decisions. Didn't you ought to raise this?"

"Maybe," Eleanor said, "except Avalon's trying to get to know him better. We need some inside information."

"How is she?" Elliot whispered, drawing his head close.

Eleanor's gaze wandered, before she spotted her chatting to Peter, dazzling in her dress with its light chiffon tiers fluttering around her knees.

"She's over there, look," she smiled in adoration, "and the man she's speaking to is Peter Summerville, who I'd also like you to meet."

The air felt warm as the sun continued to drip down its rays. With everyone huddled in their own little groups, Eleanor broke away, determined to track down the Merrimans. Flitting through the rose arch to the end of the garden, she caught a flash of Rosemary's white hair. Turning, she blazed as bright as the flowers in her bohemian tunic and trousers.

"Eleanor!" she announced, stretching out her hands. "Congratulations, my dear!"

She felt a wrench of emotion as they were reunited; Joshua, whose sweet face was bronzed from travelling, his floppy hair bleached golden. Next to him stood Alison, who shared the same long grey eyes. Stunning in an ice blue evening gown worn with a bolero jacket, she had always been an avid follower of fashion, especially in the 70s when Eleanor had borrowed her clothes.

Finally her eyes met Luke's, the same pale green as his mother's. He was accompanied by his wife today, along with their twin boys, aged eight.

For several minutes they exchanged news but as the conversation waned, they all seemed to be looking at her. Shooting a glance over her shoulder, Eleanor made sure no one was hovering, before her eyes once again locked with Luke's.

"What is it?" he said in a low murmur. "Is something wrong, Eleanor?"

"I-I wanted to talk to you about the press conference," she faltered.

Starting with Robin Whaley, it was predictable Rosemary's children would never have forgotten him; the sinister attention he had paid Luke, his hostility towards Alison and then Joshua.

"He lives here," Eleanor shivered, "though it's not just him I need to warn you about, but the other man. The blonde one who accompanied him."

"I remember," Luke muttered darkly. "You've met him too, haven't you?"

Eleanor nodded, relating the events that had brought them into contact. "I've explained a lot of this to Rosemary already, but he's *on to me*. So I have to ask; is there any way we can prove he attended that press conference?"

"For what reason?" Alison frowned. She looked as anxious as her two brothers.

"We always suspected he was the man Jake saw," Rosemary said. She placed a comforting arm around Alison's shoulder. "But it now appears there is new evidence. Isn't that right, Eleanor?" Staring deep into her eyes, she seemed to urge her to convince them.

"Someone else saw him," Eleanor confessed, "but if ever we are to resolve this, we have to recapture what happened at the press conference. Everyone had some involvement. Hargreaves handled the murder enquiry. Whaley was there to repeat their lies about the drugs... but what was Perry Hampton's role?"

"We never found out," Alison whispered, "though he practically had a coronary when *you* appeared. It was something you said... something about *following clues*..."

"The Dutch man mentioned Jake's friend, Andries," Eleanor said dazedly. Her mind started spinning, the memories pouring in so fast, she felt giddy: *his friend Andries spoke the truth, when he told you that Jake witnessed something. Just follow the clues...*

A witness. Those hastily spurted words were all it had taken to send Perry into an uncontrollable rage. She could still picture him squirming, tearing at his tie. But in the aftermath of the conference, Alison and Joshua had filled in the gaps; their horror when Whaley had turned on them.

"I guess they sussed us out," Alison shrugged. "Even that dishy journalist warned they wouldn't be able to publish a word of what you insinuated."

"Can you remember who *he* was?" Eleanor whispered in hope. "And is there a chance any of you could get in touch with him?"

"Adam Morrison," Joshua grinned. "Yeah, I reckon so! I'm getting into journalism myself soon. I think he still writes for NME."

Eleanor gazed at him with adoration. "Oh, Josh! I never did thank him for the glowing article he wrote in Jake's honour. But we were wondering if there might be archives..."

A buzz of excitement captured them, although the moment was short lived. Staring at Luke, Eleanor feared the danger she was about to bring into their lives.

"Whatever you do, be careful. This is a very dangerous man we're taking on and I should warn you, I've bumped into *all* my enemies recently... including Theakston."

Luke curled his arm around her shoulder like a long lost brother. "He's still around?"

"Lives a few miles away in Swanley," Eleanor said. "Charlie confronted him. I haven't told him *everything* yet, but I did warn him never to underestimate him..."

She never had a chance to elaborate. With a bell ringing across the garden, it appeared time had run out. Eleanor guessed they were about to be summoned to the banqueting suite.

"Come on, let's go inside," she sighed. "There's a hell of a lot more to discuss but it can wait for now. I want you to meet my new family."

The room had a baronial quality with exposed flint walls, draped with tapestries and coats of arms. In the moment they wandered in, Eleanor was gathered up by the crowd, who immediately began shepherding her towards the top table.

"Eli!" Alison gasped as he materialised by William's side. "Oh my God, look at you! It doesn't seem so long ago you were just a baby!"

Cheeks glowing, Elijah offered her a shy smile in return. "H-how's the acting going?" he stammered. "Didn't you play a Bond girl in *A View to a Kill?*"

"Yes, but only as an extra," Alison laughed airily. She gave his glossy hair a ruffle. "Take a look at the blonde bimbos hanging around in the background... You might see me."

"Wow!" William exploded, eyes widening. "Did you ever get to meet Grace Jones?"

As old friends merged with new, Eleanor could barely take it in. Guided into her seat, her head felt light as a cloud. More and more people were arriving, including Sue from the Olde House at Home. Calling across to announce that Boris would be along later, she was joined by the Harpers; familiar faces from Aldwyck who were here to celebrate her special day.

Tears pooled in her eyes. But as the buffet got underway, Eleanor, still reeling from her conversation with the Merrimans, diverted her attention to the food. Beautifully presented, it reminded her of the feast Angelo and Bryony had prepared in honour of William's birthday.

Her heart soared again as they made a toast to absent friends; to Anna, who they would always hold dear. To James, whose untimely death had denied him a chance to share in this wondrous event. Then Elijah sprung to his feet, surprising them all by mentioning Jake.

"I never knew my own father," he began shakily, "only that h-he was a talented rock musician and wrote great songs. We've got a recording and hope to see you all dancing to one of the numbers he performed with his band, Free Spirit!"

"Here, here!" Joshua and Luke chorused, rising to their feet and clapping.

"I also want to thank Charlie," he smiled, turning to him, "for asking my mum to marry him... and to raise a glass to my *new* family, to Andrew and Margaret and my best friends, William and Avalon!" Draining his glass, he was subjected to a roar of approval.

The next time Eleanor gazed at him, she felt an irrepressible burst of love. "Eli, that was so sweet," she gasped as they began to haul themselves away from the tables.

Elijah shuffled from one foot to another. "I meant every word. I also wanted to ask if we could make more copies of his tape... I left my last one in the Orangerie."

"You never!" Eleanor spluttered, clamping a hand across her mouth.

Elijah gave a shrug. "Ben left a tape in there once; creepy, electronic music to frighten Avalon. Besides that, Free Spirit were a brilliant band. I wanted people to hear how good they were..." His gaze turned penetrating. "Even those who might have killed him."

"Ssh, Eli," Eleanor breathed, pulling him aside. "Look, I'll explain everything to you soon, I promise. But for now, let's just enjoy what's left of our special day."

As Charlie left the table, he wasted no time. Catching Christopher's eye, he knew they could no longer delay their discussion. They sauntered from the banqueting room, glasses in hand, where the garden felt cool and inviting.

"So, what were you going to tell me about Councillor Dean?" Charlie quizzed.

"Ah, yes," Christopher said, reaching into his pocket for his cigarettes. "You wanted to know who else was interested in that land. Well, Rosebrook is ripe for development it seems and the land has drawn the attention of various property developers."

"Really?' Charlie frowned. "Then what would the council want it for? I'm guessing they're not about to turn it over to Peter, to set up an affordable housing trust."

"Not if there's money at stake," Christopher warned, "and I fear this *Robin Whaley* is using Peter's idea to convince the council that it is in their best interests to buy it; secure the futures of local people and you never know, maybe they will! But it is far more likely they'll put it out to tender and make themselves a nice fat profit in the bargain."

"Do I smell a whiff of corruption?" Charlie said.

"Bloody right," Christopher nodded, taking a drag of his cigarette.

As they wandered down the length of the garden, the sunlight still lingered. Sensing they were far enough away from the crowd, Christopher turned to Charlie.

"So, you want to know who else is bidding for it."

Charlie said nothing. A small part of him already knew.

"Perry Hampton appears to be the strongest contender," he added coldly.

"I knew it," Charlie hissed. "Couldn't get his claws into Aldwyck, so he's going to muscle in on Rosebrook!" His face drooped. "I half expected this, but it still makes me sodding angry. Is there any way we can stop him?"

"You could bid for the land yourselves," Christopher muttered. "Maybe that delightful Avalon can find out how much it is selling for. But I warn you, Hampton is not the only interested party. It seems Whaley approached someone else and this one's a corporate developer. Have you ever heard of a man named Theakston?"

"What?" Charlie spluttered, almost choking on his beer. Flecks of froth flew from the top of his glass as he pictured him; that tall menacing character in a black tracksuit.

But the effect this would have on Eleanor.

It had him wondering if Dominic was genuinely interested. Or could Whaley be deliberately reeling him in, to unhinge her?

"This has got to be a wind up," he shuddered, pulling himself out of his reverie.

"I'm guessing you know him too," Christopher frowned. "Hmm, a bit of a player apparently. He's cottoned on to the lack of entertainment facilities in Rosebrook and proposing the land could be developed into a leisure complex. You're up against a couple of giants here, Charlie."

"Well, thanks for sharing this, Chris," he said numbly. "I'll keep it under wraps."

Such news left him floundering. Then just as they were making their way back towards the hotel, he spotted Eleanor. Arm in arm with Avalon, they ambled past flower beds, deep in conversation. She looked so beautiful; graceful as a swan in her clinging ivory dress. He felt as if his heart would explode with the love he felt for her. And to think, her worst enemies were all vying for the same plot of land.

"Great," he muttered under his breath. *Whaley, Hampton and now Theakston, right here in Rosebrook... and on the dawn of a new life they had only just established for themselves.*

"Are you okay, Charlie?" Eleanor called as they drifted a little closer.

Exchanging a few last words, Christopher wandered off to rejoin the party. The next time Charlie turned to her though, she was gazing at him with questioning eyes.

He slipped his hands around her narrow waist and pulled her close. "Brace yourself, my love," he whispered, "the chances are we've got a new fight on our hands, but can I tell you about it later?" In truth, he didn't want anything to cast a cloud on this momentous day.

III

More people spilled into the garden to savour the last of the fading light and as the creeping dusk intensified, the flowers took on an iridescent glow. Andrew had just indulged in a sneaky joint. Sauntering from the shadows with Matt, the two of them were grinning like schoolboys. His girlfriend, Tiffany, tottered along behind them in her spiky stiletto heels.

No one took much notice of the midnight blue BMW approaching, as it swerved into the curb. The occupants gazed across at the scene.

"Oh look, Dominic, a wedding!" Pippa gasped.

Closest to the wall, she watched the guests moving around the garden, chatting and laughing, while her partner sat masked in darkness.

"Yeah," he answered softly, "know who's wedding it is, too."

Surveying the scene, he instantly recognised Peter. Then Charlie shimmied into view, accompanied by a pretty adolescent girl dressed as a bridesmaid.

"Old flame of yours?" Pippa teased.

"Far from it," Dominic muttered. "More an enemy really. Eleanor Chapman and I go back a long way..." Then at last he saw her, sylph-like and fluid as she wandered into view.

Dominic could not take his eyes off her. He had snatched one last glimpse of her on the day she had fled from London, except things were going to be different now. The next time he confronted her, it would be on a corporate battleground.

He had driven here to show Pippa the land he was interested in buying. Moving on to enjoy a discreet dinner, she had been intrigued by his plan. Rosebrook was a quiet town and desperately starved of entertainment facilities. Yet the idea of doing business here intrigued him.

Whaley was right; *Eleanor was a loose cannon who they needed to exert more control over.*

450

Dominic relished the challenge. He may have taken a shine to her partner, Charlie, but saw this not only as an exciting business venture, but a chance to gain the upper hand...

"Are we going in for a drink then?" Pippa snapped, wrenching him out of his daydream.

Dominic shot her a cocky smile. "Nah! No point rocking the boat, love... But very soon, we're gonna be spending a lot more time in this town, and *then* you can expect some fireworks!"

As his eyes settled on the back of Eleanor's head, he was reminded of the third reason he had been seduced here. His ex-wife had snapped up a house just on the other side of town; no doubt to put extra distance between himself and his kids. Establishing a foothold here presented a golden opportunity to visit them once a week.

"Game on, darling," he whispered to himself.

Eleanor turned her head and glanced towards the car. But unwilling to be detected, Dominic fired up the engine and discreetly drove away.

Eleanor, oblivious to his presence though, was pleasantly tipsy from champagne. Her cheeks were flushed, her topaz eyes sparkling like jewels, as Charlie led her back towards the doors. He was hoping for another dance, but with so many people lingering, progress was slow.

Finally, the Merrimans loomed in front of them.

"We're going to have to make a move soon," Alison said. "It's been great to catch up, only Luke's boys are getting tired..."

"It's okay," Eleanor murmured, "I understand."

"Congratulations on your marriage," Rosemary added lovingly. After kissing her on both cheeks, she turned to Charlie. "I'm delighted for you both."

As Charlie returned her embrace, he was looking forward to seeing more of them; and Joshua was about to embark on a fact finding mission to uncover the 1973 press conference.

"You deserve happiness," Rosemary added with heartfelt candour. "Elijah too..."

As if on cue, Elijah came racing out of the door with Margaret, skidding to a halt as all heads turned to them.

"Eli!" Eleanor chirped. "You know you were asking about Jake's demo tape? It's thanks to Joshua we even got that copy! He tracked it down before you were born."

"We didn't listen to much else in them days!" Joshua laughed.

"So sad you had to leave," Alison added wistfully. "It marked the end of an era. I couldn't imagine how you'd cope, living in our old caravan."

"It was a lovely retreat," Eleanor reassured her, "and I exchanged it for a bigger one... but talking of *the end of an era,* the caravan is up for sale now."

"You're not keeping it?" Rosemary frowned. "Not even for holidays?"

Charlie paused for thought. The field still belonged to the Barton-Wells family, yet he could understand her reluctance to return, now the Hamptons were in situ. Their evil would haunt them like a shadow, the threat of Elijah's near capture a terrible experience in itself.

Eleanor shook her head with a sigh.

"How much do you want?" Joshua asked. "I'll buy it! Lucy and I were thinking about getting a caravan. I've toured the world, but never been to Scotland or Wales."

Charlie looked at Eleanor, guessing what she was thinking.

"Do you know, I'd like you to have it," she said.

"No way, man!" Joshua gasped.

"Why not?" Eleanor beamed. "It's thanks to your wonderful mother here, I got a caravan in the first place; and if you talk to Adam Morrison you'll be doing *us* a huge favour!"

"Aw, Eleanor, that's so good of you," Joshua spluttered.

"It's okay," Eleanor responded, keeping her voice low. "I don't really need the money. James left me a legacy of £10,000."

Alison's eyes widened as she smiled at her in wonderment.

"Business is good too," Charlie added. "Andrew and I have never been busier, so we're happy for you to take it off our hands. Though you might need a pretty hefty vehicle to tow it out of that field! Anyone you know got a Range Rover?"

"Why not leave it where it is?" Rosemary suggested. "It can do no harm to visit Aldwyck occasionally..." She gave a clandestine smile. "You can keep an eye on the shenanigans at Westbourne House. You'll even have Auntie Marilyn next door to fuss over you."

"D'you know, that really isn't a bad idea," Luke commented.

"Just as long as Perry doesn't see you," Eleanor finished and sensing their imminent departure, she kissed his cheek. "I'll see you all again very soon, I promise."

"Lovely family," Charlie murmured as they wandered back inside.

Gathering his bride in his arms, he began to sway her gently around to the heady beat of 'Don't Leave me this Way' by the Communards.

The kids were bopping away on the dance floor beneath a shower of disco lights, a vision that brought a smile. Margaret and Holly were practically shoving each other out of the way to monopolise the floor space opposite William. He was convinced his daughter was in love with the Barton-Wells boy and with such enchanting good looks, who could blame her?

Burying his face in Eleanor's neck, he breathed in the scent of her skin, soft as silk, as his lips grazed the surface. Already he was dreaming about their honeymoon - and what a sweeter way to celebrate their love than to steal a few days in Paris? Once it was over, they would resume their lives in Rosebrook. But with the renovation of the Community Centre imminent, they were yet to be drawn into a sinister *new game* if Whaley had his way.

The last year had been turbulent, yet he sensed their struggle was far from over.

He never had a chance to voice his fears, until the party was winding down. But shortly before Midnight, most people had dispersed, leaving a small but intimate circle.

They found themselves in the company of Peter, alongside Elliot, Boris and Sue. Draped in chairs around tables strewn with streamers, they were ready to enjoy a last toast. Eleanor's bridal bouquet rested on the table top. Filled with a desire to cherish every precious memento, she had been reluctant to hurl into the crowd, loving the velvety red roses and white carnations

"Cheers," she slurred, raising her wine glass, "and here's to the future of Rosebrook!"

"And Aldwyck," Boris added, tapping her glass with a loud clink. "For I fear the future of our village is doomed..."

"In what way?" Peter frowned, lifting his eyes.

"We may have won the first battle," Elliot said, "but with Perry's takeover of Westbourne House there's bound to be repercussions. We'll probably see an end to our traditions; the Christmas fair for example, not to mention the vegetable gardens. He still plans to get rid of them you know and few people will be able to wander around the grounds any more... not unless they're paying guests. All these little customs held our community together."

"That's so sad," Peter sighed, "the reason I want to create something special in Rosebrook." He gazed tenderly at Avalon as she joined their table. "Community is essential. It draws people together in ways that make them feel they belong."

"I know," Charlie exhorted, "and we'll work together to get that land for you, Peter. Although I warn you it could be war, even with Avalon's influence."

"Robin Whaley and I are getting along fine," Avalon said. "I know you think he might betray us, but maybe we can turn this around in our own favour..."

Eleanor closed her eyes, listening to their words. She allowed her finger tips to trail over Jake's pendant, which she had wanted to wear even today of all days. Sensing the power of his spirit, she recalled the first day she had paused outside the gates of Westbourne House.

"I've got a feeling you'll get Westbourne House back," she murmured as if

453

in a trance.

Everyone fell silent, staring, as if guessing she was about to say something even more poignant. Yet how could she forget the pledge she had made on that same pivotal day?

Together we will create a society where everyone can live in safety.

And by the time Elijah, along with Margaret, William and Andrew joined the table, she felt a sudden fire erupting in her heart.

"Fourteen years ago, I swore to Jake I'd find people like us," she declared, "people who've suffered injustice and *that's* why we've got to help Peter fulfil his vision!"

"But we could be up against the Hamptons..." Charlie started to whisper.

"Then we have to bring them down," Eleanor smiled. "So let's make a new pledge."

With her hand folded around Charlie's, she pushed it into the centre of the table. Her eyes clashed with Peter's, drawing strength from their captivating blue glow.

"Let us swear we will stand up to our enemies and defeat them..."

There seemed little need for words as one after the other, all hands joined across the table.

Epilogue

October 15th 1988

Dear Mrs Eleanor Bailey

I am in receipt of a letter from your solicitors, Sharp, Bancroft and Blackmore. Whilst it has been many years since I was involved in politics, I do of course remember the MP, Albert Enfield, as well as the shocking event of his death.

I am happy to tell you a little more about his agenda, though I cannot deny, curious to know the purpose of this discussion.

Please feel free to contact me via your solicitor, so we may agree on a mutually convenient time to meet. I hope you understand my need for discretion.

Yours sincerely

Evelyn J. Webster

******

This is the end of 'Visions'
Watch out for
'SAME FACE DIFFERENT PLACE - Book 3 - Pleasures'
The start of a terrifying new conflict.

Author's Note

Thank you for purchasing my second novel, which I sincerely hope you enjoyed. I hope this inspires you to read the third book of the series, Pleasures, where the mystery continues through the late 1980s into the 90s.

Also, if you have a moment, please would you be so kind as to post a review on Amazon. Reviews are the lifeblood of authors and are always appreciated.

For further information, you can visit my website which has regular updates about my books. This also lists links to my social networks and blog, where I post articles from time to time to keep everyone up to date with my research and writing.

Helen J. Christmas
www.samefacedifferentplace.com

Books by Helen Christmas

Same Face Different Place
Decade-spanning mystery thriller series

Beginnings
Visions
Pleasures
Retribution Phase One
Retribution End Game

Available for Kindle and in Paperback

Rosebrook Chronicles The Hidden Stories
Interlocking stories linked to Same Face Different Place

Available for Kindle, Paperback and Audio

Lethal Ties
A Psychological Suspense thriller

Available for Kindle and in Paperback